JADE WAR

JADE WAR

THE GREEN BONE SAGA:
BOOK TWO

FONDA LEE

www.orbitbooks.net

Copyright © 2019 by Fonda Lee
Author photograph by Elena Rose Photography
Cover design by Lisa Marie Pompilio
Cover art © Alamy and Shutterstock
Cover copyright © 2019 by Hachette Book Group, Inc.
Maps copyright © 2019 by Tim Paul

Orbit
Hachette Book Group
1290 Avenue of the Americas
New York, NY 10104
orbitbooks.net

Simultaneously published in Great Britain and in the U.S. by Orbit in 2019
First Edition: July 2019

Orbit is an imprint of Hachette Book Group.
The Orbit name and logo are trademarks of Little, Brown Book Group Limited.

The publisher is not responsible for websites (or their content) that are not owned by the publisher.

The Hachette Speakers Bureau provides a wide range of authors for speaking events. To find out more, go to www.hachettespeakersbureau.com or call (866) 376-6591.

Library of Congress Cataloging-in-Publication Data

Names: Lee, Fonda, author.
Title: Jade war / Fonda Lee.
Description: First edition. | New York, NY : Orbit, 2019. | Series: The Green Bone saga ; book 2
Identifiers: LCCN 2019000760 | ISBN 9780316440929 (hardcover) | ISBN 9780316440905 (trade paperback) | ISBN 9780316440936 (ebook)
Subjects: | GSAFD: Fantasy fiction.
Classification: LCC PS3612.E34285 J38 2019 | DDC 813/.6—dc23
LC record available at https://lccn.loc.gov/2019000760

ISBNs: 978-0-316-44092-9 (hardcover), 978-0-316-44093-6 (ebook)

Printed in the United States of America

LSC-C

10 9 8 7 6 5 4 3 2 1

For the martial artists I've trained with and learned from.

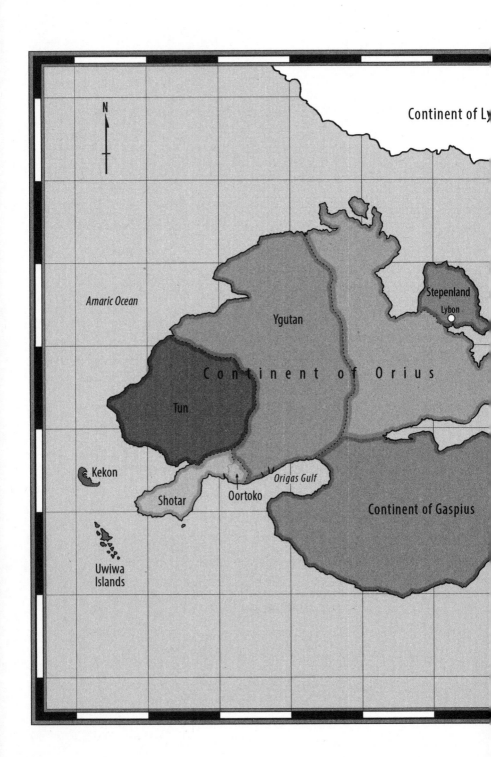

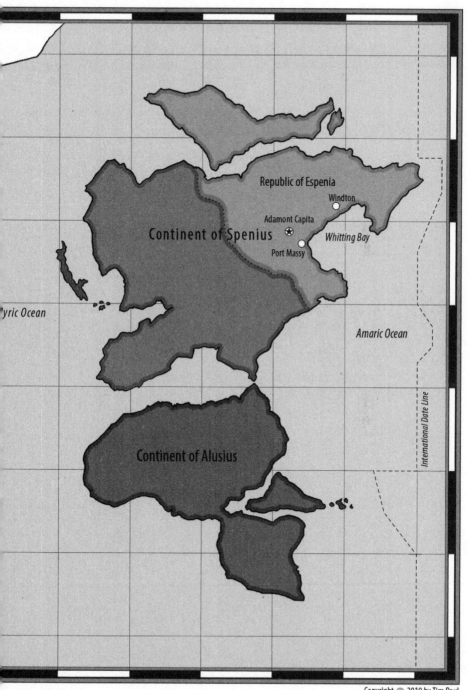

Republic of Espenia

Windton

Adamont Capita

Continent of Spenius

Whitting Bay

Port Massy

yric Ocean

Amaric Ocean

Continent of Alusius

International Date Line

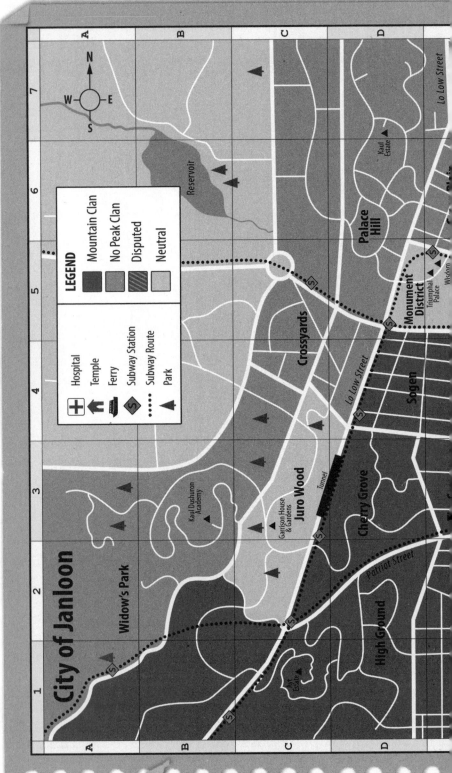

The Stump

Fishtown

Coinwash

KI-1 Freeway

Paw-Paw

The Forge

The Docks

al's Ride

Temple District

Janloon General Hospital

Financial District

Janloon Temple of Divine Return

Ship St.

The Armpit

Junko

Little Hammer

Dog's Head

Poor Mom's Rd.

Spearpoint

KI-1 Freeway

Rail Station

Summer Park

Twice Lucky Restaurant

To Euman

To Little Button

SUMMER HARBOR

Way Away Bridge

Typhoon Shelter

While every effort has been made to verify the accuracy of this map at the time of printing, territorial jurisdictions are subject to change. Travelers are strongly advised to consult local authorities for current information.

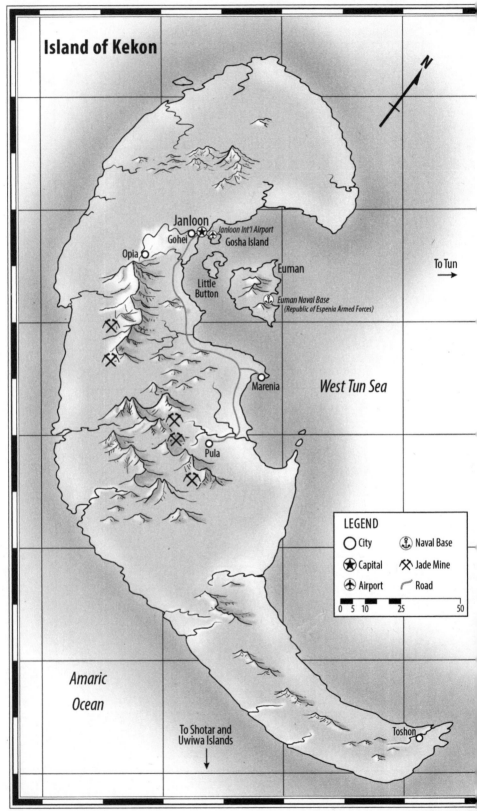

Island of Kekon

Janloon
Gohei
Janloon Int'l Airport
Gosha Island
Opia
Euman
Little
Button
Euman Naval Base
(Republic of Espenia Armed Forces)

To Tun

West Tun Sea

Marenia

Pula

LEGEND

◯ City   ⚓ Naval Base
★ Capital   ⛏ Jade Mine
✈ Airport   〜 Road

0 5 10   25   50

Amaric
Ocean

To Shotar and
Uwiwa Islands

Toshon

Copyright © 2019 by Tin

The Green Bone Clans

Along with Their Associates and Enemies

The No Peak Clan

KAUL HILOSHUDON, Pillar
KAUL SHAELINSAN, Weather Man
EMERY ANDEN, a Kaul by adoption, recent graduate of Kaul Dushuron Academy
KAUL LANSHINWAN, former Pillar of the clan, elder brother to Hilo and Shae; deceased

KAUL SENINGTUN, the Torch of Kekon, patriarch of the family; deceased
KAUL DUSHURON, son of Kaul Sen, father of Lan, Hilo, and Shae; deceased
KAUL WAN RIAMASAN, widow of Kaul Du, mother of Lan, Hilo, and Shae

MAIK KEHNUGO, Horn of No Peak
MAIK TARMINGU, Pillarman to Kaul Hilo
KAUL MAIK WENRUXIAN, wife of Kaul Hilo, a stone-eye

WOON PAPIDONWA, the Weather Man's Shadow, former Pillarman to Kaul Lan
HAMI TUMASHON, Master Luckbringer
JUEN NURENDO, First Fist of Maik Kehn
LOTT JINRHU, a Finger of the clan

YUN DORUPON, former Weather Man of Kaul Sen and Kaul Lan; a traitor
AUN UREMAYADA, mother of Emery Anden; deceased
HARU EYNISHUN, ex-wife of Kaul Lan
TEIJE RUNO, a second cousin of Hilo and Shae
KYANLA, housekeeper of the Kaul estate

Other Fists and Fingers

VUAY YUDIJO, Second Fist to Maik Kehn
IYN ROLUAN, a senior Fist
VIN SOLUNU, a senior Finger talented in Perception

HEIKE, DUDO, TON, Fingers of the clan, former classmates of Emery Anden

DOUN, YONU, TYIN, HEJO, Green Bones reporting to the Pillarman

Notable Lantern Men

EITEN, proprietor of the Cursed Beauty distillery, a former Fist maimed by Gont Asch

MR. UNE, proprietor of the Twice Lucky restaurant

MRS. SUGO, proprietor of the Lilac Divine Gentleman's Club

MR. ENKE, real estate developer, president of Enke Property Group

The Mountain Clan

AYT MADASHI, Pillar

REE TURAHUO, Weather Man

NAU SUENZEN, Horn

AYT YUGONTIN, the Spear of Kekon, adoptive father to Mada, Im, and Eodo; deceased

AYT IMMINSHO, adopted elder son of Ayt Yu; deceased

AYT EODOYATU, adopted second son of Ayt Yu; deceased

GONT ASCHENTU, former Horn of the clan; deceased

WAUN BALUSHU, First Fist to Gont Asch and Nau Suen

IWE KALUNDO, Master Luckbringer

VEN SANDOLAN, president of K-Star Freight, a Lantern Man of the clan

VEN HAKUJON, a senior Fist of the clan, son of Ven Sando

KOBEN ATOSHO, a child, born Ayt Ato, son of Ayt Eodo

SEKO, a Fist of the clan, manager of White Rats

MUDT JINDONON, an informer; deceased

Ti Pasuiga

ZAPUNYO, jade smuggler, leader of Ti Pasuiga

IYILO, Zapunyo's bodyguard

SORADIYO, rockfish recruiter and manager

BERO, a jade thief

MUDT KALONUN, a jade thief, son of Mudt Jin

Others in Kekon

HIS HEAVENSHIP PRINCE IOAN III, current sovereign of Kekon

Son Tomarho, chancellor of the Royal Council of Kekon, a No Peak loyalist
Guim Enmeno, minister of Home Concerns, a Mountain loyalist
Mr. Kowi, a member of the Royal Council, a No Peak loyalist

Tau Marosun, professor of foreign studies at Jan Royal University
Master Aido, private trainer in the jade disciplines
Durn Soshunuro, Pillar of the Black Tail clan
Dr. Truw, a Green Bone physician
Grandmaster Le, head instructor at Kaul Dushuron Academy
Toh Kitaru, news anchor for Kekon National Broadcasting

Representatives of the Espenian Government
Gregor Mendoff, Republic of Espenia ambassador to Kekon
Quire Corris, secretary of international affairs for the Republic of Espenia
Colonel Leland Deiller, commanding officer of Euman Naval Base
Lieutenant Colonel Jay Yancey, executive officer of Euman Naval Base

In Port Massy
The Kekonese-Espenians
Dauk Losunyin, Pillar of Southtrap
Dauk Sanasan, wife of Dauk Losun, his "Weather Man"
Dauk Corujon, "Cory," son of Losun and Sana

Rohn Torogon, the "Horn" of Southtrap
Mr. and Mrs. Hian, host family to Emery Anden
Shun Todorho, "Tod," a Green Bone, Cory's friend
Etto Samishun, "Sammy," a Green Bone, Cory's friend
Ledt Derukun, "Derek," Cory's friend
Sano, a doorman at the grudge hall

The Crews
Blaise "The Bull" Kromner, Boss of the Southside Crew
Willum "Skinny" Reams, top foreman of the Southside Crew
Moth Duke, a foreman of the Southside Crew
Carson Sunter, a coat in the Southside Crew

Joren "Jo Boy" Gasson, Boss of the Baker Street Crew
Rickart "Sharp Ricky" Slatter, Boss of the Wormingwood Crew; in prison
Anga Slatter, acting Boss of the Wormingwood Crew, wife of Rickart Slatter

JADE
WAR

CHAPTER

1

Heaven Awaiting

It was madness to rob the grave of a Green Bone. Only someone with little regard for his own life would consider it, but if one was that sort of person, then tonight was the moment of opportunity. The cool, dry days of late winter had not yet given way to the incessant rain of spring, and low clouds obscured the rising moon over the tops of the trees in Widow's Park. The streets of Janloon were unusually quiet; out of respect, people were forgoing their usual activities and staying home, hanging ceremonial spirit guiding lamps in their windows to honor the passing of Kaul Seningtun—national war hero, patriarch of the No Peak clan, the Torch of Kekon. So even though Bero and Mudt had taken the precaution of carrying no light, there was no one to take notice of their arrival at the cemetery.

The groundskeeper, Nuno, met them at the gate five minutes before the official closing time. "Here." He thrust a black garbage bag at Bero. "Be quick. Night security doesn't arrive for another half hour." The three of them were alone, but Nuno spoke in a hurried whisper. His eyes, in the sun-shriveled hollows of his face, darted fearfully about the shadows of the shrubbery and tombstones. Thieves were the lowest sort of scum on Kekon, and grave robbers were lower than that. A bullet to the back of the head, the bill for the expense sent to their relatives—that was the lawful punishment they could expect to receive by morning if they were caught.

Bero took the plastic bag from Nuno. Ducking next to the stone wall, he pulled out two blue shirts and caps embroidered with the logo of Heaven Awaiting Cemetery. Hastily, he and Mudt put on the shirts and set the caps on their heads. Nuno led them at a brisk walk up a switchbacked hillside path to one of the largest, most prominent memorials on the grounds. A new plot had been dug in front of the looming green marble monument. Tomorrow, Kaul Seningtun would be laid to rest next to his grandson, Kaul Lanshinwan, former Pillar of No Peak, murdered and buried sixteen months ago. *Sixteen months!* A frustrating eternity for Bero to scheme and wait for his jade.

Nuno had dug the new plot himself that afternoon; a tractor with a backhoe attachment still rested next to the grave. Bero stood at the lip of the neat rectangular hole in the ground. A breeze stirred the disturbed grass at his feet, raising the pungent smell of damp earth. A shiver of excitement traveled up Bero's spine. *This* was what he'd needed all along: for someone else to do most of the work for him. The first time he and Mudt had snuck into the cemetery with shovels, they'd been interrupted by a group of other drunken teens stumbling around after dark and scaring each other; the second time, it began pouring rain and they barely made a dent in the soggy earth before nearly being caught by security. After that, Bero figured they had to be smarter; they had to come up with a better plan and wait for the right time to act.

To Bero's surprise, Mudt crouched down and jumped into the empty grave first. The boy looked back up, wiping his hands, his ferrety eyes bright. Bero slung the duffel bag he carried off his shoulder and took out the tools he needed. He passed them down to Mudt, then followed, the soles of his shoes thudding on freshly exposed dirt. For a second, the two teens glanced at each other, awed at their own conspiratorial daring. Then together, they began to attack the wall of the pit with shovels, burrowing like moles toward the neighboring coffin.

Nuno stood watch near the tractor, chewing a quid of betel nut and pretending to be taking a casual break from the hard work of grave-digging. It was uncommon for him to need to bring out the backhoe; most Kekonese were cremated and entombed in columbaria or buried in small plots dug by hand. Due to space considerations, even wealthy families like the Kauls, who could afford full plots, were buried with only a foot of space between caskets, so it was not long before Bero's shovel struck a hard surface in the wall of soil. Stifling a shout of triumph, he redoubled his efforts. Dirt flew; it streaked his sweaty hands, and when he paused to wipe his brow, it left muddy tracks across his face. Bero did not feel any fatigue at all, only exhilaration and nearly unbearable anticipation; surely it was because his rightful jade was so close now, calling to him from within the coffin of the man he had killed.

"Kaul Lan used to be the Pillar of the No Peak clan," Mudt said in a hushed but eager voice, speaking for the first time since they'd arrived. Mudt was only fifteen, three years younger than Bero, and his arms were skinny; he labored at their task, and his narrow face was flushed in the near dark. "He would've had more jade than just about anyone, wouldn't he? More than the Maik brothers, even." A vengeful glint shone in Mudt's eyes. He had his own reasons for wanting jade.

"You can bet on it, keke," Bero answered, without shifting his attention.

An anxious edge came into Mudt's whisper. "How can we be sure the jade's even here?" Except when taken by an enemy in battle, a Green Bone's jade passed to his family. Warriors were often buried with some ceremonial portion of their green, but Kaul's casket might contain only a few gemstones, or nothing at all. Given the intense cultural and religious stigma against stealing from the deceased, and the death penalty it carried, the effort and risk of grave robbing was rarely worth it, even for the most jade-fevered criminals.

Bero did not reply to Mudt; he couldn't offer any reassurance other than that when he got a certain feeling, he always listened to it. He had that feeling now, like fate was smiling at him. The capricious tides of fortune pulled people this way and that, but Bero thought they took special notice of him, that he rode higher on them than most. Ah, he'd had plenty of bad luck in his life from the minute he'd been yanked squalling from his short-lived mother's womb, but then again, he was alive when many others he knew were not—and now he was close to jade.

The side of the casket was visible now. What had once been a burnished cherry surface shone dull brown against black earth. The teenagers put down their shovels and tied kerchiefs tightly over their noses and mouths, then pulled on heavy work gloves. Bero picked up a cordless reciprocating saw. "Hold up the light," he said, his voice muffled by the cloth. Mudt's narrow penlight came on; he played it over the side of the coffin. When Bero started the saw, its shrill chatter nearly made him jump and drop the power tool on his feet. Mudt's flashlight beam shook wildly before steadying again. Heart pounding against his ribs, Bero made a plunge cut into Kaul Lan's casket and began to saw.

He cut out an area roughly the size of a television screen, then turned off the saw and set it down. With Mudt's help, he hauled the piece of wood away. Dust and polyester batting came free and swirled in the air. An object dropped into the dirt at their feet. With a shout of elation, Bero dropped to his knees, barely restraining himself from seizing what he saw glinting like unearthed treasure under the flashlight beam: a string of jade beads, each stone flawless and brilliantly green, separated from its fellows with short black spacers on a silver chain. A powerful Green Bone leader's ornament and weapon, a part of his very identity. A priceless object that could not be bought except with blood.

Mudt recovered his senses first; he grabbed Bero's shoulder and said, "It was sewn into the lining. There might be more." They dug around further in the damaged upholstery and almost at once found two leather forearm cuffs, studded with gems. Kaul had also worn a belt, heavy with jade; perhaps it was here as well, hidden elsewhere in the coffin.

Before they could search further, Nuno appeared at the edge of the grave, looking down from above them, his leathery face twitchy. "You have to get out. I sent the guards to check a broken lock on the back gate, but they'll come back. We need to clean up this mess."

"Throw down the duffel bag," Bero called.

Nuno did so. Bero and Mudt pushed the cut piece of casket wood back into place and packed as much of the damp soil around it as they could. It pained Bero deeply to think of the other jade stones they might be leaving behind, but it was best to get away now, with what they had. He'd learned some painful lessons from being over-ambitious in the past. Careful not to touch the jade with his bare skin, he wrapped the precious finds in several layers of burlap and stowed it in the duffel bag along with their tools. Bero wiped his caked hands on his pants, slung the bag over his shoulder, and reached out a hand for Nuno to pull him out of the grave. The groundskeeper stepped back, his stained lips drawing away from his teeth in disgust. "I'm not getting near stolen jade." It was only because Nuno had fallen into a considerable amount of debt that they'd been able to bribe him at all, with enough money that Bero had entertained long second thoughts over the amount of stashed shine he'd had to sell over the course of months to fund this venture.

Bero had Mudt lace his hands into a step and boost him out of the pit. When he'd scrambled safely back to his feet, Bero looked down at the younger teen, standing in the dirt with his arm outstretched, and for a moment he was tempted to leave Mudt behind. Now that he finally had his jade, why split it with this boy? But Mudt might give him away if he was cast aside. Besides, he had thick blood, and he had been useful so far—Bero had to admit that.

He crouched down and helped Mudt out. Nuno started up the backhoe and used it to pack the disturbed soil back into place. When he was done, the grave looked much as it had before. A keen eye inspecting the site would notice footprints in the dirt and an irregular, loose wall, but they weren't counting on scrutiny. Bero and Mudt untied their kerchiefs and wiped the sweat and mud from their faces as Nuno led them briskly back down the hill. It was fully dark now, and no one was paying attention to them, but if someone had been, they would've seen what appeared to be a trio of cemetery mainte-nance workers finishing up for the day.

At the gate, Nuno said, "Give me back those shirts and hats, quick." They tore off the soiled disguises, stuffing them back into the garbage bag. "You got what you came for, didn't you? Damning your souls and all." Nuno spat. "Now, about the other half of the money."

Bero nodded and crouched down to unzip the side pocket of the duffel bag. From behind, Mudt swung with all his strength, hitting Nuno in the back of the head with the rock clutched in his fist, then shoved him to the ground. Bero stood up with a compact pistol in his hand and fired twice, putting the first bullet in Nuno's forehead and the second in his cheek.

Both boys stared dumbstruck for three or four long seconds after the sharp report of gunfire faded. Rolled over, Nuno's eyes were fro-zen open in alarm and surprise; the entry wounds were surprisingly small, and the blood was already being sucked up by the dry ground.

Bero's first thought was that the plan had worked surprisingly well and he was right to have kept Mudt around after all. His second was that it was a good thing the groundskeeper wasn't a large man or they would've had a real problem moving him. The two teenagers were panting and pouring sweat from exertion and fear by the time they dragged the body into a shallow hollow under the nearby shrubbery. Bero dug hastily through Nuno's jacket for the man's wallet. "Get his watch, too," he hissed at Mudt. "Make it look like a robbery." They snatched the key ring from the groundskeeper's pocket, then kicked leaves and branches over the body and ran for the gate. As Bero cursed and struggled with the lock, Mudt bent over, gasping, hands on knees, the rolling whites of his eyes visible under the greasy mop of his hair. "Holy shit. *Holy shit holy shit holy shit.*"

The gate swung open at last. They pulled the heavy metal bars shut behind them and Bero clutched the duffel bag tight as they sprinted into the cover of Widow's Park ahead of the guards' sweep-ing flashlights, toward the lantern glow of the city below.

2

The Passing of the Torch

Kaul Hiloshudon stood at the head of the vast assembly of mourn-
ers who'd come to offer their final respects to his grandfather. There
were a great many people paying close attention to him today, and
they would notice if he seemed distracted or agitated, so he kept his
eyes fixed firmly on the coffin draped in expensive white cloth and
moved his lips dutifully to the penitents' chanted recitations. Still, he
found it difficult to pay attention to the service, impossible to gird his
sense of Perception against the presence of so many enemies.

His grandfather had lived a long and important life. Kaul Sen had
fought for the liberation of his country, and later, through politics
and business and the great clan he built, he'd shaped the nation of
Kekon in lasting ways. At the ripe age of eighty-three, he'd passed
away quietly in the middle of the night, sitting in his usual chair by
the window of the family house. A sign of favor from the gods, surely.
If, in the final years of his life, with dementia and declining jade

tolerance, Grandda had become a cruel, unbearable old man made bitter by regret and loss, who had nothing but unkind things to say about the leadership of the No Peak clan passing to his least favored grandchild—well, that was something the average citizen did not know. For two days and nights, a great public vigil had been held in the Temple District, and it seemed to Hilo that half the population of the city had turned out for the funeral. The other half was probably watching the event on television. The death of the Torch of Kekon marked the end of an era, the passing of a pivotal generation that had secured Kekon's freedom from foreign occupation and rebuilt its prosperity. Every public figure of importance was here to take part in such a profound commemoration—including Ayt Madashi.

The Pillar of the Mountain clan was standing on the other side of the crowd, in a long, white jacket and white scarf, surrounded by her own people. Hilo could barely see her from where he stood, but he didn't need to; he could Perceive the distinctive density of her jade aura easily enough. The irony of her presence at the very place where Hilo's elder brother Lan lay turning to dust in the ground would've enraged Hilo if he'd allowed himself to dwell upon it, but he did not; he had no intention of giving his rival that satisfaction.

Yesterday, Ayt had issued a public statement praising Kaul Sen as a national hero, a father of the country, and the beloved comrade and friend of her late father, Ayt Yugontin—let the gods recognize them both. She expressed sadness over the recent strife between the clans of these two great men; she hoped the unfortunate disagreements could be overcome so the country might move forward in the spirit of unshakable unity once demonstrated by the patriotic wartime brotherhood of the One Mountain Society.

"Bullshit," Hilo had said. He did not for one second believe that Ayt Mada would ever abandon her goal to kill him and his family, to destroy No Peak and take unquestioned control of the country's jade supply. Blood scores were not erased by press releases.

"It's a good public relations move," Shae had said. "Reminding people of Grandda's partnership with her father and thus associating herself with the legacy of all Green Bones."

Beyond that brief analysis, his sister had spoken little in the past seventy-two hours, even outside of the official two-day silent vigil. Hilo glanced at her standing beside him, her spine straight but the puffy circles under her eyes still visible under the white mourning powder that dusted her face. Her normally sharp jade aura seemed muted. Shae had loved their grandfather, had always basked in his favoritism. She'd wept bitterly upon his death.

Hilo returned his attention to the crowd. Other top leaders of the Mountain clan were in attendance; standing near Ayt Mada was a short man with slicked hair—Ree Turahuo, the clan's Weather Man—and next to him, a man with coarse features and a closely trimmed salt-and-pepper beard to match his hair. Hilo knew relatively little about Nau Suenzen, who had succeeded Gont Aschentu as Horn of the Mountain, but rumors and spies told him that Nau possessed a reputation as a devious guerrilla fighter who'd conducted sabotage missions and assassinations for Ayt Yu during the Shotarian occupation. He'd been only twenty-three years old when the Many Nations War ended. He did not appear, either from his unassuming appearance or the coolly bland texture of his jade aura, to be half as powerful or impressive as his predecessor. Hilo suspected this was itself a deception to be concerned about.

The Deitist penitents in white funerary robes—two dozen of them, for such a large crowd and such an important funeral— concluded the long religious ceremony with several refrains of *let the gods recognize him*, which were echoed multitudinously by those gathered. Hilo closed his eyes, focusing his fatigued Perception as he scanned through the mental noise of thousands of breaths and beating hearts. There: Unseen somewhere behind the cluster of Mountain clan members was the familiar cloudy jade aura of a man he'd once called his uncle. The former Weather Man of No Peak, a traitor to the Kaul family. Yun Dorupon was here, and he was grieving.

"Don't bother. We won't get to him today," Shae said in an undertone. Perhaps she'd seen the look of concentration on his face, or simply Perceived his animus, but Hilo was surprised. He hadn't thought that she'd noticed Doru, that she was paying any attention at all.

She was right, of course; they could not act in violence in the presence of penitents on the day of their grandfather's funeral, but more pragmatically, there were too many of the Mountain's warriors present—hundreds of their Fists and Fingers arrayed across from No Peak's own. When Hilo widened his Perception, the auras of all the Green Bones in attendance created a heavy buzz of jade energy like the ceaseless chatter of a busy street. The clans were making a show of strength with their respective numbers, but today they stood in truce to honor the same man.

The huge gathering began to disperse. Hilo braced himself for the long, unavoidable task of putting on a solemn countenance and accepting condolences from the clan's inner circle of influential loyalists—Lantern Men, politicians, prominent Green Bone families. Earlier on, some disquiet seemed to be going on near the entrance to the grounds, and Maik Kehn had sent one of his Fists to investigate. Now Kehn appeared at Hilo's side and said in a low voice, "There's talk about a dead body being found in the cemetery last night."

Hilo's mouth curved. "Only one? Did the others get up and leave?"

The Horn snorted—as much of a laugh as Hilo ever got out of him, though his broad shoulders rose in amusement. "The grounds-keeper was discovered shot in the head near the gate. Over his debts, they say. Doesn't seem all that important, but you know how some people are, crying bad luck over a fly in a cup of hoji."

Hilo nodded. There ought not to be any negative news to taint the Torch's funeral. "Talk to the cemetery manager and quiet it down." He glanced reluctantly at the long line of well-wishers he had to face. He could no longer Perceive either Ayt or Doru anywhere nearby. "Tell Tar to give me an hour; then I'm going home, no matter how many ass kissers are still here."

Two and a half hours later, Hilo arrived back at the Kaul estate. There were cars parked all the way up and down the long driveway and in the roundabout; the public funeral was being followed by a private reception reserved for family members and the highest-ranked Green

Bones of No Peak. Through the half-open car window, Hilo could hear music and smell barbecue coming from the courtyard. Living into one's eighties was supposedly a cause for celebration; it was considered as a sign of achievement in the Divine Virtues and a mark of the gods' approval, guaranteeing admittance back to the fold of Heaven on the promised day of the Return. Hilo thought it was one of those beliefs that must've made more sense in a time of warfare and poor medical care, but nevertheless, now that the official mourning for Kaul Sen was over, the white drapery had come down and the more informal gathering had a somewhat festive air. It was bound to go on for some time.

Maik Tar drove the Duchesse Priza straight up to the front of the main house. Hilo's Pillarman put the car into park and turned over his shoulder. "Those people you agreed to see today, Hilo-jen, they're still here. You want me to send them in to you, or get rid of them?"

"Where's my sister?" Hilo asked. "Did she come back already?"

"She's waiting for you inside."

Resigned, Hilo stubbed out his cigarette in the ashtray. "Send them in."

Tar cast his boss a sympathetic glance. "I'll save you a plate of food. You want anything in particular?"

"Some of the smoked pork." Hilo got out of the car, walked into the house, and reluctantly went into the study. It had once been Lan's favorite room, and Hilo still did not feel entirely comfortable in it. He had finally made some changes—removing some of the bookshelves and putting in a television and a larger minibar, bringing in more comfortable armchairs—but every time he used it, the officious room reminded him unkindly that he'd never been the intended Pillar of the clan.

So ordinarily, when he met with his own subordinates, Hilo preferred the kitchen or the patio, but those were not private at the moment, and he had to admit that the study communicated a sense of formal authority that made it more appropriate for meeting with the clan's stakeholders and petitioners—people with whom he knew he needed to downplay his youth and street reputation and emphasize his family's power and legacy.

Shae was already in the room, sitting in one of the leather armchairs. She'd washed off her face powder, redone her makeup, and changed into a dark skirt and beige blouse, but her eyes were sunken and tired, and seemed almost accusing. *Didn't you love Grandda at all?*

"You don't have to stay," Hilo told her. "I can handle this myself."

Shae said, "What if a Lantern Man asks you to pressure the Royal Council regarding the upcoming bill on limiting fuel surcharges?"

Hilo narrowed his eyes. "No one will ask me that."

"You're right," she said. "There is no upcoming bill on fuel surcharges. I made it up just now." Her smile was thin, and her needling held little of its usual thrust. "I'll stay."

Hilo frowned but refrained from replying, only out of consideration for her grief. It was true that he didn't know the business and political issues of the clan as well as she did, but pointing it out was the sort of cutting unkindness that his sister must've inherited from Grandda.

Hilo had barely taken off his tie and unbuttoned his collar when Tar knocked on the door and opened it to admit a man accompanied by a woman with a baby in her arms. At the sight of them, Hilo brightened at once and went to embrace the man warmly. "Eiten, my friend," he said. "Your daughter's grown huge! Is she really only nine months old? She could wrestle a two-year-old to the ground."

Eiten could not return the Pillar's embrace, nor raise clasped hands to his forehead in the traditional respectful salute, but his eyes shone with pride at Hilo's words and he tilted into a slight bow. He wore a crisp, white, short-sleeved shirt that covered the stumps of his missing arms, and soft, slip-on black sandals. "She's a terror, Hilo-jen; she cries for hours and refuses to be put down for a minute." He shook his head morosely but did not sound at all unhappy.

"Of course she's destined to be as green as her da," Hilo said. He saw Eiten's wife nod and smile. The old belief that fussy infants grew up to be better warriors used to apply only to boys, but these days, twenty percent of the students in Kaul Dushuron Academy were female; there were women Fists and even a woman Pillar—a colicky baby girl was cause for pride, not consternation. "I only worry she'll be too green to be married," said Eiten's wife. Hilo caught her gaze flickering briefly toward Shae before dropping.

"Maybe by the time she grows up, people won't think that way anymore," Shae said with a small smile.

"The Weather Man is right, and besides, it's too early to worry about that now," Hilo said, placing a hand on Eiten's shoulder and leading the family toward the chairs. A brown monkey scampered behind Eiten's heels. When Eiten sat down, it jumped onto the armrest and sat perched beside him alertly, scratching its chest. Hilo pulled a few bottles of soda from the mini-fridge and placed them on the coffee table. At a word from Eiten, the monkey hopped onto the table, uncapped one of the soda bottles, inserted a straw, and carried it back to its master. Eiten slid one foot from his sandal and held the neck of the bottle firmly between his toes. A jade bracelet hung from the ankle he rested across his opposite knee.

Hilo sat down across from his former Fist. His voice took a serious turn. "How're you managing? Is there anything else you need from the clan that would be of help?"

"You've done a lot for us already. Life has been hard, but it's gotten easier since we got Zozo; he opens doors, he buttons my shirts, he even wipes my ass for me," Eiten said with a chuckle. A Finger in the clan had given Hilo the useful lead about a Shotarian organization that trained monkeys to aid the disabled (there were a lot of war veterans in that country), and Hilo had had a Lantern Man make the arrangements.

Eiten bent forward to sip from the soda straw. When he straightened back up, he matched the Pillar's gaze squarely. "When Gont Asch took my arms, you promised me that you would kill him and take his jade—and you did as you said. You told me to stay alive for one year, so I could see the clan's vengeance, and see my child be born, and after a year, if I still wanted to die, you would honor my wishes yourself." The man's voice turned rough but did not waver. "A year has passed and I'm sitting in front of you, Hilo-jen. If I asked you to fulfill your promise to me without question, would you still do it?"

Eiten's wife clutched their sleeping child tight and bent her head, biting her lips. Her husband did not look at her or the baby; his eyes remained on Hilo, who Perceived a strange and poignant insistence in the hum of the man's jade aura. "Yes," Hilo said. "As I promised."

Eiten nodded. His aura relaxed and settled; he looked over at his slumbering daughter and his face softened in obvious adoration. "You were right, Hilo-jen; I have things to live for now and don't wish to die anymore." But it had been important, Hilo understood, for the man to know that the option had been there, that the decision had truly been his, and that the Pillar's word could always be counted on. Eiten looked back at him. "Still, I don't want to spend the rest of my days idle and dependent. I used to be a first-rank Fist of No Peak. I realize that I'm not of any use to you anymore, but if you'll hear me, I've come to ask you for a favor."

"Ask for whatever you need," Hilo said. "I'll happily grant it if I can."

"My father-in-law makes hoji. His distillery is small, but it produces some of the best liquor in the country, and he sells it to upscale stores and restaurants. He wants to expand into a bigger location, but he's getting old and needs a partner to run the company. I realize this would be a small thing to the clan, but I ask for the Weather Man's office to offer patronage for me to take over my wife's family's business. My body may not be whole, but my mind is, and I think I could find satisfaction in growing the company, as a Lantern Man of the clan."

Hilo turned to the man's wife with a smile. "What do you think of this idea, Mrs. Eiten? Does your husband have what it takes to be a world-class hoji maker?"

"We've both helped my father with the distillery for years, and he's always wished we would take it over at some point," said Eiten's wife, speaking quietly but confidently. "But my husband was a Fist, devoted to you and the clan, so of course that came first. I'm grateful he's alive at all—thanks only to you, Kaul-jen—and I feel in my heart that this is our second chance. He would do well at it, and once our daughter is older, I would help too, of course."

"You said you needed a new location," Hilo said, speaking again to Eiten. "The entire lower level of the Double Double is being renovated and expanded. We could make space for your distillery, and there's an ample cellar. Would that do? You'd supply hoji to all the betting houses on Poor Man's Road."

Eiten's eyes widened. "Hilo-jen, that's far more than we could expect…"

"I need someone I trust in that part of the Armpit district," Hilo went on. "There's always the risk that the Mountain will try to take back what we won from them last year. The Horn sees to it that the area is always protected, but I'd feel better if I had a trustworthy Green Bone inside the premises, keeping his eyes open and one ear to the ground. Could you make your fine hoji and still serve the clan, Eiten-jen?"

Eiten swallowed thickly and nodded. "The clan is my blood, and the Pillar is its master. Thank you, Hilo-jen. I will always be one of your warriors, in any way you ask of me."

Hilo grinned and stood up; the others stood with him. The motion woke the baby, who rooted for her mother's breast and began wailing at a piercing volume that made Hilo wince, then laugh. "Go on; you need to feed your little demon. We can sort out the details later."

"Gather your father-in-law's past five years of financial records and send them to the Weather Man's office along with the details of the patronage request," Shae said. "Then we can move it along quicker."

Eiten and his wife reiterated their gratitude. The brown monkey drank the last bit of peach soda in its master's bottle and scampered close behind his heels as the family departed.

Seeing Eiten doing as well as could reasonably be hoped for, and being able to fulfill his request, improved Hilo's mood considerably. The next two meetings were straightforward. The minor Black Tail clan had sent a representative to deliver condolences in the form of money and flowers, and to express Black Tail's unwavering and continued friendship. ("He's likely heading over to Ayt Mada right now to say the exact same thing," Shae said after the man left.) Then came a business associate of their grandfather's, wanting to write a hagiographic biography of the Torch of Kekon, with the Pillar's permission and the clan's final approval, of course. Hilo was pleased with their progress and looking at his watch when Mrs. Teije was shown into the room.

Immediately, he had a feeling that he would not enjoy this conversation. Behind him, he felt a subtle shift in Shae's aura that suggested she felt the same way. "Aunt Teije," Hilo said, kissing the woman on one dry cheek, "it's been such a long time." *Not nearly long enough,* he thought, glad that the woman wore no jade and couldn't Perceive any of his true sentiments.

"Auntie," Shae said, also faking a warm welcome. Mrs. Teije was sixty years old and the wife of their father's cousin. Kaul Sen had had only one older sister who survived until adulthood; she married a man named Teije Jan and had four children by him. The Teijes were related to the Kauls and outnumbered them; this fact alone should have made them one of the most powerful families on Kekon, but no Teije had ever achieved anything noteworthy or held a position of real leadership in the clan. Only a handful of them had graduated from the Academy as Green Bones; to Hilo's recollection, two had made it as far as being junior Fists. The rest of the Teijes were an assortment of minor Lantern Men and jadeless civilians—some with an education and respectable jobs, some not, almost all of them having advanced further than they might otherwise have on account of their connection to the name Kaul.

"The gods play favorites," Hilo's grandfather had once said at the dinner table. "They took from one side of our family to give to the other. So be kind to your cousins; if the Teijes had more brains or thicker blood, who knows where we'd be?"

Mrs. Teije was a plump woman with short, coarse hair and a tight-lipped expression that suggested she was constantly trying to swallow something unpleasant in her mouth. In a wheezy voice, she said, "Kaul-jen, Kaul-jen, may the gods shine favor on you. You are my only hope," and sank into one of the chairs, dabbing at her eyes with a crumpled tissue.

"What's the matter, Auntie?" Hilo asked.

"It's my good-for-nothing son, Runo," Mrs. Teije said. "He's gotten himself into some trouble in the Uwiwa Islands. Only the gods know what he was doing in that sinful place to begin with, but because of some terrible mistake, he was arrested and thrown into prison."

Hilo suppressed a sigh and composed his face into a reassuring expression. "Aunt Teije, no wonder you're so upset, but if it's a mistake as you say, I'm sure it can be resolved, and we can pay to have Runo released. How much is the bail amount?"

"Ah," said the woman, looking embarrassed, "the bail has already been paid and he was released two weeks ago." When Hilo looked confused, she continued in a rush, "We didn't pay it; our family was collecting the money, but before we could do so, we heard that the bail had been posted by a wealthy stranger and Runo released to his custody."

"Who's the stranger?" Hilo asked.

"His name is Zapunyo," said Mrs. Teije. "They say he is a bad man, a smuggler. A *jade* smuggler." She looked as if she would spit, if she wasn't in the Kauls' nicely carpeted study. "My son is being kept as a 'guest' of this man, who will not release him. We have tried to negotiate, to offer money, but this Zapunyo says he will only talk to the Pillar of the clan."

Aunt Teije left her chair and knelt in front of Hilo, grasping him by the hands. "Please, Kaul-jen, you must get Runo back. He has a troublesome, wayward heart, but he is a good boy. My husband refused to come to you—curse his stubbornness! 'If we ask the Kauls to help us with our own matters, they'll always look down on us,' he says, but I don't care. I know that you're as big-hearted and caring as your grandfather—let the gods recognize him."

Hilo winced inwardly at the comparison but patted the woman's clutching hand. He did not look at Shae, but he could feel her aura prickling warily as she watched the exchange. He considered Mrs. Teije's plaintive face for a long minute before making up his mind. "Don't worry, Auntie. I'll do whatever I can to make sure Runo is freed and returned to you. What would the No Peak clan be without the Teije family? I'll go to the Uwiwa Islands myself to speak to Zapunyo."

Mrs. Teije let out a sob and touched her clasped hands to her forehead over and over. Hilo raised her to her feet and showed her out, rubbing her bowed back with his hand. Then he closed the door and turned around to face his sister, who had not moved from her spot in the chair near his. Shae didn't look pleased. "You shouldn't have raised her hopes like that."

Hilo dropped into a seat across from her and slid down low into it, legs outstretched. "What was I supposed to do? Send her away thinking we'd let that Uwiwan crook take her son without consequence? He's a member of the family after all, a Green Bone."

Shae squinted. "You're not seriously going to risk your own life for Teije Runo." Runo had been three years ahead of Hilo and Shae at the Academy; he'd been good at singing, relayball, maintaining a revolving list of girlfriends, and not much else. He'd graduated with a single jade stone and earned another during his two years as a Finger before deciding to travel and see the world while seeking his fortune. According to clan gossip, as a Green Bone for hire, Teije had guarded mining and oil-drilling projects in war-torn parts of the world and spent time as a personal bodyguard to some rich oligarch in Marcucuo. Hilo had not seen the man for years and had no desire to; he had no respect for any person who used his jade abilities for personal gain and gave nothing back to the clan to whom he owed his green.

"I couldn't care less about Runo myself," Hilo said, "but you know this isn't about him at all. Clan war has been good for the jade smuggling business, and that scavenger Zapunyo has gotten fat and bold in the past couple of years. With the news out of Shotar these days, he's got even more reason to think the black market's going up." A separatist conflict had broken out in Shotar between the country's government and a pro-Ygutanian insurgency in the easternmost province of Oortoko. The major world powers were likely to get involved and escalate the armed crisis—which meant greater demand for jade, from both legitimate and illegitimate military forces around the world.

"Hilo," Shae said seriously, "Zapunyo is trying to force a meeting under his terms, in his country, where he has the corrupt government and the police on his payroll. You'd be walking into certain danger if you went there. It's not worth it, not for the sake of that useless ass Teije Runo."

"But he's *our* family's useless ass," Hilo said, standing and stretching. A muscle in his shoulder twinged, and he rolled it out with a grimace. The outward marks of the vicious beating he'd taken at the hands of Gont Asch and his men more than a year ago had long since faded, but his body still insisted on offering unwelcome reminders. "How does it look, to have an Uwiwan holding a Kekonese Green Bone hostage, one of our own blood relations? Zapunyo knows we won't stand for it. This is his way of getting my attention."

"Send Kehn or Tar to deal with him."

Hilo shook his head. It was the Weather Man's job to counsel the Pillar with a shrewd and logical weighing of costs and benefits, so Shae was only doing her job in advising caution, but she had never been on the military side of the clan and so there were things she didn't appreciate. Hilo had not established his personal reputation by remaining behind and sending others to handle important matters; he was not about to lapse now, not when he was relying on his notoriety as the former Horn to carry him as a wartime Pillar. "I need to talk to Zapunyo myself," Hilo insisted. "A misunderstanding between friends is okay. A misunderstanding between enemies isn't."

Shae seemed about to argue further, but at that moment, Tar knocked on the door and opened it just far enough to stick his head through and say, "It's getting dark, and this thing in the courtyard's wrapping up. What do you think, Hilo-jen? You still want to talk to Anden?"

A change came over Hilo; his mouth turned down and his shoulders stiffened, as if a weight had fallen onto them. "I'll talk to him," he said quietly. He looked at Shae. "Alone."

Tar departed. Shae got to her feet. "I'm the one who convinced you to speak to Anden in the first place. You wouldn't listen to me for months, wouldn't even say his name, and now you want me out of the room." She fixed her brother with an indignant and suspicious glare. "You're going to try to threaten or cajole him back into the clan, back into wearing jade. I know you, Hilo."

"I want to talk to him alone, Shae." Hilo's voice was hard now. "What happened that day was between us. We should have the chance to talk about it properly."

The Weather Man regarded him for a long moment, her aura bristling. Then she walked past him to the door, exited wordlessly, and left the Pillar alone in his brother's empty study.

CHAPTER

3

Exile

Emery Anden sat on the bench under the cherry tree in the courtyard of the Kaul estate, nursing a bottle of lime soda and avoiding
eye contact with the other funeral reception guests. The long tables
laden with food were adorned with garlands of white heart blossom
flowers, and a harpist installed in the garden strummed melodiously
sentimental and uplifting music. The courtyard was crowded, but
the ongoing murmur of conversation remained respectfully muted.
The only thing that marred the tasteful event was the temporary
blue plastic fencing on one side of the courtyard that cordoned off
the construction site where the Weather Man's residence was being
stripped down to its frame and renovated.

Anden could not claim to have been close to Kaul Sen, but the
man had been his adopted grandfather and had given him everything: made him a part of the Kaul family and sent him to be educated at Kaul Dushuron Academy in the same manner as the Torch's

own grandchildren. Ever since he was a child, Anden had assumed he would one day repay the patriarch by becoming a first-rank Green Bone of the No Peak clan. Now Grandda was dead, and Anden's debt to him would remain unpaid.

The late-afternoon shadows thickened and the crowd thinned and still Anden waited. He got up to get another soda from the beverage table and was aware of all the shoulders and chins that turned, all the interested and unkind eyes that followed him. Most of the upper echelon of No Peak was here. They knew who Anden was and what he had done last year: helped to save the clan from destruction, then on the day of his graduation, refused to wear jade and been publicly disowned by the Pillar.

With a jolt, he recognized a few of his classmates from the Academy—Lott, Heike, and Ton—standing together near their families. They were speaking to each other and casting glances in his direction. An echo of old feeling, numb with disuse, stirred in Anden's chest. Lott Jin was leaning casually against a table. He had not lost his slouchy, restlessly idle manner, but he appeared to have been working out over the past year; his shoulders were broader, filling out his gray suit jacket, and he'd cut his hair so that it no longer hung in front of his hooded eyes.

Anden averted his gaze, heat climbing into his face. There were times now, after living in Marenia for over a year, that he enjoyed his day-to-day life and could push away the memory of his disgrace. Being back in Janloon, in this house and among the clan again, dragged him back to the days and weeks after his exile and reminded him of everything he'd given up.

Anden returned to his seat on the bench by the tree. To his horror, Ton crossed the courtyard. Lott and Heike stayed behind, watching but not approaching. "Anden," Ton said, touching his forehead in informal greeting. He cleared his throat. "It's been a while. I'm glad to see you looking well."

Anden reluctantly raised his eyes to his former classmate's face. "It's good to see you, Ton-jen," he said. Ton nodded and fiddled with the two jade rings on his left hand in nervous habit. He was a Finger in the clan now, answering to the Horn and his Fists, patrolling and defending No Peak territory, maintaining the clan's tenuous advantage over the Mountain. Ton looked as if he was fishing for something else to say to break the awkwardness, but Maik Tar appeared and bent to speak quietly to Anden. "He's ready to see you."

Anden got up, set his empty soda bottle on the bench, and followed the Pillarman into the house. At the entrance to the study, he paused, wanting another second to prepare himself, but Tar pushed the door open and Anden had no choice but to step inside. Tar closed the door behind him, shutting out the background sounds of the people still mingling outside.

The Pillar was sitting in the largest of the leather armchairs. Kaul Hilo seemed both the same and different from the last time Anden had seen him. He still possessed a youthful appearance, still exuded the casually insolent charisma that Anden had seen manifest as generous warmth with his friends and fearsome menace with his enemies. But the mantle of Pillar left no man unchanged; there was a stiffness to Hilo's eyes and mouth now, a grimmer, more controlled aspect to his manner that Anden had seen little evidence of before.

Anden looked for Shae, but she was not in the room. She was the only member of the clan that Anden had been in regular contact with over the past year. He'd hoped that she would be here. Anden swallowed. He brought his clasped hands up to his forehead and tilted into a formal salute. "Kaul-jen," he said. "I'm sorry for the loss of your grandfather."

There was a time not long ago when Hilo would've risen and embraced his cousin warmly, kissed him on the cheek, and smiling, led him to the nearest chair. "Andy," Hilo would've scolded, "don't act like that; take the pole out of your ass and come sit down."

The Pillar did not do that. He remained seated and said, with cool remonstration, "He was your grandfather too, Andy, in every way but blood. He brought you into this family."

"I haven't forgotten that," Anden said quietly.

"Haven't you?" Hilo sat forward and picked up the package of Espenian-branded cigarettes lying on the coffee table. He tapped one out for himself and put it in his mouth, then to Anden's surprise, held the box out to his cousin. Anden sat down and took a cigarette without meeting the Pillar's eye. Hilo lit his smoke, slid the lighter across the table to Anden, then leaned back in his chair again. "What have you been doing with yourself, Andy?" His voice was soft and reproachful. "Shae tells me you're living in Marenia. A nineteen-year-old man trained as a Green Bone, living in a village with jadeless fishermen and seniors."

Anden hid the flush of his face by looking down as he lit his cigarette. "I have a job there," he answered. "It's steady work and I can support myself. In another month, I'll have saved up enough money to rent my own place so I won't be a burden on your ma anymore."

Hilo's eyes blazed with sudden ire. "And what about the guards set to watch over you? Will your salary from working in the furniture shop cover the expense of them as well?"

Anden flinched at Hilo's tone. "Kaul-jen, the clan shouldn't make any special allowance for me. You need every Green Bone you have in the war against the Mountain. No one's come after me in Marenia, and if they do, it's only right that I bear that risk myself."

"Don't be stupid," Hilo said. "You killed Gont Asch; you turned the war last year. You think Ayt Mada will ever forget that?" Hilo sat forward again. "She knows you could become one of the most powerful Green Bones in the country."

Anden muttered, "Not if I never wear jade again. It would be against aisho to—"

"Ayt will find a way around aisho if she wants to. She doesn't need to send Green Bones with moon blades against one jadeless man in a fishing village. She hasn't whispered your name because there's no gain in it for her right now. Who knows, maybe she thinks that if she waits awhile, she can turn you."

Anden's head shot up. "I would never turn to the Mountain, not if my life depended on it. I may not be a Green Bone, but I wouldn't betray the clan to our enemies."

"Did you say that to the man who approached you last month?"

Anden did not reply, but the hand that held the cigarette shook a little. A stranger, a bald man, had come up to him in the supermarket and said, with a confidential smile, "I admire what you did, refusing to put on jade and become one of those Green Bone killers. You're obviously a young man with integrity. Even in this small town, people know who you are. If you ever need help finding a job or a place to stay, or could use a favor from a friend, you should feel free to call me." The man had handed Anden a business card with a phone number.

"Shae looked into it. He has ties to the Mountain," Hilo said. "They're being patient, but sometime soon, they'll make sure you have some unexpected trouble, and maybe you'll call the number on the card. And if you don't, you'll have some worse trouble down the line."

Anden took a quick drag on his cigarette and ground it out. He saw now why he'd been asked here at last: The Pillar might not have forgiven him, but neither did he want a member of his family, disowned or not, to be left vulnerable and potentially manipulated by the enemy.

"Andy," Hilo said, and though his voice was still hard, there was a pained edge to it that made Anden finally meet his cousin's eyes. The Pillar's mouth twisted as he ground out his own cigarette. "You're my brother; if you'd come to your senses, if you'd asked to return at any time this past year, if you'd spoken to me and admitted you made a mistake— the way I admitted I was at fault too—I would've forgiven you at once. I'd have welcomed you back; how could I not? But you never did that. You stayed away from the family and wasted a year of your life."

"You said you never wanted to see me again," Anden mumbled.

"Who doesn't ever say the wrong things when they're angry?" Hilo snapped. "You humiliated yourself that day, humiliated the clan, and insulted me in doing it."

Anger and resentment rose and dispelled Anden's guilt. "Would you have welcomed me back even if I refused to wear jade? Or am I only worth anything to you as a Green Bone?"

"You were meant to be a Green Bone," Hilo said. "You're fooling yourself if you think otherwise. Shae took off her jade and went away; she tried to pretend to be someone else and look what happened. If she hadn't done that, maybe everything would be different. Maybe it would still be Lan sitting in this room instead of me. Refusing to wear jade, you're like a goose that won't go near water." Hilo blew out a harsh sigh. "Don't try to tell me that you don't think about it."

He did; of course he did. The memory of jade, of the power it had given him, the ecstatic terror of that last battle when he'd killed one of the most powerful Green Bones in Janloon—sometimes it stirred in him a longing that was almost sexual in its intensity, in its sheer animal hunger. Anden's eyes dropped involuntarily to the top of Hilo's shirt, the first two buttons left undone as usual. Looking at the long line of jade stones studding his cousin's collarbone, Anden felt conflicting fear and yearning pull his insides taut. He still wanted to be a Kaul.

Yet stronger than the craving loomed the specter of madness and a life lived in constant terror of himself. Whenever he contemplated the idea of putting on jade again, black memories forced themselves into his mind: his mother's screams of insanity before her death from the Itches; Lan on the last day Anden had seen him alive—worn down, volatile, and weakened from carrying too much jade and drugging himself with shine; and Anden himself, after the battle with Gont, waking up in the hospital parched and feverish, half-mad with a thirst for jade and killing.

He shook his head. "I won't do it, Hilo-jen. Jade will turn me into a monster. I'm still grateful to the family and loyal to the clan; I'll do anything you ask of me—except wear green."

Hilo did not reply at first. Anden did not dare to say anything more, and the silence stretched between them. When the Pillar spoke again, his voice was resigned, devoid of the anger that Anden realized had been a sign of how much he'd wished for a different outcome between them, how dearly he'd hoped it would not come down to what he was about to say. "I'm sending you to Espenia. Shae's made all of the arrangements. You'll leave next week."

Anden stared, not believing it at first. "Espenia?"

"You're no use to me here if you won't be a Green Bone. You can't stay in Marenia; I won't have you guarded day and night so you can carve rocking chairs and pick seashells on the beach while the Mountain decides when to make a move. If you won't wear jade, you'll need to do something else with your life. You'll go to Espenia and get an education there."

"I've never been to Espenia," Anden protested.

"You're half-Espenian. You should learn about that country, learn the language," Hilo said. Anden was so astonished he couldn't speak at first. Hilo had never pointed out his foreign side, never suggested that Andy was not truly Kekonese and a full member of the Kaul family.

This sudden change, perhaps more than anything else, was so hurtful that Anden lost the rest of his composure. "You want to be rid of me," he choked out. "You're exiling me."

"Godsdamnit, Andy," Hilo snarled, "for the last time: Will you kneel and take your oaths again to me as Pillar, then put on your jade and be a Green Bone, a part of this family?"

Anden clutched the arms of the chair, his jaw so tight he could feel the pressure in his eye sockets. If he opened his mouth, he wasn't sure what would come out of it, so he didn't let himself speak. Hilo stood up. He walked over to the side of Anden's chair and stood over him, his spine tense and his shoulders angled slightly forward, as if he wanted to reach down and grab his cousin, to embrace him or hurt him. Anden felt tears pricking the backs of his eyes. "Please, Hilo-jen," he whispered. "Don't send me there. I hate those people and that country."

"You might like it when you get there," Hilo said. "You won't be all alone; the clan has connections, and they'll take care of you while you're away from home. After a couple of years, you'll have options, and we'll talk about them then."

He supposed he could refuse. He could disobey Hilo a second time, insist on staying in Marenia. Even if a dull, routine life was all he could hope for there, at least he would be on Kekon and not in some foreign country. But he was certain that Shae could not help him further if he did that. He would truly be out of the family. Kekon was ruled by the clans; as a pariah, his future prospects were slim. With Hilo standing so close to him, he could sense the edges of his cousin's jade aura, could Perceive the reluctant determination behind his words. Hilo had made his decision. He was the Pillar and, with the death of Kaul Sen, the indisputable final word in the Kaul family.

Anden got up and touched his clasped hands to his forehead in salute. "Whatever you say, Kaul-jen." His voice was dull. He didn't dare to look at Hilo again as he turned and left the study.

In a daze, he walked down the hall and saw Shae sitting on the steps of the main staircase in the foyer. She looked strange sitting there by herself in the near dark, still in her business clothes, hands around her knees. She stood up when she saw him. Out in the lamplit courtyard, workers were bringing the leftover food into the kitchen and taking down the tables. They could hear cars departing from the driveway. "Anden," she started.

"You said you would talk to him," Anden blurted in accusation. "You said you'd find a way for me to come back home. But it was your idea to send me to Espenia, wasn't it?"

Shae blew out a breath. "It's what we decided was best. You'll be safer there, you'll gain some experience and skills. Espenia is our largest military ally and trading partner; it'll be an advantage in the long run for you to have spent time living and studying there. Afterward, when it makes sense for you to come back—"

"Did you think about what *I* want?" He was certain now that Hilo wouldn't have done this to him without the Weather Man's urging. "Maybe going away was something *you* wanted to do, but I don't *want* to leave Kekon. I don't care about Espenia or an Espenian education. I was never much good at studying anyway, only—" *Only jade.* He'd been a prodigy when it came to the jade disciplines.

Shae reached out and laid a hand on his arm. "You're still young. You don't know what else there is yet."

Anden jerked away. "I wish I'd died that day in the fight with Gont."

Shae dropped her hand. "Don't say that." Her reply was sharp, but Anden didn't care that he'd upset her. He spun and left the house. He heard his cousin take two steps after him before she stopped and let him go.

CHAPTER

4

Dead Ends

Well, that is very bad fucking news," said Maik Kehn.

The manager of the Heaven Awaiting Cemetery lost the color in his face. His throat bobbed in a fearful swallow. "Maik-jen, we will, of course, arrange for reburial in a steel casket. The remains appear undisturbed; only the—"

"They weren't after the body," Maik grumbled. "They got what they wanted." It was not the murdered groundskeeper that had raised suspicions, but the black garbage bag found near him, containing two heavily soiled cemetery staff uniform shirts and hats. That had motivated an examination of the last grave the groundskeeper had dug—Kaul Seningtun's—and led to the discovery of the loosely repacked dirt wall and Kaul Lan's damaged casket behind it.

"Double the number of guards you have," Maik told the manager, "and tell no one of this. Understand?" The man nodded vigorously. The Horn felt no need to threaten him further; the cemetery would certainly not want word to get out that it had been infiltrated by grave robbers on account of a bribed staff member. Already the manager was tugging anxiously on his earlobe, perhaps to ward off bad luck, perhaps contemplating cutting off the ear entirely and sending it to Kaul Hilo to forestall the Pillar's reaction. Kehn made a mental note to himself to increase the clan's own security in Widow's Park. Then he made two phone calls.

The first was to his girlfriend to let her know that he couldn't see her today, as he would be occupied with clan business. Lina took the news with aplomb. She was a kind and practical woman, beautiful in a simple way, robust and curvy in just the way Kehn liked, and most importantly, she was not a Green Bone. Being the Horn of No Peak consumed most of Kehn's waking hours; he didn't need jade in his bedroom as well. He'd seen how Tar's relationships flamed out. Kehn had met his girlfriend through his sister, Wen. Lina was a teacher at Janloon City College and came from a large family; she had her own life and career and friends, and little nieces and nephews to keep her busy, so she wouldn't be overly resentful that the Horn's first priority was always the clan.

"Will you still be able to come to my grandma's eightieth birthday party on Fifthday?" Lina asked him over the phone. "My parents would be delighted if the Horn made an appearance."

Sometimes it amused Kehn that people now invited him to all sorts of events and considered his presence a sign of clan favor and prestige. As a child, he'd rarely been invited to anything, as no one wished to associate with the disreputable Maik name. The Maik family's rise was something of a fairy tale within No Peak, spawning admiration and jealousy and an increasing number of social obligations. "Maybe," he said noncommittally.

Kehn's second call was to his brother.

Tar swore long and vociferously and then said, "We'd better tell him together."

Kehn agreed; he was already thinking about how best to break the bad news to his boss. Hilo-jen expected to be told important things right away, but he also didn't like to be informed of problems without hearing what was being done to solve them. Otherwise, he might step in and handle it himself. Although Kehn appreciated the Pillar's continued involvement in the military side of the clan, it would be impossible to command as Horn if his own Fists kept going straight to Hilo-jen the way they used to. Over the past year, Kehn had begun making more of an effort, where possible, to keep the Pillar from the Horn's job.

So later that afternoon, he started the conversation off on a positive note. "I finished assigning the new Fingers we got out of the Academy this year," Kehn said. "Put most of them in the Docks and the Armpit, where the Mountain's more likely to try something. Also Junko and the Forge, where we're seeing trouble with smuggling and shine dealing. Handed out promotions too—about half of the big Academy class we took in last year went up to third or second rank."

Hilo nodded and asked for details, but didn't crack a smile. The Pillar had been morose ever since Kaul Sen's funeral. Perhaps the old man's passing bothered him more than he let on. Or maybe Kehn's mention of the Academy graduates reminded the Pillar of his kid cousin Anden, whom he'd had to send away.

After they'd discussed business a while longer, Kehn and Tar shared a glance. Tar motioned for the waiter to refill their water glasses. Hilo ate the last crispy squid ball on the plate, then looked impatiently between the Maik brothers. "Stop acting like nervous schoolgirls and get around to it, then. What haven't you told me?"

Kehn explained that the Kaul family gravesite had been robbed. He could usually keep calm and say things matter-of-factly even in bad situations, so it was better that he did the talking instead of Tar, even if the matter would likely fall to his brother to deal with in the end. As Kehn spoke, Hilo grew unnervingly still and quiet. The three of them were in a private booth in the Twice Lucky restaurant during the middle of a Firstday afternoon, so there was no one around to overhear, but Kehn could not help casting a glance around, in case there were other Green Bones in the dining room who might Perceive the Pillar's jade aura flaring like a grease fire.

"I've posted people around Widow's Park," Kehn said. "We're talking to anyone who knew the dead groundskeeper and getting the word out to our informers—not giving them details, but we'll have them watching. Maybe someone in the Mountain is trying to lay claim to Lan-jen's jade."

"I can't believe it was the Mountain," Tar put in. "What kind of Green Bone would stoop so low? Or be so shoddy as to leave a body and discarded disguises almost in plain sight?" He palmed a few of the roasted nuts from the dish in the center of the table. "If the Mountain wants to start something with us again, there are a thousand other ways for them to do it. Ayt's a cunning bitch, and who knows about Nau, but they wouldn't touch a dead man's jade."

The Pillar still hadn't uttered a word or moved. Kehn said, "Whoever the thieves are, if they try to move that amount of jade on the black market, we'll know about it."

Hilo spoke at last. His voice was chillingly soft at first. "The only people who knew that Lan was buried with his green have the names of Kaul or Maik. Except for the *dogfucking piece of shit* who ambushed and killed him. Some hired goon, some *nobody.*" The Pillar's voice rose to a shout and his hand came down hard on the table, making the plates jump. His aura churned so violently that both of the Maik brothers had to resist the urge to edge back from the table. "We thought he was long gone from the city or that the Mountain already killed him, but he's still alive. And *he has Lan's jade.*"

The Maiks were silent. Tar would not look the Pillar in the eye. A year ago, Hilo had tasked the Pillarman with locating the remaining owner of the machine gun left at the scene of Lan's murder. Tar had accomplished nearly all the other things Hilo had set him to, mercilessly rooting out dozens of the Mountain's informers and jade-wearing criminals from No Peak's territories—but that particular bit of clan justice remained undelivered.

"The Mountain may not have been behind this." Hilo pinned his brothers-in-law with his stare. "But they sent assassins after Lan and *someone* in that clan knows who the thief is. It doesn't matter who you have to go through—*find the fucker.* And tell me once you do."

––––––––

Maik Tar rededicated himself to the task the Pillar had given him. There had been two Fullerton machine guns and the body of one teenager discovered at the pier on the night of Lan's murder. Some months ago, after considerable legwork, Tar had identified the dead young man as a member of a robbery ring based in the Docks and run by a Mountain informer named Mudt Jindonon. There was a good chance the surviving assassin had been part of that same gang. The problem was that Mudt Jin was dead; Tar had already killed him last year.

Someone in the Mountain, however, had provided Mudt Jin with jade, shine, and the information that had enabled him to run his criminal enterprise in No Peak territory. Before he'd died, Mudt had given up a description of an unnamed Green Bone. It might have been any one of several men who'd answered to Gont Asch, none of whom Tar could get to easily now, but given Hilo-jen's renewed insistence, he picked up the trail once more. Hilo had assigned him two more men, so he had four Fingers who reported to him directly, and through his brother, he could call upon No Peak's wider network of spies as well. All of these he brought to bear on his goal.

Initially, Tar had been skeptical about being removed from the Horn's side of the clan, but now he was pleased with his arrangement. Some of his work as Pillarman was routine and administrative, but the rest was sensitive and vital to the clan. Tar was glad he did not have his brother's job, managing hundreds of clan members and never filling Hilo-jen's shoes. This role suited him much better. He didn't have to deal with the layers of clan hierarchy or handle interactions with Lantern Men or the public; he answered only to the Pillar, who trusted him implicitly.

It was no small task, to ambush an enemy Green Bone in his own territory—and to take him alive, no less. Tar planned the operation down to the smallest detail. His target was a junior Fist in the Mountain named Seko, who had an elderly mother who lived in the Commons district. A fake phone call was placed to Seko early on a Fourthday morning, informing him that his mother had collapsed on the sidewalk on her way to the grocer's and been taken to Janloon General Hospital in the Temple District. Seko rushed off at once.

At an intersection on the road between Little Hammer and the Armpit, he was met by an erected construction barricade. Two cars drove up behind his, blocking his escape. Had the man been any less distracted with worry, he might have Perceived the ambushers' approach; as it was, he was entirely taken by surprise. Gunmen in the first car peppered his tires with bullets and blew out his rear windshield. Seko burst from the car with an enraged shout, running for the barricade and vaulting Light to clear it, but Tar had anticipated this and had in place two of No Peak's Green Bones who were most skilled in Deflection. They hurled a combined wave that slammed into Seko in midair and knocked him to the asphalt like a flung doll. The Fist lay stunned, his energy spent in Steeling himself against the impact. He hadn't had the chance to pull his gun from the glove compartment of his car, nor did he have a moon blade on him—only his jade-hilted talon knife. Before he could draw it, Tar's men pinned him with Strength and tore his weapon away. They bound him hand and foot, gagged him, and threw him into the trunk of one of the cars.

Tar was pleased by how smoothly everything had gone. Seizing the man had taken less than five minutes. Kehn's patrols had ensured that the avenue had been cleared, so no property had been damaged and no civilians harmed beyond the minor inconvenience of the road closure. Janlooners were used to occasional incidents of clan violence, but the intense street war last year had sapped their patience to its limit; the Pillar would not want unnecessary disruption to cost No Peak any more public goodwill.

Tar was tempted to stop by a pay phone to call Hilo-jen with the good news but decided that would be premature. He'd wait until he had substantive information to share. Besides, he needed to beat morning rush-hour traffic before it began in earnest; already the streets were filling with bicycle couriers and delivery trucks. Taking smaller roads, he drove deep into the Junko district. He could hear muffled thumps and bangs from the back of the car, but he wasn't worried. The trunk had been thoroughly reinforced with enough steel that even the Strength of a man with twice as much jade as Seko would've only succeeded in denting it. Sure enough, the noises ceased after a short time, leaving only the Perception of the man's panicked heartbeat and the shrill texture of desperation emanating from the compartment.

They took their prisoner to an old nightclub that had originally been built as an air-raid shelter fifty years ago but had stood empty for the past several months; it was scheduled to be demolished and replaced with a condo building. Seko's wrists were bound with chains and attached to a rope tied to a ceiling support beam. He hung with his arms pulled over his head, the toes of his combat boots barely resting on the floor. Tar studied the man. Seko wore dark clothes, jade bolts through his ears, and a jade ring in his nose. He had a short, neatly trimmed goatee and an arrogant face; even in his dire situation, his lips twisted in a humorless smirk.

"So you're Maik Tar," said Seko. "Kaul Hilo's hound dog."

The smirk left Seko's face as Tar ripped the jade ring from his nose and the bolts from his ears. The Fist bellowed in pain. Tar motioned for his men to stand by the door, then broke the two smallest ribs on both sides of Seko's body. "If you've heard of me, then you know that's just an introduction."

"Where's my ma?" Seko wheezed, in quite a different voice. "Is she all right?"

"Of course," said Tar. "She's probably getting back from the grocer's now. What do you think we are, animals? In the No Peak clan, we don't break aisho. We don't use jadeless people as our puppets and tools." He spat at Seko's feet. "You were good about never using your name and covering your tracks in No Peak territory, so it took me a while to catch up to you. I've found most of your little rats by now, but you're going to help me find the rest."

"You're going to kill me no matter what I tell you," Seko pointed out.

Tar shrugged. "Sure, but wouldn't you rather die quickly and spare your ma from suffering? You don't want to hang there for days, going through jade withdrawal on top of everything. I'd rather not see it myself. You're not one of those shine addicts you kept on your leash; you're a Green Bone of the Mountain—you've got some self-respect, don't you?"

Seko's head hung between his straining shoulder blades. He nodded.

"Good, now we understand each other, you fucking pussy." Tar rolled the man's jade in the palm of his hand. "Here's the thing, see: The Mountain's never answered for Kaul Lan. Someone gave two assassins information about his habits, handed them Fullerton machine guns, and sent them to the Lilac Divine. I've done a lot of asking around, and I'm figuring that was you."

After a moment, Seko nodded again without raising his head. Tar contained the excitement he felt and said, "They worked for your mole Mudt Jin, didn't they?"

"They were a couple of punks who held up trailer trucks of fancy handbags and wallets and shit," Seko said. "Just two jade-fevered kids. We didn't figure them for anything."

"What were their names?"

"How the fuck should I know?" said Seko. "I don't remember their names."

That was not the answer that Tar wanted to hear. He had a bad feeling that Seko was telling the truth, but he broke another two of the man's ribs and said, "You'd better give me more than that, you goatfucking bastard. Or I'm going to change my mind about letting you meet the gods in one piece." Seko hung limp, breathing shallowly through a slack mouth, twisting slightly on the rope. Tar left him and went outside to give the man some time alone in the dark to search his memory. Sometimes people remembered more after a good long ponder.

Outside, because he hadn't had breakfast yet, he walked down the street to the bakery on the corner and bought a bag of round walnut paste cakes and a carton of sweetened milk. Junko was primarily an industrial district, full of brick and gray concrete, not very attractive, but No Peak was strong here; the businesses had white lanterns hanging over their doors or in their windows, and people on the street dipped in salute when they saw the jade around Tar's fingers and neck. Tar returned to the building and shared the food with Doun and Tyin, two of his Fingers. Traditionally, the Pillarman was an administrative role in the clan and did not command Fists or Fingers, but in a time of war Kaul Hilo had made certain changes to the position. He'd given Tar and his men responsibility for finding and eliminating enemy agents in No Peak territory, and now he called upon the small team for whatever special tasks he needed accomplished that would otherwise be an additional burden on the Horn. To minimize confusion with Kehn's organization, Tar was going to suggest to the Pillar that his people be called something other than Fingers, but he was not sure what yet.

He was tipping the last of the cake crumbs into his palm when his Perception startled with the sudden awareness of something harsh and wrong. Tar tensed, alarmed, scanning in every direction until he realized that what he was sensing was coming from inside the building: a stampeding heartbeat, blinding pain, a blast of terror and triumph. Tar threw open the metal door and was astonished to see Seko jerking and sputtering, blood pouring from his neck down the front of his black shirt. Tar drew his talon knife and cut the rope holding the Fist up; the man collapsed like a sack, his mouth working instinctively for air, but his eyes bright with scorn. Tar bent over him, spitting curses. He could sense the prisoner's life flooding out like tidewater. He tried to stop it by directing his own energy into clotting the man's wound, but Channeling had never been Tar's strongest discipline, and in seconds, Seko was dead. His bloodstained hands, still bound in chains, clutched a small, flat blade.

Too late, Tar understood his mistake. He'd stripped the man of his talon knife and his jade and thought him helpless. In a determined feat of strength and willpower, the Mountain Fist had managed to bring his feet up to his hands and extract the plain blade hidden in one of his combat boots. Then he'd pulled his body up on the chains and cut his own throat.

Tar kicked and stomped on the corpse in a blistering fury. When he calmed down, he could not deny he was impressed. For a warrior who'd lost his jade to still outwit his enemies and die on his own terms—Seko's mother ought to be proud to have a son who was so green.

That did not change the fact that Tar was now, to his great embarrassment and frustration, at a dead end in terms of finding the remaining assassin and the missing jade.

As usual, Kehn was more stoic and levelheaded about the situation. "We just have to wait until he shows up again," he said over the phone. "Sounds like this thief is a reckless kid with an ungodly amount of stolen green. No one with that much jade stays hidden for long."

His brother's common sense made Tar feel better, but only temporarily; the following week, the Mountain stole across the border from Spearpoint and took revenge for Seko in an attack that left one of Kehn's men dead and put Tyin in the hospital for two weeks. Because a storefront was damaged by gunfire and two civilian bystanders injured by wide Deflections, the incident ended up as front-page news. The headline, *No End in Sight to Clan Violence*, was printed above the photograph of the dead No Peak Green Bone in a pool of blood in front of the shattered window of a Jollo Plus Mart.

CHAPTER

5

Every Advantage

There must be some misunderstanding, Kaul-jen," said Mr. Enke. The stocky, gray-haired Lantern Man wore a disgruntled frown, and though he was careful to keep his voice respectful, the glower he fixed on Shae from under his bushy eyebrows was indignant. "My company has been the leading commercial real estate developer in Janloon for over a decade. I've been a Lantern Man of No Peak for twenty-five years and my family has always paid clan tribute. Two of my sons are Green Bones; one is a Fist who followed your brother when he was Horn and now answers directly to Maik Kehn. How could this contract go to a smaller firm, one that has barely any history with the clan and is not even fully Kekonese?"

"The other company's bid promised earlier completion at a lower cost," Shae said from across her desk. "The clan values the loyalty and friendship of our long-standing Lantern Men, but the contract was awarded on the basis of merit."

Mr. Enke made a sputtering sound of disbelief. Slightly behind and to her left and right, Shae could sense Hami Tumashon and Woon Papidonwa shifting uncomfortably at her words. "I'm not sure how you define *merit*, Kaul-jen," said Mr. Enke in a temper now, "but I ask: What is the purpose of the clan if it does not look out for the interests of its most loyal members? Can the friendship of the No Peak clan be so easily broken by unreliable numbers on a piece of paper? Are we not Kekonese anymore, but Espenians, selling ourselves to the lowest bidder?"

"With the Weather Man's permission," said Hami, speaking out of turn but clearly intent on reining in the situation, "perhaps we can reach an accommodation." Shae's lips tightened, but she nodded, and Hami went on. "Mr. Enke, the clan has to look out for the interests of the country as well as its Lantern Men; we can all agree on that point. Smaller firms should be given a chance to succeed, and foreign investment is good for the national economy. That isn't to say that No Peak values you and your family's allegiance any less. In fact, we hope to see your company continue to grow by investing in equipment and personnel. If the Weather Man agrees, we would negotiate a reduction in tribute payments to support you in this."

Hami looked to Shae, who inclined her head stiffly. "That seems reasonable."

Mr. Enke did not look entirely satisfied by this concession, but after a few moments of silent consideration, he grumbled, "Very well. I've trusted in the clan of the Torch—let the gods recognize him— for too long to let this one unfortunate experience get between us." The way he eyed Shae made it clear that he did not trust *her* in the same way. "We'll take advantage of the lower tribute you've extended and do our best to put together a more convincing bid next time."

After Woon closed the door behind the departed Lantern Man, Shae turned to Hami and said, "Why did you speak without my prompting? You offered him too much prematurely."

"You appointed me as Master Luckbringer to speak my mind," said Hami gruffly as he stood and walked to the door. "So I'm speaking my mind now: You mishandled the situation. The Enke family is an old and influential one in the clan. Even if you had good reasons for your decisions, you made them feel disrespected." He paused and spoke over his shoulder. "Right now, Kaul-jen, you need the support of the Lantern Men more than a hundred million dien of cost savings." Hami pushed through the door of Shae's office, letting in a brief wave of noise—ringing telephones and clacking typewriter keys from the cubicles across the hall—before the door closed firmly and the man's proud jade aura receded down the hallway.

Shae slumped back in her seat. Hami was right; her defensive response to Enke and cold talk of merit had struck the wrong note and forced the Master Luckbringer to step in and offer a solution before she did. She'd come across as a naive young woman, overly influenced by her foreign education, not a properly experienced Weather Man of a Green Bone clan. Finances she understood, strategy and politics she was learning, but clan leadership required managing not only the vast scope of No Peak's business concerns but the seemingly irreconcilable interests and expectations of its people. "What was I supposed to do?" Shae demanded aloud, hearing the exasperation in her own voice.

Woon didn't react to her change in tone; they'd worked together closely for too many long, late hours over the past year for her to maintain the same professional demeanor with him as she did with Hami or anyone else in the office tower on Ship Street. The Weather Man's Shadow looked down at his folded hands, then cleared his throat. "I can only say what I think Lan-jen would've done. He would've called Mr. Enke into his office and, out of consideration for his status in the clan, given him a chance to match the lower bid. If the Lantern Man couldn't do so, then he would explain that regretfully he had to give the contract to the other developer, but he'd ask what the clan could offer to help his business become more competitive."

Shae stared gloomily out the rain-splattered windows. She'd spent the past six weeks grieving her grandfather and almost, for a short while, forgotten how much she missed Lan.

Woon leaned forward in his seat, elbows on knees. "The clan is a big, old ship—powerful but difficult to steer, Shae-jen. I know you want to make changes and improvements, but you should do so carefully. In times of uncertainty, people look for reassurance that they can count on things being done in the way they've come to expect. They'll talk about how you wronged the Enke family. They're still talking about how you wronged Kowi Don."

"I won't run the office on cronyism the way Doru did," Shae replied, with some heat. "Kowi Don wasn't qualified to be hired as a Luckbringer just because he's the son of a councilman."

Woon inclined his chin. "You're sitting in that chair because you're a Kaul."

He said it simply, with no rancor at all, but Shae winced at the truth. She was well aware that she still had a long way to go to prove herself on Ship Street. The clan had barely escaped destruction last year, and even though the street war had settled into something of a stalemate, the Mountain was larger and remained in a stronger financial position. No Peak was dominant in some sectors, such as real estate and construction, but the boom in housing and infrastructure development that had occurred in the decades after the Many Nations War had slowed; meanwhile, several of the industries where the Mountain held a greater share, such as manufacturing, retail, and transportation, continued their healthy growth. No Peak had to expand operations more aggressively if it hoped to prevail in the long run, and every action Shae took as Weather Man might improve or worsen the clan's position relative to its enemies. Her voice and shoulders fell. "We need every advantage we can get, no matter how slight," she insisted. "That's driving all my decisions, even if some of them upset people."

"Trust is also an advantage," Woon said.

"You don't believe the clan trusts me?"

"You're extremely hardworking and smart, Shae-jen, anyone can see that," Woon said, with surprising vehemence for someone normally so soft-spoken. "And you're a Kaul. So the clan trusts you on those levels. But Lantern Men are loyal to the clan because of what it can do for them, and lately, you've been shutting doors instead of opening them."

Shae sat silently for long moment. Thick clouds laden with spring rain hung over Janloon; from a distance the sky and the sea were the same indistinguishable shade of flat gray-blue. "I'm grateful I have you, Papi-jen." She meant it. If Lan had not been killed, Woon would've been the one sitting in this office as Weather Man, yet he'd devoted himself tirelessly to being the Weather Man's Shadow, her chief of staff, never expressing bitterness or complaint. Woon was not unusually cunning or clever, he did not have a forceful personality, but like Lan, he seemed made of such a steadfast and dependable fiber that Shae understood why he'd been her brother's longtime friend and aide. She put a hand on his arm. "It's been a long day. Go home; no need to wait for me."

Woon stood, dislodging her hand from his arm, and she Perceived his jade aura pulse with some sudden, stifled emotion. "I have work to do as well," he said. "Take the time you need, Kaul-jen; I'll drive you home as usual afterward." The former Pillarman had left Lan alone on the evening of his murder. He had not gone home early in all his time as her Shadow.

When Woon had gone, Shae went through paperwork at her desk for another couple of hours. Her reflection emerged in the darkening windowpanes as the lights of downtown Janloon came on, transforming the skyscrapers into luminous columns. The phone rang, and she picked up the receiver. "Kaul-jen," said the slightly nasal voice of Ree Turahuo on the other end, "I'm glad I caught you still at the office. I was hoping we might have a frank discussion between Weather Men."

Shae put down the report she'd been reading; the phone cord stretched as she pushed her chair back from the table. "Ree-jen," she said, her voice calm and dispassionate. "What would you like to discuss?"

"Next month, the board of the Kekon Jade Alliance is scheduled to finally reconvene and hold a shareholder vote on whether to recommence national jade mining operations," Ree said. "How do No Peak and its allies among the minor clans intend to vote?"

Shae said, "The Pillar is considering all the factors. He hasn't yet made a decision."

"Come now, Kaul-jen," said Ree, his voice sharpening, "don't play games. We all know that your brother leans on your counsel in all these matters. You're the one making the decision. Do you plan to prolong this needless suspension, or return the country to normal?"

"The mines can begin operations again once all possible measures have been taken to prevent another abuse of power on the part of the Mountain clan," Shae said. "I haven't fully determined to my satisfaction if the Royal Council's reforms are sufficient." She smiled to herself, wishing she could see or Perceive the other Weather Man's reaction. A national scandal had resulted when financial discrepancies she'd discovered in the KJA's records nearly two years ago had revealed that the Mountain had been secretly taking jade above quota behind the backs of the government and the other Green Bone clans. Ayt publicly maintained that negligence and operational issues were to blame, but few people believed that line, even within her own clan. The Royal Council had passed legislation instituting ownership restrictions to prevent the Kekon Jade Alliance from falling under single clan control, mandated annual independent audits, formed an oversight committee, and taken a number of other measures intended to safeguard the country's jade supply and ensure its transparent management. Meanwhile, for the past eighteen months, the mines of Kekon had sat idle. No new jade flowed into the national coffers; official exports had stopped; thousands of Abukei mine workers had gone on government assistance.

Ree said tightly, "If the vote does not go through, the matter will go back to the Royal Council for gods-only-know how long. We'll lose out on the upcoming dry season and this terrible disruption to the country's economy will last another year. Is *that* what you want?"

"I want the Mountain to be held accountable for its transgressions." The longer the mining suspension lasted, the longer the public would be reminded of the Mountain's crimes.

A pause. Ree's voice changed, took on a shrewd quality. "You will eventually run out of jade to sell to the Espenians. How much can you really afford to empty No Peak's stores?" In the momentary silence that followed, Shae could picture Ree's smug expression. "Yes, of course we know you've been selling your own reserves, and that's why the foreigners haven't yet made a bigger stink. I imagine the Royal Council and the people of Kekon would be interested to know that No Peak is bolstering its finances by selling jade directly to the Republic of Espenia."

"I imagine our official allies the Espenians would be interested to know about the Mountain's secret contracts to sell jade to their enemies, the Ygutanians," Shae replied coolly. "Especially if Espenian soldiers are deployed to fight in Shotar against rebels who're trained and supported by Ygutan. They're hardly going to be pleased to see Kekonese jade worn by soldiers on the other side of the battlefield."

"This is pointless sparring, Kaul-jen," Ree snapped. "You may believe that it is to No Peak's advantage to continue dragging out the KJA scandal, but consider our mutual dilemma. The constriction on the jade supply has done nothing but encourage smugglers and raise the rate of violent crime. The people have had enough of bloodshed and economic disruption; they're worried that the crisis in Oortoko will turn into a war between foreign powers and spread through the region. They expect Green Bones to defend Kekon if that happens—do you think they feel confident we're doing that, Kaul-jen?"

Shae did not answer.

"We're not Fists, you and I, who see the world only in black and red," Ree said. "Neither is my Pillar, though I certainly can't speak for yours. Ayt-jen proposes a meeting between our clans. One with all the proper assurances."

CHAPTER

6

The New Green

Bero felt like a new man, like the man he was always meant to be. He no longer had to sleep on the floor of his aunt's apartment; he had his own place now, on the third floor of a ten-story tenement house in the Forge. It wasn't much to look at; his door sagged, the plumbing was old, and the walls were thin. His neighbor, Mrs. Waim, was a cranky old lady who smelled of herbal throat lozenges and banged on his door in complaint whenever he played music or made too much noise. None of that mattered. When Bero woke up each day around noon, he went into the bathroom and gazed into the mirror at the jade hanging around his neck. With his shoulders squared and his head cocked, he turned this way and that, examining his reflection from different angles. He picked up a talon knife and held it poised. He liked what he saw. Strength. Power. Respect.

He tied off his arm with a rubber tourniquet and shot up two doses of SN1 each day, like clockwork, marking them off on a wall calendar. He'd been told by Mudt—not the boy Mudt Kal, but his father, Mudt Jin, now dead—that missing an injection or taking an extra one could mean a fatal overdose. When the shine hit his brain, Bero felt invincible. Some good things did come from foreigners, and shine was one of them. Why spend an entire childhood training at some draconian martial school when there were modern methods? The jade energy humming through Bero's veins was hot and sharp, better than anything else in the world, better than money or sex. The taste he'd experienced two years ago, when he'd gotten his hands on jade for a mere few minutes—that had been nothing. His whole life prior to now had been a dull, colorless, half-conscious dream from which he'd finally awoken. When he walked down the street, he felt as if he glided like a tiger through a herd of cattle.

In the evenings, he went to an underground training club in Coin-wash called the Rat House. It was one of a few hideouts in the city where people with unsanctioned jade congregated to self-train, inject SN1 safely, and show off the green that they could never display in public. Usually, Bero would find Mudt there as well, and the two of them would practice Strength on the concrete blocks or running with Lightness against the brick wall. Their abilities were inconsistent; Bero might leap a straight meter on one day but jump barely higher than normal the next. This frustrated but didn't discourage him. He hadn't expected to be good right away. It was a matter of more jade and more practice before he'd be able to rival Green Bones.

After a couple of hours, Bero would have a drink at the bar, then start to work the dimly lit seating area, selling shine. He had regular customers who bought from him every week, and he made good money so he didn't have to keep any other sort of employment, unlike Mudt, who'd moved in with some distant relatives and lied about his age to get a job as a stocker in a shoe store. Most of the people in the Rat House were men in their early to mid twenties from the low-income parts of inner northeast Janloon—the Docks, the Forge, Coinwash, and Fishtown. Some sported gang tattoos. Others, Bero suspected, were on the wrong side of the law for other reasons besides illegal jade ownership. And a few appeared to be otherwise respectable individuals with day jobs, who for some reason were willing to risk their lives to be green. No one in the Rat House was formally trained, and many were not trained at all; they needed SN1 on a daily basis to maintain the jade tolerance that Green Bones developed after years of effort. It made for a reliable client base.

Bero's untrained sense of Perception seemed to work intermittently. It did not extend very far, but he could usually tell when others in the same room were wearing jade because they seemed to glow in his mind differently. Every once in a while, he would look at someone and pick up flashes of emotion or intent. It didn't take much skill in Perception, however, for him to sense the borderline hostile curiosity directed at him as he went around the club. When he was out in the city, Bero kept his jade hidden under the turned-up collar of his shirt or jacket and stayed as far away as he could from Green Bones who might notice him and ask questions, but here in the Rat House, people saw the amount of jade he wore. They wanted to know how a teenage boy had gotten his hands on so much.

They never asked. The cardinal rule in the Rat House was that no one asked where and how another person had obtained their jade. Stolen, scavenged, bought on the black market, it didn't matter—the one thing everyone here had in common was a death sentence if they were ever caught by Green Bones of the major clans, who were, fortunately, still too busy fighting each other to pay much attention to anyone else. The Rat House was the one place where unsanctioned users could talk freely, test their powers, and boast loudly and drunkenly of overturning those that kept jade in the hands of the elite few.

They called themselves the new green.

For the most part, Bero felt that all was finally right in his world except for the fact that he was bound to run out of shine soon. His initially sizable cache was dwindling as he used it up and sold it. So when a man Bero had seen around the Rat House a few times motioned him over one night and said, "Hey, why don't you and your friend sit and have a drink with me. I've got a business idea for you, one I think you'd like to hear," Bero called Mudt over and pulled up a chair.

The man had a narrow, darkly tanned face, and his hair, with the sides shorn close to the skull and the center teased up with hair gel, made it seem even narrower. He appeared Kekonese but might have been of mixed blood, and he spoke with a foreign accent. He was perhaps thirty years old and he said his name was Soradiyo.

"What is that, some kind of shottie name?" Bero said.

"Some kind of shottie name," Soradiyo agreed, without expression. He gave the boys an evaluative stare. "You're not afraid to be wearing that much jade?"

Bero squinted. The man across from him had a jade aura, that much Bero could tell, but Soradiyo wore his green out of sight. Whoever he was, he didn't want to draw any attention to himself, not even here in the Rat House. "It's my jade, I'm going to wear it," Bero declared. "If the Green Bones get me, they get me. Everyone's got to die someday."

"We've got more jade than some Fists," Mudt added fiercely, his cheeks flushing. "I don't care how long it takes, I'm going to train until I can take on *any* Green Bone."

Fatalistic bravado was typical among the new green, but lately, words like that were spoken less often and in lower voices. Bero had heard that a couple years ago, many frequenters of the Rat House had been informers for the Mountain clan, granted their jade and kept in shine by Green Bones under Gont Asch who wanted to sow agents inside No Peak territory. Since Gont's death, the Mountain had pulled back, and No Peak slaughtered the new green whenever they could find them. The Kauls offered amnesty to any of the Mountain's agents who came forward, surrendered their jade, and provided the names of their accomplices. Many took the offer, figuring it better to lose one's jade and keep one's head than be hunted down by Maik Tar and his men.

Soradiyo raised his glass, giving them a thick-lipped smile that was somehow encouraging and condescending at the same time. "Belief is the first step toward making your dreams come true," he said.

Bero snorted with impatience. For some reason, he felt the urge to impress this man, even though he disliked him. "So what do you want to talk to us about?"

Soradiyo moved his chair out of the way of the drip from an overhead pipe. The Rat House had no windows; the ceiling and walls were water stained, and by two or three o'clock in the morning, the air was thickly clogged with the stench of sweat and cigarette smoke. "I'm a recruiter," said Soradiyo. "I look for people who have two things: jade, and something wrong with the part of the brain that's supposed to make them fear death."

"Way to sell the job," Bero said.

Soradiyo gave a sharp laugh. "I'm asking if you want to be a rockfish." A jade smuggler—the sort that moved gems out of the country. "The pay's in money and shine, and eventually, in green. You'd make more than you ever could selling shine. A lot more."

Bero asked, "You work for someone?"

"I'm a sworn man of Ti Pasuiga. You know what that means?" Soradiyo bared his teeth in a smile at their affirmative silence. The things he had said no longer seemed like exaggeration; association with the largest, most notorious jade trafficking ring could indeed deliver a daring man to fabulous wealth or an undignified death.

Soradiyo rapped misshapen knuckles idly against the tabletop. "Business is good; there's more demand than ever and money to go around. But it's too risky to keep relying on the Abukei." Jade-immune aboriginals who didn't give off an aura and didn't suffer the dramatic and sometimes fatal effects of excessive jade exposure were the natural gem mules in the black market jade trade, but they were easy to identify and subject to suspicion at any border exit. Soradiyo opened his wallet and took out cash to cover their drinks. "Fortunately, these days, with enough shine, anyone can carry jade. You might even pass as Green Bones." He stood up and picked up his jacket. "Think about it. I'll be back here the same time next Fourthday, and you can tell me whether you want to get out of this shithole and play with the big dogs."

After Soradiyo left, Mudt wiped his nose on the sleeve of his shoulder and said, "We don't need that barukan asshole. We've got everything we need already. We got this jade ourselves." He tapped the jade cuffs he wore cinched on his upper arms. "We can train here until we're good enough to take on anyone. Good enough to take on the Maiks."

"You talk too much," Bero snapped, and got up to get another drink. He passed a table of people drawing knives across their forearms, practicing Steel. One of them cursed in pain and fell off his chair when the blade bit into flesh.

The problem with Mudt, Bero thought, was that he had too many opinions; he didn't know when to shut up. The kid wouldn't even *have* any jade or shine if it wasn't for Bero. Bero had planned the night at the cemetery. He'd *killed* for his jade. Twice. Mudt hadn't done that. At the end of the day, he was a hanger-on, not truly deserving of green.

CHAPTER

7

The Weather Man's Persuasion

Jan Royal University, situated on the western edge of Janloon, is the oldest academic institution on Kekon, having withstood periods of war and occupation over the span of its distinguished three-hundred-year history. Some of the weathered stone buildings that Shae walked past dated all the way back to the unification of the island at the end of the Warring Sisters period. Others, like the Foreign Studies Department building, were gleaming modern structures of steel and glass and concrete. Shae entered through the double doors and slipped into the back of the lecture hall, taking an empty seat in the last row. The class was already in progress; Maro was writing on the blackboard and did not see her come in, but when he turned back around to face the class, his eyes found her and a small smile tugged briefly at his mouth before he addressed the students paying attention to him. "Last week, we discussed the aftermath of the Many Nations War and how the economic and political collapse of the Tun

Empire, followed by decades of civil conflict and reform, allowed Ygutan to fill the power vacuum left on the Orius continent. We'll be shifting our focus for the rest of this term to the postwar policies of the Republic of Espenia with regards to Shotar and Kekon, and how that is directly related to current events."

Shae was interested in the lecture, and Tau Maro was an engaging speaker—organized, knowledgeable, and enthusiastic about the material—but Shae could not keep her mind from returning to the prior day's phone conversation with Ree Tura. She was surprised when the hour was over, and disappointed that she'd been unable to pay better attention. Maro wrote a closing question on the blackboard. "Your assignment this week is to write three pages on the following topic: How does the recent ratification of the Pact of Friendship and Mutual Noninterference between Tun and Ygutan affect Kekon?"

When the students had gathered their belongings and dispersed from the lecture hall, Shae rose from her seat and walked to the front of the room. "I hope you didn't mind me coming early to watch," she said. "You're a very good teacher."

Maro finished erasing the blackboard, then glanced around at the empty seats before leaning in to plant a kiss on the corner of Shae's mouth. His short beard tickled her cheek, and she caught a whiff of aftershave mingled with the scent of the chalk dusting the lapels and shoulders of the brown suede jacket he wore over a white shirt. "I don't mind at all," he said. "You look nice. Where are we going for dinner?"

Spring rains had washed the campus sidewalks clean and made the wide lawns green and lush. Students on bicycles streamed past them as they left the university grounds. Shae did not have a car and driver waiting; she'd taken a taxi straight from the office on Ship Street, pausing only to refresh her makeup and exchange her blazer for a sequined red shawl. She began to hail another cab, but Maro said, "At this time on a Fifthday, it'll be faster to take the subway. You don't mind, do you?" She assured him she did not.

Standing on the subway platform, talking casually about the lecture, the university campus, and the recent weather, Shae felt some of the tension from her work week slowly unknotting. She rested her eyes on Maro, on his reassuringly unhurried demeanor as he allowed the first, overly crowded train to pass and waited for the next. Maro's short beard made him look older and more serious than he truly was, but he had a soft mouth and watchful eyes, and large, handsome hands. He was the most pleasant surprise that had happened to Shae all year. She had not been looking for a relationship. Sometimes she thought about Jerald with nostalgia and wished for companionship, but she had little room for any sort of social life outside of No Peak responsibilities. With her grandfather's death and funeral, and recent demands at the Weather Man's office, she hadn't seen Maro in over a month. "I'm sorry that it's been so long since we got together," she said.

Maro shook his head. "I know things can't have been easy for you lately. I've been thinking about you but didn't want to intrude, knowing there was already so much public attention on your family." He hesitated, then slipped his hand into hers and gave it a squeeze. "I'm glad you're able to get away tonight."

They went to the Golyaani Kitchen, an upscale dining spot in North Sotto, not far from the apartment where Shae used to live when she'd first moved back to Janloon. She'd been wanting to take Maro there for some time. The waiter showed them to a corner booth where Shae ordered a cocktail and Maro chose a midrange Shotarian whiskey and a glass of water. "So. How *are* you doing these days?" he asked her.

"Better than I was. I miss my grandfather…but he wasn't really himself in the last year of his life. He used to be such a force of nature." Shae stirred her cocktail pensively. "I like to think that he's awaiting the Return in the afterlife with my father and my brother, and they're all much happier and more peaceful now." She paused to take a long sip of her drink, determined not to be melancholy on what ought to be a lighthearted evening. She reached across the table and laid her hand over Maro's large one; his jade aura was like a light blanket, full of interesting wrinkles and pleasant to touch. "How're things at work?"

"The usual," Maro replied, letting her change the subject. "I'm teaching three classes this semester. And I'm still trying to get my foreign studies trips funded. The bureaucracy in academia never ceases to astound me." A sigh of wry resignation. "With events in Shotar being in the news so much, I've also been called to Wisdom Hall a lot lately."

When Shae had first met Maro at a Kaul Dushuron Academy alumni event six months ago, she'd determined immediately that he would be a valuable acquaintance. As Weather Man, she needed to be current in her knowledge of international relations and trade. At age thirty-three, Tau Marosun was one of the youngest faculty members in the Foreign Studies Department at Jan Royal University and a political advisor to the Royal Council. The fact that the accomplished young professor was attractive was a noteworthy but secondary consideration. She asked Maro to sit down with her over dinner a few weeks later, hoping to build a professional relationship and gather additional names from his network of experts in the field. They'd talked for four hours, beginning with his academic areas of expertise but soon ranging into everything from Janloon's restaurant scene, to foreign films, to budget traveling.

Afterward, Maro had shyly asked if he might see her again.

The Golyaani Kitchen served upscale traditional Tuni food alongside a large and varied drink menu, and on a Fifthday evening, the surrounding tables were occupied by the young professionals who populated the North Sotto district. Hanging pot lamps illuminated the stylish brick hearth, black tabletops, and shelves of decorative rustic bottles filled with dried spices. Their meal arrived: smoked liver sausage, spiced eggplant stew over rice, quail baked in a clay pot. Shae was pleased when Maro exclaimed appreciatively over the dishes and complimented her selections. She watched him ladle the eggplant stew onto both of their plates. Maro did everything with a certain subtle deliberation: outlining the topics of his lecture before the beginning of class, pausing before speaking, taking the time to smell whiskey before drinking it. He was completely unlike Jerald. Shae's previous boyfriend had been athletic and exuberant, vigorous in bed, a funny, charming, ultimately shallow and insensitive young Espenian military officer. Maro was intelligent and opinionated, but unpretentious, valuing thoughtful conversation and new experiences. He was also unlike most Green Bone men Shae was accustomed to; he wore two jade studs pierced conservatively through his left ear, but he had never been a Finger in the clan. Indeed, he seemed to have little interest in clan affairs, asking after them only insofar as they were important to Shae and to the extent that they related to national politics and world issues.

"What's the Royal Council been asking you?" Shae asked.

"Exactly the sort of thing I ask my students," Maro said, a touch ironically. "But in far greater detail than a three-page report." Shae recalled the question he'd written on the blackboard at the end of class: *How does the recent ratification of the Pact of Friendship and Mutual Noninterference between Tun and Ygutan affect Kekon?*

"So how would you answer your own essay question?" she asked him.

Maro took a bite of quail, chewing and swallowing before replying. "I would say that Kekon is going to be in an unprecedentedly difficult position. The Tun-Ygutan pact isn't surprising. Tun has too many of its own problems to oppose Ygutan, and the Ygutanians are content to leave their largest border undisturbed so they can concentrate on attaining control of the entire Origas Gulf. That's entirely unacceptable to Shotar and to Espenia. The ROE is bound to commit more military resources to the region, and to Kekon in particular."

Shae nodded. "We'll be caught between the Espenosphere and the Ygut Coalition." Kekon was officially allied with the Republic of Espenia and hosted the largest Espenian naval base in the region on Euman Island. The Kekonese, however, generally did not care for the Espenians more than any other foreigners. They were geographically closer to the continent of Orius than that of Spenius, and they had such a long enmity with Shotar that it was hard to imagine the two countries being on the same side simply because they both had alliances with the ROE. Shae's mind returned to the vexing conversation she'd had with Ree Tura. The world outside of Kekon was exerting forces that derailed even a blood feud between the Green Bone clans.

"It's a politically charged situation," Maro agreed, "but maybe an opportunity as well, for our country to play a bigger role on the world stage." He took a sip of his drink; when he set the glass down, he said, "For most of our history, we've been an insular, tribal, and isolationist island, trusting in jade and Green Bones to keep us safe. But all that's been changing. Jade brought the world to our doorstep, and now we have to take part in that world."

Shae thought about her cousin, now in Espenia. She'd been certain she was doing the right thing, convincing Hilo to send Anden to study abroad. No Peak was in need of more people who had lived and worked outside of Kekon, who understood the rapidly changing world that Maro spoke of. Anden had not believed her, though, had blamed her, even. Shae paused in her meal and settled her gaze on Maro. "I can't help but wonder," she said with a smile, "how someone ends up as a leading professor of foreign studies after graduating from a hidebound Green Bone clan institution like Kaul Du Academy."

Maro grimaced as he leaned in. "I almost didn't," he admitted. "Graduate, that is. I struggled with the jade disciplines and wanted to drop out as a year-five, but that wasn't an option. I'm the only boy in my family." It was an enduring belief among Kekonese that every family of quality had jade in it. An only son would be expected to receive a martial education and wear green. Maro pursed his lips thoughtfully, then finished the whiskey in his glass. "Looking back now, I'm glad I went through the training. I think I'm a stronger person because of it. But at the time, it was hard. Fortunately, my academic grades pulled me through, but I was never really cut out to be a Green Bone. Not like certain people who graduate Rank One." He gave Shae a teasing prod with his elbow. "I remember you from back then. I was a year-four when you came in as a year-one. You don't remember me, do you?"

Shae was embarrassed to admit that she did not. "That's okay, I wouldn't expect you to," Maro said. "I was a bookworm and didn't make much of an impression at the time. Everyone knew who you were, though. You and your brother being in the same class, it was hard to miss you."

"I'm mortified by the idea that you remember me as a ten-year-old."

Maro laughed—a surprisingly rich, pleasant sound. "I'm relieved you don't remember me as an awkward teenager at the bottom of the Academy pecking order, or there's no chance you would be having dinner with me now. I know we haven't known each other all that long, but...I think you're wonderful." Color rose in Maro's face and he briefly turned his attention to straightening his napkin. "You're beautiful and intelligent, forward-thinking, and open-minded. I think it's a great thing that you've become the Weather Man of No Peak. Anyone like me can talk about change, but you can actually make it happen."

Shae did not know how to respond. Maro's words put a flush of warmth in her chest, but she was not sure she deserved his unreserved confidence. The clans were still at war, the KJA suspended, smuggling was on the rise. The Oortokon crisis was drawing in Espenia and Ygutan, and as Maro himself had said, Kekon was bound to be affected by any regional conflict between the major powers. She felt unprepared to handle so many threats to the clan and the country, and already her decisions had made her enemies. "It's not that simple. The clan is a big, old ship that's hard to steer." Shae heard herself repeating Woon's words to her from yesterday. "Even as Weather Man, I'm not sure if I can make enough of a difference."

Maro tilted his chin down, eyebrows raised in a skeptical expression that Shae imagined he used on students who provided a poor explanation for turning in their term papers late. "Your grandfather—let the gods recognize him—helped the country to open up and become prosperous after the Many Nations War. The Green Bone clans might be the most traditional Kekonese cultural institutions, but progress has come out of them before." He took both of Shae's hands in his own and gazed at her with an utmost seriousness that made it hard for her to meet his eyes without her face growing hot. "You were the youngest in your class at the Academy, but you beat out everyone else in the rankings, even your own older brother. I've heard people say that you lead the clan as much as he does now. You were born and trained for your role. Who could possibly make a difference, if not you?" When he had strong opinions about a subject, Maro was an undeniably convincing rhetorician, and despite her recent bouts of self-doubt, Shae could not help but smile and wish to believe everything he said.

As the waiter cleared their finished dishes, the Lantern Man chef and owner of the Golyaani Kitchen came out of the kitchen and over to their table to pay her respects. She was a short, round-faced Tuni woman who must've been born or raised in Janloon because she spoke Kekonese flawlessly. "Kaul-jen," she said, touching clasped hands to her forehead and saluting deeply, "it's an honor for my humble establishment to serve you. Was the food to your taste tonight?" Shae assured her that it had been a superb meal. Maro took out his wallet to pay the bill and was promptly admonished, "No, no, there's no charge; you're a guest of the Weather Man and we're a loyal No Peak business."

Shae rose to leave, but Maro remained seated. "I insist on paying," he said, looking not at the owner but at Shae. "I'm not part of the clan so the restaurant doesn't owe me anything, and even though I know you could eat at any number of places without charge any night of the week, I would like to buy you dinner. It's a small thing, but please let me pay for the meal."

The restaurateur looked questioningly at Shae, who hesitated. If she accepted the gallant, if awkward gesture, she would've visited the Golyaani Kitchen not as the Weather Man of No Peak patronizing a clan business with a guest, but as Maro's companion. Already, she could imagine the rumors and questions that would begin to travel through the more gossipy circles of the clan.

There was something so artlessly charming about Maro's request, however, a genuine earnest desire to go through the motions of courting her, that she couldn't say no. She nodded to the Lantern Man owner of the Golyaani Kitchen and smiled at her date, sitting back down to let him settle the bill. "Thank you, Maro."

Outside, the concrete was damp with the typical drizzly Northern Sweat of monsoon season, but the moisture had cleared away the smog and Janloon smelled uncommonly fresh. They walked arm in arm down the sidewalk, talking, Shae nostalgically pointing out small things about her old neighborhood: the bookstore with the parrot in the window, the food stall that sold paper cones of sweet roasted nuts, the new neon theater signs that had appeared since she'd moved away. They stopped outside the window of a record shop, and Shae was impressed to see a selection of vinyl soundtracks from Espenian film musicals, several of which she'd watched during her time as a student in Windton. She'd developed a fondness for them; they were always full of costumes and laughable melodrama.

Maro put an arm around her waist. She liked the feel of it, the soft pressure against her hips. "Have I mentioned that you're not what I expected?" he said.

"What do you mean?" Shae leaned into his side. Letting Maro pay for dinner had stripped her guard; she felt warm from drink and food and company. It had been a long time since she'd enjoyed such a leisurely evening and been so pleasantly distracted from clan war and business.

"When people hear the name Kaul, they think *war hero*, or *jade prodigy*, or *heir to the great Green Bone clan dynasty*," Maro said. "Not *shameless fan of silly romantic musicals*."

"There's nothing wrong with silly romantic musicals," Shae protested.

"Of course not," Maro said with mock seriousness. "I'm not going to argue such an important issue with you. Not when you could kill me with your little finger."

"Now why would I do that and ruin a perfectly nice evening?" she teased.

Maro's smile faded and his expression turned hesitant. Their banter had been meant in good humor, but had nevertheless highlighted the one inescapable disparity between them. As they continued walking down the street, Maro fell silent for an uncomfortable minute. "Can I tell you a secret?" he asked. When Shae nodded, he confessed, "I've never been in a duel. I was challenged once, over some stupid drunken argument, but managed to delay it and not show up the next day. That's why I have no more and no less green than I graduated with from the Academy." Maro paused on the sidewalk and turned toward her, his face shadowed under the streetlight, his expression uncertain. "I don't think of myself as a coward, but... I'm not a clan loyalist, and winning jade has never been important to me."

If either of Shae's brothers had ever run from a fair duel, their grandfather would've whipped them for the disgrace. Of course, that had never been necessary; Hilo was more likely to be beaten for causing too many needless duels than anything else. In most other parts in the world, dueling (if two men firing pistols at each other from across a field could even be calling dueling) had gone out of fashion or been made illegal long ago, but in Kekon, winning contests was still the most prestigious way of earning jade, and jade was inextricably tied to social status. Dueling was simply expected of a Green Bone man and was a common way of settling disputes even among non–Green Bones.

"I never expected I'd fall for a woman as green as you, a *Kaul* no less. I think at least half the motivation for men to wear jade is to impress women, and it's obvious I don't have a chance in that regard." Maro gave a soft, self-deprecating laugh. He took a step closer, narrowing the space between them, and lowered his face. "But I have. Fallen for you. Even though I realize I might not be the sort of person who's acceptable to your family."

Shae pictured what Hilo's reaction would be to hearing a Green Bone confess that he'd never fought to earn or defend his jade— skepticism, astonishment, disdain—and she was seized by an abrupt surge of proud and protective affection for Maro. "I think it's the opposite of cowardice to be true to who you are," she said. She leaned forward and kissed him.

The heat of their mouths collided. Shae shivered as she felt Maro's jade aura ripple with pleasant surprise and then hum with sparking lust. Answering desire rose and tugged at Shae's navel, shockingly strong and insistent. It had been a long time since she'd taken a man to bed—not since she'd split with Jerald and returned to Kekon two years ago. She clutched the lapels of Maro's jacket and rose onto the balls of her feet, kissing him harder, more insistently. Maro wrapped a hand around the back of her head, his fingers tangling in her hair, and curled the other arm around her waist, tugging her body closer to his own. Arousal lit between them.

Shae pulled away with a sucking gasp, suddenly struck by the worry that they would be seen. Here in No Peak territory, the clan's Fingers and informers were always nearby; word might reach Hilo by midnight that the Weather Man had been seen kissing a strange man on the street corner. "A taxi," she whispered urgently, and stepped to the curb to hail the nearest one.

In the back seat of the cab, she draped her legs over his, and Maro bent his head down to hers; his mouth moved eagerly over her jaw and ear. "Do you want to go to your place?" The Weather Man's house was still under renovation, and Shae didn't want to bring Maro into the main house, where she might have to introduce him to her brother. "No," she said, sliding her hands under his jacket, feeling the heat and musculature of his back. "Let's go to yours."

Maro lived in a four-story walk-up apartment in a historical part of Sotto Village populated by art studios, curio shops, and tattoo parlors, interspersed here and there with new eateries and buttressed by infill housing. The cab let them off in front of the building, and they ran up the stairs holding on to each other. On the landing, they fell to kissing once again. Maro tried twice to fit his office key into his apartment door before he cursed and laughed and finally succeeded in letting them in. The inside of the apartment was spacious, and tidier than she'd expected, clearly the home of an intellectual bachelor, undecorated but full of shelves for books, magazines, and videocassettes. Shae did not pause to pay attention to any of it beyond a cursory glance; they staggered into the single bedroom and pulled off each other's clothes, dropping them to the floor. She pressed one hand to the small of Maro's back and cupped his scrotum with the other. Her nipples rubbed against his chest; the slight scratchiness of his hair against her intensely sensitive skin made her quiver, as did the pulse of their jade auras, mingling and coalescing together like melding body heat.

They sank toward the bed. Shae pushed Maro's hand between her legs as she stroked and fondled him, then shifted down to take him in her mouth. He tasted good—clean, but with that indescribable masculine odor. When he started gasping and thrusting, she pulled away. "Do you have a—" she began, but Maro handed her a condom so quickly that she broke out laughing. She opened the packet and unrolled it over him, feeling him shiver with anticipation.

"Get me close with your mouth first," she whispered, and pressed his shoulders down toward her hips. He went to work eagerly, and not without skill, and when Shae felt as if every muscle in her body was strained on the utmost verge of clenching, she drew her legs up in open invitation. She gasped aloud as he entered her, grabbing his ass in encouragement. She tried to hold back, to draw out the delicious climb, but several hard thrusts sent her careening over the edge, spasming and shuddering, her legs locked around his waist as the waves of her climax rolled through her and into him, spurring Maro into a wild abandon. In minutes, his jade aura spiked as he crested. Maro cried out, head thrown back, spine arching above her.

They collapsed together. Maro kissed her shoulder and rolled aside, arms wrapped around her. "Thank you," he murmured into the crook of her neck, his breath warm against her skin.

When Shae awoke the next morning, she felt completely alert and clearheaded, as if the sex had swept through her system like a long overdue cleansing typhoon. Maro was still asleep. As she gazed at his long frame stretched out on the sheets, it occurred to her that he was a beautiful sight but also remarkably naked. Lying next to him in all of her jade—choker, bracelets, earrings, anklets—she felt almost improperly overdressed. It had never even occurred to her to remove them.

She thought about staying where she was, sleeping in, making love again, walking out into Sotto Village for brunch. Instead, she got up stealthily, wiped herself down with a towel from the bathroom, then retrieved her strewn clothes and put them on. Dim sunlight framed the drawn curtains in Maro's room, and by their light she noticed things that she hadn't the night before. Travel photos and prints of antique maps on the walls. An orange cat sunning itself on the windowsill. On the dresser, a framed photograph of two little girls—perhaps six and four years old.

"My nieces," Maro said, answering her unspoken question in a sleep-thickened voice from the bed behind her. "It's a photo from last year, though. I have more recent pictures, but I haven't put them in frames."

Shae sat down on the edge of the bed and put a hand on his leg. "I had a wonderful time."

Maro reached out a hand and took her by the wrist. "Do you have to go so soon?"

She nodded and stood up reluctantly. "I have to sway the Pillar."

———

Shae found her brother in the training hall behind the Kaul house, finishing up a morning practice session with Master Aido. She could Perceive his heartbeat, his breath and exertion, before she slid open the door. Tightly blindfolded and relying only on his sense of Perception, Hilo was weaving and slashing, the talon knife in his hand a blur as it scored the hard leather guards protecting Aido's torso, arms, and neck. The master moved astonishingly fast for a man with gray hair, his own knife darting out now and again to test Hilo's Steel.

Aido had been a faculty member at Wie Lon Temple School many years ago, before he had a personal falling out with the grandmaster and left to become a private trainer in the jade disciplines. Like jade-wearing physicians, teachers were not beholden to any one clan; Aido used to coach Green Bones in both the major clans, but these days, he limited his client base primarily to the upper echelons of No Peak, to avoid potential conflicts of interest. There was a good living to be made as a trainer; Green Bones who intended to advance on the Horn's side of the clan paid handsomely to continue developing their prowess after graduation, and even those without strong martial ambitions were advised to at least be diligent about maintaining their abilities, lest they end up weak and slow, potential targets for others. It was easy to slide backward in one's jade proficiency, in the same way that it was easy to gain weight—slowly and insidiously.

The kitchen timer on the counter rang. "Much better," said Master Aido, lowering his arms. "Your knife work is confident again and you're not slowing yourself down by over-Steeling." Hilo did not look satisfied; he tore off the blindfold and stalked to the water cooler. "Kaul Shae-jen," Aido said, nodding to Shae in greeting as he passed her on the way out. "You should call to get an appointment on my calendar as well. My month is filling up fast."

"I'll be sure to do that, Aido-jen," Shae said.

Hilo finished draining his paper cup of water and tossed it into the trash bin. Wiping a towel over his neck, he glanced at Shae standing by the door, then turned away from her and leaned his hands heavily on the counter, a pall of gloom over him. "I'm not sure I'll ever be the same."

It had taken Hilo many long months to recover from his injuries last year, and despite all the urgent demands on the Pillar's time and attention, he seemed obsessed with building himself back into fighting shape. Shae knew that he had at least two other coaches on retainer besides Master Aido. She suspected that her brother's preoccupation with his martial fitness was a way for him to avoid the parts of the Pillar's job that were uninteresting or difficult for him. His fighting prowess as a Green Bone—*that* was one thing he could understand and control.

"You don't need to be the best talon knife fighter anymore," she said. "You have men to fight for you."

"Strong men don't fight for weak men." Hilo walked past her to the door. "Have you had breakfast?"

At the patio table, Kyanla brought them bowls of steamed eggs in broth and a plate of pastries. Shae told Hilo about her conversation with Ree Tura and Ayt's proposal for a formal meeting. "They want to discuss the terms of a truce."

"A *truce*." Her brother made a face. "That bitch has got some nerve."

Shae took a bread roll and broke it in half. She called to mind Maro's words from last night, the confidence he'd tried to instill in her. *You lead the clan as much as your brother does. You can make a difference.* "I think we should agree," she said.

To her surprise, Hilo did not react immediately. He chewed quietly for several seconds, then said, "Why?"

"I think you know why, Hilo. We're at an impasse. Tar kicked off another bout of back-and-forth bloodshed, but it's already petering out. The press coverage has been particularly harsh because everyone knows that by this point, the fighting is pointless. A year and half of open war has sapped both our clans; neither of us is strong enough to win."

"Ayt tried her damnedest to finish us off last year and failed," Hilo growled. "Now she comes crawling to us hoping for a truce? Why should we let up when we have the advantage?"

"We don't *have* an advantage," Shae said. "We don't have the resources or manpower to control the entire city even if we did take down the Mountain. You said it yourself: This war is a boon for criminals and smugglers, and the situation will only get worse so long as the clans keep losing people on both sides. How much longer do you expect we can keep grinding it out for street territory?"

She'd made her point too argumentatively; Hilo gave her a dark look and said, "From what I hear, maybe longer than you can hold on to the office on Ship Street." Shae grimaced but didn't look away.

Hilo rubbed a hand over his eyes. "I'm not stupid, Shae," he said less harshly. "I *do* look at those reports you put on my desk, once in a while. Jade mining's halted, tourism's down, our war expenses are high, people are upset—I get it. But do you believe for one second that Ayt's suddenly become a different person, that she's willing to live peacefully from now on?"

Shae wrapped her fingers around the warm bowl of broth. It wasn't hard to recall the Mountain Pillar's words to her last year, the utter certainty with which she promised the destruction of No Peak. "No," Shae said. "Ayt's staked everything on her vision of one-clan rule."

"Then no truce will last," Hilo said. "The Mountain will only use it as an opportunity to build up their strength, to hit us in a worse way later."

Shae nodded slowly. "It goes both ways, Hilo," she said. "We need to build up our own strength, to plan a longer game. We can negotiate now and not forget they're the enemy."

Hilo slumped back in his chair with a snort of disgust. "People have the brains of chickens. A year ago, the public was on our side, blaming the Mountain for hoarding jade and starting the war. Now they want to forget it all, give Ayt the keys to the KJA again, and have us hold hands nicely."

"Most people aren't Green Bones," Shae reminded him. "It's not personal for them. They're worried about the slowing economy, about crime and smuggling, and especially about the separatist crisis in Oortoko turning into a war between the Espenians and the Ygutanians, right here in the East Amaric. We're going to have the two largest military forces on the planet surrounding our small island, the world's only source of jade." Shae studied her brother's glum expression and added, "*That's* why people don't care about clan grievances anymore. They don't just want us to stop fighting; they want us to cooperate to defend national interests. If we don't, we may be dooming the clans *and* the country. That's why we have to agree to meet with the Mountain." In a quieter voice, "You know it's what Lan would want us to do."

"Lan wanted a lot of things that he didn't get." Hilo fell silent and stared out across the courtyard. The mornings were warm now, the springtime garden burgeoning with peonies and azaleas in pink and white. Shae waited; she and Hilo had sat out here many times over the past year—in discussion, fierce argument, or silence—and she'd come to recognize the particular feel of his jade aura when she'd finally said something to convince him. Pushing Hilo too hard with factual arguments would only make him irritable and defensive; he needed a genuine and personal reason to justify his choices.

"I have to discuss it with Kehn," Hilo said at last. He ate the rest of his bread roll in two quick bites and wiped his mouth with a napkin. "Tell Ree that we'll talk. Set a time for after I get back from the Uwiwa Islands."

CHAPTER

8

Family Matters

Kaul Maik Wen rushed to find her husband in their bedroom, packing up a few belongings for his trip. "Hilo," she gasped. She hadn't meant to sound alarmed, but he must've Perceived her agitation because he dropped his wallet and talon knife on the bedspread and took her by the arms. "What's wrong?" he demanded. "Are you all right?"

"I'm fine," Wen said. To tell the truth, she felt exhausted most of the time and had barely kept her breakfast down this morning, but that wasn't why she'd come running up the stairs. The square envelope and the papers clutched in her hand shook as she held them out to Hilo. "I found this among the papers that you asked me to box up from the study."

Hilo and Shae had left Lan's bedroom and his study untouched for so long that upon moving into the main house, Wen had taken it upon herself to deal with the situation. She'd liked Lan a great deal and mourned that she would never know him as a brother-in-law, but the dead no longer had any needs. Better to take care of those who were still living. Wen had moved the furniture out of the bedroom and repainted it; she planned to turn it into a nursery. As part of her encouragement that Hilo change the study to his liking, she'd placed Lan's belongings and papers into boxes and moved them out. At first Hilo had resisted. "Just leave it; I'm not going to use that room anyway," he told her. Eventually, he'd seen the necessity and, being more than happy to let her handle it, had asked her to at least sort through the boxes and hang on to anything important before storing or discarding the rest. This morning, she'd been doing just that when she'd found the unopened envelope.

It was addressed to Lan, postmarked two weeks prior to his death. The return address was a postal box in Lybon, Stepenland. Wen handed her husband two pieces of folded paper, dense with hand-writing, and a photograph of a six-month-old baby.

"What is this?" Hilo asked.

"Your nephew," Wen said. "Eyni was pregnant when she left Kekon." Wen pointed to the top of the letter, drawing his attention to the writing: *I can't think of any other way to tell you this: He's yours. I'm sorry I didn't tell you earlier, but I wasn't sure who the father was. It was obvious after he was born—he has your nose, your eyes, even your expressions . . . that Kaul look. You know what I mean. His name is Nikolas, and he's a beautiful, healthy baby.*

Wen watched Hilo's eyes travel in disbelief down the rest of the letter. She'd already read through it and knew how it ended. *I know this is a shock. I'm not sure what to do now. Even though things didn't work out between us, I still want Niko to know his biological father. Maybe we should talk about me returning to Kekon. I wouldn't blame you if you don't want anything more to do with me, but I've never stopped caring about you. Please write back.*

Hilo put down the letter and studied the photo. "I don't really see the resemblance she's talking about," he said at last.

Wen snatched the picture from him. "You're blind," she exclaimed. True, the baby in the photo looked much as all babies did—round-faced, wide-eyed, sweet and soft—but he was so obviously Kaul Lan's son that Wen wanted to splutter indignantly at her husband. "You have to write back to Eyni."

Hilo made a face and sat down on the edge of the bed. No one in the family had been in touch with Lan's ex-wife since she'd left. Surely, though, she must've heard of his death. "She's not going to want to hear from me," he said. "Eyni and I never got along very well. What am I supposed to say to her now?"

Wen crouched down next to her husband's legs and stared insistently up into his face. She knew that Hilo had never been fond of his brother's wife, but what did that matter? His personal feelings about Eyni weren't nearly as important as doing what was right for this young child. As soon as Wen had laid eyes on the photo of Nikolas, she'd felt her heart melting. "Tell her she can come back to Janloon," Wen said. "She's willing to return, but she needs the Pillar's permission."

"She'd want to bring that foreigner back with her, the one she cheated on Lan with," Hilo said, with an edge in his voice.

"Even so, I'm sure Lan would've set aside the issue of honor and allowed them to return if it meant bringing his son back to Kekon." Wen shoved the letter and the photo back onto Hilo's lap. "Write back to Eyni and tell her that we discovered her letter just now. Tell her that she's forgiven and that she's welcome to come home and raise her son in Janloon, where he can know his family. Niko must be two years old by now. It's not right for him to be living so far away, growing up in a jadeless culture and surrounded by foreigners."

Hilo rubbed a hand over his eyes, but he nodded. "You're right," he said. "I won't ever be able to think of Eyni as my sister, but I'd put up with her and that man-whore she ran off with, for the sake of the kid." He folded the letter and tucked it back into the envelope but kept looking at the photograph. Wen could see him trying to internalize the idea of this baby being his nephew, who he hadn't even known existed. "Maybe you should be the one to write to Eyni," he suggested.

Wen saw right away that it was a better idea. "Of course," she agreed, standing up. "She'll be more likely to welcome the assurances of another woman. I'll write back to her today and ask her to come visit, so we can meet the baby."

She could see Hilo warming to the idea now; it was like watching clouds in the sky break apart beneath sunlight. He smiled in that boyish, lopsided way that Wen knew she could never adequately capture on camera or in a drawing, though she had tried. Hilo handed the letter back to her but tucked the photograph into his shirt pocket. "When you write to Eyni, let her know that I'm willing to put the past behind us. When she returns to Janloon, she'll have the clan's assistance. We'll help her get a house, a job, whatever she needs. She'll believe it more coming from you than me. And of course, I'd treat Lan's son like my own."

Wen put her arms around Hilo's neck and gave him a grateful kiss. Her husband could be shortsighted and stubborn; sometimes he hung on to strict principles or personal grudges that clouded his better judgment, but he possessed the most valuable quality in any person, especially a clan leader, which was the ability to put others first, no matter the prevailing opinion or the personal cost.

Hilo wrapped an arm around her waist and placed the flat of his hand against her abdomen. "When can we tell people? After the old man's funeral and everything else that's been going on lately, we need some good news around here."

"Let's do it as soon as you get back," Wen said. She was struck by a sudden pang of fear that her words might've tempted misfortune to befall his trip. She tightened her grip around Hilo's neck and confessed, "I'm worried. I think your sister's right; it's not worth it for you to go to that place."

"I'll have Tar with me," Hilo said lightly.

"So I'll have to worry about both of you."

Hilo gave her waist a reassuring squeeze. "The Mountain wants me dead. I'm in danger every day right here in Janloon. Why should you be especially anxious about this?"

Wen said, "Ayt is proposing a truce because she can't afford to kill you right now. If she did, it would plunge the city into further violence at a time when she doesn't have the public support or strength in warriors to handle it. You're safer here."

"I see you've been talking to Shae," Hilo said, with a touch of amusement and irritation. "The two of you have obviously thought things through, but you should trust that I have too." Hilo stood up and finished packing a change of clothes and toiletries into a travel bag. "This crook Zapunyo relies on being inconspicuous. He pays off the government and the police of the Uwiwa Islands in order to be able to run his jade smuggling ring. If he wanted to get rid of me, do you think he'd go to the trouble of luring me onto his turf to do it there? An Uwiwan criminal murdering a Kekonese citizen, the Pillar of a Green Bone clan, would be international news. He'd lose his impunity; both countries' governments would hunt him down. He's not going to risk everything he's built for that."

Wen didn't argue, but she couldn't shake her apprehension as she watched Hilo stow his wallet and passport. She was accustomed to being left behind; as a child, she'd stood outside the entrance of Kaul Dushuron Academy, watching her brothers walk ahead where she could never go. She'd seen them grow into powerful men, earning jade and scars and respect in the clan that had once shunned them.

She'd come by her own victories. When she was fourteen years old, her brothers brought home a friend. This was a rare event; the Maiks received few visitors. Kaul Hilo was sixteen, the same age as Tar, and already people in the clan were saying he was the fiercest of the Torch's grandchildren, that he was sure to one day become the Horn. On that evening and many others to come, Hilo ate dinner cheerfully at their meager table in Paw-Paw instead of his family's grand house in Palace Hill. He was respectful to their mother and teased Kehn and Tar as if they were his own brothers. When Wen's mother snapped her fingers at Wen to refill their guest's teacup, she shyly hurried to do so. Most people avoided looking at or speaking to Wen for longer than necessary; they tugged their earlobes to ward off the stone-eye's bad luck. Hilo turned to thank her, and paused. His eyes rested on her face for a prolonged moment, then he smiled and returned to the meal and to conversation with her brothers.

Wen finished pouring tea and sat back down, hands in her lap, eyes on her own plate. Her face felt as if it were on fire with a feverish certainty she'd never had in her life. *That's the boy I'm going to marry.*

She had a great deal to be thankful for now, she knew that. Even being a stone-eye no longer troubled her, as it allowed her to do useful things to help the Weather Man in the war against No Peak's enemies. And hopefully there would be more joy in her life, soon. Yet the familiar feeling of being left behind—a queasy and helpless resentment lodged deep in the pit of her stomach—it never stopped being hard to take. "Don't underestimate this man," Wen whispered. "Promise me you'll be careful."

Hilo picked up his sheathed talon knife and strapped it to his waist. "I promise." He looked at his watch, picked up his bag, and gave her a quick kiss on the mouth. "I'm going to be a father. I know that changes things."

CHAPTER

9

The Uwiwan and His Half Bones

It took just under two hours for the ten-seater turboprop plane to fly from Kekon to Tialuhiya, the largest of the thirteen Uwiwa Islands. It had been wet and overcast in Janloon when Hilo left; he stepped out of the airplane into tropical heat and blinding sunlight. Waiting for them next to the tarmac were two white rental cars with drivers, which Hilo had asked Tar to arrange, alongside a welcome party of ten armed men, which he had not, but was unsurprised to see.

Tar and his man Doun descended first; they flanked Hilo as he stepped off the plane's folding stairs. One of the ten strangers came forward to meet them. He was tall and his features did not look Uwiwan, but he was so tanned it was hard to tell. A thick gold chain with five green stones hung around his neck. "Kaul Hiloshudon, welcome to Tialuhiya," he said in passable Kekonese. "Pas Zapunyo has sent us to meet you and ensure that you're conducted safely to his personal residence, where it will be his pleasure to host you."

Hilo looked the man up and down, then drew his eyes over the others arrayed behind him. They were all dressed similarly, in khaki pants and silk shirts, dark sunglasses, and green gemstones set into heavy necklaces, chunky rings, and metal bracelets. Hilo's lips fought down a smirk. "We'll drive in our own cars," he said. "You can escort us."

In addition to Maik Tar and Doun, Hilo had brought with him three of Kehn's men: the clan's First Fist, Juen, and two Fingers, Vin and Lott. Hilo had been deliberate in his choices. Juen was one of No Peak's best warriors, whose fighting skill could be counted on if anything went wrong, but he was also No Peak's most operational man in Janloon. Hilo wanted the chance to speak with him on the plane, to keep abreast of what was happening on the ground and how Kehn was performing as Horn. Vin had been a Finger for two and half years and was on the cusp of being promoted to Fist. Hilo had heard that he was one of the most talented Green Bones in No Peak when it came to Perception. Lott was only a junior Finger who'd graduated from the Academy last year, but he was the son of a top No Peak Fist who'd been murdered by the Mountain at the height of the clan war. Hilo had taken a personal interest in Lott; he would use this trip to get a better sense of the young man's potential.

Hilo got into one of the rental cars with Tar and Lott; he sent Juen, Doun, and Vin ahead in the other. Zapunyo's men climbed into their three identical silver sedans; one vehicle led the way, the other two brought up the rear. The conspicuous convoy traveled for thirty minutes, first down a long, flat highway with sugarcane, tea, and fruit plantations stretching off to both sides in the shimmering heat, then up a winding, pitted road, into hills dotted with goats, roadside craft stands, and sun-withered laborers in broad straw hats. Several of the workers flashed crooked-toothed smiles and waved at the cars, then continued staring after them as they passed. The Uwiwans, Hilo thought, had the cunning look of a race that knew they were dependent on the might and wealth of outsiders and hated themselves for it. They could be the friendliest sort of people during the day, then steal your wallet and cut your throat in the middle of the night.

Here and there, Hilo saw faded road signs written in Shotarian. Even the newer signs in Uwiwan were full of Shotarian loanwords, in the same way most Uwiwans had singular Shotarian or Shotarian-influenced names. Like Kekon, the Uwiwa Islands had been occupied by the Empire of Shotar prior to the Many Nations War. Unlike Kekon, there was not a pebble of jade in the entire archipelago, and no Green Bone clans to wage a long rebellion against the foreigners. Uwiwan opposition had been swiftly crushed and Shotarian rule ironclad for seventy years. After its defeat in the Many Nations War, Shotar was forced to relinquish the Uwiwa Islands to its people, but independence had yielded mixed results at best. Now the impoverished country was internationally known for cash crops, beautiful tourist beaches, and jade smuggling.

"Kaul-jen," Lott spoke up as they drove. "Who are those men who work for Zapunyo?"

"They're barukan," Hilo answered. "Shotarian gangsters."

"So much bluffer's jade on that lot, it's like they raided a costume shop," Tar scoffed.

"Don't get cocky," Hilo said sharply. "Where we're going, there'll be several of them for every one of us. Just because of their tacky looks, you think they're not dangerous?" He was still displeased with Tar, for his recent carelessness and failure to find Lan's killer and recover the family's stolen jade. The Pillarman fell into a silent sulk, his aura scratchy.

The wheels churned a long plume of dust as the cars turned onto a gravel road that crested a ridge and sloped into a shallow valley between two hills. The convoy circled a man-made lake surrounded by a garden of broad-leafed greenery and stone Uwiwan idols set among plantings of tropical flowers. At the end of the road on the far side of the lake sprawled a red two-story plantation mansion in the old Shotarian colonial style: large square windows below a gabled clay roof, a wide front balcony supported by stone pillars, single-story wings fanning out on either side of the central structure. The cars pulled up in front of the entrance.

Hilo had noticed the lookout towers with rifle-carrying sentries along the approach to the estate, and he counted many more guards around the house, in addition to the escorts who'd met them at the airport. As he got out of the car, he saw electronic locks on all the doors as well as security cameras and motion sensors discreetly tucked into every crevice of the traditional architecture. Zapunyo's residence was a lavish fortress. The lead barukan who'd spoken to them earlier went ahead of the group and held open the door. Hilo motioned Vin to walk next to him as they took the front steps into the house. "How many?" he asked in a low aside.

"Twenty-two people in and around the house, Hilo-jen," Vin whispered. "Fourteen of them with jade, but... not nearly as much as they're pretending to show off."

Hilo nodded in satisfaction at having his own assessment confirmed. "Stay alert," he said, and Vin nodded. The Finger's sense of Perception was indeed excellent; most of the gemstones conspicuously worn by Zapunyo's barukan bodyguards were inert, decorative nephrite—*bluffer's jade* as the Kekonese called it. When he'd met the tanned leader, Hilo had noticed that only one of the five green stones on the man's necklace was true jade. However, to anyone who was not a Green Bone and could not discern the incongruity in jade aura— which would be nearly all Uwiwans—the barukan looked as intimidating and dangerous as the best warriors on Kekon. Though there was not a Fist in No Peak who would wear his jade in such a clumsy manner, on dangling chains and bracelets, impractical for actual combat.

The posturing did not, as Hilo had already reminded Tar, mean the men were not a threat, but it did arouse the Pillar's contempt. In Shotarian, the word *barukan* traditionally meant both *guest* and *stranger*, and was used in reference to an unwanted but unavoidable visitor, such as an inspector from company headquarters or an opinionated mother-in-law. In the past twenty years, however, the word had become synonymous with Keko-Shotarian gangsters. During the foreign occupation of Kekon a generation ago, hundreds of thousands of displaced Kekonese were forcibly sent, or willingly migrated, to Shotar. Their descendants were a marginalized minority in that country, and many turned to illegal jade and lives of crime.

The Kekonese call the barukan *half bones* and view them with disdain and pity.

The half bone mercenaries employed by Zapunyo escorted Hilo and his men up a wide, curving marble staircase, through a spacious drawing room with a grand piano and tall bookcases, and out a set of open glass double doors onto the balcony overlooking the private lake. Zapunyo sat under a yellow shade at a large cast-top patio table, eating lunch. Three young men dined with him. The one to his right was the eldest, perhaps twenty-five. The other two were seated on the left; one man looked to be twenty, and the youngest was a teenager of about sixteen. They were obviously Zapunyo's sons.

The barukan leader stopped at the foot of the table. "Pas," he said, using the respectful honorific common to both Shotar and the Uwiwas. "Your guests have arrived."

"Much thanks, Iyilo." The smuggler looked up but did not rise. "Kaul Hiloshudon, Pillar of No Peak. I've been looking forward a long time to our meeting in person. Please sit. Have something to eat." Zapunyo spoke accented but clear Kekonese in a leisurely paced, slightly hoarse voice. He was a short, dark man with crooked front teeth and a stunted look that suggested poor nutrition in childhood. Reliable sources said he was diabetic; his mother had also developed the disease in her forties and died from it. Zapunyo wore a loose yellow silk shirt and a pale blue kerchief tied around his neck; a thin mustache twitched over dry lips. He appeared entirely Uwiwan, like a roughened plantation foreman, but it was well known that Zapunyo was half-Kekonese. His paternal bloodline and small doses of SN1, injected alongside daily insulin, gave him the jade tolerance necessary in his line of work. He wore no jade himself.

There was a single chair and place setting directly across from Zapunyo and his sons. Hilo sat down in it. Tar stepped back to a corner of the patio, and the other four Green Bones positioned themselves watchfully behind the Pillar. Zapunyo's barukan bodyguards took up similar places behind their boss. Hilo could not help but smile at the comical tableau: The two men faced each other across a table spread with plates of tropical fruit, marinated vegetables, and cured meats, with a dozen heavily armed attendants standing around silently behind them. Zapunyo had arranged this scene as a meeting between kings of equal rank. With his sons arrayed alongside him, the Uwiwan signaled that he was the one who held state here.

A servant came out and filled glasses with citrus-infused water. Hilo did not touch either the water or the food, not because he thought Zapunyo would poison him, but because he did not entirely trust the water sanitation in the Uwiwas. He leaned back in his chair. "Where's Teije?"

Zapunyo was spooning out the flesh from a quarter wedge of papaya with a small silver spoon. "I suppose enjoying himself by the pool." He put a mouthful of pink pulp in his mouth, mashed, and swallowed, then dabbed the corner of his mouth with his kerchief. "Your cousin for sure knows how to have a good time. Are you aware of how he got in trouble with the police? First, he walked into a nightclub wearing jade; you can't do that here. Then he tried to have three women in the same night when the limit is two. He's very lucky that I heard of his situation. The prisons in this country, they can kill a man with disease before he ever gets a chance to stand in front of a judge. I wouldn't want such a misfortune to cause bad relations between our countries."

"You can put him back in that cell for all I care," said Hilo, "except that I'd feel bad seeing his poor mother cry. All your stalling and mincing of words to get me here in person—you're obviously under the impression that we have something to discuss. I came because I'm honestly curious to hear what a scavenger like you could possibly have to say to me as Pillar."

Hilo had thought the smuggler would show some anger, or at least bristle, but Zapunyo merely nodded as if this was exactly what he'd expected. "You Green Bones, you have an old way of thinking," he said, fixing Hilo with small, beetle black eyes. "I suppose some Kekonese still believe that jade comes from Heaven, that you're descendants of Jenshu and closest to the gods out of all races. I've heard those stories myself. So you cling to jade, you hold on to it so tight, as if it were your very souls that might be snatched. Instead of thinking in an open-minded way about how you can share this wonderful gift you have with the rest of the world."

"And that's what you do," Hilo said sardonically. "Share jade with the world."

"I'm an entrepreneur," said Zapunyo. "I see the need and I fill that need. If there is demand for something, and the normal suppliers are not doing a good job, then of course that is where there is a business opportunity. My Kekonese father, he gave nothing to me and my mother, nothing but pain and sorrow, but because of him, I learned to take care of myself. And from my blessed mama I learned to share what little I had with others. So that's why I wish to talk with you."

Hilo looked out across the glimmering lake and wondered how much of Zapunyo's wealth from black market jade dealing it had taken to construct this artificial oasis in the hills, to build, man, and fortify his property, and to pay off all the required officials. Zapunyo called his organization Ti Pasuiga—*The Tribe* in Uwiwan. He had jade-wearing subordinates and enforced oaths of loyalty from those in his employ. The smuggler might disdain Kekonese ways and beliefs, but that didn't stop him from taking on the trappings of clan to suit his own purposes. Hilo turned back. "You baited me here to make me a business proposal. So make it."

Zapunyo speared some pickled green beans and slices of eggplant onto his plate. "My business, like any other, relies on people. But it is hard to find and keep workers when Green Bones are so quick to kill anyone who tries to take even a little jade out of the country. A clan as powerful as No Peak, you have more important things to concern yourselves with. Your territories in Janloon must be defended against enemies; you need men and money to do that—so why spend any energy on things that don't hurt anyone? There is no reason at all for us to be against one another. I am not a greedy man. I was born poor, and even now, I'm content to take only the scraps from Kekon and even to share what little I make."

Hilo nodded. "You want me to stop killing your rockfish, in

exchange for a cut of the profits you make off the black market jade you smuggle from our shores."

"You accept tribute from all sorts of businesses, Kaul Hilo. Do you look down upon the money that comes from a brothel as opposed to a grocer? Kekon sells jade to the governments of Espenia and its allies—is their money better than mine?" For the first time, a hint of dangerous affront rose in the smuggler's slow, dry voice. He turned his head to either side to indicate his sons. The eldest was eating heartily and noisily, glancing up now and then from his plate, but seemingly unconcerned by any of the conversation. His two brothers glowered at Hilo like dogs with their hackles raised. Zapunyo said, "My sons here have much more than I did growing up, a much better life. It is a comfort to me to know that one day they will take over the business, and if anything bad should happen to me, they would remember my enemies. Getting older, I think less and less about myself and more and more about how I want to pass what I gain in this life to my children and my children's children. Do you have children yet, Kaul-jen?"

"No," said Hilo.

"Gods willing, perhaps you will someday soon be so blessed. Then you will understand that I am just like any other father and business-man. You, Kaul-jen, you want your family and your country to be safe and prosperous—and jade is what makes that happen." Zapunyo waved vaguely to indicate his house, his sons and attendants, the whole of the Uwiwa Islands. "You cannot say that we are so different, can you?"

Hilo pushed his untouched plate out of the way and shifted forward in his seat. It was a small movement, there was no outward threat in it at all, but his Green Bones, and the barukan guards with any sense of Perception, tensed at the change in his jade aura. "The two of us have as much in common as your barukan have with Green Bones. *Nothing.*" The Pillar spoke in a voice soft with scorn as he laid an unmoving stare on the Uwiwan. "Jade is only a *thing* to you, to be stolen and sold. It's why you don't wear any of it yourself. You wanted to speak your mind to me in person, and I can appreciate that. I came for the same reason, so I could tell you in the simplest terms: Stay off Kekon. You're no Lantern Man and you'll get no accommodation from No Peak. If desperate Abukei want to risk their lives ferrying jade to you, that's one thing. But there's a difference between a dog that picks garbage outside your house, and one that jumps through your window to steal from your table. One is a nuisance you can ignore; the other is a problem and has to be killed.

"I know you have agents in Janloon recruiting Kekonese criminals to be your rockfish. I know you land boats on remote parts of the coastline and send bands of pickers to scavenge from the mine sites. My orders to my Fists and Fingers are to kill any of the thieves they catch. Don't get me wrong; I understand your position. The last couple of years have been good for you. The mines suspended, the Mountain and No Peak at war, and now, the conflict in Shotar that will raise the black market even more. But don't think jade makes your posse of half bones into a clan, and don't imagine for a second that money makes you a Pillar." At last, Hilo felt Zapunyo's anger, saw the man's mouth below his mustache tighten into a wrinkled line. Hilo's upper lip curled. "You should get out of the smuggling business while you're on top. Go any further, bring your stink to Kekon, and you'll lose it all. Green Bones can't be bought with your dirty Uwiwan money."

"Money is money—all if it is dirty, and anyone can be bought." The country cordiality that Zapunyo had displayed before was suddenly gone; his small eyes were hooded, and he had the look of a mongoose with needle-sharp teeth. "It was my mistake to think you might be a sensible man, a smart man. We both know you have enemies I could go to instead."

Hilo laughed. "Go ahead and try. Ayt Madashi would just as soon snap your neck. The Mountain murdered my brother and went to war with my family to control Kekon's jade. If Ayt won't compromise with other Green Bones, you think she'll deal with *you*?" Hilo stood up, smoothly and quickly. Iyilo and the other barukan nearest Zapunyo moved their hands toward their guns; Hilo felt Tar and his men shift forward, their auras humming. Hilo said calmly to Zapunyo, "You bailed out my worthless relative and showed him hospitality in your own home, so even though I'm a Green Bone and you're a jade thief and by all rights I ought to kill you, let's say there's no need for us to ruin this pleasant afternoon. We've had a good talk; now we know where we each stand. Anything that comes afterward, even if it's unpleasant, should come as no surprise to either of us."

Zapunyo did not move from his seat. He put a final slice of cold, seasoned meat into his mouth and his jaw ground back and forth as he stared at Hilo with eyes made squinty by unforgiving years of dust and sun. The smuggler laced his stumpy fingers and rested them across his stomach. "Of course, I'm disappointed," he said. "I did the clan a great favor, I invited you into my house and offered you food and drink, and I've been given no thanks. You Green Bones put such importance on your honor, but if you won't extend courtesy to others, you'll be left behind in the world. It's true, what you say, though: There's no need to ruin this lovely afternoon. I am not a prideful man, Kaul-jen, and what little pride I have, I am used to swallowing. That's how it is when you start off with nothing in life and learn never to take anything for granted."

Zapunyo waved his hand nonchalantly toward the patio doors. "You are welcome to take your cousin Teije and be on your way back to your country. Iyilo will see you out."

They found Teije Runo, as Zapunyo had said, lounging beside the pool behind the mansion, a drink in one jade-ringed hand, a slender young woman in a bathing suit stretched out on her stomach on the towel next to him. A record player on a stand turned out Espenian jiggy songs. Hilo walked up and stood over the man. Teije stirred and removed his sunglasses; apparently, he'd been dozing. He stared at Hilo for several befuddled seconds, then clambered hastily to his feet, setting down his drink and straightening his swim trunks. "Cousin Hilo," he exclaimed, spreading his arms in delight and surprise.

Hilo struck the man across the face. Teije stumbled and let out a pained exclamation. Hilo hit him again, sending the man sprawling.

Teije's foot caught his drink glass; it toppled over and broke. The young woman in the bathing suit shrieked and scrambled away, shouting in Uwiwan as Hilo kicked Teije viciously in the side. "Kaul-jen, please, wait, stop," Teije wheezed, crawling away from the Pillar on hands and knees. Hilo followed; he kicked his relative in the stomach and the crotch, then hit him several more times in the face and body.

Teije Runo was not a small man—he was half a head taller than Hilo, with broad shoulders and long arms, and he kept himself fit—but he put his arms over his head and curled into a ball as Hilo's blows descended. The woman ran screaming into the house. Iyilo stood to the side and watched, as did the other barukan and Hilo's own men. Tar snickered in amusement. When Hilo was done, none of Teije's bones were broken, but his oiled body bloomed with bruises and he moaned piteously.

"Get up and put on your clothes," Hilo said. "We're leaving."

CHAPTER

10

A Ridiculous Waste

They left Zapunyo's estate fifteen minutes later. The barukan in their silver cars did not escort them this time; Hilo did not ask, and Iyilo did not offer. The darkly tanned half bone stood at the front entrance, watching their departure, his expression carefully guarded. As Hilo got into the car, he Perceived the unmistakable pulse of hostility in the bodyguard's jade aura. Iyilo might be a hired Shotarian goon, but he and those like him had reason to resent and hate people like the Kauls. Jade and lineage made Green Bones the historical heroes and unofficial rulers of Kekon; the same traits made the barukan criminals and outsiders in Shotar. Hilo was quite certain that, if given the word by Zapunyo, Iyilo and his men would be eager to prove themselves just as worthy of jade as their Kekonese guests, by killing the whole lot of them.

This time, Hilo took Tar, Vin, and Teije in the first car with him and sent Juen, Doun, and Lott in the other. Teije, thoroughly cowed and blotting his lip with ice wrapped in a paper towel, was silent throughout the drive. Tar rolled down the windows and said, "Did you see how that runt and his barukan dogs couldn't even look us in the eyes back there? They let us walk right out. If they're the toughest men in the Uwiwas, it's no wonder this country is such shit."

Hilo did not respond; he'd chastised Tar once already today and didn't want his Pillarman further distracted. Tar sometimes ran off his mouth when he was feeling insecure. He was loyal and fierce, but he didn't have a strategic mind. As Hilo had said to Wen, Zapunyo would not have tried to harm them on his own estate. Too risky for him, too much exposure.

Hilo tilted the car seat back and closed his eyes. He appeared as if he was resting, perhaps trying to take a nap. The sun beat down on his face; the inside of his vision was a wall of red that colored even his sense of Perception as he extended it, scanning, fully alert. As they entered the airport road, Hilo sat up and opened his eyes. Five police cars and two motorcycles were parked in front of the runway where their small charter plane lay waiting. "Vin," Hilo said.

"Twelve men," the Finger said at once. "Hilo-jen . . . they're here to kill us."

Hilo nodded, but Teije Runo, speaking for the first time since they'd left Zapunyo's estate, exclaimed in a panicked voice, "They're here for me. They think I'm jumping bail."

"They don't give a shit about you," Hilo said. "They're on Zapunyo's payroll." Two of the officers motioned for them to pull over; Hilo told the driver to obey. The other car pulled up behind them. Hilo turned around to speak to Teije. "You stay in the car," he ordered. "I promised your ma I'd bring you home safe, but disobey me, and I'll break her fucking heart."

Hilo got out of the car. His Green Bones followed. "Hands up! Put hands up!" one of the police officers ordered through a bullhorn. The fact that he addressed them in broken Kekonese was another sign that he knew exactly who they were, that this had been arranged beforehand. Hilo raised his empty hands over his head and began to walk forward.

"Stop!" the officer with the bullhorn shouted. He sounded frightened. "Stop now! This is final warning!"

Hilo did not stop, but continued ahead with slow, deliberate paces. "You understand Kekonese?" he called out. "You can't stop us from getting on that plane. But I'm giving you a chance to leave. Green Bones don't kill those without jade. Unless they break our laws or side with our enemies."

Hilo's Perception clamored with galloping heartbeats. Behind him, he could sense the tension in his men, their jade auras straining forward like horses behind the starting gates, and in front of him, the stench of fear and grim determination. Hilo slowed. "Even if Zapunyo owns this island, and you have to take money from him, it's not worth your lives," he called out. He took another step forward. The police opened fire.

Hilo was already moving; he thrust his arms down sharply, unleashing a wide, descending Deflection that swept over the hail of bullets like a vertical gale wind. The scared policemen had overcompensated and fired wastefully. All of the initial shots—at least thirty—had been directed at Hilo. It was what he'd intended when he walked out alone; focused fire was more easily Deflected. The volley of disrupted gunfire tore up the tarmac well short of its target, though a few bullets sailed close enough that Hilo flinched with Steel.

His Green Bones rushed in. Tar's and Juen's auras blazed with Strength and Lightness as they bounded over the row of squad cars, Tar landing amid the cluster of officers with drawn talon knife, Juen warping the roof of one of the vehicles as he dropped onto it in a crouch, straightened up with a pistol in each hand, and began firing precise shots into the line.

Doun, Vin, and Lott were not far behind their Fists. Two of the Uwiwans turned and fled toward the airplane; Lott drew a pair of slim throwing knives he carried sheathed against the small of his back and hurled them together along with a razor-thin Deflection that deftly parted the trajectory of the blades. They sailed through the air like twin prongs, catching one man between the shoulders and another in the back of the neck.

Hilo strolled into the melee, talon knife in hand; he seized one man and cut his throat from behind. Another policeman abandoned his empty handgun and swung a black truncheon at Hilo's skull with whistling force. Hilo slid his head under the arc and slashed the man across the inside of the forearm. The truncheon fell from the man's nerveless grasp and Hilo caught it in his left hand before it hit the ground. With a burst of Strength, he twisted his weight into a strike that smashed the Uwiwan across the knees with the length of the steel, then he uncoiled and slammed the butt of the weapon into his opponent's chin, breaking the man's jaw as he fell.

Hilo looked around for the next adversary, but there was nothing left for him to do. His men were accustomed to fighting other Green Bones, and this had not been anything similar to that. Their opponents were poorly trained and had no real abilities; they were not even Kekonese. Looking around at the bodies, Hilo was struck by a swift and powerful hatred for the smuggler Zapunyo—nearly as strong as what he felt for his enemy Ayt Mada. The Uwiwan criminal kingpin sat safe in his luxurious stronghold, guarded by barukan who might have been a real contest for Green Bones, but he did not risk them or himself. He had ordered corrupt policemen to see to it that Hilo was killed resisting arrest.

Such a ridiculous waste.

Some of the men on the ground were not dead, but since none of them posed a threat any longer, Hilo told his Fists to leave them. They went back to the cars and gathered their belongings as well as Teije Runo, who blanched when he saw the scene and let himself be led meekly to the plane. The Kekonese pilot was an associate of the clan; he had not radioed in the disturbance, instead waiting patiently as instructed.

Juen's shoulder had been grazed in the gunfire, and Doun had taken a bullet clean through the calf. "I was careless, Kaul-jen," he said, grimacing in pain but looking embarrassed to have been injured in such a one-sided battle. Hilo found the first aid kit in the airplane's cabin storage and passed it back but told the pilot to take off immediately. The twin-engine aircraft sped down the runway and lifted into the sky, leaving the bloody tarmac and lush green fields of Tialuhiya far below.

————————

On the way home, Hilo checked on Juen and Doun. He made sure their bleeding was under control and that they were kept hydrated with the soda in the onboard cooler. Tar was in a more relaxed mood now; it seemed their violent exit had purged some of his earlier frustration. He stretched out across a row of seats and napped. Hilo went to sit beside Lott, who was in the farthest row back, staring out the window at the ocean below.

Hilo said, "I've only met one other Green Bone who can throw knives that well, and direct them with Deflection no less."

"My father, I know," said Lott, still staring out the window. The young man was upset and confused, that much Hilo could tell from the persistent churning of his jade aura, though like a typical teenager, he pretended otherwise.

"You're not much like your da in other ways," Hilo said.

The young man's shoulders stiffened. "I'm sorry if I disappoint you, Kaul-jen."

"That's not what I said," said Hilo. "Your father was as green as they come, one of my most fearsome and loyal Fists, let the gods recognize him. But he could be cruel for no reason and he didn't care for most people. You don't seem that way to me."

"I killed those men, didn't I? I know you brought me along to see how I'd perform."

Hilo was certain the young man would never speak to the Pillar of the clan with such candid resentment under other circumstances, but he'd taken a life for the first time and was emotional, not knowing the proper way to react. There was no proper way, Hilo knew; people reacted differently. Some threw up, some were exhilarated, others felt nothing.

"You only killed one of them," Hilo said. "The one you got in the neck, yes, but the other one will live." He wasn't certain that was the case, but if it made Lott feel better, there was no harm in saying so. The Finger didn't answer or even turn his head.

"Lott-jen, look at the Pillar when he speaks to you," Hilo demanded, his voice sharp.

The young man flinched, in the way of a boy accustomed to punishment, and turned quickly toward Hilo with guilt in his eyes. His expression flickered briefly between doubt and defiance, but he dared not meet Hilo's commanding stare; he dropped his gaze and murmured, "Forgive my disrespect, Kaul-jen."

Ever since he'd first met Lott, Hilo had noticed him to be a moody, sulky sort of teen, which could be forgiven for a short while, but the man was a Green Bone now; he had to learn how to behave. Hilo's eyes did not shift or lose their sternness, but after another minute had passed, he said in a much gentler voice, "I'll always forgive a friend, because otherwise how could people be honest with each other? I didn't bring you on this trip to make you prove yourself. I brought you because you stood in front of me ahead of all your classmates last year and took your oaths first—that's something I'd remember. When it comes to which brothers I want to get to know, which ones I want fighting next to me if it comes to life or death, that sort of thing is important."

Lott did not look back up, but after a second, he gave a nod and his jade aura settled into a grudging but calmer hum. Hilo turned around in his seat and reached into the cooler to pull out two mango sodas; he opened them and handed one to Lott, who accepted it and drained half the bottle.

Hilo said, "Those men you fought today—you didn't know them and they'd done you no personal offense. That's why it bothers you to have killed them. It's only natural to feel that way; if we didn't, we'd be no better than animals. There are some people who are like that, of course, even some Green Bones, but thankfully not too many."

Hilo drank from his own soda bottle. "People are born selfish; babies are the most selfish creatures, even though they're helpless and wouldn't survive a day on their own. Growing up and losing that selfishness—that's what civilization is, that's what sets us above beasts. If someone harms my brother, they harm me—that's what our clan oaths are about. Those men weren't your enemies—they were *our* enemies. You can understand that, can't you, Lott Jin?"

The Finger hesitated. "Yes, Kaul-jen."

Hilo put a warm hand on Lott's shoulder and left it there for a moment, then rose and went to another seat to give the young man space to be by himself and think. When he'd been Horn, Hilo had considered it a vital part of his job to see to it that new Fingers were coached along, and that those with the most promise were noticed and mentored. He was still unsure about Lott, but he was glad that he'd had this chance to speak to the young man personally; sometimes those few words mattered.

Hilo finished his soda and set the bottle on the empty seat next to him. He leaned his head next to the small window and stared out to the distant horizon. The noise and vibration of the propeller plane droned in his skull. Midway between the Uwiwa Islands and home, there was nothing to see but ocean and more ocean separating Kekon from its nearest neighbors. On the other side of that seemingly endless expanse of water lay the country of Espenia and the city of Port Massy where Anden was now living.

Hilo glanced across the aisle at his blood cousin Teije Runo, still morosely icing his bruised face, and felt a savage desire to push him out of the airplane and watch him fall a long way into the ocean below. When he turned back to the window, Hilo was frowning, and his frown grew deeper and more pensive than the one he'd tried to ease off Lott.

CHAPTER

11

~

Port Massy

The week after his adoptive grandfather's funeral, Anden boarded an eleven-and-a-half-hour flight out of Janloon International Airport. He felt as if he were entering the cell that housed prisoners on the night before execution. Only, instead of a shoebox-sized shrine and a penitent to guide meditation prayers that might ease his conscience in preparation for the afterlife, there were stacks of tattered gossip and lifestyle magazines and stewardesses moving through the circulating haze of cigarette smoke to offer blankets and hot tea.

Anden took a sleeping pill and knocked himself out for most of the trip. When he awoke, the plane was coming in for a landing, and groggily, he opened the window shade to get a first glimpse of the foreign city he'd been exiled to. Like a vast, spiky beast asleep under a blanket, the metropolis of Port Massy lay sprawled beneath a thick layer of fog, tinted orange by the late-afternoon sun. Steel and concrete skyscrapers jutted up in dense clumps on the tidal banks where the great Camres River emptied into Whitting Bay and met the North Amaric Ocean. Anden searched for landmarks he'd seen in photographs and on television: the Iron Eye Bridge, the Mast Building, the Port Guardian statues. Even up until now, he had not really believed that he was leaving Kekon, but at last it seemed real, and when the landing wheels of the airplane bumped against the tarmac, his heart answered with a thud of awe and fear.

In the baggage claim area, he picked up his suitcase and stood nervously scanning the crowd until he saw an elderly Kekonese couple holding a sign with his name written on it. He approached them and said, "Mr. and Mrs. Hian?" They looked at him in surprise, as if he was not who they had been expecting. The man had gentle eyes and a short, wiry gray beard that was darker than his hair; the woman had a wide, rosy face with surprisingly few wrinkles for her age.

Anden set his bag on the ground and said, "I'm Emery Anden. Thank you for opening your home to me. May the gods shine favor on you for your kindness." He touched his clasped hands to his forehead and tilted into a respectful salute.

If the couple had been initially confused by Anden's appearance, they were put at ease by his fluent Kekonese and respectful manners. "Ah, it's no trouble for us; we like to host students," said Mr. Hian, smiling now and touching his forehead in greeting. His wife did the same, and asked, "How was your flight? It's very long, isn't it? We've only been back to Kekon twice since we moved here; that flight, it's too long! My old body can't take it anymore." Her husband tried to take Anden's suitcase, which Anden quickly insisted on relieving him of, and the couple led the way out of the airport to the short-term parking lot.

Mr. Hian drove, with Mrs. Hian in the front passenger seat. It was the smallest, oldest car that Anden had ever been in, with brown fabric upholstery, a faux wood dash, and windows that only rolled down halfway. Anden sat in the back, staring out at the passing streets and buildings. The air was humid, but nothing like Janloon's fragrant sweat; the dampness here felt cool and ashy. Steam rose from grates in the sidewalks as people hurried past storefronts with mannequins displaying bright, tinselly clothes. Buskers drummed, largely ignored, on upturned metal pails outside a train station. Double-decker buses spewed black exhaust. The largest city in Espenia seemed a sunless and unfriendly place, a picture of frenetic activity against a sepia canvas of brick and concrete. And everywhere he looked, he saw Espenians.

"So, do you have family in Espenia?" Mr. Hian asked casually.

"No," replied Anden, and because he recognized the seemingly mild question for what it really was—an inquiry into his ancestry—he said, "My father was Espenian, but I was born in Kekon. This is my first time here." It felt strange to even speak of his father, some foreign serviceman he'd never known and had no desire to. Even more strange to think he was in the man's homeland.

Mr. and Mrs. Hian lived in a part of the city called Southtrap on the lower side of the Camres. It was a working-class, largely immigrant neighborhood with multistory brick apartment buildings packed close together in a manner that reminded Anden of the Paw-Paw or Forge districts in Janloon. His host family lived in one of the better homes: a yellow, two-story row house facing onto a busy two-lane street. Anden carried his suitcase into the house and up the narrow staircase to the guest bedroom, which overlooked an alley in the back. It was about the size of his dormitory room at the Academy, much smaller than the bedroom he'd become accustomed to in the Kaul family's beach house in Marenia. It was homey, though; the bedspread was thick and soft, and a watercolor print of a misty mountain hung on the wall above the headboard. A vase on the dresser held three sprigs of blue fabric flowers.

Mrs. Hian made a proper Kekonese dinner of blackened chicken in milk, sautéed greens, and noodles with garlic sauce. Anden was immensely grateful for the familiar food and had no trouble eating several servings to show his appreciation. "Eat as much as you can," Mrs. Hian encouraged him. "Espenian food is not very good. I always tell my son to come home for dinner more often, but he's so busy and the traffic is too difficult. That's why he's losing weight." The Hians had two sons. The eldest, which Mrs. Hian was referring to, lived in the north part of the city but worked in sales for a medical equipment company and traveled a great deal. He was the one who'd brought his parents over to Espenia a decade ago. Their younger son was studying to earn his doctorate in history at Watersguard University in Adamont Capita. "A useless degree," Mr. Hian sighed. "But children do what they want."

After dinner, Mrs. Hian cleared the plates and Anden brought out the gifts Shae had instructed him to give: a bottle of expensive hoji, an envelope of cash in Espenian thalirs, and a green ceramic teapot, wrapped with newspaper to keep it safe during the journey. The hoji and money were mere tokens; Anden was sure that the couple would be paid on a monthly basis for housing him. The teapot was more meaningful. Mr. Hian lifted the lid. The circular insignia of the No Peak clan was stamped on the inside. A gift of something green, marked with the symbol of the clan, connoted the friendship of Green Bones and conferred status on the recipient. Presented to a person outside the clan, it meant a favor had been done and would at some point be returned.

The couple thanked Anden warmly and put the teapot on a shelf in the kitchen next to photographs of their sons. Mr. Hian offered Anden a glass of the fine hoji and they enjoyed it together at the dining table. "Are people in Kekon worried about the war?" he asked.

Anden was initially confused. For a moment he thought his host was referring to the clan war between the Mountain and No Peak. "You mean the conflict in Shotar," he said, once he realized otherwise. "I think so. I haven't been keeping up with the news very well, though." He didn't explain that he'd spent the past year keeping his disgraced head down in a sleepy coastal village.

"The Oortokon War is being talked about a lot here," said Mr. Hian. The eastern province of Shotar known as Oortoko (Ortykvo in Ygut) sat along the border of Ygutan and had long been a disputed area populated by many ethnic Ygutanians. Three months ago, an insurrectionist militia proclaimed the area independent of Shotar. The Shotarian government rejected the unilateral declaration and sent troops to the region to suppress the rebellion, only to find themselves facing a well-equipped fighting force not-so-covertly trained and backed by the Ygutanians. The Shotarians appealed to Espenia for help.

"If Espenian troops are sent to fight the rebels in Shotar, it may turn into a war against Ygutan." Mr. Hian shook his head with concern. "My nephew tells me that Kekon will also be affected because the Espenians will use it as a base, and they will demand jade for their soldiers."

"I'm sure he's right," said Anden. "The people working in the Weather Man's office would know what's going on." Mr. Hian's nephew was a senior Luckbringer in the clan's Ship Street office tower; he'd been an Academy classmate of Kaul Lan and Woon Papidonwa and had vouched to Shae that his uncle would take care of Anden while he was in Espenia.

"What about you, Anden?" asked Mrs. Hian curiously. "Are you of rank in the clan?" She did not say "a member of the clan" or "part of the clan." The majority of people in Janloon could claim to be affiliated with one of the Green Bone clans, but being "of rank" was different—it referred to a position of status and usually meant someone who wore jade.

Perhaps Mr. Hian's nephew had told them that Anden was a graduate of Kaul Dushuron Academy. They must be confused by the fact that they had not seen any green on him. Anden hesitated; he didn't want to lower his hosts' regard for him, but he didn't want to be dishonest either. "I was, but my cousin is the Pillar and he decided I should come to Espenia to study." For an instant, he pretended to himself that he was referring to Lan instead of Hilo, and suffered a pulse of self-pity and grief; he would not be in this situation at all if Lan were still alive.

The Hians nodded, no doubt sensing there was more to Anden's story, but refraining from inquiring further. "You're lucky to have a family that's so powerful and able to sponsor your education, even if it means sending you to the other side of the world," said Mr. Hian. "You must be very tired, though. We should all go to sleep."

"Mr. Hian," Anden began, but the man raised a hand to interrupt him.

"Your cousin put you in our care," said the old man. "While you're here in Espenia, think of us as your family. Ask anything of us that you would ask your own kin."

Anden nodded. "Uncle, do you like living in Espenia?"

Mr. Hian scratched his beard and looked thoughtful. "Well enough," he replied. "Of course, it's not Kekon. The food, the language, the Espenians and their ways will always be a little strange to us. But there are good things about it as well. And most importantly, it's where our sons are. Your home is always where your family is." His wife nodded in agreement.

Anden's long, drug-induced nap on the airplane flight made it so that he couldn't fall asleep when he went to bed. The dorm at the Academy, the Kaul residence in Janloon, and his room in the Marenia beach house had all been quiet spaces separated from the bustle of the city. Now he could hear people and cars and sirens and other urban noise all night, right outside his window. Anden lay awake for several hours, feeling utterly miserable.

———

Shae had enrolled him in the Immersive Espenian for Speakers of Other Languages (IESOL) program at Port Massy College. The spring term began the following week. Mr. Hian showed Anden where to take the bus and rode with him the first day. Anden knew a total of about thirty words in Espenian, mostly from pop culture; there'd been a class at the Academy, but he'd only taken one semester before dropping it in favor of a supplemental Deflection elective. At the time, he couldn't see how speaking Espenian would be of any use to him. Proficiency in the jade disciplines was far more important if he was to become a Fist of No Peak.

There were fifty students in the program, hailing from all over the world. There were four Tuni and two Shotarians in the class, but Anden was the only Kekonese. The teacher was a bearish woman with hair the color of wheat. When Anden answered her question about where he was from, she initially thought he said, "Callon," a city in Stepenland. The students were seated together at round tables and encouraged to get to know each other. Anden decided that he would be polite, but he was not here to make friends—which was just as well since during the lunch break, social groupings quickly formed based on ethnic background. Anden might've tried to join in at the table of Tuni youths, but he did not, as he was instinctively distrustful of them; the Kekonese view themselves as superior to neighboring races.

In Anden's mind, there were two ways to deal with his situation: give in to despair and sleepwalk through the year, or grit his teeth and prove that he could conquer this punishment. Despite the fact that he was clearly starting out as one of the least proficient students, he was determined to work harder than all the others. Book studying had never been a strength of his and so he was not surprised that reading and writing Espenian proved to be a constant struggle, but he soon discovered that he was much better at picking up on spoken language. Whenever he could, he sat in the campus food court, on public benches, or at bus stops, and eavesdropped on nearby conversations, sometimes echoing the words in his head, forming them silently in his mouth. He clung to the idea that the sooner he graduated, the sooner he would go home.

Over the following months, when he was not in class or studying, he tried to make himself useful to his hosts. His time spent working at the furniture store in Marenia had made him handy with tools and chores; he fixed a sagging door, caulked drafty windows, and turned some discarded boards into a shoe rack. He accompanied the Hians on errands and carried things.

"*We* should be paying *you* to stay with us," Mrs. Hian exclaimed. "We've had students room with us before, but most of them want to explore, to go out and enjoy themselves in the city. You work too hard."

Their neighborhood, Anden discovered, was like a quilt—there were several distinct cultural enclaves side by side within it. Many families of Kekonese descent lived in the dozen square blocks around the Hians' row house, but Anden could cross a road and find himself in an area that was entirely Tuni, where the residents shouted out to their children in that guttural language, and the eye-watering smoke of clay-pot cooking rose from portable hearths on every front stoop. The rest of the broader Southtrap district, which extended west to Lochwood and east to Quince, was lower- and working-class Espenian.

One afternoon, Anden missed his bus, and as it was a warm spring day by Port Massy standards, he decided to walk back to the Hians' home. It took him nearly two hours, but he was proud to be making his way alone in this foreign city and gaining a better understanding of its layout. Along the way, he grew thirsty and stopped into a convenience store on the corner to buy a soda and bag of nuts. He counted out the copper Espenian coins on the countertop. The shop owner, a large man with a mustache, said something cheerful that Anden took to be a pleasantry. As he was still not confident in anything that came out of his mouth, Anden merely nodded and smiled. This was a recurring problem—on first appearance, he could pass for Espenian, and it was invariably awkward and embarrassing when strangers tried to speak to him.

As he made his way toward the exit of the store, two men came in. They didn't stop to browse for merchandise, but went straight up to the counter and began speaking to the owner in an initially cordial tone that quickly turned rough and threatening. Anden paused at the threshold and turned back in time to see the shopkeeper open the register and nervously count out a stack of cash, which he handed to one of the intruders. His eyes darted briefly toward Anden, as if hoping for a stranger's assistance. Anden stood indecisive, one hand on the door. These were not his people; he did not know what was going on and did not want to get into a bad situation.

The amount of money surrendered was apparently insufficient because more sharp words were delivered. One man grabbed the two nearest store fixtures and pulled them forward, spilling candy bars and sunglasses across the floor. The store owner let out an angry shout of protest. The second man seized him by the hair and banged the owner's forehead into the top of the cash register with a painful-sounding clang, then shoved him violently backward. The shopkeeper crashed out of sight. His two assailants left; Anden backed out of the way as they pushed past him. One of them paused long enough to snarl directly in Anden's face, "What're you looking at?"—it was the first time Anden so clearly understood something said in Espenian—but the other man hurried them both out the door, which jangled shut behind them.

Anden's pulse was galloping. He felt as if he should've done something, but he wasn't sure what. He knew instinctively that it would've been a bad idea to get in the way of the two men, but he didn't know what a person was supposed to do here in Espenia when he witnessed trouble. In Janloon, he would've run out and reported the incident to a Finger in the clan, or a Fist if he could find one.

The shopkeeper groaned and began pulling himself to his feet behind the counter. He did not seem badly hurt, and Anden, with a distinct sense of shame but a desire not to have to interact with the unfortunate man further, pushed through the exit and escaped down the street.

Mr. and Mrs. Hian were distressed by how late he was and berated him for not phoning them to be picked up. They became more upset when he explained how he'd walked home and what had happened along the way. "Those men are in the Crews. They work for Boss Kromner," Mrs. Hian exclaimed. "Don't go there from now on!"

Anden wasn't bothered by the idea of certain parts of the city being off limits; in fact, it was oddly reassuring to realize that there were clans and territories in Port Massy, just as there were in Janloon. With that in mind, he suspected that the shopkeeper had been a Lantern Man of sorts, and the two men had been sent to collect on delinquent tribute payments. He was glad he had not foolishly interfered in an unknown clan's business, but he was troubled by the situation because it struck him as remarkably coarse. In Kekon, it was rare for Green Bones to treat even the most troublesome Lantern Man so badly. The clans were enmeshed in every aspect of society; failing to pay reasonable tribute meant losing the clan's patronage, which would make life difficult in a myriad of ways. An unreliable Lantern Man might find it hard to open a bank account, buy a house, or put his children in school. There was no need to threaten or injure him.

Anden thought about this as he tucked into Mrs. Hian's gingery fish soup. "Why doesn't the store owner go to this Kromner and ask for some lenience?" he asked. He was certain that a not-insignificant percentage of his cousin Shae's job as Weather Man was negotiating accommodations with Lantern Men, albeit at a higher level than that of corner store owners.

Mr. Hian chuckled, then turned serious once he realized that Anden was not joking. He stood up and rummaged in the cardboard box on the floor that held an accumulating stack of discarded newspapers, until he pulled out an edition of the *Port Massy Post* from a week ago and flipped through it to the page he was looking for. Mr. Hian put down the paper and pointed to a black-and-white photograph of a heavyset Espenian man in a dark suit and tie, getting out of a black ZT Toro with a woman in a long white fur coat. Anden was still not good at reading Espenian; the headline had something to do with police corruption.

Mr. Hian said, "This Blaise Kromner—he's a bad man. A criminal. He's known to sell drugs and to deal in women. His people do all the work so he is never caught, but he has a nice car, nice clothes, and is always going to parties and being photographed. Do you think he cares about the store owner, or even knows who he is?" Mr. Hian folded the newspaper up and put it back in the bin. "Anden-se, the Crews aren't like clans. All they care about is money. They never give, they only take. That store owner pays and pays, but gets nothing."

Anden received another shocking cultural education two weeks later, this time much closer to home. He was returning to the house in the evening, carrying a bag of groceries he'd gotten for the Hians, when he heard shouting from one of the open windows across the street.

This was not uncommon; there was a Kekonese couple living there that fought like animals all the time, sometimes screaming at each other late into the night. The man's voice could be heard clearly. *"I ought to kill you, you fucking cunt!"* There was a crash, more shouting from both parties, then abruptly, the woman burst from the front door in her nightclothes and ran, it seemed to Anden, straight into traffic.

Anden envisioned her being smashed like a loose goat on the freeway and flying off the hood of an oncoming car. A bicycle swerved out of the way and the young man riding it leapt off with a startled curse. Anden dropped his bag of groceries and started forward even though he knew in that instant that there was no way for him to do anything in time.

The young man who'd been riding the bicycle lunged and grabbed the distraught woman. In a burst of Strength and Lightness, he dragged her back to the sidewalk. Cars shot past a hand's breadth away, honking loudly. The woman's astounded husband—shirtless, drunk, and enraged—ran up yelling unintelligibly. He staggered as the bicyclist turned and threw a Deflection that hit him at the knees. As he stumbled forward again, another Deflection caught him in the midriff and he sat down hard, as if he'd been clotheslined at the waist.

The wife ran sobbing into a neighbor's house down the street, not even bothering to thank her defender. After a minute, the husband got to his feet and retreated back to the house, muttering curses but keeping his murderous glare averted.

Anden found his voice. "You're a Green Bone," he shouted in Kekonese.

The young man across the street looked over, pushing the disheveled hair off his forehead as if to see Anden better. He laughed, showing a broad flash of white teeth. "And you're a fool islander," he shouted back. He dusted off his pants and gathered his bicycle.

Anden stared, his mouth open in astonishment. He couldn't see any jade worn on the man's body, but it must be there. The Green Bone swung his leg over his scuffed bicycle and glanced back at Anden, still standing on the sidewalk, groceries spilled behind him.

"You didn't think there was anywhere else in the world where people have jade?" The man waved mockingly and pedaled off, calves bunching, ropey shoulders leaning over the handlebars. Anden stared after him until he was out of sight.

Possibly, he thought, not everything in Espenia was strange and unbearable.

CHAPTER

12

~

Necessary Actions

The meeting between the Pillars of the Mountain and No Peak clans was held in the town of Gohei, roughly seventy-five kilometers from the heart of Janloon. The last time Kaul Hilo and Ayt Mada faced each other in person had been a year ago in Wisdom Hall, in a negotiation that had spanned the course of several days under the jurisdiction of a mediation committee arranged by the Royal Council. Unlike that event, which had been a public performance that both clans knew would not result in any real agreement, the event in Gohei was known only to a handful of Green Bones in the top leadership of both clans. Gohei was controlled by the minor Black Tail clan, which had no tributary status or formal allegiance with either the Mountain or No Peak, so the proceedings would take place on neutral ground. The meeting would happen over the course of a single afternoon. Each clan paid for the presence of two senior penitents from the Temple of Divine Return. All these details were arranged between the Weather Men and signaled that the discussions would be taken seriously.

Hilo, Shae, Kehn, and a small group of their closest aides—Tar, Woon, and Juen—arrived in Gohei shortly after noon and were met at the house of the Black Tail clan's Pillar. Durn Soshunuro, his wife, and three of his four children greeted the visitors with great respect. The only one not present was Durn's oldest son, who was waiting somewhere away from the premises—an understandable precaution that no one would begrudge the family for, given the slim but danger-ous possibility of the negotiations breaking down in dramatic fashion and the hosts being blamed or caught in the center. Durn's uncle had been a wartime comrade of Ayt Yugontin and Kaul Seningtun but had afterward eschewed living in the big city, preferring to reside in the countryside. With Ayt's and Kaul's blessings, he formed his own small clan and took jurisdiction over Gohei, which at the time was a farming community that also acted as a trading post with the Abukei tribes and a stopping point for travelers on the way to Janloon.

Following Janloon's decades of expansion, Gohei had since become more of a far-flung suburb—Hilo had seen barely any break in the urban landscape on the drive here—and Durn Soshu was highly motivated to remain on good terms with both the Mountain and No Peak, knowing that his own clan's continued independence relied on it. Even it if was only a matter of time before Black Tail became a tributary entity, Durn was a wise enough Pillar to want that transi-tion to occur peacefully. He had seen what bloodshed the big clans were capable of and wanted to avoid his family—only half of whom even wore jade—ever being on the receiving end. So he put his entire home at the disposal of the visitors and arranged the large sunroom to be the meeting place, with the proper number of chairs in their positions and a jug of cold citrus tea and glasses already set in the cen-ter of the table. Two of the penitents stood in the corners of the room and the other two were situated in the front and back halls so there was nowhere on the main floor not within spiritual purview. Hilo thanked Durn graciously and Woon discreetly handed Durn's wife a green envelope in consideration for the trouble they had gone to.

It was a good thing that Hilo had already spoken at length with Shae and Kehn and had mentally prepared for the meeting during the car ride, because Ayt Mada and her people arrived only a few minutes later. When they entered the room, the number of jade auras crowding Hilo's mind seemed to dim the sunlight pouring in from the large windows. It was the first time he'd gotten a close look at Nau Suen, the new Horn of the Mountain, and his eyes and Perception lingered a little longer on the man who'd stepped in to replace Gont Asch. Nau was tall and lean, and though he was in his early fifties, he looked like the sort of person who would get up at sunrise to run five kilometers before breakfast. Perhaps because of his prior career as an instructor at Wie Lon Temple School, Nau carried his jade stacked on his wrists, on leather bands similar to the sort used by students. An unblinking gaze and cool, probing jade aura suggested that very little escaped his notice.

Ayt Mada appeared unchanged and straightforward in appearance, wearing a pair of blue slacks and a white blouse, but commanding in the intensity of her assured stare and dense aura. "Kaul-jen," she said, and seated herself comfortably in one of the two chairs pulled up close to the table. Wordlessly, Hilo sat down in the seat across from her. The Horns and the Weather Men took their seats slightly behind their Pillars, and the remaining Green Bones stood watchfully against the walls. Durn and his wife came in with plates of light snacking foods—sliced fruit, small nut paste buns, salty dried meat cakes—and poured cool tea into glasses. Durn's youngest child, a girl of about eight, followed close behind her parents. With the nodded permission of the Pillars, Durn made a point of also pouring his daughter a glass of tea and letting her help herself to the snacks, so there was no suspicion of anything wrong with the food. Durn saluted deeply to both Ayt and Kaul, then drew the long window shades for privacy and silently withdrew.

Ayt spoke first. "I trust your Weather Man has explained to you why we're meeting."

Hilo narrowed his eyes at the condescending insinuation that he needed even the simplest things explained to him. So be it if Ayt viewed him a simple thug; he saw no reason to dissuade her of the opinion. He leaned back in his chair and popped an entire nut paste bun into his mouth, taking his time to chew and swallow. "We're here because you expected to be in control of the city by now, and for everyone with the name of Kaul to be feeding worms, but that hasn't happened." He spread his hands and gave her a cold smile. "Talk is for when violence fails."

The Pillar of the Mountain said, with a flash of impatience, "If one of us could've won this war with moon blades, Kaul-jen, we'd have already done so. Now we've placed ourselves, and the country, in an untenable position. There's no money entering the national coffers from jade exports. The Oortokon conflict will become a contest between the major powers, who're greedily eyeing Kekon's inactive jade mines for their military forces. If we continue in this way, we'll undermine the national government, drain the jade stores of both our clans, lose the support of the people, and make our nation a vulnerable target for foreigners. The public knows this, the Royal Council knows it, the smugglers like Zapunyo know it. So now it is up to us to avert this disaster."

Hilo regarded the other Pillar shrewdly. "If the KJA starts up again, it has to be with all the new rules in place. All the jade that's mined goes through the official body so there's no *theft* on anyone's part." His lips curled slightly. "I should say, no *further* theft. You haven't repaid the Kekon Treasury for the 'financial discrepancies' that the audit turned up last year."

Ayt was not ruffled. "Let's not open those books again, Kaul-jen. No one cares about balance sheets from three years ago. You drop the subject of the alleged misappropriations, and we'll take a lower share of KJA allocations for the next three years. Our Weather Men can figure out the exact percentages in order to satisfy the board of directors."

Hilo shrugged; he had never expected that the Mountain would account for the jade it had already stolen, so this was as far as he figured Ayt would go. "Fine. So that's the KJA. As for the smuggling: Ti Pasuiga has crooks working in the city and all over the country.

Zapunyo doesn't care about clan territorial borders and neither will the foreigners. A truce means both of us have to agree to take an equal part in going after the black market—stamping out the rock-fish and the shine dealers and the foreign gangsters that've sprung up like weeds while we were busy fighting each other. If one side puts in more effort, it would be too easy for the other to take advantage and move in on undefended territories."

Ayt inclined her head. "My Horn will cooperate with yours to make sure we're jointly committed in our efforts against smuggling. We agree it has to be eliminated. We won't move on any of your territories, so long as the currently disputed districts are fairly divided."

"Fairly divided," Hilo repeated scornfully. There was no division that would satisfy both sides; three days in Wisdom Hall last year had made that abundantly clear. No matter which parts of the city were conceded to which clan, one could argue endlessly that the split was incorrect and should be done another way. The thought of giving up *anything* to the Mountain made Hilo furious, but he knew there was no way to deal with it except quickly and bluntly. "That depends on whether we're talking about area or value."

"Value," said Ayt.

Hilo grimaced; he could've guessed as much. He turned over his shoulder to consult briefly with Shae, then turned back to Ayt. "We keep Poor Man's Road and the rest of the Armpit." The city's largest gambling houses were not merely the clan's most profitable and symbolic conquest, they were a strategic complement to No Peak's companies in the hospitality sector.

"Then we reclaim Spearpoint south of Patriot Street and take Sogen," Ayt answered smoothly and at once, having clearly anticipated her rival's priorities.

"Three-quarters of Sogen," Hilo countered. "Everything west of Twentieth Street." That would preserve a No Peak zone on both sides of Haino Boulevard and create a buffer for Old Town. It was still a major concession, especially since Tar and his men had fought so hard to win that district last year. Behind him, Hilo could Perceive his Pillarman's unhappiness, but they'd come in expecting to lose something. Hilo said, "Both of our Weather Men will have to do the math and agree."

"Of course," Ayt said.

Hilo said, "And you hand over Yun Dorupon."

"He's living unguarded in the town of Opia," Ayt said, without blinking an eye, as if she were telling him the time of day. "You can have your spies confirm." Hilo felt Shae's aura shift slightly, but he himself did not react.

"One last thing," Hilo said. "My cousin Anden. You know he isn't wearing jade. So long as that's the case, no matter where he is, no one from the Mountain goes anywhere near him. He's studying abroad now, but the world's getting to be a smaller place every day. Anything suspicious happens to him, I'm going to blame the people in this room. We shouldn't have to spell out aisho as if it's for preschoolers, but that's the way things seem to be these days."

Ayt seemed amused. "So long as I'm Pillar and Emery Anden remains jadeless, we won't interfere with him, or take vengeance for the death of Gont Asch." Ayt's expression was icy, but the corner of her mouth twitched upward. "Do we have an agreement, Kaul Hiloshudon?"

Hilo had never imagined he would be in this position. *Dead*, yes, he had imagined that countless times—but not this, sitting within arm's reach of his enemy and calmly negotiating for peace. He was not a true Deitist believer in the afterlife, but he imagined the spirits of everyone who had died on the clan's behalf hovering accusingly behind him: his brother Lan, his many Fists—Satto, Goun, Lott, to name just a few—and dozens of Fingers who'd sworn their loyalty to him, most of them young warriors cut down in the prime of their lives.

For a second, Hilo felt almost physically sick with self-loathing. How had Shae convinced him to agree to this? She was always pushing him to make calculated, sensible decisions—but sensible was not always *right*. He knew Ayt could Perceive the flare of emotion in his jade aura, just as he could sense easily enough that behind her composed expression, her hatred for him had not diminished in the least. She was acting as much out of necessity as he was.

"Yes," Hilo said. "Under Heaven and on jade."

"Under Heaven and on jade," Ayt agreed, repeating the words, lifted in shorthand from the traditional closing of the longer Green Bone oaths. They sealed the decisions reached in the meeting, making them the official word of the Pillar, the will of the clan. With the intent of the pact in place, it would be up to the clans' Weather Men to negotiate all the specific details.

Ayt turned slightly over her shoulder to address her Horn and her Weather Man. "Before we go, I'd like to speak to Kaul Hilo-jen alone for a few minutes," she said. Ayt turned back around to face Hilo, her expression even more inscrutable than usual. "As one Pillar to another."

Nau Suen and Ree Tura rose from their seats and left the room, taking their aides with them. After a moment of hesitation, Hilo glanced at Kehn and Shae and nodded that they were to leave as well. Both their jade auras buzzed warily at the unusual request, but they stood and exited, the rest of the No Peak men following. None of the Green Bones went far; Hilo could Perceive them all standing just outside, ready to return at a second's notice from their Pillars.

Ayt's demeanor shifted, turned almost casual. She leaned onto the table with one elbow and placed a few slices of fruit and a meat cake onto a small plate, the sleeve of her blouse falling to her elbow and revealing silver-mounted coils of jade stones. "Let's speak frankly, Kaul-jen," she said. "You don't want to be Pillar. You're not suited to the role like your grandfather and your brother."

Hilo said in a very cold voice, "I haven't forgotten you're the reason I'm in this job."

"And I haven't forgotten that you massacred dozens of my Green Bones and murdered Gont Asch. We both used whatever methods and ruses we deemed necessary in a time of war. Unexpected losses were to be expected." Ayt stood up, taking her plate with her to the window and opening the shade enough to look out at the countryside:

low green hills cut into neat terraces, laborers working in the distance, a muddy pickup truck passing an oxcart on the road behind Durn's property. Slowly, Ayt ate the food on her plate and turned around, the light from the window framing her, shadowing her face. "Kaul Lan was born and trained to be the Pillar; you were not. Do you really believe you can succeed at diplomacy, at business, at anything where you don't have a talon knife in your hand?

"Set aside blind vengeance and find it in yourself to think dispassionately for a minute, if you're capable of doing so. I didn't order your brother's death, and I'd hand his killers over to you if I knew who and where they were." Her voice lowered and for the first time that Hilo could remember, Ayt spoke to him in a tone approaching reasonableness. "A merger between our clans is still possible. It would be better for everyone: no more fighting in the city, no more vying for every bit of business and political influence. Together, Green Bones could wipe out smuggling, control the jade and shine trade, and present an unassailable force against encroaching foreigners."

Ayt stepped away from the window. "There are two things even your enemies say about you, Kaul-jen: You always keep your promises, and you're a natural Horn. Nau Suen is too old to be Horn of the Mountain for more than a few years. You can serve both yourself *and* the country: Pledge to end the blood feud and join our clans, and you'll return to your rightful place, ruling the streets, keeping jade out of the hands of criminals and smugglers, being the Green Bone you're good at being, the sort that leaves a trail of blood in his wake, like you did on Tialuhiya."

Hilo sat back and tilted his head slightly to one side. "You're an unusual sort of person, Ayt-jen," he said at last. "I wonder what it's like, to think like a machine and not care about anyone."

Ayt's manner hardened instantly at Hilo's words. Her thick jade aura rolled like a wave. She did not raise her voice, but it emerged slow and deadly. "Don't presume you know me, Kaul Hilo."

Hilo rose from his seat in one smooth motion and stalked forward. "I know a few things about you. You whispered the name of your own brother. You colluded with a traitor in my clan and seeded criminals in No Peak territory. You stole and sold jade behind our backs. You're the reason Lan's dead. You tried to have me assassinated, and you tried to convince my own sister to kill me. Are those enough things, Ayt-jen?" He glanced at the penitents standing unmoved in the corners of the rooms, as if suggesting they ought to be listening carefully to his accounting of her sins. Each of Hilo's words came out as distinct as a slowly drawn knife cut. "I will *never* swear oaths to you."

Ayt's expression simmered with a scorn that suggested she was fed up with predictable reactions. "I'm extending a hand instead of a blade. Refuse it, and it won't happen again."

"So we understand each other," Hilo said. "It's obvious you're still dreaming of one-clan rule in Kekon, which means that truce or no truce, you're going to have to kill me eventually." Hilo shrugged, but there was nothing nonchalant about the motion. "If I don't get to you first."

Ayt's mouth moved imperceptibly, but her powerful aura bathed Hilo in the furnace heat of a menace as unforgiving as a wildfire. "I've tried enough times to reason with the stubborn Kaul bloodline." She adjusted one of the coils of jade on her arm. "Ree Tura will work with your Weather Man to arrange how we announce the agreement between the clans to the Royal Council and the public. I'm sure the people of Kekon will be relieved and pleased by our change of heart." The Pillar of the Mountain strode past him, set the small plate down on the table, and left the room.

CHAPTER

13

After the Show

A formal press conference was held two weeks later, the morning after Boat Day, on neutral ground in the Monument District. The grand ballroom of the historic General Star Hotel had hosted foreign heads of state, government officials, diplomats, and dignitaries of all stripes, but Hilo doubted it had ever seen two clan Pillars and this many Green Bones within its four walls. Through the expanse of windows behind the raised platform, one could see the west side of Wisdom Hall, and beyond a row of blossoming trees, the tiered roof of the Triumphal Palace. No one in attendance, including the journalists sitting in the front rows of chairs, could fail to grasp the significance: The announcements being made today were as consequential to the country as anything that came from the official government.

The show was not just for the press and the public, but for the clans themselves. Hundreds of high-rank members of the No Peak clan—Lantern Men, Luckbringers, Fists—occupied the left side of the room. Mountain clan loyalists dominated the right side. A dozen penitents in long green robes stood along the walls and in the corners as peace insurance.

Kaul Hilo and Ayt Mada sat side by side at the raised table. A microphone had been placed in front of each of them. Shae and Kehn sat at a slightly recessed table next to Hilo; Ree Tura and Nau Suen mirrored them on Ayt's side. The highest leadership of the two largest clans in Kekon, that for nearly two years had striven to destroy each other, were seated together to face the Kekonese people and to declare peace.

Both sides had agreed to have Toh Kita, a well-known news anchor from Kekon National Broadcasting, moderate the press conference. Speaking into the cameras, Toh introduced the Pillars, who needed no introduction to anyone in the room. Then Hilo and Ayt took turns reading aloud the joint statement that laid out the terms of the truce: new territorial jurisdictions, resumption of mining activities under the reformed auspices of the Kekon Jade Alliance, cooperation to combat the escalating problems of shine dealing and jade smuggling. Both Pillars finished by reiterating their duty and commitment not only to the constituents of their clans but to the nation.

A limited number of prescreened questions from the press were submitted and read out to the room by Toh. Ayt was asked what measures she would take within her clan to ensure that "financial oversights" would not occur again. The Pillar of the Mountain replied that she took the concerns of the Royal Council and the public very seriously. Ree Tura had resigned from his post and a new Weather Man would be appointed within the month. Hilo was unsurprised at this; Ree himself did not react in the slightest. He was near retirement anyway, and had no doubt expected to figuratively fall on his sword for the clan.

A question was posed to Hilo. "Kaul-jen, with today's agreement, are you hereby declaring that you will no longer seek personal vengeance for the death of your brother?"

"There's been death on both sides," Hilo answered. "My grief isn't any less, but I know that vengeance is not what my brother or my grandfather—let the gods recognize them—would want the clan to be focused on. We have to move on."

It was not, strictly, an answer to the question, and this was noticed by the Fists in the room who knew Hilo well. But Shae and her people had prepared extensively for this event, and it was perhaps a sign of experience gained on both their parts that the Pillar was staying so unerringly on script.

The final question asked if the Pillars had anything to say about the current crisis in Oortoko and whether they felt the geopolitical tension between Espenia and Ygutan put Kekon in danger. "The interference of foreign powers in Shotar is deeply concerning," Ayt said. "Although we stand by our long alliance with the Republic of Espenia, we must make it clear that we will not be taken advantage of by any nation."

"Kekon is an island surrounded by bigger countries, and we're the only place in the world with jade," Hilo said. "We've always been in danger. But we've always had Green Bones."

On the face of it, the Pillars sounded very much in accord as Toh brought the press conference to a conclusion. Onstage and in view of all the spectators and cameras, Kaul Hilo and Ayt Mada stood at the same time and, facing each other, touched clasped hands to their foreheads, saluting each other with all respect. As Hilo met the other Pillar's steady stare, a moment of almost amiable congratulations passed between them: They'd both played their parts well. Their jade auras burned against each other like hot coals and molten steel.

Tar and Woon were waiting to escort them away from the stage. Woon put a steady hand on Shae's back and guided her toward the rear exit where their cars were waiting, but Hilo paused along the way to speak to Chancellor Son Tomarho. The corpulent politician looked pale and overworked these days; he appeared to have gained even more weight and he wheezed a little as he caught up to the Pillar. Son's time as head of the Royal Council had been plagued by clan violence, economic concerns, and now international military escalation and foreign pressure. While ostensibly representing the interests of the common people, the overwhelming majority of councilmen were affiliated with one of the major clans; for two years, open war between No Peak and the Mountain had bred a tense and factional political environment in which the tide of political fortune might be swayed by the outcome of street battles between Green Bones. Trying to lead such a divided political body was surely not good for one's health. Son had less than two years left in his six-year term, and Hilo suspected the man was already looking forward to leaving office.

"Chancellor," Hilo said, forcing a smile and putting a hand on the man's large shoulder. "Peace between the clans, like you wanted. And both of us still alive."

Son cleared his throat uncomfortably. "Ah, yes, well. It's true that was not always a foregone conclusion. I speak gladly for the Royal Council in commending you and your Weather Man on this achievement; the entire country is thankful and relieved." Son touched his hands to his forehead and bent into a salute. "A great day, Kaul-jen."

"What a miserable day, to end a miserable month," Hilo grumbled after dinner. He spooned coconut rice custard into small bowls and passed them down the table as Kyanla cleared away the used plates. "At least I got Teije back."

"An accomplishment that was surely worth getting yourself and everyone in No Peak banned for life from the Uwiwa Islands," Shae said drily. "Zapunyo's made sure that scenes of dead Uwiwan policemen are all over his country's news programs and some international ones."

"Shae," Hilo admonished, glancing at their mother.

To everyone's surprise, Kaul Wan Ria spoke up and said, "Everyone knows the Uwiwans are all crooks; even their police are crooks. To think what might've happened to poor Mrs. Teije's son if you hadn't rescued him. You saved your auntie's life, Hilo-se; she would've died of a broken heart if her son had come to harm, and so far away from home. I hope he learns his lesson and stays in Kekon from now on." She began to push back from the table.

Wen got up to help her. "Don't you want dessert, Ma?" she asked.

"No, you should eat it. You need it for the baby."

After dinner was a time for the Green Bones in the family to discuss clan issues. Hilo recalled that as a child, he would be shooed away to play, while Grandda, Doru, and their inner circle remained in the dining room, smoking and drinking hoji, and his mother retired to her room to read or watch television.

Hilo walked around the table behind Kehn's and Tar's chairs to give his mother a hug before she left. Full family dinners were rare in the Kaul home these days. "Everything okay with the guesthouse? It'll be a lot nicer once we fix it up; we're going to put in new floors and appliances. I know you like it in Marenia, but you should live closer once the baby arrives." Since Lan's death, it seemed to Hilo that his mother had aged and shrunken; he'd hired help to take care of the family's beach house, bring her groceries, and check in on her, but it would be safer to have her behind estate walls, and a grandchild might give her some purpose.

His mother patted him on the arm. Hilo didn't press his argument. She might be reluctant to give up the peaceful solitude she'd grown used to on the coast, but he was her eldest son now, and she was sure to obey him; he simply needed to be gentle about it.

Once his mother had departed, Hilo sat back down and ate his dessert, giving Shae another remonstrative look for her deliberate tactlessness. Securing the peace agreement between the clans had been a significant public victory for the Weather Man's office; Hilo knew his sister had been working long hours for weeks, spearheading the detailed negotiations. But that didn't excuse her talking down to him, in front of his own men and his wife, no less.

"You want to know what Ayt Mada said to me in Gohei?" Hilo looked around the table before settling his gaze back on Shae. "She told me to give up now. To kneel and take oaths to the Mountain, because I'm not Grandda, and I'm not Lan, so No Peak's fucked."

"Hilo-jen," Kehn said, scowling, "she's trying to make you doubt yourself. Just because you're not the Torch, or because you're different from Lan-jen—let the gods recognize them—doesn't mean you can't be a strong Pillar, or an even better one. For myself, I can't be the

Horn that you were; I can only be my own sort." Everyone looked at Kehn, a little surprised by his honesty and thoughtfulness.

"I wouldn't have made you Horn if I didn't think you could do a good job," Hilo said. "So there's a difference. I never had either Grandda's or Lan's blessing."

Wen placed her hand on Hilo's leg. "You have us."

Hilo nodded. "That's true, and maybe that's the one thing I have that Ayt doesn't. We're all family at this table, so I'm not ashamed to admit that I need the help of every one of you. For my part, I promise to listen to what you have to say, even when I don't agree or if I make a different decision. And when I do, it's the word of the Pillar, and you have to respect that." This last part was directed at his Weather Man, who glanced at him sideways with an appropriate amount of grudging guilt for the sarcastic way she'd spoken earlier.

"So," Tar said, cleaning his teeth with a toothpick, "are you going to tell us the real plan now?"

"What we agreed to in Gohei *is* the real plan," Hilo said firmly, "to everyone in the clan except those at this table. I want you to make it clear all the way down the ranks. We'll hold to the borders we've agreed to. No more raids or attacks on their territory, no more taking Mountain blood or jade without family approval." *Gods in Heaven, I sound just like Lan,* Hilo thought unhappily.

"We'll stick to our part of the bargain," Hilo said, in response to Tar's skeptical face, "because we need the Mountain to do their part in going after the smuggling. One clan can't protect the country's mine sites and coastline. So we have to do this; we have to make peace for now. Because it's obvious from what happened on Tialuhiya that Zapunyo has every intention of reaching into Kekon, and that uwie midget is ambitious enough to think he can take on Green Bones. He'll hide inside his mansion and use others—cops, crooks, addicts, anyone he can pay or intimidate—to do his work. That means he'll have rats all over Janloon, if he doesn't already."

"We've got rats of our own," Tar reminded the Pillar.

"Not enough of them." Hilo directed his words to both of the Maik brothers. "We need White Rats wherever our enemies are, and that's not just on the streets here in Janloon. We have to be watching every which way for the Mountain's next move—Ayt will try something clever, come after us in some way we don't expect and that doesn't make her look bad for sitting next to me, smiling on camera. And we need people we trust or own in the Uwiwa Islands, close to or inside Ti Pasuiga, feeding us information about Zapunyo's business so we can take it apart."

The Maik brothers nodded. Shae said, "Zapunyo's hardly the only one who's interested in the country's jade mines. And some of the other interested parties have armies. We ought to be more worried about the Ygutanians and the Espenians than about Zapunyo."

Kehn leaned his crossed arms on the table. "The Ygutanians wouldn't dare come after Kekon, not with the Espenians camped out on Euman Island."

"That's not stopping them from buying jade off the black market from dealers like Zapunyo, or under the table from Ayt Mada, who's already established shine factories inside Ygutan to support her secret contracts," Shae pointed out. "The Espenians think of Kekon as *their* jade source, and it'll be a problem for us if they decide their wartime supplier isn't secure or reliable enough."

"The Espenians are full of shit," Tar exclaimed. "They can't handle the jade they already have. Look at what's going on over there. They're going to ban jade outside of military use. Even the ROE special ops guys aren't allowed to wear it for more than three years of service, because of what being addicted to shine does to you—fucks you up, gives you cancer or something, I don't know. There's more jade around this dinner table than in one of their platoons." Tar began to pull out a cigarette, but Hilo took it from him. He wanted to have one too, but Wen said smoky air wasn't good for the baby. He poured Tar a glass of hoji instead.

"Anyway," Tar said, grudgingly accepting the drink, "if those thin bloods tried to occupy Kekon, they'd never hold it. It'd be too costly for them, and the spennies are all about money."

"They're our largest trading partner and military ally," Shae said. "If we intend to grow the business side of the clan, we need access to that market. There're ways they can pressure or control us without resorting to invasion. They're already trying."

"Then it's a good thing I have a Weather Man who speaks Espenian and stays on top of it," Hilo said. "The Espenians can be placated or bought, like what you did last year."

Shae snorted. "You make it sound so simple." To Hilo's amusement, she and Wen exchanged a glance that might've been commiseration. "That's what I get for being the Weather Man at a family dinner table full of former Fists."

"Come on, Shae, don't be like that." Hilo prodded her arm. "You could balance things, bring someone into the family from the Ship Street side of the clan. I'm sure Ma would like it if you brought Woon Papi home for dinner. He comes from a good Green Bone family, doesn't he? And with business sense too."

To Hilo's delight, his sister blinked. Color began to rise in her face. "Woon-jen is the Weather Man's Shadow," she said stiffly. "Our relationship is entirely professional."

Hilo chuckled and the Maiks hid smiles. "I'm sure it is for you," he agreed. "Ah, Shae, how can you be so smart in some ways, and so dense in others? I'm guessing it's because you've already got someone else in mind. Have any of the clan's families succeeded in pitching an eligible son at you?" He could tell that his wide, teasing grin was starting to embarrass and infuriate her, and it improved his mood considerably—not because he wanted to get into a fight, but because it made him feel oddly nostalgic for their many childhood battles. Besides, she had acted so superior with him earlier.

Hilo stacked the empty dessert bowls. Kyanla came from the kitchen to clear them and brought out a pot of tea. As Wen poured for everyone at the table, Hilo leaned back in his chair. "Enough of that fun stuff," he said. "We made peace with the Mountain today, like I said." The smirk vanished from Hilo's face and he spoke in a voice of complete seriousness. "So when we make our move, we can't do it halfway. We can't injure them and start another bloody war. We have to cut the tree down all at once. That means we have to figure out how to do it. When we act, we have to be strong—in our people, our businesses, everything. Ayt was plotting for years before she showed her hand. That was good for her; she almost got what she wanted and she hurt us badly, but we're still here and now it's our turn. Everyone here is kin, so we all know what happened on that stage today was for show."

Hilo paused and looked around the table. No one said anything. Their gazes remained on him and their jade auras hummed evenly and without surprise. "The Mountain has weaknesses we don't know about," he said. "Otherwise, they would never have agreed to a truce. We have to find out what those weaknesses are. Even if it takes time. Then we'll plan how to kill Ayt Madashi and her followers and destroy her clan."

Hilo awoke rested but vaguely anxious the following morning. The conversation at the dinner table last night had tumbled about in his mind before he'd fallen asleep. Perhaps other people in Janloon would go about more happily today, knowing the clans were officially at peace, but Hilo felt no different. As Horn, he'd seen Fists duel for jade, pimps and drug dealers knife each other for the best street corners, dogs and vagrants fight over food. One thing he knew for certain was that stalemates and compromises always broke down. Lasting peace came from unequivocal victory.

Even as he thought about how to eventually bring down the Mountain for good, he had no doubt that on the other side of town, Ayt Mada was likewise scheming to do the same to him. He did not yet know how to go about crippling the Mountain so thoroughly that he could be sure it would never again threaten his family. It seemed an insurmountable task, one he wasn't certain even his grandfather or Lan would've known how to achieve, and yet No Peak's ultimate survival depended on it entirely. On top of that, now there were other adversaries and threats for him to think about as well. Too many pieces—all of them shadowy, instead of out in the open.

He curled himself around Wen and wrapped his arms around her gently bulging belly. If he concentrated, he could Perceive the tiny life inside her—a faint, rapid drumming, like the heartbeat of a mouse nestled under his wife's familiar energy. It delighted and aroused him, to think of Wen growing his child in her body. He began to fondle her, gently but a little impatiently, cupping her swelling breasts, rolling the dark nipples under his thumbs, running his hand along the curve of her hip and over her buttocks and between her legs. He pressed the heat of his erection between her thighs. Wen rolled over and smiled sleepily at him, squirming closer. He pulled her nightgown over her head, turned her onto her side, and made love to her, perhaps a little more carefully than he ordinarily would, because of the baby, even though she said there was nothing to worry about.

Afterward, as he lay on his back, considerably more relaxed, Wen said, "Maybe Tar's right and Espenia's not likely to invade Kekon directly, but people are nervous. For years, we've been happily taking foreign money to build the country, but now for the first time the average person is realizing what it means for foreigners to have what's always belonged to us." She propped herself on her elbows next to him. "They're starting to wonder if our decisions have put us in danger. Maybe by trading our jade, we've lost our souls or angered the gods. When people are scared, they make bad decisions."

Hilo shifted onto his side to face her, puzzled. "Why do you always do this? When we were all talking after dinner yesterday, you stayed quiet and didn't say anything. Later, we're lying in bed, and you want to talk clan business. If you have things to say, why not say them at the time?"

Wen looked away and rested her chin on her folded forearms; to Hilo's surprise, she looked a little hurt by his question. "It wasn't my place; I'm not a Green Bone."

"You're not like my ma, either, leaving as soon as the talk starts. You're not a Green Bone, but you're my wife. Everyone here is family; you should just talk if you want."

Wen was quiet for a moment. "I'd rather speak to you alone." She turned to face him again, her head pillowed on one bent arm. "When it's just the two of us, I can say anything that's on my mind. I know you'll listen even if you don't agree. I talk to a lot of ordinary people: small business owners, contractors, office workers, students." Wen had turned a talent for interior design into a job consulting for clan-affiliated properties, and she was taking classes at Janloon City College to further her career. "So I'm only telling you what I'm hearing out there."

Hilo pulled her near and pressed his face against her chest. "When the baby comes, you'll have a new job to occupy you so you won't have time to worry so much about mine."

"I'll always worry," Wen said. "Even though I know there's no man greener than my husband. Every time I see all this"—she ran her fingers down Hilo's collarbone and chest, gently tracing each jade stud—"no matter how proud I am, I think of the danger you're in, of how many enemies we have."

"I will never let any of them near you," Hilo promised. "Or our children."

They kissed and touched each other for a while longer, and just as Hilo was thinking he ought to get up because he had a thousand things to do, Wen spoke quietly. "Eyni replied to my letter. I wrote her a long message and mailed it right away. I gave her news about the whole family and asked her to come visit with her boyfriend and son. I knew it would take time to get a letter to Stepenland and back, but still, she took over a month to reply and wrote only a few sentences."

Hilo sat up with his back against the headboard. Wen rarely sounded so aggrieved; she was generally of a warm and caring disposition, but when she was upset, she could be extremely stubborn and cagey about the specifics of her displeasure. He had to prod her to elaborate. "So? What did she say?"

"She thanked me for taking the time to write but told me not to contact her again." Wen sat up beside him, her eyes flashing with hurt. "Why would she say something like that? We'd met before. We weren't close friends when she was Lan's wife, but only because we never had the chance to get to know each other. I can't make sense of her rudeness."

"I told you, Eyni was always stuck-up like that." He'd always considered his sister-in-law to be a shallow, selfish woman—someone who liked nice clothes, theater, wine, and the status of being a Pillar's wife but who didn't fit into the Kaul family at a deeper level. He'd done his best to show respect to his brother's wife, but had gotten the distinct sense that she looked down on him, thought of him as an uncouth kid (which he supposed he had been), and she'd never made an effort to talk to him. Lan must've appreciated her cultured intellect and pretty face, but Hilo had been unsurprised and secretly relieved when the marriage ended.

"*You* have to write back to her this time," Wen insisted. "If she won't show me the courtesy of a proper response, she'll at least have to acknowledge the Pillar of the clan."

"I thought we talked about this," Hilo said, but seeing the determined look on his wife's face, he relented. "I don't think it'll make a difference, but all right."

Wen nodded, satisfied, although obviously still vexed. "If she won't make the effort to come here, you should go see her in Stepenland. Even if it's a long trip, it would be worth it." At Hilo's doubtful expression, she said, "You always say yourself that meeting face-to-face is best."

CHAPTER

14

Old Warrior's Mercy

Three days after the press conference, Shae took only Woon and Hami with her on a trip out of Janloon. They arrived in the village of Opia late in the afternoon. As was typical during rainy season, a thick mist had rolled off the mountains, obscuring the canopy of trees overhead and reducing visibility on the winding single-lane road that led into the township. Opia consisted of a few dozen wood and clay buildings resting at odd angles to each other, dug into tenacious positions on steep slopes. Chickens sat on the corners of low, corrugated aluminum roofs. A barefoot boy with a yellow dog stared at the three Green Bones as they stepped out of Shae's red Cabriola LS; with a shout, he turned and ran out of sight down a narrow cobblestone path.

Woon came and stood next to her. Shae glanced at him for a little longer than usual. Ever since Hilo had teased her at the dinner table, she couldn't help but wonder whether her brother was right, whether

Woon had developed feelings for her that she'd failed to see or had dismissed as dutiful protectiveness. It was strange to see her chief of staff out of business attire and wearing a moon blade at his waist; he didn't look like his normal, Ship Street self. Perhaps, judging from the uncertain expression in his eyes, he felt the same way looking at her.

Woon had suggested bringing some of the Horn's people with them, but Shae had declined. She felt this was almost a personal errand, a responsibility of the Weather Man's office. The two sides of the clan depended on each other, but there was a sense of competition between them as well.

The boy with the dog must have spread word of their arrival, because the residents of the small houses came to stand in their doorways. "Green Bones! Come see," Shae heard the children whispering excitedly. The men and women wore plain or checkered cotton shirts and watched with silent, wary respect, touching their hands to their foreheads in salute as Shae and the two men passed. Opia seemed like a place from another time, or perhaps simply a place that time had carelessly bypassed in its relentless march. The thick fog that obscured even nearby features of the landscape made it seem all the more remote and eerie. It was hard to believe they were only a ninety-minute drive inland from the metropolis of Janloon.

Hami was turning his head from side to side, alert. With the pistol bulging under his leather jacket and the sheathed talon knife strapped to his belt, Shae could easily imagine what her Master Luckbringer had looked like as a Fist prior to his corporate career. "Seems the Mountain was telling the truth," he said. "No other Green Bones anywhere nearby."

Shae's Perception told her the same thing; she stretched it this way and that through the subdued energies of the townspeople until she found the one familiar jade aura she was searching for, lying straight ahead in a brown, wooden slat house at the end of the street. There was something slightly different about it, but she could not place her finger on what.

Shae walked up to the cabin and pushed the unlocked door, which swung open on rusty hinges. She stepped into a small room lit by a single lightbulb hanging from the ceiling.

"Uncle Doru," she said.

The former Weather Man sat in a chair beside a square folding card table in the kitchen area. He was huddled in a brown bathrobe worn over a sleeveless white undershirt and gray track pants. A girl of about thirteen, the daughter of a townsperson, Shae guessed, was bending over, pouring steaming water into a foot bath. At Shae's entry, she gave a start and dropped the towel she'd been carrying.

"Shae-se," Doru rasped. A smile cracked his lined face. "It's good to see you." He looked over her shoulder. "Ah, Hami-jen, and Woon-jen. This is much better than I expected."

Shae turned to the girl. "Leave," she ordered. The teenager looked to Doru uncertainly. He said, fondly, "Yes, go back to your parents, Niya-se, and thank you for all your kindness to an old Green Bone these past weeks. The watchful gods will surely shine favor on you and your family."

The girl set down the empty water bucket and hurried out of the small house, her eyes at her feet the entire time. Shae watched her go. The knobs of the girl's spine and the small mounds of her adolescent breasts showed under the fabric of her thin shirt.

Shae turned back to Doru. "You're a wretch."

"Not for long, Shae-se. That *is* why you're here, isn't it? To hand out the clan's justice." Doru eased his feet into the hot water and sighed. "It's cold up here at night, much colder than in the city, even though it's not very far away. I remember this kind of cold, but I used to be a younger man, so it didn't bother me as much." A nostalgic softness came into Doru's eyes. "During the war, the main camp of the One Mountain Society was perhaps...ah, eight kilometers south of here." He gestured vaguely off into the distance. "It was over difficult terrain, though, and the road from Janloon wasn't nicely paved the way it is now. The village of Opia was our waypoint. Shae-se, there are no greater patriots on the island of Kekon than these simple country people. They hid us from Shotarian soldiers, they tended our wounds, they hiked food and supplies into our camp. They were the first Lantern Men, truly—more so than all the company executives these days, the ones who used to send me gifts of fancy pens and bottles of hoji."

"And they hid you away even now," Shae said. She glanced around the small kitchen and sitting area. There was only one bedroom attached to it, with a single narrow bed. Beyond the grimy lone window, the sky was growing dark.

Doru shrugged. "Only as long as they were able. I knew the Mountain would eventually sell me back to No Peak. I cooperated with them for years, using my position as Weather Man and the influence I had with Kaul Sen and Lan—let the gods recognize them—only in the hopes of achieving a peaceful solution for us all. Once I was out of No Peak and peace was no longer a possibility—what further use was I to anyone? I'm very grateful, however, that you were the one to come for me and not that brute Maik Tar."

Shae stared at the man who'd been her grandfather's closest friend and advisor, who'd been a fixture in her family since before she'd been born. Yun Doru seemed even more fragile and shrunken than the last time she'd seen him jade-stripped and captive in his own house over a year ago. His hair was thin and nearly white, his eye sockets were recessed deeply in his long face, and his skin was an unhealthy pallor dappled with deep shadows in the light of the single bulb.

"I'm dying, you see," Doru said with utter indifference. The moment the words were out of his mouth, Shae knew it was true; she could Perceive it now in the sickly limpness of his jade aura. "Cancer of the liver. In the late stages, I'm told." The former Weather Man smiled wanly. "I hope you didn't bargain much in exchange for my life. It's worth very little, and now that Kaul Sen has joined our comrades in the afterlife, I'll be relieved to finally follow after him. You've come to do an old warrior a mercy. I would ask, though, that we have a few minutes to speak alone."

Shae hesitated, then said to Woon and Hami, "Wait outside."

"Shae-jen," Woon protested, but Shae gave him a strong look to show she meant it. "Wait outside, like I said. I'll handle this."

Hami said to Doru, with pity and disgust, "You're getting better than you deserve."

The two men stepped out the door. Shae and Doru were alone. Doru took his feet out of the bath and dried them with the towel the girl had left. The window had fogged from the steam, and Shae could smell the herbal scented salts. "I want you to know," Doru said, "that I had every intention of keeping my promise to you. I would've willingly remained a jadeless prisoner in my own home to keep company with Kaul Sen in his final days." Doru's lips trembled, and Shae felt the pulse of grief in his enfeebled aura. "He was a great man, the greatest Green Bone of our generation, and a dear friend—let the gods recognize him. I broke my word to you only because he insisted I do so, and I have never disobeyed him in anything."

Doru slid his bare feet into slippers, and with painful creakiness, he stood and walked to a battered yellow armchair, tying his bathrobe around his waist. He looked so frail in that moment that Shae had to quell a strange urge to go help him. "What did you give to the Mountain when you went to them?" she asked.

"Nothing, Shae-se—though not from lack of trying." Doru lowered himself gingerly into the armchair, wincing at some unseen pain. "I went to Ayt Mada when the Mountain seemed poised to win the war because I hoped to bargain for your safety. I volunteered my knowledge of No Peak's businesses and offered to aid in the financial and operational merger after the Mountain was victorious—on the condition that you be spared from harm. I asked the same for Anden, because I knew you would want it. Ayt refused. After the way you angered her, she had no intention of letting you live.

"I cannot tell you how relieved I was when Hilo turned the street war, even though it meant there was no place or need for me. The Mountain allowed me to remain here in Opia to tend to my health. At first they set guards, supposedly for my protection, but in truth I was a prisoner—more to my own failing body than anything else." Doru coughed—a long, deep, wracking sound—then he looked up at her with a clear-eyed and serious expression. "Shae-se, even in this place, I hear things—and I always read the clouds. When I heard that the clans were declaring a truce, I was thankful, believe me. But so long as Ayt Mada rules the Mountain, you will never be safe."

Shae felt his words turn her hands and feet cold. "What should I do?"

"To hold on to power, one must deny it to others. Ayt has no heir. There are prominent families in the Mountain that hope to succeed her, who are following behind like a pack of wolves waiting for a stumble. The Iwe family is in the loyal inner circle, and the Vens are wealthy, but the Koben family has the strongest claim and the most to gain. Ayt is a strong Pillar, but she is still human, and a woman. Find a way to ally with her successor. It will be up to you, Shae-se, to end the war between the clans, to find a way back to real peace." Doru coughed again; it sounded like pneumonia. "Beyond that, I have only the advice of an old Weather Man to a young one: Listen to everyone, but read the clouds for yourself."

Shae's voice felt abruptly tight in her throat. "Do you have any-thing else to say, Doru-jen?" The time had come; she put her hand on the hilt of her moon blade but did not draw it yet.

Doru reached around his neck and lifted off a chain with four jade stones. He held the gems in his wrinkled, long-fingered hands for a moment, his eyes glistening. "This jade was your grandfather's," he said. "It belongs in the Kaul family." He set it down next to him on the small wooden side table. His familiar jade aura dissipated like smoke coming off a black log; only his slow heartbeat and wheezy breath remained in Shae's Perception.

Shae felt heavy in her limbs. This encounter was not going as she'd envisioned. She'd hated Doru for years. Coming here, she'd imag-ined acting swiftly and with cold righteousness to correct the mistake she'd made by sparing him before. She had not expected to find him sick and suffering, most of the way to his grave already. It was time to act, but still she remained standing where she was, unable to move. Doru was a devious old pervert and he had committed treachery at the highest level of the clan, but as he folded his hands in his lap and gazed up at her with calm expectancy, she remembered that he had been an uncle to her, that he was Kaul Sen's best and dearest friend.

An ache built in her chest, one that seemed to spread to her limbs and turn them to lead. She couldn't kill Doru. Her grandfather—let the gods recognize him—would never forgive her.

The former Weather Man let out a strangely satisfied sigh. "Ah, Shae-se, I'm afraid you've something to learn from your enemy Ayt Madashi. To lead a Green Bone clan, there are times you need to be as cold as steel." Doru shifted in his chair and opened the drawer of the side table. "Still, it makes me glad to think that, even after all the ways I've lost your respect, you have some softness in your heart for your old uncle after all. You were your grandfather's favorite, and mine as well; I've never wanted to cause you any trouble or heartache." Shae realized what he was about to do an instant before he took out the pistol, put the barrel in his mouth, and pulled the trigger.

The door of the small house slammed open and Woon burst in, moon blade drawn, jade aura blazing with alarm. He made some exclamation that Shae did not hear; the reverberation of the gunshot had turned her world silent. Doru's body had been flung back against the seat and it slumped there now, long limbs slack, wizened head lolled sideways on the thin neck. Bloody bits of his skull and brains were sprayed across the back of the armchair. Shae's heart was stampeding so hard she could feel the beat in her throat. Doru had acted so quickly and unhesitatingly, she hadn't even Perceived it coming. To her surprise and shame, she felt tears prick the backs of her eyes.

Hami came in and stared at the body but said nothing. It was obvious what had happened. Shae had failed, but Doru had accepted the clan's justice nevertheless.

"Collect the jade on the table; it belongs to the clan," she said. She couldn't bring herself to approach the body and claim it undeservedly for herself. Shae turned away and walked back out the door. She heard Woon following after her, but Hami lingered behind. She had damaged his respect for her; she understood that. The huddle of villagers gathered outside shifted back at her appearance, making room as she walked into their midst. "Who's the headman of this town?" she asked.

A bearded, middle-aged man in overalls and a flat cap came forward. Warily, he touched his clasped hands to his head and bent forward in salute.

"Thank you for showing an old Green Bone kindness and hospitality in his final days," Shae said, clearly enough for those gathered to hear. "If his presence was any hardship on you, I offer my clan's gratitude and apologies."

The headman glanced around at his fellow townspeople before turning back to Shae. It was dark now, and she could not clearly read his expression in the light of the kerosene lamps that hung from wooden poles in front of the scattering of houses. "We've always fed and sheltered any Green Bone who needs our help," the headman said. He didn't ask about what had happened in the cabin. It was a custom engrained by past decades of war and occupation: The country folk of Kekon aided and harbored Green Bones without speaking of it to others and without asking questions—the better to protect themselves from torture by Shotarian soldiers. The people of Opia held fast to tradition.

Shae placed an envelope of cash into the headman's hand. It was sure to be more money than the town had seen in years. "Bury him in the mountains, near the old rebel camp south of here," Shae told the villagers. "Mark his grave with the words, *Here lies a Green Bone warrior of Kekon.*"

Rats in the Celestial Radiance

Once a week, Wen spent the afternoon in the Celestial Radiance Bath & Tea House, a women-only facility one block west of Twentieth Street in the Sogen district. This part of the city used to be Mountain territory; during the clan war, No Peak conquered the area, but nearly three months ago, Hilo had ceded it back to the Mountain as part of the truce negotiation between the clans. None of this seemed to affect those who worked at or frequented the Celestial Radiance. The owners had two lanterns—one white, one pale green—and they swapped out which one hung in the front window depending on the current jurisdiction. They paid token tribute as required, and the bathhouse had not incurred any damage during the periods of street violence. The Celestial Radiance was a social spot for wives, and a place sought out by tourists to relax after sightseeing in the nearby Monument District. It was not high value, and Green Bones would not suffer the disgrace of attacking a women's bathhouse any more than they would be seen fighting over a daycare or a funeral home.

So even though Wen was technically three hundred meters inside enemy territory, she was not concerned. The bodyguard who'd driven her here held open the car door, and Wen stepped out of the green Lumezza 6C convertible that her husband had bought for her as a wedding gift. A beautiful car, if not very practical. She was sweating by the time she crossed the short walkway and tiled steps to the entryway; being seven months pregnant during summer in Janloon was an unpleasant ordeal. Once inside, she checked in at the front desk and was shown to a changing stall, where she undressed, stowed her belongings, and entered the adjoining private room where she settled herself onto the cushioned table for a full-body scrub and pre-natal massage. Five years ago, working for secretary's wages at a small law firm and living in a cramped apartment in Paw-Paw, she would never have indulged in such luxuries. There were perks to being the wife of the Pillar. It was not a position to which she'd ever aspired; she'd expected to remain the wife of the Horn—a place with status, but more anonymity, and requiring considerable emotional fortitude and self-sufficiency, as the Horn's job was dangerous and unpredictable and called him away at all hours. Lina possessed such admirable qualities, which was why Wen had introduced her to Kehn.

Being the wife of the Pillar on the other hand, meant visibility. It required Wen to accompany her husband to high-profile events, host clan functions, and be photographed. Wen was well aware that every time she appeared at her husband's side in public, judging eyes settled on her, the petty minds behind them thinking that surely Kaul Hiloshudon, second son of No Peak and Pillar of the clan, could've done better for himself than a stone-eye wife, a supposed bastard with a disreputable family name. Pretty enough, perhaps, but there were more beautiful women.

Wen would not allow herself to be Hilo's weakness, to be exploited or used against the family by anyone inside or outside of No Peak. She took pains to know all the people in the upper echelons of the clan, particularly those who might be resentful of the Maiks' rapid rise in status. She dressed impeccably; she took care of her body. Her health was very important. She hoped to eventually return to interior design work, but for the next few years, she had greater responsibilities as a wife and mother. The clan was not just people and jade and money. It was an idea, a legacy that connected the past with the present and the future. The family's strength was a promise. Lan was dead and his son was far away (although Wen hoped that would soon change). Shae was not about to have children any time soon. Kehn and Lina were not yet married, and Wen was not sure what to do about Tar. The Teijes shared blood with the Kauls but were of no consideration. Knowing that her contribution to the clan was crucial and hers alone gave Wen a sense of anticipatory satisfaction even greater than the normal glow of an expectant mother. The baby kicked Wen in the ribs and rolled like a small mountain across her abdomen. The masseuse smiled and said, "Your child is already so athletic, Mrs. Kaul."

Feeling refreshed after her spa treatments, Wen took a brief dip in the mineral pool, showered, and dressed in soft lounge pants, a tank top, and fleece robe. She went into the teahouse and sat cross-legged at a low table in one of the many screened nooks intended to create a sense of calm and retreat from the bustle of everyday life in the city. Lush potted ferns and broad-leafed plants created a modest indoor garden, and a stone water fountain burbled pleasantly in the background. Most of the other women in the teahouse were older than Wen; some stayed contentedly to themselves with a book or newspaper, others chatted with friends or played circle chess or cards. Wen ordered a sesame pastry and a glass of chilled spiced tea with lemon. The server, a plump, grandmotherly woman, smiled knowingly at Wen and brought her the entire lemon, cut into delicate wedges on a small white dish. Superstition held that sucking the juice of an entire lemon each day guaranteed a masculine child. So did taking daily walks at dawn (dusk for a female child), eating spicy food, and conceiving on designated lucky days (as determined by fortune charts cross-referencing the birthdates of the father and mother). Wen was not the superstitious sort—what was the point when one was already a stone-eye?—and she left praying to the gods to her sister-in-law, but she smiled and thanked the woman anyway, waiting until she was gone to dispose of the lemon in a nearby planter. The sex of the baby was already set; why sour her mouth for nothing?

A slight woman of about the same age as Wen approached and glanced around nervously before sitting down at the table. Wen said in a low voice of concern, "How have you been, Mila? How's your daughter?" The woman looked away, tugging at her long sleeves. Wen was struck with pity for her.

Mila said in a mumble, "I've sent her to stay at a friend's house for a few days."

"That's good," Wen said gently. "You're doing everything you can to keep her safe. That's all a mother can do." When Mila rubbed her eyes and nodded, Wen said, "What do you have?"

The woman removed a manila envelope from her handbag and passed it under the table to Wen, who tucked it into her own tote bag without looking at it. Mila twisted her hands together in her lap and said in a hurry, "The new Weather Man, Iwe Kalundo, took over the office last week. He's been busy holding one-on-one meetings with all the top Lantern Men in the clan. I saw his schedule for the whole month lying open on his secretary's desk and made a photocopy of it."

"Thank you." Wen slid Mila an unmarked envelope of cash, which vanished quickly into the woman's purse. Akul Min Mila worked as a low-level department secretary in the Weather Man's office of the Mountain clan, also located in the Financial District, five kilometers north of Kaul Shae's office on Ship Street. She was married to a violent drunk who regularly beat her and their eight-year-old daughter. Her husband came from a well-connected family within the Mountain; Mila feared retribution if she told anyone within the clan. She was secretly saving up the money that No Peak paid her for the information she stole from the office so she could take her daughter and run away to her only relatives, who lived in Toshon, all the way in the south of the country.

As the rat stood up to go, Wen said, "Mila, don't rush or take unnecessary risks. You've survived this long already; make sure that when you leave for good, there's no suspicion."

The woman hesitated, biting her lip and looking at Wen with a sort of cornered gratitude. Then she nodded, turned away, and left. Mila was not very knowledgeable about the Mountain's business and did not always know what to look for, copying whatever she saw lying around when the opportunity arose. Some of what she gave to Wen was useful, much of it was not, but she was motivated. Wen was cautiously optimistic this time; the detailed meeting schedule of Ayt Mada's new Weather Man would shed light on the Mountain's business priorities and biggest constituents.

Wen sipped her spiced tea and rubbed her swollen feet. Over the past year, she and Kaul Shae had found and cultivated a handful of informers. It was as Hilo had said to Kehn and Tar at the dinner table: No Peak needed rats everywhere, not only on the street, and not only on the Horn's side. The women's bathhouse was perhaps the most invisible place in the city for Wen to meet spies; she rarely saw Green Bones here, and those she did see—stressed young women needing a break from keeping up with their male peers—had their facials or massages and left without lingering in the teahouse. The owners were well aware that they were located on a territorial border and had absolutely nothing to gain from betraying either clan and risking their advantageous status as a business of no disputable importance. And while the Weather Man of No Peak could not spend a suspiciously large number of hours receiving spa services, no one batted an eye at the indulgences of the Pillar's wife.

Wen had considered telling Hilo what she was doing. Perhaps it would prove to him that she was serious and capable of being fully involved in the clan's matters, and even if he did not approve on principle, he would have to see the enormous usefulness of her actions and come over to her thinking. Hilo was accepting of people as they were; he had never once made her feel shame for her parents' well-known disgrace across both major clans, her rumored illegitimacy, or her condition as a stone-eye. For that, she loved him ferociously. She hated to keep secrets from him. But for Kaul Hilo, there was a stark division in the world that determined a person's duties and destiny—a line drawn with jade.

When she became pregnant, Wen reluctantly came to the conclusion that her husband would not condone even the minimal risk she was taking by meeting informers in the Celestial Radiance. In addition, being honest with Hilo would mean exposing Shae's orchestration, and the Weather Man was entitled to the secrecy of her methods and sources of information. As long as Hilo thought his wife's bathhouse visits were simply innocuous pampering and good for her health and that of the baby, he would see no reason to prevent them. The potential value of what she and Shae might learn about the clan's enemies was more important than Wen's peace of mind, and the relationship between the Pillar and the Weather Man could not be risked. The family's survival depended on it. The Pillar was the master of the clan, the spine of the body, but a spine that was not well supported would sag and break. Wen's late brother-in-law, Kaul Lan, had been a good Pillar, but dragged down by a senile grandfather, a treacherous Weather Man, and a faithless wife. He'd tried too hard to carry the clan on his own, hadn't claimed help when he should have, had kept his sister and his cousin out of the clan at the time he needed them the most. He'd made every effort to be strong, and it had made him weak. Wen would not let that happen to her own husband.

She relaxed on the cushions and read a book for fifteen minutes until she saw her second informer pad into the teahouse in slippers, smelling of bath salts. A woman in her late fifties, Mrs. Lonto was a hairdresser who had owned and run her salon in the wealthy, Mountain-controlled district of High Ground for thirty years. Over the decades, she'd heard all manner of stories, rumors, and gossip circulate among her clientele, which consisted primarily of the wives, mothers, and other female relatives of the Mountain's highest-rank Fists, Luckbringers, and Lantern Men. Not only were Mrs. Lonto's clients keenly, jealously aware of the social standing, fortunes, and alliances of the various powerful families in the Mountain, more than a few of them whispered harshly about Ayt Mada, the one woman who controlled the lives of their men more than they did.

Mrs. Lonto had come to the Celestial Radiance regularly for years, and she had approached Wen instead of the other way around. One day, she'd seen the Pillar's wife coming out of the mineral soaking pool and said, "Mrs. Kaul, I'm very sorry to disturb you, but…" The woman's face trembled in desperation. "My son has caused offense against your clan, and I don't know who to turn to for mercy." The salon owner's troubled eldest son had robbed a store at gunpoint in No Peak territory for money to buy drugs. In the process, he shot and wounded two innocent bystanders, including the uncle of one of No Peak's senior Fingers. Fortunately for Mrs. Lonto's son, he was apprehended by the Janloon police and thrown into jail before the clan got to him, but the offended Finger in No Peak had every intention of seeking out the robber upon his release, and if not killing him, at least handing him such a savage beating that he would beg to be returned to prison.

Mrs. Lonto was taking out a loan against her hair salon to pay for her incarcerated son's addiction treatment, but despite knowing many people in the Mountain, she refused to ask for financial help or protection for her son from anyone in the clan. Her grandson by her daughter was nine years old and applying for entry to Wie Lon; as he was a borderline case, Mrs. Lonto was afraid to draw any attention to the taint of drug use and criminality in the immediate family, as it would completely destroy his chances. After hearing Mrs. Lonto's story, Wen spoke to Kehn, who spoke to the Finger in No Peak, who was persuaded to renounce his grievance in exchange for a formal apology and the offender's ear in a box. (Luckily for everyone, the uncle had made a complete recovery.) Now, Mrs. Lonto looked to be in a heartened mood as she sat down across from Wen and told her that her son's rehab was going well and he been clean for four months. Wen congratulated her; it was nice to know the money No Peak paid to secure the woman's eyes and ears in High Ground went to some charitable use. "I'm sorry, Mrs. Kaul," Mrs. Lonto said. "I don't have much to say this week. There hasn't been much news, and business has been quiet. People have gone to the coast because of the heat."

"That's all right," Wen replied. "I still want to speak with you about some events that happened in the past, that I think you might know about." When the older woman nodded warily, Wen folded her hands on top of her rounded belly and said, "Tell me everything you know about the Koben family."

———————

Wen made three further visits to the Celestial Radiance Bath & Tea House over the following two weeks to meet with additional informers who could corroborate and expand upon what she heard from Mrs. Lonto. She had a few casual conversations with the most gossipy relatives in Lina's large and well-connected family, and she made a visit to the national library and archives in Wisdom Hall to examine some public records. Wen conveyed everything she learned to Shae, who combined it with other information she possessed of the Mountain's business dealings to gain a better understanding of their enemy's situation.

According to Mrs. Lonto and others, when Ayt Eodo, second adopted son of the clan patriarch, Ayt Yugontin, was murdered on the orders of his sister, Ayt Madashi, he left behind a wife who did not grieve him. Eodo's marriage had not been a happy one, for several reasons including the fact that he was a hopeless philanderer. His widow might've found it in herself to feel some more sadness if he hadn't been assassinated naked in his mistress's apartment— insulting to her even in death. She returned to her parents, dropped her married name, and raised her then four-year-old son under her family name: Koben.

The Kobens were a large family of moderate status in the Mountain clan. They counted among their ranks nearly two dozen Green Bones, including several Fists, many more Fingers, a few teachers, a doctor, and a penitent. Other members of the family were midlevel Luckbringers or small business Lantern Men, or held other respectable jobs connected to the clan. Although they were generally dependable people, they were no superlative leaders or talents. Some described them as stingy and stubborn, with more guts than brains. At one time, it seemed their star had been on the rise, when one of their own married into the great Ayt family, but upon Eodo's death, they counted themselves lucky the marriage had been a disaster and were quick to make it clear to the new Pillar that they had never liked the man anyway.

Koben Atosho, born Ayt Ato, was Ayt Mada's only nephew. He had few memories of his late father and had been raised with no love for him. He was now nine years old; in the coming year he would finish primary school and be admitted to Wie Lon Temple School to begin his martial education. With this milestone, the Koben family hoped the Pillar would recognize the boy as Ayt Yu's grandson and her potential heir, and consequently, that the Koben family's prestige would rise within the clan.

The two main obstacles to their aspirations were named Ven and Iwe. The Ven family was smaller than the Koben family but one of the wealthiest in Kekon. The patriarch, Ven Sandolan, owned the largest freight shipping company in the country. He had three sons and two daughters; the eldest son was a respected, high-rank Fist. Ven Sando was an influential man in the business world, and also not afraid to be critical of his own clan when he believed criticism was called for.

The Iwe family was not as numerous as the Kobens or as wealthy as the Vens, but Iwe Kalundo had just become Weather Man of the Mountain. Iwe was thirty-six years old and a longtime friend and colleague of the Pillar; he had worked under Ayt Mada back when she had been Weather Man herself. The Iwes were pleased by speculation that Ayt saw her Weather Man as her most likely successor. It would go a long way toward removing their poor reputation. They were less gifted in jade ability but as prone to the Itches as the infamous Aun family, and were suspected of being shine addicts.

––––––––––

Shae explained the situation at the family table after dinner the following Seventhday. "Ayt faces pressure to clarify the line of succession in her clan, but she's understandably avoiding the issue. The Koben boy's only nine—too early for anyone to judge his abilities, and Ayt's had no part in his upbringing. Iwe Kalundo's brand-new in his job. Ayt surely plans to be Pillar for a long time and wants to keep her options for a successor open; naming an heir now would only undercut her authority by raising the status of some other family."

Hilo rolled an unlit cigarette between his fingers, eyes narrowed in thought. "You say Doru thought the Kobens had the strongest claim."

"The others seem like long shots," the Weather Man replied. "The Vens have wealth and influence but no legitimate claim, and they're outside of Ayt's favor; they were slow to declare their allegiance after Ayt became Pillar, initially supporting her brother until that wasn't an option anymore. She might want to hang on to the Ven family's money and support, but she's unlikely to let them anywhere near the leadership."

Shae took a sip of tea and pushed the rest of her dessert toward Wen. "The Iwes, on the other hand, are completely loyal to Ayt and wouldn't talk to us if we approached them. Iwe Kalundo's personal reputation is entirely solid, but his father died of the Itches and there's been shine addiction in his family. There are a lot of people in the Mountain who wouldn't support the leadership of the clan going to that bloodline."

Kehn scratched his eyebrow and frowned. "It's what the Pillar thinks that matters," he pointed out. "If Ayt trusts Iwe enough to make him the Weather Man and he does a good job, maybe she won't care what the other families say."

"Maybe," Shae replied slowly, "but the Kobens have far more people *and* the Ayt family connection." Succession in a Green Bone clan was not strictly hereditary, but there was a strong historical and cultural bias in favor of keeping it within family.

"The boy doesn't have any blood in common with Ayt Yu *or* Ayt Mada," Tar said, throwing up his hands. "If that's the strongest claim, it still seems pretty fucking weak."

"Which is why it's not a foregone conclusion," Shae said. "I can see why Doru would suggest forming an alliance. If we were on friendly terms with the Koben family, it could strengthen their position by suggesting to both clans that peace would continue under their leadership. And with the Kobens on our side, Ayt might think twice about openly coming after us." The Weather Man made a grudging noise. "It makes sense, as a defensive move."

Wen looked around the table. Then she spoke to her husband, in a mild but meaningful way. "Doru was a good strategist. He obviously thought a great deal about how to bring the clans together." She touched Hilo's knee. "That was what he wanted, what he tried to arrange behind Lan's back: unification. So now we know what *not* to do, if we want something different."

Kehn and Tar and even Shae seemed surprised at Wen asserting herself in the discussion, but Hilo smiled at her approvingly. "It seems that old weasel Doru was a help to us in the end after all." He turned to Shae. "Find a way for me to meet with Ven Sandolan."

CHAPTER

16

~

Not a Thief

Anden became accustomed to the routine of his life in Port Massy. The summer days lengthened and grew hot and muggy, although the city more often than not remained overcast and colorless. Despite himself, Anden grew to be on cordial terms with his classmates, and he got to know a few of the Hians' neighbors. On two other occasions, he saw the Green Bone on the bicycle—once speeding by in the opposite direction on the other side of the street, once standing on the street corner talking to a trio of other young men while Anden passed on the city bus.

Anden was inordinately curious and wanted to ask the man a thousand questions. When he mentioned his encounter to the Hians, they said, "Ah, that's Dauk Corujon. He's going to law school; we're all very proud of him. Yes, of course he's green; he's a true Kekonese son. How many Green Bones are there here? In our neighborhood?" Mr. Hian shrugged. "Thirty? Forty? Who knows."

Anden was amazed. Shae had studied in Espenia but had never mentioned anyone wearing jade. He suspected she had never come across any during the time she resided in graduate school housing in the college town of Windton where there was no significant Kekonese community. Port Massy contained twenty times the population of Windton, and showed its roots as a trading hub in the people, food, and goods that could be found from every part of the world. Riding the bus every day, Anden had heard many different languages spoken, and he imagined it would be possible to survive in Port Massy without actually learning Espenian, by sticking closely with one's own people. Now that Anden knew there were Green Bones living near him in secret, he kept trying to spot them. He studied ordinary-looking men and women in the grocery store, standing in line at the bank, strolling down the sidewalk. He queried Mr. and Mrs. Hian frequently.

"Mr. Tow? Of course not. Can you imagine him as a Green Bone?" Mrs. Hian snorted. Later on, "Oh, yes, the Ruen family— all Green Bones. Ruen-jen has been teaching the jade disciplines for years." They were amused by his extreme interest, not fully appreciating that Anden had been surrounded by Green Bones all his life and from his first day in Port Massy had found the absence of them one of the most disquieting things about Espenia. Conversely, discovering their covert existence in the Southtrap neighborhood was oddly reassuring.

No matter how hard he looked, however, he didn't see any jade on display—no piercings, no rings or bracelets or gem-studded belts. It was entirely bewildering. In Janloon, jade was an unmistakable mark of status—it commanded respect in the darkest alleys of the Coin-wash district and the boardrooms of the highest skyscrapers in the Financial District. Green Bones wore their jade openly and proudly and would not think to hide it unless they had some desire to appear especially modest or unassuming.

It made social interactions in Espenia difficult, Anden felt, not even knowing who to address as *jen*. "This isn't Kekon," Mr. Hian reminded him. "The Espenians don't appreciate that jade is part of our culture. They would think we're trying to threaten them or stand out as different. Showing off jade would only be asking for trouble."

As fascinated as Anden was by the unusual jade subculture, he didn't make any special effort to meet the neighborhood Green Bones or to find out where they trained and socialized. He was, after all, not a Green Bone himself—a fact that still stirred a sense of shame in him every time he thought about it, although the feeling had diminished over the months. Far away from Janloon, his disgrace within the No Peak clan was unknown and he wasn't reminded of it constantly the way he had been back home. Here in Southtrap, where a person couldn't tell who was and wasn't green, it didn't seem to matter as much. He had no expectation that he would become personally involved with Green Bone matters ever again—until he made an understandable but serious mistake.

With the student allowance Shae had provided for him and Mr. Hian's help in perusing the classifieds section of the local newspaper, Anden had purchased a secondhand bicycle, which he kept chained in the alley behind Mr. and Mrs. Hian's row house and hoped to use more often now that the weather was agreeable and sometimes even sunny. One afternoon late in the summer, he rode his bike to a nearby park, where he settled under a tree to complete the week's assigned readings. He ended up dozing off afterward. When he awoke, he gathered his belongings, fetched his bike from the rack, and headed back to the Hians' home.

He'd gone no more than half a block when he heard yelling and glanced back to see a man chasing after him and waving his arms. Anden stopped and put a foot down. His pursuer caught up; he was a man in his early twenties, not much older than Anden himself. His face was a splotchy pink and his large teeth were bared in anger. "What're you doing? That's my bike!"

Anden looked down and saw that, indeed, he had taken the wrong bicycle. It was nearly identical to his own, but the red paint was new and unscratched, the tread on the tires still pristine. The owner seized the handlebars. "You thought you could steal my new bike?" He launched into an accusatory tirade in Espenian too rapid for Anden to follow.

"Sorry." Anden's face burned with embarrassment as he got off the bike. "Sorry. Mistake."

The man shoved Anden aside roughly. "You've got to be the dumbest thief around. You have any idea who I *am*? Don't you even speak Espenian?"

Anden's grasp of the language was far from perfect, but he understood enough to know he was being accused of thievery. At first he was astonished; then a surge of angry defensiveness flooded up his neck and into his head. Thieves were the lowest sort of people; being called a thief was worse than being called a coward or a degenerate. Men in Kekon were killed for less. Who would say such an abusive thing to a complete stranger, without giving the other person any chance to explain? "No steal," he protested vehemently. "I said mistake."

"Yeah, sure, nice try. Get out of here, go back to wherever you came from, you dumb fuck." The man began to push his bike away. Anden stood dumbfounded for a second. Then he took several quick strides and grabbed the back of the bicycle seat. The man spun back around, his mouth open in outraged surprise.

"I didn't steal your bike." Anden enunciated each word. "Apologize."

"Are you kidding me?" shouted the man. "You sound like a keck— is that what you are? You want your fucking face smashed?" He dropped his bike to the ground and faced Anden with fists upraised.

Anden experienced a moment of severe doubt. All he'd wanted was for the man to take back what he'd said; no one deserved to be roughly treated and slandered over such a simple error. He wasn't keen to fight this man, but he couldn't think of any way out that didn't involve retreating—which was not acceptable, as he was the one who'd been so badly insulted. In Janloon, if he'd had friends with him as witnesses, he might've tried to reschedule the contest to a later time and place—sometimes, cooler heads prevailed in the interim—but he had no idea what the dueling customs were in Espenia, and it didn't look as if the other man was about to back down.

Anden took off his glasses and put them in the side pocket of his school bag before setting it down on the grass next to the sidewalk. He raised his fists and fell into a poised, evenly weighted stance, still wondering why it had come to this at all. Why couldn't the other man have simply accepted his apology for the mistake and moved on?

The man's eyes widened in surprise, then narrowed in angry menace. "Oh, you're asking for it now, you cocky little—" He rushed forward and swung at Anden's head.

It had been some time—his final Trials at the Academy, to be exact—since Anden had fought, and he was initially slow to react. He barely fended off the man's opening barrage of punches, and though he saw the obvious opportunity to counterattack, he'd overcompensated for his sluggish reflexes by retreating too far out of striking range and couldn't move fast enough to close the distance before his opponent squared up to face him again. Anden shook his head, frustrated at himself; Hilo would've cuffed him hard about the head for being so sloppy. As he was thinking this, his adversary popped a perfect jab through his guard and hit Anden in the cheek.

Pain bloomed in Anden's face. Being struck seemed to snap an entire childhood of martial training back into place; he lowered his chin and shoulders and ducked under the next blow, burying a fist in the man's side. His opponent grunted in pain and made to fling an arm around Anden's neck in a headlock. Anden dropped the point of his elbow into the man's thigh and shoved himself backward, dodging under the grip and sending the Espenian stumbling ahead. The man recovered his footing immediately and came back at Anden with an onslaught of heavy blows. Most of them battered Anden's raised arms but a few connected with his stomach and sides with eye-watering force, and one popped him in the mouth hard enough to cut his lip on his teeth. There was little finesse to the man's fighting, but there was plenty of speed and power, and the brash instinct of someone who'd been in more than his fair share of scraps before. He was larger than Anden, and angrier, and in this blunt physical contest, those two things gave him the advantage.

It occurred to Anden, in a sudden surge of panic and shame, that he—the youngest member of the Kaul family, schooled at one of the best martial academies on Kekon—was about to be beaten by an Espenian street brawler.

Anden gasped with pain but held his ground; arms still tucked close against his head, he popped his elbow up and clipped his opponent in the chin. Planting his shoe in the man's abdomen, he kicked him back with as forceful a thrust as he could muster. When the Espenian regained his balance and came forward again, Anden backed up hastily, as if reluctant to engage with him again—not an altogether false sentiment. He felt his heel touch the edge of the sidewalk. As the other man committed his weight to the next blow, Anden jumped back off the curb. He caught the man's outstretched arm and pulled. It was not a forceful move, just a sharp tug at the wrist, but with their combined momentum, the Espenian went forward; his leading foot landed off the curb and he went staggering headlong. Even so, he was nimble and wouldn't have fallen; Anden had to solve that by punching downward as his opponent's upper body tipped, connecting hard with the side of the face, scraping ear to jaw.

The Espenian put his hands out, breaking his fall as he landed on the asphalt. Anden wasted no time; he struck the man again, then kneed him in the chest. His opponent tried to throw his arms around Anden's legs; Anden dodged aside and kicked him in the ribs. The man finally rolled into a ball, groaning in pain, and Anden leapt upon him, straddling him across the chest and holding a fist poised over his swollen face.

"Do you want to stop?" The man didn't answer, so Anden hit him in the mouth hard enough to cut his knuckles on the man's teeth. "Do you want to stop?" he asked again, and was relieved when this time the Espenian nodded. "Say I'm not a thief," Anden insisted.

"Wh-what?" the man slurred through puffy lips.

Anden drew his fist back again. "Say I'm not a thief."

"Fine, fine, you crazy fuck! You're—you're not—"

Several arms grabbed Anden around the arms and chest and hauled him off the man and back onto the sidewalk. Anden looked around in surprise and confusion to see a small semicircle of gathered bystanders; two large men had pulled him away, and another person squatted down to check on his downed opponent. Anden shook off the restraining hands. Why had they interfered? Clearly, he'd won fairly; the other man had been on the verge of conceding.

One of the bystanders appeared to be Kekonese. Anden called out to him in his native language, "What's going on? What's the problem?" but the man looked at him with stony displeasure.

Anden's opponent crawled to his feet. "You're dead, you hear me?" His voice was a deadly snarl. "I don't know who you think you are, but you step on Carson Sunter, you step on the wrong crewboy. I'm going to find you, and I'm going to *kill you*." He spat a glob of blood onto the sidewalk at Anden's feet, then turned and stumbled away, retrieving his bicycle and leaning on it for support as he disappeared down the street, snarling profanities.

The small group of spectators dispersed, none of them willing to look at Anden. Again, Anden spoke to the Kekonese man, who he was sure he'd seen around their neighborhood. "What happened? Did I do something wrong?"

To his astonishment, the man responded in Espenian. "What did you do that for? You want to give all of us a bad name? Beating a man up over a bicycle?" In an added rush of Kekonese, "Are you trying to be one of those clan goons from the old country?" Shooting Anden a parting look of disdain, he turned away and left, leaving Anden on the sidewalk.

———

When Anden walked in the front door, Mrs. Hian let out an appalled gasp. "What have you been doing?" she exclaimed, sitting him down in a chair at the kitchen table and rushing to fetch ice and salve for his swollen cheek and lip. "How did this happen?"

After Anden had relayed his story, Mr. and Mrs. Hian exchanged a grim look. "This isn't good," said Mr. Hian with a worried sigh. "It may cause problems for us."

"I don't understand," Anden protested. "He insulted and challenged me, and I won the fight fairly. He conceded; people saw it. If he comes back for vengeance, he would be in the wrong."

"Anden-se," Mr. Hian said somberly. "Dueling is not allowed in this country. The Espenian courts will not uphold the result of any dispute solved by a duel, even if the parties were willing."

"That man could come back to harm you, or more likely, his family could demand money from us," Mrs. Hian explained as she dabbed Anden's bloodied face.

"Under the law in Espenia," Mr. Hian explained, "there is no such thing as a clean blade."

Anden sat in silent dismay for so long that the Hians looked even more anxious and tried their best to comfort him. Mrs. Hian got up and rubbed his back and said, "Don't feel bad; it's our fault, not yours. You were only defending your reputation and your family's name; how could you know that the rules here make no sense? We should've explained it to you, but we didn't think this would happen." Mr. Hian offered Anden a glass of hoji and a cigarette and said, "Don't worry too much."

"What do we do now?" Anden asked miserably.

Mrs. Hian's mouth was set in a worried line. She turned to her husband, who folded his arms on the small kitchen table and nodded reluctantly. "We must go to the Pillar."

CHAPTER

17

The Pillar of Southtrap

The following evening, Anden and the Hians took the bus six stops to the other side of the Southtrap neighborhood where they entered a blue, split-level house and were greeted by a woman of about fifty with permed hair and white nail polish, who welcomed Mr. and Mrs. Hian warmly and ushered them inside. "You must be Anden, the student from Janloon who's here studying," she said.

"Yes, Auntie," Anden said, and the woman exclaimed, "So polite!" and smiled at him approvingly. "Come in, you can put your shoes there. Losun-se!" she called down the stairs.

A man came up the steps, wiping his dusty hands with a rag. The sleeves of his flannel shirt were rolled up to his elbows. "Nearly done putting in the bathroom tiles," he said, unrolling his sleeves and buttoning the cuffs. "After this, I think the basement will almost be finished."

"It'll never be finished," his wife said with cheerful pessimism.

"You have no confidence," he grumbled. "Ah, the Hians are here."

Yesterday, Anden had asked his hosts, "Who is this Pillar? What clan does he lead?" He was bewildered and wondered why none of this had been mentioned to him before.

Mr. Hian had scratched his beard. "Well, it's not the same as it is in Janloon. We don't have that many Green Bones. Dauk Losunyin is the one that the others obey, and the only man around here that all of us call Pillar, so I suppose that makes him..." Mr. Hian shrugged. "The Pillar of Southtrap."

The Pillar was a heavyset, balding man with large, tradesman's hands and a friendly, agreeable countenance. Looking at him, Anden did not know what to think. This man did not strike him as a Green Bone warrior, much less as the leader of a Green Bone clan. His house was smaller than the guesthouse on the Kaul property. He gave off no great sense of power or authority; picturing him next to someone like Kaul Hilo or Ayt Mada was laughable.

"Dauk-jen," said Mr. Hian, clasping his hands and touching them to his forehead. He bent into the salute to show his great respect. Mrs. Hian did the same and handed Mrs. Dauk a plate of homemade almond paste buns. "Thank you for having us over," said Mr. Hian. "This is Emery Anden, the student from Janloon, the one we told you about."

Anden followed his host family's lead and inclined in a formal salute. "Dauk-jen."

Dauk clapped Anden on the shoulder in an amiable way. "How're you liking Espenia?"

"I... um... I'm getting used to it, jen," Anden replied.

The Pillar chuckled. "It does take some getting used to, doesn't it?" He motioned them through the kitchen and into the dining room, where he proceeded to pull up extra chairs at the oval wooden table. There was an alcove in the wall between the kitchen and dining room with a lustrous green vase that made Anden's jaw fall open, until he realized that it was not, as he'd thought upon first glance, an astonishing and dangerous amount of jade, but a decorative item made of nephrite.

Then he noticed two small matching carved statues of horses on the mantel, and a candleholder on a side table next to the sofa, all made of bluffer's jade. In Janloon, such a display of false green in one's home or business would be terribly gauche. Was it because the Kekonese-Espenians had so little real jade, and could not wear it openly, that they showed the fakes instead? Or maybe, Anden thought, they appreciated the ostentatious appearance of the inert ornaments as a visible reminder of their cultural heritage?

The front door opened and a young man walked in. It was the Green Bone that Anden had seen before, the one who'd saved the woman from running into traffic some months ago. Mrs. Dauk hurried to the door to greet him. "Coru, I didn't think you'd make it home for dinner tonight."

The young man took off his cap and gave his mother a hug. "We have guests?"

"Mr. and Mrs. Hian, you know them," Mrs. Dauk said, "and this is Emery Anden, a student from Kekon who's living with them while he studies at Port Massy College."

Anden realized he was staring like an idiot. Only now did he remember that Mr. Hian had told him the Green Bone's family name was Dauk. It had been so long ago, he'd forgotten and not drawn the connection. The quick-witted bicyclist was the son of the Pillar.

Coru's eyes widened in recognition. Then he grinned. A dimple formed in the center of his brow, and his dark eyes danced with mirth. "So we meet again," he said in Espenian. "And you still have the expression of a startled deer, same as you did the first time I saw you."

Anden blinked and said, in halting Espenian, "You surprised me both times, jen."

Mrs. Dauk exclaimed, "Coru, what kind of a way is that for you to talk to a guest?" She gave her son a reproachful smack across the back of the head. "Speak Kekonese!"

"It's all right, Mrs. Dauk," Anden said, warmth rising into his face. "I need to practice my Espenian if I'm to get any good at it. Your son was only being helpful, as he...often seems to be."

"Sana," Dauk Losun called. "How long before dinner?"

"It's ready," his wife called in reply, rushing back into the kitchen and bringing out a steel pot, which she placed on a trivet in the center of the table. "The pork stew is not quite done, but everything else is. I'll bring it out later. Don't stand there everyone; sit down and start eating!"

It was crowded around the table with six people. Dauk Sana had made more than enough food—spicy cabbage, shrimp with lemon chili sauce, and the belated vinegar pork stew, which had generous chunks of mushroom and egg in it—all of it traditional, homey Kekonese food, with the exception of the long, thick, dark salted crackers that went around the table in a basket; Espenians seemed to serve them as an accompaniment at every meal, for scooping up food like a spoon and dipping into soups and stews. Anden was seated next to Dauk Coru, who ate heartily and, like a good Kekonese son, complimented his mother on all the dishes.

Anden tried desperately to think of a way to start a normal conversation with his neighbor at the table without bringing up their awkward prior encounters. He kept glancing over, trying to see if he could spot the jade Coru wore. Anden leaned over, deliberately timing his reach for the basket of crackers so that his arm brushed close to the other man's. A tingle went through his elbow and deep into his bones; he felt a firm tug in his gut, like a steel hook on the mouth of a fish before it's yanked from the water. Anden broke into a sweat; it had been a long time since he'd been close enough to feel another's jade aura. After such an absence, his own body's unmistakable, longing reaction to the proximity of jade made him nearly dizzy. He shivered and drew his arm away.

"So, how long are you here for?" Coru asked.

"Hm?" Anden hastily pulled himself together. "Ah, two years. Long enough for me to complete the language immersion program and get an associate degree. That's the plan, anyway."

Coru took another mouthful of food without asking a follow-up question. After an unwieldy pause, Anden said, "So...Coru-jen, I hear you're a student too. You're going to law school?"

The other young man looked up at him and laughed. "Nobody calls me Coru except my parents and their friends. Everyone else calls me Cory." He wiped his hand and held it out to shake Anden's. "Now that we've met properly, yeah, I'm going into the law program at Watersguard U next fall. I'm taking this year off to do some community volunteering and save up tuition money working as a paralegal. And I'm planning to travel the country for six weeks next summer." He tilted his chin up and raised his voice so his father could hear him. "Before I'm forced to follow in my sister's footsteps."

"You have an older sister?" Anden asked.

"Three of them." Cory shook his head. "Feel free to pity me."

Anden didn't know what it was like to have so many sisters, but he too was the youngest in his family and had three older siblings, so to speak, and he said so. Cory got up from the table and took a framed family photograph from the mantel. Showing it to Anden, he said, "My oldest sister's the lawyer; she works in the federal Industry Department. Her husband's an engineer; they don't have kids, though. My second sister studied nursing; now she stays at home with her two little ones. The third one—that's her—she graduated with a degree in social work and got married just last year."

All the Dauks bore family resemblance in the shape of their smiles and the broadness of their shoulders. Anden wanted to ask if any of Cory's sisters were also Green Bones, but he'd made so many cultural mistakes and wrong assumptions in Espenia so far that he was hesitant. If the people here hid their jade, maybe it was rude to publicly ask if someone was a Green Bone. He studied the family photo appreciatively for another minute before handing it back to Cory.

"Your younger son is still at Watersguard, isn't he?" said Dauk Losunyin to the Hians. "How's he doing there? Is he still working on his doctorate?" The conversation between the four elders veered into talk and sundry complaints about their grown children, then turned to gossip about neighbors in the Kekonese parts of Southtrap. To Anden, it all seemed like talk that was far too common to be worth a Pillar's attention, but Dauk Losun propped a heavy elbow on the table and listened with chin on fist as Mrs. Hian bemoaned the increasing traffic in front of their house and expressed concern about the couple across the street, the ones who were constantly fighting.

Dauk Sana had just cleared the dinner plates and brought out tea and a tin of Espenian biscuits when the doorbell rang. Cory opened it to admit a man who stepped inside and nodded in solemn greeting to all of them. "Dauk-jens. Mr. and Mrs. Hian." He looked at Anden but didn't say anything. The man took off his hat and coat and boots. He was wearing fine black leather gloves, and he took these off as well, but instead of leaving them with his coat, he tucked them into his front shirt pocket as he joined them at the dining room table. Cory pulled over another chair and the man muttered a thanks, helping himself to a biscuit as Sana poured them all tea.

This newcomer was the first man Anden had met in Espenia that made him think: *Fist*. He was not an especially large man, but everything in his manner—his sharp gaze, the way he stood and moved and carried his lean frame—suggested the capacity for violence. Kaul Hilo had once told Anden that good Fists had the minds of guard dogs—they could be friendly, smiling and wagging their tails, but they were always alert. If you made a wrong move, if you threatened what they valued, they wouldn't hesitate to use their teeth. Without having ever met this person before, Anden recognized him immediately as someone who would fit in alongside the Maik brothers.

"I'm sorry I couldn't join you for dinner," said the man. His arrival signaled a shift in the evening; Anden suspected it had not been coincidence at all, but precisely timed. The idle chatter ceased. Chairs scraped back slightly from the cleared table; cigarettes and hoji appeared.

"Rohn-jen, you know you're welcome anytime," said Dauk Sana, but there was a subtle reserve in her voice that had not been there earlier. "How's your shoulder feeling these days?"

Rohn said, "Much better after your healing sessions, Sana-jen."

Dauk Losun gestured to Anden. "Toro, this is Emery Anden, a visiting student from Janloon. He's only half-Kekonese, but his mother was a powerful Green Bone and he was adopted into the Kaul family of the No Peak clan as their youngest grandson."

Anden was taken aback. All through this dinner he'd been under the impression that the Pillar of Southtrap knew him only as a student living with the Hians. Dauk Losunyin spoke in the same neighborly, casual tone he'd used all evening, as if Anden's history was known to everyone, even though that was clearly not true. Cory's eyebrows rose. He sat back and cocked his head, looking at Anden with heightened interest.

Rohn Toro dipped a cinnamon biscuit into his teacup. "Kaul is a famous name," he said.

"Very famous," Dauk Losun agreed, sitting back and rubbing his stomach with satisfaction after such a good meal. "I grew up in Kekon in a Green Bone family during the Shotarian occupation and was always hearing stories of the brave leaders of the One Mountain Society. Ayt Yugontin and Kaul Seningtun—the Spear and the Torch. After my father killed a Shotarian policeman, the Society helped me and my mother and sisters to escape to Espenia. Those three weeks in the hold of a cargo ship were the worst of my life. But gods be thanked, we arrived safely in our new country, with nothing but the clothes on our backs. I was fourteen years old." The Pillar gazed at Anden intently. "Young man, I tell you this so you understand that I have the highest respect for your family. I make it my business to know what happens in this neighborhood, so when Mr. and Mrs. Hian called to say they were bringing you to meet me, of course I had to ask some questions and find out more about you. Now that I know who you are, my family and I want to help you in whatever way we can."

"Thank you, Dauk-jen," Anden said, trying to recover from the sudden change in both Dauk and the tone of the conversation. He was still not sure what to expect from this unassuming Pillar, the snug family dinner, the house decorated with false jade.

"Anden-se, tell them what happened," urged Mrs. Hian.

After Anden told them of his violent encounter in the park, Dauk turned to Rohn Toro. "You know of this Carson Sunter?"

"He's a coat for Skinny Reams." Rohn said the word *coat* and the name *Skinny Reams* in Espenian. "Boss Kromner wouldn't bother himself over a small thing like this, but Reams might take issue."

Mr. and Mrs. Hian looked deeply concerned. "Dauk-jen, the Crews have no principles at all," Mrs. Hian exclaimed. "Might they come after our home, or even our sons?"

Anden was entirely lost and increasingly alarmed. "That man I fought—who is he?"

To his surprise, Cory answered. "You didn't know any better than to get into a scrap with a crewboy? They're gangsters, you know. Boss Kromner runs all the gambling, extortion, drug dealing, and racketeering on the whole south side of Port Massy, and Willum 'Skinny' Reams is his number one foreman. That man you beat up, Carson Sunter, is a coat—a foot soldier in Kromner's Crew. Not very high up, mind you—the sort of guy who shakes down businesses and carries drug money. But the foreman Reams—he might see a Kekonese thrashing a local as something else."

"Those crooks, they prey on anyone weaker, especially immigrants," said Mr. Hian. "But they leave our Kekonese neighborhoods alone because we have Dauk-jen as Pillar and Green Bones with jade to protect us. That's why you don't see them in our part of Southtrap."

"We have something of an understanding with the Crews. They stay out of our business, and we stay out of theirs," Dauk Losun explained. "But I'm afraid things will change as soon as civilian possession of jade is made illegal."

His words caused a ripple of consternation to go around the small table. Dauk Sana muttered a profanity under her breath. Her husband held up a calming hand. "We might as well accept it. There've been too many publicized stories of irresponsible usage, cases of the Itches, and now this swell of interest in jade because of the military involvement in Oortoko. The legislation to ban jade is already in the National Assembly and has the backing of the premier and the biggest Trade Societies. It's a foregone conclusion that it'll pass."

The Pillar reached under the collar of his flannel shirt and pulled out a circular jade pendant on a silver chain. He kissed the jade disc and said to Anden, "This is our Kekonese heritage. My family has worn jade for generations. Today, it keeps our people safe from the Crews and anyone else that would take advantage of us; it binds our community and is part of our identity as Keko-Espenians. Now the government tells me it's against the law? It's the law that's wrong."

His wife nodded in vehement agreement. "I may not be a doctor, but I was trained as a nurse back in Kekon and I learned enough medical Channeling from my mother to help people who come to me with problems. Now, because of this ridiculous law, they will be afraid of getting involved in something illegal, even though they've been coming for years." As he had with the other Dauks, Anden tried to determine where Cory's mother wore her jade but could not.

Dauk Losun dropped the pendant back under his shirt, out of sight. "The only thing this upcoming ban will accomplish is to make the Crews hungry for jade of their own. I can tell it's already happening; they expect a piece of any black market business in Port Massy. They're already into drugs, so naturally they'll want the shine trade too. It won't be long before we have to contend with the Crews targeting us for what we have."

Dauk Sana blew out sharply. "That day isn't here yet. Let's not get off track. Anden and the Hians came to us for help, and we can't let this silly misunderstanding cause problems for any of them. Let's ask Rohn-jen to go to Skinny Reams with"—she considered for a moment—"two thousand thalirs. I would say we can go up to three thousand, but not more."

The Pillar nodded. "As usual, my wife's smarter than I am. It's a good thing I have her to keep me focused these days. Toro, you should bring two of your greenest friends with you, and if Reams tries to bargain for higher, remind them that we know all about the Gerting job and have said nothing to the police. Three thousand and our continued silence—they'll accept that."

Anden stared around the table. He felt caught in the clutch of two simultaneous epiphanies. The first was that he had not, contrary to his own initial beliefs and those of his cousins, come to a land devoid of jade and clans after all. In Janloon, the question of who would control jade had led to open bloodshed in the streets between No Peak and the Mountain; here it was just beginning, simmering in the

Espenian underworld and the shadows of immigrant communities, but it existed nonetheless.

The second realization fell into place as he looked from Dauk to his wife, to the stranger Rohn. This small family dining table was a far cry from the formal study in the Kaul house or the top floor of the tower on Ship Street, but Anden understood now that he was looking at a Green Bone Pillar, his Weather Man, and his Horn. In Port Massy, they were something different than in Janloon. Simple people in the community, neighbors secretly helping neighbors.

He glanced at Cory. The young man soon to be a lawyer was leaned back with his chair tipped against the wall, one leg drawn up on the seat, still paying some attention to the conversation but seemingly more interested in his handful of jam-filled biscuits. Cory was smooth-skinned and tall and had strong calves from biking. He wore a T-shirt with the logo of what Anden presumed was a popular music band and seemed in all ways to be very Espenian. But he was a Green Bone; he wore jade somewhere on his body and had been trained to use it. What was his place in the clan?

Rohn Toro finished his tea and got up. "I'll find Reams and talk to him."

"Thank you, old friend," said Dauk Losun, standing up as well and seeing him to the door. "Also, sometime soon, it would be a good idea for you to pay a friendly visit to Tim Joro. What happens between a man and his wife is his own business, but when it becomes a known problem in the neighborhood that could bring the police—well, that becomes a bigger issue affecting everyone. Be sure to remind him of that, will you?"

Rohn nodded and left the house. As Dauk Sana pressed a casserole dish of leftovers into Mrs. Hian's hands, Mr. Hian gathered their jackets and again saluted deeply to the Pillar. "Dauk-jen, we can't thank you enough for taking care of this problem for us. May the gods shine favor on you."

"Don't worry," said Dauk. "Rohn Toro is completely reliable, and we've had to deal with the Crews before. Come over for dinner anytime, and bring this one with you." He leveled a mock stern finger in

Anden's face. "Stay out of trouble from now on, you hear? Now you know dueling is not allowed. There are ways to get around that, but we won't talk about it right now. I admire your thick blood, though, standing up for yourself and refusing to be talked down to by anyone. A real Kekonese man from the old country, green in the soul, not like our soft Espenian kids these days." He slid a look at his son.

From behind his father, Cory winked and said, "See you around, islander."

Anden touched his clasped hands to his forehead in parting salute. He was still reeling from everything that had happened. "Dauk-jen, are you sure this will work to smooth things over?" He was most concerned about the Hians; he couldn't bear to think he'd put them in any danger.

"Well, there's never any guarantee, but you should put it out of your mind," said the Pillar. "There's a saying, you know: When there's a problem to be solved, the Espenian tries money first, then resorts to violence. The Kekonese tries violence first, then resorts to money." Dauk Losun chuckled. It was clearly a phrase he'd quoted before because his wife and son rolled their eyes behind his back. "We're in Espenia, so in the same way the Hians are your foster parents here, allow me to act as a friend to you and your family."

Anden nodded in thanks but felt a creeping worry. He had a strong suspicion that the Pillar of Southtrap, though he might be a warm and genuine man, was extending his assistance not just out of affection for the Hians, but because of Anden's association with the Kaul family. Might he not expect that at some point, friendship and favor would be returned by the No Peak clan? He would be sorely disappointed if Anden could not provide any reciprocation.

Anden chose his words carefully. "Dauk-jen, you have my gratitude. I'm a stranger in this country and have only gotten by thanks to the generosity of those in the Kekonese community. I only wish I could speak on behalf of my cousins as well, but I'm afraid I don't hold any status in the No Peak clan—that's why I was sent away from Janloon to begin with. I'm not a Green Bone myself, but I hope that one day my friendship will be worth something more than it is now."

The Pillar seemed not in the least disappointed by this candid admission. Perhaps, in finding out more about Anden in advance of this evening, he'd learned everything there was to know and was already aware of Anden's role in the clan war and his subsequent disgrace. He extended his large, rough hand and as Anden shook it, he said, "A well-spoken young man like you? I'd bet on it. Things change. Circumstances exiled me and my family to Espenia as well, but I have no regrets."

CHAPTER

18

The White Lantern Club

Shae arrived at the White Lantern Club twenty minutes before her scheduled meeting with the Espenian ambassador and the commander of Euman Naval Base. She wanted to secure one of the best tables and to position herself as host before the foreign guests arrived. She asked the hoji master to bring up two recommended labels from the cellar as well as a bottle of imported wine and to place them in the center of the table. A few of the club's members noticed her arrival and looked intent on coming up to pay their respects. Woon went around to greet them and deftly head off any possible attempts to initiate conversation, explaining that the Weather Man was here on important business and unfortunately could not be distracted right now, but he would be glad to carry their regards to her.

Shae went into the restroom to check her makeup and wash her hands, which felt clammy. She was wearing a bold red skirt and blazer, cut in an Espenian style with wide lapels and cuffed sleeves, and a high-necked white blouse that hid her jade bracelets and choker. Her earrings were the only visible green. She took out two folded pieces of paper from the inside pocket of her blazer and reviewed them. A few important economic and political facts and figures, gathered after talking to Maro. A page of strategy notes written to herself during a recent working session with Woon. She stowed the papers. She was well armed, but still felt as if she were going into battle on disadvantaged terms.

She returned to the table. Ambassador Gregor Mendoff and Colonel Leland Deiller arrived at the same time five minutes later. Shae stood to greet them and shake their hands. "Ambassador. Colonel. I'm glad you could join me this afternoon." The words came reasonably smoothly; Shae had spent much of the past two weeks with the radio in her office tuned to the Espenian station and several hours talking to herself in Espenian, refreshing her memory of the language she'd had limited occasion to use since returning home from Windton. She spoke more slowly and deliberately than usual not only to minimize her accent, but to set the tone of the meeting. She did not introduce Woon or the other man she had with her, a translator that she hoped not to have to call upon. She assumed her guests would be familiar enough with Kekonese business custom to understand that this meant they were observers only and would not be active participants in the discussion.

Shae exchanged pleasantries with the men for a few minutes as the waiter brought out tea and appetizer plates of shrimp cake and pickled figs. Ambassador Mendoff complained about the humid weather, and Colonel Deiller, not having been in this room before, commented upon the breadth of premium liquor displayed on the wall behind the bar. The White Lantern Club was an unabashedly opulent place: stuffed red leather chairs, glass chandeliers, expensive artwork on the walls, impeccable servers in black waistcoats. Membership was by invitation only and had until recently been extended exclusively to No Peak Lantern Men of a certain level and standing, as one of the most coveted status perks granted by the clan. Women were admitted for the first time five years ago. The following year, membership by application was opened to those who were not strictly No Peak business executives, including councilmen, prominent Janloon writers and artists, and Kaul Dushuron Academy faculty members. Now there was even limited reciprocal membership privileges with the Janloon City Club on the other side of the Financial District, which had long been the old boys' social club of the Mountain clan. Even during the recent period of clan war, money was more fluid than blood. The Green Bones of the two clans might be deadly enemies, but their tribute-paying businessmen remained able to network over drinks at elite establishments.

"I trust that you gentlemen have heard the good news," Shae said, once the appetizers had been cleared and the soup and meat dishes brought out. Espenians, Shae had learned, did not typically wait until after the meal to begin important conversations. "The government suspension on jade mining has been lifted and mining operations resumed, which means that Kekon will soon begin fulfilling its regular export contracts."

"Yes, welcome news indeed," said Ambassador Mendoff. The ambassador was a bulky man with a gray mustache and congenial blue eyes. He seemed, Shae thought, to be a little bemused by her; he kept angling his wide shoulders slightly to the side, glancing at Woon on occasion. Mendoff was the former president of the powerful Shipworkers Society and had been in the ambassadorial post for six months, a reward for his enormous campaign contributions to the current premier of the Espenian National Assembly. He cleared his throat. "And may I add that this comes at a vital time, Miss Kaul. Considering the political instability caused by the civil war in Oortoko, my government sees our trade agreements with Kekon as one of the primary means of promoting security in the region."

Shae smiled at the man politely but firmly. "Ambassador, here in Kekon, the proper form of address for a person who carries jade is *jen*. You may address me as Kaul-jen, or simply as Weather Man, which is a term that sounds strange to you, perhaps, but means a great deal in my culture."

Mendoff flushed and looked uncomfortable, but Shae continued as if there had been no awkwardness. "I appreciate that ongoing jade exports are of considerable interest to you." She inclined her head to Colonel Deiller. "After all, experts say the conflict in Oortoko is poised to become the first modern jade war."

Colonel Deiller had a square face, assertive eyebrows, and the long-suffering dignity of a career military officer who'd been posted to a dozen places in the world and seen every form of bullshit there was to see. He regarded Shae with an intensely evaluative gaze, one that made her feel faintly uneasy. She suspected the man was flipping through his mental dossier, comparing her to photographs from many years ago, when she'd acted as an informant to the ROE's intelligence service. She'd been twenty-two at the time, the girlfriend of a Republic of Espenia naval officer, spoiled granddaughter of the famous war hero Kaul Seningtun. Perhaps the colonel was wondering how, in seven short years, she had become one of the most influential political and business figures on the island of Kekon.

"Our objective in Oortoko is to provide support to the Shotarian government." Deiller's voice had a heavy northern Espenian accent that Shae recognized from her graduate school years in Windton. "We're deploying military assets at their request."

"You were quick to amass naval forces in the West Tun Sea as soon as you suspected the Ygutanian military was equipping the Oortokon rebels," Shae pointed out.

"The ROE's policy is to combat any Ygutanian aggression, and it's abundantly clear that the rebellion in Oortoko is a vehicle for Ygutan to extend its territory." Deiller eyed the squid dish suspiciously and reached for the pork instead. "The premier and the secretary of the War Department have stated that we'll unequivocally defend the sovereignty of our allies." He gave her a pointed look. "Including Kekon, I might add."

Shae motioned to the server to refill the small cups of hoji. The ambassador had finished his first serving, the colonel had not. Shae had only tasted hers. "I'm sorry to say that many Kekonese don't see the rapid military buildup on Euman Island and in our surrounding waters as the actions of a trusted ally."

"I've spoken at length with Chancellor Son Tomarho," said Ambassador Mendoff, managing to sound indignant at Shae's suggestion while still retaining the smooth tone of a diplomat. "I've assured him and the Royal Council that our heightened military presence on Kekon is a necessary and, we hope, temporary measure in our joint security interests."

"Jade is in your interest," Shae clarified, setting down her soup spoon. "We all watch the news, Ambassador. Stories of Espenian special operations teams equipped with Kekonese jade... that makes people very nervous. You must remember that my country has a long history of foreigners trying to invade and occupy us. How can we trust that our Espenian allies are any different? If you wanted to, could you not use your military might and jade-wearing soldiers to take over our mines for yourselves and control our country?" Shae opened her hands in a helpless gesture, as if she was only giving voice to a ridiculous paranoia, but she was certain Mendoff and Deiller had been in conversations of that very nature with their superiors. If No Peak hadn't kept jade flowing to Adamont Capita during the KJA shutdown, or if the clan war had continued and forced the mines to remain inactive too long, the Espenians might indeed have taken military action. She said, "Don't be offended; I'm only telling you how the Kekonese mind works. We are always on guard against theft."

"It seems you're already aware of our request to the Royal Council," grumbled Ambassador Mendoff. "Nothing in this country escapes the notice of you clan people."

Shae said, "Asking for such a significant increase in jade exports as soon as the mines begin running again, while at the same time you amass forces in our territory, is not going to cause Espenia to be viewed favorably by anyone on Kekon. The Royal Council is already under severe pressure from the public to reduce jade exports and condemn the Oortokon War."

"Shotar is in a crisis situation," the ambassador insisted, leaning forward for emphasis, "and Ygutan is a clear and present threat to us all. Kekon is geopolitically important not only as the world's sole source of bioenergetic jade, but because of its strategic position in the West Tun Sea. We require your country's full support."

"You will not get additional jade," Shae said. "Neither the members in the Royal Council nor the clan representatives that sit on the board of the Kekon Jade Alliance will agree to surrender more of the country's reserves to a foreign proxy war."

Ambassador Mendoff sat back and frowned. "Excuse me, Miss Kaul-jen, but you don't speak for the Kekonese government."

"That's true," Shae said. "You will have to wait for the official answer. It will be the same as the unofficial one that you're hearing from me now. We have a saying in Kekon: 'Gold and jade, never together.' Those of us who wear jade don't hold political office, but you're not asking for gold—you're asking for jade. In that, the clans have the final say."

Shae hoped that the two men picked up on the subtle reminder: Kekon might be a small island with an undersized national army, but any attempt to exert military control over the country would mean contending with the Green Bone clans, which controlled the cities and all major industries and whose membership included thousands of trained fighters each wearing more jade than several elite Espenian soldiers put together.

The Weather Man said, "Allow me to explain, so you can communicate to your superiors: It's not that we disagree with your stance against Ygutan. But in Kekon, we believe that jade is a divine gift from Heaven. A person must train for many years beginning in childhood before they can wear it, and it is our sacred tradition that it be wielded only by those who defend others. Of course," she added, "we recognize the world has opened up and we are no longer the only ones who can possess jade, but nevertheless, it is central to our national identity. There is a large Keko-Shotarian population in Oortoko; they and other civilians will be caught in this conflict. We don't want jade to become known as a tool of war for foreigners, one that might even be used to harm fellow ethnic Kekonese."

"You're suggesting that it'll somehow tarnish Kekon's reputation and the sanctity of jade for it to be used by military personnel in an armed conflict?" Ambassador Mendoff said skeptically. "Disputes between the clans in this country have resulted in people wearing jade killing each other with *swords* in the streets of Janloon. So where's the logic in your argument?"

Shae spoke calmly but with a cold edge in her voice. "The two things you describe are entirely different. If you cannot see why, it is because you are not Kekonese."

The two men looked disgruntled. The server came to clear their empty plates; Mendoff and Deiller glanced somewhat apologetically at the men beside Shae, who had not eaten or drunk anything from the meal. The translator, a junior Luckbringer in the clan, could not help looking at the leftover food hungrily as it was taken back to the kitchen. Woon, who knew well enough to have eaten his fill elsewhere before the meeting, did not spare the dishes a glance.

Shae waited for the server to finish pouring tea, then added in a more conciliatory tone, "Do not think, however, that this means we do not support our allies. Jade is a national resource that must be managed by all of Kekon, but I would speak to you now, not as a board member of the KJA, but as Weather Man of my clan. We can offer other things of value to you besides jade." For the first time, she turned toward Woon, who immediately handed her a thick manila envelope.

Shae set the envelope down in the center of the table and observed that Colonel Deiller reached out to take it first. He removed the papers within and began to examine them. As he read, his eyebrows drew together, and though his face kept its gruff composure, his pulse quickened enough for Shae to Perceive. He handed the papers wordlessly to Ambassador Mendoff, who, after a few minutes of study, rubbed his mustache and looked up at Shae. "How did you get this?"

Shae had searched Doru's files for the information he'd compiled after his trip to Ygutan on Lan's orders two years ago. She'd questioned the Fist and the Finger who'd corroborated the report on the Mountain's activities in that country, and with Maik Kehn's permission, sent them back to Ygutan for four weeks, along with two of her own people, to verify and update their findings.

Shae asked Deiller, "Has the cormorant ever provided you with false information?"

The colonel's eyes narrowed at the use of her old code name. "No," he admitted.

Their table was discreetly partitioned from the rest of the dining floor by a wooden screen, and Woon had seen to it that the dining floor staff did not seat any other patrons within earshot, but nevertheless, Ambassador Mendoff lowered his voice. "This is evidence of large-scale SN1 production in Ygutan."

"With ample SN1, if Ygutan can secure jade on the black market, they can use it for military purposes, including equipping their puppet militia in Oortoko."

Both men appeared noticeably discomfited by the idea. Mendoff asked Deiller, "Why haven't our assets in the Ygutanian government told us about this?" he asked Deiller.

"Your spies embedded in Dramsk probably aren't aware of it," Shae said. "The SN1 production facilities aren't being run by the Ygutanian government. As much as we Kekonese oppose shine trafficking in our own country, there are some people—in clans other than my own—who have no problem producing it and selling it to anyone who will pay, regardless of political alliance."

Even before the clan war, Lan had anticipated that No Peak could use information about the Mountain's overseas SN1 manufacturing operations to damage their enemies—and that was precisely what Shae intended to do. She took the sheaf of papers and put them back in the envelope, then put a hand on top of it and looked at the two men with her eyebrows expectantly raised. "Despite our differing views and priorities, the No Peak clan wishes for our countries to remain friends, which is why I asked you here today for an honest conversation and to offer you something of value."

The two men across the table glanced at each other, apparently coming to some silent, terse agreement between them before turning back to her. "I would have to make some calls to Adamont Capita," said Ambassador Mendoff slowly, "but you've done us a great service by sharing this information. It would be worth perhaps ten to fifteen million thalirs to us."

Shae managed to hide a grimace at the sudden blunt mention of price. The Espenians were a mercenary, plutocratic people; their society was built on a long history of naval power and trade, and they treated fair commerce like a religion. They could put a price on anything, Shae suspected, certainly jade, maybe even life and death.

She leaned back and drank some tea, pretending to consider the ambassador's offer; they would likely be offended if she did not appear to take it seriously. "Clans in Kekon have a tradition," she said at last. "When an outsider has done something for us out of respect and goodwill, we give them a gift. It must be an item that's green, marked with the symbol of the clan. It means that we're grateful for their friendship, and if there's any way we can help them in the future, we'll do so."

Deiller shifted in his chair; Mendoff coughed. The idea of favors and indebtedness clearly made them uncomfortable. The ambassador said skeptically, "That's what you'd like in exchange for information of military importance?"

Shae smiled. "No, no, that isn't your custom, so of course I wouldn't expect you to follow it. The whole point of the gift is that there is no specific date or value tied to it. It's meant to symbolize appreciation and trust. But I don't need a symbolic token, and I wouldn't expect you to accept an exchange that's so undefined. I only bring it up because I would like this to be an opportunity for us to improve the bond between our countries. We are allies, as you say, but because of what's happening now, the relationship is strained. If we build bridges—profitable bridges—it would go a long way in strengthening our alliance *and* public perception of Espenia."

Ambassador Mendoff nodded slowly. His broad shoulders and pale blue eyes were squared toward her now. "You have some particular opportunities in mind?"

"There are many Kekonese companies that would like to gain access to the Espenian market. For that to happen, tariffs would need to be reduced or eliminated in certain industries such as textiles and consumer products. I'd like to see restrictions on foreign real estate investment in cities such as Port Massy be lifted so more Kekonese businesses can operate there." She decided it was best to speak as frankly as they had. "Since the end of the Many Nations War, Kekon has been opening itself up to international trade, but if you subtract our primary export to Espenia—jade—we're running a substantial trade deficit. In order to correct that, and to expand business opportunities for Kekonese companies, I would need your support."

Ambassador Mendoff and Colonel Deiller regarded her silently for several seconds. At last the colonel said, "Well, I'm a soldier, not a politician, but I will say that Kekon is the strategic linchpin of our military presence in the East Amaric. We're committed to our alliance and maintaining good relations with the government and people of this country."

"Be that as it may," said Ambassador Mendoff, "what you're hoping for isn't the sort of thing that can be accomplished quickly or easily. You might be well advised to accept fifteen million thalirs. I can advocate your issues with Premier Galtz and the National Assembly, but..."

"That's all I ask." Shae added a calculated touch of humble flattery into her voice. "I know that you're friends with the premier and have great influence on him, or so I'm told by everyone I speak to. If you're able to put in a word at the highest level that might improve our joint economic future, I'll gladly take it in place of anything else you could offer me."

"You act as if you're the final authority in this discussion, Miss Kaul-jen." Ambassador Mendoff looked uneasy. "Where's the leader of your clan? Why isn't he here?"

Because, Shae thought, *Hilo would rather do anything else but sit in the White Lantern Club cozying up to foreign diplomats.* "I have full authority to act as the Pillar's representative in these matters," Shae said. "My word in the No Peak clan is final."

19

Reunion in Lybon

When Hilo arrived in Lybon, Stepenland, he was surprised by how clean everything was. The inter-terminal airport shuttle was a punctual, silver capsule that announced arrivals and departures in Stepenish, Espenian, and another language that was probably Lurmish. The temperature was mild, almost cool, even in late summer. The people weren't unfriendly, but they seemed curt, pale, and efficient.

Hilo decided he would like to be able to drive around and see the city, so Tar rented a blue coupe from the airport car rental counter. While his Pillarman studied the map, Hilo got directions from the rental agent by showing her the address they needed to reach and having a conversation using the limited Espenian vocabulary that he possessed. When they eventually got on the road, it turned out to be easy to navigate Lybon. Compared to Janloon, the city was more like a large town, divided into four quadrants and bisected north-south by the Farstgein River. The blue outline of craggy mountains rose in the west, and picturesque tall brick houses with pointy roofs lined the wide streets, flowers spilling from the garden boxes of iron balconies. The sidewalks were narrow but bordered by immaculately trimmed green hedges and leafy trees.

Tar suggested they go to the hotel first, but Hilo shook his head; he'd slept on the plane and whenever possible he preferred to get on with whatever needed to be done.

The address turned out to be a quaint, single-story pastel green house in the northwest quarter of Lybon. Tar parked the car along the street. When they rang the doorbell, it opened almost at once. Eyni must've been expecting someone else, perhaps a delivery or a repairman, because she began to say something before she realized who was standing in front of her. Lan's ex-wife took an involuntary step back, her eyes widening.

Hilo smiled and stepped across the threshold into the house. "Sister Eyni," he said warmly, "I'm sorry for not calling ahead to let you know we were coming, but I didn't have any Stepenish coins for the pay phone in the airport. I hope we're not showing up at a bad time." Hilo shut the front door behind Tar. "This is Maik Tar, I don't know if you remember him; he was my Second Fist when I was Horn and now he's my Pillarman."

"What are you doing here?" Eyni's voice came out high. "How did you find out where I live?"

"It's easy to find those things out." It was not worth mentioning that he'd tracked her down years ago, but at Lan's direction, had never acted on the information. Eyni had changed somewhat; her face had not aged, but having a child had added to her hips and she'd cut her hair to chin-length.

Hilo took off his jacket and laid it across the back of a chair. He said, "Going back and forth by mail isn't the best way to talk about important things. You have to take the time to write it all down, then wait for weeks before you get a reply. By then, you've practically forgotten what you said before. And when you can't see the other person, it's easy for there to be misunderstandings. For example, I know you didn't mean to be rude to Wen, even though it came across that way on paper. So I thought: Instead of putting you to the trouble of planning a big trip to Janloon, which I know can be hard when you have a little kid, I'll come talk to you in person."

Eyni's eyes darted from Hilo to the door. "Lors will be home any minute."

"Good," said Hilo. "Then we can all sit down together and be properly introduced." He looked around the living room curiously. It was a small but bright space that smelled of floral air freshener. Eyni had always liked art; there were clay masks and small square watercolors on the walls and a wicker bowl on the coffee table that held fruits made out of felt, as well as, incongruously, a bright green plastic rattle in the shape of a frog. Eyni was trying to appear calm, but he could Perceive her heart beating, her distrust blaring like a red siren, and it irritated him. There were times when it was useful to inspire fear, when he needed to do so, but when he had no intention to frighten, the reaction was a bit offensive. He sat down on the sofa and, with a glance, bade Tar to do the same. Hilo picked up the rattle. "Where's my nephew?"

"He's napping," Eyni said quickly, but at that moment, a noise came from another room and Hilo got up to see a toddler standing and clutching the white metal rails of a baby gate at the end of the hall. Hilo went to the child and crouched down on his knees. The two-year-old barely resembled the plump baby in the photograph Wen had shown him; now he had the features of a Kaul—the nose and mouth, the watchful eyes. Hilo could already tell that he would grow up to be the spitting image of Lan, in the same way that Lan had resembled their father. That seemed to be the way it was, with firstborn Kaul sons. The boy stared at Hilo with great interest, entirely unafraid. His left eye squinted slightly and he reached through the bars of the gate with a chubby hand. Hilo, entranced, put his hand out to the child, who grasped his fingers.

"Hello, Niko," said the Pillar. "I'm your uncle Hilo."

Eyni pushed past him and took the rattle as she opened the gate and picked up Nikolas, who gave a squeal of protest as she shushed him and carried him back into the nursery. The boy squirmed and reached out over his mother's shoulder as he was taken away.

A sudden and all-consuming protectiveness seized Hilo. He'd only just met the child, but now he regretted that he hadn't come earlier. He should've come as soon as Wen had shown him the letter and not waited. He almost reached out to seize Eyni's arm, to prevent her from hurrying Niko away mere seconds after he'd finally laid eyes on the boy.

Eyni disappeared into the other room, then reemerged a minute later, closing the door behind her. "He *should* be sleeping," she explained. "He's been fighting naps lately. If he gets too excited, he won't settle down and then he'll be cranky this evening." She led the way back down the hall without looking at her former brother-in-law. Hilo followed at something of a distance. Once in the living room again, he said, with a greater sense of determination, "We need to talk, Eyni. It's true we didn't use to be friends; maybe I wasn't ever really like a brother to you and you weren't ever really like a sister to me, but that's not important now. We have to think about what's best for Niko. We need to talk about you returning to Janloon."

Eyni was facing away from him, her back rigid. When she turned around, her arms were crossed and her expression was tight with suppressed anger and stubborn resolve. "You shouldn't have come here, Hilo," she said. "I told your wife not to contact me again, and I didn't respond to your last two letters for a reason. I've put the past behind me."

Hilo's face twisted in a flash of annoyance. "You wrote to Lan. I saw the letter; you said you wanted your son to know his father and you were willing to move back to Kekon."

"That was two years ago," Eyni exclaimed. "I hadn't been in Lybon for long, and after Niko was born, I felt so alone and unsure about everything. I still loved and missed Lan, but then I learned through friends—*friends*, because no one in the clan even bothered to tell me—that he was dead. *Murdered.* In some ridiculous Green Bone war that had taken over the whole city."

"You'd left the family," Hilo said, without sympathy. "That's why you weren't told."

"Yes," Eyni said quietly. "It took me some time, but I finally did leave. I have a life here with Lors now. We have a home and friends. We've no reason to go back to Kekon."

"No reason?" Hilo was flabbergasted, but he forced himself to take several seconds to compose a reply; he knew that his temper could sometimes cause him to say things that could not be unsaid. In as patient a voice as he could manage, he said, "I admit I don't know much about Lybon, but I know it's no place to raise a Green Bone. There are hardly any Kekonese people here. What kind of life could Niko possibly have in Stepenland? He'll always be an outsider. He needs to grow up in Janloon, where his family is."

"Lors and I are his family," Eyni replied.

"This man, your boyfriend, he's not Kekonese. And is he really willing to raise a child that isn't his? Are you even married?"

Eyni's eyes flashed with indignation. "What does that matter? We're committed to each other and to raising children together."

Hilo was silent for a minute. "All right," he said at last. "I see how it is. Let's sit down to talk; there's no need to get angry at each other from across the room." He went to Eyni slowly, as if approaching a skittish horse, and taking her elbow, led her toward the sofa. He sat down and though she extricated her arm from his grasp, she did as he wished and sat down next to him. Hilo said, in a much gentler voice, "I think you probably remember me as Lan's kid brother. I was quite a bit younger than he was, and it's true that I didn't always have the best judgment. Who really does, at that age? But a lot has changed in the years since you left Kekon. I'm the Pillar of the clan now, and that means that when I make a decision, it'll be followed.

"You left Janloon under not the best of circumstances, and you've grown used to this foreign country, so I can appreciate you're reluctant to return. And you want to stay with your boyfriend, I understand that." He leaned forward to look into her downcast face. "Here's what I can promise: You and your family will have a good life in Janloon, better than what you have here. The clan will make all the arrangements. You'll have a house, on or off the Kaul estate—it's your choice. A car and driver, a housekeeper, a nanny for Niko, and whatever else you need. Once you're married in Janloon, I'll welcome your husband into the family. He's lived in Kekon before. Does he still work in tourism? There're plenty of foreigners in Janloon these days, and more international companies than ever before. It won't be a problem to find him a good job; he'll probably have his pick." Of course, Hilo had no intention of ever bringing Eyni's foreign lover into No Peak, but he supposed he could learn to tolerate the man's presence in Janloon, so long as their interactions were infrequent. It was an issue he was willing to compromise on, since Eyni was the sort of person who would need companionship, and no respectable Kekonese man was going to have her.

While she was contemplating his assurances, Hilo said, "Tar, why don't you get us all something to drink." The Pillarman, who'd been sitting back and watching the exchange, got up and went into the galley kitchen. Eyni looked up anxiously and made a slight movement as if to follow him, but then seemed to think better of it. She settled back and twisted her hands together in her lap. Hilo said, "There's something else to consider: My wife, Wen, is pregnant. She's due in less than two months. Niko will have cousins close to his age. He'll have aunts and uncles who love him, and in Janloon, he'll grow up as a Kaul, as the first son of No Peak." He gestured to Eyni's house and its surroundings. "Is this place so much better that it's worth giving up your son's birthright? Worth abandoning your home country?"

Tar returned with two glasses of water. Eyni's hands trembled slightly as she took a glass without looking and drained it quickly. Hilo could tell that his last words had struck a chord. Eyni might be a woman without much depth, but on some level, he knew she must be homesick. She wouldn't have left Kekon on her own if it hadn't been for the affair and the divorce, and now that Hilo was offering the forgiveness of the clan and a return to a life of status back in Janloon, it wasn't hard to Perceive the internal war raging inside her. He drank some water and waited.

Eyni held tight to the empty glass. "It's true there're things I don't like about Lybon and things I miss dearly about Janloon," she admitted at last. "But the life you're offering—life in the ruling Green Bone family of No Peak—it's what broke me and Lan apart. It's what got him killed. It's nothing but steel and jade and blood. It's not a safe or happy life… and it's not what I want for Niko."

The flare in the Pillar's aura made Tar look up with more interest. In a soft, disbelieving voice, Hilo said, "Niko is my nephew, the son of a Pillar of No Peak, the great-grandson of the Torch of Kekon. He was born to be a Green Bone. And you want him to grow up speaking another language, surrounded by foreigners, never wearing jade, never knowing who he is?" Eyni truly was a faithless woman, but Hilo felt that what she was doing now was even worse than her betrayal of Lan. "How can you justify that, as a Kekonese?"

Eyni stood, hands clenched at her sides. "You don't understand anything, Hilo. Maybe if Lan were still alive, things would be different, but you're *not* Lan. You're not Niko's father. And I'm *not* an underling of the clan who'll upend my family's life to do whatever you want."

"Watch how you talk to the Pillar, now," Tar broke in with a warning note in his voice, but Hilo silenced him with a look and a sharp shake of the head. He'd heard a car door closing outside and now he Perceived someone approaching the house.

Eyni rushed to the door as it opened. A trim Stepenish man with reddish hair stepped inside. Seeing Hilo and Tar, he stopped in surprise and confusion. Hilo rose from his seat and Tar stood with him. Eyni took her boyfriend's arm and said in Kekonese, so everyone could understand, "Lors, this is Hilo, my ex-husband's brother from Janloon. He and his friend were visiting Lybon and dropped in to say hello. I forgot to mention they were coming."

The man's posture relaxed slightly. Hilo realized that Eyni was afraid for Lors's safety. She was trying to put him at ease, to prevent him from trying to challenge the strange men in his house. "Hello," Lors said warily, in accented but reasonably fluent Kekonese. "We haven't had any of Eyni's friends from Kekon visit us before. How long are you here?"

"Not long," Hilo said. "I came to meet my nephew. Until a few months ago, I didn't know I had one. It's unfortunate you live so far away; the rest of my family would like to meet him too."

"Yes, well, it's a rather awkward situation, it is," said the man, smiling nervously and running a hand through his coppery hair. "We figured there might be some hard feelings, after all."

"None that can't be put aside," Hilo replied. He glanced at Eyni, who stood stiffly by her boyfriend's side. "I was just talking to Eyni about how much we wish you'd all return to Janloon. But she seems to prefer it here. You must've done a good sales job, to be able to lure a Kekonese woman so far from home."

Lors chuckled, put at ease by Hilo's casual and complimentary tone. "I must say, before I lived in Kekon, I'd no idea how beautiful the women were there. I don't know how I was so lucky as to get one." He gave Eyni's bottom an affectionate pat. "I've traveled to my fair share of exotic places, and I dare say she's the best souvenir I've brought back from any of them. Isn't that right, flower?" Eyni smiled in a faintly uncomfortable way, still looking at Hilo. Lors said, "Listen, Hilo—I did say your name right, didn't I? You seem like a good fellow. I just want to say that I never meant anything against your brother. I didn't even know him. It's just that Eyni and I, well..." He put his arm around Eyni, who stiffened a little more, "We were—*are*—in love. Do you have a woman at home that you love?"

Hilo gave a nod.

"Well, then, you can understand, can't you? In my country, we have a saying." Lors spoke a phrase in Stepenish, then translated it into Kekonese. "'Flowers grow even in the desert; so too there is nowhere love cannot happen.'"

Hilo's lips twitched upward. "It's nice to see that the two of you are happy together, even after such a big move and the addition of a child that you must've hoped was yours."

The man's smile wavered. "Well...families can be messy, can't they? We plan to give Nikolas plenty of brothers and sisters. He'll fit right in and it'll all work out."

"I'm sure it will," Hilo said. "But it's a shame for my nephew to be so far from his relatives and not know anything of his Kekonese heritage. So we should compromise. In a few years, when Niko's older, he can split his time between Stepenland and Kekon. Half the year here in Lybon, half the year in Janloon." Hilo was honestly pleased with the solution that had just occurred to him, and felt that it could not possibly be objectionable. It was not a perfect arrangement, not what he'd hoped for, but he'd come here knowing that Eyni was difficult. This would be acceptable to everyone. "When he's in Janloon, he'll live with me and my wife and we'll treat him like our own son. There are international schools in Janloon now, even ones that teach Stepenish and other languages. He can attend one of those until he's ten; then he can go to Kaul Dushuron Academy during the school year and return to Lybon during the holidays. He'll grow up to appreciate both countries and both cultures. A global citizen. Everyone says that's the way of the future; it'll be an advantage for him."

"That sounds like an excellent idea," said Lors. "Don't you think so, flower? Especially after we have kids of our own, it'll be awfully helpful for Nikolas's Kekonese relatives to raise him some of the time." To Hilo, "You might take your offer back if you knew how much of a colicky little monster he can be! I think it was rather hard on Eyni the first six months."

Eyni's face was rigid; she nudged her boyfriend in the ribs in an attempt to make him stop talking. Hilo said, "Tar and I will be in Lybon for a few more days. We've never been here before and want to look around and enjoy the city. Why don't we all get together for a proper dinner on Fifthday evening—I'll pay, of course—and talk about this some more, so I can tell the family the good news. Bring Niko along; we'll go somewhere casual."

The red-haired man shook Hilo's hand and then Tar's. "I dare say I'm sorry we've never met before now. Eyni, you really should've told me they were coming." In an aside to Hilo, "I don't understand why she doesn't keep in touch with relatives in Kekon. Seems to think they'll judge us. Personally, during my two years in Janloon, I found all the people I met to be good-natured and pleasant. Nothing like the stereotypes."

"I only want what's best for both our families," Hilo said.

They made arrangements to reconvene in three days' time. Hilo and Tar left the house and walked back to the rental car. "What're we going to do here for three days?" Tar asked.

Hilo glanced back at the house and lit a cigarette. "I want you to follow that man and find out everything there is to know about him. It could be useful."

CHAPTER

20

Complications

You've been quiet," Maro said. They lay facing each other, Shae's leg thrown over his thigh, his hand resting on her hip, their bodies sticky and languid. The pedestal fan in the corner of Maro's bedroom oscillated back and forth, blowing cooled air over their bare skin. The Autumn Festival had recently passed, and typhoon season this year had been mild, but still the blanket of summer lingered damp and heavy over Janloon. Shae did not want to get up to go to work.

"Something on your mind?" Maro asked.

A lot of things were on her mind—too many to choose from, all of them No Peak matters that would be difficult to explain. She ran a hand over the curve of Maro's bare shoulder. "Does it bother you?" she asked. "That I wear more jade? That I'm a Kaul?" She wondered if she sounded insecure, but with Maro she felt unguarded, removed from the day-to-day realities of the clan.

Maro hesitated. He drew his fingers up her arm and collarbone to the hollow of her throat, bringing them to rest lightly on the two-tier jade choker around her neck. "It does bother me a little," he admitted. "Men are expected to be stronger and greener than women, and it's hard not to be affected by what the world expects. People might assume I'm trying to climb to the top of the clan by being with you, when that's not true. I like spending time with you for your personality, not your family name or your jade."

Shae lowered her head and flicked her tongue over his nipple. "Just my personality?"

"And this." He jiggled one of her breasts. "And this." He squeezed her ass, and Shae gave a yelp of laughter. Maro's smile faded. "I should be the one asking you. Are you ashamed of dating me? Is that why we always come to my place, because you don't want to introduce me to your family?"

Shae was quiet for a moment. "You might not want to know my family."

"I'm not naive," Maro said. "I know Green Bones, and I know your brother's reputation."

"It's not just Hilo. The realities of the clan, of being a Kaul...you might not want to be a part of that." She traced his eyebrow with her thumb. For the past three months, whenever she made her usual weekly visit to the Temple of Divine Return and knelt to pray in the sanctum, she thought of Doru's body flung back against the armchair. "I had to kill a man recently. Someone I knew well."

Maro stiffened slightly. "I'm sure there were good reasons."

"There were, but I couldn't do it," Shae said. "I've never had to kill someone I knew so personally. When the time came, I couldn't draw my blade. Strangely enough, I'm sad that I failed him. And worse yet, I lost the respect of a person whose support I need." She was still mulling on how she'd damaged her standing with Hami. The Master Luckbringer was a former Fist; he was unlikely to forgive such a stumble. A Green Bone leader couldn't be soft or hesitant, especially if she was a woman and people were expecting her to fail. Ayt Mada had killed her father's closest friends; she had ordered the death of her own brother. She would not have hesitated in that cabin.

Shae said to Maro, "You wear jade, but you're an educated, accomplished professional and a world traveler. I wish there were more people like you. You're the modern side of the country. But Kekon's other side is all blood and steel. Somehow, as the Weather Man of No Peak, I have to be both of those things at the same time."

Maro was silent for a long minute. Then he sat up and swung his legs over the side of the bed, his back to her, elbows resting on his knees. Shae wondered if she had said something wrong, inadvertently offended him in some way, but before she could ask, Maro said, "There's a reason why I chose a career in foreign studies, and why I've specialized in Shotar in particular." He looked over his shoulder at Shae, then turned back around partway to face her. "My father was a Shotarian soldier stationed in the Janloon garrison during the Many Nations War. He fell in love with a local girl; he and my mother wanted to get married but neither side would allow it. He was sent back to Shotar along with the rest of the retreating army, and my mother gave birth to me a few months later."

Maro's voice took on a bitter edge that Shae had never heard in him before. "My grandparents told everyone that my father was a young Green Bone fighter in the One Mountain Society who'd been killed in the war. Far better to be the love child of a dead jade warrior than the bastard of an enemy soldier. To preserve the family's reputation, my mother went along with the story her whole life. She finally told me the truth while sick on her deathbed, when I was in my twenties. All my life until then, I'd wondered why, if my father was supposedly a Green Bone warrior, I was so hopeless at the jade disciplines. I figured it was my fault for not trying hard enough, for reading books instead of training." Maro raised his face toward the ceiling and laughed painfully. "To think of all the childhood insecurity I could've avoided. When I learned the truth, I was furious at my mother and grandparents. They robbed me of half my identity, just because they were ashamed."

Maro shifted closer. He tucked a strand of hair behind Shae's ear, giving her a wan smile. "I know that I can't understand what it's like to be a Kaul, or the pressures you face as Weather Man. But you don't have a monopoly on poisonous honor culture. Maybe the Green Bone clans sit at the top of it, but it goes all the way down."

Shae was not sure what to say. She felt grateful to Maro for confiding in her, but also oddly culpable. She and her family were very much responsible for perpetuating the Green Bone way of life, the cultural preoccupation with greenness that permeated every aspect of Kekonese society. "Did you ever try to find your father afterward?" she asked.

"I did." Maro leaned against the headboard. "It took me a few years to even work up the courage to look for him, but I eventually found him. After the war, he married a woman in his home country. I found out that I have two Shotarian half sisters." Maro paused, his gaze turned inward. "I went to Leyolo City six years ago for the first time to meet all of them. It was…a strange experience. I think my father never stopped feeling sad and guilty about leaving my mother, even though he had no choice because deserting the Shotarian army meant execution. I get the sense that my existence reminds him of sad times. He's nice enough, and we still keep in touch, but…" Maro trailed off. The sun was creeping up the window. Outside, Shae could hear the chime of the street tram and the shouts of the city's more industrious street hawkers. Maro said, with a happier note in his voice, "I've gotten to know my half sisters much better. They're younger than me, of course, and the older of them—those are her two girls, my nieces, in the picture."

Shae had always thought that the two children did not look Kekonese, but had politely refrained from questioning Maro about it. "They're awfully cute," she told him.

Maro got off the bed and took the framed photograph from the dresser. "That's Kullisho," he said, pointing to the older girl. "She's an avid reader and loves cats." He smiled and pointed at the younger sister. "Danallo, the little piglet, is always getting herself hopelessly covered in dirt, but she's the sweetest little girl and says the funniest things. I hope one day if I have children that they're half as good as my nieces."

Shae looked at the two cherubic faces and then back over at Maro.

How many Kekonese would not only admit to, but seek out, a foreign bloodline? Her own adopted cousin, Anden, had never shown any interest in his biological father or his Espenian ancestry. It still pained her to remember how unhappy he'd been about being sent to Port Massy at all. Perhaps things were different for Maro because he could easily pass as completely Kekonese, but then again, in their parents' and grandparents' generation, Shotarians were the most despised of foreigners. "It was brave of you to contact the Shotarian side of your family. And to make the effort to have a real relationship with them." She meant it sincerely.

Maro put the photograph back down. "The rest of my family doesn't think so. My grandmother's passed away now—let the gods recognize her—but my grandfather won't talk about it, and neither will my uncles or cousins. They think it was wrong for me to stir up something that should've been left alone." Maro sighed. He picked out his clothes from the closet and began to dress, slowly. "They have reasons other than prejudice. I'm the only one in my family who wears jade. I have a good career at the university and connections to the Royal Council. The story of my real parentage would only drag our family down. So I keep it a secret, just like my mother did."

Maro sat back down on the bed next to her. "You see? Every family has some darkness that it's afraid to share, even the ones that aren't famous and powerful." At her thoughtful silence, Maro kissed the curve of her jaw, then looked at the clock on the dresser. "It's getting late; I should get to work."

"Me too." Shae startled at the time. She got up and went to the closet, taking out the set of clothes she kept at Maro's apartment. She dressed while Maro went into the bathroom to shave and was done when he got out. "I didn't answer your question," she said, picking up her shoes. "I *do* want to have you over at my new house, now that it's finally finished. My sister-in-law is still working on decorating the inside, but I'm mostly moved in by now. Would you like to come over and have dinner sometime?"

Maro patted down his tousled hair; Shae found his rumpled professor appearance in the mornings endearingly sexy. "Even now that you know I'm a half-Shotarian bastard?" Maro said it lightly, but there was a note of worry in his voice. A suggestion that perhaps he wasn't sure he should've told her so much, made himself so vulnerable.

Shae went to the door. "My cousin's mixed blood; it doesn't matter." Years ago, she'd made a mistake by keeping the relationship with Jerald a secret, fearing her grandfather's scathing disapproval. But Grandda was gone now, and she was not afraid of Hilo's opinion, whatever it might be.

―――――――

Woon was waiting in Shae's office when she arrived, thirty minutes later than usual. He stood up as she came in, and Shae felt suddenly awkward, knowing that he suspected the reason she was late this morning and wondering if he could smell Maro all over her. He seemed unusually anxious, not his usual self. Swallowing uncomfortably, he handed her a folded piece of paper. Shae began to read it, then looked up at the Weather Man's Shadow in bewilderment. "What is this?"

"My resignation, Kaul-jen," Woon said.

"Your *resignation*?" Shae stared at him. "Why?"

The man would not meet her eyes. "You can find someone better for the position."

Shae dropped the letter and her purse on her desk. "What's this really about, Papi-jen?"

Woon's normally even aura was churning with agitation. "I think you know by now," he said hoarsely. "Don't make me say it, Shae-jen. I value our friendship too much."

Shae shook her head, fighting down a swell of panic. Her position was tenuous enough as it was. She'd been concerned about losing Hami's support but had not imagined that she might lose Woon. He had been unfailing in his duties, always dependable, at her side through every difficult situation since she'd come into this office. Woon was her right hand, as he had been for her brother Lan. She could not lose him, not if she wished to remain Weather Man of No Peak. "I don't accept this resignation, Woon-jen."

Woon looked up sharply. Shae could count on one hand the number of times she'd seen him appear angry. "I've served you as best I could," he said, his voice not quite steady. "You're being unfair, to keep me in a role I'm asking to leave."

"I need you," Shae said. "There's no one else who could take your place as Shadow, who I'd trust as much. Under other circumstances, you would've been Lan's Weather Man."

"I failed Lan-jen," Woon said, his face stricken. "I'm afraid I'm failing him again now. And that I'll fail you."

"The only way you'll fail me is if you leave." Shae stood in front of the man. "Please, Papi-jen. You know I could go to the Pillar and ask that he order you to stay. I don't want to do that. I *won't* do that. But I need you to keep helping me as you have."

Woon's shoulders sagged. "It's too painful for me, Shae-jen," he confessed. "You're Lan-jen's sister, and the Weather Man, so I would never cross either of those lines; but we spend so much time together, I can't help how I feel."

Shae could not believe this was happening. It was not that she didn't feel any affection for Woon; on the contrary, she'd come to count him as a true friend. He was almost a decade older than her, but handsome in an unassuming way, and there was no questioning his work ethic and character. She had simply never considered a romantic relationship with a subordinate. And of course she was with Maro now, so it was out of the question. The fact remained, however, that she could not afford to lose Woon Papidonwa, even if she had to hurt him.

"You're a good man, Papi-jen," Shae said. "You deserve someone who'll show as much devotion to you as you've shown to the clan and to my family." She wanted to put a hand on her friend's arm, in the casual manner that she used to, but was afraid to touch him in any way now, for fear of making the situation worse. Her mind sprinted through options: Could she offer him more pay? A bigger office? Or would that only offend him, show her to be even more callous than he already thought she was? She had only one reliable piece of emotional leverage over him, and she used it now, knowing and regretting that it would have a cruel effect on him.

"We're both in our positions because of tragedy, because we owe it to Lan to be able to face him in the afterlife," she insisted. "We managed to keep No Peak afloat during the war, but there's a lot more to do, to make the business strong enough to outlast its enemies. We're a good team, Papi-jen; we're changing the Weather Man's office for the better. We've made investments and alliances that will pay off. And the work we're doing won't just benefit the clan, but the country as a whole. Give it a year. Can you put aside any discomfort you might have around me, for one year?"

Shae stopped talking, afraid that if she continued, she'd only show her own desperation and weaken what she'd already said. She waited with held breath as indecision shifted across Woon's face. At last, eyes downcast, he nodded reluctantly. Shae breathed again. The Weather Man's Shadow opened his mouth to say something, but at that moment, there was a loud knock on Shae's office door.

Woon stepped away from her as the door opened and Hami thrust his head into the room. He glanced between them for a second, eyes narrowed, then said, brusquely, "It's happened. Espenian ground forces invaded Oortoko. It's on every news channel right now."

They followed him into the office floor's common area, where a dozen people were gathered around a television. On screen, the KNB news anchor Toh Kita was speaking to a political analyst over video footage showing convoys of Espenian military transports traveling through the hills of eastern Shotar and air support launching from the aircraft carrier RES *Massy*.

The news cut to Chancellor Son Tomarho giving a speech in Wisdom Hall. The chancellor declared that "Kekon stands with its Espenian allies" but also emphasized the need for "diplomacy, honest dialogue, and mutual respect," and he expressed deep concern about the potential for civilian casualties in the military conflict. Shae understood all that to mean the Espenians had not informed the Kekonese government before proceeding to invade Oortoko. In his official comments on behalf of the Royal Council, Son was now being forced to walk a fine line between the public interests that the Council ostensibly represented, the clans they were functionally beholden to, and the reality of the country's diplomatic alliances.

An hour after Son's speech, Ayt Madashi held an impromptu interview with reporters as she stood outside Wie Lon Temple where she was attending an alumni fundraiser. A crowd of hard-bodied young Green Bone trainees filled the background of the screen. "In my father's day, the One Mountain Society fought against the tyranny and brutality of the Shotarians. It's appalling that our jade and our security are now being sacrificed on behalf of the foreigners that killed, raped, and tortured our countrymen." The Pillar of the largest clan on Kekon was as self-assured on camera as she was in person. She spoke in the clear, precise voice of a natural orator and her steady gaze appeared to travel through the small television screen to rest on each viewer individually.

"Chancellor Son can stand with the Espenians," Ayt said, "but the Mountain clan stands for Kekon alone. We will defend it against avowed enemies or those masquerading as friends. I am not a politician. Gold and jade, never together. But if you must choose between the two, count on jade."

A few people standing near the office television began to cheer, before realizing *who* they were cheering. Shae saw them clap their hands over their mouths and glance at her in chagrin. She could not fault them. Ayt Mada, her sworn enemy, who had vowed in Shae's presence to kill everyone in the Kaul family and destroy the No Peak clan, had spoken on behalf of the nation's Green Bones and given voice to the sentiments of the people of Kekon.

Meanwhile, Kaul Hilo was nowhere to be seen or found because he was on the other side of the world. "Find the number of the hotel my brother is staying in," Shae ordered her secretary as she strode back to her office. "Then get me on the phone with him, now."

CHAPTER

21

Change of Plans

Hilo got off the long-distance call and said, "We need to go home."

Tar, who was watching a ruckets game on the hotel television despite the fact that neither of them understood the rules of the sport, said, "Our flights are booked for Sixthday and we're supposed to have dinner with the kid's mom and her boyfriend tomorrow night. What do you want to do?"

Hilo picked up the remote control and changed the channel. The news was covering the Espenian entry into Oortoko. He couldn't understand what the Stepenish commentators were saying, but they were referring to a large map of the East Amaric region, with Shotar, the Uwiwa Islands, and Kekon highlighted. Hilo mumbled a curse under his breath. Trust the Espenians to do things when they pleased, without informing or consulting anyone else.

Shae had made it clear that he needed to return to Janloon as soon as possible, but he was also determined not to leave Lybon until he'd hammered out an acceptable arrangement regarding his nephew's future. He hated the prospect of explaining to Wen that he'd flown all the way to Stepenland at her urging, leaving her in her thirty-fourth week of pregnancy, and had nothing to show for it.

Also, he found himself thinking about Lan's son a great deal, and feeling, on a deep and painful level, a kinship with the child that went even beyond blood relation. Like Niko, Hilo had lost his father when he was not even a year old. From all the stories he'd heard of Kaul Dushuron, Hilo had always imagined he would've gotten along with his father—certainly better than he'd gotten along with his grandfather. Niko would never know his father either. Perhaps it was because he was soon to become a parent himself that the thought caused Hilo to grieve for his elder brother in a way that he had not been able to two years ago, when war and vengeance and survival had been paramount in his mind. Over the past couple of days, he'd been unusually morose, unable to enjoy the picturesque novelty of Lybon.

Tar, sensing the Pillar's mood if not the underlying reasons for it, tried with the earnestness of a worried child to lift his spirits, making fun of everything unexpected they encountered—from salty candy, to Stepenish hairdos, to the fact that supermarkets closed at dusk. While Hilo spent time dealing with clan issues on phone calls with Shae or Kehn, Tar went around the town and returned to offer up daily accomplishments he hoped would please his boss: He'd found a good restaurant and made a reservation for Fifthday; through the clan's vast network, he'd made a few local connections that might be useful; he'd discreetly tailed Eyni's boyfriend to an office building near the center of town and discovered where he worked and with whom.

"You want me to call the airline and see if we can get on an earlier flight?" Tar asked now.

Hilo pinched the bridge of his nose, then nodded. Lybon was seven hours ahead of Janloon; it was early evening and the street-lights outside of their hotel room had just come on. If they took a flight out tomorrow morning, they could be back home by the end of the day. "Change the flights," he said. "Then we'll go talk to those two. We'll insist on having dinner tonight to figure everything out."

When they got to the house, Hilo said, "Stay in the car this time. You're too intimidating." Tar made a noise of incredulous protest, but Hilo said, "You look and act like a Fist. Eyni's never thought of me as anything but a goon, and having you standing around like a silent henchman won't help things. I have to sweet talk those two into seeing reason." He got out of the car and leaned back through the open window. "Wait here. I'll be back out soon and we'll go eat."

Hilo paused when he got to the front door. He could Perceive Eyni moving about inside with considerable energy and haste, and in the back of the house, a small, quiet presence that could only be the slumbering child. The Stepenish man was not home; he must be working late. Suspicion formed in Hilo's mind. In the few days he'd been in Lybon, he'd noticed that it seemed to be common for people to leave gates and doors open. Instead of ringing the bell, he turned the door knob. It was unlocked; he pushed open the door and stepped inside.

The first thing he saw was two suitcases and a folded stroller sitting in the living room. One of the suitcases was latched shut and upright; the other was open on the floor and partially packed with toddler's clothing, a stuffed monkey, and a few children's board books. Eyni's open purse lay next to the suitcase, wallet and passport visible. Cold understanding filled Hilo. Eyni came out of the bedroom, arms full with baby blankets, towels, and a pack of diapers. She froze when she saw Hilo standing in the foyer.

"Sister Eyni," Hilo said softly. "It seems you're about to take a trip."

Eyni blurted, "We're not meeting until tomorrow."

Hilo looked at the suitcases and the pile of supplies in her arms. "You're overpacking if you plan to be back in time for dinner tomorrow night. Where's that foreign boyfriend of yours?"

The blankets trembled in Eyni's arms. "He went out for a minute."

"He's tying things up at work because you don't expect to be back for a while," Hilo inferred. His voice turned hard. "Where were you planning to go? You were going to disappear without telling me; you figured you'd leave me waiting around like a fool."

"Go home, Hilo." Eyni's voice rose, pleading and angry. "I didn't reply to your letters for a reason, and you still showed up at my house uninvited. Lors doesn't know what you and the clan are like. You would've convinced him to let you have what you wanted—to take my son back to Kekon and raise him as a killer. That's right, a jade-obsessed killer destined to die young, just like his father and his grandfather. And like you."

"That's how you talk about your husband and my brother? And my father, who gave his life for his country?" Hilo's lips drew back. "What happened to you, Eyni?"

Eyni set the items down and straightened to her full height. She'd always been a proud and elegant woman, a former dancer, and now, in an effort to reclaim some of the status she'd once held over Hilo when he'd been a young Fist and she the wife of the Pillar, she lifted her chin and glared at him. "You haven't changed at all, Hilo. You always were a vicious thug at heart, an arrogant boy obsessed with jade and his own ego. You don't care about Niko; you only want to turn him into one of your followers." She breathed in hard. "Do you know that in Espenia, civilian possession of jade is now *banned*? That other countries including Stepenland are likely to follow suit? People associate jade with soldiers and mercenaries and gangsters, and that's how you want to raise my son? No, Hilo. Nothing you can offer will sway me. I want Nikolas to grow up Stepenish, with Ste-penish friends and siblings and a Stepenish education. I don't want him to have *anything* to do with you."

For one of the few times in his life, Hilo was speechless. For some seconds, he felt nothing except an initial shock, as disorienting as being stabbed in the stomach. Then hurt flooded in, and with it, rage.

"Go home to your Fists and turf wars," Eyni said. "I won't *ever* let Niko become a Green Bone." She stepped backward into the kitchen and picked up the receiver of the phone, hovering her finger over the dial. He saw her eyes flicker to the block of kitchen knives that lay within her easy reach. "Go or I'll call the police. They'll be here in minutes. You're a foreign tourist with no power or authority in this country, and if I tell them you broke into my house, they'll put you in jail."

"Let me see Niko," Hilo said. Eyni's finger moved, dialing a single number. "I'll go," Hilo promised in a low voice that bordered on a plea, "but at least let me see my nephew."

For a second, the defeat in Hilo's voice and the open hurt in his expression seemed to have an effect on Eyni. She depressed the phone cradle. Then, as if remembering her determination not to give her former brother-in-law even a sliver of leverage, she set her lips together in a line and shook her head.

From the nursery, Nikolas began to cry. *"Maaaa..."*

Eyni turned toward the sound and took two steps, and Hilo moved, with the sort of speed that only a heavily jaded Green Bone can call upon. He wrapped one arm around the front of her body, holding her in place. Pressing his palm to her back, he Channeled with all his might in one sharp, violent thrust. Eyni's head snapped back; the top of her skull smacked Hilo in the chin. His jade energy tore through her with the destructive precision of a metal shaft and she died without uttering a sound.

Hilo's vision wavered. He sank to his knees on the kitchen floor, still holding Eyni as if in a lover's embrace. The energy blowback of her death crashed over him and then washed out, leaving him momentarily dazed and rattled. He'd cut the inside of his lip on his teeth where her head had smacked into his mouth, and the sharp tang of blood on his tongue along with the droning sound of the telephone dial tone near his ear brought him back to himself. He reached up and set the telephone receiver back into its cradle. Standing up, he lifted Eyni and carried her to the sofa. He laid her down lengthwise on the cushions, then stood back, wiping sweat from his brow with the cuff of his sleeve.

She didn't look pained or awkward in death, just soft and limp, and he arranged her arms across her stomach so she looked even more natural. Hilo walked back into the kitchen and took a long drink of water directly from the kitchen faucet. Then he stood with his hands leaning against the counter and stared for a long minute at the body of the woman on the sofa. She hadn't suffered or struggled at all, had not even seen death coming, which only showed that she was still an ignorant and haughty person at heart, to not understand her own position clearly and anticipate what Green Bones were capable of—what *he* was capable of—when grievously pushed and insulted. He'd gone to every length to meet her more than halfway, offered every reasonable allowance, kept his temper so firmly in check—all to no avail.

Hilo had never liked Eyni and always thought Lan was wrong to let her and her lover walk away with no consequence in the first place, but looking at her now, he felt sad. He knew Lan would not have wanted her killed, even for the sake of his own son.

"*Maaaa*," came the cry again, from the room down the hall. Hilo followed the sound; he stepped over the child gate blocking the way and went into the nursery where he found Niko standing up, holding on to the slats of the crib. He was calling out in an impatient but not tearful way, and when Hilo came into the room, he stopped making noise and stared up at his uncle with wide eyes and an open mouth. Hilo lifted the child out of the crib and set him on the ground. The boy sat down, picked up a toy car and began pushing it along the carpet. Hilo crouched down next to him. "Car," Niko said in Kekonese, then sang a nursery song in Stepenish and looked to Hilo for approval. Hilo smiled and held out his hand. "Come with me, Nikoyan." The name came to him at once, a perfect Kekonese name. He led the boy out of the nursery and into the living room, opening and closing the child gate for him to pass through. Niko went to Eyni. "Ma ma ma," he said.

"Your ma is sleeping," Hilo said gently. He placed the supplies Eyni had been carrying into the smaller suitcase along with the child's other packed belongings, then shut and latched it. He searched inside the open purse and found Niko's birth certificate tucked inside Eyni's passport; when he unfolded it, he saw that the field for the father's name had been left blank. He refolded the certificate and tucked it into his jacket pocket. He knelt down and pointed to the toy car in Niko's hand. "Would you like to go for a car ride?"

The boy's expression brightened. He stopped trying to rouse his mother and held out his arms to be picked up. Hilo kissed the child on the top of the head, then scooped him up in one arm and picked up the suitcase with the other. He carried Niko out of the house and to the car where Tar was still waiting. Hilo threw the suitcase into the rear seat, then got in the front passenger side, holding the two-year-old in his lap. "Niko-se," he said, "this is your uncle Tar."

"It's nice to meet you, Niko," Tar said, ruffling the toddler's hair. "You're a good-looking boy." If the Pillarman was surprised to see Hilo emerge alone from the house with the child, it showed only as a shift of alertness in his jade aura, a beat of hesitation as he looked at the Pillar questioningly.

Hilo said, "We need to call the airline to transfer your plane ticket to Niko. And I need to find a typewriter to fill in his birth certificate, so he can board the plane with me. You'll have to stay behind to deal with the boyfriend. Be quick and careful about it. He's not so bad; he shouldn't suffer at all."

Tar nodded, then handed the car keys to Hilo. "You'd better put the kid in the back seat and take the car back to the hotel. I'll wait here. See you in a few days."

———

Six weeks later, Wen gave birth to a healthy baby boy. Hilo brought his nephew into the room where Wen was resting. Kaul Rulinshin, three hours old, lay on his mother's breast. Bouquets of chrysanthemums and yellow heaven's breath flowers—symbolizing joy and good health—had been sent by the clan faithful and crowded every available surface in the room.

"Baby," Niko exclaimed. "Little baby." He had begun to string Kekonese words together into short sentences. After several frustrated tantrums, he no longer tried to speak Stepenish.

Hilo swung the toddler up in his arms and set him on the edge of the bed. After sixteen hours of labor, Wen's eyes were ringed with exhaustion but shone bright with triumph. Hilo leaned over and placed a kiss on Wen's brow, then on the baby's head, breathing in his son's indescribable sweetness. Niko reached out to pat the infant's wispy hair. "That's your little cousin," Hilo told him. "The two of you have to take care of each other from now on."

Lost and Found

A well-known figure in the ancient history of the Tun Empire is a man named Ganlu, who was a warrior, healer, religious philosopher, and advisor to Emperor Sh'jan the Third. Ganlu is described in Tuni historical texts as a bearded foreigner who came from the Island in the West. Accounts differ as to the date of his arrival, but it is said that when he saw the vast plains of the Great Basin of Tun he fell to his knees and praised the gods, famously exclaiming (in a phrase that would later be appropriated by various Tuni rulers and generals as justification for imperial expansion): "Glorious land, where a man can walk for his whole life and never reach the sea!"

Ganlu traveled for many years. In the wake of recent famine and war, the Tun countryside was plagued by lawlessness and banditry, against which common villagers were often helpless. Wherever Ganlu went, he confronted crime and immorality, taught martial skills to the ordinary people, treated sickness and ailments with his healing touch, and espoused a philosophy of peaceful living, neighborly obligation, and communion with the divine spirits of the land, rivers, and sky. His teachings formed the basis for krajow, the Tuni fighting arts, and greatly influenced the Shubai religion.

Eventually, the traveler's reputation reached the ears of the emperor, who summoned Ganlu and his disciples to the palace and asked him to become a royal advisor. Ganlu refused three times before consenting, each time asking the emperor to offer evidence of his virtues as a monarch. Ganlu's acumen as a counselor and the founding of his schools of krajow are recounted in further legends, which differ in detail but hold in common that Ganlu derived extraordinary power and wisdom from an enchanted stone given to him by his forest goddess mother and which he wore close to his heart at all times. It is said that Ganlu lived until the age of one hundred and seventy; upon his death, his spirit went into the stone, which was kept in the Imperial Palace so that the emperor could continue to consult it.

While historians agree that Ganlu was a Kekonese Green Bone and that his teachings bear considerable resemblance to both Abukei folklore and pre-Deitist spirituality, only recently have they concluded that he was most likely the third son of the king of Jan during the early part of the Three Crowns period in Kekonese history.

Kekon has no record of this man, other than a royal genealogy set down at the time with an unnamed reference to "a young prince, lost."

The Grudge Hall

Anden played relayball twice a week now, with Dauk Corujon and a group of his friends, in the grass and dirt field behind the neighborhood high school. One day, two weeks after the dinner at the Dauks' house, the Pillar's son had ridden by the Hians' home while Anden was outside, standing on a stepladder and fixing a broken gutter. Instead of speeding past as he usually did, Cory stopped his bicycle and called up to Anden. "Hey, islander, you play relayball?"

Anden wiped his hands on his pants and came down the ladder. "Yeah."

"Are you any good?" Cory asked, not in an arrogant or scornful way, merely curious. The young man looked Anden up and down.

"I played on the team at the Aca—" Suddenly, he didn't want Cory to know he'd gone to the Academy, that he'd been trained as a Green Bone. "At my school in Janloon."

"What position did you play?"

"First guard."

Cory nodded. "Fifthday evening, all right? I'll come get you." He pushed his bike forward and pedaled off again before Anden could say yes or no.

At the first game, Cory introduced him to a group of similarly aged young men and said, "Look here, crumbs, this is our new first guard, Andy."

"Anden," Anden corrected quickly, and perhaps more forcefully than he'd intended. He smiled to soften the unintended rudeness and said in a friendlier voice, "I go by Anden." He hadn't meant to strike yet another awkward note with the local Pillar's son, now that they'd finally had a conversation of more than twenty words and he was being brought into Cory's group of friends. It was just that back home, his cousin Hilo was the only one who ever called him Andy; it seemed strange for someone else to do so.

Anden discovered that he was one of the better players. Relayball was the primary national sport in Kekon, but here in Espenia, only the Kekonese and Shotarian communities played the game, so the most athletic members of Cory's informal league had other pursuits that they took more seriously—bootball, ruckets, swimming—and they came to the Secondday and Fifthday games at the high school field purely for recreation. There was a lot of joking and mock feuding, and Anden found it hard to follow all the Espenian slang that was tossed around, but soon the gatherings became the highlight of his week. He didn't quite fit in, but that was fine, he was used to that. At least he was becoming an accepted member of the community. No matter how busy he was with schoolwork, the Hians always encouraged him to go. "It's good that you're finally making friends," they said.

Cory played the position of finisher. He was the best player, and the unofficial organizer and leader of the neighborhood league. At first, Anden assumed that could be attributed to the fact that he was a Green Bone and the son of the Pillar, but he soon came to realize that the young man stood on his own feet. Cory never spoke of his father's dealings, and even after two months of seeing him twice a week, Anden had not figured out where he wore his jade. As far as Anden could tell, Cory never employed his advantages of Strength or Lightness while on the relayball field. Even so, he always placed himself and Shun Todorho, the other Green Bone who regularly showed up at the games, on opposite teams, so all would be fair. He didn't argue about points either. More than once, when a game grew heated, Anden heard him say, with a laugh, "We're just here to have a good time, crumbs." Contrary to the stereotype of the Kekonese being quick to fight, Cory never seemed to take offense, nor to give it either. He seemed to get along with everyone. Even when he called Anden, "you fool islander," he did so lightheartedly and with a teasing wink that could not be construed as mean-spirited.

Anden had a hard time imagining how Cory would fare as a Finger in Janloon. People would not know what to think of a Green Bone who was so easygoing, who seemed so quick to please.

They played throughout autumn, when damp wind billowed the relayball nets and the evenings grew cold enough for them to need hats and gloves. One Fifthday, they were finally driven off the field by the first real winter storm; the ever-present clouds over Port Massy darkened to the color of slate and began dumping icy sleet over the city. People ran between cars and buildings with briefcases and newspapers held over their heads. The clumpy turf behind the high school turned into a soggy marsh. Anden slipped during a pass and landed hard on his back in a puddle of freezing slush. He'd never experienced such cold before in his life. He decided, as he rose with his teeth chattering, all his extremities numb, and his glasses too smeared and fogged to see through, that it was no wonder the Espenians were a people who'd sailed all over the world, if their homeland was so inhospitable.

Cory called a premature end to the evening; everyone hurried for their homes. Anden dreaded trying to bike back to the Hians' house in such weather. "This won't last long," Cory said to him and two of the other remaining players as they huddled under the high school's covered back entranceway. "Let's run over to the grudge hall to warm up and get something to eat while we wait it out."

They hurried two blocks through Southtrap to a rectangular, gray building that from the outside looked not unlike a school or library. The large white sign over the front entrance read KEKONESE COMMUNITY CENTER in both Kekonese and Espenian. Anden had passed it many times and walked through the doors out of curiosity one Seventhday morning. Inside and to the right he'd discovered a tiny Deitist shrine with a framed poster print of the mural of Banishment and Return hanging on the wall in front of a couple dozen faded green kneeling cushions and a row of blackened incense candles. To the left was a cafeteria-style kitchen behind an area of clumped tables and armchairs occupied by elderly people playing circle chess or reading out-of-date newspapers and well-used books taken from the unstaffed Kekonese-language library, which consisted of several bookcases crammed against the back wall. Down the hall, there was a small fitness room with exercise equipment and a schedule of classes posted on the door. The drop-in hourly daycare was manned by two teenagers.

"The community center?" Anden asked skeptically, his lips numb with cold as they ran across the slicked street through a gap in traffic. He didn't think the place would be where a group of young men would want to spend Fifthday evening. "That's what you meant by the grudge hall?"

One of Cory's friends, Ledt Derukun, snickered, but the other, Shun Todorho, said, "That's just the front of the place, crumb. The grudge hall's in the basement; you get in from the back." They jogged around the rear of the gray building to a set of unmarked metal doors, where to Anden's surprise an erected portable metal awning sheltered a long line of people—mostly men, but women as well—young and old, rubbing their arms and stamping their feet against the cold as they waited to get in. Cory led the way to the front where the door attendant, a muscular man in a fleece-lined raincoat said, "Cory, it's been a while." He nodded to the other two. "Derek, Tod, good to see you."

"Hey, big Sano," Cory said, clasping the doorman's hand and bumping his shoulder with his own. "Miserable night, but maybe that'll mean a lot of people tonight, yeah? My folks in there?"

"Sure are." The man pushed the metal door open and stepped aside to let them enter ahead of all the others waiting. Anden was surprised; it was the first time he'd seen Cory take advantage of his status as the Pillar's son. The doorman stopped Anden before he could go in. "Not him," Sano said in Kekonese, eyeing Anden with disapproval before saying to Cory, "You know the rules about outsiders in the grudge hall. Thirddays only, and it's twenty thalirs."

"He's one of us," Cory said. "Straight off the island, even. Plays relayball like a pro."

"That true?" asked Sano, speaking to Anden. "You're Kekonese?"

"I was born in Janloon," Anden said. "My family sent me here to study."

Cory said, "It's true. You can even ask my da; he'll vouch for him."

Sano raised his eyebrows. "How about that," he said, and let Anden pass.

Inside, the warm smell of food hit Anden at once. They were in a large open room with exposed ceiling beams and a concrete floor— it appeared to have been originally built as the community center's garage. From portable cook stations situated behind long white tables, people were serving up spicy noodles in soup, hot fried bread, and Kekonese pastries on trays. There were also cheese-stuffed potato cakes and the sour sweets so ubiquitous at Espenian sporting events. A line was already forming where a cask of hoji had been rolled in and set on a low platform. "Let's go downstairs and snag a place to sit, first," Tod suggested.

They crossed the room and went down a flight of stairs. Anden was having a hard time reconciling what he'd seen in the uninspiring front part of the building with the liveliness of the rear half now. In the basement, small bar tables and stools were crowded along the brick walls; people were claiming spots by draping jackets over their chairs. Tod and Derek found seats for the four of them near the loudly chugging radiator. Anden followed more slowly, distracted. An area roughly the size of an indoor ruckets court was cordoned off with blue rope and bordered with bench seating. In the center of the bare space, a cockfight was occurring. Bettors leaned over the barrier, shouting in excitement or groaning in disappointment as one of the gamecocks fell beneath its opponent's steel spurs in a feathery melee.

Cory led the way to the table where his parents were sitting, eating steaming noodles from disposable plastic bowls and talking to Rohn Toro—the man Anden had begun to think of as the Horn of Southtrap—and two others that Anden did not know, but suspected must also be Green Bones. Cory said, "Well, relayball season's over; we finally got rained off the field and decided to come here. I brought my crumbs." He smiled and shook hands with the other men around the table, who clapped the Pillar's son on the back affectionately, asking him whether he was excited about going to law school.

Dauk Losun beamed when he saw Anden standing behind Cory and motioned him over. "My young friend from Janloon! You've never come to the grudge hall before, have you?"

Anden shook his head. A commotion rose up as the next cockfight got off to a rousing start. The Pillar raised his voice to be heard. "Now that we know you, you're welcome anytime. We keep some of the old ways from the island, you'll see. Some of it is serious, but most is in good fun."

Rohn Toro said, "Everything is sorted out over that little incident, by the way. Just so you know not to worry."

"I'm glad to hear that, Rohn-jen," Anden said, relieved. "I never wanted to cause trouble for anyone."

"From what *I* hear, you're a great help to the Hians, more so than their own sons, who are too busy to visit." Dauk Sana clucked her disapproval, then patted Anden on the arm. "Have you eaten? You absolutely must try the noodles Mrs. Joek makes."

Anden and Cory rejoined Tod and Derek at their own table, then took turns going upstairs to fetch food and drinks. Anden's wet clothes were soon dry; the basement was warm, and as more people arrived and filled the space, it grew somewhat uncomfortably stuffy, yet no one seemed to mind. The cockfighting appeared to be the main attraction, but people were also playing cards, drinking, and socializing. Anden overheard several nearby conversations heatedly discussing Espenia's involvement in the Oortokon War. Two young women sidled over to their table, looking sly. "Hey, Cory." One of them pouted. "Why don't I ever see you anymore?"

"Aw, Tami, you're seeing me now, aren't you?" Cory slapped her ass and pulled her into his lap. She gave a squeal of mock indignation and draped her arms over his shoulders.

Anden looked away uncomfortably. He slurped another mouthful from his steaming bowl of noodles, which were indeed well worth Dauk Sana's recommendation, and turned to Tod. "I didn't know this place existed. Is it always like this?"

"No, only on certain evenings." Tod glanced at Cory, deferring the explanation to him, but the Pillar's son seemed distracted, so Tod turned back to Anden and said, "When it's not a grudge hall, it's a training gym."

Anden looked around and saw the folded blue gym mats leaning against the wall in one corner, the stacked wooden blocks and closed equipment bins. "A gym for Green Bones," he said.

The chatter in the hall abruptly died away. The girl hopped reluctantly out of Cory's lap and hurried back with her friend to their own table. A few oblivious teens in one corner of the hall continued chatting, but several nearby adults shushed them so remonstratively that they fell silent. Anden turned around on his stool to see that the latest cockfight had ended, and now two men were stepping over the blue ropes. They took off their boots, then their shirts, and handed them to friends standing on the other side of the cordon before facing each other.

It was easy to hear the scrape of chair legs as Dauk Losun pushed his seat back. There seemed to be nothing to distinguish the Pillar from those around him—his seat in the room was not better than anyone else's; he wore a red sweater vest and wiped his mouth with a paper napkin as he stood up—yet no one else spoke a word as Dauk cleared his throat and said, "Orim Rudocun, you've been offered a clean blade by Yoro Janshogon. Do you accept?"

"Yes," said one of the men, who was of slightly heavier build than the other. Neither man actually carried a blade. They touched their clasped hands to their foreheads in brief salute but did not pause to offer up any prayers to the gods.

The challenger, Yoro, launched himself at the other man with an angry shout. It was over quickly. Yoro drove his shoulder into Orim's chest. They staggered together into the blue ropes, bringing the cordon down with them as Yoro dragged his opponent to the ground by the neck. They rolled about in a tangle for a minute. Orim flailed and caught Yoro a blow across the face, but the slighter man ended up on top and clamped his hands around his rival's throat. Snarling, he shook the other man—the back of Orim's head smacked against the concrete floor with a sound that made everyone in the hall flinch—then he jammed crossed forearms against Orim's windpipe, leaned his body weight forward, and began to press with all his might. Orim sputtered and kicked and clawed at Yoro's arms. No one in the hall made a move. A few worried murmurs began to rise.

Seconds passed; Orim's face turned purple. Dauk Losunyin stood up again and said, in a stern and concerned voice, "Mr. Orim, do you yield? Raise your hands if you do."

For a moment, Anden thought that Orim would refuse and consent to be choked to death. Then, reluctantly, he opened his hands in a gesture of submission. Yoro spat in disdain, then released him, stood up, and strode away to gather his shirt and boots, staunching his own bleeding mouth with the back of his hand. Orim lay on the ground gasping. Two of his friends lifted him to a sitting position and, taking him under the arms, helped him out of the hall.

Someone righted the rope cordon. The Pillar sat back down. Anden caught a glimpse of Dauk; he looked relieved as he leaned over to say something to Rohn Toro. People turned back to their tables and conversation returned to the hall.

"If you can believe it, Orim and Yoro used to be good friends," said Derek.

"Business partnership gone bad," Cory explained, in response to Anden's questioning look. "Orim says Yoro cheated him out of ten thousand thalirs. Yoro says he did all the work while Orim was doing the deal with Yoro's girlfriend behind his back." Cory unwrapped a sour sweet and popped it into his mouth. He offered another to Anden, who shook his head—he couldn't understand why anyone liked the taste of those things. "My da was worried about this duel going all the way," Cory said, in a lowered voice. "It doesn't happen often, only once in while over really serious things, but it's a good thing Orim yielded. No one wants the police to come snooping."

Anden felt stunned by what he'd seen. Not by the duel itself, despite all the odd differences in custom, but ever since his encounter in the park with the crewboy Carson Sunter, he'd been careful to try and learn all the rules in Espenia. "I thought dueling was illegal," he said.

"Crumb, *everything* in Espenia is illegal." Derek laughed. "Even cockfighting."

Cory patted Anden's arm in a reassuring manner that surprised Anden and made his face warm a little. "Naw, it's only that the law is complicated. And more often than not, negotiable."

"True words from an aspiring lawyer," Derek said.

"Shun Todorho!" came a shout from the center of the room, where a young man now stood in the place where the clean-bladed duel had happened minutes earlier. "Tod, where are you?" He pointed through the crowd at Anden's table, then crossed his arms in a posture of mock offense. "I've been hearing some talk that your Deflection is better than my Lightness. Care to test that bit of bullshit?"

A round of foot-stomping applause ran through the grudge hall. Cory smacked Tod on the back encouragingly and shouted back at the other man, "He's only had two drinks, Sammy, you sure you don't want to wait?" Shun Todo raised his glass and drained the rest of it dramatically, then slammed it down on the table and rose with his hands held up in a show of acquiescence to the crowd's demands. "Etto Samishun," Tod growled. "For your arrogance, I offer you... an *ass kicking*." More foot stomping and cheers as Tod climbed over the blue rope. In contrast to the sense of deathly seriousness of the preceding duel, the mood in the grudge hall was now jovial; everyone could tell that this contest was benign, the typical sort of social challenge that Kekonese threw down all the time.

The challenger, Sammy, crouched in a posture of exaggerated readiness. Tod, smirking a little, faced the audience and strode around a little with his arms raised to urge them to make more noise, which they did with so much enthusiasm that Anden was reminded of an Espenian sporting event and could not help but think the whole display rather crass and un-Kekonese.

Tod whirled and threw a spear of Deflection at Sammy, who leapt Lightly out of the way with a taunting shout. The Deflection buffeted some of the people nearby, who clutched their drinks and hung on to their tables and chairs. A plate of food went flying. Tod unleashed two more Deflections in quick succession that Sammy was hard-pressed to dodge—he bounded straight over Tod's head and landed behind him.

Cory whooped and shouted, "Get him, Tod!" Their friend spun and feinted high, then sent out a low, wide Deflection that at last caught the other young man at the knees in midleap and sent him sprawling to the ground. Sammy rolled over and held up his hands, grinning and mock cowering while Tod made a show of pretending to jump on him and finish him off. The people in the hall cheered.

The two Green Bones clapped each other on the shoulders good-naturedly before climbing back over the rope and returning to their tables amid praise. "That was toppers," Derek said when Tod sat back down, and Cory added, "Mass toppers, crumb."

Anden nodded along in agreement, though in truth, he hadn't found the contest to be particularly impressive. The style with which Tod and Sammy employed their jade abilities was different and some of it seemed inefficient. Tod's Deflection had precision but little power; Sammy's Lightness was nimble enough, but lacked the speed it might have with more Strength. All in all, it had been at the level of what one might see from year-fives at the Academy.

These were ungenerous thoughts, Anden chided himself. The Green Bones here did not receive a full-time education in the jade disciplines. What little jade they carried, they had to hide at all times.

They had to train in secret, in the stuffy basement of a community center instead of the sprawling campus of a school like the Academy. Any pride or status they could claim on account of being green could only be garnered here, within the Kekonese community, on nights like this.

All evening, Anden had found the grudge hall strange and a little overwhelming, and now he understood why: The place was like a distillate of Kekonese culture—the food and hoji, the cockfighting and gambling, the social life, the tradition of clean-bladed dueling, and the celebration of jade abilities—all crammed together under one roof in one evening. It gave Anden the oddest feeling. It was both acutely Kekonese and not Kekonese at all.

More food and drink was had, more conversation. Another cock-fight was played out. At the urging of friends, other Green Bones got up to challenge each other to contests of Strength and Steel. After a time, Tod, who had to work the next morning (he was an assistant manager at an electronics store) stood up to go, and Anden, already worried that the Hians might be concerned about him being out so late, put his drink down and followed suit. Cory said to them, "It'll be freezing cold and black out there by now. Let me see if my da is heading out anytime soon. Maybe he can give us all a ride."

Anden did not want to bother Dauk Losun, but Cory had no compunction about going over to ask his father, who said, "Sure, no problem; no need for me to stay any longer."

Before they could take their leave, however, Mrs. Joek, the noodle lady, rushed down the stairs into the grudge hall and hurried to the Pillar's table. "Dauk-jens," she exclaimed, "there are police officers here. Two of them."

In the crowded basement, her words were heard immediately. Conversations died on the spot; heads turned anxiously toward the Pillar's table. To Anden's surprise, Dauk Sana got up from her place at the table immediately and went upstairs. Her husband did not follow; he raised his voice and said calmly but loudly enough to be heard, "Everyone, stay where you are and keep enjoying yourselves. Don't worry." To his son, "You and your friends, go back and sit down."

Anden sat back down. The room was thick was unease and shuffling murmurs. Anden saw Rohn Toro rise from his seat and move to stand in the corner of the room near the door. He removed the black gloves from the breast pocket of his shirt and pulled them on, then leaned against the wall, arms crossed.

Dauk Sana returned a few minutes later, speaking loudly in accented Espenian as she descended. "Of course, yes, food license, liquor license—I can show you, officers." She reached the bottom of the steps. Two Port Massy police officers followed her, boots clomping loudly, the brims of their black caps and the shoulders of their uniforms beaded with ice. "Not a restaurant or bar," Sana went on. She had been calm a minute ago, but now she acted extremely nervous, wringing her hands. "This is just a party. A neighborhood party."

The officers squinted around the basement. "A party, eh?" said the older one of them. "What's the occasion? What're you kecks up to down here? Fighting? Jade trading?"

Sana looked horrified and insulted. "No, of course not. Maybe you've been watching too many movies? Just because we're Kekonese you think we all wear jade like gangsters?" She gestured around at the tables of people—men and women, young and old. "We can't get together to eat and drink and have a good time in our own community center on a stormy night like this, without being suspected?"

The younger of the two officers looked a little abashed at this, but the older one strode to the center of the room and snorted at the sight of bloodstains and feathers on the ground. He lifted the blanket that had been thrown over one of the benches and peered down at the gamecocks in their cages. Straightening up again with a smug look, he said, "Cockfighting's a criminal offense, ma'am. The fine is two thousand thalirs, and we could shut this whole building down."

Sana sucked in a breath. "Please, officers," she said, "we will pay the fine. We don't have much money, but we understand there are consequences to breaking the law. We'll all pay." As if on cue, one of the men at the nearest table took off his felt hat and began passing it around the room. All those present pulled out their wallets and deposited money into the spontaneous collection fund. Sana appeared on the verge of tears; she twisted the end of her scarf in her hands and said to the officers, "We have to hold some cockfights in here once in a while, to satisfy the older people, especially. You see, it's not illegal in our home country. They bring their gamecocks and I can't say no all the time. Please don't revoke our licenses for this small thing." She gave them a pleading look. "The community center is the heart of our neighborhood, it serves everyone. There's a shrine and library and daycare upstairs. There are people—some very old or very young—who come here for a meal and company when they have nowhere else to go. And yes, sometimes parties go on in the basement, but the worst that happens is some drinking and cockfighting."

A girl of about ten years old ran up to Sana with the hat full of money. Sana thanked her, then took the hat and counted out the cash on the nearest table. "There's two thousand four hundred and fifty thalirs here," she said, stacking the bills. "More than required, but we'll pay extra. We just want to keep our community center open." She pressed the money into the hands of the older policeman and smiled at the younger. "Please, officers. We all appreciate how hard you work."

The officers looked around the room, at the wary and hopeful expressions of the watching Kekonese. Their eyes passed over Dauk Losunyin's table with no special attention. The Pillar, like everyone else, was listening to what was going on, but he was slouched in his chair, his large hands folded, drawing not the slightest attention to himself. Rohn Toro had not moved from his spot against the wall near the door.

"I'm going to let you off with a warning this time," said the older cop, as if he'd considered the issue and come to a reluctant decision. With a show of deliberation, he stowed the money in his inside jacket pocket. Sana sagged in visible relief. "Thank you; you are very kind," she murmured gratefully.

"You kecks better keep your noses clean and be careful about staying within the law from now on," said the older cop. "Jade's illegal. You should all know that by now. If you get caught wearing or selling it, that's jail time."

Sana nodded vehemently. "We are worried about jade, too," she insisted. She began to lead the officers out of the grudge hall and back up the stairs. "The Crews, they run rackets in this part of the city, and there are rumors that they want to get their hands on jade now. All Kekonese people know such a dangerous substance shouldn't be worn by ordinary people—certainly not criminals. That's why we need the police." To the younger cop, "Do you like Kekonese food? Would you like some noodle soup, before you have to go back out into the cold?"

Their voices faded up the stairs. Slowly, the tension in the grudge hall dissipated. People relaxed and normal conversation returned once it was clear that the police officers were gone. Rohn Toro waited a minute, then sat back down.

Dauk Losun came over to their table, smiling and congenial once again. "They'll be back. This happens every few months, in the same way." He smiled and patted Anden on the shoulder. "You look worried. Don't be. The Port Massy police are like another one of the Crews: expecting payment and giving little in return."

Anden nodded, though he didn't really understand. It had never occurred to him to be fearful around the city police in Janloon. When his cousin Hilo had been Horn, he had often met with the police to instruct them on where to go after petty crime, which street gangs were causing trouble, where they ought to conduct drug raids—so Anden had always thought of the police as civil servants who were useful to the clans, not a hindrance to them. Apparently, in Espenia, there were a multitude of subjective rules and regulations that even the Pillar of Southtrap was careful to insulate himself against.

"I should stay a little longer, to make sure everything is fine," said the Pillar. He fished his car keys from the pocket of his sweater vest and handed them to his son. "It's late though, and I don't want the

Hians to worry about Anden. Drive your friends home and come back to pick me up."

———————

The Pillar's car was a green station wagon parked in the back lot. Cory started the car and blasted the heater on its defrost setting while Anden and Tod scraped the front and back windshields free of ice. In the car, their breaths steamed together as Cory pulled into the street and drove first Derek, and then Tod, back to their homes. The crusty wipers scraped against glass, and the car's headlights gleamed on wet pavement as he navigated to the Hians' house on the other end of Southtrap.

On the street corner, a block away from the house, Cory pulled the station wagon over to the curb. He shut off the engine and turned to face Anden. His eyes were bright with reflected streetlight, but his expression was suddenly unreadable in the dark. "You're wondering where it is, aren't you?" he asked. "My jade."

Heat rose up Anden's neck. In answer, he forced himself to look into the other young man's eyes. Cory unzipped his jacket. Shrugging out of it, he turned in the driver's seat to face Anden and lifted his shirt. The streetlight overhead illuminated his bare torso. Anden swallowed. His eyes traveled down Cory's chest, to the trio of jade studs pierced through the man's navel.

Anden tried to pull his eyes away but couldn't; his gaze continued traveling, down the line of thin dark hairs that disappeared under Cory's waistband. The skin of Cory's arms was goose-pimpling in the cold. Anden thought that perhaps he should say something, that maybe Cory wanted him to, but he was afraid to open his mouth and say the wrong thing.

Cory didn't speak either. He reached across the front seat and took hold of Anden's wrist, pulling it forward, until the tips of Anden's cold fingers brushed bare skin. Slowly, Anden flattened his palm against the man's abdomen. His pulse was pounding in the palm of his hand. In the close quarters of the car, he could suddenly hear his own breath, loud and unsteady.

Cory's gaze was hungry now. He moved Anden's hand across his bare stomach, as if guiding a blind reader over braille. When Anden touched the hard, smooth pieces of jade, an intensely delicious and slightly nauseating sensation, like that of an overripe sweetness, hit him in the back of the throat and fell into the pit of his gut. Cory's jade aura throbbed into him, hot with desire, like a black rock baking in the sun. Anden wanted to press himself against it, to clutch it greedily, to let it envelop him, but his body remembered the taste of jade energy the way an alcoholic remembers his last drunken blackout—with a crooning, desperate longing and visceral repulsion. He wanted to lose himself in it; he wanted to jerk away. The two impulses collided; Anden froze, his arm trembling. His eyes found Cory's, and he saw the confusion in his friend's expression resolve into understanding. Gently, the young man let go of Anden's wrist. He dropped his shirt back into place and pulled on his coat.

Anden drew his hand back to his own side, his face burning with regret and embarrassment. "Sorry," he mumbled.

"You've worn jade before," Cory said. "You were trained as a Green Bone at one of the schools in Janloon, weren't you." It was a question delivered as a statement, but beneath it, another question.

After a moment, Anden gave a nod. "I suppose that wasn't hard to guess." With difficulty, he raised his gaze. "You're wondering why I don't wear it anymore."

Cory did not answer at first. "You don't have to tell me, crumb."

Anden stuffed his fists into the pockets of his fleece jacket. His breath steamed in the suddenly claustrophobic confines of the station wagon. Without looking at the other man, he began speaking. "In my last year at the Academy, my family was at war with another clan. One of my cousins, the Pillar…was murdered." He had not spoken of Lan in over a year. "Even before I graduated, I wanted to do whatever I could to avenge him and help win the war. I…I killed a man. Someone important. A few men, actually." The words coming from his mouth sounded vague and insubstantial; he couldn't imagine anyone hearing them could appreciate their meaning, certainly not someone as removed from the situation as Cory Dauk.

Cory nodded slowly. "You don't want to be a killer."

Anden looked up, a little surprised. That wasn't it at all. Sometimes it was necessary to take lives; every member of his family had done so when it was called for. He tried to think of how he might be able to explain it better, to communicate how this was different, how deeply it had affected him, how tragic and elating and painful it had been. "I don't want to enjoy it," he said.

Cory regarded him for a long moment. He rubbed his hands together for warmth, then scooted over on the car's bench seat; he was suddenly inches away from Anden, his gaze more restrained but still insistent. "You're the most interesting person I've met in a long time, islander." He leaned in and kissed Anden on the mouth.

Cory's lips were chilled, but his tongue was not. It slid, for an instant, over Anden's bottom teeth. The kiss was over quickly, so quickly that Anden had a hard time believing that it had happened at all. When Cory pulled back, Anden acted almost without thinking—he reached forward and grabbed the other man by the front of his coat.

The second kiss lasted long enough that Anden felt the blood rushing into his head, their hot breaths mingling and steaming the windows, the warmth of Cory's jade aura slipping over his skin. When they broke apart, Anden managed, "I...I thought you liked girls."

Cory laughed. "I do." He leaned in again, his lips pursed to one side. "And I like *you*, crumb. You're a paradox. You look as if you walked out of a magazine ad but you're so damn...*Kekonese*. It's kind of sexy." The bridge of Cory's nose scrunched up, his expression teasing as he slid a hand up Anden's leg. "You're not like the rest of us kespies."

"Kespies?" Anden said.

"Kespenians. You know, Kekonese-Espenians." Cory began rubbing his hand on the crotch of Anden's pants. Anden sat very still, not daring to move, though it seemed all the heat in his body was flowing down into his groin. Cory unbuttoned the top of Anden's pants and slid a hand under his waistband. Cold fingers found their way into his pubic hair, began touching and encircling his stiffened cock.

Anden made an inarticulate noise. Excitement and terror rose in him. "Wait, I..." he gasped, but did not get any further; Cory unzipped Anden's pants in one swift jerk and pulled back, lowering his face into Anden's lap. Anden could not truly believe this was happening. It seemed somehow inappropriate to let Cory do this—he was the son of the local Pillar, to whom Anden was indebted—yet it also seemed wrong to try and stop him. Then he felt Cory's mouth—the sudden, exquisite, flooding heat made Anden's eyes roll back in his head—and he could no longer think clearly about anything.

It was over too quickly, for which Anden blamed himself. He would've wanted it to go on longer, but in a way he was relieved, if also disappointed. He felt as if he'd just experienced one of the most memorable moments of his life thus far, even though the release itself had not exactly been ecstatic. Furtive and unexpected, thrilling, a little uncomfortable. Cory drew back and wiped a hand over his mouth. Anden shivered with the shock of cold air on his wet, exposed crotch. He buttoned himself up quickly, still at a loss, feeling entirely out of control.

Cory said, "You've never been with a man, have you?"

Without quite meeting the other man's gaze, Anden shook his head. He was twenty years old and had never been intimate with anyone. There was one time, on a Boat Day three years ago, when several of the students at the Academy had gone to a bar and gotten drunk and one of his female classmates had kissed him for a long, booze-scented minute, putting her tongue in his mouth, but he didn't count that.

Cory leaned in and touched his lips lightly to the side of Anden's mouth, in a strangely tender, chaste action. He said, "Okay. We'll go slow, then," which made Anden want to laugh out loud, a little hysterically, because everything that had happened this evening had been, in his opinion, anything but slow. The windows of the car were fogged. Large flakes of white snow had begun to fall. Just down the street, the lights in the Hians' house were still on. Anden imagined Mrs. Hian waiting up past her bedtime at the kitchen table to make sure he made it back to the house safely in the storm, and he said, "I should go." He thought he ought to say something else, but what?

"See you around, islander," Cory said, smiling a little. Anden got out of the car. He drew his coat around himself and walked down the sidewalk. The headlights of the station wagon turned on and fell across his back, throwing his shadow against the wet pavement. As he reached the front stoop of the townhouse that had, after eight months, finally begun to feel like home, he heard the car start, and Cory drove past, tires plowing through slush, before the taillights of the car turned the corner.

CHAPTER

23

~

Scrap Pickers

Bero stood on loose ground near the top of the slag heap. Below him on the slope, the jade pickers were like ants, each one a dot crawling on the black hill of rubble, headlamps set to their dimmest setting as they worked in the dark, searching. Everything was a trade-off between the need for haste and care. They had to work as quickly as possible, but too much light and noise might give the crew away. With every minute they stayed, the risk of being discovered by a patrol increased, but searching for jade scrap was a patient, painstaking task. The pickers turned over each rock, prying them loose from the ground, feeling and examining them, rubbing them against the hems of dirt-encrusted shirts and holding them to the light to peer closely for the subtle glint that suggested an otherwise nondescript stone held precious jade encased within.

A headlamp flickered twice. Bero leapt Lightly down to the man who'd signaled. He was getting the hang of Lightness, could call

upon it consistently now and better control his height and speed.
Lightness and Strength were the easiest disciplines for a novice to
grasp, so he'd been told, because they were cued by physical actions
everyone was familiar with. He hadn't managed to Deflect anything
except by accident, and the one time he and Mudt cornered a stray
dog and tried to kill it by Channeling, it turned on them and bit
Bero on the leg—he still had the scar.

The scrawny Uwiwan man—all the pickers were scrawny Uwiwan men; Bero had a hard time telling any of them apart—held up
a rock the size of a small peach. "Jade, good jade," he said, which
were probably the only two words he knew in Kekonese, and the only
two necessary. He held it against his cheek for emphasis. Jade was
an amplifier with no detectable energy of its own; the pickers always
pressed the rocks against their skin—they put the smaller ones in
their mouths if they could—hoping to feel a tingling reaction in
their bodies, a rush of energy, a heightened clarity in their senses. It
was not a perfect indicator; the jade was often shielded by outer layers
of dense rock, and the desire to find worthy pieces was so great that
the pickers often imagined their own reactions. Besides, they were
so doped up on shine that their perceptions of jade were muddled
anyway. Without it, they risked getting the Itches if they stayed in
the job too long.

Bero took the stone from the man. It was brown and dirty, utterly
ordinary looking from the outside. With a thick white paint pen, he
wrote 1124—the man's work number, written on the top of his headlamp and on the laminated card that hung on a lanyard around his
neck—on the surface of the stone. When the rock reached the Uwiwa
Islands, it would be cut open with a rock saw. If there was jade inside,
a note would be made in a ledger and the man would be paid, relatively handsomely, for his find. There was perhaps a one in twenty
chance this would happen—it was more often the case that there
was nothing inside, or that the jade was of poor quality, with flaws
that made it unusable, or that a glimpse of lustrous green turned out
to be nothing but inert nephrite, useless for anything but imitation
or decoration. Real Kekonese jade was one of the rarest substances in

the world, and the mines run by the Kekon Jade Alliance took all the real finds. These were merely the scraps.

But the scraps had worth enough. They were worth ferrying crews of impoverished Uwiwans by boat to Kekon's shores, and then by truck into the densest jungle regions of the island's mountainous interior. Worth hiring local supervisors like Bero and Mudt and paying them with money and shine, and if they stuck around for more than a year, with their own cut of jade. Last summer, Bero and Mudt had been brought into a room in a disused gym along with a couple of other new rockfish initiates. In front of Soradiyo and each other, each man pricked his bottom lip with a clean knife and kissed a slip of parchment paper with his name written on it. The papers were held together over a candle, burning their wet blood and sealing their pledges of loyalty and silence to Ti Pasuiga.

Bero pretended to take it seriously, but he smirked to himself. They were acting like kids joining a secret club, even though they were only here to get money and jade—same as what everyone wanted. Nothing secret or special about that.

Soradiyo, their barukan manager, usually met them in the Rat House and gave them three to four days' notice of a nighttime scavenge so they had time to trek out to meet the loads of pickers when they were trucked in. Sometimes the weather or advance warning of a Green Bone patrol caused a change in plans and the job was canceled or delayed, in which case they had to pitch a tent and wait in the forest, eating dried food and grousing until conditions improved and the operation could proceed. Their job was to supervise the pickers—specifically, to make sure that none of them tried to steal any of the jade they found. A poor laborer might try to hide a bit of jade in his pockets or inside his cheek or up his ass crack, in the hopes of selling it himself for far more than he was paid by Soradiyo. Jade-wearing foremen could Perceive unsanctioned auras among the workers. A first attempt resulted in a warning. A second in death. Bero hadn't had to kill any workers yet, but Mudt had. He'd had to shoot a man in the head last month, roll his body into the trees.

Bero took the marked stone and climbed up the overlooking ridge with short, Light jumps to the metal rolling bin, half-full of similar stones, each marked with workers' numbers. Mudt guarded the bin tonight and kept watch next to the three military trucks splattered with mud and covered with camouflage-patterned tarps. Bero dropped the rock into the bin; it clattered amid the others. "How much longer have we got to do this?" Mudt griped, rubbing the outside of his arms and stamping his feet. Winter was the best time to scavenge because it was usually dry, but high in these mountainous areas, it was bitterly cold at night, cold in a relentlessly damp and clingy way. "This is a miserable job, keke. We could be back in the city right now, practicing. And fucking *warm*."

"And working for shit wages in a gas station or shoe store or something? You're grumpy because of the cold, but this is good money, keke. And if we keep doing it for three more months, we get *jade*." Bero's eyes ran covetously over the rocks in the bin. "No other job is going to give us that."

"We *have* jade," Mudt retorted. "We haven't done anything with it except watch over these poor, dirty saps and freeze our asses off in the jungle. What do we need more jade for?"

"What *for*?" exclaimed Bero. "What do you think?" That was like asking why a person needed more food, or more money, or more women. You could never have too much; that was why the Green Bones were always fighting each other. Sometimes Mudt asked the stupidest questions.

"We should be training. We should be going after No Peak," Mudt groused again, but Bero had stopped listening because he thought he'd heard something in the forest. The slag heap was entirely exposed, but dense, dark foliage surrounded them on all sides. He tried to reach out his sense of Perception. Staring into the darkness, his heart began to race and the night suddenly seemed to be full of danger.

"They're coming," Mudt whispered in sudden, certain fear. An instant later, Bero sensed it as well: swiftly approaching jade auras that could only belong to Green Bones. He couldn't tell how many there were or how long it would be before they arrived. In his mind, they seemed like bright missiles flying through the darkness toward him.

Bero shouted, "The trucks! Get to the trucks!"

He seized the rolling metal bin and dragged it toward the nearest tarp-covered vehicle. He threw open the back but didn't bother to take the time to lower the metal ramp; with a heaving of Strength, he tried to lift the rocks inside. The container must've weighed at least a hundred kilograms; it wobbled and nearly upturned but Mudt ran to help him, and together, they wrestled the fruits of a night's scavenge into the back of the vehicle.

Mudt ran to the top of the slag heap and broke open two flares, which sizzled and burned with painful red light and drew the attention of every picker below. "Green Bones!" Mudt yelled. "Run! Run!"

The pickers began to scramble up the hill in a panic, clawing with hands and feet, dislodging loose stones and sending them tumbling noisily down the slope. The first pickers to make it to the ridge dove into the trucks like rabbits into a burrow, eyes wide and white in their dark faces. They gibbered in frantic Uwiwan, begging the Abukei drivers to start driving, while their fellows shouted and cried for the trucks to wait. Bero stared down the hill. The pickers who were too far away, who knew there was no way they'd reach the trucks in time, were running toward the forest, hoping to scatter and hide among the trees. They were right to be afraid. At first, the clans had beaten the pickers and shipped them back to the Uwiwas, but that had not been enough to dissuade the scavenging; now the usual response was to snap the necks of any foreign thieves. Along with their jade-wearing supervisors.

Bero sprinted for the nearest truck. Mudt had already climbed into the one behind it. "Go, go!" Bero shouted, even as two pickers leapt for the open tailgate. One of them made it in; the other stumbled and fell as the truck shot forward, spraying him with mud as it left him behind. Bero stuck his head out of the window and looked behind them to see half a dozen figures emerging from the trees. They were moving so quickly their bodies seemed blurred, but Bero could see that they carried guns and moon blades.

If he had not been so terrified, he might've been awed. The scene looked like something out of a movie, one in which the Green Bone rebels flew out of the jungle and ambushed the Shotarian soldiers in their camp. Except that this was not a battle, but a crackdown. Gunfire broke out along with distant screams as the Green Bones began to sweep the slag heap for pickers. Nothing to be done for those poor bastards. Bero swiveled around to face the front again—just in time to see three men burst from the trees ahead and land in the road in front of them.

"Keep going, keep going! Run them over!" Bero screamed at the driver, but any further words caught in his throat as he watched the three men plant themselves in a line and throw a massive low-sweeping Deflection in unison. It tore across the surface of the narrow, pocked road like an amplified wave, flinging dirt and gravel up into the truck's windshield. The truck's tires skidded violently. The driver tried desperately to straighten them, but the vehicle spun nearly ninety degrees and careened off the path. It banked in a precarious, stomach-lurching jolt, then toppled sideways into the gully full of rocks and bushes.

Bero was flung against the side door; his hip and shoulder slammed into the metal, and he heard a crack that he hoped had not come from any of his bones. The driver landed heavily on top of him. In the back, Bero could hear thuds and cries from the trapped Uwiwan workers. A few sickening heartbeats passed, then the door of the truck was flung open so hard it was nearly torn from its hinges. Several hands reached in and yanked out the driver, screaming, then reached back in and latched around Bero's legs. Bero shouted and kicked, but his flailing, imprecise Strength did not prevent him from being pulled out of the overturned vehicle like a hooked tuna being dragged from the water.

Bero was dropped facedown on the road. He struggled to his knees as Mudt was deposited roughly next to him. A nauseating sense of dreadful familiarity rose in Bero's throat; this was like that time nearly three years ago when he'd been caught and beaten by the Maik brothers. He had a crooked face and a limp to remind him of that encounter every day, and he had a terrible feeling that he was unlikely to get off as easily this time.

Mudt spat dirt from his mouth. "Now we're fucked, keke. This is all your fault."

Bero blinked grit from his eyes. The lower half of the upended truck was blocking the road; the other two trucks had been forced to stop behind it. Green Bones were dragging pickers out of all three vehicles and killing them with chilling efficiency. In minutes, they were dead, thirteen in all. Bero suspected the other seven in the crew were lying on the slag heap some distance behind. He considered leaping up and running for his life. With Lightness and Strength on his side, he might make it, though probably not. He was just about to give it a go anyway, because what did he have to lose at this point, but one of the Green Bones must've Perceived his intentions because a pair of rough hands seized them by the backs of their necks. "Do anything stupid and you die, you barukan piss rats."

"We're not barukan," Bero protested angrily.

A man approached. He was older than the others, his closely cropped hair receding to either side of a sharp widow's peak, but his trim body moved with the lean economy of a grizzled wolf. His piercing eyes did not seem to blink very much. "Zapunyo doesn't send his hired barukan to supervise the scavenges, not anymore," the man explained to the other Green Bone. "He needs them to run his operations in the Uwiwas and to guard his compound. The local jade-fevered shine addicts are a lot more expendable."

"Should we kill them, then, Nau-jen?" asked the other Green Bone, his grip tightening.

The Horn of the Mountain studied the two kneeling teens. In the dark, Bero could not see much of his expression, but the man's aura was like a low, simmering heat off baked bricks. The Horn's searching gaze settled upon the jade encircling Bero's neck and Mudt's arms. "That's a lot of quality green for a couple of punks like you." His voice had the coarse, demanding quality of a military sergeant. "How'd you two scavengers come by it?"

Bero was quite sure he was going to be executed, but he lifted his head proudly and defiantly. "I won this jade. I took it from Kaul Lan's body myself."

There was a moment of stunned silence from the nearby Green Bones. Then they burst into raucous laughter that echoed over the idling engines of the stalled trucks. Nau Suen didn't laugh, but he let his men do so. After the chuckling had died down, one of the Fists said, "These new green, as they call themselves, are worse than the barukan. Every one of them would have you believe they won their spoils in a pitched battle when not a single one of them can use jade worth shit."

Nau Suen turned a stern look toward the Green Bone who'd spoken. "We hooked half of these sorry miscreants on jade and shine in order to use them against No Peak. Why should we be surprised now that Gont Asch's discarded tools have been picked up by an opportunist like Zapunyo?" His men fell into chastised silence.

Nau looked back down at the two teens. "We're not going to kill these two. We're going to send them back to their employer as an act of goodwill." He motioned for Bero and Mudt to be released. Bero blinked, not quite believing it enough to be relieved. Nau said to them, "Listen carefully. Tell the barukan Soradiyo that as long as I keep finding and catching his scrap-picking crews, he won't make money. Zapunyo won't be pleased. Your manager might even soon be out of a job in the worst possible way. Let him know that Nau Suen, Horn of the Mountain, would like to discuss bettering his career options."

"You're going to buy out Soradiyo?" Bero asked, suddenly interested now that he'd recovered from his fear. Mudt shot him an urgent look that screamed, *Shut up, you want him to change his mind about letting us live?*

The Horn looked at Bero closely and curiously, as if he were a strange species of frog that had been discovered in the rain forest. Bero found the man's gaze unnerving and began to think that maybe Mudt was right; maybe he should've kept his mouth shut the whole time. He'd heard rumors on the street that Nau Suen was so skilled in Perception that he could read minds. Which was stupid, everyone knew that was impossible, but nevertheless, Nau's stare was so penetrating that Bero's skin crawled.

The Horn said, "Ask another question and I'll rip your tongue out. You're a dog, a messenger, that's all you are." Nau leaned in close and spoke into Bero's ear. "But you're not lying. You actually do believe you're wearing Kaul Lan's jade. Which means that sooner or later, you'll wish I'd done you the favor of killing you tonight."

Nau straightened and turned away. "Let's go," he said. "Get these trucks out of here." Several Green Bones combined their Strength to haul the lead vehicle upright, then Nau and his Green Bones got into the three trucks, taking the bin of jade scavenge with them. A few paused to roll the bodies of the pickers into the gully, one by one. With a rumbling spray of dirt, they drove off, leaving Bero and Mudt still kneeling by the road to wait for morning and make their way back down the mountain alone.

CHAPTER
24

The Inheritance

Shae walked from the Weather Man's residence to the main house. Even though it was an hour before dawn, the lights were on in the kitchen. Kyanla was stirring a pot of hot cereal at the stove. Hilo sat at the table, cutting a nectarine into bite-sized pieces with a paring knife and putting them on a plastic food tray in front of Niko. The toddler pushed them around, depositing more of them on the floor than in his mouth. Hilo grumbled with weary patience.

Shae stood in the entry of the kitchen. Whenever she looked at Niko, she still felt a jolt—an echo of the shock on that evening three months ago when her brother had arrived back in Janloon with an exhausted two-year-old child in his arms. "Does he always wake up this early?" she asked.

"Pretty much," her brother said, eating the rejected fruit pieces himself. "Since I had to be up early anyway, I thought I'd let Wen sleep in. She was up half the night with Ru."

"We have to go," Shae said.

Hilo wiped his hands on a napkin and got up, leaving Kyanla to take his vacated spot. The boy ignored the housekeeper's attempts to reinterest him in breakfast and held his arms out to Shae to be picked up. "Auntie, auntie."

"Not now, Niko," Shae said, with a stab of guilt, as she placed a consoling kiss on the top of his head. Despite the shock of both his existence and his arrival, she'd loved the little boy almost at once. It was impossible not to see his resemblance to Lan, not to feel a mingled pang of sadness and joy every time he made an expression that reminded her of her dead brother. When Niko was fussy, clingy, and confused, when he began to follow her and tearfully hug her legs, she loved him all the more, wanted to comfort and protect him. She suspected he had taken such a strong liking to her because she was the one in the family most similar in appearance to Eyni.

A nondescript car and trusted driver were waiting for them at the front door. They couldn't take Hilo's Duchesse Priza or any of the family's more recognizable vehicles. The two of them sat in silence as the car drove down dark streets.

Shae said, "What do we tell the clan about Niko?"

Hilo lit a cigarette and rolled down the window. "That he's Lan's son. That he was born overseas without our knowledge and brought back to Kekon after his mother died. What else do they need to know?"

"No one will believe it's that simple."

"Let them believe whatever they want," Hilo said harshly. A tense silence swelled between them. Hilo turned his head to the window and blew out a stream of smoke. When he spoke again, the anger had gone out of his voice. "I know what you're thinking, Shae, but it didn't happen like that. I tried to work things out differently. You remember Eyni, what she was like."

"She used to be Lan's wife," Shae said quietly. "She was Niko's mother."

Shae had not been close to Eyni, but they had been on cordial terms before Shae had left for Espenia. She struggled to even remember the woman clearly now, to describe her better in her own mind, so that when she knelt in the sanctum of the Temple of Divine Return and asked the gods to recognize her father and her grandfather and her eldest brother—all of them gone from this world to await the Return—she could pray consideration for her former sister-in-law as well. When she finished naming those who'd passed on, she pleaded forgiveness for her brother. What Hilo had done went against the Divine Virtues, but Lan's son would be cared for and loved, she promised it on her soul. And hadn't the family suffered enough already? *Don't punish us further*, she begged.

Hilo finished his cigarette and rolled the window back up. "Would you rather I'd given Niko up?" When Shae failed to answer, he leaned back in his seat. "That's what I thought."

They arrived at the harborfront. It had not been easy to arrange a meeting with Ven Sandolan, president and chief executive officer of K-Star Freight and patriarch of one of the country's most prominent Green Bone families, in a place where there was no chance of the conversation being observed by members of either the Mountain or No Peak clans. The deck of a private yacht moored in Summer Harbor was probably as neutral and secure a location as could be expected.

Ven Sando was an avid boater and known for taking his fourteen-meter-long motorboat *Inheritance* out every Sixthday morning. They were on the water by sunrise. Ven Sando came accompanied by his eldest son, Haku, a first-rank Fist in the Mountain. Haku manned the cockpit while the elder Ven stood at the railing with his tanned face turned toward the ocean, his gray hair blasted back by wind and salt spray, expounding to his guests on the horsepower, speed, and fuel capacity of the *Inheritance* and how he'd once spent four weeks sailing along the coast of Tun. Shae listened politely, if impatiently, as Ven toured them around the boat, beaming with pride as Hilo ran a hand appreciatively over the furniture and the built-in wet bar behind the helm.

Ven Haku steered the craft around the far side of Gosha Island before cutting the engines, leaving only the sound of water slapping gently against the hull and the distant rumble of airplanes taking off and landing from Janloon International Airport. A thin layer of haze sat over the city's waterfront and diffused the morning light, but overhead, the late autumn sky was blue and cloudless except for the fading contrails of recently passed fighter planes, coming or going from one of the several Espenian aircraft carriers in the area. Shae pulled her sweater tight to cut the chill.

"This isn't the first time I've had members of the No Peak clan aboard." Ven Sando possessed the cheerfully overbearing manner of a man who felt he'd earned every penny of his wealth and a belly paunch that suggested he saw no reason not to enjoy it. He gestured them into the boat's lounge and settled comfortably into one of the white deck chairs. "About eight years ago, I met Kaul Sen at a fundraiser for the Janloon Arts Council and offered to take him and a few others on a cruise around Little Button the very next morning. He was such an interesting man, wonderful company, your grandfather. Relations between our clans were much more cordial at that time. Kaul Sen and Ayt Yu had differences, but there was always respect back then."

Hilo's smile approximated his usual easy and open expression but did not quite reach his eyes. "I hope our clans will be on such friendly terms again someday." He seated himself across from Ven. Shae positioned a deck chair slightly to the right and behind her brother; Ven Haku mirrored the position next to his father. Hilo ran a meaningful gaze over the meeting's participants and their surroundings. "Here we are, the Mountain and No Peak, so it would seem this is a good start."

"I'd like to agree with you," Ven said mildly, folding his hands over his stomach, "except that I'm not the Pillar and can't speak for my clan. And neither are any of the other members of the Mountain that you've been talking to." Ven's eyebrows rose in wary inquiry. "It seems as if No Peak is a cock courting many hens."

Four months ago, following the discussion at the Kaul family dinner table about Ayt's potential successors, Shae had sent a large bouquet of glory hibiscus and dancing star lilies, symbolizing prosperity and friendship, to the office of Iwe Kalundo, to congratulate him and his family on assuming the office of Weather Man of the Mountain.

Six weeks later, shortly after his return from Lybon, Hilo had paid a visit to Kaul Dushuron Academy and met with Grandmaster Le. That week, nine-year-old Koben Ato was offered admission and a full scholarship to attend the Academy—an uncommon occurrence, reserved for prospective students demonstrating unusual early talent.

The Academy's obvious attempt to poach Ayt Yu's grandson from Wie Lon Temple School was met with a flat decline by the Koben family—they would be insane to defect from the Mountain's feeder school and the alma mater of the entire Ayt family, no matter how generous the financial incentives—and the bouquet sent to Iwe garnered only a curt note of polite thanks, but both actions accomplished their purpose of drawing attention to the Iwe and Koben families, inflaming speculation that No Peak was looking past the current Pillar of the Mountain and toward the next one. It had been Hilo and Shae's intention that Ven be aware of these actions before their meeting.

Hilo spread his hands unapologetically. "I want to be on good terms with whoever leads the Mountain after Ayt Madashi. Our clans declared peace, but I don't trust Ayt to keep it. I'm thinking of my own family, of course. Ayt whispered my name and is the reason my brother is dead, so I won't sleep well until she's stepped down or been moved aside by a deserving successor."

Ven sat forward. "That's the whole problem right there," he said, with conspiratorial vehemence. "Ayt *has* no succession plan. She became the Pillar by killing the rightful male heir, and now she's too old to have children even if she could find a man who would dare to marry her." Ven's voice gained heat. "The Mountain wouldn't be facing this problem if our Pillar was a man with a wife who could give him sons. The clan needs a strong Green Bone family bloodline that can be trusted for generations." He gestured to Hilo. "You have that in No Peak, to your credit. We don't. We're being led by a childless woman pursuing her own ambitions—that's how low the once great clan of the Spear of Kekon has fallen."

Shae was astounded. Even Hilo's eyes widened slightly. Ayt Mada was their enemy, and Shae would not have hesitated to describe her as power-hungry, but they had not expected to hear Ven speak of his own Pillar in such an openly disrespectful manner. Shae's first reaction was suspicion; was Ven trying to ingratiate himself with them? Or was he truly so guileless?

Ven held up his hands as if to check his own tirade. "Don't misunderstand me," he said hastily, glancing at Shae sideways before returning his attention to Hilo. "I don't have anything against women being Green Bones and holding positions of responsibility in valuable supporting roles. But the Pillar is different. The spine of the body, as we all say. Ayt has made misstep after misstep: allowing jade and shine to be used by common criminals, inviting public scandal upon us, and getting us into a costly street war that, if you'll forgive me for saying so, most people in the Mountain thought we should've easily won." Ven puckered his mouth. "When I raise valid criticisms— unselfishly, I might add—she stubbornly refuses to address them. My very life might be in danger if that woman knew I was conversing with you." Despite this statement, Ven did not seem fearful to be voicing opposition. Shae suspected that K-Star Freight was too big and important to the Mountain, and the Ven family too well known and powerful, for Ayt Mada to simply whisper their names and make them disappear, no matter how condemnatory Ven was.

"I'm glad we're having this meeting, Ven-jen. You're obviously the right person for me to be talking to." Hilo leaned back in his deck chair, angling himself more directly toward the Vens with a subtle shift of his body. He seemed to expand and relax, as if he'd occupied this very seat on the boat countless times in the past, and his voice took on the quality of contented camaraderie established at once between new friends who've discovered they grew up on the same street corner. The change occurred so smoothly and naturally that Shae found herself feeling as if she had suddenly become an uninvited guest sitting uncomfortably apart from the three men, who now possessed a familiarity they had not shared mere seconds ago.

Hilo's voice lowered. "I'm glad to learn there are people in the Mountain who want change as much as you and me, Ven-jen, but speaking as an outsider, it seems to me the Koben family doesn't have any strong leaders, just a little boy. I'm not patient enough to wait twenty years for things to improve, and I can tell you're not a complacent person yourself. Naturally, I was curious about the new Weather Man, but from asking around, I hear the Iwes follow Ayt Mada blindly."

Ven snorted. "That's true, and also there's too much thin blood in that family."

"In these uncertain times," Hilo said somberly, "cooperation between the clans is important to the country. That's why I wanted to meet with you in private, to see if we could help each other. The Ven family is known and respected by everyone, on the business side and on the streets. That old saying, 'Gold and jade, never together'— it sounds nice, but who can argue that we don't need both for our families to be truly strong?" Hilo fixed the overweight businessman with a stare of strict confidence. "You're obviously a man of principle, and maybe it's not your wish to take on so much responsibility, but since this issue in the Mountain clan affects not just my own family but all of Kekon, I feel that I have to be honest. No Peak would gladly recognize the leadership of the Ven family. I can't think of anyone I'd rather see succeed Ayt Mada."

Ven's jade aura gave a perceptible pulse of gratification, but he let out a dramatic sigh and waved a hand vaguely over his shoulder, dismissing the idea as if he'd been told it so many times already that he was tired of having to disappoint people. The gesture struck Shae as so contrived and self-important that she was forced to mask a stab of deep dislike. Ven said, "I'm flattered, Kaul-jen, I truly am, but I have a company to run, and besides, I'm getting to be an old man, nearly retired. People always expect the Pillar to be green." The only jade Ven wore was a heavy gold watch with a jeweled case. "Wearing so much jade—that's for young men. It would suit the clan best to have a leader who's in his prime, who has the right image but also the backing of family resources and social capital. Myself, I'm content to simply be the voice of age and wisdom in the background."

Shae looked past Ven Sando to his son. She saw Hilo's eyes shift in that direction as well. Ven Haku was about the same age as they were; he was said to be a reasonably good Fist and popular among his peers and subordinates, in no small part because he was not shy about flaunting his family's wealth by throwing parties and rewarding those under him. He wore his hair gelled back and his jade studded on a bold black leather choker around his neck, like a gem-encrusted dog collar. He sat partly slouched, with an alert but slightly scornful expression on his face, and even the low, steady buzz of his jade aura seemed to emanate privilege and insolence. For a strange, disconcerting moment, looking at Ven Haku and his perfectly unlined face, Shae was reminded of the Hilo she'd known six or seven years ago.

Ven Sando intended to install his son as Pillar after Ayt Mada was gone. Hilo looked between the elder and younger Ven and inclined his head with a half-concealed smile. "A dutiful son and supportive father working together? I'm not sure any clan has ever been so fortunate." Hilo's jade aura, normally so bright and expressive, hummed as smoothly as a wide river, betraying almost nothing. "I'd like to help bring about such a change. But Ayt Mada and I sat together in front of both our clans and the public and declared truce. I don't break my promises, not even to my enemies. I have to make that clear before we talk further."

Ven Sando gave Hilo a shrewd look. "No one wants another street war between the clans. But you wouldn't have asked to meet unless you had something to give besides encouragement."

Hilo's manner hardened a touch, into formality, and he spoke more slowly. "Ayt Mada will never step down willingly. She'll have to be forced out. When you move against her, No Peak will offer you our friendship and complete support, against those who might be resistant or who would take advantage of the transition when it comes about, and there are always those people. That's not a small thing and I don't promise it lightly. There are also the people who need to have practical reasons to accept a new leader. There are things that my Weather Man can do to help you persuade them."

The prompt caught Shae off guard for an instant; she'd begun to think with some annoyance that Hilo had forgotten she was even there. "K-Star Freight is one of Kekon's largest and most profitable companies, so I imagine you already hold a great deal of sway in the Mountain," she said to Ven, laying the flattery on a little thick. "Even so, some of your potential supporters might be encouraged if they knew there were financial incentives involved. No Peak's influence in certain industries might be of interest to those who can't normally take advantage of it. There are even parts of our business where we would be open to discussing purchase offers or partnerships...if the clans were on friendlier terms. Naturally, that's information we expect you would share judiciously."

Ven appeared to consider all of these assurances before blowing out a heavy breath, as if coming to a difficult but inevitable decision. "What we're talking about would not be easy to accomplish. Ayt carries a great deal of jade and surrounds herself with those who are loyal to her. It would take time and planning to bring about the sort of change we want to see. But knowing that I have the promise of your friendship, Kaul-jen—it fills me with determination to fix what's wrong with the Mountain, and to put things right between our clans."

So there it was: Ven would secretly garner the support for a coup within the Mountain clan. If successful, such a thing would almost certainly end in the death of Ayt Mada and her inner circle. No Peak would quietly back the usurpers with bribes, payouts, and financial concessions in addition to, when the time came, the might of their Fists and Fingers to help put down Ayt's supporters. Afterward, the Ven family would control the Mountain, and there would be true and lasting friendship between the clans, not merely the cynical truce that currently existed.

Hilo said, "I look forward to the future, Ven-jen."

Ven clapped his hands together, then ended the meeting by getting up, going to the wet bar, and pouring two glasses of hoji. "Surely you already know this, Kaul-jen, but within the Mountain clan, you have a bloodthirsty reputation. And your lovely sister is said to be a cold-hearted Espenian sympathizer. It just goes to show what sorts of lies people spread about their enemies. I can see for myself that you're an upstanding and reasonable man, just like your grandfather, someone who's easy to work with." He and Hilo drank in recognition of their new alliance.

Ven Sando offered to sail them around some more and host them for lunch, but Shae played the part of the Pillar's anxious aide by suggesting it was best that they return before anyone in No Peak became concerned by their absence. As the president of K-Star regaled the Kauls with a few more sailing stories, interspersed with the occasional anecdote about the freight shipping industry, Ven Haku steered the *Inheritance* back to the private dock where the Kauls' car and driver were waiting.

When the Pillar and his Weather Man were alone together in the moving vehicle again, Shae could no longer contain herself. "Ven Sando might be the most conceited, insufferable boor I've ever met," she exclaimed.

"Does it make you feel sorry for Ayt?" Hilo grinned broadly and stretched his legs out into her side of the seat well, propping his shoes on top of her feet. She kicked them off, as if they were still children bickering over space in the back of Grandda's car while Lan growled at them from the front to leave each other alone. Hilo threw an arm over his sister's shoulder. His mood had changed completely from the earlier dark car ride, and the easy friendliness he'd shown to the men on the boat had vanished; his lopsided smile was bright and feral. "Ven and his son put together would be less than half the Pillar that Ayt is. This is how we *win*, Shae. We get the Mountain to tear itself apart under Ayt's feet."

There were times Shae was forced to admit that perhaps Grandda would've better appreciated his younger grandson's qualities if there'd still been a Shotarian occupation force around that needed to be destroyed. She said, "I'll think of how else we can give the Ven family our support."

CHAPTER
25

Interception

Maik Kehn steadied himself on the deck of the motorboat as it sped up, throwing white spray into the air as it jumped the swells of the cargo ship's wake and pulled up alongside the much larger vessel. Kehn did not particularly like being on the water, especially given the cold drizzle of rain flying in his face; he would much rather be on the familiar streets of Janloon—the noisy, dirty streets that he and his Green Bones ruled. But the clans needed to protect and patrol far beyond the city these days—up in the mountains, along the coast, even hundreds of kilometers out to sea. Kehn suspected that he might be the first Horn, at least in his generation, to hijack a ship in international waters. That was part of his job, though, adapting to the enemy's moves—and he'd learned from Kaul Hilo to always lead from the front.

Juen, his First Fist, fired the grappling hook, which went sailing over the railing of the cargo ship and caught, tethering their motorboat. Unlike some large men, Kehn had no difficulty with Lightness; seizing the taut rope, he swung his feet onto it and ran halfway up its length like a lizard on a thin branch, crossing the last few meters to the ship's deck in a bound. He landed quietly, talon knife drawn.

Two men armed with handguns were running toward the railing. To his surprise, Kehn sensed jade auras, shrill with hostility and alarm. At the sight of him, they stopped and opened fire. The Horn leapt straight for the guards, releasing tight twin Deflections that cleared his path as he went airborne and landed between them. He clamped onto the barrel of the nearest weapon with his left hand, twisting it away from the gunman with a burst of Strength as he hurled the man on the right backward with a Deflection that sent him crashing across the rain-slicked deck into the nearest metal wall of stacked containers.

Kehn tossed the gun overboard; its former owner drew twin triangle-headed *durbh* daggers—fighting knives of the Uwiwa Islands—and came at the Horn with vicious, swift stabs. Kehn hooked and controlled the man's left wrist with his talon knife and caught the blade of the right-hand dagger with his Steeled hand. His opponent reacted instantly, letting go of the weapon and driving his fist into Kehn's solar plexus with enough Strength that the air went out of Kehn's lungs with a painful grunt. He felt the telltale flex in his opponent's jade aura as the man gathered himself to Channel a lethal blow.

Kehn battened his torso with Steel; the *durbh* blade he'd caught in his hand cut sharp into suddenly unprotected skin. Dropping it, he Channeled first, fast and quick, a nonlethal jab to the heart, just enough to shock. Grabbing a fistful of the man's shirt, he let out a bellow as he shoved, then yanked forward hard, whiplashing his opponent's face into a head butt that connected with an audible crack. The Horn dug his shoulder into the limp man's chest and heaved, sending him over the ship's railing and tumbling into the white-capped water far below.

Kehn turned around. His Fists, Juen and Iyn, and two Fingers,

Lott and Dudo, had leapt to board the ship right behind him, leaving one Finger, Ton, behind to man the motorboat. Iyn was stalking after the second guard as he tried to stumble away from her with a broken leg. As she drew her moon blade, Kehn ordered, "Leave him alive for now." It occurred to him that he shouldn't have thrown the other one into the sea; now the man's jade, even if it was not much, was at the bottom of the ocean. At least it was no longer being worn and used disgracefully by a hired half bone cur.

He strode down the deck of the ship between fifteen-meter-tall walls of red, orange, and blue shipping containers uniformly stacked like his nephew's building blocks. The three-hundred-meter-long cargo vessel was too large for him to be able to Perceive everyone aboard, but he knew his Fists and Fingers would split up to sweep the ship; they would find and kill any additional barukan guards and round up the crew. Kehn wrapped his hand in the hem of his shirt, putting pressure on it to stop the bleeding as he headed toward the bridge.

Twenty minutes later, the captain and his officers were gathered together in the ship's dining room. The captain was a man of about forty with a curly orange beard and sideburns—Captain Bamivu eya Kijdiva, according to his nameplate—an Ygutanian, like several of his officers. The crew, which had been rounded up and placed in the mess hall, was mostly Uwiwan. Though Kijdiva acted admirably calm, sweat stood out on his brow and Kehn could Perceive his heart beating much faster than normal. He obviously didn't know anything about Green Bones and thought his ship had been attacked by pirates who might steal his cargo or harm his crew.

"Don't worry, no one will be hurt," Kehn said. Either the man did not understand or was not put at ease by the assurance. "You speak any other languages?" Kehn asked. "Uwiwan? Espenian?"

The captain spoke passable Espenian, which was fortunate as Lott also had a decent grasp on the language, having studied it during his years at the Academy. That seemed to be popular these days; with more foreigners and foreign businesses in Janloon, it was useful even for Fingers to know another language besides Kekonese. Kehn asked

Lott to translate. "Tell him we want to see the ship's registration and freight manifest."

After some back and forth, the requested documents were brought over from the bridge. The MV *Amaric Pride*, owned and operated by an Ygutanian company but registered in the Uwiwa Islands, had left Tialuhiya two days ago, bound for the northern port city of Bursvik in Ygutan. Normally, ships bound for Ygutan went south around Shotar and through the Origas Gulf, but the waters near Oortoko were currently a war zone full of Shotarian, Espenian, and Ygutanian warships.

Kehn frowned as he flipped through the manifest. The ship was carrying nearly twenty thousand tons of cargo—apparel, consumer goods, canned fruit. There was no way to search it all. The captain asked a question, and Lott said, "He wants to know if we killed those men, the four guards."

Juen and the others had encountered two other barukan as they took over the ship. "Those men worked for a smuggler in the Uwiwa Islands," Kehn said to the captain, not answering his question. "Do you know what they were guarding?"

The captain swallowed. "I didn't ask questions," he said, through Lott. "I was paid for their passage. It's typical for us to have four to ten paying passengers aboard. I don't know what's in the boxes; I never see any of it. I just move it."

Kehn left the captain and officers under Juen's guard and went back up onto the deck with Lott. The sky was still spitting weak, intermittent rain, but the sun had come up now. The barukan that Iyn had left alive was tied to the railing, his leg bent at a disturbing angle, his face a sickly hue. Iyn had stripped him of his jade. The Fist was sighing with disappointment as she leaned against a nearby container, pulling the links of the gemstone necklace apart and flinging the nephrite pieces into the ocean, pausing only to pocket two pieces of real green. Junior Fists like Iyn were the most anxious to prove themselves, vying with their peers to gain additional jade, territory, responsibility, and Fingers to command. Kehn made a mental note to himself to give her another chance to earn jade sooner rather than later. He'd come to realize that the bulk of the Horn's role was managing people, and although he wasn't naturally gifted with the personal warmth and magnetism of his predecessor, he tried to always pay attention to those under his command and be strict but fair in his decisions. After two grueling years in the job, he'd become more secure in his own leadership and knew his warriors respected him.

Standing in front of the injured barukan man, Kehn said, "Do you speak Kekonese?" When the man nodded, the Horn got straight to the point: "Which container is it in?"

"I don't know," the man said. "Zapunyo doesn't pay me to know things. Kill me and be done with it."

"I'm not going to kill you," Kehn said. "Your leg is badly broken, but it's a clean break; if I ask the ship's doctor to come out and set it, you'll heal and be able to walk again. Or I can have Lott and Iyn here turn it into pebbles in a skin bag, and your other leg as well, then drop you back off in the Uwiwa Islands as a cripple to see what use Zapunyo has for you then."

The little color remaining in the man's face drained out. "If I tell you anything, I'm a dead man. Do you know what Zapunyo does to people who steal or rat? Who break the silence of Ti Pasuiga?" His teeth began to chatter as the wind chilled his wet clothes and sweat-drenched skin. "First, he cuts off the feet, then the hands, and finally the head, and he has the parts buried in different places so you won't be whole even in the afterlife."

"That's because he's an animal," said Kehn. "We can get you away from Zapunyo. How do you think we knew about this shipment if we didn't already have informers that we protect? Also, we have the support of the Espenians; they're at war and want to stop the smuggling as well, to prevent their enemies from getting any stronger. You want to start a new life somewhere far away from Zapunyo's grasp? Or you want the other option? I'm going to have a smoke while you think about it." Kehn paced away.

He did, indeed, light a cigarette and walk out of sight to enjoy it. Behind him, he heard Iyn say, "I'm inclined to break your other leg just for wasting Maik-jen's time. He's a patient man, but he doesn't like to talk much, so he's being extra generous with you and you're not taking it seriously, you barukan dog fucker."

Lott said, "Iyn-jen, there's no need to insult him when he's in that state." Speaking to the man in a concerned tone, he added, "Personally, I hope you decide to cooperate. I don't see what loyalty you owe to Zapunyo that's worth this much suffering, and I don't really want to make things worse for you, although naturally I'll do it if that's what I have to." This was said with just the right amount of sympathy, reasonableness, and cold certitude. Kehn made a satisfied noise to himself; Lott Jin had had a shaky beginning as a Finger, but following Hilo's instruction that he be placed under the tutelage of good mentors, the young man had come a long way and his attitude was much improved.

While Kehn waited, giving the captive a few more minutes, he considered how to propose marriage to Lina. He knew she would accept, as they had spoken of it already. It was the right time; he was an oldest son and hoped to father children of his own soon. As a generally private man, he would personally prefer a small, simple wedding but knew that would not be possible; the marriage of the Horn would be a clan event. All the political considerations and turns of fortune that affected the Kaul family affected the Maiks as well.

When Kehn finished his cigarette, he returned and demanded an answer. Shivering violently now and utterly defeated in spirit, the man directed them to the container that he'd been ordered to protect. It was hard to believe that the barukan were actually Kekonese by blood, Kehn thought, because they were weak willed, but that was a natural consequence of being born and beaten down in a cowardly place like Shotar.

Kehn summoned the ship's doctor to see to the man's injuries. Crew members were brought out to operate the shipboard crane to move the indicated six-meter-long container off its stack. When the corrugated blue metal box was opened on deck, Kehn saw it was packed full of cardboard cartons. The first several boxes they inspected contained hundreds of individually poly-wrapped items of clothing—exercise pants, tank tops, swimwear—straight from the garment factories in the Uwiwa Islands. Then Iyn noticed that some of the boxes appeared to have an extra bar code on the side. Kehn opened one of them and held up a woman's blouse with small green buttons down the front. The buttons were made of jade and the blouse was false—it didn't even open at the front. The whole box was filled with jade, disguised as mere ornamentation. Nestled in layers of fabric and mixed in with thousands of items of clothing, the gems would easily evade casual inspection until someone on the receiving end in Ygutan took delivery on behalf of a fictitious retailer and collected a fortune in jade.

"That Uwiwan is a clever dog," Kehn admitted in a grumble, standing among a mess of boxes, plastic, and fabric. He left his Green Bones in charge of the continuing search and went to the bridge to order the captain to change course; the MV *Amaric Pride* would be docking in Janloon's Summer Harbor.

CHAPTER

26

~

Setting Expectations

The news was vaguely reported in the Ygutanian papers and not at all outside that country's borders, but according to the translated articles Shae received from the clan's contacts in Ygutan, several targeted bombings had occurred in the past week, destroying chemical factories near Dramsk, Nitiyu, and Bursvik. The Ygutanian Directorate was blaming the attacks on Shotarian loyalist groups from Oortoko, backed by the Espenian government. The articles did not reveal who owned or operated the facilities nor what they were producing that would make them the targets of sabotage, but Shae already knew. The Espenians wouldn't offer to pay for something if they didn't plan to use it; she'd met with Ambassador Mendoff and Colonel Deiller in the White Lantern Club eight months ago, and now the Mountain's lucrative shine-producing facilities were destroyed.

Ayt Mada must be furious. A satisfied smile crept onto Shae's face and hovered there before sliding off. No Peak had not acted against the Mountain's operations directly, but Ayt was sure to deduce who had sold the information to the Espenians. Shae did not for an instant regret what she'd done; she'd dealt a staggering financial blow to the Mountain without risking any No Peak lives or businesses, prevented vast quantities of the poisonous drug that had killed Lan from ever reaching the black market, and strengthened the alliance with the Espenians without giving in to their demands for more jade. It was precisely the sort of cunning victory that her grandfather would've been proud of. The only problem was that Ayt was sure to retaliate. Shae didn't know when or how it would happen, but the Mountain would find a way.

Shae called Woon into her office and asked him to arrange another meeting with Colonel Leland Deiller. "Tell the colonel we have additional information of military interest to him."

Woon sat down in front of her desk. After his attempt to resign as her chief of staff, several weeks of unspoken awkwardness had lingered between them, but it had faded under the pervasive necessity of their working relationship. Shae was glad that Woon seemed comfortable around her again. She was grateful they were still friends, even if things were not the same as before. "Maik Kehn's discovery of jade being smuggled from the Uwiwa Islands to Ygutan on commercial cargo ships," Woon inferred. "You believe if we hand over that information to the Espenians, they'll shut it down, the way they destroyed the shine factories in Ygutan."

"Kehn and his Fists got lucky with a tip-off on that one ship, but they can't possibly patrol the entire West Tun Sea. The Espenians can, and do," Shae said. "Even though we have informers and agents in the Uwiwa Islands, we have little power there—less ever since Hilo caused a publicized bloodbath. Espenia, though, provides the bulk of that country's foreign aid; they could force the Uwiwan government to crack down on Zapunyo's activities when no one else can."

Woon nodded. "We get them to solve our problems."

"Ayt Mada's nationalistic rhetoric aside, we have interests in common with the ROE," Shae said. "We don't want jade or shine on the black market, and neither do they."

"Because they want it all to themselves," Woon said. "You have to be careful, Shae-jen. Working with the Espenians is like sleeping next to a tiger—it seems like a good idea until the tiger gets hungry, and the Espenians aren't a subtle people. There's over a hundred thousand of them on Euman Island now, and we're fielding complaints from Lantern Men about Espenian soldiers on shore leave in Janloon causing problems in casinos and brothels. The news is reporting rising civilian casualty figures in Oortoko, and the world is blaming it on Espenian involvement. Given public opinion these days, we don't want No Peak to seem too cozy with the foreigners."

Shae couldn't disagree, especially since she knew some people, inside and outside of the clan, already viewed her as an Espenophile for her foreign education. Meanwhile, Ayt Mada was capitalizing on the Oortokon War, excoriating foreigners in general and Espenians in particular, raising her own public profile and popularity.

Shae could understand people's temptation to buy into Ayt's bellicose arguments, but she couldn't agree with it. Ayt's calculated sentiments led down a well-worn path toward ethnocentric isolationism. Kekon had come from that centuries ago but could never return to it, not with modern technology and global trade and people such as Maro. "You're right to be cautious, Papi-jen," Shae said to her aide, "but you encouraged me to open more doors for our Lantern Men, and Espenia is where we can do that."

"What you say makes sense," Woon said slowly, "but the more ties we have with that country, the more leverage they'll have over us as well. They may use that in the future, in ways that we don't know about yet and that might be costly to us. And how do you know the foreigners will even come through? Mendoff and Deiller haven't yet delivered on anything you asked for in the White Lantern Club."

"Which is why I'm doubling down," Shae said. "The Espenians treasure their reputation as direct and honest businesspeople, and they view indebtedness and poverty as moral failings. Providing them another gift before they've repaid me for the first will make them uncomfortable. They'll be motivated to fix that imbalance soon."

Woon stood and took his leave. "I'll arrange the meeting as you requested, Shae-jen, but I'll keep it quiet. Not everyone in the clan agrees with us."

That evening, Shae had Maro, Hilo, and Wen over for dinner at her house. She'd considered inviting Maro to a family meal at the main Kaul house, but perhaps meeting the entire family, including the children and the Maiks, would be too much at once. Besides, the main house was the Pillar's residence, and she thought that might send the wrong signal as to the nature of this get together. She ruled out meeting at a restaurant where people might see them and start speculating about when the Torch's granddaughter would be getting married and having children.

Shae had never seriously taken to cooking, but with Kyanla's help, she put together what she thought was a presentable meal of pickled radish salad, ginger egg soup, and baked red chicken glazed with chili sauce. She'd instructed Hilo to show up fifteen minutes before Maro, because she wanted to talk with him first and make a few things clear.

"I'm not bringing my boyfriend home for your inspection," she told her brother, when he and Wen arrived and Wen went into the dining room to help Kyanla set out plates. "Maro seems to think that because he doesn't wear much jade and isn't a member of the clan, I'm reluctant for him to meet my family. That's not true; I meant to do this much earlier, but with all our schedules—he's been traveling, we've been busy, and now with Niko and Ru to take care of—there hasn't been any time. So we're finally getting a chance, but it's *just dinner.*"

"What are you so nervous about?" Hilo said, with a teasing smile that irritated her because she was not nervous, she simply wanted to set expectations. "You think I'm going to interrogate him? Make him fight me? Wen and I are just glad to have an excuse to get away from the kids for a few hours."

The Fingers who guarded the gates of the Kaul estate had been told to admit Shae's boyfriend when he arrived. Maro showed up wearing a new shirt under his suede jacket and bearing an expensive bottle of premium hoji. He kissed Shae chastely on the cheek and saluted Hilo deeply to show proper respect. "Kaul-jen."

It bothered Shae more than she thought it would, to see Maro acting deferential toward her brother. "Shae tells me that you're a professor, so I ought to call you Dr. Tau," Hilo said with a smile, "but we're all friends here, so I'll drop the formality if you do." He accepted and admired the gift (tactfully neglecting to mention that the Cursed Beauty distillery was owned by his former Fist and thus the Kaul family could get as much of this hoji as it could want) and, putting a hand on Maro's shoulder, led him inside to introduce him to Wen.

Dinner was more relaxed than Shae had anticipated. The food had turned out fine—quite good, even, no doubt thanks to Kyanla's help. Hilo was perfectly casual and disarming in the way that he could be when he wished, and Shae was grateful for her sister-in-law's presence because Wen kept the conversation going by warmly asking Maro about his teaching work and his published papers on postcolonial Kekon-Shotar relations. Maro had recently returned from a two-week trip to Leyolo City, where he'd given a series of guest lectures at the Imperial University and conducted some research at the national archives. Shae knew his frequent professional trips were also covert opportunities for him to visit the Shotarian side of his family.

The only truly awkward moment of the evening came about inadvertently, when Wen asked Maro, with genuine interest, "Maro-jen, since you're a respected advisor to the Royal Council, would you ever consider pursuing a career in politics yourself?"

Maro took a sip of hoji before answering. "The thought has crossed my mind," he admitted. The long-standing prohibition against Green Bones holding political office meant that he would have to voluntarily give up his jade to run for the Royal Council, a hardship that dissuaded the vast majority of Academy graduates from government ambitions. "I enjoy teaching and research, but I also want to make more of a difference in national policy."

"Maro's been getting involved in nonprofit work, addressing humanitarian issues related to the war in Oortoko," Shae mentioned.

"That's very admirable," Wen said with a smile. "And the fact that you speak Kekonese, Espenian, and Shotarian—that must be quite an advantage in your career."

Hilo refilled their guest's hoji cup and said, encouragingly, "With Chancellor Son retiring next year, we could use more No Peak councilmen in Wisdom Hall."

Maro did not respond right away; he rubbed the back of his neck uncomfortably. "I don't have plans to run for public office any time soon, but if I did, I would do so as an independent." He glanced at Shae and then at the Pillar. "I know it would be more difficult to win without the backing of one of the major clans, but I'm not a tribute-paying Lantern Man and I don't come from an established Green Bone family. I wouldn't feel comfortable accepting the clan's support and creating the appearance that my relationship with Shae is motivated by personal political gain." He placed a hand on Shae's arm but continued speaking to Hilo. "The biggest reason, though, is that I think it's important there be more voices in government that aren't clan affiliated."

Hilo's eyebrows rose, very slightly. Shae's eyes jumped between her brother and her boyfriend. The contrast between Hilo and Maro was stark. Hilo sat relaxed in his chair, one elbow resting on the table, taking up space in his usual casual manner. Maro sat upright and intent, seemingly older, warier, more deliberate in posture and speech. "Independents can be bought or cowed," Hilo said, in a perfectly neutral voice. "Does having them in the Royal Council really make any difference?"

"If there were enough of them, it would," Maro insisted. "There are things the clans accept as sacrosanct, that perhaps ought to be more closely examined for how well they actually serve society. SN1 prohibition, clean-bladed dueling, the Kekon Jade Alliance."

Wen made an attempt to derail the impending collision by saying, brightly, "Hilo often complains about all the reading he has to do for the KJA meetings, and how slow and boring they are."

"They're also economically inefficient," Maro went on, failing to take the conversational escape Wen offered him. "There's a case to be made that jade ought to be treated like any other resource, with supply and demand dictated by the open market."

Hilo snorted. "Then the foreigners would try to buy up every pebble."

"Is that objectively such a bad thing?" Maro asked, as if prodding a student's thesis argument. "The KJA constricts the global supply of jade, which artificially inflates prices and funnels capital into the illegal secondary market instead of adding to our own GDP. With the availability of SN1, we're moving rapidly toward a time when jade is less and less exclusive to Kekonese." When Maro warmed to a subject, he spoke faster, his voice taking on a tone of academic discourse. "Our economy is developing and diversifying; we have other industries and resources. Our fastest-growing exports are manufactured goods, textiles, and metals. So why do we continue to treat jade as far more important than the others, something that has to be regulated by a national cartel and defended with violence? Only because of our deep-seated historical and religious biases."

Hilo looked at him in a funny way. Unlike Shae, he was not used to Maro's habit of challenging accepted beliefs for the sake of robust debate. For a moment, Shae could sense her brother assessing Maro coldly: What kind of a Green Bone, what kind of Kekonese man, would devalue jade and all that it represented, in front of the Pillar of the clan, no less?

"Maro's good at playing devil's advocate," Shae said quickly but firmly, putting a hand on Maro's arm in affection and restraint. "Which is why he's thought of so highly as a teacher, for always challenging his students. He could argue you into believing a black cat was white, or a white cat black."

Hilo gave them a thin smile. "That doesn't change the color of the cat, though."

The confidence in Maro's manner faltered. Shae glimpsed embarrassed resentment color his face. She had forgotten how quickly Hilo could put other men in their place—with a glance or a word, and without even trying—and she was furious at her brother in that instant. Scholars might be respected, but Kekonese parents prayed to have at least one son bring honor to the family as a Green Bone warrior. All of Maro's degrees were mere paper next to the jade of a man like Kaul Hilo, and for a fleeting moment, Shae could see the reminder of that fact stamped across his stiff expression.

Maro forced a smile. "I do argue too much, even outside the classroom. Shae is patient with me, but sometimes I have to remember that not everyone appreciates it."

Perceiving either the man's discomfort or Shae's anger, Hilo's manner changed immediately; he waved off Maro's explanation and said with a short laugh, "Shae, patient? I've never seen it. You must bring out a better side of her." He sat forward and clapped Maro on the shoulder in a lighthearted way. "Don't take anything I said as a criticism; I've never had patience for politics myself, but I'm sure you would succeed in it no matter what, and I'm glad my sister's found someone who's a match for her in brains and strong opinions."

Wen asked, "Do the two of you have any plans for Boat Day this year? We're going to take our boys to the harborfront for the ship sinking. We haven't been to see it in years."

The momentary tension dissipated, and conversation veered back into lighter territory as they finished their meals and lingered to enjoy tea. Maro gracefully took leave of their company before the hour grew too late. He saluted Hilo again, less formally this time, and thanked him for spending time with them this evening. At the door, he turned to Shae with a relieved and rueful expression, as if to say, *Well, that wasn't so bad—we survived, didn't we?* then gave her a kiss on the mouth. "Will I see you sometime soon?" he asked in a lowered voice.

"Soon," she promised him.

Wen said she needed to return to the main house to nurse Ru and put him to bed but told her husband he didn't need to hurry. "Let's have tea together next week, if you have the time, sister," she said, embracing Shae on the way out. "Fourthday or Fifthday would be best; I have a class on Secondday and I'm going to the bathhouse on Thirdday. It's been weeks since my last massage."

"We could build you a pool or a sauna here at home," Hilo suggested. "It would save you all these trips."

"It would take up too much space," Wen told him. "And I like getting out of the house." Wen's small children occupied most of her time and attention, but she still managed a handful of informers who occasionally carried information through the Celestial Radiance to No Peak's ears.

"Next Fifthday, then," Shae said. "I'll call you when I get home from work."

After Wen departed, Hilo helped to stack the dishes in the kitchen sink, then stepped out the door into the courtyard, lighting a cigarette. When Shae followed and stood next to him, he said, "That was a nice dinner, Shae." She was about to thank her brother when he added, "He's a little odd, but I like him well enough. At least he's Kekonese."

Shae's reply took a sharp turn into indignation. "What did I say to you beforehand? I didn't invite Maro over to get your approval."

Hilo turned to her with a frown. "Don't yell at me, Shae. You invited me to come over to meet your boyfriend, and I was happy to do that. You wanted me to take it easy on him, to not treat it like a big deal, so that's what I did. I already said it was a nice dinner; Wen and I had a nice time. You introduce me to someone and then expect me not to say a single word?"

Even though Hilo was unaware of Maro's true parentage, Shae was incensed on her boyfriend's behalf. "'At least he's Kekonese?' What does *that* mean?"

"Exactly what I said, is all," Hilo snapped. He ground out his cigarette with more force than necessary. "Maybe that wasn't the right way to put it," he admitted grudgingly. "All I'm saying is that I'm glad we won't have another issue like we did in the past. Maro's too idealistic, but he seems like a man with a good heart. He's not anywhere near as green as you are, but there aren't that many men who are, so that's no surprise. As long as he makes you happy, that's what's important. Do you love him?"

Shae was thrown by the sudden question. The contrast between Hilo's bluntness and apparent reasonableness made her unsure. "I think so," she answered, almost without thinking.

Hilo said, "If you're not sure you're in love, then you're not."

Of course that would be something Hilo would say. Shae knew for certain that she loved the time she spent in Maro's company, their long conversations, the warmth of him next to her in bed, the way he was everything that No Peak so often was not: peaceable, thoughtful, open-minded. When she was with him, she felt valued and attractive. She could imagine a future unfolding before them. But she had been cautious ever since Jerald.

"I think we're getting there," Shae said. "I wish we could spend more time together. The clan doesn't leave room for much else."

Her brother's posture slackened. "I know," he said, and rubbed a tired hand over his eyes. Looking at him, Shae lost some of her irritation and could not help but feel a pang of sympathy. Hilo was the most hands-on Pillar anyone had ever known. He still left most of the business and political matters to her, but she'd seen him sitting at the kitchen table in the evenings, forcing his way through industry reports and highlighting the parts he needed to ask her about. He dutifully attended the meetings she arranged with corporate executives and councilmen, compensating for lack of business experience and knowledge with the undeniable force of his personal presence. Although he'd gradually given Kehn a great deal more autonomy, he still went out into the streets and talked with his Fists and Fingers, met with Lantern Men, and reviewed every aspect of No Peak's military activities, which had shifted and grown to include patrols in motorized boats and stakeouts in the mountainous wilderness.

Ayt Mada could command respect as a leader with her public poise and canny rhetoric. Hilo could not do that, but he managed the vast No Peak clan in the same way he'd built his following as Horn: through thousands of conversations and personal interactions with his people, painstakingly accomplished one at a time. It was an effective but grueling way to be the Pillar. And now he also had two small children to take up all the rest of his energy.

"I've no problem with Maro," Hilo said, "but I don't want any secrets or surprises. If it gets serious, if you want to marry him and bring him into the family, you have to tell me. You have to ask me properly."

"Because you're my older brother?" Shae said, smirking a little.

"Yes," he said, with a touch of anger and a glare that said she was being difficult. "I'm the Pillar," Hilo said. "You don't do something that affects the whole clan without the Pillar's say so. I went to Lan to ask for his permission before I married Wen."

"And what if he'd said no?"

"He didn't. Why would he do that?" Hilo's aura was crackling with irritation now. "Just because you're my sister and the Weather Man, you think the rules don't apply to you? Kehn came to me properly. So did Woon. Of course I said yes to both of them."

Shae blinked. "Woon...asked you if he could...?"

Hilo blinked back at her. "You didn't know?" He gave her an odd, almost pitying look. "Shortly after New Year's. He came to see me and brought his girlfriend. They hadn't been together long, maybe four or five months. But the families know each other, and they seem happy together. As happy as Woon ever seems, that is. It's hard to tell with him."

New Year's had been eight weeks ago. Shae had been talking to Woon in her office that afternoon. "Why didn't he tell me?" she asked, more to herself than to Hilo.

"He was probably planning to and forgot," Hilo said, though Shae could tell he didn't believe that was the reason. Woon did not forget anything.

"We're Kauls; all our decisions are clan decisions, even the ones that seem private," Hilo said. "You think I didn't know that people would talk about the Maiks, about Wen being a stone-eye? Of course I knew. I gave Kehn and Tar every chance I could to earn green and prove their worth to the clan. I got Lan's blessing to marry Wen. You've got to do the same with Maro, because he's not going to be a force in No Peak. He's a nice person, but the clan's not for him. I'm sure he'll go far in his own world, and he'll have a good life if he's with you, but he won't be at the table after dinner when we talk clan business. Ever. He has to know that going in, I'll have to have that talk with him if and when you come to me. I think he already knows it about himself, so I don't think it will be a problem. But we're getting ahead of ourselves; tonight was just a dinner, like you said, so let's end the subject for now."

"Let's do that." Shae heard her words come out sour and a little numb. She wanted, more out of instinctual habit than anything else, to be angry at Hilo, but nothing he'd said was untrue.

Hilo yawned. "I should go. Ru's going to wake me up before dawn." He gazed out across the garden. "How's Andy?"

The question came so completely out of the blue that Shae had no response at first. Their cousin had been in Espenia for more than a year, and Hilo had not once asked about him. Whenever Shae mentioned she'd spoken to Anden on the phone, or gotten a letter from him, Hilo listened but never replied. His question now was delivered as simply and unexpectedly as a coma patient opening his eyes and asking what time it was.

"He's doing well, I think," Shae said. She tried to recall the most recent long-distance conversation she'd had with Anden, perhaps a month ago. "He says he's getting good grades and the family he's staying with treats him well. He's made friends and is even playing relayball. He tells me there are people wearing jade in Port Massy, if you can believe it. Among the Kekonese immigrants, there's a small, informal clan of sorts, and Anden's gotten to know the local Pillar and his family." Shae shook her head incredulously. "I can't believe he traveled thousands of kilometers from Kekon to find himself among Green Bones again."

"I'm not surprised." Hilo spoke quietly. "Green isn't easily rubbed away."

———

The following morning, Shae arrived in her office on Ship Street to find Woon waiting for her, looking unusually agitated. She felt a flash of worry—perhaps things were not all right between them after all, perhaps that was why he hadn't told her about his engagement, and he had somehow learned that Hilo had informed her last night—but then her aide handed her a copy of the *Janloon Daily* newspaper, opened and folded over to the bottom of the second page. Shae's eyes fell on the headline: *Weather Man of No Peak Was an Espenian Spy.*

Shae stared uncomprehendingly for a moment, then read the rest of the article in mounting disbelief. It cited confidential sources and documents proving that seven years ago Kaul Shaelinsan had been in the employ of the Espenian military as a civilian informant. Over a period spanning eighteen months, she had cooperated with the Espenian intelligence services to advance foreign economic and political interests in Kekon. In return, she'd been handsomely paid and granted a student visa to attend graduate school in Windton with her boyfriend, an Espenian military officer of Shotarian ancestry. A number of anonymous clan insiders testified that this betrayal on the part of his favorite grandchild had rendered the late Kaul Seningtun heartbroken and caused a rift in the Kaul family that preceded the Torch's physical and mental decline.

The newspaper began to shake in Shae's hands. She threw it onto the desk and wrapped her fingers around the edge of the table. "This is Ayt Mada's doing," she whispered. Only yesterday she'd been smug about using the Espenians to deal a blow against the Mountain's operations. She'd wondered when and how Ayt would respond, and now she had her answer.

At the height of the clan war, Ayt had dug into Shae's background, had used her own spies and sources to discover everything she could about Shae's past in an effort to sway her into turning against Hilo. Now she'd fed that information to the press. Shae's decisions as Weather Man had already garnered detractors, and the Oortokon War, which had been going on for eight months with many casualties and little discernible progress, had fanned public hostility against foreigners and Espenia to a high point. Ayt had calculated her attack to be perfectly destructive.

Woon spoke from behind her. "How should we respond, Shae-jen?"

Shae released the death grip on the edge of her desk and turned around. If she ignored the public revelations, her silence would condemn her. If she denied them, Ayt would pounce on her lies. Her mind was racing, considering how to contain the damage, how to regain the upper hand she'd held only yesterday afternoon, but beneath the calculation, a trembling fury was growing. She'd expected Ayt to strike in some way, but she'd failed to anticipate that the blow would be so swift and personal, that her own past would be used as a weapon against the clan.

"We have to issue a statement as soon as possible," Shae said. "Find out who these reporters are and what their ties are to the Mountain. Call the editor in chief of the *Janloon Daily* and tell him I want to talk to him immediately. We need to shut this down."

CHAPTER

27

~

Purely Practical

Hilo opened the drawstring on the small black cloth bag that Kehn dropped on his desk and lifted out a handful of small jade buttons. He rolled the gems in his palm and looked up questioningly at his Horn. Kehn said, "I had six Fingers and a dozen volunteer senior students from the Academy working for days, going through boxes of clothes from the latest cargo ship we seized—the third one in as many months. You'd think we'd opened a fucking sweatshop. Only, taking the clothes apart instead of putting them together." Kehn looked as if he'd come straight from the Docks; his hair was windblown and the collar of his shirt was sweaty from the heat. He unslung his moon blade and propped it up against one of the chairs but didn't sit down. "That's just one of the bags; I had Juen bring the rest of the jade to the Weather Man's office for safekeeping."

Hilo dropped the buttons back into the bag. "That Ygutanian

shipping insurance company is still phoning every day, no matter how many times I tell them to go fuck themselves."

"Shae-jen is handling it. Starting with suing their clients for transporting stolen national assets." Kehn shrugged his large shoulders. "She has a lot to deal with right now, though."

"I heard you dropped a barukan man overboard and sunk his jade to the bottom of the ocean without thinking," Hilo said, and grinned when Kehn looked a little embarrassed.

"It was probably only a piece or two anyway," Kehn grumbled, but Hilo stood up, pulled out half a dozen of the jade buttons from the small sack, and went around the desk to lift the flap of Kehn's jacket and drop the gems into the Horn's inside pocket.

"That should cover your loss," he said, straightening the jacket back into place. His brother-in-law muttered a protest, but Hilo said, "Don't question me as Pillar; you deserve it. Besides, you'll be a married man soon; think of it as an early wedding gift." It was encouraging to see Kehn come into his own as Horn. Secretly, Hilo wished he could've led the raids himself, but he knew that was unreasonable, and he was glad this was Kehn's victory alone. He was also pleased to see Kehn and Shae working together in a way that the Horn and Weather Man usually did not. That was the way it ought to be, the military and business sides of the clan cooperating instead of opposing each other, unlike how it had been with him and Doru.

There was a knock on the door and Tar put his head through to say, "There are people here to see you, Hilo-jen." Niko toddled past Tar's legs and into the study. He had the run of the house and was always getting underfoot. The boy put his arms out to be picked up. Hilo scooped him up and swung him back and forth a few times, making him giggle, before handing him to Kehn and saying, "Go with your uncle Kehn; I'll play with you later."

Holding the squirming child in one arm, Kehn saluted one handed and began to withdraw. Before he left, Hilo said, "What about the Mountain? Are they keeping up their end of the bargain?"

Kehn paused at the door and grunted an affirmative. "So far, it would seem so. Nau Suen and his Green Bones have caught half a dozen scavenging crews so far this year." At Hilo's wary silence, he added, "Don't worry, Hilo-jen, we're keeping an eye on them."

After Kehn left with Niko, a man and a woman entered. Hilo had never met them before, but he'd heard of their terrible misfortune and knew who they were. Mr. Eyun was the co-owner of a local packaging firm and a minor Lantern Man in the clan; he and his wife had five children. The eldest, a girl, was sixteen years old. The couple saluted Hilo in silence and sat themselves down woodenly on the sofa across from him. Hilo motioned for Tar to remain in the room, then closed the door before sitting down across from the Eyuns and inquiring gently, "How's your daughter?"

"She'll live," Mr. Eyun said hoarsely. His wife's face trembled with the effort of holding back her emotions. Both of them appeared to be in a state of shock.

Hilo motioned for Tar to offer the visitors some water. "Is there anything the clan can do to help your family right now?" Hilo asked. "You don't have to worry about medical expenses; that's already taken care of. Is there anything else you need?"

"Vengeance," Mr. Eyun whispered fiercely, his voice breaking. "The Espenian dogs who did this deserve worse than death."

Hilo had nothing but sympathy for the poor Eyun family, but he knew this would be a difficult conversation in which he could not promise everything that he would want to. "The two soldiers have been taken into custody by their own government and are being held in the base on Euman Island. They can't be touched right now."

Mrs. Eyun began to cry, and Mr. Eyun burst out angrily, "The lawyers say that the Espenians have negotiated for the soldiers to be tried in civil court and to serve their sentence in their home country. They offer us money as compensation. For beating and raping my daughter—*money!*" Mrs. Eyun clutched her husband's arm and wept harder, but Mr. Eyun, flushed and maddened, seemed not to notice her as his voice climbed. "The Royal Council can't stand up to the Espenians, but I thought I could count on the clan to deliver justice. You were the Horn and now you're the Pillar. You're supposed to be the fearsome Kaul Hiloshudon of No Peak. Are you saying that even you're toothless against these foreigners, these animals?"

Hilo gave Mr. Eyun a minute to regain control of himself, then he said, calmly but a little coldly, "Because of your grief, I'm not offended by anything you say. If these two men were Kekonese, they'd already be in far worse shape than your poor daughter. Unfortunately that's not the case, and with all that's happening in the world these days and all the foreign powers our country has to deal with, there are limits to even what the clan can do."

Hilo placed a box of tissues in front of Mrs. Eyun. "I said those men can't be touched *right now*. Sometimes we have to wait for justice, but the clan doesn't forget offenses. Let's see what happens. I can't make you any promises, but I'm a parent myself so you should know that I consider the crime against your family to be unforgivable."

Mr. Eyun's mouth trembled and he lowered his face; Mrs. Eyun wiped her eyes with a handful of tissues. Hilo said, "My advice is to take the money that the Espenians offer; take as much as you can get from them. It may feel like dirty money that's being used to bribe you out of what you really deserve, but don't think of it that way. Let them feel as if they've made amends—that's how their people do it—and use the money to take care of your daughter and the rest of your family."

Hilo's tone was kind as he said this, but also firm. Tar showed the heartbroken parents out the door, and the Pillar asked for a couple of minutes to be by himself. He felt bad about not being able to give the Eyuns greater assurances, but the Oortokon War and the large ROE military presence on Kekon was like a weeping sore on the bottom of one's foot; it seemed like no one on Kekon, not even the Green Bone clans, could take a single step without feeling it and wincing at the trouble and pain it added to even the simplest tasks. Just last week, following a conversation with Eiten in the Double Double, Hilo had sent Kehn to shut down a dozen illegal money-changers taking advantage of the foreign servicemen frequenting the casinos on Poor Man's Road, as well as to bolster security in the Armpit following a string of drunken incidents.

"Do you want me to send in Hami and the others, Hilo-jen?" Tar asked. Hilo grimaced and was greatly tempted to say no, but if he did, the problem waiting outside his door would not go away and would only get worse, which it seemed likely to anyway. "Fine," he said.

Tar admitted four men into the study. One of them was Hami Tumashon, the Master Luckbringer of the clan. Hilo recognized another as Councilman Kowi by his turnip-shaped head. The other two were senior Lantern Men whose names Hilo did not remember offhand. They saluted Hilo respectfully; Mr. Kowi said, "Kaul-jen, may the gods continue to shine favor on No Peak. We know you're very busy, especially with two small sons at home, so we appreciate you taking the time to meet with us to hear our concerns."

"You're right, it's been very busy; you all have children, so maybe you remember how it is. Thank you for coming to my home instead of forcing me to make the trip to Wisdom Hall or somewhere else." A reminder to everyone in the room that he had not even wanted to take this meeting and had acquiesced only on account of Hami, whom he liked and respected. Hilo sat down in one of the armchairs and his guests seated themselves as well. Without any further preamble, Hilo said, "So what is it that you're here to ask me?" He already knew the answer, but he wanted them to have to speak their minds out loud, to justify themselves to the Pillar.

The men glanced at each other before Councilman Kowi said, "Kaul-jen, it's about your sister. Given the scandalous revelations of her past...She shouldn't continue as Weather Man."

"Why's that?" Hilo asked.

The councilman looked uncomfortable but said, "I want to say first of all that I have absolutely nothing against the Weather Man personally; I'm only concerned for the reputation of No Peak. I'm afraid it looks extremely bad for the clan, Kaul-jen. The main thing is that she was an agent for the Espenian military and sold them information that might've been of national security importance. And today, the *Janloon Daily* printed an interview with her former lover, an Espenian soldier of Shotarian blood. She was still involved with him while living in Espenia, less than four years ago." Mr. Kowi spread his hands, indicating how self-evident the problem was. "How can she be trusted in the second-highest position of No Peak?"

Hilo saw the two Lantern Men nodding along, and he shifted his eyes to Hami. "You're sitting in this room as Master Luckbringer, Hami-jen, and have many years of experience on the business side of the clan. In your opinion, is the Weather Man running Ship Street badly?"

Hami glanced at the other men before shifting in his seat and clearing his throat. "No, I wouldn't say that. She's made some... debatable decisions, but that's not the same thing."

"But you asked for this meeting and you're sitting here. So you agree with them."

"I share their concerns about the way this affects No Peak's standing," Hami said. "Councilman Kowi has always advanced the clan's interests in Wisdom Hall, and Mr. Orn and Mr. Eho are two of the clan's highest Lantern Men. When they came to me to request an audience with you, I thought it was important that you hear from them directly. I'm not advocating for any specific decision on your part as Pillar." Hami might be known for his straightforward honesty, but he was certainly savvy enough not to presume above his rank, nor to speak poorly of his own Weather Man in front of people who were not Green Bones.

Hilo said to the two Lantern Men, "You think I should replace the Weather Man?"

"Kaul-jen," said the older of the two men, whom Hilo recognized now as Mr. Eho, "this is a purely practical decision. Along with the Pillar and the Horn, the Weather Man is the face of the clan. Since this information about her past has emerged, the press and the public have been questioning if she's still secretly working for the foreigners, serving their interests instead of ours. They've been calling her Espenia's charm girl. Very crude. The thing is, the Oortokon War has turned opinion against Adamont Capita. The Weather Man's past is a problem for No Peak."

"She could resign and continue to assist the Weather Man's office in a less visible role," added Mr. Orn, whom Hilo also recalled had recently declared an intention to run for the Royal Council himself. "We simply need someone more publicly suitable to be a business leader."

Hilo ignored him and said to Mr. Eho, "Who's calling her that?" When the Lantern Man blinked in confusion, Hilo repeated himself. "Who's been calling my little sister a whore?"

"I...I never said..." Mr. Eho stammered, looking suddenly contrite, even a little bit frightened, as if he was just now remembering that Kaul Hilo had a prior reputation of his own.

"Don't bother to answer," Hilo said. "I know who. Ayt Mada's set up the whole thing to make herself out as a patriot. She's smearing Shae in order to weaken No Peak."

"Still, you can't deny the facts," Councilman Kowi argued.

"No," Hilo said, "I don't deny them. My sister made some mistakes when she was young, but everyone does. She had a foolish romance with a foreigner, but that's over, and any communication she has with the Espenians these days are for No Peak's gain, on account of the oaths she took to me as Pillar. If she's doing her job as Weather Man, there's no problem."

"Kaul-jen," Mr. Eho exclaimed, "don't you care how this *looks*, what people think?"

Hilo gave Eho, Orn, and Kowi a briefly withering glance, then laid a hard, flat stare on Hami, as if to say that naturally the others could be forgiven for wasting his time, but he'd expected a Green Bone to know better. The Pillar was the spine of the clan; he didn't make decisions to please others. Certainly not jadeless politicians.

Hami's aura drew in, and he said, with some defensiveness, "It would be irresponsible for me as Master Luckbringer not to point out the consequences this might have on No Peak, and on your own leadership, Kaul-jen. Your grandfather and most of his comrades are gone—let the gods recognize them. When people look at Green Bones today, they're not looking at the heroes from the Many Nations War. They're seeing young leaders who grew up with wealth and foreign influences and wondering whether they're green enough to defend the country the way their parents and grandparents did."

Hilo leaned forward and swept an unimpressed stare around the circle of men. "My grandfather kept his old crony Yun Dorupon in place as Weather Man for decades, long after he should've retired and no matter how many pubescent girls he fucked, and I didn't see you putting up much of a stink about it. I made the decision to put my sister on Ship Street, and I'm not going to oust her now just because Ayt Mada is digging up shit and feeding it to the newspapers." He stood up; the meeting was over. Reluctantly, his visitors stood as well. Councilman Kowi and the two Lantern Men were visibly dissatisfied, saying nothing as they saluted stiffly.

Hilo said, "I like that you speak your mind, Hami-jen, as long as you keep using your good sense to serve the Weather Man." The Master Luckbringer dipped into a wordless, terse salute and left along with the others. When they were gone, Hilo paced several circles around the study, cursing under his breath. Then he picked up the phone on the desk and dialed the Weather Man's office, reaching Shae's secretary. "Tell my sister we need to talk."

CHAPTER

28

Not That Stupid

Bero's prospects, which had seemed so promising last year, had been stalled for months, ever since the Mountain raided the scavenging operation and murdered the Uwiwan work crew. It had taken him and Mudt the rest of that miserable night and another two whole days to walk down the mountain and hitchhike back to Janloon. When they finally arrived, hungry, sore, and bedraggled, and told Soradiyo that Green Bones had killed the pickers, stolen the trucks, and taken the jade, the barukan manager's face had turned purple, and he looked fit to kill both of them on the spot.

"All the fucking jade you're wearing, and you couldn't Perceive them in time to get out of there with *anything*?"

"We got out with our lives," Mudt muttered.

"Yes, how *are* you alive?" Soradiyo asked, his eyes narrowing with suspicion. "Why didn't Nau snap your necks?"

"He sent us back to give you a message," Bero said. "Says he wants to talk. Says you're not going to make money at this rate. I think he wants to buy you out."

Soradiyo's narrow face seemed to lengthen further with his scowl. "Get the fuck out of my sight," he told them.

Bero thought their next job would be an opportunity to make up for the prior disaster, but it turned out to not even be a scavenge; they were trucked out to a windy cove on the remote west side of the island to help pack motorized fishing boats with raw jade stones hidden under ice and seafood. Apparently, the clans were unofficially running the coast guard and patrolling Kekon's waters so vigorously that it was becoming increasingly difficult to sneak jade offshore. Soradiyo was splitting up his shipments to the Uwiwa Islands and sending half a dozen boats in different directions at the same time, hoping that at least a few would get through. Bero could smell rotting fish on his clothes, his skin, and his hair for days afterward.

The next scavenge job Soradiyo scheduled for them was canceled due to a tip-off about a Green Bone patrol in the area, and then the torrential spring rains arrived, rendering the mountains inaccessible and shutting down both legal and illegal jade mining activity for three months.

Bero expected to return to work once summer came around, but Soradiyo did not contact them. The barukan manager seemed distracted and was becoming difficult to pin down in person. The one time Bero found him in the Rat House and demanded an explanation, he said testily, "Soon, soon, all right? I've got other things going on, things that might solve a lot of our problems," but refused to further elaborate. Bero became frustrated and impatient.

Mudt's attitude did not help. "I told you from the start, keke, we don't need that unreliable barukan asshole. It was a bad idea to begin with, but fine, we did it, we're still alive and we made enough money to last awhile. The clans are hitting the smuggling harder and harder, and Soradiyo's going to end up as worm food, so it's better we get out now while we can. Get back to training seriously, and then to going after Maik."

"I don't give a fuck about the Maiks," Bero snapped.

Mudt yelled at him, "Maik Tar killed my da."

"Your da had it coming," Bero said, "messing in a clan war, and you'll end up the same way if you don't shut up."

The next day, however, Bero felt a little bad for having spoken so harshly to Mudt. They had been through quite a few harrowing times together, he and Mudt. They had stolen jade and risked death together. They were each alone, and so they were friends, of a sort. He was surprised to realize that he did not want to lose the kid, that deep down, he kind of liked him. So he called Mudt up, and they went to play pool in the basement of the Rat House. Bero said, "I didn't mean what I said about your da. We'll get Maik. I'll help you get that fucker back for what he did. And then we'll take his jade for ourselves, the same way we took Kaul's. You and me."

Mudt looked up with eagerness in his small black eyes and was a lot more cheerful after that. They hung out and trained, and Bero went back to dealing shine, but still he hoped that Soradiyo would call with some other work, or a new opportunity would materialize, because despite what he'd said to Mudt to make the kid feel better, Bero had no intention of going after the Maiks for the sake of some foolish sense of revenge that wasn't important to him.

When Soradiyo finally called them up to meet in the Rat House, he clapped Bero and Mudt on the backs and spoke to them in a perfectly friendly way, as if there had never been any problems between them. When they'd all had a few drinks and gone through the usual conversational bullshit, Bero said, "We've been working as rockfish for more than a year. Where's the jade you promised we'd be earning by now?"

Soradiyo spread his hands. "You're getting it soon, keke." He seemed to have picked up some Kekonese slang and mannerisms since Bero had first met him. "But the rainy season doesn't count. That's vacation time. You've got another couple months to go."

Bero scowled. "So you've got more work for us, then?"

For the first time that Bero could remember, Soradiyo appeared nervous. He wetted his lips and leaned in to speak so that no one could overhear them. "Yeah, but it's not a scavenge," he said.

"What is it, then?" said Bero. "Packing rock, again?"

"It's what you call a whispered name. Can't wear jade to do it either, because it's not just *any* name. We've been offered the chance to go on the offensive. To go into the tiger's lair, so to speak. I need a couple of kekes who're fearless and want to make a shitload of money."

"Who are we going after?" Mudt leaned in, sounding interested for the first time.

"First, I have to be sure you're both up to the task. We've got a plan to get you in, do the job and get out, no problem. Still, it's going to be—"

"Not interested," said Bero.

Soradiyo sat back, surprised by his quick refusal. "It's a big opportunity. If you don't take it, I'll give it to Mo and Shrimps." They were another pair of his rockfish managers.

Bero shrugged. He didn't care to explain that he'd already been down this road. Every time he'd had a run-in with Green Bones, he'd been lucky to escape the encounter alive, and far from gaining what was promised, his fortunes had taken a nosedive. He'd had enough near-death experiences for someone who was only twenty years old, and he'd learned by now that there were easier ways to get jade than trying to kill a Green Bone directly. He finally knew what it was like to wear jade and walk around with a secret sense of power over all the weaker people around him—but the Green Bones could take it all away from him in an instant, leave his body floating in Summer Harbor.

"Give me another scavenge job. I'll even pack fish like last time, but I'm not taking off my jade for anything, and I'm not doing any whisper work, not if it involves Green Bones," Bero said. "I'm not that stupid."

Soradiyo got out of his chair. "Wait, what about me?" protested Mudt, but the barukan threw down some money for the drinks, gave both of them a scornful, disappointed glance, and walked out of the Rat House.

Opening and Closing Doors

The Lantern Man Mr. Enke was back in Shae's office. His overall demeanor was considerably more amenable this time because he was asking for money. "The Oortokon War is having a terrible effect on Janloon's real estate market," Enke said. "My company needs to diversify our holdings. Property in Port Massy is a reliable, high-return investment. And this particular development is good value for its location."

"And you want the clan to loan you the capital," Shae concluded.

Mr. Enke extracted a file folder from his briefcase, placed it on the table, and opened it to a page with a financial summary detailing his request. "With the assistance of the Weather Man's office, Enke Property Group could purchase a forty percent stake in the development."

Moneylending was one of the most common activities on the business side of the clan. Of course, Mr. Enke could go to an independent bank to ask for a loan, but banks were purely financial institutions, operating within a limited scope. A relationship with the clan meant that Mr. Enke had access to innumerable business connections throughout Kekon and beyond it, the assurance that Green Bones would protect his properties from criminals and rivals, and preferential interest rates that reflected the fact that he had two Academy-trained sons who wore jade and served the clan as Fists. He would resort to the open market if No Peak did not give him as much as he hoped for, but like most Lantern Men of standing, he went first to the clan.

Shae studied the figures on the paper in front of her, then handed the file folder over her shoulder to Woon. She regarded Mr. Enke silently while her Shadow perused the papers. If Woon had any concerns, he would give a subtle signal—a cough, a clearing of the throat—to indicate that she ought to hold off on her decision. She Perceived in the even hum of Woon's aura that he was satisfied with what he saw. Mr. Enke, however, could not tell; faced with the intimidating silence of the Weather Man and the stoic expression of the aide behind her, he continued talking. "I've sent my most experienced scouts to Port Massy, and they've all reported back that the area of Lochwood is desirable. Well served by transit, rapidly gentrifying, walking distance to the Port Massy College campus and major shopping districts. The development will be mixed use: condominium apartments with ground level commercial space and—"

Woon closed the file folder and handed it back to the Weather Man, who placed it on her desk and said, "Mr. Enke, the Weather Man's office would be pleased to extend our patronage."

Mr. Enke broke into a smile and touched his clasped hands to his forehead. "Kaul-jen, I couldn't be more pleased to have the clan's approval. May the gods shine favor on No P—"

"I'd like you to buy the entire development."

The Lantern Man blinked. "That's far more than..."

"You'll have to adjust your calculations," she said. "The clan is willing to finance your acquisition of a controlling interest in the project. As you say, it's a good investment."

Mr. Enke cleared his throat. "I would like to take advantage of your generosity, Kaul-jen, but there are regulations in Espenia strictly limiting foreign ownership of property."

"I've recently received reliable assurances from the Espenian ambassador that within three months those regulations will be relaxed for investors of certain preferred nations—Kekon being one of those." It was not everything Shae had hoped for in terms of trade concessions, but it was a good start. The Espenians were stingy, but reliable. "Move now to purchase the forty percent stake as you planned, and buy out the rest next year."

Mr. Enke opened and closed his mouth, then said, "My current tribute rates…"

"Would normally go up, but there's a way we can work around that," Shae said. "It's becoming more common for Kekonese graduates to further their education by going to study in Espenia. It was unusual when I did it five years ago, but these days, many families encourage their children to gain some international experience. My younger cousin is in Espenia right now, living with a host family. Once these apartments are built, you can rent them out to Kekonese students studying in Port Massy. Charge them half the market rate for the area. In exchange, the clan will screen potential tenants from No Peak families and cover the difference in your income. Our subsidy will offset your tribute obligations, and you'll be guaranteed renters who've been backed by the clan."

Mr. Enke licked his lips warily. His bushy eyebrows drew down until they touched. "Kaul-jen," he said slowly, "can I count on this being a binding agreement with the Weather Man's office?"

Normally, such a question would be unnecessary; the Weather Man's word guaranteed fulfillment of the contract. But Mr. Enke was not sure Shae would remain in charge of Ship Street long enough to deliver on their arrangement. Since the scandal over her past connection to the Espenian military intelligence services had broken six weeks ago, she had been persistently disparaged in the media and there had been calls for her resignation.

Shae gave no sign that she shared Mr. Enke's doubts. "Woon-jen will have a memo of our conversation drawn up in writing and sent to you by the end of the day," she said.

Satisfied, Mr. Enke promised that he would have an updated financial proposal to the Weather Man's office by the following week. Woon showed the Lantern Man out the door, then took the vacated chair in front of Shae. "You're hoping to turn this into a human resources advantage," he said.

"Opening doors, as you say," Shae replied.

Woon nodded slowly. "Offering incentives for families in the clan to send their children to college in Espenia could benefit No Peak in the long run, but only if they put their education to use for the clan. What's to stop the students we send there from being lured away by the bright lights of Espenia? We might lose much of our potential talent overseas."

"In addition to subsidized housing, we'll pay their tuition. But only if they return to Kekon and work for the Weather Man's office for three years after graduation." She expected very few, if any, sponsored students would be so foolish as to renege on a promise to the clan, not when they had families in Janloon whose lives and livelihoods depended on No Peak's continued favor. "Councilman Kowi's son would be a good candidate," she added.

"I'll be sure to convey that to the Kowi family." Woon stood up to go but paused at the door, looking back at her with worry. "Is there anything else you need right now, Shae-jen?"

Shae had been trying to act normal all morning, but she was certain that Woon, who knew her well, could Perceive the emotional turmoil in her aura, no matter how composed she managed to appear outwardly in front of the Lantern Men and the rest of the office. At least he would assume that it was attributable to the verbal attacks mounting against her, including the fact that Ayt Madashi spared no opportunity to declare that as a patriotic Green Bone clan Pillar, *she* would never allow a former Espenian spy near the leadership of the Mountain. With the Heroes Day holiday only two weeks away, Shae expected things to only get worse, not better.

She did not want Woon to suspect that there was anything else troubling her beyond that. "No, Papi-jen," Shae said, doing her best to sound unconcerned, even a bit optimistically smug. "I told you Ambassador Mendoff would come through on his debt, didn't I?"

After Woon had departed, the phone on Shae's desk rang and she nearly jumped. It wasn't the call she'd been expecting. Maro said, "I don't mean to bother you at work, but I saw the newspaper this morning and just wanted to call to see if you were doing all right."

Shae felt a fist close in her chest at the sound of Maro's voice. She glanced at the clock and closed her eyes; she couldn't talk to him right now. "I'm fine," she told him. "This isn't even close to the worst thing Ayt Mada has done to my family."

It was, however, proving to be effective. Shae had issued a public statement declaring that her consultative work with the Espenian government had ended years ago and categorically denying any conflicts of interest that would compromise her loyalty to No Peak and to Kekon. She'd responded to the attacks in greater length in an interview with Toh Kita on KNB. She'd criticized and pressured the editorial staff of the *Janloon Daily.* All to no avail; the *Daily's* owner had, unsurprisingly, family and business ties to the Mountain and, also, papers to sell. Jerald's smiling face had stared up at Shae this morning from the black-and-white newsprint. Some industrious reporter had tracked him down in the city of Loruge, south of Adamont Capita, where he now worked as a mortgage broker, but they'd paired the tabloid-style interview with an old photograph of him dressed in his ROE Navy officer's uniform.

"All of this is such bullshit," Maro burst out over the phone. "The things they're saying about you are completely unfair. It's short-sighted, misogynistic, anti-foreigner hysteria. Don't give in to what they want. You deserve your place as Weather Man no matter what they say." She'd never heard him so upset and angry. "Isn't there anything I can do to help?"

"There isn't," Shae said. "This is clan war again, in a different way. My brother and I will handle it. Just . . . stay clear of the whole mess and don't talk to any reporters." Ayt and the press did not know about Maro or his family background, and she wished to keep it that way. She wanted to say more but said, "I have to go. I'll call you back later."

"All right," Maro said. "Stand your ground. I love you."

Shae swallowed, glad that Perception did not work through telephone lines. "Me too."

The phone in Shae's office rang again twenty minutes later. This time, it was the call she'd been awaiting from the doctor's clinic. The nurse on the other end of the line came to the point quickly. "The urine sample you dropped off yesterday tested positive."

"Are you sure?" Shae asked.

"Yes," said the nurse. "You're pregnant. Would you like to make an appointment to see one of our obstetricians? We have available times as early as next week."

"Not right now." Shae thanked the nurse and hung up. She sat in silence for what felt like a few minutes that might've in reality been much longer, because she had the strange and nauseating sensation of everything around her—the office noises, the energies of the people nearby, the very movement of the air—coming to an ungraceful momentary standstill.

Shae picked up the phone again. She had a sudden impulse to call the clinic back to demand a retest because maybe there had been a mistake after all, but she knew that was mere denial. Instead she dialed her secretary and told her to reschedule the rest of her appointments for the day, as she was not feeling well. Shae got up, took the elevator to the ground floor, walked across the spacious lobby of the clan's office tower, and out the front doors of the building.

Outside, she began walking west. It was a hot but soggy day; people streamed in both directions along the sidewalk, wearing summer clothes but carrying umbrellas. Shae walked for thirty minutes, until her feet ached in her black pumps and sweat plastered her blouse to the small of her back under her blazer. Rain fell, not steadily but with insulting indifference, scattered fat droplets that flecked the asphalt and landed noisily on awnings, car hoods, and garbage lids. Where Ship Street ended, Shae turned right and kept going, out of the Financial District, until she passed between the stone pillars and through the treed courtyard of the Temple of Divine Return.

Shae went straight to the front of the sanctum and knelt on one of the green prayer cushions. Rainwater from her damp hair left speckles on the stone floor as she touched her head to the ground three times and whispered, in a litany that she had repeated so many times that she barely had to call it to mind consciously, "Yatto, Father of All. Jenshu, Old Uncle. I beg you recognize my grandfather Kaul Seningtun, the Torch of Kekon, gone peacefully from this earth to await the Return. Recognize my brother Kaul Lanshinwan, taken from us before his time. Have mercy on the soul of Yun Dorupon. Give peace to the spirit of Haru Eynishun. Above all, guide and protect those of us who remain in this world, especially Wen and Niko and Ru, and my brother Hilo, for whom I also beg your forgiveness." Shae fell quiet, trying to put her churning thoughts and emotions into words. From the front of the room, the steady burning energy of the meditating penitents filled the white spaces in her mind.

She spoke aloud, almost in a demand. "What do I do now?"

She couldn't believe she was pregnant—not intellectually, though she had no reason to doubt the clinic's verdict. When her cycle was late, she'd assumed that the stress of dealing with the public scandal had something to do with it. She and Maro had taken precautions. She was an educated professional woman, she was the *Weather Man*. She would've placed an unplanned pregnancy well below sudden assassination in her internal ranking of things that she considered likely to happen to her. The timing, she mused despairingly, could not be worse.

Shae had never been able to say if she wanted children. She loved her two nephews dearly but didn't feel a maternal longing of her own. There was no room for the feeling; her position in the clan was all-consuming, and she'd been beleaguered in her role from the start. Perhaps if things were different, the urge to have children would happen naturally. But nothing in her life, it seemed, happened naturally—only as unavoidable blows, like those of a sledgehammer.

There was no precedent for a woman with children in the leadership of a Green Bone clan. Ayt Mada had no offspring of her own and continued to pointedly ignore those who questioned her about the succession. After Lan's death and the ouster of Doru, it had been difficult for No Peak to accept a young woman as Weather Man, but it had been a desperate time of clan war, and Shae was a Kaul. She still wore the label of being the Torch's favorite grandchild, she was backed by respected men like Woon and Hami, and few people dared to challenge her brother.

Those advantages would not help her now. She was already under attack for her past supposed misdeeds; she couldn't walk into a boardroom or into Wisdom Hall pregnant out of wedlock with the child of a man from a family of little standing in the Green Bone community. Ayt and the press would dig into Maro's past, would question his parentage and his many trips to Shotar, would flay open his family's history and discover that he was the bastard of a Shotarian soldier. Maro was not a Kaul; he was barely green. He was not equipped to handle the animosity and scrutiny, the risk to his professional career and to his safety. It would ruin his life.

As for her? It was true that the clan was a big, old ship, but for two and a half years, she'd thrown herself sweating against the wheel, straining No Peak toward the growth and change required to survive enemies at home and the threats of the modern world beyond. Her efforts were beginning to take effect: She'd gotten the clan back on solid financial footing, made advantageous military and trade agreements with the Espenians, expanded the clan's operations and opened up opportunities. If she was ousted from her position by personal scandal, everything she had accomplished might be undone. Woon and Hami were capable, there was no doubt of that, but they had not lived abroad, they were not as strategic as Ayt Mada, they would not know how to stand up to Hilo or persuade him. And it was worse than that: Shae's brother had appointed her Weather Man and stubbornly kept her in the role against all opposition; her shameful

downfall would cascade through the clan, would become an indictment of the whole family and affect Hilo's standing as Pillar.

All of these thoughts sank from Shae's mind through her body and
settled like a pile of rocks in the pit of her stomach. She'd assumed
business leadership of the clan because she'd been forced—by her
own actions and her brother's death—and when the days were long
and the work difficult, she told herself that she was doing it for Lan
and for her grandfather. Deep down, she knew herself better than
that. She wanted to be the Weather Man.

Shae gazed up at the high ceiling of the sanctum and closed her
eyes. She waited for an epiphany, for a sense of spiritual peace to fill
her and guide her with certainty. She stretched out her Perception
and tried to sense a message in the croon of jade energy that vibrated
through her flesh and bones. She felt nothing from the gods, except
perhaps a distant watchfulness, and within herself, only a turbulence
swirling and coalescing finally into resignation and purpose.

She got up and left the temple.

CHAPTER

30

~

Heroes Day

Wen alone went with Shae to the clinic early on a Secondday morning. They took one of the family's nondescript cars, leaving both Wen's conspicuous Lumezza convertible and Shae's red Cabriola in the garage. Wen could always say that she was going to the doctor for a prenatal checkup and that Shae was the one accompanying her. At twelve weeks, Wen was clearly showing her second pregnancy. She was still nursing Ru, so between her enlarged breasts and swelling belly, her body was a collection of soft maternal curves. Shae felt as if they were doing something wrong, perhaps inviting bad luck, for Wen to be an accomplice to terminating an unborn life when she was carrying one of her own. "You don't have to come inside," she told her sister-in-law. "You're doing me enough of a favor driving me there and back. That's all I'm asking for."

"If it were me, I'd like another woman to be with me," Wen said. "Why should we have to go through hardships in life by ourselves?"

She parked the car in the nearly empty lot. It was still dark; the clinic didn't open for another two minutes.

"It seems unlucky for you to be here," Shae said.

Wen cupped her hands around a thermos full of ginger tea, which she drank every morning to help settle her stomach. A wry smile curved her lips. "I've been called unlucky my whole life. I'm not afraid of bad luck any more than a bird would be afraid of feathers."

They went inside and Shae checked in. Getting an abortion was neither particularly easy nor particularly difficult in Janloon. Clinics varied in repute and there was a moderate cost, but the main restriction was that a woman had to obtain the consent of her husband if she was married, or that of a male relative if she was not. This rule was regularly circumvented for an additional fee. Shae had filled out the necessary paperwork in advance and forged Hilo's signature next to her own at the bottom. The young woman at the reception counter looked at the forms, then at Shae, and her eyes widened. Shae suspected the receptionist did not see heavily jaded Green Bones come through the clinic very often.

Wen went with her into the room and then held her hand during the whole procedure, which took less time than Shae had expected. Afterward, as she rested in a pleasantly sedated state, Shae said, "You were right. I'm glad you're here." She almost added, "Please don't tell anyone," but caught herself before she said it, realizing how insulting and laughable it would sound. She already knew that her sister-in-law could be trusted with secrets.

Wen drove them home. Shae felt relieved, if somewhat damaged. She thought of Maro—his earnest expression, his thoughtfulness, his genuine optimism and belief in her—and a band of sadness and guilt cinched around her and made it momentarily hard to breathe. The two of them had not discussed having children, but the way Maro spoke so fondly of his nieces, she was certain he wanted a family of his own eventually. She hadn't called him or returned any of his several messages since they had spoken on the phone in her office three days ago, before she'd known for certain what she had to do. And what she still had to do. She was terrified that if she spoke to him, something in her voice would give her away and he would know, or that hearing his concern or seeing him again would rob her of her conviction.

She leaned her head against the car door. "Do you think less of me now?" she asked.

Her sister-in-law stopped the car so abruptly that Shae had to put a hand against the dash. Wen pulled the car over to the curb and put the gear shift in park. She turned to face Shae, her eyes flashing. "Shae-jen, I'm ashamed to say this, but there was a time when I didn't trust you very much because I wasn't sure you were the sort of person who would put others ahead of yourself." She fixed Shae with a steady, almost unnerving stare. "You could've resigned your position to marry your boyfriend and have a child. It would create a miserable scandal for a while, but then you'd be free to live a much easier life. But where would No Peak be without you as Weather Man? How could my husband be Pillar without your counsel? What would become of the valuable work we've done together, and in the future how could I do anything in the clan at all without you?" Wen declared, almost angrily, "I could never forgive you if you decided to be so selfish. So how can you believe I would think any less of you for being responsible instead?"

Shae was a little taken aback. "But you have children."

Wen put the car back into gear and began driving again. She finished the dregs of her tea and spoke matter-of-factly. "We each serve the clan in the way we're best suited. Look at Ayt Mada and how alone she is. We must never be like that."

Before she'd left Kekon to pursue a degree at Belforte Business School in Windton, Espenia, Shae had lived for three weeks in a room in the Tranquil Suites Hotel on Euman Island. Jerald had been discharged two months ago and was awaiting her back in his home country, and after the most recent screaming family argument, Shae could not bear to be around her grandfather and could not stand to look at Hilo's face, so she packed her bags and moved out of the Kaul house.

Lan was the only one to come see her the night before her departure. He took the ferry from Janloon and knocked on her hotel room door to offer to take her to dinner. Shae said she didn't care where they went, so Lan suggested a nearby noodle shop. "After tomorrow, you'll be eating Espenian food, so let's have something homey tonight," he said. The restaurant was on the main thoroughfare of the port town. Neighboring bistros and bars had signs and menus written in Espenian, and on a pleasant summer evening, off-duty Espenian military personnel crowded the open-air patios and conversed loudly on the sidewalks. There were no lanterns hanging in the shop windows; Lan and Shae were not seated or served ahead of everyone else. Shae's flight was not until tomorrow, but she already felt as if she were in a different country.

Lan did not seem irritated at not being recognized and saluted. As they waited for their meals, he took in the environs with thoughtful bemusement. "I wouldn't be surprised," he said, "if this is what the whole world looks like one day—an unrecognizable blend, cultures and people mixed together. Where will jade and clans and Green Bones fit in, I wonder?"

"That's for you to think about, not me." In retrospect, she'd been rude to her brother, but at the time, her jade was locked in a bank safe and she was still moody and ill from withdrawal.

"You should eat more," Lan said, when he saw that she hadn't finished the food in her bowl. "You have a long, tiring trip ahead of you, and then you'll be alone in a foreign country."

"I won't be alone," Shae countered. "I'll be with Jerald."

Lan looked at her compassionately. "We're always alone with our own decisions." Her brother had been Pillar for a year, and in that time, he'd grown more somber and forthright, had seemed to age in a way that widened even the nine-year gap between them. "You can make a rational, well-informed choice, and still be unprepared for what it means. You're the youngest in the family, and a woman, and a Kaul, and none of that makes life easy on Kekon, but in Espenia, you'll start out below everyone else. You'll have to fight for every scrap of respect that you're used to getting at home."

"Did Grandda send you to make a final attempt at discouraging me?" Shae asked.

Lan's remonstrative stare made Shae avert her eyes. "No," he said, coldly enough to make her feel ashamed. "I've said that I support your decision, but I'm your older brother, and the Pillar, so that gives me enough extra life experience to tell you that no matter where you go, others will try to define you. Unless you define yourself."

"I'm twenty-four years old, Lan," Shae said. "I can take care of myself."

"I know you can," Lan said sadly. The waiter came to clear their dishes. A swollen orange moon was rippling in the narrow stretch of water that separated Euman Island from the skyline of Janloon, which Shae would soon watch fade from her airplane window and would not see again for two years. "Just try not to forget who you are," her brother said.

———

While several countries mark the end of the Many Nations War (Victory Day in Espenia, War's End Day in Tun, Liberation Day in the Uwiwa Islands, to name a few), Kekon's national holiday commemorates the defeat of Shotarian occupation forces on the island and restoration of the country's sovereignty fifty-two days prior to the signing of the international armistice. The official name of the holiday, Triumph of the Nation's Heroes Over Foreign Oppression, is rarely used on account of its unwieldiness; it is referred to simply as Heroes Day.

As a child, Hilo had enjoyed Heroes Day, because in addition to being a day of patriotism, it was a celebration of Green Bone culture. Kaul Du Academy and Wie Lon Temple School opened their doors and put on public demonstrations of the jade disciplines. Movie theaters played a marathon of the adventure films about Baijen, the legendary Green Bone warrior. Veterans like his grandfather and late father were praised and honored. In the evening, there was a parade and fireworks. Afterward, Hilo went to sleep smiling, feeling like a prince.

As Pillar of the clan, he dreaded Heroes Day, and more so this year than any other. He was expected to make numerous public appearances and graciously accept the respect-paying of countless people while maintaining an appropriate solemnity out of memory for those slain in Kekon's struggle for freedom. This year, he expected the holiday would be underscored with the tension of current anti-foreigner sentiment and would make the scandal over Shae's past all the worse for No Peak. No wonder his sister was staying at home and not making any appearances today. She claimed to be feeling unwell, but he wouldn't have blamed her if she'd simply said that she'd rather skip the shitshow and the inevitability of having to see Ayt Mada's smug face.

"Forget the garbage Ayt and the newspapers are spewing," Hilo had told her. "You have to get Ship Street under control. Hami was in the room with the men who came to see me. He didn't speak against you, but he didn't stand up for you either. That's not good, Shae."

His sister seemed pale and much quieter than usual. "I'll handle it," she said.

"If your people are behind you, it doesn't matter what any of those other fuckers think, but they have to be behind you."

"I said I'll handle it," Shae repeated. "Do you trust me?"

"I don't have a choice, do I?" Hilo had no intention of caving to pressure from inside or outside of the clan, but what if things got so bad that Shae no longer had the credibility to run the business side of No Peak? He didn't want to contemplate the possibility of having to remove his sister from her post; he was certain that was exactly what Ayt Mada was hoping for. Three years ago, the Mountain had tried to weaken Lan's position by targeting Hilo for assassination; now they were doing the same to him, undermining him by going after Shae.

Hilo went on the offense. Ten-year-old Koben Ato had recently fallen ill for a week from a potent stomach virus, a fact that was known only because the boy had begun his training at Wie Lon School as something of a minor celebrity. When questioned by the press about Shae's past, Hilo answered that the outrage ought to be focused instead on the more serious past misdeeds of clan leaders who were known for killing their own relatives. Hilo hoped out loud that Ayt's nephew's illness was nothing more sinister; perhaps the Koben family ought to be worried about the child meeting as untimely a fate as his father.

His efforts deflected some of the attention, but had little effect otherwise. The idea that Ayt Mada would target a child was shocking but unfounded, and even though it reminded people of her past fratricide, in today's political climate, it seemed murdering one's way into power was more easily forgiven than sleeping with a foreigner. No Peak remained in an infuriating position and Hilo did not yet know what to do about it. It sat near the front of his mind all of Heroes Day morning as he walked through Widow's Park with a large contingent of No Peak clan faithful, laying flowers and fruit on the Kaul family memorial and the graves of other Green Bones slain during the overthrow of Shotarian occupation during the Many Nations War. This part of his schedule was actually pleasant, as he had his family with him. Wen had dressed the boys in suits—even Ru wore a tiny vest and clip-on tie that he'd already spit up on—and people were exclaiming over how handsome they were, which pleased Hilo to no end. Niko ran between the gravestones, dirtying his shoes.

The afternoon, however, was an ordeal. Wen and the children went home, and Hilo was driven to the Monument District where His Heavenship Prince Ioan III would make a grand public appearance in front of the Triumphal Palace. In portraits, the prince was depicted as a regal and stately man, but in person his heavy brow and small chin gave him the appearance of perpetual squinting confusion. He performed his ceremonial and charitable duties with good-natured enthusiasm, though, and had produced two sons and two daughters, so was quite popular with the public. When he came out of the palace and waved to the crowd, they cheered loudly.

As was custom on Heroes Day, the leaders of the Green Bone clans were in attendance to demonstrate their fealty to the monarch of the country. They each in turn climbed the steps of the palace and knelt before the prince, declaring the service and loyalty of their clans. The traditional event was a ceremonial reminder of the nation's modern founding, when the jade warriors who triumphed over foreign occupation had, in accordance with aisho, eschewed political power and ushered in the reestablishment of the monarchy and the Royal Council.

Hilo smirked when Ayt Mada strode up the marble steps and lowered herself like a tiger consenting to be patted by a child. The prince was a figurehead with no real power, but once a year, people took heart and patriotic pride in the knowledge that even the most powerful Green Bones, the ones who commanded true influence in society, were united and subservient to Kekon itself. That reassurance was particularly relevant now, with a foreign war raging not far away.

Hilo followed after his enemy and knelt on the palace's landing, touching his forehead to the marble. "Your Heavenship," he said. "I, Kaul Hiloshudon, the Pillar of my clan, pledge No Peak to your service. May you live three hundred years under the favor of the gods."

Once that part of the pomp was over with, the prince's retinue escorted His Heavenship down the street to the public gardens behind Wisdom Hall, where he blessed the unveiling of a new statue commemorating the famous wartime partnership of Ayt Yugontin and Kaul Seningtun—the Spear and the Torch of Kekon. Hilo was required to be in attendance at this event as well and to stare at the bronze cast of his grandfather as a much younger man, standing straight and proud next to his comrade and gazing off into the distance, presumably at Kekon's glorious future.

Upon last year's declaration of truce between the clans, someone in the Janloon city government had apparently thought it a good idea to commission public art to mark the reestablished harmony between Green Bones. Considering that the clans were currently engaged in a contest to undermine and ruin each other—a contest the Mountain appeared to be winning—the whole affair struck Hilo as ironic.

After the prince and a few other officials had said their words, Ayt took the microphone and spoke eloquently about the sort of man her adopted father had been—a brilliant general, an honorable Green Bone, and above all, a principled patriot. "My father believed that with jade comes great responsibility, and that Green Bones owe their loyalty to country above all else." Ayt let her words hang in the air as her eyes moved over the assembly of people and settled on her rival Pillar, standing near the front and scheduled to speak next. Hilo felt the weight of his enemy's stare and the pressure of her thick aura bathing him in an unwelcome spotlight.

Ayt said, looking directly at Hilo, "The allegiance to a higher cause, to the safety to the country, takes precedence over even the treasured bonds between friends and relatives. A strong leader must be capable of setting aside sentiment and making painful decisions for the good of many." Ayt's message was clear: Everything she had done to become Pillar of the Mountain—including murdering her ineffectual playboy of an adopted brother and her father's old guard—she had done for the greater good of the clan and country. Kaul Hilo, in contrast, by stubbornly siding with his unworthy sister, was no great leader.

Ayt turned back to the crowd and declared, "My father, if he were alive, would despair to see that foreign interests have once again invaded our country, this time with the help of those who ought to be the staunchest defenders of our nation. As the daughter of the Spear of Kekon, as the Pillar of my clan, I am deeply concerned."

Shae had prepared a speech for Hilo to give; it contained innocuous Heroes Day platitudes and some touching and amusing stories about Grandda. Hilo had come to this event determined to stick to the text and not respond to Ayt's goading, but his aggravation mounted steadily as Ayt continued talking. "The Weather Man of the second-largest clan in the country is in thrall to foreign people and ways. Her past actions prove that she is of weak character, not fit to be called Kekonese, and not to be trusted in a position of power and influence. It's time for my counterpart to listen to the concerns of the public."

Ayt Mada was co-opting what was supposed to be a feel-good speech about her father into a pointed indictment of her rival. A few members of the Royal Council in attendance at the statue unveiling ceremony were shifting uncomfortably. Among the public who'd gathered to watch, some were nodding, others were listening stone-faced or staring at Hilo, waiting for his reaction. Hilo's eyes were slits; he kept his expression stiff but knew his suppressed fury was Perceivable to any Green Bone nearby.

"Hilo-jen," Kehn grumbled from behind Hilo's shoulder in a low, uneasy voice, "we don't have to stand here listening to all this shit. We could leave right now."

Hilo did not answer his Horn; he could sense Ayt Mada's aura humming in smug curiosity. Could she provoke him to explode in a temper in front of everyone? Would he finally bend to the pressure and remove Shae as Weather Man, making No Peak appear guilty and weak, or stubbornly refuse and watch his clan's reputation plummet and his own hard-won fitness as Pillar come into question?

He did not Perceive Shae's approach until she was right behind him. Her aura prickled like static against his, and when he turned in surprise, he saw that she was cutting a straight path toward him. Her hair was drawn back in a tight clasp, and in the sun, the jade gleamed at her throat. Her pale face was set as firm as a mask. She paused as she came alongside him but barely glanced in his direction.

"I thought you weren't feeling well," Hilo said. "What are you doing here?"

"Ending this," the Weather Man said, and stepped forward past him with the suddenness of a leap from a subway platform. He realized what she meant to do a second before she spoke, but by then, she had crossed half the space to the podium.

"Enough," Shae declared, loudly enough to disrupt Ayt midsentence and be heard by those nearby. There was a ripple of astonishment through the crowd, and in the space where Ayt's searing aura met Shae's like lava pouring against rocks. Shae continued advancing, implacably, cold as the moon. "You've insulted and slandered me enough. You've called me a poor granddaughter, an unfit Weather Man, unworthy of jade, a traitor, and a whore."

She stopped; the heartbeat of silence that fell was blistering. "Ayt Madashi, Pillar of the Mountain, I offer you a clean blade."

The Two Thrones

Following the Three Crowns era in Kekonese history, which ended with the self-destruction of the Hunto royal line, the two conquering kingdoms—Jan in the north and Tiedo in the south—sought to maintain peaceful relations in the time-honored way, by exchanging royal children. The second son of the royal house of Tiedo was sent to the court of Jan. The monarch of Jan had three children but only one son, so the eldest daughter was offered up instead as a hostage to Tiedo.

In Tiedo, the captive Jan princess and the firstborn prince fell deeply and fortuitously in love and were married. Once the prince succeeded his father, however, his wife pressured him to attack her homeland of Jan in a bid to rule all of Kekon. Historians debate how much she was driven by political ambition, blind confidence in her husband, or ill feelings toward the family that had traded her away. The new king was initially hesitant, but after his younger brother in Jan perished in a suspicious training accident, he acted on his wife's encouragement and declared war.

Their rival, the prince of Jan, was intelligent but sickly. Though it was rare for women to be trained as Green Bones at that time, his younger sister was allowed to learn the jade disciplines. She married a warrior who would become a famous general in the Jan army, and she subsequently became a key figure in the military campaign against her sister and brother-in-law from Tiedo. The final victory of Jan, two hundred years later, unified the island under one monarchy with its capital city located on the northern coast, where it remains to this day. Although the strife between the northern and southern kingdoms extended long past the lives of its instigators, this segment of Kekonese history is still known as the Warring Sisters period.

The Kekonese hold an overall negative view of this era, as the prolonged conflict weakened the country and reduced the population of its jade warriors, allowing successive foreign invaders to gain a foothold on the island. Nevertheless, judging by the disproportionate number of Kekonese novels and movies set during this time, the love story between the traitorous Jan princess and the Tiedo prince is considered one of history's great romances, and the resulting war between the two sisters recounted as one of its tragic dramas. Kekon's most famous classical play about this period, *The Two Thrones*, begins with an oft-quoted line that harkens to Deitist philosophy regarding the origin of earthly conflict: "Out of small resentments, spring great wars."

CHAPTER
31

Stand Your Ground

The duel was set for the following morning, as it would be uncouth to spill blood on a national holiday and detract from the planned Heroes Day festivities. The combatants would meet in Juro Wood, halfway between the Ayt and Kaul residences. Shae knew that she ought to go to bed early, but the idea of sleep seemed impossible considering this might be her last night alive. Around midnight, with the popping of the parade fireworks still sounding intermittently over the city, she crept into the prayer room of the main house and knelt on the stiff cushion in front of the small shrine. The dark certainty, the sense of cold purpose she'd felt earlier was nowhere to be found. All she felt now was nauseating fear and dread.

Shae was a heavily jaded and skilled Green Bone who had graduated at the top of her class at Kaul Dushuron Academy. Now she spent most of her days behind a desk or in meetings. She maintained a routine of daily morning practice and semiregular private coaching sessions, but unlike Hilo, she had not been training diligently to keep her martial abilities at a peak. If she'd had any inkling she would be in this situation, she would've booked Master Aido solid for the past six months. Ayt Madashi wore more jade and had killed more men in single combat than any woman Green Bone in recent history. Years had passed since her violent ascension to Pillar; perhaps Ayt had gotten lax as well. Shae hoped that was the case but was not optimistic.

She bent her head. "Old Uncle in Heaven, judge me the greener of your kin tomorrow, if it be so," she murmured in prayer to Jenshu the Monk, the One Who Returned, the patron god of Green Bones. She paused. "And if you judge otherwise, at least give me credit for a dramatic attempt."

The genuine surprise on Ayt's face that afternoon had given her one pure moment of satisfaction. If the Pillar of the Mountain had considered the possibility of Shae challenging her with a clean blade, she must've dismissed the idea. Her target was a young woman in an office—not a testosterone-driven and jade-hungry male Fist. Not someone eager to die.

Two seconds of mutual disbelief had hung between the two women, and then Ayt's jade aura had swelled ominously as she leveled a stare at Shae that seemed to vanish the presence of all the stunned people watching them. Ayt put down the papers of her speech. In the unnatural silence, the microphone magnified the rustle of the pages. The Pillar of the Mountain stepped out from behind the podium and said, in a clear, firm voice that needed no amplification, "I accept."

After he'd gotten over the initial shock of what she'd done, Hilo had been, unsurprisingly, furious. Not even the Pillar could reverse a challenge between two willing parties once it was issued and accepted, but from the explosive roar of his jade aura Shae thought Hilo might try to kill her himself before Ayt got around to it. In the Duchesse after escaping the ensuing hubbub, he'd struggled to find words. "What the *fuck*, Shae?" he shouted.

"It's the only way," Shae whispered, numbed by what she'd done. The only way to quash the scandal, to erase all doubts, to silence Ayt Mada and anyone who accused her of being too Espenian, overly influenced by foreigners, a naive woman who was not trustworthy. It didn't matter if Hilo kept her in the role or not; after Ayt's damaging accusations, she would never again be taken seriously as Weather Man unless she answered the critics unequivocally.

"Stop this stupidity while you still can," Hilo had ordered. "Take back the offer of a clean blade. You're green enough, sure, greener than most men, but you can't expect to beat Ayt Mada, not unless you have some trick you're not telling me about, or you've been secretly training at night all year." From Shae's silence, he deduced this was not the case and exploded again. "Are you trying to get yourself killed, then? Aren't you supposed to be the smart one?"

In truth, Shae had felt a terrified urge to retract the offer as soon as it left her mouth, but the familiarity of Hilo's temper jolted her back into the state of inescapable logic that she'd summoned earlier. Reneging on the challenge would destroy whatever standing she had left and irreparably shame No Peak. Hilo, who'd fought many duels in his life, knew this, so the fact that he'd even suggested it was oddly touching. "It's done, Hilo," she said. "I can't back out."

"She's right," Kehn said from the driver's seat. "Ayt's the one who caused offense. Also, no one in No Peak has actually seen the bitch fight. Shae-jen has as good a chance as anyone."

"I didn't ask for your opinion," Hilo snarled at his Horn, something Shae had never seen before. "Ayt's always searching for ways to get at us. Now she has a clean blade and the chance to cut off my little sister's head with everyone watching. She's got to be fucking ecstatic!"

Shae had to admit there was a painful irony to the situation. Four years ago, she'd been ambivalent about even returning to Janloon; now she was sacrificing a relationship, a pregnancy, and most likely her own life to defend her position and reputation as Weather Man of No Peak. She was not usually the bold and reckless one—that had always been Hilo's role in the family.

How things change. Then again, all the actions Ayt Mada had publicized as evidence of her weak character—dating a foreigner, working for the Espenians, taking off her jade, and leaving the clan to be educated abroad—had been rebellious declarations, attempts to prove herself equal or better than her brothers. She wanted what she was told by others she couldn't have, was willing to dramatically self-immolate rather than accept terms forced upon her. So no, some things had not changed after all.

The door to the prayer room slid open and Hilo came in. Shae did not get up or turn around to face her brother, but to her surprise, he knelt beside her and touched his head to the ground the customary three times. She had never even seen him come into this room before.

"I didn't think you believed in the gods," she said when he straightened.

"I don't," Hilo said, "but the feeling's mutual, so maybe they won't hold it against me." His jade aura was still humming at a higher pitch than usual, but he was calmer than he had been. Perhaps Wen had talked to him; she always seemed able to smooth her husband's thoughts. Shae could hear her sister-in-law's footsteps upstairs, pacing with Ru to settle him down, and she could Perceive Niko's soft energy, asleep. She thought about how she might not live to see either of her nephews grow up, and an ache bloomed in her chest.

Hilo muttered, "If this is supposed to be peace, I think I prefer war."

Shae glanced at him. "Ayt had us in a bind, and she knew it. Whether I resigned or not, No Peak would be damaged. We would be seen as weaker than the Mountain. Tearing me down would've been only the start." She faced the shrine again, chin raised. "No matter what happens tomorrow, we'll have taken that leverage away from her."

"As if that'll do us much good if you're *dead*." Hilo turned to her with a ferocious glare. "You didn't listen to me; you never do. You did your own crazy thing as usual. So now you have to go through with it and *win*." He seized her upper arm in a painful grip and forced her to meet his eyes. "It's true what Kehn said. You have a chance to put Ayt Mada in the ground. We both know that anything can happen in a fight, and a duel is fought in here"—he tapped the center of her forehead with a forefinger—"before blades are drawn. So tell me you'll do it, Shae. You'll cut off Ayt's fucking head and put an end to all this."

Shae felt her bones prickling from the insistent pressure of her brother's aura. She forced a swallow out of her shrunken throat. "I'll do it," she said, her voice muted but steady. "I'll win tomorrow."

Hilo released her and stood up, his fierce expression unchanged. "Then stop sitting in here pretending to talk to the gods. Go to bed and get enough rest. Or else get your moon blade and practice, put your mind in the right place." He opened the door. "I'll be in the training hall."

In the morning, Shae rose and dressed in comfortable pants, fitted nylon top, traditional leather vest, and soft-soled shoes. She tied her hair back and examined herself in the mirror, debating how much of her jade to wear. Combatants hoping for every modicum of advantage wore all their jade into a duel, but that meant losing it all if one was defeated. Green Bones who were heavily jaded and thus gained little additional martial benefit from carrying their entire arsenal might be advised to think of their jade more prudently, as family wealth that they'd rather see passed on to family members instead of adorning the body of an enemy. Notwithstanding the promise of victory she'd made to Hilo in the prayer room last night, it was in Shae's nature to be realistic about her chances. After a long moment of consideration, she removed her earrings and bracelets, leaving in place her anklets and two-tier choker.

She selected her best moon blade—twenty-nine and a half inches in length, with a slightly curved twenty-and-a-half-inch single-edged blade of the finest tempered Da Tanori steel and a hilt stippled with small jade stones. She was not remotely hungry, but she cracked an egg into hot porridge and forced herself to eat. She looked around at her surroundings, thinking that the house was nice and Wen had decorated it well—hardwood flooring and dark furniture with clean lines contrasted with the soft throw pillows, light walls, and creamy drapes.

The place was too large for one person, though. Shae thought of Maro, of all the ignored messages now filling up the tape in her answering machine, and her throat closed, making it impossible to finish the last bites of her breakfast. Guilt and regret swelled and settled below her gut like bloat. She ached, more desperately than she'd expected, to see Maro's face, to hear his voice, to seize the chance to tell him that she did in fact love him. She knew that at last, when it was too late. She wished she'd thought of writing him a letter, but there was no time to do so properly, and speaking to him now would be of no good to either of them; she didn't think she could explain herself, and Maro—idealistic, rational, argumentative Maro with his two jade studs and skepticism of clan culture—he would not understand. Maro had never dueled, had walked away rather than spill blood or risk his life to satisfy traditional notions of Green Bone honor. He'd tell her to do the same.

She washed and dried her single bowl and spoon, put them away, and turned off all the house lights. Then she walked outside to where Hilo and the Maiks waited by the Duchesse.

The drive was quiet. The darkness under Hilo's eyes suggested that he had not slept any more than Shae had the previous night. He did not speak, and the Maik brothers, taking their cues from him, didn't either. The morning after a holiday, traffic was light, and it didn't take long to get to the Garrison House & Gardens in Juro Wood. Shae suspected that Ayt Mada had chosen the location for the symbolism. The Garrison House was a colonial mansion of red tiles and white colonnades; the residence of the Shotarian governor during the occupation period, it had been spared from destruction and turned into a national historic landmark containing a museum and public gardens. Shae and Ayt would be facing each other on the lawn, with the country's most visible symbol of past foreign domination looming in the backdrop.

Creeping warmth in the air promised a hot day to come, but the sky was thick with clouds and a layer of summer smog hung low over the city, creating a diffuse, sunless gloom. As the Duchesse pulled up to the curb in front of the public gardens, Shae saw an enormous crowd bordering the lawn. Some people carried cameras and others had spread blankets on the ground. For a second, Shae thought they had interrupted some public event and would have to move the location of the duel. Then it dawned on her that the duel *was* the public event. Of course, dueling was not uncommon—but this was not a common duel. News of Shae's challenge had created a storm of overnight attention. Clean blades between the Pillar and the Weather Man of the two largest clans in the country was dramatic enough, but moreover, there had never been a duel between two women of such high rank in their respective clans. Only in the postwar generation, with the country's population of male Green Bones depleted, had it become more commonplace for girls to be trained to wear jade. These days, one in five graduates from the nation's martial schools were female, but most men still scorned to duel a woman, and duels between women, even Fists, were often smirked at as something of a joke.

This contest would not be a joke. Shae and Ayt Mada would be making history, no matter the outcome. Social progress, Kekonese-style, Shae mused. Equal opportunity to die by the blade.

She closed her eyes for a minute before getting out of the car. Even when the mind is determined, the body objects vehemently to the possibility of injury and death. Shae's hands had gone clammy, and there was a tightness in her chest that she tried to alleviate with controlled breaths. She wondered if her thudding pulse was as Perceivable to every nearby Green Bone as it was to her. It occurred to her that her classmates from Belforte Business School in Windton would be horrified and flabbergasted by what she was about to do. Oddly, the thought made her smile.

Tar got out and opened the back door for her and Hilo; the spectators edged forward eagerly but kept a respectful distance from the intimidating presence of No Peak's leaders as they stepped out onto the lawn. Seconds after their arrival, a long, sleek, silver Stravaconi Monarch pulled up behind the Duchesse. Ayt Mada emerged, along with her Horn and two Fists. Ayt appeared unruffled by the presence of the crowd; she nodded casually toward the Mountain loyalists who called out and saluted her. She was wearing a black tank top and comfortable silk pants with a tied drawstring. Her hair was pulled back into a tight ponytail. A pair of sunglasses perched on top of her head. As she walked to the center of the lawn, she removed them and handed them to Nau Suen, who tucked them into the breast pocket of his shirt as if he regularly held on to the Pillar's sunglasses during duels. Ayt looked as if she were stopping by the event in between running Sixthday errands, except for the fact that she was carrying her thirty-two-inch jade-hilted moon blade slung over one shoulder. All of her jade sat in its usual place, coiled in silver bracelets up both her arms.

The time had come. Shae drew her moon blade and held it out to Hilo. Her brother turned his head to stare across the lawn at Ayt and her people. He turned back slowly, looked down at Shae's blade, and spat on the white metal for luck. Shae opened her mouth to say something—she was not even sure what—but Hilo dropped his hands onto her shoulders. His grip and aura fell on her like a warm lead vest. Leaning close, he brought his cheek next to hers and whispered into her ear. "Four cars full of our Fists and Fingers are on their way here, to block off the Lo Low Street tunnel and every road out of this place. There are others headed to the Ayt mansion, to the Factory, to half a dozen other Mountain properties in the city." His voice was soft and chillingly devoid of inflection. "Some blades can't be cleaned."

The iciness of Hilo's words ran down Shae's back in a wave of abrupt understanding. Unlike her, he had not been awake all night worrying or praying; he'd been making military preparations. If Shae fell under Ayt's sword, Hilo would not allow their enemies to leave the grounds alive. He would break the immutable law of the clean blade; he would take forbidden vengeance on her killer and plunge the clans, and the entire city, back into all-out war.

Shae was horrified. She was risking her life to clear her name and her clan's reputation by solving a dispute of personal honor in the old way, the Green Bone way, under the eyes of Old Uncle and in adherence to rules that all Kekonese held as inviolable stricture. Duels were traditionally meant to contain personal feuds and prevent them from escalating into family or clan vendettas. Breaking the pact of the clean blade would be unacceptable; it would put all the fault for the resumption of war squarely on No Peak. Hilo was a Green Bone to his core and the Pillar of the clan; for him to so flagrantly break the moral code they lived by—it would ruin *everything*. It would make a mockery of the jade warrior honor she was dueling to uphold in the first place.

Before Shae could put any of these thoughts into words, Hilo stepped away from her, his expression dark and unreadable. He turned and walked to the corner where the Maik brothers waited, and Shae was alone in the center of the lawn, save for the impatient red intensity of Ayt Mada, standing across from her, moon blade already drawn, waiting to begin.

Shae scrambled to regain her focus. She wondered for an instant if Hilo was bluffing—if this was his twisted way of motivating her to survive the duel—but she had no time to dwell on the idea. An anticipatory hush had fallen over the crowd; she heard the clicking of camera shutters around her. Innumerable heartbeats were rising in her Perception, loud and seemingly in time with her own, all of them eager and waiting. Standing out from the general multitude were the jade auras of Green Bones from both clans who'd gathered to witness this event, one that was supposedly a matter of personal honor between two people, but that everyone knew was far more than that. Janlooners wanted the clans to hold to the truce, to respect territorial lines and cooperate to combat crime and smuggling and current international pressures, but they had nevertheless come out enthusiastically at a moment's notice to see blood spilled between the Mountain and No Peak.

Shae faced her opponent and touched the flat of her blade to her forehead in salute. Ayt did the same. Gone was Ayt's casual demeanor. There was a frightening quality to her stillness now, an almost reptilian poise in the way she stood erect and regarded the younger woman, waiting for her to attack first. In Shae's acutely sharp Perception, Ayt was a column of red energy, the inside of a coal furnace, its painful heat blotting out everything else. The longer she stared at it in her mind, the more unassailable it would seem; she would lose her nerve. Shae gathered her Strength and rushed in with a burst of speed, moon blade flashing downward in an opening diagonal cross slash aimed at opening Ayt Mada's torso from left shoulder to opposing hip.

Ayt slid left at the edge of the weapon's reach, deftly deflected Shae's next cut, and spun low to the ground, hair whipping around her neck, her extended blade a blur of steel. Shae launched herself Light, barely evading being taken apart at the knees, and came down with a hard chop from above. Ayt braced the blunt backside of her weapon against her left palm as she blocked Shae's attack head-on. For an instant, white metal rang against white metal, Strength clashed against Strength, the jade auras of the two women vibrated with impact; then Ayt's blade disengaged, changed direction like the darting tail of a fish, and shot a deadly path to Shae's throat.

Shae jerked her head out of the way and threw her Steeled arm up in instinctive defense; Ayt's moon blade sheared against her raised forearm, the razor edge parting skin but stopping short of muscle and bone. With her attention on Ayt's weapon as it passed inches from her face, Shae nearly failed to Perceive the Channeling blow that Ayt thrust with her left hand. It drove toward Shae's center like a sharpened metal rod, aiming to punch through heart and lungs.

Shae twisted her torso out of the way, battening herself with Steel, her rib cage shuddering with concentrated jade energy as she sucked in the deadly momentum of Ayt's energy and countered in blind desperation: a quick, jabbing Channeling strike to the sternum, followed by an unaimed Deflection that nevertheless blasted her opponent in the midsection. Ayt stumbled backward several feet, lips parted in a grimace. Shae saw the Pillar's eyes widen and her normally perfect composure fissure as the realization struck them both at the same time: Shae stood a chance of winning. In the opening seconds of the duel, anyone could see that Ayt Mada was a superlative jade fighter, a powerful, deliberate combatant, well deserving of her reputation, but Shae was fast and talented and perhaps most importantly, a dozen years younger, a Green Bone in her physical prime.

A moment of emotional stalemate seemed to pass between them. Then Ayt's jade aura lit with the violence of an exploding star, just as a surge of adrenaline and odd elation caught feverish hold of Shae's brain. Ayt came at her with weapon upraised and lips curled back, and with a wild cry of effort, Shae flew Light at her, blade slicing across in a deadly horizontal blur.

It became difficult for anyone watching the contest to follow the movement of the opposing moon blades as the duelists sent them singing against each other, seeking open angles, striving with equal ferocity to connect metal with flesh. Spectators murmured in alarm and scrambled to the edge of the lawn to make more space for the fighters as they raged across the field. Shae's reality telescoped to the desperate purity of the fight. Her conscious mind all but shut down; only Perception, training, and reflexes could possibly save her from the onslaught. She saw Ayt's face contort in a snarl of impatience as she lashed out with a flurry of darting, unpredictable slashes meant to overwhelm and confuse her opponent's sense of both sight and Perception. Cuts rained down on Shae's arms and torso; her Steel trembled under the strain of constant flexing and her lungs heaved like bellows, scalded with exertion. She sensed rather than saw the impending killing blow—an upward thrust that would pierce the hollow of her throat. Instead of blocking with her own blade, she threw a tight Deflection, just enough to shift Ayt's aim; the stab passed inches from her left cheek as her own blade lashed out for her enemy's neck.

Ayt barely twisted away from the lethal maneuver; Shae pressed the attack with a quick upward slash, and a bloody gash opened across the side of Ayt's head, bisecting her left ear and taking half of it clean off.

Shae heard the collective intake of breath from the watching crowd a split second before she Perceived her opponent's pain and rage. A slashed ear was a minor injury compared to the killing blow Shae had intended, but there are few things in Kekonese culture more symbolic than a missing ear. Ayt touched the blood on the side of her face in disbelief. For a fraction of a second, Shae was equally astonished. Some part of her had not expected Ayt to be a mere mortal, a woman of flesh and blood like herself, someone who would bleed if cut, someone who could be killed—and then she snapped back to her senses. She was tiring rapidly and could not keep fighting like this much longer; these brief seconds while Ayt was unbalanced—she had to take immediate advantage of them, win while she had the chance.

Shae sidestepped and committed to the momentary opening, throwing her weight into a cleaving, decapitating strike. Far from still being distracted by her superficial injury, Ayt seemed to have been anticipating the move; she shifted her position and met the attack head-on, slamming her own blade into the path of Shae's weapon with so much force that Shae felt the impact reverberate through her frame and clatter into her teeth. For an instant, they were both rooted in the concussion of the blow. Ayt's roaring jade aura crashed over Shae like a tidal wave; the churn of their desperately grappling energies filled every bit of her Perception. Faster than a striking cobra, Ayt's left hand shot out and seized Shae's sword hand, crushing down on the meat of her thumb in a grip of extraordinary Strength. With a twist, she forced Shae's weapon downward and vertical, and with Steeled forearm, knocked the blade out of her opponent's weakened grip. It happened in less than a second: Shae's moon blade went flying, and Ayt sliced across with her own weapon, snarling as she threw Strength into a disemboweling cut.

Shae Steeled for all her life was worth. It was not fast or hard enough; pain lanced across her abdomen like flame along a line of blasting powder. A sudden hot wetness flowed down the front of her pants as if her bladder had given out all at once. When she looked down, she saw blood running down her legs as if a waterfall faucet had opened up above her navel.

She felt faint; the reality of impending death emptied her mind. Time elongated and turned the world strangely still. In the periphery of her Perception, she sensed Ayt Mada's murderous triumph descending along with the executioner's swing of her blade. With every particle of remaining wherewithal left to her, Shae staggered backward and fell to her knees in the grass, arms wide. "Ayt-jen!" she cried out hoarsely, her head thrown back. "I concede!"

She closed her eyes; at any second, she would die. "I concede," she declared again. She could barely recognize her own voice; it seemed to be coming from someone else. It was hard to think, to grasp words and string them together into a final effort, a thin, calculated lifeline. "You are the greater Green Bone warrior, truly a worthy daughter of the Spear of Kekon. My life and my jade are yours for the taking. If you're merciful enough to spare me, it'll be only so I can follow your example and continue contributing what little worth I have to the good of Kekon."

A heartbeat passed. Another. The pain of the stomach wound was unbearable; she wanted to slump to the ground in the damp grass and curl feebly around her injury, but she held herself still. With her eyes closed, she Perceived Ayt's flicker of hesitation; the blade paused in its descent. Less than ten meters away, Hilo's jade aura roared like a monster in a pit, its reckless, savage intent unmistakable. Shae opened her eyes and looked into Ayt's maddened face, the left side of it smeared with blood, and then past the other woman's shoulder. Two large cars were blocking off the two-lane road up to the Garrison House & Gardens. Another two had pulled up along the curb behind Ayt's silver Stravaconi. A dozen No Peak Fists were coming out of the vehicles. The watching civilians were looking fearfully from Ayt to Shae to Hilo, to the surrounding soldiers of both clans, whose hands had gone for the hilts of their weapons.

Despite the agony in her torso and the clamor of her own panicked heartbeat, Shae met her opponent's eyes and saw the fearsome expression shift into bitter understanding as Ayt too Perceived the arrival of Hilo's warriors, the sudden dangerous shift in the air. Even now, facing death, Shae was desperately playing what cards remained to her. With the attention of the entire country on them, she had fought bravely and well, in true Kekonese fashion defended her reputation and that of her clan, and ultimately conceded the duel to the better warrior. There had been a moment of opportunity for Ayt to take Shae's life fairly in battle—but that moment was lost. Clean-bladed dueling was an honorable tradition; striking down an opponent who'd surrendered was not.

Killing Shae now, as she knelt injured and disarmed, would show the Pillar of the Mountain to be merciless and bloodthirsty, would publicly confirm that she was who Hilo had been reminding everyone she was—the woman who'd seized power by having her own brother murdered in his sleep. The sort of person who would behead a defeated opponent on her knees might do anything, might break aisho in other ways, might even harm a child. Ayt's image as the patriotic warrior stateswoman, which she had been carefully cultivating for over two years as she rebuilt the reputation of her clan, would be ruined. And Hilo would seize the justification he needed—if he needed any at all—to turn the scene into a bloodbath.

Shae's blood soaking into the dry dirt raised a pungent metallic smell that stung her nostrils. With shaking fingers, she fumbled for the clasp of her jade choker and broke it. The twin strings fell from her neck, sliding from her skin as easily as blood from a vein. She held it out to Ayt, her arms shaking even from the small effort. She could Perceive the uncertainty, the frantic calculation, behind the burning gaze the other woman fixed on her. Ayt was furiously debating whether to eliminate an enemy now or preserve the moral high ground, and she could not be certain whether Kaul Hilo would go so far as to break the pact of clean blades, not to mention the truce between the Mountain and No Peak, and send them all careening back into clan war. Ayt's eyes narrowed. Shae's mind rang with the crowded Perception of all the people watching and waiting with growing alarm and held breath.

Ayt lowered her blade. She reached out and seized Shae's jade in her fist. When she spoke, she raised her voice so all those nearby could hear. "You've acted disgracefully in the past, Kaul Shaelinsan. Nevertheless, it would be a waste to kill a fellow Green Bone at a time when Kekon needs every one of us." The Pillar of the Mountain wiped the length of both sides of her moon blade against the thigh of one silk pant leg. "My blade is clean."

Noisy exclamations of relief and appreciation erupted from the sidelines. The collective fever pitch of tension from the auras of the waiting Green Bones settled back to a wary hum. Ayt leaned in, close enough to speak to Shae alone. Shae stared at her jade in Ayt's grip with curious horror, as if it were a part of her own body—a severed hand, her heart, her entrails—that the other woman was holding between them. The left side of Ayt's head was grisly where part of the ear was missing, but she paid it no heed. "I promised you before, you foolish girl, that you would live to see your clan in ruins," Ayt whispered. "It would be dishonest for me to kill you until then." She turned calmly and walked into the posse of congratulatory Mountain fighters.

The jade withdrawal and blood loss hit Shae simultaneously, like a typhoon ripping her violently off the face of the earth. Everything fractured and tilted away as her weakened body collapsed beneath her. Dimly, she was aware of a great deal of commotion: Hilo and the Maiks crouching over her, the family's Green Bone physician, Dr. Truw, pressing down on her wound and Channeling into her, forcing tingling warmth into her shivering limbs. Other people speaking as if from a great distance: "Get her into the ambulance." Shae inhaled the smell of the grass pressed under her cheek and let unconsciousness drag her away from it all.

CHAPTER

32

⌒

Overdue Conversations

Shae required a blood transfusion and twelve days in Janloon General Hospital before the surgeon and Dr. Truw cleared her to return home. At her request, no one but immediate family had been allowed to visit her while she was in the hospital. Addled with painkillers and shaking with jade withdrawal, the last thing she wanted was to answer questions from reporters, be seen in this state by any of her Ship Street colleagues, or even to guiltily face Maro. As a result, when she got back to her own house, she felt utterly disconnected from the world and overwhelmed by how to even start getting her footing back. Although she'd been trained at the Academy and had fought and killed before, by Green Bone standards, and by Kaul family standards in particular, she'd enjoyed a relatively safe existence: spoiled by her grandfather, protected by Lan, groomed for the business side of the clan, living abroad in Espenia, then working on the top floor of an office tower. She had never been so near death before, and it humbled her.

Now she stood naked in front of the mirror in her bathroom. A long pink scar, fading to white at the edges and puckered by stitches, ran across her abdomen, distorting the shape of her navel. It still gave her pain when she twisted or bent at the waist. A dull jade withdrawal headache sat at the base of her skull and every muscle in her body felt leaden. She still had her jade earrings, bracelets, and anklets, which Hilo had brought to her in the hospital when she was strong enough to wear them, but her neck was pale and bare without her two-tier jade choker.

Shae dressed and called Woon on the phone. He came over immediately, and in a mutual flood of relief, they embraced each other in the doorway. "Shae-jen," Woon said, his voice unsteady, "I understand why you acted as you did, but at the time, I thought I was about to lose you as well. If that had happened, I think I would've gone to the Pillar and begged for death."

"Don't ever think such a thing, Papi-jen," Shae said, a little shaken by his words. They went into her kitchen. Shae leaned heavily against the table as she pulled out a seat; Woon put a steadying hand under her elbow and helped her into it. "How bad has it been, Shae-jen?" he asked, his brow deeply creased with concern.

"Withdrawal?" Shae grimaced. "It's manageable, and it won't last long." She was achy and exhausted and felt at times as if there were cobwebs over her eyes and ears, but she was not incapacitated. She still had her jade abilities. Withdrawal symptoms felt worse piled on top of her physical injuries, but they weren't nearly as severe as they would've been if she'd lost all her jade, and she knew from experience they would pass within a few weeks.

Woon took what she'd said to mean something different. "I'll bring you jade from the clan's stores," he said. "How much do you need to have a new choker made?"

Shae shook her head. "I don't want a new one." There was nothing to stop her from drawing from the Kaul family's reserves of wealth to replace the jade she'd lost in the duel, but after nearly dying in the most public manner possible, she felt as if it would be dishonest, personally diminishing in some way, to be seen wearing a new choker made of jade she had not fought for. It would seem as if the near-fatal stand she'd taken had no lasting impact, as if what she'd lost that day could be so easily restored. Ayt Mada could not grow back the missing portion of her ear. Shae would carry the absence of her jade openly, like a scar.

Woon looked unsure at her refusal, but understanding how personal the decision was, he accepted her explanation without argument. Shae asked him to tell her what had happened over the past twelve days. The Weather Man's Shadow had been staunchly holding her place on Ship Street. The decisions that had to be made, he'd made in a way he judged she would approve; all other questions and requests he'd dealt with by saying the Weather Man would answer them upon her return.

Woon had done one thing she had not anticipated: He'd gone to Hami Tumashon and asked the Master Luckbringer if he intended to resign from his position. The two highest-ranking men in the Weather Man's office had had a respectful working relationship stretching back years, to when Woon was Lan's Pillarman, and Hami a senior Luckbringer under Doru, but Hami had not taken the question kindly, seeing it for what it was: an accusation of disloyalty.

"Only the Pillar or the Weather Man can ask for my resignation, Woon-jen," Hami had answered coldly. "I'm tempted to offer you a clean blade, but I think we can agree that any other duels would be anticlimactic at this point." The Master Luckbringer continued to manage the day-to-day activities on Ship Street with all of his usual competence, but after the confrontation, he and Woon spoke little beyond what was necessary.

When Woon had filled her in on everything she needed to know, Shae felt as if it wouldn't have been so bad to have stayed in the hospital a few more days. "I can't thank you enough, Papi-jen," she said. "And I'm sorry that I left you with so much to deal with at a time when you should've been happily planning your wedding." Woon was to be married in a few months. Shae had not met his fiancée but had seen a very pretty photograph of her on the man's desk.

Woon's jade aura shifted at the mention of the wedding. "It was hardly anything compared to what you went through. Besides, Kiya and my mother are doing all the work; I only need to show up." He added, "However, the next time you challenge Ayt Madashi with a clean blade, if you could be more considerate about the timing, that would be appreciated." Woon's sense of humor, when it made an appearance, was so deadpan that Shae wasn't sure whether to laugh.

When she returned to Ship Street the following day, she felt physically stronger and less muddled after having slept for fourteen hours in her own bed. An abrupt silence accompanied her arrival into the building. As she walked from the elevator to her office, people stopped in their conversations and paused in their work. Shae's Perception was sluggish from the combination of jade loss and days of convalescence, but she sensed the wave of trepidation that spread down the corridor.

A man on her left brought his clasped hands up to his forehead and dipped into a formal salute. "Kaul-jen," he called out. "Welcome back."

The woman at the desk next to him followed suit, as did another, and the Luckbringers near them stood up from their chairs and went to the doors of their offices or the entries of their cubicles and saluted the Weather Man as she passed. Shae saw tenuous smiles on their faces, congratulatory and consoling in equal measure. She'd lost the duel and the majority of her jade, but she'd defended herself and her clan from slander. She'd fought as well as anyone could've expected and shown herself willing to die for personal and family reputation. In those most critical aspects, she'd put to rest the question of her integrity and fitness as a Green Bone leader.

Shae's secretary jumped up and followed her into her office. "Kaul-jen, Councilman Kowi and two Lantern Men have been coming into the building for the past two mornings and waiting in the lobby to speak to you. Do you want to see them or should I send them away?"

"I'll see them," Shae said. Behind her, people went back to their work as if there was nothing out of the ordinary.

Kowi and the two Lantern Men were admitted to Shae's office. The pretense of the meeting was to give her an update on the goings-on in the Royal Council during her absence, particularly the national budget, and the question over what Kekon's stance ought to be regarding refugees from the Oortokon War, which had been going on for nearly a year. Shae knew the true reason for their visit. They had taken a risk by going to Hilo to advocate her removal as Weather Man. Now that it was clear they had failed and she was to remain in her post, they were here to forestall disfavor.

"Kaul-jen," Councilman Kowi said, saluting deeply and nervously. "I speak for all of us in expressing how relieved we are to see you well." The two Lantern Men echoed his sentiments vehemently. Shae accepted their well wishes graciously and entertained twenty minutes of discussion on Council matters. At last, Kowi cleared his throat. "Kaul-jen, my family's ties to No Peak go back generations, so it goes without saying that my allegiance to the clan is ironclad and I personally hope to be working with you for many years."

Mr. Eho, the Lantern Man, said, "In this day and age, the news cycle moves faster than ever, and things are printed in the newspapers or spoken on the radio before the truth is even verified. I'm ashamed to say that perhaps I jumped to conclusions based on some of the recent negative talk, but I should never have lost faith in the clan and in the Weather Man's office."

"I'd be willing to publicly declare my regrets to the Pillar for any misunderstanding," said Mr. Orn contritely and earnestly, though his pained expression suggested obvious reluctance. A missing ear would not look good on someone hoping to run for political office.

Shae let a silence come to rest in the room, for long enough that she could Perceive the anxiety of her visitors rising. She looked at each of them in turn, her face impassive; none of the men met her gaze for more than a few seconds before glancing away. She crossed her legs and folded her hands over one knee. "That won't be necessary," she said. "My grandfather taught me that if a friend asks for your forgiveness, you should always give it." Her guests relaxed considerably, their shoulders coming down, smiles beginning to appear on their faces.

Shae added, before any of them could begin to speak, "He also taught me that if you have to give it again, then they weren't a friend to begin with." She rose smoothly from her seat to end the meeting. "I know I can count on your friendship and allegiance from now on."

Shae spent the next few days getting caught up. On Fifthday morning, she called Hami Tumashon into her office. "Hami-jen," Shae said without preamble, "it's time we talked about your future in the Weather Man's office and in the No Peak clan."

Hami's expression turned stiff and wary, and his jade aura began to bristle defensively. Shae went on, "We haven't always seen eye to eye during the time I've been Weather Man. At times you've challenged my decisions or made it clear that you felt I acted incorrectly."

"I've spoken up when I've thought it necessary," Hami said brusquely. "I did the same when Yun Doru was Weather Man. He was too parochial, but the truth is that the clan was comfortable with him, because he was an old-timer, a comrade of the Torch. You don't have that luxury. Even if I agree with the general direction you're taking the clan, I have to point it out when you act in ways that are ill considered or that cost respect for you and for No Peak."

"You're right to do so," Shae said. "As much as your honesty wounds my pride sometimes, I have to admit you're the one person in No Peak who best straddles the different sides of the clan. You have the presence and cold instincts of a Fist but the brains and experience of a good Luckbringer. You see the need to change with the times but also the importance of staying true to our core as Green Bones. That's why I called you in here: I want you to move to Espenia, to start up a branch of the Weather Man's office in Port Massy."

Whatever Hami had been expecting when he'd been called into Shae's office, it was not this. As he was too stunned to reply at first, Shae continued. "Despite current political sentiments, the reality is that we're tied to Espenia economically. They buy our jade, have military bases on our soil, and now our business interests in that country are growing more than ever. We can't manage it all from Janloon. I need someone there. Someone who I know is loyal to the clan, who is adaptable to new ways but will run the business like a true Kekonese."

Hami was obviously still trying to process the idea. Cautiously, he said, "What support would I have from Janloon?" He wanted to know if Shae was serious about expansion, or if this was simply a convenient excuse to send him overseas and into functional exile.

"As much as I can give you," Shae said. "You would choose a handful of Luckbringers to help you start the branch office. We have connections in Port Massy to help you hire additional staff locally. You would report directly to me as you always have. The clan would pay for your family's relocation and living expenses. You have two children, don't you, Hami-jen?"

Hami nodded. "They're four and six years old."

"If you accept, I ask that you commit to the assignment for at least three years. Your children would attend school in Port Massy and become fluent in Espenian, but still be young enough to attend Kaul Du Academy when you return to Janloon."

She could see Hami weighing her offer. As Master Luckbringer, the man was at the height of his career; there were few avenues for further advancement. No doubt he'd expected to stay in his role on Ship Street for another decade or more. But he was still relatively young, only forty-one years old—the idea of being paid to live abroad and start a whole new division of the clan's operations was appealing. "My wife and I have talked about the idea of spending time overseas," he admitted.

"There's something else for you to consider," Shae said, knowing it might dissuade him but must be addressed. "Civilian possession of jade is now illegal in Espenia. You would have to give up your green. You could store it safely here in Janloon, or we would find a way to make sure it's covertly transported to you in Port Massy, but you can't wear it while you're in that country. If you were only going to be there for a short while, we could obtain a visitor's waiver, but you'll be living there. Wearing jade would expose you and the clan's businesses to too much legal risk."

Hami winced. He'd left the military side of the clan a long time ago, and Shae doubted he'd been called upon to employ his jade abilities in a martial capacity for years, but the idea of losing one's jade was appalling to most Green Bones. Even though this would be a temporary measure of his own choosing instead of a permanent loss brought about by an enemy, Shae could see him questioning whether he could stand to live in a place where he couldn't wear jade, no matter how good the pay, the professional challenge, and the family enrichment.

Hami looked to her. "You've taken off your jade before. How bad was it?"

Shae considered the question before answering honestly. Her own recent symptoms had abated considerably, but the memory was fresh. "Withdrawal isn't pleasant, but it's not as bad as most people think," she said. "You'd go through it here at home, under medical supervision, so it would probably be over in a couple of weeks. Being without jade is different when you're in Espenia. I'd never ask for such a thing from any Green Bone in Kekon, but over there, when you don't see green anymore, after a while you stop missing it altogether."

"Like being deaf in a country of deaf people." The Master Luckbringer mulled the idea for a minute. "I can't make such an important decision right away. I need to talk to my family."

She nodded. "Give me your answer by next Fifthday."

———

Shae left the office an hour after lunch and took a thirty-minute subway ride to meet Maro on the campus of Jan Royal University. She brought a book to read along the way but couldn't focus on any of the words. She'd been longing terribly to see Maro again, but she dreaded the conversation to come. When she'd finally mustered the courage to call him, part of her had hoped that Maro would hang up the second he heard her voice and make it easy on her. No such luck; there'd been several heartbeats of silence from the other end of the line, and then he'd said, in a voice with no emotion she could read, "I can meet you after my last class finishes today."

"I'll come to where you are," Shae offered, as if, ridiculously, this small consideration on her part could compensate for the weeks she'd been out of contact.

At the height of summer, the city subway was humid and odorous, but the campus was pleasantly green and generously shaded. Shae spotted Maro sitting at an outdoor table behind the Foreign Studies Department building's cafeteria. His back was to her. He had a book open on the table but wasn't reading it; the pages lay undisturbed in the hot, still air. Shae felt a powerful desire to walk up and put her arms around Maro's shoulders, to pretend that nothing had happened, that everything was the same as before. And yet in the same moment, the idea struck her as impossible, awkward, inappropriate, like draping her arms over a stranger. The ease she felt around him— the escape and acceptance he represented, that she realized she'd made of him—that feeling was gone. She could sense it even from this distance.

She walked around the table and sat down in the chair across from him. Maro took her in: dressed in her usual business attire, ugly new scars hidden, her throat bare and pale where her distinctive jade choker used to be. A strange expression crossed his face—a mixture of hurt confusion, affection, anger, and relief that seemed to twitch his features in several indecisive directions before he forced it into a cautiously neutral smile. The smile of someone trying to be civil to another driver who's smashed into their car. "I'm glad you're okay," he said slowly. "And I'm glad you came to see me."

"I'm sorry," Shae said. It seemed to be the only way to start.

"*Why?*" The single word came out strained, but there were so many things that it could be referring to that Shae was not sure how to answer. Maro lowered his voice. "Why wouldn't you return any of my calls? Before, or after, you did it?" For a second, Shae was struck by uncertainty—did he mean the abortion, or the duel? But he didn't know about the former, so it was the duel. "Why did you make me find out about it from the *news*? Why wouldn't you even talk to me?"

"I'm sorry," Shae repeated. "A lot of things happened quickly. I knew that if I talked to you, I'd lose my nerve and not be able to do what I had to."

"What you *had* to?" Maro asked, skepticism strangling each of his words. "You *had* to volunteer for a dramatic public death?"

"I was being discredited and forced out, Maro. The Mountain was using me to undermine and weaken No Peak." She'd promised herself she would not give in to defensiveness, but she heard it creeping into her voice anyway. "I had to put a stop to it. On the phone, you reminded me that I deserved my position. You told me not to give in."

Maro shook his head. "A duel wasn't what I had in mind! You could've been killed."

Shae said, "Yes, but I wasn't. I'm still here. Still the Weather Man."

"But if you *had* been killed—and you almost were—you wouldn't even have *spoken* to me beforehand. That's..." Disbelief and anger contorted his expression. "That's not how it's supposed to work between people who care about each other. How could you not even talk to me about it?"

"What would you have said?" Shae asked. "Would you have supported my decision? Or would you have told me not to risk my life? To avoid the duel by not showing up?"

She regretted her words almost at once. Maro's eyes widened, and then his face crumpled softly. "Yes," he said. "I suppose that's exactly what I would've said. I would've told you that you're above that kind of thing, above using violence to prove yourself. No matter the public pressures, I would've reminded you of what you once said to me: that it's brave to be true to who you are."

Shae said quietly, "This *is* who I am."

Maro reached a hand partway across the table but did not touch her. "It's not who you are when you're with me." When she didn't meet his eyes, he nodded sadly. "But I don't really know you, do I? All the time we've spent together, I was seeing what I wanted to and what you wanted to show me. Your other side, the *greener* side—I don't know that person at all."

Shae's face felt hot, as if Maro had slapped her. "I never meant to lie to you or shut you out. I tried to warn you that there're things about the clan and about me that you wouldn't agree with."

"Whether I agree with them or not, you shouldn't have kept me in the dark like that!" Maro's voice rose and he forced it down again, with effort. "You're right—maybe there are things in your life and your family that I'm never going to be able to accept. I've thought about them, before—how couldn't I? I wondered if I would have to join the clan to be able to marry you, how we'd ever raise a family with the demands on you as Weather Man, whether my Shotarian family would ever be able to meet yours...there were so many things that I knew we would have to talk about, but I always assumed we *would* talk about them. We'd be truthful with each other about the challenges, and we'd get through them together." He searched her face with pained eyes. "That's the only way I want a relationship with you—if we're completely honest with each other. I know you can't tell me everything that you do as Weather Man. I can live with that, but things that affect your safety, our *lives*...I deserve that much, at least. Can you *promise* not to keep important things from me?"

Shae was lacking enough moisture in her throat. She certainly couldn't tell Maro about the abortion, not now, not with him already hurt. What else might she have to do in the future that she wouldn't be able to explain? "In the last few years, I've done things I never thought I would," she admitted hoarsely. "I'm not sure what I can promise anymore."

Maro's silence lasted for an interminable minute. It seemed to Shae that he was receding from her, shrinking to the end of a tunnel. Maro drew his hand back to his side of the table and looked away, across the green lawn of the campus, the line of his bearded jaw flexing. "I don't know where this leaves us, then."

Shae managed to say, "As friends, for now. If that's something you'll still accept from me."

Maro closed the book on the table, one finger tucked between the pages to hold his place as he stood up. His lips formed the shape of a weak smile, but one entirely without cheer. "Of course. Who in all of Kekon would be unwise enough to refuse the friendship of the No Peak clan?"

CHAPTER

33

Not a Safe Place

During his second year in Port Massy, Anden took a part-time job at a hardware store, stocking shelves, manning the cash register, assisting customers with home improvement projects. He still had his usual course load to manage, but he wanted to earn some extra money. He could help out the Hians with some of their monthly expenses, save some cash for the future, and have a little extra to spend. Financially, he'd relied on the Kaul family all his life; now that his prospects in the clan seemed so low, he felt as if he ought to be better prepared to pay his own way through life. Also, he would rather be doing something besides studying. Working at Starr Lumber & Supply would improve his ability to speak Espenian, so in truth, it could be considered part of his education. He could now navigate public transit and read signs and hold conversations with strangers. It was satisfying to feel self-reliant. Anden had never understood why, years ago, his cousin Shae had gone abroad and distanced herself from the clan; now he thought he had a better idea.

He'd continued meeting up with Cory Dauk and his relayball friends at the grudge hall all throughout the winter and the dreary wet spring. When he first told Mr. and Mrs. Hian where he was going on Fifthday evenings, he was surprised that they didn't seem to approve. He would've thought they would be happy he was spending more time with friends in the neighborhood. Instead, Mrs. Hian said, in a tone that suggested Anden might be making a poor decision, "Anden-se, that place is not a good influence on young people. So much violence. It gives people a bad impression of us."

"I have great respect for the Dauks," Mr. Hian put in, sliding Anden a gaze of paternal concern, "but the grudge hall...I wouldn't spend time there myself. The cockfighting and gambling and dueling—those things are against the law. What if the police raid the building and you're caught doing something illegal? You could have your student visa revoked."

It occurred to Anden that if that happened, he would be deported back to Kekon immediately and Hilo would have no choice but to take him back in. He didn't voice this flash of wry optimism to the Hians. Instead, he promised them that he would never engage in gambling or dueling of any kind.

"But there are always a lot of Green Bones there," said Mrs. Hian, persisting in her concern. "It's not safe."

In Janloon, it was common knowledge that the safest places to be were those frequented by Green Bones. Excepting unusual circumstances of clan war, there were few spots less prone to trouble than establishments like the Twice Lucky restaurant or the Lilac Divine Gentleman's Club. So Mrs. Hian's worries made no sense to Anden until he remembered that the proposed law Dauk Losun had spoken of last summer had been passed by the National Assembly and jade itself was now another thing that was illegal in Espenia.

He often forgot this fact. He could accept that a great many things were different in Espenia than they were in Kekon, but the idea of banning jade was as hard for Anden to imagine as forbidding the use of cars or money—of course, not everyone could or should have those things because they were dangerous in the wrong hands, but trying to do away with them altogether would be ridiculous. How would society function?

Anden reminded himself that he was reacting with a narrow Kekonese mind-set. Other places in the world had gotten by for thousands of years with no jade at all and so the availability of it now was a new and harmful thing. The recent prohibition against civilian ownership and selling of jade had not changed anything so far as Anden could tell; no Green Bone that he knew of was giving up his green on account of it. All the new law did, Anden thought, was promote a negative view of Kekonese people.

Mr. Hian was thinking of a different threat besides law enforcement, however. "The Crews have left our neighborhood alone for a long time, but the Bosses—they see there's gambling and money-lending going on here that they don't control. And jade." Mr. Hian frowned deeply. "Dauk-jen said it wouldn't be long before the understanding broke down. You don't want to be caught in the middle if anything bad happens between Green Bones and Boss Kromner's Crew."

This rationale Anden could better understand. Civilians were always better off steering clear of conflicts that did not involve them. Seated in the Hians' kitchen, he grew quiet and pensive. He didn't want to cause the Hians any worry on his account, but he couldn't give up going to the grudge hall and meeting with Cory.

Seeing this, the Hians relented. "You're our guest, and we feel as responsible for your safety as if you were one of our own sons, but it's not up to us to tell you what you can or can't do; you're a grown man who can make his own decisions." Mrs. Hian sighed. "You grew up with Green Bones, so naturally you want to be back among them, and who are we to say no? We only want you to be careful." Anden gratefully promised them that he would be and that they needn't worry.

It was not, in truth, that he wanted to be back among Green Bones, as Mrs. Hian had assumed. Although he enjoyed the food and drink, the displays of jade ability, and the generally convivial atmosphere of the grudge hall (punctuated on occasion with the genuine and deadly serious settling of grievances), it was, as he'd already learned on his first visit there, not really like Kekon at all. At best, it was something entirely different, at worst, an exaggerated facsimile of a working-class Kekonese tavern. If anything, it made him miss home more than ever. What he truly wanted came after his visits to the grudge hall, when Cory would offer to drive Anden back to the Hians' but instead drove the two of them to his own apartment.

Cory did not own the place he lived in, which was a one-bedroom condo only ten minutes away from his parents' house. The Dauks kept it as an investment property and were planning to renovate it and put it back on the market once Cory went to law school in the fall. It was drafty, the furnace was noisy, and the hot water heater badly needed replacing, but these were minor discomforts. Anden was forced to admit to himself, with some embarrassment, that he would probably follow Cory anywhere the other man asked him.

After that first time in the car, Anden had spent the entire following week thinking about his friend, about the pale skin of Cory's torso illuminated by streetlight, about his teasing eyes and quick smile, his shapely hands and mouth. When the weather was still bad the following Fifthday, Cory phoned the Hians' house to ask if Anden wanted to meet up at the grudge hall again, and Anden said yes. Afterward, he said yes to going to Cory's apartment. And he said yes to everything else that Cory suggested that night and on the other nights that followed.

Cory was the same in lovemaking as he was in everything else— spirited, good-humored, eager to please and easy to please in turn. For this, Anden was grateful because he felt acutely that he was the opposite: torn between the nearly unbearable force of his awakening desire and the self-consciousness of his own inexperience and nerves. Cory did not take himself too seriously in anything: He played music in the bedroom and danced in his underwear; he gave Anden gently teasing advice about what to do in bed; he admitted that when he was with men he preferred to be the receiver, but he wasn't insistent, suggesting they should be open-minded and figure out what Anden liked. When they were together, Anden could feel Cory's jade almost as acutely as if he were wearing it himself; every sensation was heightened to an exquisite pitch. Cory's aura was as light and sunny as he was, like whipped cream or spring sunshine, gently sweet and addictive, as exciting and tangible to Anden as the sweat on his friend's skin or the smell of his hair. Sometimes Anden wondered how much of his newfound appetite was for Cory himself and how much of it was the amplifying effect of the other man's jade, but the combination was utterly intoxicating.

They saw each other every week, and sometimes more than once a week, if they could manage to sneak away from their respective obligations. Anden, who'd never in his life skipped class or showed up late for work, found himself cutting it close on a regular basis. Whenever his mind was idle, it drifted to thoughts of Cory, to erotic remembrances and anticipation of their next meeting, which was never soon enough, even if it was tomorrow, or in an hour.

He wondered if this was love.

Relayball started up again with the spring. They'd lost a few players and gained a few others, but Anden was part of the regular group now; others wanted him on their team, said hello to him around the neighborhood, showed friendly interest in him, and asked him questions about school or work or what it had been like growing up in Janloon.

Then summer arrived, and Cory got ready to leave on his long-anticipated travels, which would take him through the major cities along the coast of Whitting Bay, backpacking into the scenic wilderness of northeastern Espenia and back down into the heartland of the country before ending in Adamont Capita where he would begin law school at Watersguard University.

"Come with me," he suggested to Anden.

"I can't." Anden wanted to. The idea of six weeks alone with Cory was appealing in the extreme. But he was already registered to continue with the IESOL program through the summer, he didn't have either the funds or the days off from work, and he wasn't about to abuse the generosity of either the Hians or his cousins by asking them for money. Also, he imagined the Dauks would suspect his reasons for suddenly wanting to leave behind his obligations and travel alone with their son.

"What would your parents think, if they knew about us?" Anden asked.

Cory made a face. "What does it matter what my parents think?" In Kekon, queerness was considered a natural, if unfortunate permanent condition afflicting unlucky families, not unlike stone-eyes and children with birth defects. Cory explained that in Espenia it was commonly thought of as a sign of weak character, similar to addiction and indebtedness—a situation that some susceptible people were predisposed to fall into if not careful, but might recover from. "Bad luck can be turned around," was Cory's wry assessment of the prevailing attitude among Keko-Espenians. "Look, crumb," he explained to Anden, "I know my da. He's a traditionalist from the island, like you. What he cares about is that his son wears jade. He'll let me get away with just about anything else, but wearing jade, being true to our roots—that's an absolute must for him. I suspect at some point, my ma will start making noises about me getting married and having kids, but come on, I'm twenty-four! Plenty of time to think about that later."

The summer days were long and hot and smelled of dock fumes and piss. Seagulls wheeled in the sky and left shit on lawns. Tourists crowded the transit system. The streets swelled with traffic and street vendors, petty crime and road construction. Port Massy was an expansive world-class city in a league above even a burgeoning metropolis like Janloon; after living in it for sixteen months, Anden still felt as if the place completely defied familiarity. At times, it seemed to him that the sheer size and cultural scope of Port Massy only made his life shrink, made him want to take refuge in the routines and people he felt he could trust.

The Fifthday evening before Cory's departure, they played relay-ball as usual in the high school field. Anden was keenly aware of his friend's presence at all times. He felt as if he were a small planet caught in the gravity of a star, circling at a helpless distance from its radiance. He watched Cory scramble and leap for passes, laugh and joke, push his hair out of his eyes, and perform the silly dance he did when he put the ball between the point posts. Anden fumbled the next pass and the ball flew into the net. He cursed under his breath.

When they went to the grudge hall afterward, Sano, the doorman, clapped Cory on the back and said, "Last we'll see of you for a while, heh? Travel safe, and don't forget about us in Southtrap when you're a big shot attorney." Downstairs, Cory's friends had pushed several tables together. Derek's mother had baked a cherry spice cake, and people were signing messages in a notebook for Cory to take with him. Anden had no idea what to write in the book, so when it was his turn, he wrote, in careful Espenian: *Thank you for your friendship this year. You made me feel at home in Port Massy. Good luck in law school!* and then felt wretched about it. He turned to look for Cory again and saw him with his arm thrown over Derek's shoulder, laughing uproariously at something Sammy had said. Jealousy stabbed into Anden like a talon knife to the gut. At Watersguard, Cory would be immersed in new experiences and surrounded by new friends, confident young fellow Espenians. Anden turned away and took a piece of cake.

There were no duels in the grudge hall tonight, merely the usual entertainments. Dauk Losun and Dauk Sana were nowhere to be seen, perhaps so Cory could enjoy one of his last nights in Port Massy away from the watch of his parents, but Rohn Toro was present, sitting by himself at a small table by the door, quietly enjoying a drink and nodding to people who touched their foreheads in silent salute as they passed him.

"Did you hear about Tim Joro?" Anden overheard a man nearby talking to two others. "Died from a sudden heart attack. Only fifty-four years old. He was always drinking and getting in trouble with the law, though, so I guess I'm not surprised."

"What about his poor wife?" asked a woman.

"Moved back in with her parents." The conversation continued in more hushed tones. Anden glanced again at Rohn. Occasionally, someone would slide deferentially into the empty chair opposite the man and lean forward to speak to him quietly. Rohn's expression rarely changed; he would nod a little or ask a question, but he maintained the serenely impassive look of an animal at rest, alert even in its own lair. The people who came to speak to him did not linger or make social talk; they left so that others could come in their turn. Something about the understated gravity in these small interactions made Anden think of home, of the safety he'd always felt and taken for granted in No Peak territory.

Cory came up behind him and grabbed him in a bear hug around the shoulders. "Hey, crumb, it's toppers in here tonight," Cory said, letting go innocently. "You doing all right? Have you tried the cake? You want another drink?"

Anden turned around, forcing a smile onto his face. "No, I'm fine. It's a great party." His voice fell. "I'm happy for you. I'm just… wishing Adamont Capita wasn't so far away."

"I told you, it's only a three-hour bus ride, crumb," Cory exclaimed. "It'll be easy for me to come home to visit." Anden didn't feel comforted by this, but Cory said, "Come on, gang along with the rest of us." He led Anden back to the cluster of their usual relayball friends and cheerfully announced, "Hey, did you all know Anden's an uncle now?"

Abashed by the attention but proud nonetheless, Anden produced the wallet-sized photographs that Shae had sent him. One was of Niko sitting on the floor of the kitchen in the Kaul house wearing a green T-shirt and blue shorts, holding a plastic toy talon knife in one hand and a half-eaten cracker in the other. He was holding the cracker out, as if offering it to the photographer, probably Wen. The camera appeared to have caught him by surprise—he stared out of the photo with a slightly bewildered expression, crumbs on his chin, one eye squinted in a way that made him look so similar to Lan that it was sometimes painful for Anden to look at the picture.

He'd been astonished to learn of Niko's existence. Every time he thought about this boy he'd never met, he felt a deep pang of sympathy. Niko was an orphan too, brought into the Kaul home in the wake of tragedy (his mother and stepfather were killed in a terrible house fire, Shae had explained). No doubt he'd felt as lost and confused as Anden had been. If only there was some way he could reassure Niko, tell him not to worry, because unlike Anden, he was a Kaul in both blood and name.

The second photograph was of baby Ru, eight weeks old, though he must be nearly eight months by now. Anden had asked for more recent photographs in his last letter, but it took so long to get them, and he was not about to bother the Weather Man over such a small thing. Ru was cherubic and had a lot of dark hair; he held one pudgy fist cocked by his head and the other extended, as if in a fighting pose. It made Anden smile. His friends in the grudge hall exclaimed appreciatively over the photographs and handed them back. "They're so cute!" exclaimed Tami, the flirtatious young woman who Anden had learned was studying at Port Massy College to be a dental technician.

Derek said, "Are you going to share your own news, Tod?"

Tod looked around the circle and squared his shoulders. "I enlisted yesterday."

A brief silence followed this announcement. Cory said, "Good for you, Tod." Sammy said, "Yeah, that's toppers."

Tami's friend, Ema, asked, with a touch of concern, "What do your parents think?"

"My ma's worried about me being deployed in Oortoko, but she supports me. My da's against it, says it's a betrayal for me to fight on the side of the Shotarians after what they did to Kekon and to our family." Most Kekonese-Espenians came from families who'd fled the Shotarian occupation of their parents' and grandparents' generation. Many had distant relatives who'd been part of the One Mountain Society, who'd been tortured or executed.

"I don't see it that way at all," Tod said, a little angrily. "The occupation was thirty years ago, and besides, I wouldn't be fighting for the Shotarians, I'd be fighting for Espenia, to keep the 'guts from thinking they can take over the world. The recruiter I've been talking to said that they're really interested in getting more kespies like us to enlist."

"I've been thinking about it too," Sammy admitted.

"It's the only legal way to wear jade now," Tod pointed out. "And if the immigration records show that at least one of your parents came from Kekon, you'll be put on the fast track to special forces. If you make it in, you'll get a medical exemption: low or no SN1 dosing, no three-year restriction. And you won't be prosecuted for having worn jade prior to your service."

"You won't be able to wear any of your own jade, though," Cory pointed out. "I've heard they start everyone at square one. Even if you already have training in some of the traditional disciplines, they want to build you up their own way."

Tod stuffed his hands into his pockets and said, "I think it's worth it. I'd like it if people saw us as patriots, you know? If they realized that jade can be used for good, to serve Espenia."

Those two things, Anden might've pointed out, were not the same at all, but he held his tongue. This was the most bewildering conversation he'd heard during his time in Port Massy. A Green Bone serving the government that banned his jade? Willingly leaving his home to fight in a faraway country for people to whom he owed nothing, in a way that was almost certain to kill jadeless civilians and break aisho? It was astonishingly un-Kekonese.

Anden knew, from discussion at the Hians' dinner table and from the Kekonese-language newspaper that they subscribed to, that Kekon was hosting more than a hundred thousand ROE soldiers on Euman Island and providing economic and logistical support to the war effort, and still the Espenian government was pressuring the Royal Council for more. The Kekonese were understandably angry. Shae had been vilified for her former military ties to Espenia and been forced to defend her reputation in a near lethal clean-bladed duel against Ayt Mada—something Anden could barely imagine and felt a little sick even thinking about. The foreigners and their war were causing nothing but trouble for his cousins in No Peak.

Anden was sad to admit he'd lost some respect for Tod.

Cory apparently did not feel the same way. "I think it's toppers what you're doing, Tod. I hope that—" He didn't finish because a sudden motion caught his attention. Rohn Toro had leapt to his feet and was standing stock-still, his eyes unfocused in the way that Anden knew to be the expression of a Green Bone concentrating intensely on something in his Perception. A muted burst of rattling noise, like the popping of a dozen firecrackers, came from the street above. Gunfire.

Rohn tore up the stairs like a demon. A wave of confusion, then worry, then fear swept through the enclosed space of the underground grudge hall. Several people began to scramble for the stairs toward escape, but Cory reacted, just as he had when Tim Joro's wife had run out into the lanes of speeding traffic. "Don't go up there!" he shouted, in an urgent and commanding voice that Anden had never heard him use before. "Stay here, everyone." He looked to Tod and Sammy. "Green Bones will go first. Don't come out until one of us says it's safe."

Three men and a woman—Anden had seen them in the grudge hall before but didn't remember their names—rose from their seats and joined Cory, Tod, and Sammy as they ran for the stairs. Most of the people nearby moved aside to let them pass, but a few still tried to follow or push ahead of them. Protesting voices started to rise. At the foot of the stairs, Tod spun around and threw a wide, shallow Deflection that swept through the hall, knocking off hats and upending drink glasses. "Stay here, we said!" The Green Bones raced up the stairs.

Anden stood rooted to the spot for a second. Then he ran after them. He couldn't say why he did so; he wasn't a Green Bone, and he wasn't armed with anything except a compact talon knife. He didn't think about any of that. The only thing on his mind was the fact that Cory was disappearing up the stairs without him.

"Hey, islander, where are you going? They said to stay put!" Derek shouted after Anden, but neither he nor anyone else moved to actually stop him. On the main floor, Anden saw Mrs. Joek and the other food vendors crouched underneath their tables in fear. Rohn Toro was nowhere in sight. Anden caught up to Cory, who turned, eyes widening with astonishment and alarm. "What are you doing?" he hissed. "Go back downstairs with everyone else!"

A muffled, agonized groan came from behind the metal doors. "Sano," Tod said. He ran to the entrance and threw it open. The large doorman was slumped against the brick wall, gurgling, bleeding from a profusion of bullet wounds. Tod fell to the man's side. "Oh shit. *Shit*." One of the other men ran to help Tod pull Sano inside. A slick red river trailed after them across the concrete floor. "If only my ma was here, maybe she could do something…" Cory's voice was trembling. "Can anyone else do medical Channeling?" The others shook their heads, panic on their faces. Anden's hands closed helplessly; in the Academy, he'd learned the basics of Channeling for first aid, but it was no good to him now. Tod tried anyway, but Anden could see it was already too late; there was too much blood loss and the light was already going from Sano's eyes. Mrs. Joek began to crawl out from under her table, muffling sobs in the crook of her elbow. "No, stay there," Cory ordered her.

"Let's check the front," Sammy suggested. His voice was a hoarse whisper. "Where the fuck is Rohn?" They hurried to the unmarked interior double doors that led into the front of the building, the community center proper. Anden followed, even though Cory shouted at him again over his shoulder to stay behind. The community center was dark, the tables, chairs, and bookshelves discernible as shadowy outlines. The front windows of the building had been blown out by gunfire; shards of glass glittered on the carpet and the streetlight illuminated the bullet holes in the door and walls. A figure stood in front of the building, looking out at the street, framed by the jagged outline of the shattered window. The air from a nearby grate billowed Rohn's coat; otherwise, he was as still as a lamppost.

"Rohn-jen," Cory said as they came up cautiously behind the man, staring at the damage. Rohn held up a black-gloved hand to stop them. "They're coming back for another pass." Three cars barreled around the corner, engines roaring. A second later, machine gun fire clattered to life.

Cory fell upon Anden and dragged him to the ground as Rohn, Tod, Sammy, and the other Green Bones threw overlapping Deflections that sent the bullets veering into walls and furniture, into the ceiling where they shattered the lights, and into the floor where they gouged chunks out of the carpet. Anden hit the ground with his shoulder. He heard someone else let out a shout, of anger or pain. "Stay down!" Cory ordered, then his weight was gone as he leapt up to try and help the others.

Several items came flying through the broken windows and tumbled across the carpet. Anden, still on the floor, blinked at the red flame that rolled toward him: a lit rag, stuffed into the neck of a glass bottle full of liquid. In seconds, Anden realized, the flame would reach the gasoline and the homemade explosives would go off and light the building on fire.

Anden lunged forward and grabbed the bottle. He felt a sharp jab in the knee as a piece of glass cut into his skin. Scrambling to his feet, he ran for the broken window. He hefted the bomb to hurl it back out into the street. The burning fabric fell across the back of his hand and he cried out in pain. His throw fell short; it spun end over end toward the sidewalk.

A gloved, speed-blurred hand snatched the burning object out of the air like an intercepted relayball pass. In a burst of Strength and Lightness, Rohn Toro flew toward the black cars as they fled down the street, showing their taillights. Rohn heaved the lit bottle; it sailed like a missile over the top of the rear car, breaking on the hood and igniting in a small wall of fire as gasoline sprayed the windshield. The car swerved and its front right tire ran up onto the curb of the sidewalk. The grill struck a fire hydrant with a crunch of metal. The front doors flew open and two men stumbled out of the car.

Rohn strode up, drawing a revolver from the inside pocket of his jacket. He put two bullets in the chest of the driver. The other man swung up the Fullerton submachine gun he'd used to pepper the building. Rohn shoved him back hard with a left-handed Deflection; the shooter was thrown against the open door of the black car. Rohn shot him in the head. The man slumped to the asphalt, and Rohn put another bullet in his face. Rohn looked down the street; the other two cars were gone.

Anden turned around, clutching his hand, trying to see through the spots of red in his vision and the grit on his glasses. Cory had grabbed one of the other explosives and yanked out the rag; with Steeled hands he was snuffing out the flame, grimacing with pain and intense concentration as he suffocated the fire between his palms. One of the other Green Bones was disarming another unbroken bottle in the same way, but the others were desperately battling fires. One bomb had shattered against the concrete wall outside and was burning itself out, but another had broken against a table inside and lit the carpet on fire. One more had rolled into the room with the Deitist shrine and exploded; a fire raged in front of the replicated mural, igniting the frayed kneeling cushions.

Anden grabbed the nearest thing he could find—a wooly blue area rug from the daycare center—and threw it over the fire in the shrine, stomping it out with his shoes. The woman Green Bone ran into the room with a kitchen fire extinguisher, and after fumbling with the thing for a moment, sprayed foam over the remaining flames. She ran back out to help Tod and Sammy, who were dousing the other fire with buckets of water. In a few minutes, the community center was dark again. Anden staggered back into the main room. The faces around him were streaked with sweat and some were bleeding from glass cuts; hair and clothes and hands were singed. "Seer's balls," Tod gasped, bent over with his hands on his knees. "Those were crewboys—Kromner's people. Those *fuckers.*"

Rohn Toro stepped back through the broken window as the sound of sirens rose distantly. "Anyone with jade needs to leave now before the police arrive," Rohn said. "Split up and lie low for a while. Don't talk to any cops; you don't know anything about what happened here. I'll call and leave messages when it's safe."

"All the people still downstairs in the grudge hall—we need to get them out," Cory said.

"I'll take care of that," Rohn said. He turned to Anden. "You stay and help."

Anden nodded dumbly, though he had no idea why Rohn thought he would be useful. Cory protested, "Don't pull Anden into this; he shouldn't even be here."

"He already is," Rohn said. "I'll take him back to the Hians' house afterward." The sirens barreled closer; still, Cory hesitated. "If you're caught here now," Rohn growled, "you won't be going to Watersguard."

Cory looked as if he wanted to argue further, then closed his mouth. "Cory, you should go," Anden urged him. The Pillar's son gave Anden a distressed look, then turned to the others. "Okay, you heard Rohn-jen."

The six Green Bones left in a hurry, parting ways on the sidewalk and disappearing down different streets. Rohn turned to Anden. "I need time to get everyone out the back of the building before the police have a chance to detain and question them. The cops who show up might not be as easy to handle as the ones we regularly see; if they get a chance, they might harass and threaten people into pointing out who in the neighborhood's a Green Bone, maybe even point to the Dauk family." Rohn's eyes raked over Anden's face. "I need someone to go out front and delay the police for a while. Can you do that?"

Anden said, "I'll do it, Rohn-jen."

Rohn nodded and clapped him once on the shoulder with a gloved hand. Anden felt the momentary pressure of the man's jade aura, then Rohn strode back through the wreckage.

Anden went out to the front of the building and ran down the block toward the sound of the approaching sirens. When he saw the red-and-blue pulse of the squad car's lights, he stepped off the curb and waved his arms urgently. The vehicle came to a stop in front of him. Anden brought a hand up to shield against the glare of the headlights as the door opened and a middle-aged policeman stepped out. He had a thick mustache and squinty eyes—not one of the cops Anden had seen collect from the grudge hall before. "What seems to be the problem here?" the officer demanded. "Were you the one who called in a report of gunfire in the area?"

Anden had no idea who had called but he nodded at once. He understood why Rohn had given him this task. Anden wore no incriminating jade and looked Espenian. He could pose as a concerned non-Kekonese bystander, not anyone that might be connected to the grudge hall and to the Dauks in any way.

Out of spontaneous inspiration, Anden spoke with a mild Stepenish accent. "I saw three cars racing up and down the street." He had never been to Stepenland and did not speak a word of the language, but a few of his classmates in the IESOL program were Stepenish. A Stepenish accent was distinctly recognizable and easy to affect, and as Anden's Espenian had greatly improved but was not perfect, it would serve to hide the only obvious indication that he was Kekonese. "They were going too fast, and the people inside were waving guns and shooting out the windows."

"Typical bloody Southtrap goons," the police officer grumbled. "Did you see which direction they went?"

Anden nodded and pointed west, away from the community center. "That way. About five minutes ago."

The officer nodded in thanks, got back into his squad car, and drove in the direction Anden had indicated. Anden doubted he would be misled for long. In short order, he would discover the bodies of the dead men, the burned car, the bullet casings in the street and the shattered windows of the community center. But Anden had done as Rohn had asked: He'd bought time.

Anden waited until he was sure the squad car was gone and there were no others on the way. Glancing around to ensure he was truly alone and unwatched, he walked quickly, but not too quickly, back toward the community center, circling around the building to the grudge hall entrance at the back. Rohn Toro was closing the metal door. He was alone, and all the cars in the lot were gone. It appeared as if he'd succeeded in clearing out the building and sending everyone home. "I sent the policeman toward Fifty-Fourth Street," Anden said as he hurried up to the man. He looked down at the puddle of blood next to the grudge hall door. "What about Sano?"

Rohn said, "Mrs. Joek took him to the hospital. It was too late, though."

Anden muttered, "Let the gods recognize him."

"My da used to say that. But I don't think there are gods in

Espenia. Not our gods, anyway." Rohn began walking purposefully away from the building, crossing the parking lot and entering one of the nearby alleys. Anden followed. The sound of another siren rose up—perhaps the police officer had circled back and discovered the bodies and the car by now.

Rohn Toro stopped and turned to the brick wall beside them. He felt around the surface with his gloved hands, then closed his fingers around a slightly protruding brick. He pulled and it came loose, revealing a small, hollowed-out space. Carefully, the Horn took off his black leather gloves, folded them neatly, almost reverently, and pushed them into the small crevice. He replaced the brick so that all that was visible was the slight unevenness between it and its neighbor.

Rohn grimaced and leaned heavily against the wall for several seconds, as if suddenly nauseous. Anden recognized the signs of discomfort for what they were: jade withdrawal. Rohn Toro's jade was stitched into the lining of his leather gloves. When necessary, he could remove and hide them in a secret location until he had occasion to return and retrieve them. If he was stopped and questioned by the police later tonight, they could strip him naked and not find a bit of green on him.

Rohn straightened away from the wall. Hesitantly, Anden offered a hand to help the man; he had seen Rohn's abilities tonight and knew it could not possibly be easy to live as a Green Bone in this way, putting on and taking off so much jade at an instant. Rohn was not young either, perhaps fifty already—how could his body handle it? But the Horn was steady now; he gazed at Anden and his mouth moved with wry embarrassment, as if the younger man had witnessed him in a moment of vulnerability, fly open and pissing against the wall.

They continued down the unlit alleyway.

CHAPTER

34

⌒

The Clan's Friendship

The two months following the attack on the grudge hall were the worst that Anden had spent in Espenia, even worse than when he'd first arrived and been bereft with homesickness. Cory was gone; he'd called from the train station to say goodbye. He explained that he'd wanted to come over to see Anden in person, but it was too risky; not only were Kromner's crewboys still about, the police had begun randomly stopping Kekonese residents on the street and searching them for jade. The Dauks were glad their son was getting out of the city.

"I'm sorry I didn't listen when you told me to stay downstairs," Anden told Cory morosely over the phone. "I just wanted to help."

Cory was silent for a few seconds, then he sighed. "You know, I worry about you, islander. For a guy who seems so responsible, you sure do manage to get into trouble." An announcement came over the speakers at the train station, and Cory said, "I have to go, crumb.

I'll be back for Harvest'Eves break. Don't do anything stupid while I'm gone, okay?"

After they hung up, Anden was not only despondent at Cory's departure, but troubled by their conversation. After leaving the grudge hall that night, he and Rohn had walked three blocks away from the scene of destruction before Rohn hailed a taxi and instructed it to take them to the Hians' house. Mr. and Mrs. Hian were relieved and dismayed when they opened the door. While Anden ran the burn on the back of his hand under cold water at the kitchen sink, Rohn explained what had happened.

"Why did you have to get involved?" Mrs. Hian berated Anden as she rummaged bandages and a tube of antibiotic cream from the drawer. "You're a visiting student, why didn't you stay in the basement with the others where it was safe? You should've let the Green Bones handle it. If you'd been hurt or killed, what would we tell your family?" She was near tears.

Anden was mute with guilt, but Rohn said, "Don't be so hard on him; he couldn't help it. He's green in the soul, like Dauk-jen said. In fact, he was a great help." Rohn told them about how Anden had diverted the police for long enough that Rohn could get all the people safely out of the grudge hall. The Hians reluctantly agreed that was indeed a good thing to have done. Rohn drank some hot tea and got up to leave, saying that he had to work the next morning. It was sometimes hard for Anden to remember that Rohn Toro was not actually a clan Fist, that he had to earn money in an ordinary job, running a small moving company with a couple of friends.

As soon as Rohn left, the Hians insisted, "Anden-se, what happened tonight is going to cause big problems. Don't go anywhere near the grudge hall or the Dauks' house from now on; just go to school and work and back home again right away. If the police recognize you as the person who misled them, they'll want to question you."

Anden did as he was told, but over the next several days, he kept recalling Cory's look of alarm that night, the way he'd pulled Anden down to the ground away from machine gun fire, and how he'd gotten angry at Rohn and told him not to involve Anden at all: *He shouldn't even be here.*

Thus far, Anden had thought of Cory as the leader in their relationship, himself as the follower. Espenia was Cory's country, this was his city and his neighborhood; he was three years older than Anden; he was more socially gregarious and more sexually confident and experienced. None of this had bothered Anden, had indeed made Cory only more attractive and alluring. But for the first time now, Anden also saw himself as the weaker of the two of them. Mrs. Hian was right; Cory was a Green Bone and Anden was not. When he'd rushed into danger, the Pillar's son had been forced to protect him. If their relationship lasted, would this always be the case?

Anden was deeply troubled by the idea. He'd been born to a Green Bone family, adopted and raised by Green Bones, and trained at a Green Bone school. All his life he'd been taught to stand up not only for his own honor and reputation, but that of his family and clan, and to defend those who were weaker, those without jade who fell under the clan's protection. Even as an exile from No Peak, even without jade, he hadn't yet faced the reality that *he* was now one of those people who needed defending. Everyone Anden had ever been close to, everyone important in his life, was a Green Bone. He had no template for how to be a member of the Kaul family, indeed, how to be a Kekonese man at all, without jade. He had a sudden vision of Cory one day following in his father's footsteps and becoming the Pillar of Southtrap, with Anden relegated to being his secret lover, a vulnerable boyfriend who never fit into Espenia on his own terms, and the thought made Anden feel, for the first time in nearly a year, a fresh pang of shame over his situation.

It didn't help his mood that he'd lost the parts of his routine that he'd come to enjoy the most. Relayball was put on hiatus for two weeks following the incident, and afterward, he couldn't muster the enthusiasm to attend knowing that Cory wasn't there. The grudge hall was indefinitely shut down; Anden snuck by the building once during the day and saw police tape crisscrossing the broken front entrance.

The Port Massy police questioned the residents of Southtrap but learned very little. No one claimed to have been there at the time that the shooting happened. No one said anything about why the community center had been targeted. That same night elsewhere in Southtrap, Kekonese businesses had been vandalized and walls were spray-painted with slurs, but no one pointed out the obvious to the police: that the crimes were racially motivated, that Kromner's crewboys were targeting the Kekonese for their gambling operations and jade.

Anden heard rumors from Derek and Tami and a few others he managed to run into occasionally on his way to and from school and work. Dauk had sent Rohn Toro with a few of his men to retaliate against Kromner's Crew. Two bookmaking operations were attacked and robbed, and two crewboys suspected of being among the drive-by shooters were found dead with broken necks. In response, the attacks on Kekonese businesses and civilians increased: The barbershop that Mr. Hian had been going to for eight years was set ablaze; an elderly Green Bone was ambushed and beaten outside of his home and his few pieces of jade stolen; a local shopkeeper falsely suspected of being a Green Bone was attacked at a bus stop. No arrests were made.

The Hians' eldest son, a perpetually harried but well-meaning man in his early forties whom Anden had met over several polite but shallow interactions in the past, came over to the house to try to convince his parents to move out of the neighborhood and into the suburbs. Anden sat upstairs in his bedroom trying not to eavesdrop, but there was no avoiding it.

"Southtrap's turning into an ethnic ghetto," their son argued. "Wouldn't you rather live somewhere with more space and less crime?" But the Hians insisted that they did not want to move. They liked the location, they had friends here; where else could they walk to a Kekonese grocery store? Maybe, Mrs. Hian complained, if their sons were considerate enough to give them grandchildren while they were still alive, they would have a reason to move; otherwise, what was the point?

––––––––––

Dauk Losun called and asked if he and his wife might pay the Hians a visit one afternoon. He explained that they would like to invite the

Hians to their home, but the police knew that Sana was connected to the grudge hall and suspected the couple was not telling the whole truth about the shooting and arson, so they were paying extra close attention to their part of the neighborhood. The Dauks did not want to put Mr. and Mrs. Hian to any trouble, however, so they would bring something to eat. And could Anden please be there as well?

The Hians nervously agreed, although Mrs. Hian cooked a large amount of food anyway, so when the Dauks arrived with white plastic bags filled with half a dozen takeout dishes, there was far too much to eat. Extra chairs were brought into the Hians' kitchen. Anden saluted the Dauks respectfully, but he was on edge. Why had the Pillar asked to see him? Did it have something to do with Cory? Did he know about them? Would he place the blame on Anden and forbid them from seeing each other?

"How is Coru?" Mrs. Hian asked the Dauks. "Has he settled into AC now? Have his law school classes at Watersguard started yet?"

"They started this week," Dauk Sana said, passing out paper plates and plastic cutlery. "He sounds happy there, but that's Coru—always free spirited. He hasn't had to work hard yet, so we'll see. I'm just glad he's safely away and busy."

Anden had forgotten that law school had already begun. Cory hadn't phoned him from Watersguard, not yet. He was probably busy. Moving in, student orientation, new classes...Still. A curl of hurt turned the food in Anden's mouth tasteless.

As they ate, Dauk Losun asked, "How are you all doing? Has there been any trouble lately?" He listened, nodding sympathetically, as Mrs. Hian talked about how the neighborhood wasn't safe anymore and how their son wanted them to move away. Mr. Hian said, "Kromner's thugs are hurting innocent people and businesses, and the police do nothing."

Dauk Sana said, "It's because they're paid by the Crews to look the other way. We have some of the police in our pocket, it's true, but they have more. At the end of the day, Kromner and his men are Espenians, and we are foreigners, so the police take their side. And so do people in general, because they're told by the news that Kekon is harming the war effort in Oortoko by hoarding all of the world's jade, even though that's not true. Sometimes they even confuse us for Shotarians."

Mrs. Hian cried, "What can be done, Dauk-jens, if the law won't allow people to wear jade to protect the community, but the police can't be trusted? It is so unjust."

Dauk Losun's expression was grim. "I'm afraid this question has been keeping me awake at night for months."

"It's true," his wife said. "He has to take anxiety pills."

Anden listened to all this with a growing sense of anger and disgust. In Janloon, the combatants in a clan war would not attack blameless civilians, not even if they were Abukei or foreigners. If either side started doing that, what was to stop a society from losing all sense of aisho and descending into savagery? And the police! They had taken tribute from the grudge hall—Anden had seen it with his own eyes—yet they did not protect it. Dauk Losun had likened the local law enforcement to another clan, but they were not a clan at all, simply another predator, like the Crews. Meanwhile, it was the Kekonese who were persecuted and treated like criminals simply for wearing jade to defend themselves and manage their own affairs.

Dauk Losun's heavy frame seemed to sag into the kitchen chair. In a resigned voice, he said, "I've been in this country for forty-five years. In truth, I'm almost Espenian. Maybe that's why I prefer to solve problems quietly, with money and influence. But all these years, I also knew we could back up our words with force if needed, because we were the only ones with jade, and the only ones who could use it.

"But times have changed for the worse. With jade now illegal, the Crews no longer see the need to respect us. They know we can't retaliate against them without making ourselves vulnerable to prosecution. The experienced Green Bones from the old country, the ones to really fear, like Rohn Toro—they are few and aging, and the younger ones who were born here are not as well trained or serious. Look at my own son for example, as much as I love him. Or someone like Shun Todo, who has talent in the jade disciplines but is too Espenian—he wants to leave home and join the military." Dauk shook his head. "I'm worried there's no longer any way for us to stand up to tyrants like Blaise Kromner. Rohn is the greenest man in this city, but he's only one man. And I lie awake at night afraid they'll get to him; sooner or later, they'll kill my good friend. It seems we have no choice but to agree to whatever terms the Bosses lay on us: paying their protection rackets, shutting down our grudge hall, letting their drug dealers and pimps into our neighborhood."

No one was eating anymore. Mrs. Hian covered her mouth in distress and her husband put a comforting hand on her back. Anden had been picking heartlessly at his meal, but now he noticed that the Dauks were both looking at him. Slowly, Anden met the Pillar's eyes. Dauk Losun continued speaking to the Hians, but his gaze remained on Anden. "I've thought long and hard about the terrible situation we're in, and now I have to ask something of our young friend, Anden. And because you're his host family, I must ask it of you as well."

Dauk Losun said to Anden, "You're from the old country, and your family rules one of the most famous and powerful Green Bone clans in Kekon. I still have friends on the island and rumors reach even across the Amaric Ocean, so I've known for a long time that you're more than you say you are. You and your cousins went to war against a stronger enemy that might've destroyed your clan, but you prevailed."

When Anden had first met Dauk Losun, he'd thought him too homey and unimpressive a man to be called Pillar. Now Dauk's wrinkled eyes were steely and unwavering. Anden understood what was being asked of him; he recalled that he'd anticipated this since that first time he'd dined at the man's table and accepted his help.

Dauk said, "The Kaul family has far greater resources than we do. Jade, money, people, even influence over governments. Perhaps they have no reason to care about what happens here in Espenia, but if there's a chance they would offer their friendship in some way, it might help us now, when we have nothing else to rely on."

Quietly, Anden said, "Dauk-jen, if I had sway over my cousins in the No Peak clan, I wouldn't be in Espenia."

Dauk Sana held up a finger and made a skeptical noise in her throat. "I've seen and heard enough about you to believe that your cousins, if they have any sense or cunning at all, wouldn't throw you away. How can you be sure they didn't send you to Espenia for other reasons? They're your family, after all."

Mrs. Hian stood up from the table and took the green ceramic teapot from the kitchen shelf, the one that Anden had brought with him and given to his host family on behalf of the clan on the first day he'd arrived in Espenia—a token of the clan's friendship, the promise of a favor to be returned. She placed it in front of Anden, and said, "For the sake of the Kekonese community, Anden-se. If you have any affection for us, as we have for you, we beg you to please try."

CHAPTER

35

~

Stranger Allies

A year after the Republic of Espenia entered the Oortokon War, the secretary of international affairs made his first visit to Kekon as part of an eight-country state tour. He was welcomed by a formal military procession in front of Wisdom Hall, as well as a crowd of silent antiwar protestors and scathing editorial commentary from the Kekonese press. On the last day of his three-day visit, the secretary held a closed-door meeting on Euman Island Naval Base with Chancellor Son Tomarho, selected members of his cabinet in the Royal Council, and the top leadership of No Peak. The government of the ROE had learned over time that political power on Kekon was openly underwritten by the jade warrior class, and nothing in that small country was ever accomplished without the backing of at least one of the major Green Bone clans.

Hilo tried to leave the dealings with politicians to Shae whenever he could get away with it, but he couldn't reasonably refuse a meeting with such a high-level Espenian diplomat without appearing to be deliberately insulting the ROE, something his Weather Man would counsel him against in no uncertain terms for a variety of reasons. Hilo, Shae, and Kehn were transported by private helicopter from Janloon to the airfield at Euman. When they arrived, they were met by the commanding officer, who Shae recognized and introduced as Colonel Leland Deiller, and his executive officer, a man by the name of Yancey, who escorted them across the grounds.

As they walked past a large training field, the low collective hum of unexpected jade auras caught Hilo's attention. Two lines of soldiers carrying heavy packs of gear faced a smooth ten-meter wall. At a signal from their instructor, the first line sprinted forward, turned their backs to the wall, and crouched in readiness. The second line raced toward their comrades, who boosted them into the air in one simultaneous heaving of jade-fueled Strength. The heavily laden soldiers flew Light and hoisted themselves to the top of the wall—at least a majority of them did, a number did not make it and fell back to the ground. Those who succeeded turned around and used their own Strength to seize their fellows at the peak of their bounds and haul them up alongside.

Yancey noticed Hilo's interest and explained, "Cadets of the Navy Angels, the most elite special ops division in the ROE military. Only thirty percent of those recruits will make it through basic IBJCS training." Yancey had to nearly shout to be heard over Euman's stiff wind.

At Hilo's questioning glance, Shae translated both the officer's words and the unfamiliar acronym. Hilo had heard of the Integrated Bioenergetic Jade Combat System—the long and sterile term the Espenians used to describe their version of the jade disciplines, adopted and modified from what they knew of Kekonese methods—but he had not actually seen it before. Kehn muttered, in a low aside, "You've got to hand it to the Espenians. They know how to cook scraps into a meal." A Green Bone skilled in Lightness could get over the wall unaided. From their auras, it seemed the Espenian soldiers wore only as much jade as a middling graduate of Kaul Du Academy, but IBJCS trained them to act together to amplify their collective effectiveness. Kekonese culture revered the prowess of the superior jade warrior, accorded respect to the victors of duels, celebrated the heroism of patriotic Green Bone rebels in times past—but the Espenians took jade and issued it as military equipment with unsentimental uniformity. Hilo's mouth twitched in a grimace of distaste. He was certain it was no coincidence the Green Bone visitors had been escorted along this path and allowed to witness the demonstration on the training field. Whatever the Espenians wanted to talk about this afternoon, they were underscoring their message by situating it in the center of their military presence on Kekon and prefacing it with a reminder that they, too, could use jade.

They reached the main building and were shown into a large, if spartan, meeting room, containing office chairs around a gray table, and the flag of the Republic of Espenia hanging on one wall. Secretary Corris, whom Hilo recognized from media photos, was already in the room, engaged in a conversation with another man that Shae whispered quickly was Ambassador Gregor Mendoff. The secretary and ambassador broke off their discussion and came over to shake hands. Quire Corris was a typical broad-chested, blue-eyed Espenian man who Hilo thought looked almost the same as Mendoff, without the mustache. Like many Espenians, he spoke animatedly, barely pausing long enough for the translator standing at his elbow to finish relaying his words, but there was also a certain reserve in his manner, a calculating, mercenary quality in his frank gaze. It wasn't that the Espenians were greedy, precisely, Hilo thought, but they always seemed to be holding back some human warmth, shrewdly considering how to make the deals to get what they wanted.

Chancellor Son and a handful of other members of the Royal Council were also present. "Kaul-jen," said Son, saluting him. If Secretary Corris and the other Espenians were surprised at either the Pillar's youth relative to the other men in the room, or the deference paid to him by the official head of government, they were careful not to show it.

Besides the leaders of No Peak, there was one other individual in the room wearing jade: General Ronu Yasugon, senior military advisor to the Royal Council, and perhaps the only person in Kekonese government who could be said to be an exception to the ironclad cultural and legal prohibition against jade in political office. This one violation was deemed acceptable because, like medicine, martial education, and religious penitence, joining the Kekonese military was one of the few ways for a Green Bone to honorably renounce clan oaths and pledge loyalty to another calling. Unlike those other professions, however, jade-wearing individuals could not go into military service straight after graduation; they were expected to spend at least one year as a Finger. The clans made certain that most of the young jade talent went first to them; after a certain period, less promising Fingers were subtly or not-so-subtly encouraged to serve their country in uniform. General Ronu was an exception; he'd left the Mountain as a junior Fist to begin a military career eighteen years ago, and he wore more jade than most officers—a watch with six stones set into the steel band. He saluted Hilo, and the Pillar touched his forehead in greeting. "General."

When everyone was seated, Secretary Corris began the meeting by talking about what a pleasant and productive visit he'd enjoyed, and thanking the government and the people of Kekon for being such generous hosts. He spoke at length about the importance of Kekon-Espenia relations and the premier's commitment to continued strengthening of the political, economic, and military alliance between their two nations. "As different as our history and cultures are, we have one crucial thing in common," said Corris, pausing to allow the translator to catch up. "A fierce sense of national pride and independence, and an equally fierce loyalty to our friends and allies."

Those were at least two things, not one, Hilo felt like pointing out, but Ambassador Mendoff nodded and smiled in agreement, and the Kekonese listened politely to the foreigner's hyperbole. Corris cleared his throat and said in a graver tone, "As you know, gentlemen—and ladies," he added with a quick glance at Shae, "the Republic of Espenia has committed considerable resources to defending the sovereignty of Shotar against Ygutanian expansionism. Unfortunately, at this point in the campaign, it's clear that we still have a long way to go to win the war in Oortoko."

This was a rather significant admission. The Espenians, ever confident in their military might, had anticipated victory in Oortoko within a year. The eastern Shotarian province, however, was proving to be a difficult battleground for them. The terrain was hot, arid, and mountainous with plenty of places for the rebels to hide their camps and blend in among the civilian population. The ROE was unparalleled in the world in naval strength and also boasted a massive quantity of ground troops and bombs, but they were not accustomed to guerrilla warfare against entrenched enemies.

Colonel Deiller spoke up. "Due to the nature of the military engagement, small, nimble, special operations teams are proving the key to success in the Oortokon conflict. The physical and extrasensory advantages afforded by bioenergetic Kekonese jade allow our elite forces to operate with greater precision and effectiveness, thus minimizing civilian casualties."

Hilo's eyes narrowed in impatience. Was this entire meeting another of the foreigners' attempts to persuade Kekon to sell them more jade? Shae had already made it clear to Mendoff and Deiller that the Kekon Jade Alliance would not be increasing quotas.

Secretary Corris raised his hands. "Now, I understand the issue of jade exports has been discussed at length before, and although my government is disappointed we can't see eye to eye, we appreciate the pressures you face from prevailing public sentiment about the preservation of your natural resources. What we haven't fully discussed yet is the potential for Kekon to provide military support in Oortoko."

A frisson of discomfort traveled through the Kekonese side of the room. Chancellor Son leaned forward and placed his ample elbows on the table. "Secretary," he said, speaking slowly for the translator, "we're honored by your visit and we value the relationship between our nations, but you must understand: We are a small island nation. We've never committed aggression against other countries. In fact, as General Ronu can explain, our military is not designed for such things."

Ronu was sitting slightly behind and to the left of the chancellor. At the sign that he'd been given permission to speak, he straightened and said, "We maintain a modest force of sixty thousand active-duty personnel to defend Kekon's surrounding waters, airspace, and borders." It was, indeed, a small number even for a country of only twelve million people. The military was accorded nominal respect, but hardly considered a vital national institution by the Kekonese.

"I think that's rather understating the matter, isn't it, Chancellor?" said Ambassador Mendoff, once Son's and Ronu's words had been smoothly relayed into Espenian. "Your official army includes several thousand personnel equipped with bioenergetic jade. And your real combat strength lies in the civilian population. When you take that into account, it's no exaggeration to say you have the largest reserve force of jade-enhanced soldiers in the world."

The discomfort deepened. Chancellor Son tugged at the collar of his shirt and glanced at Hilo, who was the only other person on the Kekonese side seated directly at the table in a position to speak with the same authority as Son. Slightly behind and to either side of him, Hilo could sense the aura of his Weather Man crackling with wary vexation and the rumble of displeasure from his Horn. The Espenians were astute—they understood that Kekon's actual fighting capability was to be found in the ranks of the Green Bone clans—but their arrogance was staggering and offensive.

Hilo hated diplomatic bullshit. He considered letting Shae speak in his place; she was used to dealing with the foreigners and would no doubt give a tactful response. Instead he leaned forward. The Kekonese politicians around the table edged back. Fixing a look on the foreign secretary, the Pillar said, "Those jade soldiers, as you call them, live by a code that you wouldn't understand." Though his face retained a mild friendly neutrality, there was an edge to Hilo's voice that made the translator hesitate a second before relaying his words. "Green Bones defend Kekon and fight for the clan they swear oaths to, not for any foreign government."

"You're the leader of your clan, Mr. Kaul-jen," said Secretary Corris, without missing a beat. "So I assume it's up to you to decide what your clan's interests are. And from what I understand, it would seem they're aligned with ours. Your people have been partnering with us to combat illegal jade and drug trafficking, seeking investment opportunities, and lobbying for reduced barriers to international business between our countries. Unlike the other prominent clan leader in this country, whose public rhetoric has been downright antagonistic and jingoistic, your family seems invested in continued good relations, which we greatly appreciate. That's why we're making an effort to maintain an open dialogue with you." No Kekonese person in the room had failed to notice that Ayt Mada and representatives of the Mountain clan were not present.

Secretary Corris continued, "Premier Galtz, myself, and the secretary of the Industry Department are prepared to pass several of the trade reforms you've been asking for. We've already lifted restrictions on foreign real estate ownership, and we're looking at reduced tariffs on Kekonese imports in select industries and a streamlined visa approval process for Kekonese expatriates working or pursuing higher education in Espenia. Of course, certain Kekonese companies and organizations that inspire our confidence would be deemed preferred partners." The secretary inclined his head to make it clear that his statement applied to the people in this room.

Hilo was somewhat surprised; the Espenians were not as ignorant about the clans as he'd assumed. They were offering something that would give No Peak an advantage over the Mountain, and they knew enough to understand how valuable that was to the Kaul family. Hilo suspected that if he turned to consult with his Weather Man, she could quantify the value in terms of dien—but there was no point. Everything was a transaction to the Espenians—and some prices were too high to pay.

Hilo laid his hands on the table and said, "My Weather Man has been working hard to expand our businesses, so naturally we'd like to see all those things you mention come true." Shae had once told him that the Espenians interpreted the word *no* merely as the starting point for negotiation, so he paused to make it absolutely clear that he meant what he said next. "But as Pillar of my clan, I will never send Green Bones to fight for strangers, no matter what you offer."

The secretary appeared unperturbed by Hilo's blunt refusal. "Kekon is the linchpin of our strategic presence in the East Amaric. If we can't count on your military contribution to this vital effort, then it's all the more important that we have your staunch political support."

Chancellor Son let out a cough. "Kekon is hosting more foreign troops on our soil than at any time since we achieved independence in the Many Nations War. That is *considerable* support."

"It's to our mutual benefit," said Colonel Deiller. "The presence of ROE forces on Euman Island acts as a deterrent to aggression in this region and ensures your country's safety."

"A few months ago," Hilo said in a soft, almost placid voice, "I spoke to a couple whose sixteen-year-old daughter was raped by Espenian soldiers. Ask Mr. and Mrs. Eyun if the foreign troops gambling, whoring, and getting drunk on shore leave in our city streets is good for *safety*."

Ambassador Mendoff winced in distaste. "Tragic, isolated incidents notwithstanding," he said, undeterred, "what we're concerned about is Kekon's willingness to stand firm on issues of regional security, namely, acting as a reliable bulwark against the growing threat of Ygutan."

"Ygutan's aims are to expand its territory and extend its influence in any way possible," added Colonel Deiller. "The Directorate in Dramsk and their body of religious leaders, the Protecks, are preaching a vision of manifest national destiny in which the Ygut Coalition stretches across the continent of Orius from the Amaric to the Ullyric Ocean. If, God forbid, Oortoko falls to the Ygutanians, Dramsk will be emboldened to commit further acts of aggression. Kekon's proximity to the Orius continent, its unique resources, and its strategic position in the West Tun Sea would make it an obvious target."

The Kekonese politicians exchanged sullen glances but did not respond to Deiller's assertions. An attack by Ygutan was possible, but Hilo was certain the Espenians were overstating the danger. The truth was that an Ygutanian victory in Oortoko would have a far more certain and immediate consequence for Kekon: It would cause the ROE to panic and pour even more military resources into the region, to assert control over Kekon before their enemies did, all in the stated interests of "defending" their allies.

"We're aware," said Secretary Corris, "that there's a growing desire from the civilian population, and from some parts of your government, for Kekon to increase its humanitarian involvement in the war, particularly in regards to admitting and resettling refugees."

Chancellor Son nodded warily. Mounting civilian casualties in the Oortoko region had captured the public consciousness; people were moved by the plight of the ethnic Kekonese in the region—those who'd been relocated to Shotar generations ago, oppressed and discriminated against by Shotarian society, and were now suffering in a bloody contest between foreign powers. Even the prevalent stereotype of Keko-Shotarians as mixed blood, nephrite-wearing barukan gangsters had not discouraged grassroots calls to repatriate Oortokon refugees. *That*, Hilo mused cynically, was the undeniable power of television. At what other time in history had the Kekonese ever bothered to care about what was happening to people overseas?

"The human sentiment is understandable, but it poses a security risk that we're not sure you've fully analyzed," said Ambassador Mendoff. It irritated Hilo that the Espenians kept changing who was speaking, so he was forced to continue shifting his attention. Secretary Corris was supposedly the highest-ranking person on their side, and it seemed the others were in agreement with him, so why was it necessary for them all to take turns jumping in unprompted?

As if to underscore Hilo's thoughts, Colonel Deiller said, "Ygutanian agents are prevalent in Oortoko, and our intelligence has confirmed that there are ties between the rebels and Keko-Shotarian organized crime groups. Unless Kekon is vigilant about guarding its borders, it risks Ygutanian infiltration, which would be an unacceptable danger to our military assets here."

"*Your* assets," Chancellor Son echoed dubiously.

"It's in your interest to take this threat seriously," Colonel Deiller responded. "Currently, there are no restrictions on travel within Kekon. Civilians move freely between Euman Island and the rest of the country. That would change if there were Ygutanian agents within your population who could steal military information, sabotage our facilities, or send bombing coordinates to Dramsk. They might even work to undermine your government and install a more Ygutanian-friendly regime. The best line of joint defense against such unacceptable risks is to prevent them from entering in the first place."

No one replied for a moment. Then Hilo's mouth curved into a humorless, sardonic smile. "You want us to keep out other foreigners, in order to protect the ones that are already here."

Secretary Corris pursed his lips to one side and gave a small shrug that, while not in overt agreement with Hilo's statement, was ample confirmation. "What we want is the assurance that our allies in Kekon will do their utmost to influence public policy and legislation in a way that preserves the long-term strength of our relationship and our mutual security. We want to feel confident that you'll stand against other, more shortsighted, rabble-rousing voices—and we'd like to help you do that, by making it economically advantageous to remain our friends."

Hilo nodded, then stood up. The Espenians had said everything they'd intended to say, and he was tiring rapidly of the long-winded sugary political talk, not to mention the continued pretense that this was anything but a bribe, made at the highest level. Gods in Heaven, he'd been a Fist and then the Horn for years before he was Pillar; he knew all about the delicate balance of threat and inducement required to get what one wanted from reluctant assets. Shae and Kehn stood up with him, and after a beat, Chancellor Son and the other Kekonese politicians did so as well. Secretary Corris followed their movement with faintly raised eyebrows.

"Ayt Madashi is my enemy," Hilo said, "but that doesn't mean you're my friend. I'll deal with you and your government so long as it benefits No Peak. But you're still visitors here. Don't ask for too much, or presume to control Kekon. Other foreigners have tried before you."

When the translator had finished repeating Hilo's words, Secretary Corris smiled, showing a flash of white teeth, and to the surprise of everyone in the room, raised clasped hands and touched them to his forehead in the traditional Kekonese salute. It was done with just the right amount of deliberation to be a pointedly casual retort without being overtly mocking.

"May the gods shine favor on your clan, as they say in your country, Mr. Kaul-jen," said the Espenian diplomat. "Or as they say in mine: 'May you see and bear the Truth.'"

"Fucking Espenians," Hilo said, after dinner that evening.

Kehn grumbled in agreement and pushed back his empty plate. "Dealing with them is like wrestling a creature with many heads. One head's smiling at you, another's stealing your food, a third's taking a bite out of your ass." The Horn crossed his arms. "They knew we wouldn't send Green Bones to fight on their side in that hellhole. They only said it so they could be more forceful asking for what they thought they could really get."

"Spennies—they'd line up to sell their own mothers just to see who could get the best price." Tar was leaning back with a contentedly lazy look on his face, having spent the afternoon with his sometimes lover Iyn Ro instead of on Euman Naval Base.

"You could've let me mention a few things in that meeting," Shae said to Hilo, a little sourly. "Such as the fact that the proposed trade agreements benefit their economy as well. Manufacturing capacity in Espenia has been shifted to the war effort and they need foreign trade to meet consumer demand. So it's not as if the leverage they're trying to apply is one-sided."

"There were already enough people in that meeting trying to sound like the smartest one in the room," Hilo replied. "The bottom line is we're stuck: Most people hate the foreigners being here and want to suck on Ayt's teat every time she whips out another of her speeches, but we've tied ourselves to their godsdamned money."

Shae crossed her arms in response to Hilo's squint. "You're looking

at me as if it's my fault the Espenians are demanding and unscru-
pulous. Yes, they'll try to take advantage of us, they'll make offensive requests, they'll bargain for the most they can get out of every
situation—that's their way. But they're still our strongest edge over
the Mountain." The destruction of the Mountain's shine factories in
Ygutan five months ago had dealt Ayt a serious financial blow. Shae
was keen to press the advantage by cutting off their rival's other overseas investment options, especially in Espenia, where the Weather
Man's office was focusing on expansion. "The Mountain is still in
a stronger position than we are with their core businesses in Kekon.
But if we secure trade agreements that benefit us and lock them out
of the Espenian market, *we* could be the larger clan in five to ten
years."

Hilo approved of Shae and her people eking out every economic
victory they could over the Mountain—anything to weaken Ayt
Mada's position as a leader and strengthen internal opposition against
her—but he was not willing to wait five to ten years for results.
K-Star Freight was prospering, raising the Ven family's prominence
in the Mountain, but Ven Sando's opposition to his Pillar had not yet
spawned any concrete action that would see Ayt feeding worms in
the Heaven Awaiting Cemetery.

"Ayt's been too quiet lately," Hilo mused. Perhaps she wasn't as
eager to make public appearances now that Shae had cut off half
her ear, but Hilo wasn't so optimistic as to think she had been dissuaded by her failed attempt to oust Shae and bring down No Peak
in the process. More likely she was simply gathering her resources for
some other attack. "Money's not enough; we need to keep stirring the
Mountain's shit so it doesn't settle. Have you dug into the Iwe family,
like I asked?"

Shae frowned at the way Hilo changed the subject, but she said,
"There's nothing on Iwe Kalundo. He wears two jade rings on his
smallest fingers, and a band of three stones on his left wrist, and has
never had any problems so far as anyone knows." Shae opened her
hands and turned them up. "*But*...his aunt nearly died of an SN1
overdose two years ago and doesn't wear any jade now. Both Iwe's

youngest brother and his cousins are addicts, and they use the same supplier—a dealer in the Crossyards who's rumored to quietly sell the highest-quality shine to Green Bones."

Hilo eyed his sister, impressed. "How did you find this out?"

"Rats are everywhere these days," Shae said, so smugly that Hilo smirked. Gossip about drug addiction and vice was not exactly the sort of intelligence he'd imagined the Weather Man's network would be able to deliver, but if Shae was exercising some creativity in her role, he wasn't about to complain.

Wen smiled and spoke up. Long gone, it seemed, were the days when she would hold her tongue except when she and Hilo were alone. "If we know who to look for, it shouldn't take long for Kehn's Fingers to find this dealer."

"Do it quietly," Hilo said to the Horn. "Tell me when you've found him, but don't act unless I say so. You have enough to do already, handling the raids on Ti Pasuiga."

Kehn's wife, Lina, came back into the dining room with Ru, his diaper freshly changed, and handed him back to Wen. She kissed her husband goodnight and said that she was going back to their house to finish marking term papers. Kehn nodded, gazing after her with the obvious besotted look of a newly married man. Hilo smiled to see it. The wedding last month had been a lavish event befitting the Horn's status, and between Lina's enormous extended family and all the Fists and Fingers of No Peak, it had taken up most of the General Star Hotel. Tar made a teasing face of mock disgust and threw a napkin at his brother.

Kehn tossed the napkin back at Tar, his usual gruffness reasserting itself as he returned his attention to the table. "Our attacks on Ti Pasuiga—there's good and bad news," he said. "The good news is that we've killed dozens of Zapunyo's rockfish, confiscated hundreds of kilos of raw scrap, and about five hundred million dien worth of cut jade."

Not for the first time, Hilo envied his brother-in-law. The duties of the Horn were difficult and dangerous, but simpler and more tangible. "The bad news," Kehn went on, "is that clever dog Zapunyo keeps getting more creative. I've seen jade disguised as buttons and children's toy marbles, packed in frozen seafood, or hidden in canned goods. We catch some of it, but the Espenian navy catches more. Another reason why Shae-jen is right. We need to stay in bed with the foreigners if we want to put that Uwiwan dog out of business."

Tar shook his head at the irony. "The spennies start a war that grows the black market for jade. We get them to help us shut down the smuggling that they caused in the first place, and in return they expect us to be grateful and do their bidding like children."

The political demands of the Espenians, the constant threat of the Mountain, the dirty schemes of Ti Pasuiga—any one of them was more than enough to have to deal with, but they were all connected in inextricable ways that made Hilo frustrated and uneasy. "It's getting late," he said. "That's enough talk for tonight."

Kehn and Tar departed for their own homes. Niko came down the stairs to say that he'd had a nightmare and didn't want to be alone. Wen handed Ru to Hilo and rose with a pregnant groan to settle the boy back to bed. The Pillar and the Weather Man were left alone in the dining room except for the drowsy child in Hilo's arms and the sound of Kyanla doing dishes in the kitchen. Shae appeared deep in thought; Hilo noticed that she'd developed the habit of rubbing absently at her bare throat where her two-tier jade choker had once rested.

Shae dropped her hand and turned to him. "I'm going to Espenia for a couple of weeks," she said. "I've been thinking about what Anden told me over the phone, and I think we should meet these people, these Green Bones in Port Massy. One thing was clear from the meeting on Euman Island today: The Espenians have leverage over us because they have people here, and they know more about what's happening in our country than we know about what's going on in theirs. It seems everything the Espenians do affects us in some way, and from what Anden's said, their largest city is turning into a battleground for jade, just like here at home. I need to go over there and learn more."

Hilo considered her words. "No," he said after a minute. "You need to stay here. There's too much political bullshit going on with the Royal Council, the KJA, and the Espenians these days. You can't afford to be gone from Kekon that long in case something happens, and now that you have the support of the clan back under you, the *last* thing you should do is leave Ship Street and travel to Espenia again." The Weather Man opened her mouth to argue, but Hilo said, "I'll go."

Shae did not mask her surprise. "You...will?"

"I'm the Pillar; if this could be as important as you say, I should handle it in person. You keep telling me that our advantage is in Espenia, that we need to invest there. I'm going to that country to see it for myself." Part of the problem, Hilo thought, was that foreign people and businesses had always been Shae's thing. Now they were too much a part of No Peak's fate, indeed Kekon's fate, for him to leave them entirely to his sister's attention. Hilo had always found that when things were unclear, when he couldn't immediately see the right action to take in a confusing situation, he needed to get closer. Talk to the right people, understand it all better. The solution was always there on the street, somewhere in plain sight.

Ru began to fuss, and Hilo stood up to walk around and calm him. "Besides," Hilo said quietly, "it's been a long time since I've seen Andy. Too long, I think."

CHAPTER

36

What You Deserve

Bero and Mudt sat on the floor of Bero's apartment, drinking and practicing their Channeling on a pair of rats that Mudt had lured and captured in a plastic bucket in the alleyway behind the building. "I say we learn how to make shine ourselves," Bero said. "Then we can sell it and save what's left of the good stuff for ourselves."

"Sure, keke." Mudt opened a bottle of beer and took a large swallow from it. "You got a lab to synthesize chemicals?"

"We're not the fucking Espenian military," Bero scoffed. "You can make street shine if you can get syrup." The main ingredient in SN1 could be found in small quantities in plant-based remedies that had been used since ancient times as a health aid; if you could steal or smuggle prescription medicine out of a hospital or pharmacy, you could distill it into "syrup" and amplify its potency with industrial chemicals.

Bero hovered his hand over the bucket on the ground. If he closed his eyes, he could Perceive the rats more clearly, as thrumming hot spots of energy. Trying to visualize his own jade energy as something he could extend beyond his own body, like a sharp weapon held in his hand, Bero Channeled into one of the rodents with a two-fingered jab. The animal fell stunned onto its side, legs twitching in pain, but not dead. "Godsdamnit."

Mudt handed the beer bottle to Bero. "Have the rest."

"I thought you liked this stuff."

"Not anymore. It's cheap Ygutanian shit." Mudt put his hand in the bucket, his face tight with a concentration that looked almost angry, and touched the other rat. It gave a little jump, staggered in a circle, and keeled over dead. Bero scowled and drank the rest of the beer. Since when had Mudt gotten better than him at Channeling? Had he been practicing?

Bero admitted there had not been much else to do for the past three months. They hadn't seen or heard anything from Soradiyo. The ungrateful barukan sheep fucker had cut them out and was probably giving all the jobs to Mo and Shrimps now. Which meant that Bero once again needed to think about how to bolster his income stream. "I already have clients who buy from me, regular," Bero went on. "All we need is to set up our own supply." He wiped the back of a hand over his sweaty brow; the last typhoon of the season had brought down the lingering summer heat but also knocked out the power in Bero's building, so none of the fans were working.

Mudt said, "Your clients don't come to you for the weak stuff cooked with drain cleaner that'll make you go blind. They come to you for *quality* shine." He turned to Bero, his small eyes dead cold. "Shine you stole from my da's storeroom after he died."

Bero stared at him. *He's drunk.* But Mudt's gaze was steady, his face flushed from anger, not booze. Bero growled, his voice a low threat, "Are you calling me a thief?"

It was a cliché, posturing thing to say—the sort of challenge that started bar brawls—and Mudt just laughed in an oddly high giggle. "That's real funny, keke. We *are* thieves, remember? We're the lowest of the low." His voice took on a strange edge. "But *you*...you're something else. My da gave you work and paid you good money, and then when everyone was looking to have you killed, he saved your life. And you took his shine for yourself and you sold it, and you pretended the whole time like you cared to help me avenge him, but you never did. You only kept me around because I was useful, but you never intended to pay my da back for anything he did for you. You'd never stick your neck out for anyone but yourself. You've got jade, but you don't know what to do with it because you've got nothing to live for. I might be a thief, but at least I've got *reasons*. You've got nothing. You *are* nothing."

It was the longest speech that Bero had ever heard the teenager give. Bero stared at Mudt with astonishment. Then he exploded. "Who the fuck do you think you are, talking to me like that? You think I need you? If it weren't for me, you wouldn't even *have* jade. *I* came up with the plan to get Kaul's jade; *I* got us into the Rat House; *I* got us the scavenging work—everything's been my idea all along, *you're* the one who's nothing and you're saying that *I'm* nothing? I ought to—"

Bero lurched up to grab Mudt by the throat, but the boy leapt up and scrambled out of Bero's grasp. Bero lunged after him, but suddenly the ground seemed to tilt under his feet; he staggered and fell against the sofa. A wave of dizziness swept over him and his head swam. He hadn't had that much to drink yet, definitely not more than Mudt, and Mudt was standing with no problem, watching him impassively, expectantly.

In one sharp instant of clarity, Bero realized what was happening. He stared at the empty bottle of beer he'd knocked over on the floor. He remembered that he'd once told Mudt why his face was crooked—had explained with regret and yet some pride that he'd almost managed to steal jade straight off a drunken Green Bone by drugging his drink, years ago.

"You fucker." Bero tried to shake the descending curtain out of his head; he blinked and cursed and crawled forward toward Mudt with murder on his mind. "You shit-eating little rat *fuck*." Bero's stomach churned and convulsive spikes of pain shot through his guts. He tried to summon his focus; with a snarl of effort, he unleashed a feeble Deflection in Mudt's direction. It went wide, knocking a lamp off a table and sending it into the wall with a crash. Mudt didn't even move.

Bero curled on the carpet, sweating, clutching his stomach, tongue lolling. Through a fog, he saw Mudt approach and stand over him with something in his hand. Bero couldn't see what it was until his betrayer bent down and jabbed him in the thigh with it. Mudt depressed the syringe, shooting a triple dose of concentrated SN1 into Bero's veins. Enough to send his heart into convulsions. Enough to kill him.

Bero tried once more to wrap his hands around Mudt's skinny neck, but the teenager used his Strength to break Bero's grip easily. He sat on Bero's chest, pinning his arms, and as Bero's eyes rolled and his mouth worked frantically, Mudt removed the string of jade from around Bero's neck and placed it around his own. Bero's world dimmed. The poison in his drink, the overdose of shine in his blood, the jade being torn away from him—he couldn't tell which of the three was most rapidly robbing him of the ability to move, to speak, to think.

Mudt stood back up. "I'm not sorry for you," he said, but he sounded hesitant, as if he were saying it to convince himself. He stared at Bero for a long moment, then said, with greater conviction, "You'd have done the same to me if you were in my place. You're only getting what you deserve."

Bero's fingers clutched at Mudt's ankle. Mudt stepped out of reach, and Bero flopped and rolled after him on the ground like a fish flung onto the deck of a boat. He heard Mudt walking away, and then he heard the sound of the apartment door opening and shutting. Mudt was gone, and he had taken Bero's jade and left Bero to die. *Mudt!* That greasy little kid, that nobody, that boy who'd worked in the Goody Too and had always seemed so dim. He'd been killed by *Mudt*, who was supposed to be weaker, supposed to be the sidekick, and who had become the only person Bero might've called a friend— and the irony of it was such that Bero was overwhelmed by the desire to laugh and to scream and to bash in the boy's skull.

With this last surge of hate, Bero crawled to the apartment door and heaved himself against it; the loose lock popped and he fell across the threshold, and then it seemed he was being dragged backward down a very long, dark tunnel.

CHAPTER

37

~

Threats and Schemes

A large insulated shipping container marked to the attention of the No Peak clan was discovered in a boathouse in the Docks on the basis of an anonymous tip. The box, normally used to transport frozen seafood, contained the dismembered body of an Uwiwan man—arms, legs, hands, feet, cock, torso, head. One of the Fingers, Heike, leaned over the water and lost his latest meal; Lott kept his gorge down as he peered at the grisly sight before taking a hasty step back. "Who was it, Maik-jen?"

Kehn closed the lid on the body; it seemed indecent to look at the parts for long, particularly as he thought it likely the man had been alive for at least part of the time that they were being separated. "One of our rats in Tialuhiya," Kehn said. "My guess is the one who tipped us off on the *Amaric Pride*." Kehn was not the sort of person to openly show the full extent of his disappointment or anger; it had been his habit since he was a boy to be the calm one, to keep Tar out of trouble, or if they were already in trouble, to get them out. Now, however, he stormed out of the boathouse under a dark cloud. Establishing and maintaining informers in the Uwiwa Islands was painstaking work and a significant investment of time and money on the part of the Horn's side of the clan. In Kekon, No Peak had ample resources and influence, but it was not easy to recruit, control, and protect White Rats in other countries. When, despite all efforts, some of them were discovered by Ti Pasuiga and grotesquely punished, it scared all the others, and No Peak could not effectively retaliate.

Kehn stewed on these troubles and thought about how to bring them to the attention of the Pillar. "We've lost rats before," he explained the following day over lunch in the Twice Lucky, "but they just disappear. This is the first time Zapunyo's rubbed our face in it, sending us a body in pieces like that. Smugglers used to be mostly a nuisance, but Ti Pasuiga is well organized and feared in those islands, and now it's not afraid to offend us directly. That Uwiwan cur has gotten too bold."

"He's frustrated," Hilo said, passing the plate of duck skewers to Tar. "Zapunyo has plenty of dirty money and cheap lives, but if he can't get jade out of Kekon and move it to buyers, he doesn't have a business. The Ygutanians, the Oortokon rebels, and the barukan who're supporting the rebellion because they hate the Shotarian government—those are his biggest customers, and with the heat you've put on his routes through the Origas Gulf and East Amaric, he's stuck."

The Pillar seemed less upset about the slain rat than Kehn had expected, or perhaps he was simply preoccupied, thinking about his upcoming trip to Espenia. While he was gone, the Weather Man would be in charge of No Peak, and although Kehn liked Kaul Shae well enough, she worked behind a desk and had no real understanding of the military side of the clan. He was accustomed to being able to consult with Hilo-jen about every aspect of the Horn's responsibilities. "Zapunyo's starting to look to other markets," he said. "He already brews SN1 to keep his scrap pickers and rockfish and polishers from getting the Itches; it's natural that he's also making it to sell for profit, especially now that the Mountain's factories in Ygutan are gone. We've heard he's trying to partner with other groups—drug cartels, arms dealers, prostitution rings—to distribute jade and shine in other parts of the world."

"Why can't the Espenians get the Uwiwan government to deal with Zapunyo?" Tar asked. "They know where his mansion is; why not just kill him?"

"The Uwiwan government is a corrupt black hole," Hilo said. "Parts of that country are lawless, and half of the foreign aid that goes into that place disappears."

"Ti Pasuiga pays the police more than the government does," Kehn said. "And Zapunyo makes himself out to be a generous man, giving money to the local towns to build roads and schools and temples. He's practically untouchable in that country. We may be harming his business, but as long as he's alive, he'll keep being a problem for us." Kehn scratched his jaw. "Hilo-jen, we have to think of how to whisper his name."

Hilo barely reacted to his Horn's pronouncement. Kehn expected the Pillar had already thought about this but not come to any satisfactory conclusions. "We have enemies here at home that we've been trying to put into the ground for years. We can only handle so many things at one time," Hilo said.

Two weeks ago, on the Pillar's discreet instructions, the Janloon city police had arrested and interrogated the shine dealer Shae had spoken of and Kehn's Fingers had quietly tracked down. The man cut a deal by naming several high-profile Green Bone clients, including immediate relatives of Iwe Kalundo, the Mountain clan's Weather Man. No Peak made sure that news of both the arrest and the clients who'd been named was leaked to the press. Ayt Mada was not the only one who could use the media to paint her rivals in an unflattering light. The story had reignited a public debate about the evils of SN1, but more importantly, renewed concerns about the leadership of the Mountain clan possibly falling to the Iwe family.

Meanwhile, No Peak had solved some of the problems it was

having on Poor Man's Road by offloading it onto their rivals. On Hilo's orders, Kehn's Green Bones had shut down prostitution in the gambling triangle of the Armpit district; pimps were forcefully run out and warned not to be caught anywhere near the casinos. Instead, the No Peak chance houses put up posters and distributed leaflets advertising the strip clubs and brothels in the nearby Mountain-controlled districts of Dog's Head and Spearpoint. Rowdy Espenian servicemen were migrating their money and troublesome disorderliness into Mountain territory; recently a group of three drunken foreign sailors had gotten into an altercation with some Green Bones of the Koben family and wound up in the hospital, which forced Ayt Mada into the humiliating position of having to publicly support the imprudent Kobens while quietly paying off the Espenians.

Kehn admired Hilo-jen's tactical cunning, though he could not help but think that the Pillar's preoccupation with destabilizing the Mountain was like trying to light wet grass on fire: They were making a lot of sparks and smoke, but so far no roaring flames had erupted.

Perhaps Hilo was thinking the same thing because he pushed his plate of remaining food aside and said to Tar, "Have someone in the Koben family killed. Not the kid or his mother, but a Green Bone man, someone close to them. Not by you or any of your men; the job has to be hired out, and it can't be traced back to No Peak in any way. Make it an obvious thing, not an accident."

"The kid's ma has a brother who wears jade, and an uncle," Tar said.

"That's good," said Hilo. "Either of them would do. It's better if he dies, but even if he doesn't, it's okay. So long as they don't know who to blame." The Maiks nodded; the Kobens were numerous but not very clever; now that they seemed to be ahead of the Iwes, perhaps they could be provoked into useful violence, as they had been against the drunk foreigners. Tar began to ask a question, but Mr. Une, the Lantern Man owner of the Twice Lucky, came around to pay his respects and they chatted with him pleasantly for a few minutes. After the smiling restaurateur saluted and withdrew, Hilo answered his Pillarman. "No rush on killing one of the Kobens; sometime after we get back from Espenia is fine."

As they got up to leave, Hilo put a hand on Kehn's shoulder. "I haven't forgotten what you said about Zapunyo. Losing some rats is expected, but you're right to be angry and offended by this. We have a lot of things going on right now, but I agree we have to move stronger on Ti Pasuiga. We'll think about it some more, when I get back."

Tau Maro returned from a lunch-hour meeting with the board of directors of Four Virtues International feeling both cautiously optimistic and deeply frustrated. The grassroots charitable organization was only a year old but had already exceeded its initial public fundraising goals and was getting considerable positive press; on the other hand, efforts to lobby Wisdom Hall on key issues such as refugees were meeting with little success. When it came to business and politics, it was still exceedingly difficult to accomplish anything in a timely manner without clan support. There ought to be a word, Maro mused, for the particular combination of persistent hope and inescapable difficulty that seemed to prevail in all aspects of his life— from climbing the academic ladder, to policy and nonprofit work, to matters of the heart.

He walked into his office to find three men waiting for him. Two of them were young enough to be undergraduates, but he did not recognize them as students in any of his classes. The third man, sitting in Maro's desk chair and swiveling it around slowly, had a jade aura but was not wearing any of his jade in plain sight. In Janloon, that was the equivalent of showing off the jacket bulge of an illegal pistol; it could only mean that he was not entitled to his green and was a criminal of some sort.

Maro stood in the doorway of his office, tamping down suspicion and alarm. "I'm sorry, this isn't your office," he said.

"We're looking for Dr. Tau Marosun," said the man in his chair.

"Who are you?" Maro asked, keeping his voice even.

"A half-shottie bastard," said the man, speaking in perfect Shotarian. "Just like you." Maro tensed as the uninvited guest rose from behind the desk and walked up to Maro with a partial smile on his narrow, tanned face. There was no menace in his manner or hostility in his aura, but Maro took an involuntary step back as the man gently closed the office door and said, "It's okay, Dr. Tau. I'm not trying to offend you. I know how prejudiced the Kekonese can be, and I understand you don't want your colleagues to know the real reason you make so many trips to Leyolo City." The man hadn't given a name. He looked like a villain straight out of a Shotarian crime movie, Maro thought. Lumpy knuckles and a cruel mouth. Maro stared at him with a rising sense of disbelief, and despite himself, a frisson of fear.

The stranger said, "You have to look out for yourself, after all. It's not easy to get ahead in this city unless you're a stooge of one of the big Green Bone clans. Men like yourself don't get the consideration they deserve." He noticed Maro glancing at the two younger intruders and said, "Don't worry about them; they can't understand Shotarian. Say, Dr. Tau: Are you still fucking the Kaul woman, or are things over between you two?"

Maro's head jerked around to stare; his unease took a sharp turn into anger. "If you people think you can bribe or blackmail me, you're wrong," he said. "I don't have any special knowledge of the No Peak clan, and even if I did, I wouldn't give it to you for any price or threat. Go ahead, tell everyone I'm of mixed blood. Start a xenophobic scandal, like you did with Kaul Shae. I'm not afraid to lose my job; I'll let my work speak for itself."

The narrow-faced man raised his hands in a mock placating gesture. "Relax. Do I look like I'm from the Mountain clan? My friends and I had nothing to do with those nasty accusations against your girlfriend. We don't want any information from you."

"Then what *do* you want?" Maro demanded.

"An introduction," said the stranger. "That's all. Like I said, we're not from the Mountain. You know the Kaul family personally. We would like to set up a meeting."

A chill traveled through Maro's body. He yanked open his office door. "Get out," he said, trying and failing to keep his voice from trembling. "And don't ever come back."

The man replied, with sudden ice in his voice, "You're not being reasonable. What do you owe to No Peak, that's worth refusing our request so rudely? Think about it." With a jerk of his head, the man motioned to the two teenage thugs he'd brought along with him. They shrugged and moved away from the wall they'd been leaning against. The leader said, in an offhanded way, still speaking in Shotarian, "Remember that we know a lot more about you than you know about us, Dr. Tau. Consider that before you do or say anything else hasty."

The men left unhurriedly. Maro shut his office door and fell into his chair. He shuddered, unnerved, to find the leather still warm from the stranger's body heat.

CHAPTER

38

~~

Not the Real Thing

Mudt walked into the Pig & Pig pub in Coinwash and sat down at the counter. "A plate of the battered shrimp and a glass of the Brevnya ale." The bartender eyed Mudt skeptically on account of his age, but seeing as he appeared to be a heavily jaded Green Bone, he asked, "You want a regular glass or the extra tall, jen? It's only five dien more on Seconddays."

"The extra tall then," said Mudt. The battered shrimp and the beer arrived, and Mudt took his time enjoying his meal. He was in a celebratory mood; today, for the first time, he'd combined Lightness and Steel—he'd run to the edge of the roof of his apartment and leapt a full twenty meters to the top of the building next door. He'd hit the concrete, rolled, and collapsed on his back, his heart pounding with adrenaline and all the breath knocked out of him, but uninjured, with not even a bruise. All his long hours of obsessive practice were starting to pay off. He knew he was still a long way off from being able to take on someone like Maik Tar, a Green Bone with years of training. He would need to bide his time and also think of some way to gain an unexpected advantage, the way he had when he'd drugged Bero's drink.

Mudt could not help but feel remorse for murdering Bero, and even after all these weeks, he missed the other teen's company and wished he had someone to talk to, to share his success today. He was still haunted by the way Bero had lain on the floor twitching in those last minutes, eyes rolling with impotent rage. But with each fortifying swallow of ale Mudt took, the feeling diminished. There wasn't any room in this world to be soft. Look at the Green Bone clans. A real Green Bone wouldn't give a second thought to killing an enemy and taking his jade. That was the sort of person Mudt needed to be if he was going to achieve his eventual revenge against Maik Tar and the No Peak clan.

Mudt ordered another extra tall glass of beer and reassured himself with the knowledge that the world had suffered no great loss from Bero no longer being a part of it. Mudt had even heard his father once say, "I think he's a sociopath." In their world, that was not necessarily a bad thing. Mudt had looked up to the older teen for a long time. Unlike Mudt, Bero had seemed so confident and tough, not afraid of anybody. Mudt admired that about him.

The jade around Mudt's neck felt warm and heavy. It moved and rolled on his skin like something alive, that *gave* life. He'd had to increase his daily dose of shine to carry it all. Fortunately, he knew where Bero kept his stash hidden, and unlike Bero, he also knew how to get more. He might, at one time, have told Bero, if Bero had ever bothered to ask him.

The pub was slow at first, but more people arrived as the night went on. A group of five college-age girls arrived, dressed in short skirts and high heels. They were on a mission to get their friend, who had just been dumped by her asshole boyfriend, properly drunk. "A Green Bone," one of them exclaimed, flashing a coy smile at Mudt after she'd ordered her drink from the bar. "I haven't seen you before, but you must be a Fist. Are you new around here?"

"He's not a Fist." An older girl rolled her eyes at her friend's naïveté. "He's too young. That can't be real jade."

"It *is* real," Mudt said, his face warming. He'd never been noticed by women before, had barely ever had any conversations with them. His head buzzed from the booze and his stomach felt bloated with fried food. With this much jade, his sense of Perception was distracting, overwhelming. The girls seemed like furnaces of energy standing close to him—he had a hard time focusing on their faces. "Do I look like some barukan poser? Every bit of green you see is the real thing."

The older of the two girls said, "How did you get it then, since you can't even be twenty?" She feigned intense interest. "Did you win it in duels? Is your family name Kaul?"

Her friend laughed. The girls wore perfume and makeup and they were as pretty as models on television, even as they laughed at him. Twin surges of embarrassment and anger flooded Mudt's brain. People treated Green Bones with *respect*. That was the way it was supposed to be, the way it had always been. They wouldn't dare to question Green Bones about how they'd earned their jade or speak to them in a condescending way, the way these girls were speaking to him.

But not everyone who wore jade these days was worthy of deference. They could be found in Janloon, or on television, or in gossip talk: new green and barukan and foreign gangsters and Espenian soldiers who killed even women and children.

Mudt had jade, but he was not a Green Bone; he had not been raised or trained as one and so he was not convincing as one. He had a wary, twitchy, cowed manner that became apparent to anyone who spoke to him for a few minutes. On some deep and shameful level, he knew this about himself, and he knew the girls at the bar could sense it too. In that instant, he remembered how Bero had stood up to the disbelief and laughter of the Mountain Green Bones on that night in the forest when Mudt had been sure they were both going to be killed. Bero had been selfish and reckless, but he hadn't been afraid.

Mudt turned to the girls and blurted, "What makes you think the

Kauls are so special? You want to know where I got my jade? I won it. I took it off the body of Kaul Lan himself."

The two girls stared at him. Mudt saw that he'd gone too far. He might as well have stood on the counter and proclaimed himself the reincarnation of Jenshu. Unlike Nau Suen and the Mountain Green Bones, no one here was amused by new green bravado; they did not want to be seen associating with him. The girls began to edge away as if he'd admitted to a contagious disease, their eyes darting around to see if there were any real Green Bones in the pub who had overheard and would come over to break Mudt's legs for his blasphemy.

Quickly, Mudt laughed loudly and smiled. He was not practiced at smiling, so it came out as an overly toothy grimace. "You should've seen the look on your faces," he exclaimed.

"You're drunk," the older girl said, not smiling at all, and pulled her friend away to rejoin their party.

Mudt admitted that he might be, at that. He paid his bar tab and left before he could say anything else foolish. The bartender had only been at this particular establishment for a month, but he had sharp ears and was not new to the neighborhood, not by a long shot. After Mudt was gone, he went into the back of the kitchen and used the employee phone near the restroom to place a call.

A Meeting of Pillars

Anden went to Port Massy International Airport with Rohn Toro to meet Kaul Hilo when he arrived. The flight was an hour late. While they waited, Rohn bought a cup of coffee from the food court and browsed the spinning racks of paperbacks in the convenience store in the terminal. Anden sat in one of the molded yellow chairs near the gate and tried unsuccessfully to read a magazine. He hadn't seen his cousin since the day of their grandfather's funeral, when the Pillar had essentially banished him from Janloon, and their last words to each other had been curt and painful. When Anden had phoned home and spoken to Shae, explaining the situation and the Dauks' request for assistance, the last thing he had expected was for her to phone back two weeks later and tell him that Hilo was getting on a plane and coming to Port Massy himself.

It had taken another month to secure all the necessary travel papers and free up the room in Hilo's schedule. In the meantime, the leaves turned golden in Port Massy and the sky darkened to a creamy gray. Harvest'Eves decorations went up: garlands of acorns and dried apples, dolls and pictures of Straw Jack, rows of yellow candles in windows. Flyers and signs littered the streets and walls of the city; grocers and restaurants advertised feasts of corn cake and fatted rabbit; stores proclaimed the year's steepest retail discounts.

In Southtrap, the Crews continued to target Kekonese people and businesses. After the body of one of Boss Kromner's midlevel drug dealers was found floating in the Camres River, three gunmen burst into a restaurant where Rohn Toro was eating. The Green Bone sensed them coming and escaped out a back door, but whenever Anden saw Rohn now, he was almost always wearing his leather gloves. He was wearing them now, even here in the airport. He kept his peaked cap pulled low and he often paused in whatever he was doing, his eyes going momentarily distant as he cast his Perception about for threats.

To pass the time, Anden tried to engage the man in conversation. "Do you have family coming to visit you over the Harvest'Eves holiday, Rohn-jen?"

Rohn looked up briefly from the travel guide he was flipping through. "My daughter is coming for a few days." Anden had not been aware that Rohn had a daughter or any family at all; he'd known the man for as long as he'd known the Dauks but had instinctively treated him with a certain respectful distance and so knew little about him as a person. "She's older than you. Lives in Evenfield, near her mother. I'd like to see her more, but that's up to her, not me." Evenfield was five hours away by train or bus. Rohn appeared pensive for a moment, then shrugged. "Maybe there was once a time I could've been a better family man, instead of what I am. But I owe the Dauks. They're the closest thing I have to family now."

The flight from Janloon arrived at last, and the passengers began to disembark. Hilo and Maik Tar were two of the first people off the plane. Anden stood up nervously and went to greet his cousin. They stopped ten paces from each other, as if struck by the same simultaneous hesitation. "Kaul-jen," Anden said, lowering his gaze and touching his clasped hands to his forehead in salute. He raised his eyes again. Hilo looked slightly older than Anden remembered; his expansive energy seemed a little more contained, though perhaps that was because Anden was seeing him here, in the middle of a bustling airport in a foreign country, where he appeared like just another jet-lagged traveler. Hilo carried his jacket over one arm, and the buttons of his blue shirt were done up all the way, hiding the jade studs on his collarbone that Anden had always seen prominently displayed. He was not smiling, but as Anden watched, a reluctant softness came into Hilo's eyes. His mouth moved in an indecisive way, as if torn between a painful grimace and a grin of pleasure. Hilo crossed the rest of the space between them and greeted Anden with an unrestrained embrace. "Andy," he said, and kissed his cousin firmly, once on the cheek.

A wave of unexpectedly strong relief washed over Anden and weakened his knees. The smoothly humming intensity of Hilo's jade aura so close to him was more blindingly familiar than even Hilo's voice or the smell of his clothes—the faint odor of cigarette smoke mingled with the indescribable spicy fragrance of Janloon that made Anden feel instantly homesick. Anden began to stammer something in reply, then he remembered his role. He stepped back and greeted Maik Tar, who also embraced him warmly if less exuberantly, and then he turned slightly over his shoulder and said, "Kaul-jen, this is Rohn Toro. He's the…" Anden realized he didn't know if Rohn had an official title in the clan, indeed, if any Green Bones besides Dauk had titles. "Think of him as the Horn. Among Green Bones here in Port Massy, he's second only to his good friend, Dauk Losunyin, whom we're going to see."

"We don't stand much on ceremony here," Rohn said, in his usual even, wary voice, "but I'm honored to welcome you to Espenia, Kaul-jen." He began to bend into a salute, but Hilo surprised him by extending his hand and shaking Rohn's in a firm and friendly way. The two men's gazes met over their jade auras, and Anden saw Hilo immediately recognize Rohn Toro in the same way Anden had recognized him when he'd first walked into the room at the Dauks' house after dinner—as a certain sort of man every clan must have.

"I've heard a lot about Espenia, but this is the first time I've been here myself," Hilo said, smiling now, in a manner that was amiable and disarming yet subtly formal. "I'm a guest in this country, so I'm grateful to be welcomed and hosted by my cousin's friends." He nodded to Tar. "This is my Pillarman and brother-in-law, Maik Tar." Rohn and Tar greeted each other with perfectly equal shallow salutes, like a meeting between two dogs of the same size.

"It's good of you to come on nothing but Anden's word," Rohn said to Hilo.

The Pillar's smile stayed stiffly in place as he said, without looking directly at his cousin, "Andy wouldn't ask me here for no reason. Who can we trust, if not our family?" and Anden knew that even though Hilo was glad to see him, he was not entirely forgiven.

After Hilo and Tar claimed their baggage, Rohn Toro led the way out to the short-term parking area and a rented black town car. Rohn explained to the visitors that Dauk Losun had arranged for them to stay at the Crestwood Hotel in downtown Port Massy. Would they like to go directly there to rest for a while? Hilo was looking through the window with interest as Rohn drove the car out of the airport and onto the freeway. No, Hilo said, he'd slept on the plane and didn't need to go to the hotel right away if it meant keeping another Pillar waiting; they ought to go meet with Dauk Losun now.

Rohn drove through the center of Port Massy, intentionally taking a longer route to give the visitors a chance to see some of the cityscape. Hilo remained silent for much of the ride, but several times, he nudged Maik Tar and remarked on this or that interesting sight: the world-famous Mast Building, the garish orange buses, a familiar brand name on a billboard. Anden wanted to tell his cousin a thousand things; he felt a strange compulsion to act as a tour guide and point out tidbits that he hadn't known when he'd first arrived in Port Massy but had subsequently learned and that the Pillar might appreciate—but he was tentative, no longer sure how familiar to act with his cousin, whether his comments would be welcomed or scorned.

Anden turned partway around in his seat and remarked, "That's

Port Massy College, Hilo-jen. Those arches are the entrance to the campus." As they entered Southtrap, he said, "The place I live is about three blocks that way. If you have time, maybe you could meet the Hians—they're the couple who've been hosting me." Hilo did not answer, but when the car came to a stop in front of the Dauks' home a few minutes later, he leaned forward and gave Anden a pat on the shoulder before opening the door and getting out. Anden stayed put for a second, feeling foolish. He'd lived in Port Massy for nearly two years, he'd done well in his studies, could speak and read Espenian, had a part-time job that paid a reasonable wage. He had friends and a home of sorts. Yet in the presence of Kaul Hilo, he felt like an anxious boy again. He hadn't realized until now how much he still craved his cousin's approval and forgiveness. It must've been obvious not only to Hilo but to everyone in the car. Anden got out and followed the other men.

Dauk Losun and Dauk Sana greeted the visitors at the front door. Cory was there too, home from Watersguard University for the two-week-long Harvest'Eves break. Fortunately, after fruitless months of surveillance, the police appeared to have given up on staking out the Dauks' home, or perhaps they too were taking a holiday break. The Dauks had gone to some effort to make their modest home look presentable to an important visitor. The counters and the banister gleamed from polish; new, brighter lights had been put in over the kitchen; a vase of fresh flowers on the dining table scented the air pleasantly. Dauk Losun was more formal than usual; instead of his typical sweater, he was wearing a gray shirt and a red tie with a gold clip, and he was not quite his normal unassuming self. He greeted Kaul Hilo with a respectful salute, saying how pleased he was to meet the Pillar of the great No Peak clan in person and inquiring as to his flight. From behind his father's shoulder, Cory flashed Anden a quick smile, which Anden barely acknowledged with one of his own before averting his gaze. He'd spent months impatient to see Cory again, but right now he was too unbalanced by his cousin's presence and the strangeness of different parts of his life coming together under one roof.

Hilo quickly put his hosts at ease by smiling his lopsided smile, complimenting them on aspects of their house, and joking about the food served on Kekon Air. As they entered the dining room, Anden saw his cousin's gaze fall on the statues and vases carved from bluffer's jade. A smirk tugged at the corner of Hilo's mouth, imperceptible to anyone but Anden; it was gone in an instant. When Dauk Losun brought out a bottle of fine hoji and opened it to serve in advance of dinner, Hilo told them about one of his Fists who'd been maimed in a battle and lost his arms but now ran one of the best hoji distilleries in Janloon. Was Dauk a hoji connoisseur? Hilo would be pleased to send him a case. Maik and Rohn stood silently near their bosses, watching the exchange and each other with respect and subtle caution.

Dauk Sana, wearing a high-collared, matronly green dress, brought out dish after dish of food to the dinner table, apologizing for the meagerness of the meal even though it was obvious that she'd been slaving in the kitchen all day to cook a dozen dishes. Hilo said that his own mother could not have done so well, which made Dauk Sana beam with pleasure. "I had plans to make one other seafood dish and a sweet cake, and I would have, if my daughters had been here to help, but one lives far away, another is home with a sick child, and the third is traveling for some sort of industry conference." She sighed and said, "At least Coru was good enough to lend a hand in the kitchen this afternoon." She doled more food onto her son's plate with obvious affection. "The youngest child is usually the most helpful."

Hilo seemed to consider this comment as he regarded Cory, no doubt Perceiving him to be a Green Bone like his parents and Rohn. Anden felt a tremble in his stomach, a sudden, ridiculous protectiveness. Hilo smiled in a teasing, friendly way and raised his hoji glass to Dauk Coru. "The youngest is also the most spoiled, the one who gets away with anything."

Cory laughed a little uncertainly and glanced at his father. "I'm not sure that's true."

From across the table, Dauk Losun said, "Do you have children, Kaul-jen?"

Hilo said, "I have two sons. They're one and three years old. My wife and I are expecting a third child."

Dauk Losun and Kaul Hilo were separated in age by thirty years. "The gods favor you, Kaul-jen, to have given you two sons already and perhaps a third on the way," Dauk said.

"The third will be a girl," Hilo said. "That's how it seems to be in our family."

"Nevertheless, a blessing."

After dinner, Dauk Sana cleared the empty dishes and leftovers to the kitchen. There was still plenty of food left; Hilo, Anden, and the Dauks had dined heartily, but Maik Tar and Rohn Toro, seated next to their respective Pillars, had eaten little and spoken less. It was their unstated but mutually understood role to remain observant and on guard. This was a friendly meeting, but nonetheless one between clan Pillars that did not know each other.

Cory stood up to help his mother clear the table. Anden got up as well, wanting to be helpful and feeling suddenly out of place at the table of Green Bone men. In the kitchen, Cory put a stack of dishes on the counter and whispered, "Your cousin's not what I expected."

"What did you expect?" Anden asked.

"Someone like you but a lot older. Serious and intimidating. Black suit, sunglasses, carrying half a dozen knives on his body. Jade on gold chains hanging off his neck and wrists."

"You've been watching too many of those idiotic Shotarian crime movies."

Cory laughed softly, a sound that always made Anden's heart skip a little. "Do you think he's really going to do anything to help us with the Crews, or is he here for some other reason?"

Anden felt oddly accused, as if he was expected to know the Pillar's mind, and it was his fault the Dauks had gone to so much trouble to prepare for this evening. "I don't know," he said.

Dauk Sana took a fresh pot of tea back out to the dining table. "When are we going to get together?" Cory whispered, now that they were alone in the kitchen. He put his hand on the small of Anden's back and slipped his fingers under the waistband of Anden's pants.

Anden moved away, extricating himself. How could Cory think about that right now, with his parents and the Pillar of No Peak sitting in the room next to them? "Maybe Secondday," he said, when he saw the faintly hurt expression on Cory's face. "We'll talk later."

They went back into the dining room. Tea and cigarettes and glazed quartered plums were on the table. Maik and Rohn had edged their chairs back, so that they sat slightly behind the two Pillars. Anden stood in the doorway for a second, unsure of where he ought to place himself, but Maik Tar hooked the leg of Anden's empty chair with his foot and moved it deliberately next to his, so it was clear that Anden was expected to sit on the Kaul side, behind Hilo.

Anden did so. To his surprise, Sana's and Cory's seats remained where they were at the table, on either side of Dauk Losun. Dauk said, with an air of casual explanation, "Kaul-jen, I hope you don't mind if I ask my wife and son to remain a part of our conversation. We're usually not formal around here, and even though the people in our neighborhood call me Pillar, it's more as a sign of respect than an official title. Someone has to lead the community when needed. It's my honor to hold that responsibility, but I'm not ashamed to admit that most of the time I rely on the straightforward good sense of my wife. My son is the only one of our children who wears jade. He's like a bee that sips from every flower—he's known and liked by everyone, and, Heaven help me, he's also a lawyer-in-training, so I like to keep him close."

Anden had rarely heard Dauk Losun speak at such length and so humbly. With this opening, however, Dauk was setting the terms of the conversation and signaling his own standing as a man of influence. He was like a leopard facing a tiger; he possessed far less jade, less wealth, and less power in his country than Kaul Hilo held in Kekon, but he was a Green Bone leader in his own right and not the sort of man who would be pushed around by a visitor in his own home.

Hilo said solemnly, "I would never question how another Pillar runs his clan, especially not in another country. I know how important it is to have good counsel on your side."

Dauk relaxed a little. There was no denying, Anden thought, that Kaul Hilo knew how to take the right tone at the right time. During the dinner he'd been the perfectly cheerful guest, complimentary, quick to smile and laugh. Now he sat almost unmoving, his attention cool and animal steady. "I have a lot of questions about Espenia, Dauk-jen, and about jade in this country. Ever since I became Pillar, my attention has been focused at home. That was out of necessity. Also, I came from being the Horn, so that's where I feel most comfortable. But like you, I have good counsel on my side, and thanks to that I've come to realize that jade is an international issue now, and the threats to Kekon and the Green Bone way of life stretch from across the ocean."

Dauk Sana said, "Many of the Kekonese in this country are from families that came here to escape the Shotarians. We held on to some of the old ways but sadly also lost touch with our kin back on the island. Some families, like mine, brought jade with them, and that was never a problem because we kept to ourselves. Now it seems the world is changing and everyone is turning against us."

"We haven't made connections with our countrymen overseas either," Hilo said. "We Kekonese have never been good at looking beyond our own shores, but my friends and my enemies have taught me that needs to change. That's why I wanted to come in person to meet you, Dauk-jen, and to learn how we Green Bones might help each other."

Three hours of intense discussion followed. The Dauks told Kaul Hilo about the secretive life led by Green Bones in Port Massy, explaining that they could not openly wear jade and had to train in the disciplines covertly, using their abilities to handle affairs in their own community and to defend themselves from the predatory Crews and on occasion the hostility and mistrust of Espenians, which had only increased in recent years due to the strained relationship with Kekon over the Oortokon War and Espenian government propaganda about the dangers and evils of civilian jade use. They spoke of how they had kept the grudge hall running for a long time by paying off the Port Massy police but now the greatest threat came from the

Crews, who saw the opportunity to expand their protection rackets, gambling, and drugs into neighborhoods that the Kekonese had long controlled—and to steal jade.

The hour grew late. Dauk Sana brought out more tea and a bowl of roasted nuts. She opened the windows to clear the air as the dining room grew hazy with smoke. Outside, it had turned dark some time ago. Hilo asked increasingly specific questions: How many Green Bones were there in Port Massy? Were they organized? How many could Dauk reliably call upon if needed? What was this Boss Kromner like? What about his foreman, Skinny Reams? How many coats did he command? What were their main businesses? Who were their rivals? This was a side of Kaul Hilo that Anden knew about but had not witnessed in person before: the mind of a Horn at work.

Anden saw Cory slide slowly lower into his chair and his eyes lose focus, his attention drifting like a bored student in a college lecture hall. His mother prodded him to sit up, and he excused himself to go to the bathroom before taking it upon himself to wash and dry the dishes in the kitchen. Anden heard him running the water and clattering about in the other room, and stifled a flash of annoyance. He was also stiff and tired, but he didn't think it appropriate to get up and do something else when the Pillars were discussing strategy that would affect everyone. Dauk Losun did not publicly scold his son or order him back into the discussion, but Anden saw the man's mouth press together in disappointment.

At last, Hilo said, "I'd like to meet these Bosses. All of them, together, in one room."

Dauk Losun was silent for a minute. Then he spoke with obvious concern. "Kaul-jen, I doubt that'll be possible. Even if you could trick them into such a thing—and I don't think you could—the laws are extremely strict about violence, even against criminals who deserve it. It would be too risky and costly for you personally as well as for the Kekonese community. If anything were to happen to the Bosses at this meeting, the Crews would retaliate against all of us, including against innocent people in Southtrap."

Hilo leaned back in his chair. "My friend, what do you think I'm planning to do? Kill all the Bosses myself?" It was apparent, in the following moment of uncomfortable silence, that was exactly what Dauk had thought. A faint smile played over Hilo's lips; he seemed amused that despite being a Green Bone himself, Dauk had been so quick to jump to assumptions based on the stereotype of the Kekonese as instinctively violent.

Hilo broke the awkward moment with a shake of the head. "My Weather Man had to get a special government waiver for me to even visit the country wearing jade. I'm not allowed to stay in Espenia for more than twenty days; I had to declare every piece of green I carried in and I'll have to carry the same amount out." He shook his head again in amazement. "I can see how different things are here, and I don't intend to cause problems for myself. More importantly, it's not my place to whisper names or to take lives in another Pillar's territory, not when I respect him and would like to remain his friend." He smiled to show that he had not been at all offended by what Dauk had said. "There's a lot you can learn about people when you're in the same room with them. That's why I want to meet the Bosses. Or rather, for *you* to meet with them. I'm only a guest here."

Dauk Sana spoke up. "Kromner will be suspicious. There's been killing and property damage on both sides for months now. They've caused us problems, but we're not helpless, especially because we have Rohn-jen. Why would the Bosses agree to sit down with us now?"

Hilo said, "I know something of clan war, and one thing I know is that they're fought on many levels. The war on the street between Fingers goes on in one way, but the war that happens over telephone calls, and in closed rooms, and in tall buildings—that goes on in another way. If this Boss Kromner has any real skill as a leader, he won't let a little bloodshed in the streets get in the way of getting what he really wants: a piece of the jade trade. You have a little jade. The No Peak clan has much more. He'll be interested to meet with us."

Sana was disbelieving. "Are you truly willing to negotiate with the Crews over jade?"

"We'll see about that." For the first time that night, Hilo looked at his watch. "We have more to talk about, and a lot more to plan, but it's getting late." He stood up; Tar and Anden stood with him. "Thank you for a delicious meal, Mrs. Dauk. We'll meet again tomorrow; I'll buy dinner this time. You'll have to suggest where we should go for good Espenian food—I want to try some while I'm here." Hilo was his casual self again; the meeting was over.

The Dauks stood up and saw them to the door. "Rohn-jen is at your disposal while you're here," Dauk said. "He'll take you to the hotel." Hilo accepted graciously. Rohn said he would drive Anden home as well. With a backward glance at Cory, Anden got into the town car.

When they pulled up in front of the Crestwood Hotel, Hilo said to Anden, "Come inside and have a drink with us at the bar, Andy. I'll pay for a taxi to take you home afterward."

With a parting nod to Rohn Toro, Anden got out of the car and followed Hilo and Tar into the lobby of the hotel. The bar was almost empty; people were spending the night before Harvest'Eves at home with family. The Pillar dropped into an armchair behind one of the empty tables while Tar went to the bar to order them drinks. Hilo took off his suit jacket and threw it onto another seat, then undid the top two buttons of his shirt. Green glinted under his unfastened collar, capturing motes of light from the bar's chandelier lamps. He rubbed a hand across his face; he looked exhausted now, when minutes ago he'd shown no sign of fatigue. "Sit down, Andy," he said, and Anden did so, taking the seat across from his cousin.

Hilo shifted onto one hip; he took out his wallet and removed a couple of small photographs, which he passed to Anden. "Your nephews," he said, pride and affection lightening his voice despite the jet lag that was obviously crashing over him fast. "They're getting big. They fight sometimes, but all brothers fight." In one of the photos, Wen was holding both the boys on her lap on the bench under the tree in the Kaul courtyard; in the other, the boys were squeezed together riding a large toy car, Ru in front, Niko behind. Niko was much larger than he was in the last photograph Anden had seen. He looked happy and robust, more like Lan than ever.

"I told them they have an uncle going to school in another country, and that they'll get to meet him someday. Ru's too young to understand, but Niko does." Hilo sounded more tired by the minute. "Keep the photos; I brought them for you. Shae never sends the latest ones."

Anden looked at the photos another minute, then put them in his own wallet. Tar came back with drinks. "I don't know what this is," he said. "I just pointed to the most expensive-looking bottle behind the bar and asked for three glasses." It was brandy, they discovered upon tasting it. "Well, how about that," Tar said, smacking his lips. "A bit sweet, but not half bad."

"Here we are," said Hilo, "together on the other side of the world." He drank from his glass, then leaned his head back against the cushioned chair and closed his eyes for a minute. When he opened them again, he turned his chin toward Anden. For a moment he didn't speak, then he said, quietly, "You look good, cousin. Not as pale and underfed as I worried you might be. Tell me how you're doing, what you've been up to these past couple of years."

40

The Bosses

Dauk Losun sent Rohn Toro as an emissary to Blaise "the Bull" Kromner with a request for a meeting, to be held as soon as possible, between Dauk and the three most powerful Crew Bosses in the city of Port Massy. Rohn was instructed to make it clear that the Kekonese had had enough of the ongoing harassment in Southtrap and wished to sue for peace. To demonstrate his sincerity, Dauk was willing to meet at a time and place of Kromner's choosing, bringing only three attendants with him to the parley, with no additional guarantee for his own safety.

When Rohn returned, he told the Dauks and Kaul Hilo that Kromner had agreed to secure the attendance of the other two Bosses for a meeting on high ground between all the parties on Jons Island the following Firstday at dawn. Driving across the Iron Eye Bridge in the early morning, Hilo inquired as to the reason for Kromner's specific choice of time and place.

"Firstdawn is the holy hour for Truthbearers," Dauk explained from the front passenger seat, glancing at Hilo and Tar in the rearview mirror. "That's when they say the Seer ended the Seven Year Walk at the top of Mount Icana and the One Truth was revealed to him. No sin that's committed on high ground at Firstdawn can be forgiven by God. It's the safest time to meet."

"Don't they know we're not a part of their church?" Tar scoffed.

"It's not us the Bosses are concerned about," Rohn Toro replied as he drove. "We'll be unarmed and outnumbered to the point that even jade wouldn't even the odds. They're suspicious of each other. The Southside Crew is strongest, but the Baker Street and Wormingwood Crews put together would be larger than Kromner's organization. They'll all be on good behavior, though; the Espenians are more religious than you'd think. Anyone who sheds blood at Firstdawn would be turned on by all the others, not just in Port Massy, but all across the country and by the Bosses Table itself. And they'd lose all their paid influence with the police and the courts."

"It's like bringing in penitents," Tar observed. "Funny, isn't it? No matter where you are in the world, the one thing that keeps men from killing each other is a fear of what'll happen after they're dead." He chuckled and looked to his Pillar, as if hoping for some affirming response, but Hilo remained silent, gazing out the window as they drove past the amusement park, aquarium, and pier-side attractions of Guildman's Park—none of them open at this early hour—and then up a hill to Thorick Mansion, the historical pirate baron's house turned social club that was widely known to have Crew connections, as evidenced now by the fact that it had been opened and made available to the Bosses at this unusual time.

Rohn parked some distance away from half a dozen large, hulking luxury cars—including, Hilo noticed, a Duchesse Priza of the same model year as his own. Several men in black hats and long coats stood by the doors, and Hilo Perceived many more inside and around the building, all of them no doubt well armed. Before they got out of the car, Hilo said to Tar in a low aside, "Remember, Dauk is in charge of this meeting. The Espenians don't know who the two of us are, and it's better to keep it that way, so keep your jade out of sight."

He'd noticed his Pillarman feeling his bare fingers and wrists on the drive over. Tar had placed all his jade on a chain that was hanging around his neck under his clothes; not wearing it in its usual place was clearly agitating him. Green Bones often had small physical mannerisms—twisting the rings on their fingers, straightening their shirt cuffs, touching or tugging at their collar—subtle movements to draw attention to their green when interacting with other people. It was hard to notice and quell such unconscious habits. Hilo's own jade was hidden under his uncomfortably buttoned-up shirt and tie. Even though they were going to meet with foreign gangsters that Hilo considered almost as low as Zapunyo, he didn't like the feeling of dishonesty it gave him to be covering up his status and identity, as if he were wearing a mask. The ways things worked here, the prevailing culture of concealment... no wonder there was so much crime in this country.

They got out of the car and walked to the front of the mansion. The guards stopped them and patted them down for weapons. Tar looked affronted at this indignity, but when Hilo spread his arms and submitted without objection, his Pillarman did the same. The coats paid them only cursory attention, but they glared at Rohn Toro with hateful unease, putting hands on their guns and keeping some distance from him. Hilo noticed it, and it improved his estimation of both Rohn and Dauk. He didn't think of Dauk as a real Pillar any more than the mayor of Janloon would consider the headman of Opia village to be an equal in rank, but it was a sign of the older man's competence that he had the friendship and loyalty of a deputy who was so obviously feared.

One of the coats led them inside. Crystal chandeliers hung from the mansion's ceiling and ornately carved furniture rested on rich rugs illuminated by the early morning light that filtered through leaded windows. The air had the musty smell common to wealthy, old buildings. They walked into a room with a heavy oak conference table in the center and oil paintings of famous Port Massy tycoons decorating the walls. On one side of the table sat five men and one woman. Half a dozen coats acting as bodyguards for their respective Bosses were positioned near the walls or doors, standing in a relaxed manner but with their hands resting on their hips or in their pockets in such a way that their pistols were visible, watching the new entrants but also each other. The Kekonese were the last to arrive. This had obviously been by design; the Crew Bosses were bringing in Dauk the way a council of kings would receive a foreign emissary. Hilo waited for Dauk Losun to sit down in one of the empty chairs at the table before taking the seat next to him.

Blaise "the Bull" Kromner had been born into a childhood of poverty, and though he was now well fed and vain, his enemies would be unwise to forget that he had worked his way up through the Port Massy underworld with absolute ruthlessness and cunning, eliminating many rivals along the way. True to his moniker, Kromner was a beefy man with a heavily fleshed face and a reddish complexion. His features were crude, as if a sculptor had formed them in a hurry, pressing in two shallow thumb dents for eyes and attaching a rough lump of clay for a nose. In contrast to his natural ugliness, Kromner was impeccably dressed. His tailored pinstripe suit and vest fit his broad frame perfectly. The mustache over his broad lips was trimmed and his thick brown hair was neatly combed. He wore a gold watch with a crystal face and a red silk tie. The Bull controlled the gambling and prostitution south of the Camres and a substantial amount of the drug trade. Only the cartels from Tomascio in West Spenda that held sway on narcotics elsewhere in the country competed with him. Kromner was the most famous Crew Boss in the country and liked to be photographed by the newspapers when he appeared at expensive clubs, attended the theater, and dined at the finest restaurants. He was well insulated by layers in his organization, and although his word was law in the Southside Crew, he left much of the day-to-day operations to his trusted foremen.

Kromner was seated in the center chair at the table; to his leftmost side was a short, stocky man known as Joren Gasson. "Jo Boy" ran the

Baker Street Crew that controlled the more affluent northeast of Port Massy, primarily Jons Island, and he was dominant in horse racing and bookkeeping. Gasson was a round-faced man with a shrewd, squinty expression, and he was known for being stingy and private, maintaining a low profile and rarely appearing in public. He had the most policemen, politicians, and judges on his payroll, and so all the other Crews frequently went to him and paid him for his influence in society. The use of Thorick Mansion was on account of his connections.

On the right side of the table was a matronly woman with a white scarf around her throat and a cap that sat atop very curly hair. Anga Slatter looked like someone's rich but shrewish aunt, but she was the de facto acting Boss of the Wormingwood Crew ever since her husband, Rickart "Sharp Ricky" Slatter had been sent to jail on charges of money laundering. It was said that she acted in Ricky's stead in all things and communicated his decisions after visiting and consulting with him in prison. The Wormingwood Crew controlled the northwest of the city and its inner suburbs. All the other Bosses in the country had lost respect for Sharp Ricky for being so stupid as to get caught on minor charges, and for having no better system of management than to let his wife run the business. Accordingly, they paid Anga Slatter little heed.

Each of the Bosses had brought one of their foremen with them. Kromner's foreman, Willy "Skinny" Reams, sat on his Boss's left-hand side. In contrast to Kromner, he was lean and bland looking, clean shaven, in a charcoal-gray suit, holding his brimmed felt hat in his hands.

Kromner watched with arrogant curiosity as the Kekonese men entered. When everyone was seated, he swept his hand around the table as if in general introduction to everyone assembled. Then he spoke to his fellow Bosses. "You all know of the trouble I've been having in Southtrap with the Kekonese." Kromner was naturally a fast, animated speaker, and his voice was higher than one would've expected for so large a man. "Now I'm aware this doesn't affect any of the rest of you directly, so you're likely asking yourselves why Bully Blaise has put you to the trouble of coming all the way out to Jons

Island on a whip crack, at Firstdawn over Harvest'Eves holidays no less." He paused as if waiting for someone to validate this assertion by asking the question out loud. When no one did, Kromner lifted a finger anyway and said, "This little dispute is about more than a few broken skulls in K-Town. It's about the jade business. There's big money to be accounted here, and that's a matter concerning all of us Bosses." Kromner turned toward the Kekonese and took a second to study the four men before picking out Dauk Losun. "Mr. Dauk here is who the Kekonese think of as their own boss. He's asked to meet with us to work out an agreement."

All eyes turned toward the oldest Kekonese man, who sat with his elbows on the table, hands lightly clasped and his back stiff, clearly ill at ease at being the center of attention. Dauk cleared his throat and spoke in Espenian with a slight accent. "For many years, the Kekonese community has had an understanding with the Bosses. We each mind our own businesses. No matter how long we've been here or even if we were born in Port Massy, we Kekonese are still seen as unwelcome strangers in this country. We stick to our own affairs. We want to be good citizens, respected members of Espenian society. At the same time, we hold strongly to our traditions, and we ask only that they not be interfered with by outsiders. So we don't seek to interfere in anything that you do, and in exchange, we handle our own matters. This has applied particularly in the areas of gambling, protection money, and of course, jade."

Jo Gasson said, in a reedy voice, "That's not the case anymore, is it? You've opened up your gambling halls to the regular people, who're putting down money on cockfighting or dueling instead of racing or slots. That competes with Boss Kromner's businesses directly."

"It's true, we've opened the grudge hall to outsiders on certain days of the week," Dauk said. "But it's by invitation only. It's only natural that our children would make Espenian friends and marry into Espenian families, and it's no longer fair to say those who aren't a hundred percent Kekonese shouldn't be allowed to be part of our community gatherings. On those days when we open up the hall, we have cockfighting and gambling only, no duels. The fee we charge goes toward maintaining our community center and helping those in our neighborhood who need help. We're not making any effort to draw people away from your establishments."

"That's not the main issue here," Kromner said with obvious impatience. "I'm a generous man, and I'm willing to let go of small money if all you kecks were up to was a little gambling. But your not-so-secret halls aren't just cheap entertainment; they're where you people go to show off your jade and practice your fancy moves. You're running the only jade markets in town, and that's not right. The jade business is too big for you to have to yourselves."

A flush of anger came into Dauk's face, but he spoke calmly. "Jade is our cultural heritage. Our families brought it with them to this country and we keep it within our community. We don't sell it for profit. And now, with the government ban and negative public perception, we've all the more reason to keep our jade hidden, so as not to attract the attention of law enforcement. It's bad publicity for the Kekonese community when someone is caught selling jade or a non-Kekonese person commits crimes using jade or comes down with the Itches. That's why we train to use our green, and we police our own if there are any problems."

"Oh, you make yourselves sound quite innocent," said Anga Slatter, raising thin, well-plucked eyebrows. "As if you people haven't attacked Blaise's bookies, or murdered his coats."

Kromner made a huffing noise of appreciative agreement, but Dauk said, "There've been offenses on both sides; I'm not saying otherwise. But the main issue is that the peaceful understanding we've had for many years has broken down. The police attention is bad for all of us, but there are fewer of us Kekonese and we're not as powerful or influential as the Crews. We know we're not in a position to go up against you. That's why I've come here to petition you."

"Well, get on with it and say what you're offering." Kromner frowned, the ample flesh of his cheeks pulling down his eyes at the corners as they slid for the first time over to the younger man sitting next to Dauk, who hadn't spoken at all thus far. "And who's this you've got with you? Doesn't he talk at all?"

Dauk said, "Kaul Hiloshudon is a representative of one of the Green Bone clans in Kekon. He's come from Janloon at my request." The Bosses looked at the stranger next to Dauk with interest now. He was young, in his early thirties, though Kromner had a hard time guessing when it came to the Kekonese. He was looking back and forth attentively between the speakers during the conversation, and he was apparently important enough to travel with his own bodyguard, an equally young, tough-looking man who stood near the wall behind him. Kromner had to admit that there was something to be said for the kecks. They were a proud race, a don't-fuck-with-me race; the women looked haughty and the men looked like they would put a knife in your side for the fun of it if you looked at them the wrong way. Blaise Kromner liked that about the kecks; they didn't lie down easily, that was for sure, which was why he had to break their monopoly on jade or wipe their gemstone-toting toughs out of the city.

Dauk said something to the man next to him. The visitor nodded, then sat forward and began speaking in Kekonese, pausing frequently so that Dauk could translate his words into Espenian. "I understand that your organization wants to get in on the international jade market," said the young man. "Kekon is the only place on earth to get jade, and it's controlled by the Green Bone clans; anyone who wants to trade in green has to go through them. I come from one of the most powerful clans in my country and have complete authority to negotiate an agreement."

Kromner looked to Dauk. "You're saying this fellow can sell us jade?"

Dauk nodded slowly. "I will act as the go-between in this deal, but I don't want any share of it for myself. You can get jade straight from Kekon, and the price for my part in this is that we reestablish the peace in Port Massy. If the Crews agree to leave us complete control over our part of Southtrap, including the freedom to run all our businesses and our grudge halls as we see fit, then we can broker a new agreement that benefits everyone."

"That sounds reasonable to me, Blaise," said Jo Boy Gasson, who had nothing at risk in Southtrap but was sure to benefit from the legal and political graft that would inevitably be necessary in such a venture. Kromner ignored him and said, with a strong hint of suspicion in his voice as he looked from Kaul to Dauk, "I thought you people didn't sell jade to outsiders."

Dauk made a face that looked rather pained, then spoke again in Kekonese to the man next to him. Kaul replied and Dauk relayed his words. "That used to be true. It's admirable that our countrymen abroad are able to stick to tradition and keep jade to themselves. Often it's the immigrants that hold on to the old ways while those of us in Kekon have to keep pace with the changing times. The truth is, my clan is in a long-standing war with another clan and we need the money. They've been selling jade and shine in Ygutan and so they have the advantage over us. We need our own markets." The visitor waited patiently as Dauk caught up in the translation. "Any agreement we come to today would have to involve an entirely secure transaction. Our confidentiality has to be guaranteed. You see, the government of Kekon sells jade to the Espenian military, and it would be bad for my clan, which has ties within the government, to be selling jade to the Crews at the same time."

Kromner waved a hand as if to dispel the concern. "That's not a problem, we can promise that," he said quickly. "How much could you sell to us, and at what price?"

The visitor said, "That depends on whether it's raw or cut. There's a state cartel—the Kekon Jade Alliance—that strictly regulates how much jade is mined and processed in Kekon. So there's a tight supply of cut jade, and it's very expensive. Raw jade can be smuggled out of the mines, so you'd get much more for your money, but it's useless unless you have workers who can carve and polish it."

Boss Kromner addressed his foreman for the first time. "Skinny, what do you think?"

"I think we can easily rustle up enough migrant laborers, Boss," Reams said.

Dauk said, with concern, "Jade is dangerous for non-Kekonese to handle."

"We know that," Kromner retorted. "You think I'd go into a

business without knowing anything about it, without doing my research? It was Espenia that created shine, not your country. With all the soldiers in Oortoko and the war vets that'll need the drugs, you don't think we can get SN1? If Skinny says we can get the labor, it'll be no problem to keep them doped."

Dauk conveyed this to the Kekonese clan representative, who said, "Raw jade, then. So long as you understand that the quality varies naturally in any given amount of uncut rock. Usually, you can expect about a thirty to fifty percent yield of cut jade." Kaul leaned his arms on the table. "The market rate these days is ten million thalirs per kilogram."

God, Seer, and Truth, that amount of money made even the Southside Crew's lucrative narcotics trade look like small money. Even Blaise the Bull Kromner could not enter into such an expensive venture on his own, and before answering the Kekonese, he said to the other Bosses, "Now you know I'm getting into this for serious money. I'm not asking either the Baker Street or Wormingwood Crews to be a part of Southside's business, but we can all see it's serious money. If you want to be involved, now's the time to speak. If you don't, then feel free to say so, but I expect the old crewboy's courtesies that we leave each other to eat well."

Jo Boy Gasson smoothed his tie and said, "My Crew isn't interested in handling jade ourselves. Too risky, and too much heat. We're bookmakers, not fighters, you all know that. But we can front the money and handle all the financing in exchange for the usual cut. And we can pay the people who need to be paid to look the other way." It was exactly what Kromner had expected, indeed it would've been difficult to proceed without it; he nodded in ready agreement.

Anga Slatter said, "Blaise, you know Ricky is going to expect that the Wormingwood Crew should have at least part of the action in this. If we're talking about smuggling jade into the country from across the ocean, well, any shipments that come in or out of the city go through the ports, and we control the dockworkers unions. So let's figure a fifteen percent cut, in exchange for getting the goods safely through the harbor. I have to clear all this with Ricky, of course," she added, "but I'll turn on the wifely charms, and I'm sure he'll agree if you do."

Kromner was disinclined to give any percent to that fool Sharp Ricky or his woman, but he thought about it and decided that fifteen percent was reasonable to guarantee the Wormingwood Crew's cooperation and prevent him from having to spend his own people's time and energy on getting the goods through the harborfront. Kromner entertained longer-term thoughts about taking over Wormingwood completely, after he'd established himself in the jade trade and the Southside Crew was large and strong enough to make the expansion. So he intended to get the percentage back eventually and didn't quibble over it now. "Tell Ricky it's fine by me."

Throughout this discussion, Mr. Dauk and his Kekonese guest waited, the older man with a slightly anxious frown, the younger looking at the Bosses and their foremen with a strangely unmoving, but slightly off-center gaze, as if he was concentrating on something else while the Espenians talked. Kromner squinted at the man, then turned to Dauk and said, "Tell your friend that I'll pay him seven hundred million thalirs for a hundred kilos of jade rock."

Dauk's mouth puckered as if he'd eaten something sour. He relayed the Boss's words to his guest in an apologetic tone. To Kromner's surprise, the younger man did not appear offended or thrown off by the low offer; he brought his attention back and smiled. "In my country, it's the honor of an alliance that's important. The leaders assign people they trust to work out the details in a fair manner."

"Well, we're not in your country, are we?" Kromner said. "Seven hundred." He'd hoped to put himself in a stronger negotiating position by making the Kekonese uncomfortable, and was disappointed when the visitor gave a shrug.

"Everyone wants jade. I could sell to the Shotarians or the Ygutanians with less hassle, but I'm willing to come all the way here because of my Kekonese friends in Espenia who want to get along with you. Nine hundred."

They settled, after some predictable back and forth, on eight hundred million thalirs for a hundred kilograms of raw jade to be delivered in four equal shipments so as to spread out the risk of it being intercepted by Espenian authorities. Kaul explained that everything would be handled through intermediaries and the jade would be transported via cargo carrier ships that were not owned or registered by anyone with ties to the Kekonese clans. All communication going forward would be passed through Dauk Losun or those in his confidence.

Kromner was pleased with how smoothly everything had proceeded. Let the Kekonese have their area of Southtrap and their gambling halls, which were of little consequence; in the whole country of Espenia, only his Crew now had a supply of jade straight from the source. Already Kromner was thinking of the fortune he would make on the black market. Of course he would keep some of the jade to equip his own foremen and coats. The Southside Crew would become more powerful than any of the others; perhaps he would be making a move to take over Wormingwood sooner than he'd planned. After all, it wasn't as if Sharp Ricky could do a good job running his business from prison. Kromner would give the Slatters' territory to one of his foremen—Skinny Reams or Moth Duke, perhaps. Skinny was more competent, there was no question of that, but he was too independently minded; he might well take what Kromner gave him and break off his own Crew. Moth wasn't smart enough to entertain any complex thoughts, so he was more trustworthy.

The Kekonese man, Kaul, was still looking between the Bosses and speaking. He really was surprisingly amiable and nonchalant, not like the serious Mr. Dauk or that killer, Rohn. Kromner was not one to take anything at face value, however. He suspected that Kaul was merely a front man, someone young and easy to deal with, sent by those dangerous men who held the real power on that mysterious island. Kromner had never been anywhere near Kekon, but his imaginings included a shadowy council of elders, elaborate rituals, jade swords.

Again, Dauk translated Kaul's words. "Since you're foreigners, I feel I should tell you: Jade isn't like your drugs or guns, which can be easily used by weak men. In Kekon, we say that jade can make men into gods. Only the strong can wield it. You're going to have to move a lot of jade safely and secretly, making sure that it doesn't get into the hands of street hoodlums in your own territories, or spirited away by your own low-level people hoping to make extra money. Who's going to be responsible for making sure that the jade is handled properly?"

Kromner did not like the whiff of condescension he sensed in the Kekonese man's words and the way the visitor was now sitting, leaning back in his chair with a slightly hooded expression. Kromner said, "No street punk or coat in my Crew would dare skim from Southside. Not unless they wanted to take a river cruise with no boat." Anga Slatter smiled, and Jo Gasson grimaced, but the Kekonese didn't react. "I personally guarantee it," Kromner said.

Kaul shook his head. "Your word as a Boss is important of course, but it's obvious you're too important to be doing the unpleasant work in the streets yourself." He gestured toward Kromner as if indicating his fine clothes and hefty body. "In a Kekonese clan, the person who would handle the dangerous work is called the Horn. He has to be completely loyal, respected by the men he commands, and feared by the clan's enemies. He would be the one trusted to lead should anything happen to his boss. I'm asking if you have someone like that in your Crew, because you'll need to put that person in charge of the jade."

Kromner jabbed a finger at the man. "Listen, I like doing business with you just fine, but I don't need you kecks to give me advice on how to run my own Crew. Have you personally ever had to keep an organization of hundreds of people in line?" When the Kekonese man didn't answer, Kromner said, "I didn't think so. So let me tell you something: I didn't get to be the Boss of Southside by having incompetent men under me. Willy Reams here is the man for the job."

Kaul studied Willy with interest, then he turned toward Dauk. The two Kekonese men had an extended conversation in their own language. "What's he saying?" Kromner demanded.

Dauk cleared his throat and said, "He's concerned about jade getting out into the streets and hurting innocent people, especially women and children. It's against their code of honor, you see. So he's asking whether Mr. Reams really is the top foreman in Port Massy—how long he's been with you, how well he can fight, how many men he's killed in combat. I told him Mr. Reams has a reputation, but I wouldn't know for sure." Dauk spread his hands. "What can I say? My friend is from the old country—all they respect is personal strength and violence."

Willy fiddled uncomfortably with the hat in hands, but Kromner snorted. "Well, tell him not to worry his little keck head. Jo, Anga—tell him that my word *and* my men are dependable."

Jo Gasson said, "Everyone knows that Skinny Reams from Southside is as tough as they get and runs the tightest ship in town." And Anga Slatter nodded and said, "That's the truth."

Dauk repeated these words to Kaul, who looked at Reams again with intense assessment. Then he nodded. "That's what I've heard as well, through my own sources. I'm a stranger in this country and am taking a big risk with this deal on behalf of my clan, so forgive me if I seem pushy with all my questions." The clan representative spread his hands. "I'm happy with our arrangement."

After leaving Thorick Mansion, Rohn Toro drove Hilo, Tar, and Dauk back to Dauk's house, where Sana had prepared a lunch for all of them. The dining room of the house did not feel as cramped with only the five of them around the table. Dauk's son was out with friends, and Anden was either with him or working an extra holiday shift at the hardware store.

Hilo could tell that Tar wanted to ask questions, but the Pillarman knew his manners and didn't voice them aloud during a meal with clan outsiders. Hilo did his best to make idle conversation, but he had a headache from getting up before dawn and straining his Perception all morning. He hadn't understood everything that had been said between the foreigners at the meeting, but he'd observed every expression and gesture, the way the foreigners sat in relation to each other and their tone of voice, and he'd carefully Perceived the heartbeat, pulse, breath, and bodily twitches signaling subtle turns of emotion during the conversation. So even though his Espenian was not up to Shae's level, he felt that he understood the people he was dealing with.

He was glad he'd decided to come to Port Massy himself instead of sending his Weather Man; as smart as his sister was, sometimes she lacked a certain awareness when it came to connecting with people, striking the proper note with potential friends or potential enemies. Later today, Hilo planned to meet with Hami Tumashon, so the Master Luckbringer would know that even this far from Janloon, he still had the clan's support and the Pillar's notice. There was nothing more important than personal relationships; they were what made clan oaths real and not merely words that could be spoken by anyone.

Hilo glanced at his watch; it was too late to phone home to Janloon. Wen and the kids were sure to already be in bed.

When the meal was over, an expectant pause fell over the table. Hilo pushed back in his chair and said, "Dauk-jen, will you take a walk with me around the neighborhood? I haven't seen much of Southtrap yet, but my cousin tells me there's a toy store down the street where I can pick up some souvenirs for my sons."

Dauk rose from his seat, and the others moved chairs out of the way so the two Pillars could step out of the house and talk alone. The air outside was bracing, sharp in a way that stung the nostrils. Hilo cupped a hand around his cigarette as he lit it, then offered one to Dauk, who declined politely, saying that he was trying to quit. As they strolled down the street, Hilo said, "You look puzzled, Dauk-jen. I'm guessing you have some questions on your mind."

Dauk said, "I'm trying to figure out your purpose for being here, Kaul-jen."

"My cousin called in a favor from the clan on behalf of the family that's hosting him, to help you against the Crews. The deal we made this morning means that Boss Kromner gets the jade he wants and will leave you and your community alone. Isn't that what you hoped for?"

"It's not the solution I expected," Dauk replied. "Selling jade to the Southside Crew might satisfy Kromner for a while, but the Bull is a greedy man, not someone who's ever content with what he has, always seeking to have more money and power."

Hilo nodded. "A man like that can't hide what he is," he said. "A dog that was once starved will bark at anyone who comes near his food, no matter how much he has now. And he suspects everyone else to be the same way. Kromner's men follow him out of greed or fear, but no one loves a leader who cares only for his own meal."

Dauk slowed his pace. "I've done my homework on you and your family, Kaul-jen. No Peak has consistently opposed the sale of jade to foreigners. Yet today you agreed to sell jade from your clan's own stores to the Crews, who are nothing but criminals. I'm told you have a reputation as a fierce and uncompromising man, but you gave the Bosses exactly what they wanted."

Hilo slowed alongside Dauk and said, "You were expecting a more dramatic and permanent solution."

"When I was growing up in Kekon," Dauk said slowly, "the One Mountain Society could whisper the name of anyone. Even the highest Shotarian officials, police captains, generals."

"That's true," Hilo replied. "But as you've said before, this isn't Kekon. A couple of years ago, I spilled blood in the Uwiwa Islands and it ended up being a problem, as my sister is still quick to remind me. Now it's impossible for me or my Fists to get inside that country to deal with our enemies there. My Weather Man would have my head if I made the same mistake in Espenia." He smiled wryly and said, "So we have to deal with this in a different way."

"Then why make the trip all the way from Janloon personally? You could've sent a representative of your clan to negotiate a deal if selling jade was your intention all along."

"That was never my only intention." Hilo sped up again; he wanted to get out of the cold. "The clans in Kekon have been fighting illegal jade smuggling for years. My Horn and his Fists have confiscated thousands of kilos of raw jade scrap stolen from the country's mines and en route to be shipped offshore by shine-addicted rockfish. Some of it is usable, but a lot of it is of too low a quality to be worth the cost of carving and polishing. Maybe some of it could go to schools or temples for training purposes, but the last thing any Green Bone wants is flawed jade that might weaken his abilities at a crucial moment."

Hilo stopped in front of the toy store and looked in the window, grinding out his cigarette. "Most foreigners, though, unless they're Espenian military specialists, don't know the difference, and I'm guessing that Boss Kromner doesn't have an experienced Kekonese jade expert on hand. All that mediocre jade scrap sitting around in No Peak's storage—*that's* what I'm selling to the Bull and his Crew."

They went inside the store. Hilo eyed a train set but it was too large to bring home in his luggage. He bought some bilingual board books and a water gun for Niko and a stuffed tiger for Ru. The lady behind the cash register greeted Dauk by name and asked Hilo if he was visiting from out of town. She was delighted to learn he was from Janloon; her parents were from there.

As they walked back to the house, Dauk said, "Even if what you're selling to Kromner isn't high quality, it'll still make the Crews stronger and more dangerous. It's not a solution."

"It'll focus their attention elsewhere for quite a while," Hilo said. "It'll buy you time, Dauk-jen. Time to strengthen your own position—with more men and more jade."

Dauk drew to a halt in the middle of the sidewalk. "What're you proposing?"

Hilo stopped as well and turned around. "That No Peak equips you with jade—cut jade of good quality—as well as a few people to help train the Green Bones you have or will have. Your man, Rohn Toro, is not young, and you've said yourself you're short on others like him. Where does that leave you in five years? I can deal with that worry you have, by helping you build the advantage you need over the Crews."

The older man did not react at first. "You're able to move that much cut jade?"

"I have a clever Weather Man," Hilo said. "I trust her to come up with a way."

Dauk put his hands in his pockets. Then he said slowly, "One does not simply give away jade, not even to a friend." He looked at Hilo with suspicion. "All things come at a cost, especially jade. So what cost will No Peak make us pay?"

Hilo put a hand on the man's shoulder. "We only met this week, so I know that we've no history on which to trust each other. But I've done my homework on you as well, Dauk-jen. You were born in Jan-loon and you come from a Green Bone family; your father was a war hero against the Shotarians. You came here as a refugee and now the people in this neighborhood call you the Pillar. You've shown kind-ness and protection to my cousin, for which I'm grateful, and since I've been here you've been nothing but hospitable. You were able to arrange a meeting with the Bosses on short notice and to play the part I asked of you perfectly. So I like and trust you. And it's made me think that we can help each other from now on."

Dauk looked at him steadily. "You want a foreign tributary to the No Peak clan."

Hilo considered this. "Not exactly, but something like that." No Peak had a handful of tributary minor clans in Kekon, who fell under the umbrella of No Peak's resources, protection, and jade allo-cation. In exchange, they either paid tribute out of their business earnings, just like Lantern Men, or partnered with the clan to run certain townships or industries. No Peak's largest tributary, the Stone Cup clan, did not hold any street territory of its own but managed a sizable share of the construction trade, while its second largest, the Jo Sun clan, controlled most of the southern peninsula of Kekon.

"My clan is expanding our business interests in this country," Hilo said. "We're buying real estate. We have plans to export more Kekonese goods to Espenia, and we want to help our Lantern Men in the clan to grow their companies by entering the Espenian market. My Weather Man wants to send more Kekonese students, like my cousin Andy, to get an international education before they work in the office on Ship Street. We need help to do all of that. We need connections in this country, and we need partners and allies." Not just the pragmatic partners that Hilo knew the Weather Man's office was cultivating—foreign politicians, business people, educated graduates—but true allies who understood the weight of clan and jade, even if it was in their own strange and provincial way. Hilo gave Dauk Losun's shoulder a firm pat. "Don't take this the wrong way at all, but you don't come across like any sort of Pillar I've ever met in Kekon. But now I can see why you're the right sort of man to be Pillar in a place like Espenia. You stay in the background, but you make things happen. I would like for Green Bones to grow strong on both sides of the ocean. Will you and your people help in that, Dauk-jen?"

Dauk was silent for a minute. Then he said, "I hope you'll understand if I can't agree to such a proposal right away. We're a small but proud community here in Southtrap, and even though people call me Pillar, it's only out of respect. Others would have to agree, and no offense, Kaul-jen, but you're still a stranger to us. We don't know what will happen after this agreement you've made with the Crews, whether it will hold, or whether it'll only bring more trouble."

Hilo let go of Dauk's shoulder and blew into his cupped hands to warm them from the chill. Dauk did not seem bothered by the cold. "I'm not offended by your reluctance at all," Hilo assured him. "In fact, I would've had to reconsider my favorable impression of your judgment if you'd said yes right away without first talking to your wife and friends. I'll say only one other thing, and then let's get back to the house where it's warm. I don't make promises lightly. You can ask anyone who knows me whether that's true. Here's the promise I'm making to you, Dauk-jen. If you're willing to trust me and to ally with the No Peak clan, in five years, we Kekonese will have more power in this country than any of the Crews."

The Pillar of Southtrap clasped his hands together and touched them to his forehead, inclining in a salute. "That's something I'd like to bring about, Kaul-jen."

CHAPTER

41

Green as Fuck

Anden met with Hilo one last time before the Pillar left to return to Janloon. Hilo came to the Hians' yellow townhouse on a Sixthday morning, arriving alone in a taxi, wearing slacks that were casual enough for travel, dressed up with a fine new tan sport coat he'd bought from one of the expensive shops near the Crestwood Hotel on Bayliss Street. "Uncle and Auntie Hian," he said when he came in, "I'm glad to have this chance to tell you in person how grateful I am that my cousin's being well cared for." He presented Anden's hosts with a generous monetary gift and a beautiful rolled silkscreen print from a famous Janloon artist. The elderly couple were intimidated to the point of near speechlessness, murmuring their thanks and saluting repeatedly.

Hilo said, "Let's go out for breakfast, Andy."

They went to a Stepenish bakery and coffee house in Lochwood. "There was a place like this next to the hotel where I stayed in Lybon when I went to fetch Niko," Hilo explained. "I like these little pastries they make. Haven't found them in Janloon, though. Someone should set up a shop." The waitress came by and Hilo nodded for Anden to pick whatever he wanted and to place their order. "All this is going to pay off, Andy," Hilo said when the waitress departed. "Your studies, I mean."

"What do you think will happen now with the Crews?" Anden asked.

"I made an agreement with Kromner. It's risky because it means putting some of our jade in the hands of criminals. I'm only doing it because I think it'll work out for us, but you never know. From now on, I need you to keep your eyes and ears open, to tell us what you see going on, even if it doesn't seem important. Steer clear of any trouble, though. It's good that you have friends here, but they're not family or clan, and No Peak can't keep you safe when you're so far away."

The waitress returned with their order. Anden tried one of the pastries. It was sweet and flaky. Hilo took a sip of coffee, made a face, and looked at Anden sternly. "I worry about you being here. Anywhere people hide their jade isn't a good place. You know the saying, 'Too dark to see green'?" Anden nodded; the idiom usually referred to locations or situations so evil and desperate that even Green Bones did not feel safe entering. These days, it was also commonly used to describe books or movies with especially grim themes in which there was no morality and the protagonists died in the end—the opposite of the traditional adventure stories with victorious Green Bone heroes. Anden felt a stab of resentment at the irony: Hilo had banished him from the clan in a rage, had refused to speak to him for so long, but now that that had passed, the Pillar was full of brotherly concern.

"You should phone home more often," Hilo said. "Call collect; don't worry about the money."

"Hilo-jen," Anden said. He wasn't sure how to broach the topic that was sitting so heavily on his mind and decided he had no choice but to bring it up directly. "I've been working hard and my grades are pretty good. I'll graduate from the IESOL program next summer with an associate's degree in communications and a language fluency certificate. Shouldn't we talk about what happens afterward?"

Hilo was silent for a moment. Then he turned to the window next to them and tapped the glass. "You see that building over there?" Across the street, a new condominium complex was under construction. "We own it, through one of the clan's Lantern Men. And it's not the only thing we have. There are a lot of changes going on, Andy. Shae is setting up a branch of the Weather Man's office here in Port Massy. It'll manage our interests in this country and help Lantern Men who want to expand into the Espenian market. She's tapped Hami Tumashon to lead it, but they need more people—people who're familiar with both cultures. Relationships with the local Kekonese-Espenian community will be important to us; that's one reason I came here, to make some of those connections in person." Hilo said, "When you've gotten your degree, you'll work in the new office."

A dull roaring was building in Anden's head. "When you sent me to study here, you said that I could come home after two years."

"I said we'd talk about your options. That's what we're doing now," Hilo said.

"We're not talking about options. You're telling me what I'm to do, and that's to stay put." Anden's hands clenched under the table, twisting the cloth napkin in his lap. "How long do you expect me to stay here? Another year? Five years? The rest of my life? You want me to be of use to No Peak but stay in exile, so you don't have to see or speak to me more than once every couple of years?"

Hilo's eyes flashed with a sudden, dangerous light, and even from across the small table, Anden felt the hot surge of the Pillar's jade aura. Anden could not help but flinch, but he did not lower his gaze nor apologize for what he'd said. He'd applied himself diligently during his time here, had done everything that his cousins had asked of him. Hilo had embraced him in the airport and called him cousin, had sat him on the Kaul side of the table in the Dauks' dining room, had made an effort to spend time with him and shown him pictures of his nephews. All of these things had raised Anden's expectations, made him anticipate the clan's forgiveness and a place back in Janloon. Now he did not know what to think.

A painfully long, grudging minute passed as the two men glared at each other, flaky pastries forgotten, coffee cooling. To Anden's surprise, it was Hilo who sighed loudly and broke the silence first. "I should've made Shae explain this to you. It was her suggestion, not mine, but she leaves it to me to be the bad guy. Still, I don't disagree with her. Learning Espenian is only worthwhile if you apply it. You don't want the last two years to be a waste. What could you do in Janloon that would be as useful to the clan as what you could accomplish here?"

"There must be something," Anden insisted.

In a cold voice, Hilo said, "Tell me you'll put on jade, and I'll book an airplane ticket for you to fly home tomorrow."

Anden swallowed but did not say anything. He should've known it was still about this.

Hilo closed his eyes briefly and rubbed a hand across his forehead. In that instant, he looked far older than he had been just a few years ago, when he'd been the powerful young Horn of No Peak and it seemed that nothing could dent his cheerful ego. When he looked up again, he said, in a voice that no longer held any anger, "You think I'm being stubborn, that I'm punishing you for longer than necessary, still trying to force you to be a Green Bone." When Anden still didn't answer, Hilo nodded a little glumly, and said, "I can see why you'd think that, but it's not true, Andy, at least not anymore.

"Janloon's a Green Bone city. Sure, most of the people who live there don't wear jade, but it's still a Green Bone city, and you're not most people. There's no way to change things that happened in the past. If you go back to Janloon now, you'll only ever be the least of the Kauls, the one who was ruined by jade and can't wear it anymore. You'll be treated the way a recovered alcoholic or a released convict is treated—with pity. Is that what you want? If you intend to be something other than that, you'll have to figure it out for yourself. So you might as well do that here, where no one is judging you."

"Are you concerned about me, or just the family's reputation?"

"My wife's a stone-eye," Hilo said, "from a family that had a shit reputation before I made Kehn and Tar my closest Fists. You think that's what matters to me?" He sounded angry again. "You're fucking twenty-one years old, Andy, too young to be a case of ruined prospects in a green-as-fuck city like Janloon." The waitress came by and Hilo smiled at her and paid for their breakfasts. He turned back to Anden and said, "You've already settled in here, learned the language, started to make a life for yourself. What about Dauk Coru? Don't you want to stay with him?"

Anden felt his face reddening; he couldn't look his cousin in the eye. He almost blurted, "We're just friends," but managed to catch himself. The Pillar would see right away that it was a lie, and then Anden would only feel worse. Hilo didn't believe in queerness being bad luck or a punishment of the gods—the same way he didn't judge the Maiks for their family history or Wen for being a stone-eye. But Anden had never spoken to his cousin about romantic things— indeed, he'd never spoken to anyone—and his first instinct was to deny. He *did* want to stay with Cory; he wanted to see him far more often than he did now. And despite himself, he'd begun to like Port Massy, to see its muddled nature and strange customs as unique and vibrant in their own way. But he also wanted to go home, to hear his native language spoken on the streets, to be surrounded by the sights and smells of Janloon that he'd grown up with but always taken for granted. The conflict felt irreconcilable.

Anden forced himself to look up. "Cory knows I only planned to study here for two years. And he's going to be in law school for a while. We haven't talked about the future." Hilo was looking at him steadily and he felt supremely uncomfortable, but he kept talking, deciding he didn't care anymore. "I don't know if he'd want to live in Janloon, but if we were really serious, maybe he'd consider it. He's Kekonese after all."

Hilo shrugged. "In a way, I suppose."

"What's that supposed to mean?"

"Andy, your face might blend in here, but you're more Kekonese than Dauk's son will ever be. He wears jade, but you can tell that he's never had to kill for it, or fear being killed for it. He couldn't make it as a Green Bone in Janloon, you know that. You're greener in here"—Hilo tapped his chest—"and here"—he tapped the side of his head—"which is why the clan needs you—why *I* need you—to be No Peak's man in Espenia for now." There was authority but also a plain and unreserved honesty in the Pillar's words. When Kaul Hilo gave a difficult order, he did so in a way that showed he understood it was difficult; it was why his men would do anything he asked of them. Anden could not think of anything else to say.

They left the coffee shop and Hilo hailed a taxi to take him back to the Crestwood Hotel where he would meet up with Maik Tar and gather his bags before leaving for the airport. Anden didn't know how to say goodbye; he didn't even know when he would see Hilo again. He wasn't sure whether to embrace his cousin, or salute him, or turn and walk away without looking at him. As the taxi pulled up to the curb in front of them, Anden murmured, "Have a safe trip, Hilo-jen. Say hello to everyone back home for me."

Hilo placed a hand on the back of Anden's neck and drew him close for a moment. "Take care of yourself, cousin," he said. Then he was getting in the taxi and closing the door, and the cab was driving away, lost in Port Massy traffic.

Anden stood on the street corner for a long minute, then he went back into the coffee shop where he found a pay phone just inside the door. He picked up the slightly sticky receiver and dropped a coin into the slot. After three rings, Cory's sleepy voice said, "Hello?"

"It's me," Anden said. "Are you doing anything today?"

"No. Just packing." Cory was returning to AC tomorrow morning. Something in Anden's voice must've sounded strange, because Cory said, "What's going on, crumb?"

Anden rested his forehead against the top of the metal phone casing. "I'm at a coffee shop in Lochwood, on the corner of Thurlow and Fifty-Seventh Street. If you're not busy right now...do you think you could come pick me up?"

"Um, sure, okay. Just let me get dressed." A rustle of movement. "You want to do something?"

Anden said, fiercely, "I want to fuck."

A moment of silence passed. Cory said, "I'll come get you."

CHAPTER

42

A Difficult Position

Shae was astounded by how much difficulty her brother had managed to create for her in such a short amount of time. It was dangerous to let Hilo off the island of Kekon, she concluded. It seemed each time he returned from an overseas trip, it was with news of some shocking and irrevocable thing he had accomplished abroad. This time, at least, he had not recklessly killed anyone, although she expected inevitable violent consequences were still forthcoming.

"It was a good trip," Hilo told her. "I had some useful conversations."

"You sold a hundred kilos of raw jade rock to an Espenian crime boss, and you promised cut jade, manpower, and from the sounds of it, tributary clan status to some people you just met."

"Do you disagree with what I did?" Hilo asked mildly, but with a narrow-eyed expression at her tone. "I solved the problem they were having with the Crews and got exactly what you wanted: information and allies in Port Massy. A way for us to gain a stronger foothold in Espenia and grow the clan's business over there without relying solely on those swindling foreign politicians."

"By selling raw jade to a well-known criminal kingpin," she repeated.

Hilo crouched down to fix one of Niko's shoes that had come loose. "The KJA controls all official mining, and thanks to the Royal Council, there's now a shitload of regulations to keep all that activity on public record. But both the Mountain and No Peak have been confiscating jade from smuggling operations—and *that* jade isn't officially declared anywhere. All of it goes through the Horn's side of the clan—it's considered victor's spoils, same as from any battle or duel. I've got a bag of it sitting in my drawer in the study. None of that shows up in any KJA files. Nau Suen has been raiding Zapunyo's jobs the same way we have; what do you imagine Ayt Mada's doing with their share of the jade? And do you think she's given up on producing shine after you leaked her Ygutanian factories to the Espenians?" Hilo shook his head. He lifted Niko onto the swing set that had been installed on the lawn in the garden and pushed him back and forth. "I'd bet my own green the Mountain's still enriching its purse, in ways we don't know about and can't prove. It was always part of Ayt's strategy that Kekon supply both sides of the conflict."

Shae sat down on the stone bench by the pond and studied the water pensively. What Hilo said was true; one of Wen's White Rats had provided phone logs that showed Iwe Kalundo and his top Luckbringers making long-distance calls to Ygutan. Another informer reported that the Mountain's Weather Man had recently made a business trip to that country. Ayt Mada was no doubt well aware of No Peak's alliance with the Espenians and seeking to expand her clan's own businesses—legitimate and otherwise. Due to the Mountain's previous activities in Ygutan and connections such as the late Tem Ben, it made sense that Ayt was choosing to focus on the other world power with a market large enough to rival Espenia. It would not surprise Shae in the least if the Mountain was rebuilding its SN1 factories right now—perhaps somewhere less vulnerable to detection and attack, such as the demilitarized Tun-Ygutan border—or pursuing some even larger scheme.

Despite agreeing with Hilo's assessment, Shae was disturbed by the path he had set them on. "Ayt Mada's undermining the KJA, putting jade in the hands of foreigners and criminals who don't deserve it and can't control it," she said. "By selling jade to Kromner, we're following her example. We're acting no differently than our enemies."

Hilo made a noise in the back of his throat. "If it were up to me, foreigners wouldn't have jade at all, but we're way past that point, Shae. Grandda's generation went down that road thirty years ago, as soon as they let the Espenians into the country and took their money to rebuild after the war. Now look at where we are: SN1 and IBJCS and all the other shit." He leveled a faintly accusing look at his sister that suggested she was as much to blame as anyone for this, having made decisions that further entangled them with foreign interests.

Hilo went on. "Ayt will sell jade under the table to make the Mountain powerful enough to eventually destroy us and rule the country themselves. If we're not willing to make some big moves of our own, that's exactly what'll happen." He stared into the distance as he continued to push his son on the swing with one hand. "Unlike Ayt, though, I've no intention of keeping my clients. The Crews aren't a state, and their people aren't warriors. They're like the greedy sailors that landed on Kekon hundreds of years ago. They've no clan loyalty, no real brotherhood. They want jade but don't know what it means or how to handle it. We'll take the money they're offering and invest it where we need it, shore ourselves up, because the Mountain is going to come after us again; it's just a matter of time."

"How am I supposed to move that much jade across the Amaric Ocean?"

Hilo gave her a crooked smile. "Kehn and his people have experience with all of Zapunyo's methods, we've confiscated ships and containers, we have companies and people on both sides of the ocean. I'm sure my Weather Man will figure something out."

Shae grimaced. She was already deeply uncomfortable wielding the clan's influence over the Royal Council in support of the Espenians' political agenda. The agreement Hilo had made might turn into yet another area where she'd have to regularly plead the understanding and forgiveness of the gods. "The black market jade trade—we're getting into a dangerous game, Hilo."

"You have to go where your enemies are," Hilo said. "And then further."

Shae gave her brother a long look. She was accustomed to being the one who made decisions about the clan's foreign interests; the idea of Hilo acting like a cold-blooded Horn in the place where the Weather Man's office was placing its stakes made her nervous. She wished she could speak to Lan. She wanted to consult his thoughtful, steady moral compass, his broader view of aisho, his prudent mind. She imagined that if she'd been Lan's Weather Man, they would've had detailed, rational discussions before each major clan decision. Hilo was guided by his own strict principles, that was certainly true, but on his own, he took instinctive action with all the decisive military cunning he considered necessary—and filled in the rationale later. "I heard one of the Kobens was gunned down in a parking lot last week," she said.

"Anyone could've done that," Hilo replied, with a satisfied shrug. Not only had the assassin—a man with no clan ties and a long record of petty crime and mental illness—been conveniently killed by police while fleeing arrest, but Koben Ento himself had proven unexpectedly and unintentionally helpful, loudly blaming a business rival in the Iwe family before dying of his injuries in the hospital some hours later. Of course there was suspicion that Ayt herself had whispered the man's name, or that No Peak was behind it—but conflicting speculation was to be expected. The important thing was that the Mountain's various factions were at each other's throats, each convinced that the others were out to ruin them, and demanding Ayt Madashi quell the infighting by making a decision about the succession.

A group of workers passed, pushing a trolley stacked with folding chairs. Large red tents were being erected in the courtyard for tomorrow's festivities. Woon Papidonwa and his bride would be getting married at the Temple of Divine Return, but Hilo had generously offered to host the reception at the Kaul estate, as a gift to the new couple and in recognition of Woon's status in the clan. Since Shae had convinced the Weather Man's Shadow to stay on in his role, more than a year had come and gone, but Woon had not made any further mention of resigning his post, perhaps because he seemed to be much happier now. Shae was glad for him, but the feeling was not unreserved.

Niko held his arms out to be taken off the swing, and Hilo obliged, setting him down and watching the boy scamper off down the garden path. "I haven't seen Maro around lately," Hilo said. "Are things over between the two of you?"

Shae did her best to sound nonchalant. "We're on something of a break right now." She suspected that statement sounded as noncommittal and confused as the issue itself, and was disappointed that she was not as beyond caring about her brother's judgment as she'd thought she was. "We're still friends," she added. "He's coming as my guest to the wedding tomorrow."

Hilo gave her a knowing, almost sad look, as if he guessed how much the duel had cost her, more than even her jade. "If you're friends like you say, you should be honest with him, Shae."

Shae pretended not to have heard him. "Maro's been involved in a humanitarian advocacy group called Four Virtues International. He asked if you'd be willing to meet with some of the representatives who're looking for the clan's support. It would mean a lot to them."

Hilo sighed in exasperation—possibly with her for redirecting the conversation, possibly at the fact that as Pillar he was being constantly petitioned by various groups and had never ceased to find it tedious. "All right, as a favor to your...*friend*," he said. "Sometime in the new year, when things aren't as busy." Wen was due to give birth in a month. Niko came back with a fistful of colorful pebbles; Hilo made a show of admiring them, then picked the boy up to bring him indoors for lunch. "Andy's doing well," he said to Shae over his shoulder. "He wasn't happy about staying, but he understands."

Shae watched her brother's back recede toward the house. She called after him. "Would you really have done it? If Ayt had killed me in the duel, would you have broken aisho and gone back to war with a dirty blade?"

"Ayt thought I would." Hilo's aura was smooth as a river. "That's what's important."

———————

Chancellor Son was warming up at the target range of the Three Springs Leisure Club when Shae joined him that afternoon. "Kauljen," he exclaimed, with a relaxed and cheerful air. "A lovely day, isn't it?" The chancellor was three months away from the end of what had been a grueling six-year term in office and he was obviously looking forward to having more time for his family business, his grandchildren, and the game of chasso.

Chasso is a cross-country game that involves walking through a sprawling and manicured parkland, stopping at regular intervals to shoot fake birds (tufted rubber balls launched from hidden machines) with crossbow darts fired from specialized bows. Although chasso began as a foreign gentleman's game with origins in hunting and archery, in the past decade it caught on as a popular pastime for wealthy Kekonese. Janloon's most well-heeled politicians and businessmen regularly conducted business over games at the recently built Three Springs Leisure Club, located thirty minutes south of Janloon.

Shae personally found the game uninteresting in the extreme, but she understood why it appealed to someone like Son Tomarho. Devoting so much land to private recreation on an island where space was at a premium meant exorbitant, status-enhancing membership fees; the sport required reflexes, good aim, and expensive equipment but low physical fitness; and aging Kekonese men still liked to pretend they were capable warriors. She also suspected that Son enjoyed beating her at the game, as jade abilities were of minimal advantage.

Shae waited until after they'd spent the first two flushes in social chat and were hiking up a low hill against the wind to the third flush point before she decided to broach the topic she'd come to discuss. "No one deserves a break from the pressures of Wisdom Hall more than you, Chancellor Son, but it'll be a loss for the No Peak clan to no longer have such a dependable friend in the chancellor's office next year." The Royal Council had voted in Guim En, the current Minister of Home Concerns, as Son's successor. Guim was viewed as an experienced, fiscally responsible statesman with a populist streak. He was also a long-standing member of the Mountain clan.

"Guim is a reasonable man," Son said unconcernedly, planting himself at the vantage marker and lifting the chasso bow to his ample shoulder. Son raised his left arm to signal his readiness to the machine operator below. One after another, half a dozen chasso balls flew into the air from behind a row of shrubs. Son fired in rapid sequence and grunted in satisfaction as three impaled balls thudded to the lawn below.

"This is a difficult time for the country and for No Peak," Shae said. "The clans have held to peace, but only because the world around us hasn't. Can we count on Guim En to continue to pressure the Uwiwa Islands over smuggling? Will he keep holding the Mountain accountable to the KJA? Will he oppose the Oortokon Conflict Refugee Act when it's time for the Royal Council to vote?"

Son stepped aside and Shae took his place at the vantage marker. The chasso balls flew; Shae pinned two of them using the rented bow from the leisure club shop. She grimaced, tempted to cheat by Deflecting her opponent's darts at the next flush. As they hiked down to collect their points, Son said, in a considerably more somber voice, "Kaul-jen, I was there in the room during the visit from the Espenian secretary, and I'm well aware of the foreigners' security concerns. But the Refugee Act addresses a humanitarian issue. No Peak will seem heartless to oppose it." He wiped his brow and bent his large frame to pick up his downed chasso balls, which he handed to the young chasskeeper who tailed them at a respectful distance, carrying equipment and water and keeping score. "Compassion is one of the four Divine Virtues, after all."

Shae didn't disagree with Son's sentiments. Nevertheless, she said to Son, "In a perfect world, people would act in accordance with the Divine Virtues all the time, and then I suppose the Return would be in sight. But the world is far from perfect, and we both know there are trade-offs to be made."

Son turned around and jabbed one of the chasso darts into the air. "The Espenians are asking us to turn away homeless widows and orphans because they're afraid some of them might be Ygutanian spies. Should we compromise our morals on account of foreign pressure?" Son's words were indignant but his tone was resigned, and his objections were more rhetorical bluster than true disagreement. He knew as well as Shae did that No Peak was in a difficult position. The military challenges in Oortoko had made the Espenians paranoid and controlling. To their continued displeasure, the Kekonese Royal Council held firm in refusing to contribute soldiers or additional jade to the Oortokon War effort. Yet all the while, Shae had steered the clan toward business expansion and trade deals with Espenia and was opening a branch of the Weather Man's office in Port Massy. Now that Hilo had established clan ties with the Green Bones in Espenia, and knowing that the Mountain was seeking its own foreign opportunities, Shae was all the more certain that No Peak needed every bit of political influence it could hang on to, at home and abroad. It needed the continued favor of Adamont Capita. As did the whole country, for a fact, if it wished to maintain its rapid economic growth. The Son family's own textile business was benefiting handsomely from reduced tariffs.

"You've held Kekon's highest political office during clan war within our country, and now foreign war surrounding it," Shae pointed out to the chancellor. "You know all about pressure—*and* when to compromise."

Son shook his head. "These are issues for my successor to deal with now, Kaul-jen." They descended a well-landscaped pebble path into a small woodland. The afternoon was cooling fast; it wouldn't be long before the autumn chill and the dimming light drove them back indoors.

"You're not an old man yet, Chancellor Son. Look at how you're outlasting me on the chasso course." Shae paused in the middle of the path and faced the man. "On behalf of the Pillar, I must ask you for one more act of friendship to No Peak. Don't retire after the end of your term. Keep your seat in the Royal Council. You'll have plenty of time to enjoy yourself later, but stay in government for another year or two, and continue to do the good work this country needs of you." She paused meaningfully. "The clan would be grateful to you, and your family."

As a former Lantern Man, Chancellor Son knew that the clan's gratitude was not something lightly given and almost certainly meant a significant monetary reward to him and his relatives. If he remained in the Royal Council, Son would continue to act as No Peak's most senior politician in Wisdom Hall and would vote in line with the clan's interests. In the event of a tie, his status as chancellor emeritus gave him the same privilege as the sitting chancellor— to cast an additional, tie-breaking vote—which would potentially negate Guim's deciding power.

Chancellor Son pursed his thick lips. Speaking thoughtfully, but not without a touch of pride, "I suppose, after a lifetime of public service, what is one more year?" He fixed Shae with a sober, calculating gaze before hefting his chasso bow and turning back to the path. "I remain a loyal friend of the clan, Kaul-jen, but I can't hold back a tide. Most people don't understand the trade agreements or care about the Espenians' security concerns. Many don't see why we should accommodate foreigners at all. You're walking a thin line. If you keep pitting the interests of No Peak against the will of the country, you won't prevail."

Shae was not normally a heavy drinker, but she had several glasses of wine at Woon's wedding reception the following evening. Sometime after midnight, the bride and groom departed to the cheers of the guests, in a limousine festooned with red and yellow peonies symbolizing marital happiness and fertility. Shortly afterward, Shae left the party and retired to the Weather Man's residence. Maro, dressed in a pressed blue linen suit and tie, walked with her to the front door. She paused before she went inside and turned to him over her shoulder. "Do you want to come in for a little while?"

She wasn't sure if it was politeness, or drunken wistfulness, or something else that made her ask, but in that moment, she hoped he would say yes. Dozens of people had seen them leave the reception together, but having already endured and survived national public scandal, Shae no longer cared if there was clan gossip tomorrow morning.

Maro glanced away, then back at her with a hopeful but cautious expression. "For a little while," he said.

Inside, Shae took off her shoes and sat down on the sofa, rubbing her sore feet. Maro poured two tall glasses of chilled mint water from the pitcher in her fridge. Shae accepted one of them gratefully and pressed the cold glass to her forehead before draining half of it. Although the Weather Man's house was at the far end of the central courtyard, she could still hear the music and Perceive the energy of the remaining crowd like a distant background throbbing. By now, her body had acclimated to carrying less jade, but at times she felt as if her senses were softened, muted around the edges. The alcohol she'd consumed exacerbated the effect; she was tired and everything seemed slightly gauzy.

Maro sat down at the other end of the sofa and leaned back, loosening his tie and taking a drink from his own glass of water. He didn't appear as inebriated as she felt. "Your friend Woon Papi must be very dedicated to the clan," he said. "Your family threw quite the party for him."

"He was my eldest brother's best friend." *And mine.* "He deserves it."

"Well, thank you for inviting me." Maro turned the glass in his hands. "And I appreciate you setting up a meeting for Four Virtues to talk to your brother." As if trying to fill the air between them, he continued, "I've been on their steering committee for a while. They're doing good work but can only get so far without more high-profile support. It would be an enormous step for the major clans to publicly acknowledge the need for Kekon to take a more active role in international humanitarian efforts." He looked to her as if hoping for agreement. "Perhaps we can convince your brother to lend his support to the Oortokon Conflict Refugee Act."

Shae was in no mood to explain the situation involving the clan's business interests and the pressure from the Espenian government, nor suggest that she was the one holding Chancellor Son and the Royal Council accountable to questionable foreign interests. "Let's not talk politics right now," she said.

Maro tugged at his collar. "If you say so," he said uncertainly, as if

Shae had snatched away the last of their safe conversation topics. A swollen silence hung between them. Nearly five months had passed since the duel, but their relationship persisted in the awkward limbo of two objects held at a precise distance by constant centrifugal force, unable to move either closer together or farther apart. They'd spoken on the phone. They'd had lunch together a number of times. Shae still consulted Maro on questions of economics and foreign policy, and now he was hoping for the clan's endorsement of the nonprofit work that had begun to consume a greater amount of his time. They were cordial, friendly—but they circled each other tentatively, as if the other person was a fire whose warmth they craved but knew might burn.

Maro had, on more than one occasion, implied that they could get over this difficult stretch if they were both willing to trust again. Looking at him now, handsome and earnest, seeing the longing in his eyes and the slight flush in his face, Shae wished more than anything that were true. Tonight she ached for closeness—but she did not deserve Maro's trust and could not bear to regain it dishonestly. She considered thanking him for coming and politely showing him to the door. She considered pulling him over to her and fucking him on the floor of the living room. Neither option seemed entirely correct, nor fair to her friend. She did not regret the decisions she'd made, but she did regret that she could no longer look at Maro without seeing the impassable distance between the realities they inhabited.

"Shae." Maro cleared his throat roughly, then got up and moved to sit next to her. His soft aura brushed against her, brimming with conflicted desire, almost distress. He had trimmed his beard and there was tension in the curve of his jaw. "I think I understand better why you shut me out before. I've accepted the fact that you were under a lot of pressure at the time and wanted to keep me from being targeted. But I'm not sure I can do this anymore—be your friend, that is. Someone who's vaguely associated with your family, who gets invited to weddings, but isn't a part of the clan itself. It's...not a good position to be in."

A heaviness came to rest below Shae's rib cage. "I know. I tried it once myself and it didn't work out." She sank lower onto the sofa. A throbbing had begun somewhere behind her eye sockets. "You're right. I've kept you at a distance and not told you the truth you deserve. I was trying to protect you from my decisions, but it was wrong of me."

Maro's face moved in a brief spasm. "You can't shelter me. You know that I don't like Green Bone culture, but I still care about *you*. Do you remember when I said I wanted us to be completely open and honest with each other?" He searched her face. "I need to know where I stand with you. Can you just tell me once and for all: Is there any chance for us?"

Hilo's words came back to her: *If you're his friend as you say, you should be honest with him.* The pressure of a fierce and masochistic abandon swelled inside Shae's chest. She wrapped a hand around Maro's neck and kissed him. The taste and smell of him flooded into her mouth, and she sighed, filled with bittersweet ferocity as strong as the dry lingering taste of wine. When she pulled back, Shae said, "I had an abortion, Maro. I was pregnant before I fought the duel with Ayt Mada."

Maro's face went blank for several seconds, then he sat back as if he'd been shoved hard. A cloud passed over his gentle features, turning them wounded and ugly. The edges of his jade aura seemed to ripple and harden. *"You..."* His voice came out as a coarse whisper. "You kept this from me. You decided without even telling me. Just like the duel."

"You wanted complete honesty," Shae said. "So that's what I'm giving to you. I love you too." Shae looked down at her hands and found that they were clutched tightly in her lap. "You asked me if there's any chance for us, but only you can answer that question now."

Maro set the glass down on the coffee table and stood up. Shae felt the painful weight of his stare pressing down on her for a long, silent moment. She leaned her head back against the cushions. The ceiling seemed to be rotating and so she closed her eyes and did not watch as Maro turned away and left the house.

CHAPTER
43

Family Jade

Three weeks before New Year's, Hilo drove an hour inland from Jan-loon and stopped at an abandoned farmhouse indicated only by a highway marker on a flat stretch of road at the foothills of the mountains. He navigated the Duchesse's bulk up the rutted dirt path until it became too narrow and overgrown, then he got out of the car and walked the rest of the way to the single crumbling brick building. The sun had already slid behind the forested rolling peaks that dominated the sky to the west, and bats were flitting all over the empty field, flickers of heat in the periphery of Hilo's Perception. Two of Tar's men stood in a clearing behind the farmhouse, digging a hole, their shovels scraping and clanging against dry dirt, breaths steaming in the air. They paused in their work, wiping their brows with their forearms and touching their heads in abbreviated salute as the Pillar passed and ducked under the sagging eave to enter the dilapidated structure.

Inside, stark light came from an electric camping lantern hanging from a metal hook fashioned from a coat hanger. A layer of dirt, straw, and bird droppings caked the stone floor. Tar and his lieutenant Doun stood together, chatting and sharing a smoke as they waited for Hilo's arrival. Near their feet was a long lump, wrapped in canvas and tied with rope, like a badly rolled carpet. Next to the lump was a large rectangular steel container with a lid, lying open—an underbody truck toolbox that Tar had purchased from a freight equipment company.

At Hilo's entrance, Doun saluted, then bent down and cut the ropes binding the lump. He pulled away the canvas to reveal a dirty and bruised young man. The teenager had been gagged and bound, but at the sudden light, he blinked and twisted on the ground, struggling to sit up. His shrill jade aura flared, as painful in Hilo's mind as a blast of microphone feedback. Doun stood back and Hilo looked down into a thin, sweaty face and eyes wide with hate and fear. The Pillar's gaze slid off the captive's face and settled on the jade beads around his neck and then the jade-studded forearm cuffs cinched to his skinny arms. Kaul Lan's jade. It had not even been reset.

Hilo was overcome by a sense of cold rage and deep unease. Years ago, when he was the Horn under his brother, he'd been at the Twice Lucky restaurant in the Docks on a night when two teenage hoodlums tried to steal the jade off a drunken old Green Bone. Hilo and the Maiks had been there to stop them, but Hilo remembered thinking that those boys were a sign of a growing societal rot, an omen of worse to come. He felt that way even more strongly now, looking at this stranger, this nobody who had caused so much grief to the Kaul family and yet managed to go unpunished for so long. Some people believed that with SN1, jade could be worn by anyone—but that could never be true. Because if any lowlife could wear Lan's jade, then jade meant nothing. The world of Green Bones meant *nothing*. The sheer nihilistic possibility horrified Hilo to his core. The No Peak clan was like a tiger, and this thief like a rat, but even the largest, most powerful creature would fear a plague of rats, moving in the dark with sharp teeth and carrying disease. It was an imbalance in nature, a sign of an accelerating fundamental wrongness in the world that even this moment couldn't set right.

Tar had opened a duffel bag and was laying out some tools: a cordless drill, a length of plastic tubing, duct tape. Hilo crouched down. The teenager jerked away from him, straining with Strength to break his bonds. He threw a Deflection that rippled out in an unfocused wave, sending the dirt on the ground puffing against the stone walls and swaying the hanging camp lantern as Hilo dispelled the panicked effort with a casual counter Deflection. Doun came over and pinned the prisoner's shoulders to the ground to stop his flailing. Hilo undid the buckles on the cuffs and removed them one by one. He reached around the boy's straining neck and unfastened the clasp, gathering the long string of jade beads into his hand. Hilo tucked Lan's jade into his inside jacket pocket. He patted a hand over the bulge, reassuring himself that it was secure.

The thief moaned; his eyes rolled and his body shook and shuddered with the initial jolt of jade withdrawal. Hilo removed the gag from his mouth. The teen spat blood-tinged grit through broken teeth, and to Hilo's surprise, he swiveled his head to stare at Tar, his face contorted and gaze burning with a loathing that seemed larger than his skinny frame could hold.

"*You,*" the thief snarled, his voice shaking. "You killed my da. You slit his throat and threw him in the harbor. I hope you and your whole family die screaming, you soulless piece of shit."

Tar glanced over with interest, then went back to fitting a drill bit. "Who was he?"

"His name was Mudt Jindonon." The boy began to weep; ugly tracks ran down his muddy face. "He owned a store and a bit of jade, that's all. He was my da, and you killed him."

"I remember Mudt Jin." Tar nodded that it all made sense now. "Mountain spy, shine dealer, jade thief, crime ring leader. Helped to plan the cowardly murder of a Green Bone Pillar. Normally I don't like to think that bad blood runs in the family, but I guess in this case it's true."

Hilo looked at the noisily crying teenager who'd killed his brother and escaped, then desecrated the family's grave for its jade. He felt no sense of triumph, just an overwhelming disgust and pity, a heavy and impatient desire to finish something that should've been done long ago. Hilo unbuttoned his shirt down to the navel and pulled it open. He removed three jade studs from his chest, wincing a little as he worked them free. He rolled them in the palm of his hand, his own jade, won in his youth against some enemy he could not now remember. He would barely feel the loss of them now, but back then, every bit of green he'd added to his body had tasted like destiny. "Look at me," the Pillar said softly. He held out the three jade studs in his hand. "This is Kaul family jade. It's what you were willing to kill and steal for. I'm giving it to you. You'll take it with you to the grave, just like a Green Bone."

"It wasn't me!" Mudt screamed, animal fear finally blotting out his deep rage. "There was another guy! He did it—the whole thing, it was all his idea. I just went along—"

Hilo gripped the thief's jaw and squeezed, forcing his mouth open and cutting off his frantic protests. One by one, he dropped the three jade studs into Mudt's mouth, then clamped the jaw shut. Tar tore a piece of duct tape from a long silver roll and sealed the teen's lips. They wound more tape around the wrists and ankles to make the bonds extra secure, then Tar took the thief's feet, and Doun gripped him under the armpits, and they hefted him easily, placing him inside the metal box. With knees bent, he fit with barely any room to spare and could not turn over inside. Hilo caught one last haunting glimpse of the white face, stark with terror, before they dropped the lid in place. Thuds, faint screaming, and spiking jade aura shrieks emanated from inside the container, interrupting the whine of the cordless drill as Tar made holes all around the edge of the lid and fastened it in place with metal screws. Using the largest drill bit, he made a hole near the top of the box big enough to stick a finger through. Into this he inserted a length of plastic tubing through which air could flow. They didn't want the trapped man to suffocate.

Tar and Doun carried the box outside. The two men in the

field had finished digging and were leaning on their shovels, resting. When they saw the Pillar coming out of the building, they set down their tools and hurried to help Tar and Doun balance the box and lower it into the hole in the earth. Filling in the two-meter-deep grave took an hour, with all five men taking turns with the shovels while the others rested. At last, there was only a patch of fresh soil to mark where the box was buried, and poking up from the ground, a barely visible stiff plastic air tube.

Without his regular dose of shine, an addict would normally begin to feel the effects of jade overexposure within twenty-four hours. With jade trapped inside an adrenaline-overloaded body, it was sure to happen much faster than that. The Itches would set in shortly thereafter.

They collected the camping lantern and tools from the empty farmhouse. It was entirely silent out here in the country. The night sky was clear and filled with stars. None of the pollution or noise from Janloon reached them, and there were no other dwellings in sight. The nearest town, Opia, was thirty kilometers away on winding, mountainous roads. As they walked back to the cars, Hilo made a point of personally thanking the three Nails (that was what Tar called his people now, to differentiate them from Kehn's Fingers) for spending what would've been a nice evening diligently carrying out such an unpleasant task. All of them—Doun, Tyin, and Yonu—assured the Pillar that it was simply their duty to the memory of Kaul Lan, and they were only sorry that it had taken them so long to find the thief and dispense the clan's justice.

Hilo said to Tar, "You made sure the bartender who phoned in the tip was rewarded?"

"Of course," Tar said.

Between handling this and whispering the name of Koben Ento, Tar had been working hard lately. With the clan's expansion into Espenia, Hilo had some ideas for how to use Tar's small team in the future, but now was not the time to broach them. He put a hand on his Pillarman's back. "I know that sometimes I'm impatient or short-tempered with you, but only because you're my closest brother now, and I trust you with things I wouldn't trust to anyone else," Hilo said. "I'm glad I can count on you, Tar. I don't say it often enough."

––––––––––

It was the early hours of the morning by the time Hilo arrived back home. He closed the front door quietly behind him as he entered without turning on any of the lights, so as not to disturb Wen and the baby, only two weeks old, a girl of course. In the kitchen, he draped his jacket over the back of a chair and washed his hands in the sink. He was tired, but also hungry and thirsty, so he poured himself a glass of water and took two oranges from the fruit bowl and a bag of peanuts to the table. The Pillar sat in the dark, peeling and eating the oranges and cracking the peanut shells. He was rarely alone, so he relished the moment of peace and did not hurry to go to bed.

Hilo took Lan's jade from his pocket, set it on the table, and looked at it.

A stir in his Perception told him that someone else was awake in the house. He sensed Niko's approach before he heard the boy's feet padding hesitantly down the stairs and stopping at the entrance to the kitchen. The blinds were open over the patio door and the moon's glow mingled with the courtyard lights so it was just bright enough for Hilo to see his nephew's face, creased with sleepiness and mild concern. "Uncle?" he said. "Why are you sitting in the dark?"

"I got home late and didn't want to wake you." Hilo held out his arms and the boy came to him, climbing into his lap and laying his head against his uncle's chest. Even though Niko and Ru knew each other as brothers and called Wen their mother, Hilo always insisted that Niko call him *uncle* so that he'd never forget who his real father was. Hilo smoothed the boy's hair and whispered, "Stand up, I want to show you something." He set the three-year-old (almost four now, Hilo reminded himself) down on his feet and said, "Do you want to know where I was tonight, why I got home so late I couldn't tuck you into bed? I was searching for something, something that's been lost for a while, and I finally found it." He picked up the cuffs and the necklace of jade and let the boy admire and touch them. Some limited jade exposure at this young age was not harmful; indeed, it was beneficial for a child to have a basic foundation of jade tolerance before Academy age. "This was your father's jade, Niko," Hilo said. "It belonged to him when he was Pillar of the clan. One day, when you're a Green Bone, it'll belong to you. I'll keep it safe for you until then."

Niko yawned. "I'll have to grow a lot bigger first."

"A lot bigger," Hilo agreed. He picked the child up and carried him back up the stairs.

CHAPTER

44

The Man in the Middle

Willum "Skinny" Reams stood on a private boat dock under the shadow of the Iron Eye Bridge. It was a cloudy, starless spring night and the dark was almost absolute, save for the lights that illuminated the six-lane freeway that ran overhead, carrying a constant stream of traffic across the Camres River, the rush of the tires above louder than the steady lapping of the water below.

Four of Reams's coats waited for the shipment along with him. The twins, Coop and Bairn Breuer, stood next to the car that had been pulled up to the pier. Pats Rudy and Carson Sunter kept watch, hands resting on the butts of their pistols. It was not the first time Reams and his men had taken possession of a contraband shipment ferried up the river. The Camres was one of the longest and busiest commercial waterways in the world; for centuries it had been called the Silver Run, but it was also less flatteringly referred to as the Vice Canal, on account of the quantity of drugs and guns that made their way into the city of Port Massy from further upstream. This sort of event was routine for Reams, but he was uneasy tonight because of the nature of the goods. Willum Reams was a smart and ruthless foreman, well respected in the Port Massy underworld, but he was cautious by nature. Unlike his Boss, he didn't live lavishly and draw attention to himself; he dressed conservatively and drove a perfectly ordinary and reliable Brock sedan. He was a rich man, but he kept his money carefully stashed away and he ran all his jobs with a clear eye for the numbers. Boss Kromner valued him because he never forgot the first and most important job of a foreman, which was to make money for the Crew.

Reams disagreed with his Boss about getting into the jade business. There was money to be made, no question: The Southside Crew already had buyers lined up for the jade that the kecks were selling to them. Rich collectors, other Crews, private militia, mercenaries, and security contractors, even that cult in the north led by that religious nut claiming to be the reincarnation of the Seer—it seemed everyone wanted to get their hands on the green rocks. The stuff had been around for thousands of years, but people were acting as if it were newly discovered. Reams didn't trust in the wisdom of the crowd. Most people were stupid, and in his opinion, jade was too risky. It would bring down too much heat; the government thought of gambling and drugs as moral failings that destroyed the user but weren't a threat to the real power in the country, which were the Trade Societies. Jade, however, could strengthen armed and dangerous organizations that would pose a real threat to law enforcement and those in authority. Because you couldn't have jade without shine, there was bound to be a crackdown on the drug trade as well, which would jeopardize the Crew's most traditionally lucrative business.

The biggest problem, though, in Skinny Reams's book, was that dealing in jade meant dealing with the kecks. Reams could do business with the wesps and the 'guts, even the shotties and the tunks if he had to, but there was something about the kecks that he especially didn't like. They were unnatural, and he didn't trust them at all.

He could tell that his men were edgy as well; Pats came over and said, "Seer's balls, Skinny, how much longer we got to stand out here freezing our asses off? They weren't this late before. Something's wrong." Reams could understand his coat's suspicion; to reduce the risk of interception by the authorities, the entire quantity of jade had been split up into four shipments, transported into the harbor three to six weeks apart, passed under the noses of port inspection with the help of the dockworkers in the Wormingwood Crew, and delivered to Reams at different points along the river. The first shipments had gone smoothly, so there was no reason to believe that this one would not proceed in the same way, except that if the kecks wanted to screw them over, this would be their final opportunity.

At that moment, the sound of a motorboat engine quieted Pats. The boat's headlights emerged from beneath the gloom of the bridge and swung around the edge of the dock, pulling up to the pier where Reams and his men stood. A short man with a severely pronounced limp got off the boat. He appeared Kekonese, but Reams thought the two dark-skinned men with him were not. Perhaps they were from one of those tropical islands in the East Amaric, but it was hard to get a good look at them. They worked together to lift a heavy metal box onshore. The limping keck opened the lid of the box and shone a flashlight down to show Reams what was inside: unpolished rocks of varying size, cut open to reveal the gleam of the green gemstone within. "Twenty-five kilos," he said. "You want to weigh?" Reams shook his head; neither of the prior three shipments had been under weight; in fact, both had been over thirty kilos. When Reams had brought this up, the boatman had shrugged and said, "We give more, for the man in the middle to take his share."

The man in the middle. That was him, the foreman. The one who did the work and who took the risks, while the fat Bosses like Kromner stayed safe and warm indoors sipping brandy and smoking cigars on nights like this. Reams remembered the stranger who sat beside Dauk in the meeting, the young clan representative from Kekon who'd questioned Reams specifically before agreeing to the deal. The kecks weren't so uncivilized after all, if they recognized that the competence of the foreman on the ground was the key to a successful operation and threw in a little extra to make sure he was compensated for pulling everything off smoothly. So notwithstanding his skepticism of the jade trade as a whole, Reams took roughly five kilos of jade from each of the shipments and stored them away as a savings fund that he and his closest coats could move quietly on their own later without anyone knowing, not even the rest of the Crew. Insurance in case things took a bad turn for Kromner. The rest of the jade was taken to an industrial warehouse where another of Kromner's foremen, Moth Duke, and his men supervised migrants wearing lead-lined gloves who cut and polished the jade to be packed and delivered to final customers.

Reams closed up the boxes and said to Pats, "Go get the money." The coat went to the truck, returning a few minutes later with a suitcase that he set on top of the lid of the closed box and opened to reveal bundled stacks of hundred thalir bills. "You want to count it?" he asked the boatman, sneering a little.

The man shook his head. "I trust Espenians to count money." He closed up the suitcase, took it, and walked back toward the boat without another word. Reams motioned for Coop and Bairn to load the metal box into the car. They were halfway to the vehicle when two sets of headlights pulled up in front and eight men piled out of two black cars. The Breuer twins had their weapons out in an instant; Reams pulled his Ankev pistol, but then he heard Moth Duke's voice call out, with concern, "Skinny, that you over there?"

"Yeah, it's me, Moth. Tell your boys to point their Fully guns somewhere else, for fuck's sake." Duke's coats were carrying Fullerton submachine guns and aiming them all over the pier. Coop and Bairn started to lower their weapons, but Reams kept his own gun raised. "What's this about, Moth? Why the fuck are you here instead of at the warehouse waiting for us?"

"We heard there was going to be heat, Skinny, that it was a setup." Duke's large frame came striding ahead. He stood in front of his men, silhouetted by the glare of the headlights. Reams had always thought the man looked like an ape in a suit. "So we came to make sure you were all right, to back you up if the kecks pulled something. Did you get the rocks?"

"Yeah, we got them," Reams said.

"All of them?" Duke asked, and in those three words, in the particular tone of greed with which they were spoken, Reams understood in an instant that he'd been betrayed. He turned and ran for the pier. Moth Duke's coats opened fire, chopping Coop and Bairn apart with bullets. The motorboat's engine roared as it took off in a panic; lead peppered its hull and Reams got a glimpse of the keck boatman toppling backward, the suitcase in his hand tumbling through the air and overboard.

Reams flung himself into the black water. It swallowed him up with a shock of cold so painful that for a moment he thought he'd been shot dead after all. Then he felt himself sinking into the Camres, imagined his body coming to rest on the bottom of the polluted river alongside the bones of the men he'd put there over the years, and the furious instinct for survival snapped his mind back into place. Reams struggled free of the shoes and wool coat that dragged him down, then dove and swam, unable to see a thing and not knowing if and where he would emerge, not knowing if Pats and Carson or any of his other coats were still alive, but certain of one thing.

Moth Duke wouldn't dare turn on a fellow foreman without tacit approval. Which meant Boss Kromner—the man Skinny had served well and for many years—wanted him dead.

A Promise in the Park

Wen was annoyed with her husband. Of course she understood that the demands on the Pillar's time were great, and his responsibilities to the clan unavoidably took precedence over everything else, but that did not make her feel better at the moment. When Hilo was with the family, he was playful and attentive, roughhousing with the boys, chasing them, listening to the small children talk as if there was nothing else on his mind. However, when some issue in the clan needed attention, he was inclined to deal with it personally as soon as possible, which meant that anticipated family activities were never certain. A downpour the night before had brought the summer heat down to a pleasant temperature, making it a perfect day for a picnic outing, but Hilo was unable to spend time with them as he'd said he would; instead he'd been shut behind the closed doors of the study for several hours with the leaders of the minor Stone Cup clan regarding a construction workers' strike that was derailing projects the Espenians wanted completed on Euman

Island. After that, he'd agreed to see some representatives from a humanitarian aid group, and then he and the Weather Man had meetings downtown with Lantern Men all afternoon.

Wen made breakfast for her brothers and her sons, then fed the baby and packed a bag for the trip she'd planned to the park. Niko and Ru were unhappy that their father would not be coming on the adventure and were pestering Kehn for attention instead. He was often indulgent with the boys and snuck them treats when Wen wasn't looking, but when he sat down to breakfast without offering anything of sufficient interest, they fell to bickering over the same water gun, shoving each other until Ru began to cry. Kehn ignored the noise and continued flipping through the newspaper, but Tar shouted, "Hey!" He pulled the boys apart and deposited them into separate chairs at the table. "No fighting. Brothers shouldn't fight."

"He pushed me," Niko protested. "He's always taking my stuff!"

"Be quiet and listen to your uncle Tar," Wen admonished, filling water bottles.

Tar leveled a stern finger in Niko's face. "He's your little brother. You've got to be nice to him, because when you grow up, the two of you have to stick together, understand? You have to look out for each other. That way people know if they ever give trouble to one of you, they're sure to get trouble back from the other." Niko stared down at his plate, sulking. Tar said, "You don't think it's true? The men who murdered your da when you were just a baby, one of them thought he got away with it, but your uncle went after him and found him. You know what he did to that bad man?"

"He killed him." Niko had heard this story already.

Tar picked up a trio of grapes and held them in front of the boy's face. "He put jade stones in his mouth and buried him alive." He popped the grapes into Niko's mouth and clamped his hand over the boy's mouth, giving him a teasing shake before letting him go and ruffling his hair affectionately. "That's why no one messes with your uncles. So stick together; I don't want to see you two annoying your ma, fighting over some stupid thing, you ought to act better than that."

"Finish your breakfast and then we're going to the park," Wen reminded them.

Kehn offered to drive them—he had no plans besides meeting to train a few of his newer Fists, before spending a relaxed afternoon with Lina, who was pregnant and on bedrest—but Wen had promised the boys that they would take the bus. The park was only ten minutes away, just down the hill in the solidly No Peak–controlled Green Plain district. Wen regularly ran into the wives and children of other high-rank Green Bones at the playground and water park and there was never any safety concern. Kyanla had taken the day off to visit her aging mother in an Abukei tribal village outside of Janloon, so Wen carried the day bag and wrestled with the baby carriage herself. The task would be less aggravating if Jaya, at six months old, was not the fussiest of all Wen's children. She would not stand to be put down in the carriage for even five minutes. Hilo joked that she would grow up to be even greener than her brothers, but Wen responded irritably that the ridiculous superstition existed only to prevent desperately frustrated mothers from smothering their most unmanageable children.

Wen put a blanket down in a shady spot on the lawn near the play structure and let the boys run off to play while she watched the baby try to crawl toward the grass. Jaya would be her last child; she'd given Hilo a son (two sons, really) and a daughter. Kehn and Lina were married and expecting a child as well. Wen was still working on Tar, but the family's future was more secure than before. The baby was still too young—certainly Hilo would say so—but now that the guesthouse was renovated, Kaul Wan Ria could move back to Janloon and help care for the children so Wen could return to work, both as a designer and in any other capacity the Weather Man could find for her. Over the past few years, she'd continued to meet informers at the Celestial Radiance on a reduced schedule, but felt there was more she could do. She paid close attention to the clan issues that her husband and brothers talked about, and even when they'd moved on to other topics, she kept thinking about what she'd heard. She almost never forgot the face or name of a person she had met so she knew almost everyone of importance in the clan. She continued taking classes in interior design and Espenian, she perused the reports from the Weather Man's office that Shae brought over to the house for Hilo, and she read the newspaper every day, even when she was exhausted from dealing with the children and it was the last thing she did before going to sleep.

She did all this because often, as she lay next to Hilo in bed at night, he would share with her some problem he was dealing with or some question in his mind, and in that moment, she would know to say, "You should tell Kehn to assign the job to Lott Jin; he's coming up on promotion to Fist this year, isn't he?" or "You're already going to meet with the mayor next week; why not bring those two Lantern Men with you, and you can raise the issue with everyone in the room?" Hilo would consider her words and say, "That's what I was thinking too" or "I hadn't thought of that, but it's a good idea, love," and then he would wrap his arms around her, give her a kiss, and with his mind cleared, he would fall asleep in seconds.

Wen always felt the greatest sense of accomplishment in those few minutes before she followed her husband into sleep. At those times, she knew she'd been a true help to the family and the clan. All her life, she'd harbored a powerful resentment: If she hadn't been born with the deficiency of jade immunity, she might've gone to the Academy and become a Green Bone. But now she thought, if she'd been born a different person, she might not have ended up meeting and marrying Kaul Hilo and having children with him, so perhaps it was all meant to be.

Wen had prepared a picnic of cold noodle salad, pickled cucumber, fried nuts, and stuffed buns. When she called the boys back for lunch, they predictably ate only a little of it before running off again. Wen packed up the remaining food, then nursed and changed Jaya. She saw the white Duchesse Priza pull up to the curb beside the park, and for a hopeful second she thought that Hilo's schedule had miraculously cleared and he had come in person to join them. Then she saw her brother at the wheel and deduced that the Pillar was still busy and had asked Kehn to go in his place to pick them up. Wen called the boys back from where they were running around on the playground and told them it was time to go. She put Jaya in the carriage and pushed it toward the car with one hand, carrying Ru on her hip with the other. Kehn opened the door to get out and meet them.

The Duchesse exploded in a ball of fire.

One second it was there; in the next, Wen was stumbling backward, a scream strangling in her throat. Out of instinct, she seized Niko and yanked him close to her, turning her back to shield him and Ru from the heat of the inferno, which she could feel against her skin even from fifty meters away. When she looked over her shoulder, she saw that the windows and doors of the Pillar's distinctive white sedan were gone. Twisted pieces of metal littered the street; flames and smoke poured from the openings of the wreckage. Parents ran for their children, screaming.

"Niko, hold on to the side of Jaya's baby carriage and don't let go," she ordered her oldest child. "We're going to cross the street, now, quickly; stay with Mama and don't look back." Wen pushed the carriage in the opposite direction of the burning car, still holding on to Ru and making sure Niko did as she said. All three of the kids were crying with fear. All around her people were running; some running away from the scene of the explosion, some running toward it. There was shouting and distant sirens; none of it registered for Wen. Her brother was dead, she knew that. She and her children were still in danger. She walked with single-minded purpose, concentrating on maneuvering the wheels of Jaya's carriage over the lawn, until they reached the street on the other side. Her hands were coated with sweat, but she was astounded by how calm she felt. They crossed the intersection at the corner, and Wen went up to the first storefront with a white lantern hanging in its window. It was a boutique men's clothing shop; tailored suits, vests, and felt hats adorned the mannequins standing in the display window. Two salespeople were standing by the door, peering out at the smoke and commotion.

Wen scooped Jaya up in her arms, pushed the door open with her shoulder, and hustled all three of the children inside. "Who is the Lantern Man of the store?" Wen asked the nearest salesperson. A tall man with white hair came out from the back room. He raised thin eyebrows in confusion and mild alarm at the sight of Wen and the three small children. Before the store owner could utter a word,

Wen said, "My name is Kaul Maik Wen. Kaul Hiloshudon, the Pillar of No Peak, is my husband, and these are his children. I need to use your phone to call him right away. We'll need to wait out of sight in the back room of your store until he arrives to get us. If anyone comes in asking if you've seen us, say no unless you're certain they're Green Bones of No Peak." When the store owner stared at her aghast, Wen reminded him, "You're a Lantern Man of the clan so I know you're a friend who we can trust to help us in any way."

The store owner opened and closed his mouth once, then swallowed noisily and said, "Of course, Mrs. Kaul, come with me." He hurried Wen into his own office, a small space filled with fabric samples and catalogs, and picked up the receiver of his phone, which he handed to her. Wen dialed the main house. No one picked up. She depressed the receiver and called the Weather Man's office. Shae's secretary informed her that both the Weather Man and the Pillar had gone to a meeting at the White Lantern Club. Wen told her to send someone to inform them right away that something terrible had happened. She left the number of the store and hung up.

Hilo arrived twenty minutes later. By then, firefighters had put out the blaze, and a dozen of the clan's Green Bones and the Janloon city police were swarming the park and its surrounding streets. Wen remained in the back room of the clothing shop and did not go out to see what was happening or to find out if any remains of her brother Kehn had been recovered. If the bomb had gone off two minutes later, she and her children would all be dead. Her only thought now was to keep them all safe and out of sight of enemies who might still be watching the area. The store staff had brought whatever things they could find to distract the boys: paper and pencils, a package of crackers, some old catalogs, a box of chalk. Wen sat on the floor, trying to entertain Niko by drawing pictures with him. She rocked Jaya in her arms and fed crackers to Ru. When she heard the shop door bang open and Hilo's voice calling her name, Wen ran out to the front of the store and all but fell against her husband in a paroxysm of relief.

Hilo's arms were shaking as they held her, so tightly she was nearly immobilized in his grip. His face was bone white with fear. Wen had never seen her husband truly afraid before, and that more than anything made what had happened seem real. Up until now, for the sake of keeping herself and the children calm, she hadn't shed a tear, hadn't so much as let more than a quaver of emotion into her voice, but now she broke into choked sobs.

Niko and Ru ran out and clung to Hilo's legs; he bent and pulled the boys to his chest, kissing both of their heads and faces, ignoring the watching store staff and the posse of Green Bones who had followed him in. When he straightened up again, the color had returned to his face, and he said, with all of his usual quick, hard authority, "Juen, bring two of your Fingers with you and take my family back to the house. I'm trusting you with their lives."

The First Fist said, "Right away, Kaul-jen."

"Shae will meet you at home," Hilo told Wen. "I'll be back as soon as I can."

Wen whispered, "Does Tar know yet?" Hilo shook his head, looking stricken, and Wen felt the tears that had stopped threaten to start up again. Her brothers had always been two sides of one coin; nothing could come between them. How could Tar live without his older brother?

"Go home now," Hilo said gently but firmly. "Take care of the kids."

Wen seized her husband's arm with an insistence that surprised him, that surprised even herself. "Tell me that you'll find the people who did this." Inside, she was toppling, the last of her composure disintegrating in a roaring, incoherent firestorm, yet her voice emerged as a quiet hiss. "No matter who or where they are, or how long it takes. *Swear* to me that you'll find them and kill them."

She searched his face and found what she needed, the black danger in his eyes, the shock and fear that had been there darkening into the promise of violence. Hilo put his hands on either side of her head and pressed his forehead to hers. "I swear it."

CHAPTER

46

Unforgivable

§hae rushed home from the Financial District to discover that the Kaul estate had been turned into a fortress. Only immediate family members and Hilo's most trusted Fists were being allowed in or out of the grounds. Judging by when he'd left the house, Maik Kehn had driven the Duchesse Priza straight to the park without stopping anywhere in between so the only explanation was that someone had gained access to the vehicle and planted a timed explosive on it while it was in the family garage. The cowardly attack had come from within.

Shae could barely comprehend the idea. All visitors to the estate were members of the clan or known affiliates. The culprits might still be on or near the grounds. The guards and estate staff were being individually questioned. The leaders of the tributary Stone Cup clan, who'd been meeting with Hilo earlier that day, were being rounded up, as were the representatives from the nonprofit group. A couple of

Fingers had been dispatched to find Kyanla and bring her in; it was suspicious that the Abukei woman happened to be absent today of all days, though Shae could not imagine their longtime housekeeper having anything to do with so heinous an act.

Wen and the children were safely back in the main house, which had been thoroughly searched for any other source of danger. Shae was not sure if Kehn's wife had been told of his death yet. It was not hard to deduce that the bomb had been meant for Hilo; everyone in the city knew that the monstrous white Duchesse was his car. Kehn had driven it out to pick up Wen and the kids at Hilo's request; his own muscular black Victor MX Sport was in an automobile shop getting a new carburetor.

Shae's working assumption was that Ayt Mada was behind the attack. Two years of supposed peace between the clans was no reason to believe that Ayt had set aside her long-standing goal to have Hilo killed. Shae was on the phone in the study, on a conference call with Woon and her key staff on Ship Street. News about the bombing was on television, and the Weather Man's office was receiving anxious inquiries as to whether clan war was about to break out again. Shae did not have an answer, but she told her people to make it clear that no conclusions had been reached yet. She still had doubts. Ayt Mada whispered names in a considered and precise manner, sending assassins to do the work closely. A car bombing was an impersonal, covert, gutless, and thin-blooded act, likely to harm innocent bystanders and carelessly break aisho—it was not the Green Bone way.

Juen knocked on the study door and stepped inside. His jade aura was vibrating with urgency and agitation. As soon as Shae ended the call, the First Fist said, "Kaul-jen..." There was a strange woodenness in his voice. "A man just turned himself in at the gates. He claims to be responsible for the bombing."

A horrible sick apprehension dropped into Shae's stomach. With abrupt certainty, she knew she did not want to see what Juen would show her, yet she stood at once and followed the Fist out of the house to where half a dozen Green Bones were gathered on the driveway, surrounding a man kneeling on the ground. The familiarity of his aura assailed her before she saw him. Maro appeared unharmed, but his beige slacks were scuffed and his blue shirt rumpled. He was sitting back on his heels with his shoulders hunched, his gaze on the asphalt in front of him. The sight of him on his knees, guarded by men carrying moon blades, was so incongruous that disbelief overwhelmed Shae, dragged her steps to a halt and rooted her to the ground.

Maro saw her and began to climb to his feet. One of Juen's men put a hand on his shoulder and shoved him back down roughly. Shae protested, "Let him stand up," but Maro did not make another attempt to rise. He remained where he was and looked up at her with a desolate expression.

It did not make any sense. Maro could not have planted a car bomb. He and Shae had not ended their relationship on speaking terms, a fact that saddened her and filled her with regret, but Maro was not a vindictive personality. He had no clan interests, no appetite for violence, and no matter what anger he might feel toward her, he had nothing at all to gain from killing Hilo.

"They weren't supposed to hurt anyone else," Maro said quietly. "That's what they promised me. I would never have cooperated if I thought they might hurt you or the children."

If there had been something nearby for Shae to hold on to, she would've reached out to steady herself. "The meeting that you asked me to set up with Hilo months ago. That was this morning." Understanding pushed into her resisting mind like a thin blade. "That's how the assassins got in."

Maro's face crumpled like paper. "The meeting was real," he said. "None of the Four Virtues staff were in on the plan, I swear to you on my life. All I was asked to do was add a couple of fake college interns to the group at the last minute. They told me to get them through the gates to see the Pillar, that was all. They never gave me any other details."

Juen drew in a breath between his teeth. The idea of an enemy trying to strike at the Pillar in his own home was inconceivable. All of Hilo's meetings were approved by his Pillarman, Weather Man, or Horn. An aspiring murderer's hostile intentions would be Perceived by the guards and he would never get anywhere near the Pillar, nor would he escape alive. However, one or two unarmed visitors with seemingly legitimate credentials and no jade, attached to an otherwise honest party, would not raise suspicion. Once through the gates, they could find an opportunity to wander a short distance to the family garage. It was clear from Maro's wretched look that despite his complicity in the affair, he had not anticipated a planted car bomb any more than they had.

"Who were they?" Shae felt as if she'd been stabbed and the knife was lodged in her rib cage. "Who approached you?"

Maro pressed the base of one palm to his eyes. "There were three of them. The leader was half-Shotarian and wore jade hidden. I heard the others call him Soradiyo."

"Barukan." Juen spat. "I've heard the name Soradiyo before. He's a rockfish recruiter who works for Zapunyo."

The expectant stares and auras of the surrounding Fists and Fingers were like a hot physical pressure against Shae's skin. She turned to Juen. "Let me talk to him alone for a few minutes." After a second, she added in an undertone, "Please," because as Weather Man, she had no authority over Fists, and with Maik Kehn's death, Juen Nu was now the acting Horn of No Peak.

Juen shifted a slow gaze to the prisoner on the ground, then returned it to the Weather Man. He motioned for the other Green Bones to back off and take up vigilant positions elsewhere, but he himself made no move to leave. "It would be irresponsible of me to leave you alone with this man, Shae-jen," Juen said, and Shae understood this to be less an expression of concern for her safety than a reminder that as Horn, he was her equal, and had every right to hear what was said if it involved threats to the clan. Shae did not try to argue further. The inside of her throat seemed to be swelling and she was afraid it would soon close up completely. She made herself walk to Maro and kneel in front of him so their eyes were on the same level. "Why did you do it?" The whisper that emerged from her throat was dry and unrecognizable. Plaintive. "Did I hurt you that badly?"

Maro's eyes filmed with sadness. "Yes. But that's not why." He dropped his face into his hands. "They got to me, Shae. The barukan gangs are powerful in Shotar, and they're ruthless. They found out about my visits and phone calls to Leyolo City." Maro's shoulders were shaking now and his voice was muffled. "At first, they tried to blackmail me with the information. When I refused and ignored them, they sent me photos of my father. Of my half sisters and little nieces behind the windows of their homes. Close-up pictures of them in their neighborhood, at school, on the playground. I was told that if I didn't do as Soradiyo asked, something would happen to them. They would never know why."

Shae gripped Maro's forearms and pulled his hands away from his face. "Why didn't you tell me? We could've done something—protected your family, gone after the barukan..."

Maro raised his eyes and the bleak accusation she saw in them dried the words in her mouth. "Did *you* tell anyone when you felt threatened? When you realized you had no choice?" he asked. Shae could not reply. Maro had been visibly nervous the evening after Woon's wedding, wanting to talk, hoping for reconciliation. Instead of offering it to him, she'd told him the truth that she knew would drive him away.

Maro's shoulders slumped and he turned his face away. "Soradiyo promised that if I let a word out to anyone, the barukan would get to my nieces sooner or later and send me their tiny fingers one by one. Maybe it was a bluff, but I didn't dare call them on it. Even though my sisters are Shotarian, and I'm Kekonese, they welcomed me. They made me a part of their lives, of their children's lives. I could never put them in any danger." His jaw tightened, and bitterness slid edgewise into his voice. "You never brought me into your life. You kept me away, kept secrets from me, didn't even tell me when you decided to get rid of our—" He stopped, his eyes flickering toward Juen, still standing nearby and watching them.

Maro jammed his lips together. His hands clenched in his lap, the knuckles white. There was blackboard chalk on the cuffs of his sleeves, a detail that had become so familiar in the time Shae had known him that she was surprised to be noticing it again now of all times, as if it were something new. "You say you would've protected my family, but the truth is that the clans protect only themselves. Would No Peak really help strangers, especially Shotarians? You won't even go against the Espenians on the issue of Oortokon refugees." Maro shook his head slowly. "The Green Bone clans rule Kekon—but only Kekon. If the barukan wanted to go after my sisters' families in Shotar, they'd find a way. Who in Kekon would care, besides me? I couldn't take such an awful risk. I knew they'd try to kill your brother—why else would they want to get past the guards?—but you'd already chosen your clan over me; I had to choose my family's safety over yours. I had to do as they asked."

"Why did you come here?" Shae cried, almost angrily. "If the barukan are as powerful as you say, why didn't you ask them to get you out of the country?"

Maro let out a short, helpless chuckle. "Who in their right mind believes they can escape the justice of the clan? Green Bones have no equal when it comes to dispensing violent punishment. You know that more than anyone. Once your brother whispered my name, I'd spend the rest of my life as a dead man in waiting. At least this way, I had a chance to face you and explain myself in person."

The resentment left Maro's face and he gazed at her in sad resignation. "I never imagined this, Shae. Dying by the blade—that's for greener men. I would've been happy with books, and conversation, and . . . occasional silly romantic musicals. What we had together was real and perfect, for a while." He smiled weakly, then breathed a sigh that seemed physically laborious before dabbing the edge of his sleeve to his perspiring brow and looking up stoically at Juen. "Please make it quick."

Juen replied unsympathetically. "Tell us what else you know about Soradiyo and the barukan who contacted you. The men who came in today and set the bomb—who were they?"

"A couple of young men who worked for Soradiyo. I can describe them, but I don't know their names. The barukan made sure I didn't know much." There was no deception in Maro's aura. After he'd offered up what little additional information he possessed, Juen beckoned to one of the senior Fingers, Lott, and asked, "Did you reach the Pillar?"

Lott said, "He's on his way."

Juen glanced at Maro, then at his wristwatch. There was no question of the prisoner's guilt, but this was an instance not only of treason against the clan but a murderous attack against the Pillar's family. Any intelligent Fist would wait for direction from Hilo.

Shae got to her feet, overcome by sudden dread. "Is Maik Tar with Hilo?"

Juen said, "I think so."

Shae's stomach turned over. Tar would lose his mind; he would tear Maro to pieces. He'd make it last for hours or days. Maybe Hilo would put an end to it, but Hilo had just lost his Horn, a man he considered a brother, and his wife and children had nearly been killed; Shae couldn't count on him to be merciful.

Seeing the terrible realization on Shae's face or Perceiving the spike of panic in her aura, the little remaining color drained from Maro's face and was replaced with true fear.

A leadening sense of déjà vu flooded into Shae's limbs. She remembered standing in the cabin in Opia, facing Yun Dorupon. She'd told Maro about it: *I couldn't kill him.* She'd hated Doru for years but in that moment been unable to draw her blade. Now she walked toward Juen, her face a mask that hid every roiling emotion within her. "Juen-jen," she said. "If you're to be the Horn of No Peak, we'll be working together from now on. I've heard my brother and Maik Kehn speak highly of you, so I want us to start off on the right note." She forced moisture into her throat. "Tau Maro betrayed not only the clan but my personal trust. He's told us everything he knows, and there's no question he's to die. Do you disagree?"

Juen gave her a long, calculating look, but there was sympathy in it. He was not yet officially the Horn and it would be overstepping his authority to act on something so personal to the Kaul family without consulting the Pillar, but that was not the case for Shae, and

Juen had no desire or reason to oppose the Weather Man. "No, Kaul-jen. That's all true."

Shae returned to Maro and knelt back down in front of him. She had a nauseating sensation she might sink into the ground. "I'm sorry," she managed to say.

Maro nodded gratefully. He took one of Shae's hands and enfolded it in his own large ones, then brought it up to his face and laid it against his cheek as if it might offer a vestige of comfort. "Maybe I'm a coward after all," he said, "but you're not." He leaned into her touch, his beard tickling the center of her palm, and closed his eyes. Shae reached up and cupped both hands around the back of Maro's head and neck. His life pulsed beneath her touch, the wrinkled tex-ture of his jade aura warped with anguish and regret but no longer burdened by the tension of anger or fear.

Shae felt as if she couldn't breathe; she squeezed her eyes shut and imagined herself as a column of ice, a creature like Ayt Madashi, made of unwavering resolve and unflinching steel. With a stifled, incoherent cry, she gathered all the jade energy she could muster and Channeled into the base of Maro's skull. He put up no defense at all, did not raise even the flimsiest Steel. His energy yielded beneath hers; his aura tore and fled. The vessels in his brain burst and he died in seconds.

She caught Maro as he fell into her arms. She lowered him to the asphalt gently, then toppled over his body in a shudder as the blow-back of his escaping life rushed into and through her. She clung to the wave for a second, wanting to hang on to it, to follow it into whatever oblivion it was headed toward, but it slipped past her and she was still on the asphalt with Maro's body in her lap. Slowly, Shae lowered him to the ground onto his back. His eyes were still closed, and his face was inexpressibly sad, but relaxed. Shae kissed his fore-head, then both of his closed eyelids. She stood up. Juen and his men were gathered around, but they did not speak or move toward her.

She turned and walked toward the Weather Man's house. Halfway there, the memories came—slowly at first, a trickle from behind a wall of spreading cracks, growing into a torrent, then sweeping her away like the deluge from a bursting dam. Long conversations and tender moments, the fire in Maro's eyes when he was energized by an idea, the softness of his smile, the aching warmth of their bodies pressed together. Miraculously, she didn't break her stride, didn't stumble or collapse or burst into a run, but her vision swam and she could barely see her own front door when she reached it. When she was inside her own house and alone at last, Shae closed the door behind her, took three steps into the foyer, and crumpled to the ground with a long, silent, wordless howl, arms clutched to her sides, forehead pressed to the hardwood floor as if in eternal penitence.

CHAPTER

47

⌒

Back to Work

Shae barely left her house for a week. She dressed and emerged to attend Kehn's funeral, but the entire event passed in a blur of walking, chanting, and resentful silence. Hilo was devastated by his Horn's death; he kept Wen's hand tightly clasped in his own and their children within his sight at all times. Tar broke down at the side of his brother's grave and wept like a child. Afterward, his eyes were vacant and lost, as if he was no longer present, except for one moment when Shae passed near him and she felt his gaze settle on her for a moment, his aura flickering with bitterness that she had executed Maro painlessly.

Shae couldn't bring herself to speak to Tar and tell him that she, too, grieved for Kehn. She hadn't known the Maik brothers well at first, for a long time thinking of them only as her brother's lackeys, but the past few years had altered that impression. She'd seen Kehn grow into the role of Horn, had shared meals with him around the family dinner table, had come to know him as a loyal and dangerous but quietly dogged man who was at least half the reason for the productive cooperation between the two sides of the clan. Hilo had insisted that Kehn be laid to rest next to the grand Kaul family memorial instead of the small, disused patch where his ignominious father was buried, but from what Shae overheard, the explosion had not left much in the way of remains. Kehn's ashes did not take up even a fraction of the steel casket. The Horn was a dangerous role, one in which a Green Bone might expect to lose his life for the clan—on his feet with a blade in his hand. Not like this.

Shae went back into her house. Woon once again took over the job of managing the Weather Man's office in her absence. Kyanla brought meals over from the main house and left them in Shae's fridge, where they remained mostly untouched. Within days of Lan's death, she'd walked into the office tower on Ship Street and taken over Doru's office as Weather Man. When her grandfather passed away, she'd mourned deeply, but had gone back to work. Those tragedies had broken her heart, but they had not torn out a piece of her soul. This time, she couldn't function. She had no desire to get out of bed, to dress, or to eat. Nor did she care to know what was going on in the clan in her absence.

Shae had taken lives in combat before, but she had never thought of herself as a murderer, as she did now. Everything she had done to try to keep Maro at a distance from the clan and her unavoidable decisions as Weather Man had hurt and endangered him, had led to his death. She'd loved him; she wondered if he even knew that, if she'd ever told him. The world needed more people like Tau Maro, and she'd ended his life with her own hands.

At times in her isolation, she prayed to the gods, and at others she railed and cursed them bitterly. She questioned everything she had ever done; she thought about leaving Kekon again; when she closed her eyes, she saw Maro's face, so sad and full of accusation, and in helpless horror and remorse, she relived over and over again the moment of his death. She nursed a growing, burning, unquenchable hatred for the coward Zapunyo and his barukan thugs.

Years ago, she'd argued with Hilo that they had more important things to worry about than a smuggler ensconced in the Uwiwa Islands. Now she realized she'd underestimated Zapunyo in a crucial way. The Kekonese took it for granted that even during an outright clan war, civilians without jade would not be targeted. Zapunyo and the barukan were not Green Bones. They had no sense of aisho and did not care if innocents were killed along the way.

On the eighth or ninth day, Shae was not sure which, she heard the front door open and footsteps come down the hall toward her room. She thought at first that it was Kyanla again, come to leave more food that would go uneaten, but when she roused her sluggish sense of Perception, she recognized that it was Wen. Her sister-in-law knocked on the bedroom door.

"Sister Shae," Wen said. "May I come in?"

Shae considered ignoring the request, but felt as if she had no right to do so. Wen had seen her brother killed before her eyes and been terrified for her children's lives. She had as much if not more reason to be incapacitated than Shae, and yet here she was. Shae dragged herself out of bed and opened the door. She realized that she must look terrible; she had been wearing the same old shirt and pajama pants for several days, her hair was uncombed, and she suspected that if she looked in the mirror, she would barely recognize herself.

Wen took all this in expressionlessly. She pushed past Shae into the stuffy bedroom and opened a window, letting in a gust of air. Wen turned to face her sister-in-law and sat down on the edge of Shae's unmade bed. "Shae-jen," Wen said, as if they were having a perfectly ordinary conversation, "I want to go back to working for you. Not right away, but soon; I was thinking once Jaya turns nine months old. We've done some useful things together, but we both became too busy. In the future we can do better. I've talked your mother into moving back to Janloon and into the guesthouse for her own safety and to help with the children so I can go back to work part-time."

Shae felt as if Wen's words were coming from some other reality in which the events of the past two weeks had not happened. She blinked and let out a noise that might've been a laugh of incredulity if her voice had been less disused. "Why are you asking me this right now?"

"Who else would I ask?" Wen exclaimed. "You're the Weather Man, unless you're planning to resign your position." She looked at Shae shrewdly, her expression a question. "You were willing to die at the hands of Ayt Mada rather than step down. Has that changed?"

"Now's not a good time to ask me anything, Wen," Shae said.

"When would be a good time? When are you planning on coming back out?"

Shae felt a weak stir of irritation. "How can you be thinking about this right now?"

Wen crossed her arms. "I would like to hide in my room for a month as well, Shae-jen. But I can't do that. I have to take care of my children; they don't stop needing a mother just because I am suffering. I have to explain to Niko and Ru that their uncle Kehn is dead. And I have to keep up my strength for Hilo, so he can concentrate on managing the clan in this time and not worry about us." She fixed Shae with a straight glare and spoke matter-of-factly. "Kehn is gone, Tar is inconsolable. You're shut in this room. The Pillar is alone right now."

"He has dozens of people to help him," Shae muttered.

"He needs you. The family needs you, the same way we needed you after Lan was murdered, and after your grandfather died. Hilo needs you to help him lead No Peak. You didn't disappear for a week after any of those times." Wen's expression softened but remained resolute. She took her sister-in-law by the arm and steered Shae into sitting next to her. "This isn't the first time we've been hurt, but it's the first time you feel personally responsible for what happened, because your good intentions turned into so much pain."

Shae stared at the other woman. "I *am* responsible, Wen." The backs of her eyes began to burn, and she closed them for a second before fixing them in accusation on Wen. "Don't *you* blame me for Kehn's death? For the fact that you and your children were nearly killed?"

"Why would I blame you?" Wen sounded exasperated. "I blame our enemies, Shae-jen, for twisting someone who was dear to you to their purposes, for using him like a tool to try to destroy us. You may have ended his life, but you didn't cause his death. In our world, there's a difference."

"What does this have to do with you wanting to go back to work?"

Wen got up and went to look out the bedroom window. The sunlight hurt Shae's eyes, but Wen stared out into the distance steadily. "A barukan rockfish working for an Uwiwan smuggler on an island hundreds of kilometers away got to us here in Janloon, at a park in our own neighborhood. The clan has enemies everywhere now. We're not just fighting other Green Bones. We're fighting the world, Shae-jen. Which means that aisho will not protect my children."

She turned back to face the Weather Man. "Hilo has never wanted me involved in Green Bone matters. But the threats to the clan aren't just Green Bone matters anymore." Her voice was familiar in its soft and reasonable entreaty, but there was a sharp underside to it. "Our enemies are willing to use any angle to attack us. The clan has lost one of the Maiks, maybe two since Tar can barely function, but not all of them. So put me to work, Shae-jen."

Wen went to Shae's closet. She pursed her lips as she picked out a blouse and a skirt and threw them on the bed. "When you challenged Ayt Mada with a clean blade, everyone was shocked, even Hilo, but not me. We women claw for every inch we gain in this world, and you'd worked too hard for your place on Ship Street to let it be taken from you. It could still happen, if you don't get dressed and leave this room. There are always people looking for signs of weakness, for chances to steal what we care about away from us." Wen walked past Shae and out the bedroom door. "Your nephews asked if you would be at dinner tonight and I said yes."

CHAPTER

48

~⌒~

The Double Double

Bero was in the hospital for over a month. Even after the poison and the shine were purged from his bloodstream, he was too feeble to go anywhere. Weak as he already was from nearly dying of SN1 overdose, the crushing heaviness, deadening lethargy, and sweaty panic of jade withdrawal drained what little strength Bero had left. He lay half-mad in the hospital bed next to the other patients in the infirmary, alternately wishing for death and cursing all the gods and his own existence.

The doctors said that he was lucky, very lucky indeed. That much shine would've killed any typical person, but Bero's SN1 tolerance was uncommonly high—a result of regular, prolonged use of the drug—and the powerful sedative that Mudt had slipped into his drink had slowed his metabolism, so the fatal injection had not taken effect on his organs as quickly as it ordinarily would have. His neighbor, Mrs. Waim, incensed at the commotion she'd heard in the middle of her daytime soap operas, had come out into the hallway to discover him lying half in and half out of his door and, after a few seconds of serious deliberation about whether to save his life or let him die, had called the ambulance to their building.

Bero remembered none of this and, if anything, was irritated that he now owed unpleasant Mrs. Waim his life. When he was released, it was with a hospital bill for over twenty thousand dien and a simmering hatred for the world. He had his life but that was all. His jade was gone. He had no doubt that Mudt would've stolen his stash of shine so that would be gone too. He felt as thin and wobbly as a colt, helpless, empty-headed, and wronged beyond all sense in the world. It had taken him years—*years*—of wanting and striving, of planning and scheming, of daring and thick blood, to pull off what he had accomplished. Jade of his own and everything that came with it— money, respect, power, a future. A dangerous future, to be sure, but far better than what lay ahead of him now, which was...nothing.

He fantasized about tracking down Mudt, putting his head in a vise, and cranking it slowly until Mudt's eyeballs popped out of his crushed skull. He was wary, though. Mudt had twice as much jade now, and Bero had none, so any encounter between them was bound to be hopelessly mismatched even without accounting for the fact that Bero could still barely climb a flight of stairs without feeling dizzy. It was the only motivation Bero had left, however, so he followed it dumbly. When he returned to the Rat House, though, he learned that Mudt had not been back there. He went to some of their other usual haunts, places where new green met and talked, and the consensus was that Mudt had not been seen or heard from in some time. The kid had taken Bero's jade and shine and vanished entirely.

Bero returned to his apartment and did not leave. Months passed. Winter turned to spring and then to summer. He ordered in food, watched television, and slept. The limp he'd had ever since he'd been beaten by the Maiks was more pronounced, and he wore an unrelenting scowl that made his face even more crooked. At the age of twenty-one, he looked and felt like a ghoulish old man with nothing left to live for. Bero had always considered himself to be the sort of person who was not easily discouraged, but now as he lay on the sofa listlessly, barely moving except to eat, piss, or change the channel, he found himself weighing various options: stepping in front of the subway train, jumping off the tallest building he could find, getting ahold of a gun and putting a bullet between his eyes. He debated which of the ways would be quicker, more reliable, less messy. He already knew to rule out overdosing on drugs—very painful, too slow, not foolproof at all.

He counted what remained of his money. A year ago, he'd been flush with cash, but now he was almost broke. He had money left for another month of rent and no income prospects in sight. Bero made up his mind. One morning, he got out of bed, dressed in the cleanest clothes that remained to him, shaved and brushed his teeth for the first time in days, and left his apartment, being sure to close the door tightly behind him. Outside, the world was bright but washed out and blurred, made dull without jade. He went to the bank and withdrew every last dien that remained to him, then took a cab to Poor Man's Road, where the biggest and best betting houses in Janloon were located. The lights outside of the Double Double beckoned and he stood on the sidewalk gaping at them for a minute before he went inside.

In Bero's own mind, there was a logic to what he was doing. All his life, he'd ridden the winds of fortune. The elder Mudt had said that Bero had some strange luck of the gods on him and Bero knew it was true. His bad luck would turn to good, his good luck turn to bad, always the capricious gods would swing him one way and then slap him back in the other direction, like a relayball on a rope. This then, would be the final test: He would take what little remained to him in the world and throw it all to the winds of luck. He would bet every last dien he had at the card tables and the spinning wheels, and through that, he'd know whether he was meant to keep going, whether the gods still wanted him alive or not.

Bero sat down at the largest of the card tables with a glass of hoji in hand and began to play beggar's lot—a game that required almost no skill and relied mostly on luck of the draw. To his surprise, he had an initial string of good hands—a copper run, a brass and silver split, and a jade pair—but then, as was to be expected, his luck turned for the worse, dramatically. His next three hands—a copper pair, an iron single, and a robber's spread—lost him all his initial winnings, and then he kept losing, with steady efficiency. Bero took a generous swallow of hoji every time he lost, and two hours later, when he was down to a quarter of the money he'd entered with, he was quite drunk. He was having a good time now, though. He grinned with fatalistic cheer as he ordered another glass of hoji, pushed a stack of chips into the center and nodded to the dealer to deal him another hand. The dealer looked at Bero and his dwindling chips with mild concern and said, for the first time, "Are you sure?"

"Don't stop now," Bero exclaimed. He hadn't felt this alive, this full of certainty, since the night he'd taken the jade from Kaul Lan's grave. "I'm almost done, keke. Once I'm out of money, I'm going to jump off the Way Away Bridge. Or maybe the roof of this casino." He counted his chips. "The gods have only...ah, maybe five more chances to stop me." The dealer obliged, and Bero turned over his new cards. An iron single. Bero laughed and took a swallow of hoji.

The dealer cleared the cards and his throat at the same time. "The gods don't control the card tables, if you don't mind me saying. Maybe you ought to take a break from playing. Whatever's bothering you so badly, it can't be worth throwing away all your money and then your life."

"Just what I needed," Bero griped. "A dealer with a heart. That's not your job."

The dealer didn't reply, but surreptitiously, he caught the eye of someone across the room and made a hand gesture that Bero did not notice. Bero lost two more rounds of play. With a satisfied sigh, he pushed all his remaining chips into the center of the table. "That didn't take too long."

"Hold on," said a voice behind Bero. The dealer paused, and Bero turned toward the strangest thing he'd ever seen: a man in a white shirt and dark blue pinstripe vest, wearing leather slip-on sandals. The man had no arms; his short sleeves dangled empty. A small brown monkey sat on his right shoulder.

"Is this some kind of joke?" Bero said.

The armless man made a curt gesture with his chin. "Come with me," he said to Bero.

"You can't make me," Bero said, like a child. A stern, irritated expression came into the man's face. He took a step toward Bero, angling his torso in a slightly forward lean as if he were extending the arms he did not have, and pushed Bero out of his chair with a firm Deflection. Bero stumbled and nearly fell. He caught himself on the edge of the card table and blurted, "You can't do that! Leave me alone, monkey man. I haven't broken any rules. What're you hassling me for?"

"Walk," said the man, and nudged Bero with another precise Deflection that kept him upright but shoved him forward. Bero swayed drunkenly and cursed as the Green Bone escorted him across the main floor of the Double Double. Gamblers looked up from their games to watch them pass, but oddly enough, none of them seemed surprised by the strange sight. The brown monkey leapt to the ground and scampered ahead to pull the handle of a metal door that read EMPLOYEES ONLY. The armless man propped the door open with his foot to let Bero through and said, "Turn right. Second door."

Bero obeyed, perhaps only because he was curious about the unusual turn of events. He was in a red carpeted hallway. To the left he could hear the sounds of the casino's kitchen. To the right were several offices. The armless Green Bone directed Bero into one of them. Inside was a large desk, but it was very low, the height of a child's desk, as well as a black sofa, and several framed certificates on the wall that looked like awards. Behind the desk was a display shelf with a long row of bottles of hoji.

"Sit down," said the Green Bone, jerking his head toward the sofa. He pulled a foot out of its slipper, opened the bottom drawer of his desk cabinet, and took out a bottle of water, which he rolled across the floor to Bero. "Once you're sober, you'll get your remaining money back and so long as you promise not to kill yourself, I'll call you a cab. You have somewhere to go? Someone to go to?"

"What do you care?" Bero said, but he took the bottle of water and fell onto the sofa.

The man said, "Every once in a while, we get someone like you, someone who wants to put on a bit of a show for themselves before bringing down the curtains. Or maybe they're having a bad time so they come here hoping to turn things around, but make it worse instead. Some of them end up trying to jump off the roof of the casino or to blow their brains out in one of the premium suites. It's bad for business."

"So who are you, the owner? Or just the casino watchdog?"

Bero said it mockingly, but the man merely shrugged. As he had no arms, the movement appeared odd, as if his head bobbed briefly into his torso. "When you have a good sense of Perception, it's easy to notice the desperate ones. But no, I'm not the owner of the Double Double. I make hoji." He nodded toward the bottles on the shelf. Bero saw that the frames on the wall held certificates for various industry awards. "The Double Double has an in-house distillery. I run the distillery, and I'm an…unofficial floor manager at the casinos. I keep an eye on all of Poor Man's Road."

"Why don't you have any arms?" Bero asked.

For a moment, the Green Bone gave him a cold and disgusted look, as if he were regretting having interfered with Bero's original plan. Then he said, "I don't have arms because the Horn of the Mountain cut them off." He pushed his chair over so it faced the sofa, then sat down facing Bero. "I've been where you are now. I wanted to die. I begged for death. I was in too much pain and couldn't see a future for myself. But a friend spoke to me at the right time and convinced me to live. Now the man who cut off my arms is dead, but I'm still alive, and my family and business are thriving. So whatever it is that brought you here, whatever wrong you've suffered—there's something on the other side of it."

Bero muttered, "At least you still have your jade."

The man leaned forward. "At least you still have your arms."

Despite himself, Bero had drained the entire bottle of water and now he slouched, rolling his head back on the Green Bone's black sofa. He could feel a persistent pressure behind his eyes, an alcohol-induced headache made worse by hours under the too-bright lights of the casino floor. "I'm in this fix because of jade," he said. "Always because of jade." He was unable to say why he was admitting this to a Green Bone of the No Peak clan, except that he had stopped caring about anything. His only feeling was limp irritation that this man was trying to convince him to live when he had other plans. "I listened to a barukan asshole who promised me that if I worked as a rockfish for him for a year, I'd earn green. But then I lost a crew to the Mountain—it wasn't even my fault—and I didn't take the whisper work he wanted me to, so he cut me off. The fucker *cut me off.*" Bero wanted to scream thinking about it. More words rushed out of him in a drunken stream. "Then the guy I was working with, he *turned* on me, the greasy little piss rat. I *made* him, and he drugged me and stole my jade and left me to *die.* If I ever find him, I'm going to kill him in the worst way I can think of."

Bero opened his eyes and sneered at the Green Bone, daring him. "So yeah, I'm a thief and a smuggler. I worked with barukan gangsters and Uwiwan scavengers to steal jade from the mines. You still plan on keeping me alive now, *jen?*"

From the edge of the desk, the perched brown monkey stared at Bero. For a minute, the armless Green Bone did the same. Then he tapped the phone on the table with his big toe. The monkey leapt over and brought the receiver to the man's head. The Green Bone held it between shoulder and ear and dialed a number. His gaze remained on Bero the whole time.

Bero heard the click of the phone being answered on the other end. "Lott-jen, it's Eiten," said the armless Green Bone. "Can you come over to the Double Double? I have someone here in my office that the Pillar might be interested in."

CHAPTER

49

⌒☉

Cleaning out the Rat House

When Hilo arrived at the Double Double, Eiten met him at the entrance. "Who is this kid you found?" Hilo asked, as his former Fist led him across the floor and through the back doors to the adjoining distillery operations. Gamblers paused in their games to salute the Pillar as he passed. Hilo noticed a few Espenian servicemen at the bar, but they were behaving themselves. Poor Man's Road, which No Peak had fought so hard to conquer from the Mountain, had proven to be a troublesome area over the last two years, but there had been no recent incidents.

"A broke and drunk former rockfish who showed up with a story about being cheated by a barukan named Soradiyo," Eiten said. "Juen and Lott have been talking to him, but we thought you might want to ask him questions yourself, Hilo-jen." In the dim, climate-controlled storage room, they walked past rows of large casks, stacked to the ceiling on wooden frames and filled with aging hoji. Cursed Beauty distillery had expanded considerably and begun exporting product to overseas markets. Seeing his friend's business doing so well gave Hilo a small reason to smile in what had otherwise been a tragic and terrible past few weeks.

"I'm glad I can count on you to keep your eyes and ears open, my friend," Hilo said.

Eiten dismissed the comment with a shake of his head. "I owe everything to you, Hilo-jen; I only wish I could be more helpful. If this kid is telling the truth, maybe his appearance is a gift from the gods that'll help us find and punish the half bone dogs who killed Kehn."

Hilo did not dare get his hopes up so quickly, but he nodded. He already had every Fist and Finger in the clan hunting down any information about Zapunyo's agents and searching for the barukan that Tau Maro had named, but so far it had been like chasing a ghost.

Hilo regretted not taking Kehn's warnings about Zapunyo more seriously. He'd been preoccupied with inciting division in the Mountain and hoodwinking the Crews. Zapunyo, he'd treated more as a persistently offensive problem than a truly dangerous enemy. After all, smugglers and drug dealers were like weeds; if you pulled one out, another might take its place, so in a way, there was no rush. Zapunyo, however, was in a criminal class of his own. Hilo realized he'd lost sight of that fact. When the informer had been delivered to No Peak in pieces, he'd made the mistake of not treating an Uwiwan death as seriously as a Kekonese one; he should've understood the threat and retaliated against Zapunyo's transgression forcefully and immediately. That error in judgment would always haunt him.

Eiten strode ahead and Deflected open a swinging metal door that led into the large, clean concrete chamber occupied by the distillery's fermentation tanks. Juen and Lott were standing around a portable wooden table. On the table were city and country maps marked up with colored dots and handwritten notes. Sitting hunched in a metal folding chair behind the table was a skinny, pallid young man with bloodshot eyes and a sour face that looked as if it had been broken and mended at least once in his life. Juen and Lott broke off their conversation to salute the Pillar as he entered. Juen gestured to the notes and maps and said, "Here's what we know so far, Hilo-jen. Places in the city where Soradiyo goes to recruit or meet with his local rockfish, mostly illegal clubs for jade thieves and shine addicts. Also, drop-off and pick-up sites along the coast and in the mountains for Zapunyo's scrap-picking operations. Vuay, Iyn, and Vin have sent Fingers to corroborate—quietly, so we don't spook anyone before we decide to act."

One thing Hilo was grateful for was how quickly and matter-of-factly Juen had assumed the role of Horn. Juen was not an immediate relative like Kehn had been, and he needed to learn how to have a stronger presence when dealing with the public and clan outsiders, but he was an operational mastermind who could manage a remarkable number of details, and right now that was particularly useful. Hilo studied the information that his men had compiled and asked questions until he was satisfied that they'd done or were in the process of doing their due diligence.

Hilo turned his attention to the young man, the unexpected informer. There was something familiar about him, about his unbalanced face and the sullen, resentful intensity of his eyes. "You say you worked for Soradiyo," Hilo said. "Why are you betraying him?"

The young man glanced at Hilo with unease before scowling at the ground. "That barukan hung me out," he muttered. "I was supposed to be a big dog like he promised, I was supposed to get jade, but he hung me out. All the new green are pussies. So fuck them all, and fuck Soradiyo. They don't deserve what they have. They don't deserve jade at all."

Hilo wondered if the young man was still drunk; he certainly sounded it. Some of his angry mumbling was barely audible, and he seemed to be talking half to himself. If there was any Perceivable cunning or deception in him, though, it was blotted out by an impression of overwhelming black bitterness. Whenever he happened to glance at the Pillar, he twitched a little and looked away. Hilo tried to think of where he'd seen the man's crooked face, because he had a feeling that he'd come across it before. He asked curiously, "You've smuggled jade and dealt shine and worked for foreign criminals. Aren't you afraid we'll kill you after this?"

The man looked around the stark concrete room and metal tanks as if noticing for the first time that there were no windows and only one exit, and that no one from the busy casino floor would be able to hear anything that was said or done in here. He sniffed and shrugged.

There was still something disquietingly familiar about the man. Hilo had met a lot of people in his time as Horn and then Pillar, and though he could not place this one, he knew better than to let such a thing slide, not when so much was riding on one stranger's account. "Look at me," he demanded. The man tensed but did so reluctantly. "How do I know you?"

This time, the informer winced visibly, as if he'd been slapped, and in that instant, Hilo recognized him. "The Twice Lucky," he said. When the man twitched again and nodded, Hilo laughed. Juen, Lott, and Eiten were looking at him questioningly. "Years ago, the Maiks and I caught a couple of dock brats trying to steal jade off that old drunk Shon Ju," Hilo explained. "I was all for snapping this one's neck, but Lan let him go." Hilo chuckled again at the irony. "Jade fevered, like I said at the time, so it's no surprise he ended up as a rockfish. But now he's here, giving us the keys to Zapunyo's kingdom." Hilo shook his head, amused and also struck with sadness to think that Lan's optimism, his softheartedness, had come back to help at such a time and in such a way. *You have to give people a chance*, that's what his brother had said.

Hilo leaned over the small table and seized the young man's chin in a grip of iron. "I said I'd kill you if I saw you again, remember?" he said in a low voice. The man's sunken eyes widened, but Hilo released him with a quick shake and sighed. "I guess I can't keep that promise after all. Not after you've been helpful to the clan, and with Lan watching."

Within hours of the car bombing, Ayt Mada had issued a public statement condemning the attack and categorically denying the

Mountain's involvement. Five innocent bystanders, including a child, had suffered non-life-threatening injuries from the blast, and Ayt adamantly declared that this was the work of criminals, as no Green Bone of the Mountain would engage in such a reprehensible breach of aisho. She expressed the Mountain's sincere condolences to the Kaul and Maik families and vowed to aid them in any way possible to bring those responsible to justice.

It was all very convincing, Hilo admitted, and he intended to hold Ayt Mada to her public sentiments. Some of the leads he and his men had gathered led straight into Mountain territory; No Peak could not effectively go after Zapunyo's organization without cooperation from their rivals. Hilo sent Juen to meet with Nau Suen and request that the Mountain honor the truce between the clans and help, or at least not hinder, No Peak's vengeance against the foreign jade smuggler.

With Nau Suen's permission, Juen took three of his best Green Bones with him into the Factory, the Mountain training hall in Spearpoint. Hilo waited outside in the Victor MX with another half dozen men, two other cars, and no small amount of impatient anxiety. He rested his arm out the window and smoked two cigarettes in a row, staring at the clouds scudding across the sky over resting freight cars. Lan had fought a clean-bladed duel on this very spot four years ago. Hilo found it difficult to even believe that had happened in this same lifetime. *Lan shouldn't have fought,* he thought now. *We should've stormed that fucking building with everything we had.*

Juen and his men returned thirty minutes later. Hilo got out of the car to hear what his Horn had to say. "They've agreed to let us enter Mountain territory and to go after the targets we name, so long as they're part of it. We have to share everything we know about Zapunyo's organization, and Nau's Green Bones will be right there with us on any action we take within their borders." Hilo nodded; he hadn't expected to get assistance for nothing. Naturally, the Mountain would want to lay claim to the jade, money, and shine seized in their own districts.

Juen frowned. "I see why some people think Nau can read minds. He doesn't look like much, but he makes the skin crawl. He's not like any Horn I've ever met."

"That's because he's not. He's Ayt Mada's snake, and he'd slit all our throats in our sleep if he got the chance." Hilo got back into the car. "We have to move fast. Work with him."

They took out the Rat House the following evening. Anyone who saw the Pillar that night and on the several more that followed would think they were seeing the Kaul Hiloshudon from six years ago, the fearsome young Horn with his posse of warriors, studded with jade and bristling with weaponry. They would be mistaken, Hilo thought grimly. His thirty-second birthday was coming up, but he didn't look or feel as young anymore; he arrived in the Coinwash district in Kehn's Victor MX Sport instead of his signature white Duchesse, and Kehn himself was not at his side. Tar was there, however; the younger Maik had an unhinged look about him, something akin to a shipwrecked sailor or a starved animal, but Hilo could not possibly have left him behind, not in this.

In addition to Tar, he had with him Lott, Vin, and three Fingers. Elsewhere in the city, Juen, Vuay, and Iyn were leading simultaneous raids on other hideouts. Hilo paused on the street before they entered the club. "No killing until we find Soradiyo," he reminded his men.

They tore off the door and strode into the building. There were about a dozen people inside with unfamiliar jade auras, scratchy and awkward, untrained, flaring into terror and hostility as the Green Bones burst into the room. Half a dozen men leapt up from their places and drew guns, but in the close quarters, only a few managed to get off any shots before the Green Bones were upon them. Moving in a blur of Strength, Hilo slid his head out of the way of one man's aim, seized the outstretched arm, and slammed the heel of his other hand upward into the man's limb, just above the elbow, breaking the joint with an audible crack. The gun went off, drowning out the man's howl of pain. Hilo crushed the side of the man's knee, grabbed his hair as he began to fall, and slammed the crook's face into the nearest table as he went down.

Hilo took one, two steps—off a chair and then the bar top—pivoting as he leapt Light from the counter and off the nearest wall, drawing his talon knife in midair and Steeling as he came down with his full weight on the attacker he'd Perceived behind him. They crashed together to the concrete floor. Hilo pulled the man's head back and nearly cut his throat before he remembered his own admonition to leave the occupants alive. His opponent twisted around on the sticky ground, bellowing and heaving with desperate, unfocused Strength as he tried to seize Hilo in a headlock. He was a burly, powerful man and might've succeeded if Hilo didn't act quickly; he pushed the palm of his hand into the man's back, Channeling into his spine, rupturing the discs between the vertebrae. The man's torso and legs went rigid with agony and he lay unresisting on the ground as Hilo got back to his feet and brushed off his clothes.

Several other of the Rat House's denizens were unconscious or incapacitated, though Hilo suspected that a few of them did not have long to live. Tar, moon blade in hand, had severed one man's arm at the elbow and opened the belly of another who was now kneeling on the ground, feebly moaning and holding his protruding entrails. The rest of the new green were cowering on the ground with their heads to the floor, begging for mercy. Lott and Vin, their jade auras humming with alertness, were going around confiscating weapons and collecting the illegal jade—rings, pendants, belts. Hilo stood in the center of the dim room and took a good look around. The Rat House was a sorry, stuffy place—one half of it covered with mats, broken concrete blocks, sandbags, and other equipment for people to practice jade abilities, and the other half full of dingy tables in front of a surprisingly well-stocked bar. Two metal needle disposal boxes hung on the wall along with handwritten flyers with tips for safe and hygienic shine injection.

"All of you are jade thieves who don't deserve to live," Hilo announced. "Whether you worked for the Mountain, or foreign criminals, or are just too jade fevered and stupid to know any better, you're all in this situation because you didn't change your ways when you had the chance." He allowed his words to sink in as he paced slowly across the floor, examining faces, comparing them to the drawings he'd had made from descriptions and shown to every Green Bone in No Peak.

"I don't see who I'm looking for," he said, reaching the end of the room and turning around. "I'm going to give you collectively one minute to tell me where to find the barukan Soradiyo. I know he comes here to recruit scum like you as rockfish for Zapunyo's smuggling operation, so don't pretend you don't know who I'm talking about. And I want the locations of any other hideouts in the city where the new green can be found. If I get what I want in one minute, you'll lose your jade but keep your lives. If I don't, you'll lose both."

———————

Iyn Ro and her Fingers caught Soradiyo two days later. The smuggler had spent the weeks after the bombing hiding in the storeroom of a gym in a part of the Stump well known as an Uwiwan ethnic ghetto. Upon learning that the Mountain was allowing No Peak into its territories to hunt for him, Soradiyo attempted to flee the country. He would've stood a better chance of escaping detection if he'd taken off his jade, but in his haste and desperation, he failed to think of that. Iyn's search team Perceived a stowaway on a boat bound for the Uwiwa Islands. Soradiyo was jade-stripped and taken to a warehouse in the Docks where Tar took charge of interrogating him.

"The barukan are fucking pussies," Tar said, when Hilo arrived some hours later. "He gave up everything we wanted. The names of the two rockfish he hired to plant the bomb, plus details about Zapunyo's operations: the docking locations of the picking crews, the mine sites they scavenge from, how they get the jade scrap out of the country, the names and identities of the other agents in Janloon and the top people in Zapunyo's organization, the police and government officials that uwie smuggler has in his pocket, and the defenses around his mansion in Tialuhiya."

"Did you write it all down?" Hilo asked.

"Pano did," Tar said, indicating the Finger behind him, who was holding a clipboard with notes and who looked a little sick in the face after this unpleasant assignment. Hilo took the clipboard from him and read through all of it, carefully. When he was done, the Pillar nodded in satisfaction and handed it back, then told Tar and Pano to wait outside. He went into the windowless room where Soradiyo hung half-naked with his arms chained over his head, covered in blood and bruises and shaking uncontrollably from jade withdrawal. Hilo waited until the man roused his attention weakly. "Are you here to kill me?" the barukan asked hopefully, his Shotarian accent slurred through a dry throat and cracked lips.

Hilo had two four-ounce juice boxes with him; he always had a couple of them in the car, along with some snacks, for times when his sons got hungry or thirsty while on outings. The oppressive humidity of Janloon's summer was even worse here in the windowless warehouse than it was outside. The stale air stank strongly of the prisoner's piss, which stained a splotchy circle of concrete around his feet. Hilo approached the man. He unwrapped the plastic around the tiny straw, punched it into the juice box's small foil circle, and held it out to Soradiyo, who clamped his bloodied lips around it and sucked back the entire drink in one desperate mouthful. He eyed the second box in pleading, but the Pillar did not give it to him.

"One more question," Hilo said. "Who gave the order? Ayt or Zapunyo?"

"Zapunyo," Soradiyo rasped. "With the Mountain's encouragement." He struggled to shift, to take some of the body weight off his straining shoulders. "Last year, Nau Suen contacted me. He wanted me to act as the go-between for his clan to talk to Zapunyo. It wasn't like I had much of a choice; the bastard was killing my scrap pickers and rockfish as fast as I could hire them. The Mountain said it was obligated to uphold its publicly declared agreement with No Peak and do its part to oppose smuggling. But *if* the Mountain was in sole control, things might be different. Perhaps some sort of accommodation could be reached. That's what was suggested."

"And Zapunyo bought it."

"He saw it for what it was: a trade. The clans were making it too hard for us, costing Zapunyo too much. Ayt was saying that if we got rid of you, she would let us eat."

Hilo nodded. "It must sting that Ayt gave you up so quickly, that you're in here now."

Soradiyo made a motion that might've been an attempted shrug. "The price of failure. It's no big surprise. And it's not as if I'm telling you anything that you didn't already suspect."

"No," Hilo agreed. "Where do you want your body sent? Do you have relatives?"

Soradiyo closed his eyes. "Yes, in Oortoko, but because of the war, I'm not sure where they are now, and I don't want them to see me like this. Send me to my cousin Iyilo in the Uwiwa Islands. He'll bury me, and it'll serve him right to feel guilty for leaving me here on my own, and for what happened."

Hilo said nothing more. He drew his talon knife and opened the barukan's throat in one swift motion. Soradiyo's wracked body relaxed and his chin fell forward to his chest over an apron of red. When Hilo exited, he said, "Clean him up and send him back to the Uwiwas."

"That piece of scum killed Kehn," Tar exclaimed, furious emotion coloring his face. "Why'd you let him off so easy? We ought to sink him into the ocean bit by fucking bit."

Hilo silenced his Pillarman with a look that was not unsympathetic, but was stern enough to make it clear that he expected no further talking back. "Soradiyo and Tau Maro might've planned and carried out the bombing, but they were puppets on strings." Hilo wiped and sheathed his knife. "Ayt Mada is playing a long game. As for Zapunyo—I warned that Uwiwan dog that if he kept reaching his dirty hands into Kekon, I'd go after him, and that's exactly what we're going to do." The Pillar's voice flattened to an edge. "We're going to destroy everything he's built."

CHAPTER

50

Patience

Over the following weeks, the Green Bones of No Peak led a merciless city-wide purge targeting illegal jade dens used by the so-called new green, rockfish, barukan, and shine dealers. Dozens of criminals were beaten, jade-stripped, and imprisoned, if not outright killed. The two perpetrators that Soradiyo had paid to plant the car bomb fled Janloon and made it all the way to the city of Toshon on the southern peninsula before being caught by members of the local Jo Sun clan. The men begged for their captors to kill them, but the Jo Sun clan handed the criminals over to No Peak as a sign of allegiance and good will to the Kaul family. They were not alone in their thinking; the other minor Green Bone clans, the Janloon city police, and even the Mountain clan assisted or got out of the way—there was nothing to be gained from opposing Kaul Hilo's rampage.

Most Janlooners, judging by sentiment on the street and coverage in the press, approved of the crackdown and saw it as necessary. The car bombing, everyone knew by now, had been the cowardly scheme of a Shotarian gangster working for an Uwiwan jade smuggler. While the Kekonese are forgiving, even comfortable, with public violence between those of equal status, the idea of dishonorable foreign crooks striking at a great and powerful Green Bone family and injuring innocent people in the heart of an affluent Janloon neighborhood was offensive in the extreme.

Even Ayt Mada's prominence as a patriotic public figure was eclipsed by the return of Hilo's personal presence to the streets of Janloon. After nearly four years as Pillar, his youthful, violent reputation had begun to fade. Now he made no secret of the fact that he was out for blood, and people nodded in understanding. He replaced the destroyed Duchesse Priza with a gleaming new Duchesse Signa— even more intimidating than its predecessor, boasting greater horsepower and an enormous silver grille. He roamed at all hours, at the head of a pack of Fists. Wherever he was sighted, people stepped back and touched their foreheads in nervous salute.

There was a time when Hilo would've taken satisfaction in all this, but now he had only one real objective in mind that eluded him: killing Zapunyo. "It doesn't matter how many of his scrap pickers and rockfish we send to the grave, Zapunyo always has more," the Pillar growled, dropping a map of Tialuhiya onto the coffee table in front of Shae, Juen, and Tar, and pacing around the study. "Life is cheap in the Uwiwa Islands; in less than a year he could replace everything we've taken from him. Meanwhile, he's sipping papaya cocktails on the balcony over his lake."

"He can't have fruit juice; he's diabetic," Shae pointed out.

She received a predictable sneer in return for her cheek. "Can you think of a way to sneak fatal amounts of sugar into him? No? Then we need to find another way to whisper his name." He dropped back into the nearest armchair and said to Juen, "What are the options?"

Juen blew out a pessimistic breath as he picked up the blurry photographs. They showed the perimeter of Zapunyo's compound, taken from a distance with telephoto lenses by No Peak spies in the Uwiwa Islands and supplemented with sketched blueprints based on

Teije Runo's recollection of the property from his extended stay as Zapunyo's guest. Not that Teije's memory could be trusted all that much. Juen said, "It won't be easy. Zapunyo's compound has all the best security that money can buy. Watchtowers, guard dogs, motion sensors, security cameras, and of course his barukan bodyguards. He owns all the surrounding land so no one can get near him."

"There has to be a way to get someone into that fortress," Hilo insisted. "Or to buy someone who's already inside. Doesn't he have deliverymen, housekeepers, gardeners?"

"He doesn't let many people near him besides his sons, his doctor, and his bodyguards. Most of the house staff have been working for him for years and he only hires Uwiwans from local families, so he can be sure they will never betray him. A few years ago, a rival shine producer tried to have Zapunyo poisoned by his own cook. The cook was sent back to his relatives over the course of a week, in seven different buckets. No one else has ever tried."

"Then we have to do this ourselves," Tar said, with heat. "What are Zapunyo's cameras and hired goons next to a couple dozen of our best Fists? We fight our way in and kill him."

Juen said, "Even if we split up and take different flights at different times, we're not going to be able to fly in without Zapunyo getting wind of it." The Uwiwa Islands still had a standing travel ban on all Green Bones and any Kekonese nationals with suspected ties to the clans (which could be almost anyone). "We could try to get into the country by boat, the same way Zapunyo moves his own scrap pickers. That would mean at least a couple of days at sea in a private vessel. Once we get there, we'll need to get from the coast to Zapunyo's compound in the hills, three hundred kilometers inland. No matter what, the barukan will Perceive us before we get there—they'll have time to get Zapunyo to safety and to mount a defense."

Tar turned to the Pillar. "Let me do it, Hilo-jen," he pleaded. "When have I let you down before? Let me take ten Fists with me and I swear on my jade I'll send Zapunyo to the grave."

Shae spoke up. "I agree with all of you that we have to kill Zapunyo." Hilo thought his sister still looked pale and skinny enough for a stiff wind to blow her over, though for days, she'd been studying the gathered information and the photographs on the table as obsessively as the rest of them. "But we can't do this, Hilo. We can't send a band of Green Bones to illegally enter another country and assassinate someone in a bloody showdown, no matter who he is. Zapunyo is sure to do what he did last time—protect himself with local police officers that will end up dead in the fighting and on the news."

"Who cares about some crooked Uwiwan cops?" Tar exclaimed.

"It'll bring down a lot of trouble on us from the Espenians," Shae said, still speaking to Hilo. "You know our relationship with them is tricky. We've restricted jade exports and refused to contribute troops to fight on their side in Oortoko, because, as you and Chancellor Son so clearly explained to Secretary Corris, we Green Bones protect what's ours, but we don't invade other countries and kill civilians without jade. This would fly in the face of that and weaken our position with them. *And* it would undermine the diplomatic pressure the Espenians are trying to put on the Uwiwan government to take greater responsibility for combating corruption and crime in their own country." When Hilo frowned, she insisted, "And it's not just the Espenians— several other countries have banned civilian ownership of jade. A lot of ignorant people don't even know the difference between Green Bones and barukan thanks to those Shotarian gangster movies. For our own good, we have to be careful not to attract even more foreign attention. If we act reckless and bloodthirsty and show no respect for the laws of neighboring countries, it'll set us back in a lot of other ways, especially in our alliances overseas and the businesses we're trying to grow."

"The Espenians," Tar spat. "I'm sick of how we—how *you*"—he glared at Shae—"think about the foreigners' feelings with every decision. Ah, how are the *Espenians* going to like it? What about what people *here* will think? They count on the clans; do you want them to think we can't do anything against enemies overseas? If we're afraid to act, to answer an offense against the clan because of what the foreign press might say about us in the newspapers, then we're lapdogs that don't even deserve our green."

Shae turned a disdainful look on Tar, eyes narrowed at the veiled insult. "I'm not saying we give up. I'm saying we have to get to him in another way, one that doesn't involve a highly public massacre right in front of the man's plantation house in Tialuhiya."

"Shae-jen has a point," Juen said to Hilo. "Zapunyo has to pay for his actions, there's no disagreement among any of us about that. But we would risk a lot by sending a dozen or more of our best Fists to try to strike at him head-on in his own country. Those are Fists that we need, that I need as Horn here in Janloon. We can't afford to lose those lives, especially not when we know that, truce or not, the Mountain is still our enemy at home and will exploit any weakness."

Tar's jade aura was crackling with frustration, and when he spoke, he seemed almost near tears. "Then let me go alone, Hilo-jen. How can I live, otherwise? At least let me try."

Hilo turned a look on his Pillarman that was oddly gentle and also angry. "You're talking nonsense, Tar. We have to be ready to die, that's true enough, but not if it accomplishes nothing. How're you going to face Kehn in the afterlife and not look like a fool? You think I'm going to let you throw your life away? I've lost enough brothers already. What would Wen say?" Tar opened his mouth as if to argue, then closed it again as he looked away, ashamed.

Hilo sank lower into the armchair and scowled, leaning his head back. Outside the closed door of the study, they could hear the pattering footsteps of the children running up and down the stairs, and Wen calling them to eat. Hilo said quietly, "I promised my wife that I would avenge her brother and punish the people who put our children's lives in danger. If I were to say what I want to do, it would be exactly the same as Tar." Hilo's mouth hardened as he lifted his head and looked around the circle of his closest advisors. "But Shae's right. She's always had a cooler mind than me, even when she's angry. I'm also thinking about what Juen said. We've done a lot these past few weeks, but Ayt would like us to go farther than we can handle and cause problems for ourselves so she can take advantage. She's likely even counting on that, since the Mountain was encouraging the barukan to go after us this whole time. So taking out Zapunyo—we can't do it now, not this way."

Hilo's words were spoken reluctantly, but with finality. He got up, indicating that the meeting was over, but as he did so, he put a hand on Tar's shoulder. "I don't know what the way is yet, but it took us years to avenge Lan, remember? But we did it eventually. And that's not even fully done yet, not until the Mountain is destroyed. So we have to be patient."

———

Hilo was waiting in the lounge of the *Inheritance* when Ven Sando boarded his boat as usual the following Sixthday morning. The president of K-Star Freight was understandably nonplussed to see the Pillar of the No Peak clan sitting by himself in one of the deck chairs with a drink that he'd taken from the onboard minibar. Ven appeared shocked, then angry, then a little frightened. The man opened his mouth, but before he could say anything, Hilo raised a hand to forestall him. The Pillar stood up in one smooth motion. "Ven-jen, I thought we were friends."

The words were spoken with a chillingly soft disappointment. Ven Sando turned pale. "We are, Kaul-jen," the heavyset businessman protested. "Why would you think otherwise?"

"Friends don't make promises they don't intend to keep," Hilo said, walking slowly toward Ven. "The last time we were on this nice boat of yours, you gave me the impression that we would work together to create a better situation for both of our clans. That was over a year and a half ago." Hilo pursed his lips to one side. "With everything going on in the world these days, I can appreciate that things have been busy for everyone. But my biggest problem is that Ayt Mada is still the Pillar of the Mountain. My Weather Man tells me you've stopped returning her calls. I can't help but think that you're not taking our agreement seriously."

"Kaul-jen, I've been quite vocal in my criticisms of Ayt's leadership. I've had fruitful discussions about the future of the clan with innumerable influential colleagues and gathered strong support for a change in direction—I dare say a return to our more honorable roots." Ven cleared his throat forcefully and crossed his large arms.

"It takes time to prepare properly for change of such an...irrevocable nature. I've overseen more than a few major business acquisitions during my long career, and can say—"

"This isn't a corporate acquisition," Hilo interrupted. "Ayt Mada came from the business side as Weather Man, but when her father died, it only took her six days to kill her rivals and take control of the Mountain. You called Ayt an inept, ambitious woman who's made misstep after misstep. So tell me how is it that in nearly two years you haven't managed to accomplish what took her six days?" When Ven didn't answer, Hilo said, with a thoughtful but menacing sympathy, "I think you're losing your nerve. The war in Oortoko has been bad for the world, but good for the national economy. With so many foreigners needing to move things around Kekon, business is going well for K-Star Freight, so you have other things on your mind. The public and your shareholders have grown to like this supposed peace between the clans. So now you're less sure of risking your own life. Maybe you think that it wouldn't be so bad to leave things as they are, to forget that we ever talked."

Ven moved away from Hilo and went to stand at the boat's railing. "I haven't forgotten anything we discussed," he said shortly, though he sounded less sure of himself now. "But I need the backing of the clan to make a move. The Koben family has their supporters, including the Tems and the Gams. The Iwe family has its own allies. After Koben Ento was murdered"—Ven gave Hilo a deeply suspicious look—"there were people out for blood on both sides. Ayt held an urgent, private meeting with the leaders of the Koben family and somehow quieted down the crisis, but with all this tension, it's difficult to gather support for a third option. And with Guim taking over from Son as chancellor of the Royal Council, even Ayt's detractors within the Mountain don't want to show internal dissent right now."

"Spoken like a politician instead of a Green Bone." Hilo replied with rough contempt. "I didn't have the full support of my clan when I became Pillar. And if Ayt had had the full support of her clan, she wouldn't have had to kill her father's Horn and her own brother. If you want to lead, you can't wait for everyone to line up behind you."

The Pillar stalked over to stand at the railing beside Ven. "It's possible that I didn't make myself completely clear the first time around. I offered you the support and friendship of No Peak because we shared a desire to see Ayt Mada out of power and in the ground. If that's no longer the case, if our wishes are no longer aligned, then there's no reason for us to talk further." Hilo tilted his head in a musing way, his voice softening ominously. "If there's no one I can count on to challenge Ayt, then I might as well resign myself to turning over a new leaf with my old enemy and informing her of the traitors in her clan."

Ven's face went still. "You would place a death sentence on my family?"

"Your family's fate is up to you, not me," Hilo said. "Maybe if you cut off your ear and throw yourself at Ayt's feet, she'll spare your children, but I think it's safe to assume that your sailing days would be over. You picked a path that you can't turn away from. You have to follow it all the way now, or I'll *push you off.*" Hilo set the glass he'd taken from the minibar down on the ledge of the boat's railing and leaned in close to Ven, whose shoulders stiffened as the Pillar spoke near his ear. "My patience is running out. By this time next year, Ayt Mada had better be feeding the worms. Or you'll answer to us both."

Hilo put a hand on the railing and vaulted Lightly over it, landing on the dock and walking back along the pier to where Maik Tar waited for him next to the Duchesse.

CHAPTER

51

The Unlucky Ones

When Kaul Maik Wen went through Espenian customs and immigration, she put her folded jacket and the locked steel briefcase she
carried through the X-ray machine and walked through the metal
detector. A security guard at Port Massy International Airport took
her briefcase from the other end of the conveyor and asked her to
come with him. The guard led Wen into a secondary screening
area—a gray room with a couple of chairs against the wall, a metal
table, and the flag of the Republic of Espenia hanging on the wall.
Another guard joined them. They asked Wen for her passport, which
they examined. "You're coming from Kekon?" one asked. She nodded. "Ma'am, please open the briefcase."

Wen turned the combination on the suitcase lock and pushed
open the hinges to pop the latches. She opened the briefcase to reveal
a crushed velvet-lined interior filled with polished green gemstones,
some of them loose, others as jewelry—strung necklaces, bracelets,

heavy rings set in gold. The lustrous green gleamed yellowish under the airport room's fluorescent lights. One of the customs officers took a slight step backward; the other a slight step forward. "Is this—" the one with the gloves began to ask, but Wen interrupted him. "No, no, of course not," she assured the guards quickly. She laughed, as if embarrassed to have startled them. "It looks like jade, no? It's just nephrite. Very pretty, though, isn't it?" She took one of the specimens out of the case—a nephrite necklace—and held it out to one of the guards. He hesitated, but she smiled reassuringly and said, "I'm a gemstone dealer. Nephrite is our fastest-growing business. These days everyone knows about jade, and it's all the rage to look as fierce as a Kekonese Green Bone. In Shotar, they call it 'barukan style' but in Espenia, it's 'military chic.' See?" She loosened the scarf around her neck to show off the three-tier choker she wore on her neck and touched the bracelets at her wrists. "I'm traveling to Port Massy, to meet with buyers."

The guard took the necklace and examined it. "I really did think it was bioenergetic jade at first," he admitted. He passed it to the other guard. "Can you tell the difference?"

Wen could tell from the expressions on their faces that they could not. With a loupe and a trained eye, a person could see the difference between the grain structures of nephrite and true jade. Of course, contact with the latter would provoke a physiological reaction, but even without touching the jewelry, any Green Bone would be able to tell at a glance that the gemstones in the briefcase were indeed, nothing but bluffer's jade—they were not as hard or lustrous, and the hue was different, milkier and duller than real jade. These customs officials, however, were Espenians who had not grown up around the real substance. They could not tell that the gems in the briefcase were different from the gems she wore around her neck and wrists—real jade, worth countless times more than the pile of inert stones—and though they picked up and examined several of the items in the case, they didn't look closely at her choker and bracelets. Wen was counting on misdirection and ignorance—the guards' natural inclination was to pay attention to the large suitcase of gemstones, not to the few worn on her person. Some larger airports, including Port Massy International, had dogs trained to detect jade auras, but Wen had walked past with no trouble. Non-Abukei stone-eyes were rare enough that the Espenians did not account for them in their security measures. Even so, precautions had been taken: The jade that Wen wore had been treated with a slightly opaque coating to dull the color and shine and make it appear like bluffer's jade even to the experienced eye. It could later be cleaned off with nail polish remover.

The guard said, "Do you have paperwork?" Wen did; she handed them several pieces of paper on the letterhead of a jewelry company called Divinity Gems based in Janloon, with a listing of the sample items and their estimated value. She gave them her business card. One of the guards took a few of the stones and the paperwork and left the room. The other guard said, "Thanks for your patience. We have to make sure everything checks out, you understand. I thought it was real jade myself."

Wen chuckled. "If it was, I'd have to be the world's most powerful Green Bone, and I'd be traveling with a dozen bodyguards to guard a case worth millions of thalirs. My samples are worth quite a bit, but not nearly *that* much. I completely understand the need to check, though. Jade smuggling is a real problem, I'm told." She sat down in one of the chairs to wait. She knew they were examining the grain structure of the samples under magnification and likely phoning Divinity Gems to ascertain that she was, indeed, an employee. The call would go to an undisclosed phone line in the Weather Man's office. The person who answered the call would assure the customs officials that Wen was, indeed, a senior sales director who'd been with the company for four years.

Wen and Shae had discussed and discarded half a dozen different options for covertly transporting cut jade into Espenia—all of them required a combination of shipping the gems through means subject to inspection or theft, or passing them through other hands: agents who might be unreliable, who might betray them or who could not handle jade without being detected. Having been privy to Kehn's relentless campaign against Zapunyo's operations, they knew all too well the tricks of smuggling, but also the many ways they could fail. At last, Wen had declared impatiently, "This is foolish, Shae-jen. I'm a stone-eye. Sometimes the most obvious and direct answer is the best one." The Weather Man had balked awhile longer, but Wen knew her sister-in-law couldn't argue with logic.

The customs inspector returned twenty minutes later and handed Wen her passport, paperwork, and samples. "You're free to go, miss."

Wen took two nephrite rings from the case and pressed them upon the men. "Take them," she urged. "They're samples, I have plenty." One of the guards started to reach for the ring but the other shook his head and said, "We're not allowed to do that, miss." Wen looked disappointed and said, "Have a keychain then," and she gave them each a nephrite keychain with Divinity Gems etched on the side. Tucking her scarf once more around her neck, she picked up her case and followed the guard as he led her back out of the room and let her through the customs gate.

———————

Anden was waiting for her at the baggage claim area along with a lean man in a black cap and gloves that Anden introduced as Rohn Toro. Wen was pleased to see Anden. For a while, she'd found it hard to think kindly of him. She would always be grateful for the part he'd played in killing Gont Asch and saving the clan as well as her husband's life, but then he'd turned his back on the family and left— just like Shae once had. Hilo had been heartbroken about it; he never brought up the subject, but Wen could see that he still blamed himself, no matter what she said to gently remind him that he'd only ever done what was necessary.

Now, though, she was glad to see the young man. He'd become an anchor for No Peak in Espenia and was proving himself useful here. So Wen greeted him warmly and said, "You look well, little brother." Anden smiled the same small, reserved smile he'd always had and asked how her flight had been. She assured him that it had been fine.

They drove to a hotel and Wen checked into a suite. Rohn left, saying he would be back in around an hour. Anden stayed with Wen in the hotel room, waiting in the separate sitting area while she refreshed herself and changed. This was Wen's second trip to Espenia—the first, taken two months ago carrying a suitcase of nephrite but no real jade, had been a test run, to establish a travel history for her role as a sales representative of Divinity Gems and to familiarize herself with what to expect when going through customs. So she was still taken aback by how cold it was in Port Massy and was glad she'd packed sweaters and scarves. She went back out into the sitting room and pulled back the heavy drapes enough to peer outside. Port Massy, smoky and gray in winter twilight, sprawled below. She was charmed by it, by the majestic foreignness of the place, even by how much smaller the Mast Building looked in real life than it did on the post-cards. She was looking forward to exploring the city and seeing some of the famous sights.

Anden muted the television show he'd been watching and asked if she needed anything. Wen shook her head and sat down beside him, smoothing her skirt over her knees. "Anden," she said, putting a hand on his arm, "Hilo knows I'm here in Port Massy, working for the Weather Man on foreign real estate projects, but he doesn't know the other part. You must never mention to him that I was the one who carried the jade into the country."

Anden glanced at her, then down at his hands, clearly uncom-fortable with being asked to keep a secret. Wen said, "He wouldn't approve. You know how he feels about certain things. With Hilo, you're either a Green Bone or you're not."

"I know," Anden said. "He doesn't want me back in Janloon so long as I'm not green."

"That's not true," Wen said. "We all miss you at home. But your cousins have their reasons. Shae thinks it'll be good for you to have an Espenian education, to speak a second language and have experi-ence living abroad. You'll be able to put those advantages to use for the clan even if you don't wear green. Isn't that worth the hardship of being away from home for a little while, now, while you're young? Hilo...well." Wen smiled, her expression a little resigned. "Anyone without jade is somewhat like a child to him, to be kept away from the realities and dangers we're not a part of. Even me. I know he loves me and values my opinions, but I'm not in his world, not completely. If he seems distant or unforgiving toward you, it's because he doesn't know where you fit now, how to treat you when you return."

Anden turned to her with a searching gaze, serious but hopeful. Wen thought that even though Anden was not a Kaul by blood, in that moment, he looked more like Lan than either Hilo or Shae ever did. "Will you talk to him, for me?" he asked. "And to Shae-jen? Of course, I'll keep your secret no matter what," he added quickly, "but I know they listen to you."

"I will," Wen promised, touched by his earnestness. She looped an arm around one of his. "It's not so bad living here in Port Massy, is it? Shae tells me that you have a foster family here, there's an entire Kekonese neighborhood, and even relayball. You've been here for almost three years; do you feel as if you have friends here now, things that make you happy, people who you care about?"

Anden said, "Yes. You're right, it's not so bad. Pretty good, actually. I'm done with classes, and I'm...seeing someone." He flushed and seemed almost surprised at himself for the admission, but Wen only smiled; they were the two unlucky members of the family, each in their own way—who better to confide such things, if not to each other? "I would never have guessed I'd find someone in Espenia, and he's very Espenian in a lot of ways. We don't see each other as much as we used to, though." Anden's voice took a slightly troubled turn. "It's not that I'm unhappy in Espenia. But I don't think I could ever really feel at home here. And it's hard being so far away from everything that's happening in the family." He turned to her and said, "When I heard about what happened to Kehn, I felt as if I should've been there. Even though I know there was nothing I could've done, no way that I could've helped, and I wasn't even close enough to the Horn to know him very well, but...I still feel as if I should've been there."

Wen smiled sadly and rubbed at her eyes. "I have every reason to stay at home. Hilo would prefer it, and the children are little. You should see Lina's new baby—he looks so much like Kehn. I miss them all very much when I'm gone. But I feel as if I should be out here, doing something more. So it's true that you can be happy but still not satisfied."

There was a knock on the door. Anden got up to peer through the peephole, then opened the door to admit Rohn Toro and four other men who entered quickly and closed the door behind them. It was suddenly crowded in the room; Wen was thankful for Anden's familiar presence among the strange men. All of the visitors were Green Bones who spoke to each other and to Anden in Espenian, but they greeted Wen in Kekonese, saluting her respectfully and saying they were honored to meet her.

There were only two chairs at the hotel room table; Wen and Anden sat down and the five Green Bones stood around. Wen laid out the jade choker, bracelets, and three other coils of jade beads that she'd smuggled in under her clothes. After arriving at the hotel, she'd soaked them in solvent in the bathroom sink, wiped them clean of their coating, and laid them out to dry. Now they gleamed like nothing else on earth—unmistakable as true Kekonese jade.

With everyone watching, she used a pair of wire clippers and carefully separated the jade pieces, piling them next to each other on a black cloth in the center of the table. When she was done, there were two hundred equally sized jade beads on the table—nearly as much jade as what one might expect on half a class of Kaul Du Academy graduates. A veritable fortune. A reverential hush fell over all the men in the room. None of them touched the jade—so much of it in one place would be unwise for anyone to handle. Anyone but a stone-eye.

Rohn reached into a satchel he had brought with him and took out five small lead-lined boxes with hinged covers. Wen counted out an equal number of stones into each box. She closed the boxes and each Green Bone in attendance took one. They were, Wen had been told, well trusted by the Pillar in this city: Rohn and two of his captains from Port Massy, one man from Adamont Capita, and another who'd come all the way from the city of Resville. The exchange complete, they saluted her before they exited. "May the gods shine favor on No Peak," said the younger of Rohn's protégés, in accented but fluent

Kekonese. In one day, the No Peak clan had supplied the Kekonese-Espenian community with as much jade as an Espenian military platoon. These leaders would grant the jade in their possession to worthy subordinates; they had all agreed to take full responsibility for the Green Bones they trained and equipped, with the understanding that prudence and discretion were of the utmost importance if they were to exert their substantial new advantage over the Crews while staying beneath the notice of law enforcement.

Lastly, Wen brought out the steel suitcase full of bluffer's jade and handed it without ceremony to Rohn. There was no such company as Divinity Gems, but there was a recently formed Espenian firm called Kekon Imports, run by a Kekonese-Espenian businessman bankrolled in part by the recently formed Weather Man's branch office in Port Massy. Rohn would hand the case of green gemstones over to Kekon Imports, which would indeed sell them to Espenian jewelry stores. Rohn exchanged a few cordial words with Anden, then left.

With only Anden left in the room, Wen let out a deep breath and kicked off her shoes. She relaxed on the sofa and massaged the balls of her feet. Anden remained sitting where he was, but he too looked immensely relieved. It was no small thing to have surreptitiously moved that much jade across the Amaric Ocean and passed it into the intended hands.

"Would you like to get something to eat?" Anden asked her.

Wen got up, stifling a yawn and suspecting that she had about an hour left before the jet lag set in. "That would be lovely. Take me wherever you think we should go; I'm trusting you to introduce me to good Espenian food. After that, I think I'd better get to sleep early." She did have to be at the Weather Man's branch office the next morning; her official job as a design consultant on clan properties was no ruse—there would be floor plans to review tomorrow.

CHAPTER

52

This Is Serious

The Weather Man's branch office in Espenia was located on Garden Street in Port Massy, not exactly in the central financial area, but close enough to still be considered the heart of downtown. Anden rode the subway to and from work every day; it took only fifteen minutes door to door. The rent on his studio apartment was too expensive for what he got, but it was one of the nicer buildings in Southtrap and only a block away from the transit station, so he had to endure less time outdoors during the coldest months of winter.

Mr. and Mrs. Hian had assured him that he was welcome to continue boarding with them after he graduated. "Anden-se, you're no trouble at all," they insisted. "You're the best guest we've ever had, you're practically like a third son to us by now, and so helpful around here."

Anden was tempted; he was truly fond of the elderly couple. With them, he felt as if he had a home in Port Massy. He'd become accustomed to Mrs. Hian's cooking and his personal space in the guest bedroom. (The noise behind the building had ceased to disturb his sleep long ago.) But, as he explained to his hosts regretfully, now that he would be working downtown and no longer going to Port Massy College, it made sense to move to a more convenient location. Also, though he didn't mention this, the Dauks had fixed up and sold Cory's old condo unit, and now that Anden would be earning a living, he felt he should have a place of his own where Cory could come and spend the night whenever he was in Port Massy. Anden promised the Hians that he would still visit them often, which he did, more often it seemed than their own sons, bringing them groceries and helping to shovel the sidewalk during winter. He still saw some of his old relayball friends, but less often. Derek had a new job, Sammy was training regularly under Rohn Toro, Tod was gone on an eight-month-long military deployment.

No Peak had established operations in a professional office building that housed a couple of small law firms and accounting practices, an ad agency, a college test prep center, and the headquarters of a driver's education company. The name on the directory in the lobby and on the front door of the Weather Man's branch office read, in both Espenian and Kekonese, KEKON TRADE PARTNERSHIP LIAISON OFFICE. There were a total of twelve people who worked in the office, which was four more than there had been on the first day that Anden had arrived for work six months ago. Anden's official title was junior associate, which initially gave him no clue as to what his actual job would be, but he deduced that it was equivalent to perhaps an entry-level fourth- or fifth-rank Luckbringer. This was ironic and amusing to Anden; considering his grades in math during his years at Kaul Du Academy, he would never have imagined that he would one day find himself on the business side of the clan.

Fortunately, he was not expected to do much desk work. His boss, Hami Tumashon, had most recently been the Master Luckbringer of No Peak, reporting directly to Kaul Shaelinsan. Hami knew exactly who Anden was. "Kaul Shae-jen gave me the freedom to choose my own team, except she told me that I had to take you." Hami had a straightforward manner, and when he spoke, Anden could hear the Janloon accent, which he had never noticed in himself but that he now realized was distinctly different from the way Keko-Espenians such as Cory talked. Hami studied Anden and said, gruffly but without rancor, "So I'm to have a Kaul watching over my shoulder and reporting back to Janloon to make sure I'm not wasting the clan's time and money out here."

Anden said, "Mr. Hami, I just graduated from the city college and my cousins are trying to find something for me to do, that's all. I'm supposed to help you in any way I can, but if I'm not of any use to you, just tell me so." He was well aware that he had few qualifications.

One of the first tasks that Hami gave him was to recruit new staff members. "We need some locals," he explained. "Bilingual Espenian-born or Espenian-naturalized people who know the market, the culture, the way business is done around here. If you have friends in the Kekonese community here in Port Massy, start there and see if you can get some leads."

Anden paid a visit to Dauk Losunyin and explained the situation. Dauk nodded thoughtfully. "Anything I can do to help your family's business, I will," he said. The Pillar of Southtrap was in good spirits these days; his youngest daughter had given birth to a baby girl—his third grandchild—and the police were no longer monitoring him as they were too busy dealing with the violent conflict that had broken out between the three major Crews.

According to what Anden had heard from Rohn Toro, Boss Kromner had become fearful of Skinny Reams's growing status and suspected him of skimming from the new jade business. He'd sent another of his foremen, Moth Duke, to have Reams killed, but Reams escaped and allied with Anga Slatter, who knew that Kromner's Southside Crew was sure to come after the Wormingwood Crew sooner or later and saw this as an opportunity to act preemptively. Reams and Slatter gained the tacit cooperation of the Baker Street Crew, and shortly thereafter, the bodies of Moth Duke and two of his men were found in a boathouse, strangled and suffocated with white plastic bags tied over their heads. A signature Crew-style execution, meant to serve as an explicit warning to others. Kromner went into hiding south of the city.

All through the spring and summer, the highly publicized Crew battles and dramatic fall of Port Massy's celebrity crime boss were splashed across the headlines of the city's newspapers. Jade—made popular on the black market by the ongoing international attention around the Oortokon War—was blamed for the violence. Four members of the Wormingwood Crew were killed in broad daylight by two assassins reportedly moving faster than any normal human being. There were a combined eight hospitalizations for jade poisoning and SN1 overdose. The Port Massy Police Department, facing public allegations of corruption and ineptitude, cracked down on the Crews. A jade-polishing warehouse on the Camres River was uncovered and shut down, the drugged migrants deported.

With the Crews at each other's throats and the police beleaguered, there was little trouble in Southtrap for the Kekonese community. While repairs were going on at the damaged community center, the grudge hall was quietly relocated to a converted warehouse owned by Derek's uncle. When the original space was reopened, demand was such that the new location also stayed open, so there was now additional space for Green Bones to train by day, and high attendance and gambling money flowing freely by night. A week after the news broke that Boss Kromner had been tracked down and apprehended by the police on trumped-up charges of labor exploitation, Anden received a call from Dauk Losun, for no particular reason other than to inquire as to how he was doing these days in his new apartment and at his new job.

"My friend," Dauk said, "if there is anything you or your family ever need, please do not hesitate to ask. May the gods shine favor on No Peak, as they say in the old country."

A couple of weeks after Anden's request for assistance, Dauk Sana arrived at the Kekon Trade Partnership Liaison Office with a list of two dozen names. Anden introduced her to Hami and the two of them spent some time talking about which part of Kekon their respective families were from before Sana got down to business.

"Mrs. Kuni is one of my longtime clients, because of her stomach troubles. Right now, her son works in the mortgage industry but he doesn't like it very much; he would be interested in a new job. He was always good in school. His Kekonese is so-so." Dauk Sana moved her finger to the second name on the list. "This is my eldest daughter's friend from law school; she quit work to have a baby. Now she wants to work again, but her old company says they gave her job away. She's very smart, and her husband's family is Espenian military." Out of Dauk Sana's list of twenty-four names, ten people showed interest when contacted; seven were brought in for interviews, and four hired.

Hami was pleased. Apparently, Anden had shown himself to be of some use, so he was next assigned to learn everything he could about the liquor market, which included reading trade publications, going around to liquor stores, restaurants, and bars to interview proprietors, and purchasing samples of hundreds of different types of alcoholic beverages and having them packed up and shipped to Janloon for product comparison tests. No Peak thought there might be a market for Kekonese hoji in Espenia. After that, he was sent to scout commercial real estate.

Anden was surprised, as the autumn days cooled and Harvest'Eves decorations went up again, to find himself enjoying his job. His coworkers were mostly Kekonese, so he felt at ease among them, but his tasks were such that there was plenty of need to interact with outsiders, and to speak, read, and write Espenian. His duties were varied and consisted of whatever Hami needed done, so he was rarely bored, and he learned a great deal about how a small part of the Weather Man's office was run, as well as different sectors of the Espenian economy.

On occasion, he was given an assignment that Hami quietly told him came "from the greener side of the clan," which meant it was a matter of importance to the Horn, or perhaps the Pillar himself. He was told to examine phone books and government records and make some discreet calls to determine the whereabouts of two former military servicemen, recently released on parole after serving a year in prison for abducting and raping a Kekonese girl while stationed on

Euman Island. Anden made a couple of trips—one to the south Port Massy suburb of Orslow, the other five hours away to the town of Evenfield—to make certain his information was correct, as he knew the men were to be punished, possibly with death. After he reported his findings, he received an unexpected long-distance phone call from Maik Tar, asking for clarification on a few of the details and thanking him for being so thorough.

Several weeks later, Anden learned that one of the offenders had been ambushed and beaten in an apparent robbery attempt that left him paralyzed from the waist down, and the other suffered extensive third-degree burns from the fire that destroyed his house. Anden suspected that he was the only junior associate under Hami's supervision who was trusted with matters such as these, and he took that as a hopeful sign. When he'd first arrived in Port Massy nearly three years ago, he'd viewed his situation in the bleakest of terms, as a jadeless, damaged exile salvaging what few options remained to him. Only now did it seem to Anden that perhaps there was a path forward, resolving out of the fog.

Anden watched Cory standing shirtless in front of the mirror, shaving. He was humming a song, something Anden didn't know. It was a Seventhday morning in the dead of winter and there was not yet even a hint of morning light outside the windows of Anden's apartment, but Cory had to take the early bus back to campus because he had study hall that evening. He was in his second year of law school now, and busier than ever. Sometimes he would come back to Port Massy for family events but not have time to see Anden at all, so at other times, he would come into town unannounced for a day or two just so they could spend time together. "Don't come to the bus station to meet me," Cory had instructed him over the phone. "My parents don't know I'm coming and it's going to be a world of trouble to explain it if someone sees us. I'll take a cab to your place."

Anden would clear his schedule; they would have sex, watch television, talk, have sex again. When they wanted to go out to restaurants, the movie theater, or the arcade, they took the subway out of South-trap to other parts of the city—Lochwood, Quince, Athwart—where they weren't likely to run into anyone they knew. At first, Cory visited every month, but over time the intervals stretched to six weeks, then eight. Watching Cory now, it occurred to Anden that they had not discussed when he would next visit; neither of them had brought it up.

"Who else are you sleeping with?" Anden asked.

Cory looked at him in surprise, comically frozen with shaving cream on one half of his face. "Where did *that* come from?" he asked, hurt and indignant. "No one else. Not seriously."

"What does seriously mean? Is *this* serious? What we have going on?" Anden had never pegged himself as the possessive type and was surprised to hear himself speaking so fiercely.

Cory finished shaving, wiped his face off with a towel, and came. back to Anden's bed. He sprawled on the bedspread. The trio of jade studs around his navel stood out against his pale skin. "Look, law school is really stressful because we're working all the time, so when we do let loose, there are some wild parties. I've been drunk—everyone's been drunk—at a few of them, and ended up making out with a few people. And there was a one-night stand, only one, last semester, that was really stupid in hindsight. But that's it, I promise. I'm not seeing anyone else."

At Anden's silence, Cory reached out and tapped him on the chin, giving him an entreating look. "I'm with *you*, crumb. You're more *real*. I mean, you're younger than me, but there's something about you that makes you seem older. You take life more seriously. Me"—he shrugged—"I try to take things one step at a time, you know? To live for today. I don't know for certain what I want to do after law school, but I'm keeping an open mind about it." He leaned over and kissed Anden on his bare shoulder. "Right now, we've got a good thing, don't we?"

"Cory," Anden said. He was hesitant to begin the conversation but vexed by the fact that they had never even broached the subject. "Would you ever... want to live in Kekon? If I get the chance to move back to Janloon, I'd want to know if that was…something you'd consider."

Cory propped himself up on his elbows and looked at Anden intently, eyebrows raised. "Is this hypothetical or is it actually going to happen? Has your family asked you to go back?"

"It's hypothetical," Anden mumbled. "I just thought we should talk about it."

"Well, hypothetically…" Cory rolled onto his back and crossed his hands behind his head, gazing up at Anden's ceiling. "Yeah sure, I wouldn't mind spending some time overseas. Seeing where my parents are from, getting in touch with my ancestral roots, that sort of thing. I've never lived in another country. It could be a toppers life experience." His eyes danced with optimism at the idea. "Of course, it would depend on timing and circumstances, but anything's possible, crumb."

"What would your parents think?"

Cory rolled his eyes back in exasperation. "Why do you always ask that? You'd think they were *your* parents, the way you worry." He sat up and blew out a heavy breath that ruffled the hair over his brow. "Look, I've been a good kid to my folks. I've done what they wanted: I wear jade, I help out in the community, I'm going to law school. My ma will always want to keep me close because I'm the baby boy, and my da expects me to be 'successful'—which for him, is a very specific combination of being an old-school Green Bone and a wealthy lawyer." Cory laughed, but there was an edge of frustration to the laughter. He sobered and looked straight into Anden's eyes. "I want to do right by my folks, but I'm old enough to make my own life decisions, crumb. If moving to Kekon is important to you—to *us*—then we should seriously consider it." Cory leaned over and gave Anden a quick, sunny kiss, then swung his legs off the bed and stood up, stretching his long, lean body. He glanced over his shoulder at Anden as he picked up his clothes. "You've gone quiet on me again. Hey, it's not like there's some big rush to decide, right? We can talk about it more another time. It's just a matter of figuring out what we really want."

Anden thought about the conversation later and still felt dissatisfied. He wished he had been more honest and assertive in that moment, told Cory that he already knew he wanted to return to Kekon, and when the time came, he hoped Cory would come with him.

Then he remembered what Hilo had said about Cory Dauk in their last conversation, and his doubts rose. *He couldn't make it as a Green Bone in Janloon, you know that.* Was his cousin right? Could Cory be happy in Janloon? Their positions would be reversed; Cory would be the foreigner. If he wore his jade there, he wouldn't be protected by aisho—would it be too dangerous for him? Even though he was aware of and involved in his father's dealings, he had no real understanding of the way the clans worked in Kekon. And if the Dauks did not want their son to leave, might that not create bad feelings between the families, when they were now allies and Anden's cousins were relying on the good relationship with the Dauks to accomplish the things they wanted to in Espenia?

All of these worries were currently without purpose, Anden told himself. After all, he had no definite timeline, no real impetus to force the issue. Better to live a day at a time, as Cory said.

Early one morning on a Sixthday shortly after the Kekonese New Year, Anden received a phone call at his apartment. He'd gotten out of bed only fifteen minutes ago and was standing in the bathroom with his feet on the heater vent as he brushed his teeth, his reflection visible in the small fogged window that showed nothing but frosted darkness. The small television he'd turned on in the main room was recapping the week's news: mounting public and political pressure on Premier Galtz and the National Assembly to order a withdrawal from Oortoko, rising interest rates, the latest gossip about some movie starlet.

At first Anden thought the ringing he heard was coming from the television; then he realized the call must be from Janloon because who else would phone at this time? It would be early evening back home. When he shut off the television and picked up the phone, he said, "Hello?" in Kekonese; still, he was surprised to hear Hilo's voice, muted by the long-distance connection. "We need to talk to you, Andy," said the Pillar. "Shae and Juen are here in the room too. I'm putting you on speaker."

Since he'd moved to Espenia, Anden could count on one hand the number of times he'd spoken to Hilo on the phone. "He doesn't like talking on the phone," Shae had said to Anden once, apologetically. Anden suspected that more accurately, Hilo did not like to talk to *him* on the phone, to be reminded of his disgraced younger cousin being so far away. And Anden had certainly never been on a conference call with the Pillar, the Weather Man, and the Horn of No Peak all in attendance. Worried now, Anden said, "Is there something wrong?"

Shae's voice came from a distance on the other end. "Nothing's wrong, Anden."

"We need your help, cousin," Hilo said, "to get something done in Espenia."

Anden turned on a lamp and sat down on his bed. "What do you need help with?"

The Pillar said, "Killing a man."

CHAPTER

53

Sins and Compromises

Zapunyo's diabetic condition had after many years finally caught up with him and he was in need of a kidney transplant. The medical care in the Uwiwa Islands being one of the worst in the world, and money not being an issue for the wealthy smuggler, Zapunyo arranged to travel to Espenia in six months' time and pay a premium to have the surgery performed at a private hospital in Port Massy. This rare instance in which he would be leaving his fortified compound in Tialuhiya was discovered by a well-placed No Peak spy in the Uwiwas and was the opportunity that Hilo and Shae had been searching for since last summer.

Anden went to see Dauk Losunyin to ask for what he wanted. "Dauk-jen," he said, "this smuggler, Zapunyo, he rarely ever leaves his fortress in the Uwiwa Islands. He has an entire operation employing barukan, rockfish, and cheap labor to scavenge jade from the mines, take it out of Kekon, and ship it to black market buyers in Ygutan and Oortoko, and to dangerous organizations like the Crews."

Dauk nodded in understanding but said, "Boss Kromner is awaiting trial and may spend decades in prison. The other Bosses are in hiding. Why do I need to think of this Zapunyo?"

"Even if Kromner goes to jail, there'll be others who take his place. As long as jade remains illegal and coveted, there'll be criminals in this country and all over the world who'll try to get their hands on it, and Zapunyo will sell it to them. Maybe the newspapers are right and Kromner's fall means that the heyday of the Crews in Port Massy is at an end, but maybe not, or perhaps other groups will rise up and pose an even greater threat to us. The solution is to cut off the black market at the source, and that means stopping the smuggling of jade out of Kekon."

They were sitting together in Dauk's living room, the Pillar in an armchair, Anden on the sofa across from him. Sana had recently finished up with a client who'd come for a healing session, and now she was walking around behind her husband, their baby granddaughter asleep in her arms.

Dauk looked at Anden with a trace of disappointment. "Anden, you and your family are well known to us by now; why not just say exactly what you want and why?"

Anden dropped his gaze to the cup of tea in his hand, then put it down on the coffee table. He spoke carefully. "The first time I met you, I told you that I was only a student, that despite my upbringing, I couldn't speak for my cousins in Janloon. Now, I can tell you in all honesty that in coming to you today, I'm speaking on behalf of the No Peak clan." Anden held Dauk's gaze this time. "This man, Zapunyo, tried to kill the Pillar and is responsible for the death of the Horn. If my sister-in-law and her children had been in the car at the time, they would be dead as well. He's an enemy of my family who, because of his distance and resources, has gone unpunished for his actions. While he's here in Espenia, we have to kill him."

Dauk blew a long breath from his nose. "You say this man is well guarded, that even the Green Bone warriors in the No Peak clan can't get to him. So how do you propose to do so?"

"It won't be easy," Anden admitted. "My cousins have an idea, a way to get past his barukan guards, but we need your permission and your help, Dauk-jen. We need Rohn Toro."

Dauk Losun turned to his wife. "Let me speak to our friend alone for a while."

Anden was surprised; never in all the time he'd known the Dauks had the Pillar asked his wife to leave. Even more surprisingly, Dauk Sana pressed her lips together with a look of understanding. She put the baby in the stroller. "I'll go for a walk and pick up a few things at the store," she said. She opened the door and left the house, leaving Anden and her husband alone.

Dauk Losun refilled their teacups. He leaned back in the armchair and said, "Since the first time the Hians brought you to my house, I've only come to think more highly of you. I could see right away that you're the sort of young man who would be respected in the old country, someone who means every word that he says. In truth, I wish my own son were more like you—but he is who he is. I have the greatest respect for you and your family. So when you said you were coming here, I was prepared to give you whatever you asked for, because I value the friendship of the No Peak clan nearly as much as my own jade." Dauk's normally open, amiable face turned somber. "However, after having heard what you're asking for, I can't agree to help you.

"It's one thing to wear jade for one's own protection and to defend one's friends and neighbors. That is what Green Bones have always done; no law made by man can change that. We hold fast to our traditions, which others don't understand, and we're not harming anyone in doing so. And it's also true that sometimes we must punish people who hurt our community and criminals who are a threat to us. We only want what everyone in this country wants: to have a good life and a better future for our children." Dauk paused and rubbed a hand over the back of his neck. "This Zapunyo is a stranger to me. He may be a bad man, but he's done nothing to harm our community directly. We may feel the ripples of the struggle over jade smuggled from Kekon to the Uwiwa Islands, but it's an ocean away. It's not our struggle. You're asking me to murder a man I don't know here on Espenian soil, to expose my family and my good friend Rohn Toro to unnecessary danger and punishment under Espenian law."

Anden was not surprised by Dauk's response and had warned his cousins that might be the case. He said, "Everything will be planned and arranged by No Peak under assumed names. I will be the contact person, and nothing will be traceable to you. My Pillar gives his guarantee of that. The only thing we require is Rohn Toro. Afterward, the clan can get Rohn out of the country—he can hide in Kekon, or anywhere he likes—a paid vacation, until it's safe to return."

"Did you come to Espenia to escape being a Green Bone? Listen to yourself, Anden. You sound like a Fist." The older man smiled but shook his head. "I'm sorry. In this, I can't help you." When Anden sat silent and disappointed, Dauk said, "If this is so important to you, then perhaps *you* have to be the one to carry it out. Of course, I know you were trained to wear jade."

Anden's jaw tightened. "You've never asked me about this before, Dauk-jen, but I'm sure you know: I was sent here to Espenia because I refused to be a Green Bone. It's been years since I've worn jade. I don't know whether I'd be able to control it, or what it would do to me. That makes me too unpredictable to be useful in this situation. Even if that weren't the case, I swore to myself that I wouldn't put on jade again. That's the one thing I can't compromise."

Dauk was silent for longer than Anden expected. He seemed to be debating with himself. At last he said, "I understand, and I appreciate you being frank about your past. So let me do the same. It's time we talked about the one thing *I* can't compromise."

When I arrived in Port Massy with my mother and sisters, I was fourteen years old. One of my sisters, the youngest, died of pneumonia only two years later. My older sister, she ran away with a man that my mother didn't approve of, and we stopped hearing from her. So after that, it was only my mother and me. We lived in an apartment over a public laundry house. What I remember most about that place was the smell of the soap that everyone used back then—Purely's Rock Soap—and the damp. The windows were always steamed up and the paint on the walls was bubbled and peeling. In winter, you could feel the damp even more, it was terrible.

Almost all of us who lived in the neighborhood had fled the old country because our homes had been destroyed or our relatives imprisoned or executed by the Shotarians. Our parents had been proud Green Bones or Lantern Men in the One Mountain Society, but in Espenia, we had no status. We were refugees with nothing. Everyone looked down on us, even the Tuni immigrants who lived on the other side of Beecher Street thought we were lower than them. But we were proud of who we were and where we had come from, and we kept to the old ways.

When I was in my twenties, I worked as a deliveryman for an appliance store owner named Ito, who I think used to be a good man but had suffered too much and gone a little crazy. Ito was a Green Bone whose family, like many others, had brought their jade with them to Espenia but did not dare to wear it openly on the street. We were outnumbered by foreigners of all sorts and we saw theft everywhere around us. Children stole from shop carts, hoodlums stole from homes and businesses, the Crews stole from everybody. All with little consequence. We had come to a land of thieves. So anyone who had jade did well to keep it hidden. Although I was born and trained in a Green Bone family, my father and my uncles had been taken by the Shotarians and their jade taken with them. So my family was poor even by the standards of our neighborhood.

Like I said, Ito was a good man but had gone a little crazy. One day he got into an argument with a Shotarian customer. As a child in Kekon, Ito had watched his own sister raped by Shotarian soldiers and his older brother beaten until he could no longer walk or talk, so Ito hated Shotarians even more than the rest of us did, almost with a kind of madness. That evening, offensive words were exchanged, and then things got out of hand and the Shotarian man ended up dead on the floor of Ito's shop. I was the only one who saw it happen. Ito turned to me with a wild look, and in that instant, I saw that he was thinking that I was the only witness and he would have to kill me too, to make sure no one found out what he'd done. Quickly, I reassured Ito that it had not been his fault, that it had been an accident brought about by the other man's provocation. Thinking to save my own life, I offered to help Ito get rid of the body.

It was a horrible thing that we did. We cut that Shotarian's body into pieces and we paddled a rowboat up the Camres, sinking them into different sections of the river, weighed down with cement. I had nightmares about it for many years. Sometimes I still do.

Even after I'd helped Ito with this grisly task, I feared for my life. What had happened unhinged the man even more. Whenever he looked at me, I knew he was trying to Perceive my sense of guilt and wondering if I would talk. He was still thinking about killing me. Looking back, I think the stress had gotten to him and he was beginning to suffer from the early stages of the Itches. In Kekon, someone in the clan might've noticed; a caring friend or relative might've made him seek medical help, but he was alone in Port Massy and I was the only one who knew.

The police came poking around, asking questions about the Shotarian man's disappearance. Of course, no one told them anything because the police are not trustworthy and half of them take money from the Crews, but rumors began spreading within the neighborhood that Ito had something to do with it. Ito became convinced that I had started those rumors, but now he hesitated to kill me and confirm the existing suspicions about his guilt. People grew worried. A Green Bone who loses control and goes mad is a danger to everyone, especially in Espenia, where people do not understand jade and where it would only bring more negative attention from outsiders.

There was another Green Bone in the neighborhood, a young man named Rohn Toro, who was known for being a good fighter that even the Crews respected and would hire for some of their jobs. Rohn had gotten into trouble with the law before, so the police suspected he was responsible for the murder of the Shotarian man. They came to arrest him, but Rohn fled and went into hiding. For weeks, he remained in a basement and didn't emerge. Rohn and I were acquainted and lived in the same building, so I brought him food while he kept out of sight.

People began to grumble about Ito. They could forgive him for killing a Shotarian man and covering up the deed, but it was wrong for him to remain silent and let another Green Bone be accused and likely executed in his place. Ito, though, thought only of his own skin. He had a weak character and would never have lasted as a Green Bone in Kekon. Ito found out where Rohn was concealed and was about to go to the police with the information. Once Rohn was arrested and punished in his place, Ito figured he would be in the clear. All that would be left to do was to get rid of me as well.

When I realized what Ito was planning, I went to Rohn Toro and we decided to act. Together, we ambushed Ito on his way to the police station. There were two of us, and Rohn was younger and stronger in jade ability than Ito. We killed Ito and took his jade.

I had no special skills or standing in the community, except that even then, I was known as someone who was honest, and I was good at listening and speaking reasonably and convincing people to my way of thinking. With Ito dead, I went around to all the neighbors and told them what had to be done to prevent any further trouble. When the police came around searching for Rohn, over a dozen people came forward to say that Ito had been the murderer and had fled the city. Sure enough, the police found the Shotarian man's wallet and traces of his clothes and blood in Ito's shop—that was how stupid the man was—but they never found the man himself. The important thing was that they didn't come after Rohn or anyone else.

The true murderer was punished, the neighborhood was spared further police scrutiny, and a Green Bone who could not be trusted was removed from being a danger to us all. The community saw this as my doing, and they began coming to me to deal with other problems, some small and some big, and over time they began to call me the Pillar. But in my heart, I knew that even though the outcome was all for the best, the gods knew what I had done.

I'd been Ito's accomplice in covering up the murder of an innocent man. Even if he was a Shotarian, he didn't deserve to die and he didn't deserve to have his body desecrated. His family had no remains to bury and he would've gone to the afterlife in pieces. And even though Ito was surely planning to kill me, he was a man who was in pain who had shown me kindness and given me my first job and livelihood to support my mother and my young wife. I murdered him in cold blood and disposed of his body as well. The gods knew. I think they understood why I did it, and so they weren't too harsh. So I've been fortunate in my life in most ways. Except one.

Sana and I could not have children for many years. When finally we succeeded, we had only daughters. We went to the temple to beg the gods for the favor of a son who would carry the family's jade, but it was only after ten years of trying that we finally had Coru. He's a good son, but he is frivolous. I did my best to raise him as a true Green Bone, but he has a childish heart. He wants only to get along with everyone and play around. He's my only son, the one who will carry the family's jade when Sana and I are gone. I love him, but he is also my punishment, for the sins I committed as a young man.

———

Dauk stood up from his chair. "I will do what you ask. I will put Rohn Toro at your disposal to help No Peak to kill this man, this smuggler Zapunyo. And for that, I ask you to give up my son. I've been indulgent of him, but he needs to stop fooling around with men and take his responsibilities seriously. He's the only Green Bone out of all four of my children, as undeserving and ignorant as he might be of what it truly means to wear jade and how important it is to our family's identity. He's not green enough for the old country, but that doesn't matter; he can still have a good Espenian life, a career that puts that expensive law degree to use, children someday, if the gods are kind to us. He's not for you. You are sure to return to Janloon eventually, but his place is here."

Anden struggled at first to find a response. "That's Cory's decision," he said.

"I'm not talking to him now. I'm talking to you. It's as much your choice as it is his. You come here asking me to commit a crime to help your family, so it's only right that I ask you for something in return. Give up my son, and I will bend my principles, to help you and your family in this thing that you want. That's the only way I'm willing to cross this line for you."

Anden looked at Dauk, a man he'd dismissed when he first met him but had grown to respect, a leader of his community and a shrewd man, truly a Pillar in his own way and own right, a person that Anden now felt deeply indebted to. In that moment, Anden hated him.

He stood up. "You called me a man who means every word he says. I don't want to say anything I'll regret, which is why I'm not saying anything to you right now, Dauk-jen."

Dauk stood up and walked Anden to the door. "You're wise for your age, my friend."

———

It was late the following evening by the time Anden mustered up the courage to call Cory at the house that he shared with three other law students. To his surprise, it answered on the first ring and an excited female voice said, "What is it now? Just come over already!"

Anden, startled, asked to talk to Cory, and the woman said, "Oh, Seer's balls, I'm sorry, I thought you were someone else. Just a minute." She left the phone off the hook, yelling distantly, "Cory! It's for you!" Anden waited. He could hear a great deal of background chatter and then a huge cheer as if a crowd was watching a sports event on television. At last, Cory's voice came on the line. "Hey, islander!" he exclaimed. "How's everything back in P-Mass?"

Anden had a hard time speaking. "I miss you," he said.

"I miss you too. Midterms start next week, but I'll try to come back for a visit the weekend after that. You're still free to gang about, right?"

"That's why I'm calling," Anden said. "I'm going to be busy for a while."

"At work?"

"Sort of," Anden said. "Family things."

"You mean clan things." Cory paused to say something in Espenian to someone else in the house before coming back on the line. "All right, well, you can spare at least one evening, right?"

Anden's palms were sweating. He had no idea how to do this. He forced the words out. "I don't think we can get together this time, Cory. You're busy with school and I'm going to be busy too. I think... maybe it would be best if we didn't see each other for a while."

There was a long, uncomprehending pause on the other end, and then a sound like Cory picking up the phone and walking— the background noise from the distant sports game grew fainter. "What's this about, crumb?" Cory demanded in a whisper. "Are you... *breaking up with me*?" Anden couldn't answer; his throat felt entirely closed up.

Cory breathed loudly into the phone. Then he said, "My da put you up to this, didn't he? I *know* he did. And you gave in. What did he say to you, huh? Did he offer you money?"

"Nothing like that," Anden muttered.

Cory said, "You know what? *Fuck you*. You dumb island fuck." He hung up.

Anden placed the receiver back in the cradle and sat down on the floor, staring at the phone for several minutes. Then he grabbed his jacket and burst out of his apartment, out of the building onto the slushy gray streets of Port Massy. He walked for two hours, aimlessly, and at one point, he realized he was crying. Not loudly, not hard, but his vision was blurry and his cheeks were wet. When he finally arrived back at his apartment, it was past midnight. His shoes were soaked and his feet cold. He ran hot water in the bath to warm them, then put on fresh socks.

Back home, it would be midday, the springtime sun high over the city harbor, people in the streets wishing each other Happy New Year and standing on ladders to take red lights and streamers down from their eaves. Anden picked up his phone and dialed the operator to place a collect call to Janloon, so he could tell his cousins that Dauk Losunyin would help them to kill Zapunyo.

The Cursed Beauty

Eight hundred years ago, a renowned Alusian explorer named Gaubrett sailed across the sea in search of a fabled island with mountains of jewels guarded by giants. Upon successfully landing on the southern peninsula of Kekon, Gaubrett was pleased and relieved to encounter no giants but instead an Abukei village. After a tense but peaceful exchange with the village elders, the natives brought the half-starved travelers food and water, and Gaubrett and his crew set up camp by the shore. As grateful as they were, the sailors could not help but greedily notice the green gemstones hanging over the tribe's simple dwellings and decorating the bodies of the men and women. Even before the rise of the Kekonese warrior caste of Green Bones, jade was of significant cultural importance to the aboriginals, who viewed it as the divine remains of the First Mother goddess Nimuma and, being genetically immune to its effects, wore it for status and ceremony.

Gaubrett proceeded to barter a considerable amount of his ship's wares in exchange for the villagers' jade, which they seemed more than willing to trade in exchange for foreign tools and curiosities.

Gaubrett stored the acquired jade in a wooden chest in his tent, which he opened several times a day in order to admire his fortune. Once much-needed ship repairs had been completed, Gaubrett and his crew made ready to set sail. At that point, it occurred to the explorer that there was a great deal more jade to be had, and that he had come an awfully long way across the ocean to be leaving with so little compared to how much these simple savages flaunted so carelessly.

That night, Gaubrett gathered his men and led them into the Abukei village where they massacred the inhabitants and gathered every last bit of jade they could lay their hands on. In good spirits, they departed Kekon. Despite ample stores and good weather, over the following two months, the ship descended into an inexplicable madness. Shortly after Gaubrett hung two officers for treason, the crew mutinied; Gaubrett and several others were killed and their bodies tossed overboard. The storeroom lock was smashed and the jade equally divided among the crew. Two subsequent mutinies resulted in several more deaths. Half a dozen sailors threw themselves into the sea; others fell into a delirious fever and cut themselves with knives. One man was said to have pulled out his own eye and eaten it. A small group of beleaguered survivors, at last convinced that the treasure they carried was cursed, threw every piece of jade on the ship into the ocean and managed to limp their vessel into a port in southeastern Spenius. Their tragic tale quickly spread, cementing the "cursed beauty" as a faraway place of near mythical wealth and mysterious evil fortune.

Seven hundred and fifty years after Gaubrett's journey, the Shotarian general Damusaro famously disagreed with the national War Cabinet's decision to occupy Kekon, arguing, "That damned island is like a beautiful woman with a barbed pussy—very tempting, but not to be fucked." Perhaps as belated punishment for his vulgar objections, his superiors later sent him to command the Garrison House in occupied Janloon during the Many Nations War. His name was whispered by the One Mountain Society, and despite obsessive security precautions, he was ambushed and killed in broad daylight by a young Green Bone assassin named Nau Suenzen.

CHAPTER

54

~

The Body Doesn't Lie

Son Tomarho came out of the shower humming a tune and walked into the sitting room of his two-story house in the wealthy neighborhood of Green Plain. He startled to find a tall, older man sitting on his sofa. At first he had no idea who the man was, though his eyes fell immediately upon the jade carried on leather bands around the stranger's wrists. Only when the intruder said, "Chancellor Son, I'm sorry to surprise you like this," did Son recognize Nau Suen, the Horn of the Mountain, and he knew that, aisho notwithstanding, there was a better than average chance he would be dead in the next five minutes.

The former chancellor of the Royal Council had been in some tight spots in his many decades of business and political life, and he managed to keep cool and collected now, as he said, "Nau-jen, you've caught me at a disadvantage, I'm afraid. I would've been happy to meet and speak to you at a time when I wasn't so...immodest." He gestured self-deprecatingly at his semi-nudity. A towel covered his lower body, but he was otherwise unclothed. "If you'll wait, I'd prefer to put on some clothes."

"By all means," said Nau. "Take your time."

Son retreated into his bedroom and put on pants and a shirt. His mind raced. During his years as chancellor, he'd been given a government security detail, but now that he was once again an ordinary councilman on his way to retirement, he'd deemed personal bodyguards to be unnecessary. He had a home security system, and if he triggered an alarm, it would alert the security firm, which would send... what? Some guards who would get here too late and be no match for a superior Green Bone like Nau Suen anyway. No, he would have to survive by talking his way out of this, as he had more than once in his life before. Son smoothed down his wet hair so that it covered the bald spot on the top of his head, put on his slippers, and walked back out to the sitting room. He gave the Horn of the Mountain a polished but cheerless politician's smile and sat down across from him. "Are you here to threaten me?"

"Not at all," said Nau. "You're a respected and senior statesman who's served this country honorably over your many years in politics. That would be uncouth of the Mountain clan. You must forgive me for my unexpected appearance; I needed to speak to you in private."

Son relaxed only slightly. "Well, then, what can I do for the Horn of the Mountain?"

Nau sat back and drummed his fingers on the armrests. He was an intense man who seemed younger than his salt-and-pepper hair would suggest, and he had a piercing gaze that seemed not to blink as much as normal people. "My Pillar is concerned about the fate of the Oortokon Conflict Refugee Act," Nau said. "The proposed legislation has been hotly debated and has languished in committees for more than a year. Now that a bill is finally coming to a vote, it appears that the Royal Council remains nearly evenly split on this issue and you, Chancellor, might cast the deciding vote when it is brought to the floor of Wisdom Hall next month. Where do you stand on the matter?"

"There are strong arguments to be made on both sides of the

issue," Son said carefully. Some of those arguments were continually imposing themselves upon him in the form of phone calls from Ambassador Mendoff. With the Oortokon War grinding to a stalemate, the Espenians were anticipating a longer-term standoff with their enemies and were more concerned than ever with ensuring their regional allies resisted any potential Ygutanian infiltration. Son said, "In the end, I will have to weigh the best interests of the nation and vote with my conscience."

"What if I were to tell you that the Mountain clan is deeply committed to making sure that anti-immigration interests don't interfere with our better nature as a country. We would urge all members of the Royal Council to give our brothers and sisters of Kekonese ancestry in Oortoko the asylum they deserve from the predations of power-hungry imperialist foreigners. Would that sway your decision?"

"Nau-jen, I would listen to all reasonable arguments," said Son.

"What if I were to say that we could make it personally worth your while to vote for the bill?"

"I am not in the Royal Council for personal gain, Nau-jen," said Son with a strong note of indignation. "But I'm certainly willing to speak to you and to Ayt-jen about your concerns."

Nau lowered his chin and regarded Son with calm understanding. "I don't expect that would make any difference, as you've already met with Kaul Shaelinsan and promised her that in order to maintain No Peak's preferential standing with the Espenians, you will use your chancellor emeritus status to oppose the bill and make sure that it is blocked by the Council. Isn't that true? You remain a No Peak man through and through."

Son began to sweat. "If that's what you believe, then why are you here, Nau-jen? The vote is close, as you said. There are plenty of other members of the Council that you could try to sway to your position." He gambled now by interjecting a note of nonchalant disdain into his voice. "And if the Mountain clan believes it can achieve its political aims by grossly violating aisho and simply killing someone, why target a man like myself, who is so much in the public eye, whose murder would be scrutinized?"

"Because," said Nau, leaning forward, "you are No Peak's greatest political ally. Very few councilmen have the clout and influence that you do, Chancellor Son. And no one else has what you have—an arterial blockage in the left ventricle of your heart, one that your doctors are keeping an eye on because it poses a heart attack risk. I suspect that very few people know about it; you keep it quiet, naturally, but the body doesn't lie the way the mind does."

Nau stood up. Chancellor Son stumbled to his feet, turned, and tried to run. He did not make it far. Nau grabbed the fat man by the arm in a grip of Strength and pressed a hand to Son's chest. Son's heart was already thudding with fear; a light touch of Channeling was all that was required. The former chancellor clutched his chest and gasped for breath. Nau released him and he fell to the ground, his entire bulk rigid, his mouth open and working for air.

It would take only a few minutes of medical examination to conclude that Son Tomarho had died of natural causes. A few would not believe that; some members in the Royal Council might open an investigation that would reveal nothing, but people would whisper anyway, and that would serve the Mountain's purpose as well.

Nau stepped over Son's body and made his way toward the door.

CHAPTER

55

Final Preparations

The *Kekon Journal* is an independent weekly Kekonese-language newspaper published in Espenia, with a wide circulation among overseas Kekonese. Its editorial stance has long been favorable to the Kekonese government, but in recent years, and following a relocation from its original headquarters in Southtrap to a larger office on Jons Island, the newspaper has included more in-depth reporting and critical coverage of Kekon's clan system, Espenian foreign policy, and international regulation of jade, among other topics of interest.

Under the guise of an Espenian-born journalist named Ray Caido, Anden requested a personal interview with Zapunyo on behalf of the *Kekon Journal*. In his correspondence with Zapunyo's aide Iyilo, he emphasized that the expatriate Kekonese population was very interested in hearing opposing viewpoints regarding the jade trade; this would be the smuggler's once-in-a-lifetime opportunity to tell his side of the story and repudiate the negative coverage in the mainstream media. All of Anden's false credentials were meticulously supported, using the same No Peak resources that created and maintained shell companies such as Divinity Gems, and with the help of the Dauks, who were owed personal favors by the newspaper's editor in chief from a time in the past when he had gotten into some trouble with finances.

"The thing about Zapunyo," Hilo said over the phone, "is that he makes himself out to be a humble Uwiwan farmer turned entrepreneur. When I met him, he could've spent the whole day telling me his fucking sob story and lecturing me about how it's the Green Bone clans that are the real villains for making his business so difficult. If there's anything that'll lure him into a face-to-face meeting, it's a chance to talk to someone who'll listen to him."

The Pillar's assessment proved correct; after some back-and-forth correspondence with Iyilo, Anden was able to secure an interview with Zapunyo during the time when he would be in Port Massy, the day after his arrival in the city and before his scheduled surgery at Wigham-Cross Truthbearers Hospital. The meeting was scheduled to occur at the small Uwiwa Islands Cultural Heritage Center & Tea Gardens in the Quince area, which would afford a view of the Iron Eye Bridge and would present a good background for photographs. Anden would be unarmed and accompanied only by Rohn Toro, posing as his photographer. Rohn's black gloves would be carefully hidden on the premises the day before the event. During the false interview, Rohn would retrieve his gloves, put on his jade, and kill Zapunyo.

The assassination plan was formed over several conversations at the Kaul family dinner table. Secrecy was of the utmost concern, since after Tau Maro's betrayal, it was safe to assume that Zapunyo might have other spies within No Peak circles and they could not risk any word of the plot reaching him in the Uwiwa Islands. In order to throw off any suspicion, false rumors and death threats against the smuggler were deliberately set into motion, hinting at a more obvious plot that involved striking when he was in the hospital room recovering from surgery, when they knew the smuggler was bound to take extreme precautions. A new phone with a speaker, connected to a secure line that was known only to immediate family, was installed in the dining room of the main house on the Kaul estate so that Anden, waiting at designated times in his apartment in Port Massy, could be remotely brought into the discussion.

Anden found this arrangement difficult; the meetings were always midmorning in his time zone, which disrupted his day, and being able to hear but not see what was going on gave him a strange and lonely feeling. He could picture all of them in the dining room—Hilo at the head of the table, a cigarette in hand, Tar next to him, Kehn's empty chair, Wen filling teacups, Shae holding Jaya on her lap—all while Anden sat alone on his bed in his small apartment, his ear pressed to the receiver, trying to hear the muted long-distance conversation over the sound of his building's noisy central heating system. Sometimes Anden could hear the shouts of Niko and Ru playing in the other room or coming over to the adults to ask for this or that and being told to say hello to their uncle Anden on the phone before being shooed away again.

At times Anden thought it almost comical that he would have to make some excuse to leave on an early, extra long lunch break from working at the Janloon Trade Partnership Liaison Office in order to take part in conversations with his family back in Janloon, all to plot the murder of a man he had never met. He felt no moral qualms about assassinating Zapunyo, nor resentment over the efforts he was being asked to make. He understood how important this was to his cousins as well as to Wen, who always visited him on her business trips and whom he felt closer to now than he ever had while living in Janloon. It was only ironic to him that *this* was how he would finally be returning to Kekon. After the deed was done, both Anden and Rohn Toro would have to leave the country. Anden was instructed not to say anything beforehand to the Hians, or to his friends or coworkers. He had to be ready to depart quickly, and Shae would take care of the rest. If all went according to plan, after three and half years in Espenia, he would be going home.

Anden did not quite allow himself to believe it. In a way it seemed fitting, almost poetic: Killing Gont Asch had ruined him as a Green Bone and led to his exile; this deed would end his time abroad and return him to Kekon with the proof that even without jade, he was not useless, he was still a force in the clan, still a Kaul. Not long ago, it would've been all Anden wanted, but now he faced it with bittersweet melancholy. He was impatient to return home, but not happy to leave Port Massy after all. When he'd arrived, he'd seen nothing but the impersonal concrete grayness of the vast foreign city. Now he could say that he'd seen the fierce, enterprising life that pulsed like jade aura through the veins of its streets and in the marrow of its steel structures. Port Massy had been and still was the trading post of the world, a market where anything could be found, bought, and sold, a place that held a little of everything in its grasp—even jade and Green Bones, along with uncountable other wonders known and unknown—and still, somehow, was its own self, standing without compare. Anden would never think of his biological father with anything but indifference and disdain, but now he thought that perhaps the man was simply typical of his race and couldn't be too badly blamed; Port Massy owed its unique glory to the mercenary wayfaring nature of the Espenian people, and as the meeting with Zapunyo neared, Anden found himself appreciating, even admiring, the city more than he ever had before. Wen was correct; he had friends here now, an independent life that he was proud of in many ways, and he thought constantly and sorrowfully about what he was giving up.

He'd tried to call Cory again, on more than one occasion, hoping to explain things better than he had in their last conversation, but his friend refused to answer any of his calls. He learned from the Hians that Cory had taken an internship at a big law firm in AC and would not be returning to Port Massy over the summer. At times, Anden felt as if he'd made a terrible mistake, that he ought to take the bus to Adamont Capita and find Cory in person and say that he'd been wrong—who cared what Dauk Losun wanted? What did their families matter, what did law school or even the entire Amaric Ocean matter? They could run away together; it would be daring and romantic. Lying awake with his cock in his hand, Anden would groan with the childishness of the thought and with the simultaneous depressing certainty that he'd doomed himself to be alone forever; he was never going to find anyone else like Cory, who wouldn't even talk to him anymore.

At last, Anden sat down and wrote a letter, which he mused gloomily was a very cliché post-breakup thing to do, but so be it. *Cory,* he wrote, *You have every right to be angry at me, but I know that you're too good of a person to stay in a bad mood for long, and I hope that after a while, we'll be able to remain friends. Don't blame your da. It was my decision in the end. Even though it was one of the hardest things I've ever had to do, I made the choice I hope is better for both of us. I can't explain everything right now because they're "clan things" like you said, but I will soon.* Sitting at the cramped desk facing his tiny apartment window, Anden agonized over how much to justify himself, how to sound sincere without being maudlin, starting and discarding several versions of the letter before deciding, fuck it, Cory was probably going to throw it in the trash without reading it anyway. *You were my first. You made Port Massy a special place for me, and you're a better, more generous person than I am. You deserve the best of everything.*

Your friend and "islander," Anden.

Anden mailed the letter to Cory's address in Adamont Capita. Doing so was painful but took a burden off his mind, and afterward, he awaited Zapunyo's forthcoming arrival with impatience. If all went according to plan, in a few weeks he'd be on a flight back to Janloon. Of course, there was a reasonable chance he would be dead—shot by Zapunyo's bodyguards, but he had seen Rohn Toro's abilities and knew the man's reputation was well earned, so he trusted in their odds of survival. Having been trained at the Academy and raised in the Kaul family, Anden had been indoctrinated since childhood with the idea that for Green Bones, the possibility of death was like the weather—you could make attempts to predict it, but you would likely be wrong, and no one would change their most important plans due to threat of rain.

CHAPTER

56

~

No Surprise

The Sin 8 was one of the liveliest nightclubs in the Dog's Head district. On a Fourthday evening, the line of fashionably dressed twentysomethings waiting to get inside stretched down the block and around the corner. Once past the bouncers, partygoers lined up again at one of the two neon-lit bars, shouting over the throbbing beat of the music to place their drink orders. The main dance floor heaved with the crush of sweaty bodies and pulsed with strobe lights. Upstairs, those hoping to have audible conversations lounged on the clusters of red sofas or, if they were particularly well heeled, rented one of the fifteen soundproof suites with a private bar and server. One of these rooms was regularly reserved for Ven Haku, Fist of the Mountain and scion of the K-Star Freight fortune, to use whenever he wished to entertain his many friends.

Haku was leaning back on one of the sofas now, and despite the glass of hoji in his hand and a couple of pretty girls on either side of him, he wore a brooding, impatient expression. When his most senior Finger said something funny, he didn't laugh along with everyone else. After the next round of drinks, Haku motioned the server and the disappointed girls out of the room and sat forward, inducing the five other men in the room—all of them Mountain Green Bones with considerable jade and reputations—to quiet their banter and give him their attention.

"Is everyone ready?" Haku asked. "You're all clear on the plan? If anything goes wrong this week, we'll all lose our heads, so there's no room for error. We're committed now."

The men around the room nodded. One of them said, "We haven't been able to reach either Sunto-jen or Uwan-jen. We don't know whether they'll stand with us or against us."

"We have to go ahead, anyway," Haku said. His father had made that abundantly clear in their recent conversations. They were running out of time. "No matter which way Sunto or Uwan or the other Fists go, once Ayt's gone, the Kauls will support us." That was what Ven Sando had told him, and Haku had not questioned it. He trusted his father, who was a seasoned corporate executive, to handle the matter of clan alliances and getting the Lantern Men to fall in line; Haku only had to worry about the actual logistics of the coup, which was no small feat in itself.

"Just remember to kill Ayt first," Haku reminded them. "Doesn't matter how good that woman is at dueling and whispering names, an ambush from six of—"

He would've said more, but one of the other Fists interrupted, with sudden alarm, "Do you Perceive that?"

The men quieted, jade senses alert. At first, Haku discerned nothing out of the ordinary—merely the background energy din of all the people enjoying themselves in the club. That was one reason he chose to meet here with his coconspirators: It was easy for even the auras of half a dozen Fists and Fingers together to go unnoticed in such a crowded and lively environment. The club was a tributary Mountain property and there were always other Green Bones among the general throng. Haku's Perception was not especially strong, but after a minute, he realized that several jade auras were moving from their scattered positions in the building and congregating on the second floor—right outside of their room. Haku drew his talon knife and threw open the door.

"Ven Haku-jen," said Nau Suen, walking into the room ahead of a group of eight other Green Bones, "I'm too old for the clubbing scene, but I'm told that you throw good parties here."

"Nau-jen," Haku said, sheathing his talon knife and dipping into a respectful salute. His eyes darted over Nau's other men and his heart began to pound. "You startled me." Haku was not sure how the Horn did it, but Nau Suen had a way of quieting his jade aura to such a low, even hum that he moved inconspicuously even to jade senses and seemed to appear out of nowhere. "My friends and I always have this room. If I knew you were interested in joining us, I'd have invited you."

Nau glanced around at Ven Haku's comrades. "Nau-jen," they murmured in unison, touching their foreheads. Nau nodded at them, then rubbed his chin with a thumb and said, "Haku-jen, you're one of the clan's senior Fists, but I haven't seen much of you in person for months now. I think we ought to talk about all the time you've been spending at the Sin 8 in these parties."

Haku did his best to remain calm. The Horn did not know anything—could not *possibly* know anything about their schemes. The most he might have were suspicions. "I haven't been neglecting any of my duties," he said, with a note of defensiveness. "If I haven't been checking in as often, it's because I've been helping my father. He's busy with K-Star Freight these days."

"I suppose that's true," Nau said. "You're an obedient son, Ven Haku, but unfortunately a terrible liar. Your heart rate and blood pressure are up, your eyes are twitching, you're sweating. You wouldn't even pass a simple lie detector test, much less fool my sense of Perception, which is no doubt why you've been making an effort to avoid me."

Haku went for his talon knife. He lunged at Nau's throat, but two of the Horn's men were already moving. With combined Strength, they bore the young Fist to the ground and pinned him to the floor.

Haku screamed and pleaded his innocence, he tried to Deflect and Channel; two other men came over and helped to hold him down. Waun Balu, who was Nau's First Fist, said in a regretful, almost gentle voice, "Don't make it worse for yourself, Haku." The traitor did not take Waun's advice; as his head was pulled back, he Steeled for all he was worth, and so it took a full grisly minute for Waun to saw across his throat with the talon knife.

Two of Haku's accomplices tried to come to his aid, and one of them tried to escape by crashing bodily through the door. They were blocked and forced into a line against the far wall by Nau's other men, who drew handguns whose bullets could not possibly be Deflected at such close range. If anyone outside of the room heard the noise through the walls and over the pounding music, they did not investigate. No one, including the bouncers, would be so foolish as to interfere. When Haku was finally dead, Nau Suen barked in disgust, "Is it not enough that we have to contend with foreigners and criminals and with the No Peak clan? We have to fight among ourselves, and fear disloyalty and treachery from within our own brotherhood?"

The five Green Bones who'd conspired with Ven and his father dropped to their knees and pressed their heads to the ground. They were all Fists and senior Fingers, respectable fighters in their own right, but with their plotting exposed and Ven dead, they were not stupid enough to think they could stand against the clan or run from its justice. Nau said to them, "You all deserve death, for scheming to assassinate the Pillar and install that weakling in her place. Do you repent your part in this treason? Do you swear on your jade and the lives of your family members to give Ayt-jen your complete and unequivocal loyalty from now on?"

With collective vehemence, the men said that they did, and thanked the Horn for his mercy. Nau Suen studied the handful of kneeling Green Bones for a long minute. Then he pointed out three of the five. "Those three," he said, and from where they were standing behind the prisoners, Waun Balu and his men slit each of the indicated throats and pushed the bodies face-first to the floor. The two remaining survivors turned pale with anticipation of death.

Nau said, "Your three friends weren't sincere; they would've waited to seek revenge for Haku or betrayed the clan in some other way. The two of you, however, are being truthful." The Horn fixed them with a terrifying stare. "You'll be exiled from Janloon, to do work for the Mountain elsewhere in the country, and if you ever go against the Pillar again, you know what will happen to you and your families."

One of the spared men asked permission to draw his talon knife. He sliced off his left ear and laid it on the floor, head bowed and blood running down his neck. His companion swallowed. "The clan is my blood, and the Pillar is its master," he murmured quickly, and followed suit.

Ven Sando was in a senior management meeting with the leadership team of K-Star Freight the following morning when the door to the boardroom opened unexpectedly and Ayt Madashi strode in, accompanied by the Horn and the Weather Man and a small retinue. The Pillar of the Mountain looked down the long table of company executives and said, "Gentlemen, I apologize for the interruption. The Weather Man's office has received an offer of purchase for K-Star Freight from a credible and interested party, and I must discuss it with Ven-jen privately before we make the news public to shareholders."

The vice presidents murmured, looking at each other in surprise and confusion, but they departed without arguing. When they were gone, Ven rose from his leather chair at the end of the table and said, affronted, "I haven't been approached by any buyers. Besides, K-Star is not for sale." His gaze landed suspiciously on Nau Suen and the two Fists behind him, one of them carrying a cardboard filing box. If this was a business discussion, why were the Horn and his men here? Ven knew the answer, and despite his best efforts to appear normal, his hands began to shake.

Ayt motioned forward two strangers. They were not Kekonese. "These men are here to buy out your family's majority ownership of K-Star Freight. Iwe-jen has prepared all the paperwork."

Iwe Kalundo, the clan's Weather Man, was a dark, bald man with square black glasses frames. He placed his briefcase on the table and extracted a file folder with several documents, which he walked over to Ven and placed in front of the man.

Ven picked up the folder and flung it back across the table at Ayt, scattering pages. "Never," he declared. "I'll never sell. You're making a terrible strategic mistake by trying to oust me. K-Star is one of the Mountain clan's largest tributary entities, one of the largest corporations in Kekon. There aren't any other companies with the capital to buy us out, and certainly none with the world-class expertise in transportation logistics to be able to take over our operations. If I leave, my entire management team leaves with me. K-Star will fail, and so will the Kekonese freight industry. The Mountain clan *needs* K-Star and the Ven family."

Ayt Mada said, "You're admirably confident for a clan traitor who is facing death, Ven-jen. Yes, K-Star is one of the largest companies in Kekon, and that would seem to make the Ven family indispensable. But the world is much bigger than Kekon these days; I would think that someone working in the transportation business would appreciate that."

"You would put K-Star in the hands of foreigners?" Ven exclaimed in disbelief.

"Fifty-one percent of the company will be acquired by YGL Transport, headquartered out of Bursvik. I'm confident that these new owners have the operational capabilities to capably run K-Star in your absence. The other forty-nine percent of K-Star will remain under the control of selected Kekonese shareholders within the Mountain."

At the Pillar's nod, the Fist holding the closed cardboard filing box came forward and set it on the table. Ayt said, "Your eldest son, Haku—his head is inside this box. I'll spare you by not opening it, but even with your tiny amount of jade, I expect you can Perceive that I'm not lying. You forfeited his life and your own when you conspired with No Peak. I've been thinking that Kaul Hilo has been acting unusually restrained as of late, and now it's clear why. Sign the papers, Ven-jen. You come from an old Green Bone family; none of this should surprise you."

Ven's fragile mask of indignation and bluster collapsed; his chin trembled and his shoulders began to shudder. "My other children," he whispered. "They had nothing to do with this. Spare them, Ayt-jen. I'll sign the papers, I'll instruct my managers to stay on after the sale, I'll do whatever else you ask of me before I die, if only you'll spare the rest of my family."

"Your sons, no," Ayt replied. "Your wife and daughters can leave the country in exile. I'll allow you and your male children to be buried with your jade in the family plot on Kekon. That's all the accommodation I can give to a man who has betrayed his Pillar."

Iwe Kalundo gathered the strewn documents back together and showed Ven Sandolan each of the places he was required to sign.

CHAPTER

57

~

Emergencies

On the day that No Peak's spies had told him Zapunyo was scheduled to arrive in Port Massy, Hilo fed his sons dinner, then took his
own meal to the sofa in the living room and watched the news while
awaiting the call from his cousin to confirm that all the arrangements
were in place. Wen was in Adamont Capita for the week, consulting
on the redesign of the Kekonese embassy and scouting out properties
of potential investment interest to the Weather Man's office. Shae
often came over to eat in the main house, but she was still at work on
Ship Street, so Hilo was home alone with his children except for his
mother planting flower bulbs outside in the garden and Kyanla put-
tering around in the kitchen.

On the television, anchorman Toh Kita was reporting on the
recent narrow passage of the Oortokon Conflict Refugee Act, which
would make Kekon one of several nations to commit to taking refugees from the war-ravaged region on the border of Shotar and Ygutan.

Chancellor Guim was giving a speech in Wisdom Hall about the terrible human cost of foreign imperialism and the importance of Kekon stepping up as a responsible world citizen. He closed his address by expressing sadness over the recent passing of his predecessor, Son Tomarho, a devoted statesman and servant of the country, let the gods recognize him.

Hilo scowled at the screen. The Espenians were going to be unhappy about the passing of the Refugee Act. It would fall on Shae to deal with the brunt of the diplomatic fallout, but Hilo wished Chancellor Son had managed to keep his heart pumping for a while longer. He had gotten used to Son. Chancellor Guim struck him as too cagey and polished, and he was a Mountain loyalist, which meant No Peak's influence in the Royal Council was considerably diminished. The coroner said there was no question Son Tomarho had died of cardiac arrest, but Hilo wasn't one to believe in convenient accidents.

Jaya had thrown all her toys out of the playpen and was demanding to be picked up. Hilo knew he had a five-minute grace period before she threw a tantrum, so he finished his meal—a bowl of leftover ginger chicken stew—and held his daughter on his lap, trying to entertain her with a puppet. Hilo liked being a father and found it suited him. Children were completely honest and lived in the moment; they were demanding, but also easy to please, asking only for simple love and attention. He wouldn't object to having more of them, if Wen was not determined to have a meaningful career within the clan, which he supported for the sake of her happiness but still thought was not entirely necessary.

The phone rang. Expecting it to be Anden, Hilo handed the toddler to Kyanla and picked up the receiver in the kitchen. Juen said, "Hilo-jen, there are some . . . rumors going on."

Even after more than a year, there were times when Hilo heard Juen's voice on the phone and wondered, for a second, why Kehn had sent his First Fist instead of phoning himself. It never failed to give him painful pause. Hilo said, "Rumors are as common as rats; what's so special about these ones?"

"Ven Sandolan, the big businessman, the one who owns the shipping company—he's dead. Executed by the Mountain for treason. Apparently, he tried to organize a coup against Ayt Mada but his plans were discovered. People are shocked; he was one of their top Lantern Men."

Hilo muted the television. "What about his sons?"

"Dead as well, along with a number of other conspirators. They say Nau Suen and his men caught Ven Haku and some other Fists plotting at the Sin 8 nightclub and slit their throats."

"Ayt wiped out the wealthiest Green Bone bloodline in her clan? And none of the other families in the Mountain are rioting?" Hilo demanded in disbelief.

"Ayt's taken Koben Ato as her ward," Juen said. "From now on, she'll be paying for his studies at Wie Lon, training him privately at the Ayt mansion, bringing him under her wing. She isn't officially calling the kid her heir, but it's a big enough change that she's bought the support of the Kobens and everyone who's on their side."

"And the Iwe family?"

"Quiet. The word is that Ayt handed them a huge share of K-Star Freight."

"Godsdamnit," Hilo snarled under his breath, taken aback and furious at how suddenly it had happened, how quickly his designs had unraveled. Nonetheless, he was unable to contain a grudging admiration. Ayt had played her hand beautifully; after the destruction of the Ven family, no one else in the Mountain would dare to oppose her. Or the newly elevated Koben family. Hilo's meetings with Ven Sando, the behind-the-scenes payments and secret assurances, his calculated stoking of the internal divisions in the Mountain with provocations and violence, all of it building his hope for the past three years that the Mountain clan would take down No Peak's longtime enemy on its own and tear itself to pieces—all for nothing. "Why the *fuck* is that bitch *so hard to kill?*"

"Uncle," Niko said, tugging on Hilo's shirt sleeve.

"Not now, Niko."

"Uncle." This time it was not the boy's voice or the renewed tugging on his arm that made Hilo turn to look down at his nephew, but the strong surge of confusion and fear that Hilo Perceived in the boy—his little heart was beating like a drum. Niko was not a temperamental child, not the sort to get upset easily or be fearful of harmless things, but his eyes were wide with distress.

Hilo instructed Juen to learn what else he could and report back once he had more information. He hung up and said, "What is it? What's wrong?"

"Ru...he...he...we were playing, and he...he ate them!"

"Ate what?" Hilo said. "Where is he?" He followed Niko to the study and as soon as he entered the room, Hilo understood. A terrible dread dropped his heart into his stomach. A small cloth bag of jade buttons, long ago confiscated from the shipment of garments on the MV *Amaric Pride*, was lying open on the coffee table. Several small jade pieces were lying scattered or stacked on the glass surface; the boys had obviously found them in Hilo's unlocked desk drawer and had been playing with them. Ru was sitting curled on the ground in the corner behind the sofa, holding a throw pillow to his chest and face, as if, by hiding behind it, he could avoid his father's anger.

Hilo strode over and pulled the pillow away. He crouched down, gripping his son by the arms. "What happened?" he demanded, hoping the boys would grin, that it would be a joke they were playing to scare him, though he knew as soon as he saw Ru's tear-stained face that it wasn't.

Niko was the one who answered. "He swallowed them."

"I didn't mean to!" Ru blurted, his cheeks reddening. He shot his cousin a baleful glare of betrayal. "It was your fault! I was going to spit them out, but you had your hand over my mouth!"

"*Why* would you do that?" Hilo shouted at both of them. They had been taught that jade was to be worn and handled by adults, that it was not for playing with. They ought to have known better.

"We were just pretending." Niko was on the verge of tears himself.

Hilo's desire to give them both a beating was blotted out by fury with himself—he hadn't thought the boys would play in the study, he should've locked the jade in the drawer, why had he left it out so carelessly?—and a more urgent, intense fear. Jade inside a small child's body was dangerous. It could cause fever, erratic heartbeat, seizures, collapse, and death.

Hilo scooped his son up in his arms. He shouted for Kyanla to take care of Jaya and Niko as he grabbed the keys to the Duchesse and ran for the door. Niko, crying now, ran after him. "I'm coming too." He clung to Hilo's waist. "Don't leave me."

Hilo threw open the back door of the Duchesse Signa and piled both children onto the seat. Ru stared at his father with wide, frightened eyes. "Am I going to die?"

"No," Hilo said. He got in and started the car.

At Janloon General Hospital, the emergency room staff hurried Ru into an examination room. An X-ray revealed two button-sized jade stones, which thankfully had not lodged in the boy's esophagus on the way down but were now trapped inside his stomach. Ru was hooked up to machines to monitor his heart rate, blood pressure, and temperature. A white-haired doctor came in and explained that he believed the stones could be removed without surgery. Ru would be sedated and a flexible grasping tool inserted down his throat to try and extract the pieces of jade. Hilo sat next to the bed holding his son's small, sweaty hand in his own while the boy was put under anesthesia.

"Are you mad at me?" Ru asked, his voice turning groggy.

"No." He was too afraid to be angry. "I love you." He smoothed Ru's hair. The boy's forehead felt warm and damp; Hilo wasn't sure if it was a jade-induced fever or merely exertion from crying.

"I want Ma," Ru whimpered.

"You'll see her when you wake up," Hilo promised. Uncontrollably, his mind flashed to the worst possible outcome he could imagine: having to call his wife while she was thousands of kilometers away on a business trip to tell her that their son had died of jade poisoning while under his watch. He felt ill at the thought and told himself that would not happen.

A nurse had brought in a small stack of board books and a toy truck for Niko to play with, but after a cursory look, the boy ignored them. He sat on a chair next to Hilo with his knees drawn up to his chest, hugging his legs. After the initial bout of tears in the car, his eyes were dry. He stared around at everything with interest and faint hostility, but he had not spoken since they got to the hospital.

Hilo looked at his wristwatch. It was past dinnertime; they'd been in the emergency room for two hours already. It would be midmorning on the east coast of Espenia. By now, Anden was supposed to have phoned to confirm that Zapunyo had arrived in Port Massy and that all the arrangements were in place. Unable to reach Hilo at the house, he would've phoned the Weather Man's office. Shae would be wondering where he was; perhaps she was trying to reach him now.

The doctors came in and wheeled Ru away. Hilo followed as far as they allowed, then watched his son disappear behind closed doors. The white-haired doctor assured Hilo that the procedure would not take long. "You're not the first Green Bone family to have had this happen, Kaul-jen," the doctor said. "As long we get the jade out quickly, there's no permanent harm. SN1 isn't recommended for children, but we can use small doses if it looks like that'll be necessary."

Hilo thanked the doctor, then took Niko by the hand and went into the lobby of the hospital. He sat his nephew down on a chair near the bank of pay phones. "Are you hungry? Do you need to go to the bathroom?" The boy shook his head. Hilo bought him a bag of crackers and a bottle of fruit juice from the vending machine anyway, and keeping the boy in sight, he called the house. After assuring a worried Kyanla that Ru would be fine, he asked her to retrieve his address book from the study and to search up the phone number of the hotel Wen was staying at in Adamont Capita. He wrote the number on his hand, then depressed the phone hook and deposited enough coins to place a long-distance phone call. When the call was transferred to Wen's hotel room, it rang and rang but there was no answer. Hilo hung up. He called the Weather Man's office on Ship Street.

"Where have you been?" Shae sounded more flustered than he was used to hearing from her; he could practically sense the crackle of her jade aura even over the phone. When he explained what had happened, her irritation turned to concern. Say whatever else he might about his sister, but she was always caring toward the children. "Is Ru going to be all right?"

"The doctor thinks so. I'll find out soon." He said, "What have you heard from Andy?"

"There's a problem," Shae said. "Zapunyo won't meet in the room we've arranged at the Uwiwan Cultural Center. Maybe something's spooked him. Or maybe he intended to change the location all along, to throw off any potential threat. He's insisting that the interview take place in his hotel room, with his bodyguards. Otherwise he refuses to meet at all."

Hilo cursed. This changed everything. "We can't get jade into Zapunyo's hotel room," he said at last. "It's too late for that."

"Anden and I have been talking about it," Shae said. "If we go ahead with the interview, we could have a weapon brought up to the room by someone posing as a room service waiter. If it were hidden in a napkin or under a tray, and Rohn Toro could get to it before anyone questioned who'd made the order—"

"No," Hilo said. "Zapunyo's already suspicious; he would know right away."

"Then we're out of options. The interview is supposed to happen six hours from now."

Hilo's grip around the phone receiver tightened. His son was in the hospital, his wife was on the other side of the world, and his cousin was about to walk, jadeless and unarmed, into a hotel room to face one of the clan's enemies and a posse of barukan gangsters.

If he were in Port Massy right now instead of Anden, if he could walk into the room with Zapunyo, he would take whatever chance was necessary. He would attempt to smuggle a jade weapon into the room, or try to seize one off of Zapunyo's guards. He would risk his own life to stab Zapunyo through the throat with a ballpoint pen if need be.

But he was not there. There were so many things that as Pillar he could not accomplish solely with his own will and strength, that relied instead on other people, even in matters as personal as vengeance. Andy was over there, alone. The last time Hilo had asked his cousin to kill on behalf of the clan, it had driven the young man away from the family and ruined him as a Green Bone. Hilo would go to great lengths to defeat an enemy and had done so in the past, but at this moment, watching his little nephew eat the last of the crackers and brush the crumbs from his lap, he thought only of the safety of his family.

"Call it off," Hilo said.

"If we don't go through with the interview," Shae said, "Zapunyo will know it was rigged from the start. The cover we've created for Anden will be blown and we won't get another chance."

"We're not going to have Andy go through a two-hour fake interview for no gain, not when all it'll take is a single slip—someone in the room realizing that he isn't who he says he is—for him to get shot in the head. We'll have to think of some other way to get to Zapunyo," he said. "Call it off, Shae."

Hilo got off the phone with the Weather Man. He took Niko by the hand and walked back to the room where they would bring Ru once the doctors were done with the procedure. His mind was churning with anger, knowing that months of careful groundwork and scheming would come to nothing. Coming on top of the news about Ven, he felt as if surely nothing else could go wrong today, but when the doctor came into the room, he had a look of apprehension on his face that turned Hilo cold.

"Where's my son?" the Pillar demanded, in such a sharp and deadly voice that the doctor blanched.

"They're bringing him back right now," the doctor said hastily. "The procedure went smoothly, and he'll come out from under the anesthesia in an hour or so." The doctor handed Hilo a plastic container, of the sort used to collect urine samples, sealed with a red lid. The offending pieces of jade clinked around at the bottom of it. "He'll recover fully, Kaul-jen, but there's something you should know. Your son is nonreactive to jade. We expected to see some change in his vital signs as a result of that amount of jade exposure, but there wasn't any at all. He might as well have swallowed a cherry pit."

Hilo said, "Isn't he too young for you to tell for certain?"

"It's possible for children to show wide fluctuations in their responses to jade—from minimal to severe—in the first six years of life, which is why pediatricians recommend strictly limiting and supervising jade exposure in early childhood. But no response at all... We can be quite sure he's nonreactive."

It annoyed Hilo how the doctor kept saying the word *nonreactive* as if the technical term was somehow softer and kinder than *stone-eye*. When the man had come in looking so grave, Hilo had feared the worst. This news was not so bad in comparison. He was not shocked; given that Wen was a stone-eye, he'd always known this was a possibility. He had hoped, of course, that it would not be true, but now that he knew for certain that it was, he found himself accepting the idea with some indefinable combination of disappointment, relief, and parental defensiveness. So his son was a stone-eye; why was the doctor acting so serious and concerned, as if that were some kind of fatal disease? One would think that a medical professional wouldn't subscribe to the old Kekonese superstitions about stone-eyes being bad luck. Or was it because he thought Hilo would take the news badly, that the Pillar of a Green Bone clan wouldn't love his own son anymore just because he couldn't wear jade?

"There are worse things to be than a stone-eye," Hilo said, forcing a smile he did not really feel but that he hoped would make the doctor stop gazing at him worriedly from overtop his spectacles. "The important thing is that he's healthy and loved. It doesn't matter what other people think."

"Quite right, Kaul-jen," said the doctor, his shoulders coming down.

Ru was wheeled back into the room. He looked a little pale, but his chest rose and fell in gentle, even breaths. The nurse inclined the top of the bed and arranged the pillows to make the sleeping boy more comfortable before departing. Niko had watched the entire conversation between Hilo and the doctor without a word. When the three of them were alone, he asked, "Is Ru really a stone-eye?"

Hilo tried but did not quite succeed in keeping the sadness from his voice. "Yes."

"Is it because of what happened? Because I accidentally made him swallow jade?"

Hilo sighed and pulled his nephew onto his lap. "No, he was born that way. It's not anyone's fault."

Niko frowned at his sleeping cousin. "Will he be a stone-eye forever?"

"He'll always be a stone-eye, but that doesn't mean there aren't plenty of things he can do. Look at your ma, on a business trip right now, doing useful work for the family and the clan, even without jade." Hilo turned stern. "You'll have to protect him, though. Keep him safe. No more scares like we had today. Understand?"

Niko nodded. "Yes. I won't tease him anymore. I'll be a good big brother from now on."

58

⌒⌒

White Rat's Decision

When Wen returned to the Capita View Hotel, hoping for a nap after a morning of meetings and looking at flooring and paint samples, the bellman at the front desk told her that her husband had been trying to reach her for some time and had left a message and phone number for her to phone him back at Janloon General Hospital. Wen hurried up to her room. She told herself not to panic, but her hands were shaking as she used the calling card Shae had given her to place the long-distance phone call. A receptionist answered and told her to wait.

Several agonizing minutes later, Hilo came onto the line. "Every-one's fine," he said right away. "We had a little scare, that's all." He told her about what had happened to Ru. Then he put Niko on the line to say, "Hi, Ma, we miss you, when are you coming home?"

Wen assured him she would be home in three days, asked him

if he'd been practicing his reading and handwriting every day, then asked for the phone to be returned to his uncle.

"Do the doctors think this will have any long-term effect?" she asked Hilo.

"It won't," Hilo said. "The doctors say that Ru's a stone-eye."

Wen sat down hard on the edge of her hotel room bed. Her first reaction was surprise that Hilo sounded so unemotional about it, but then again, he'd had several hours to come to terms with the news, and she was hearing the diagnosis just now. Her voice came out small. "They're sure?"

"They're sure." Hilo still didn't sound upset, but there was an impatient edge to his voice, the one that he sometimes used to say, "Nothing," or "Fine," but that Wen always knew to be a sign that he was preoccupied or worried.

Wen felt unexpected tears prick her eyes. "I'm sorry."

"Don't be ridiculous," he said, then as if realizing he'd snapped at her, he said in a gentler voice, "I said everyone's fine, didn't I? That's what's important. Don't worry, and don't let it ruin your trip."

"What else aren't you telling me?" Wen asked. "I can tell there's something else."

"It's nothing to do with you at all. Clan things."

Wen glanced at the clock. "Does it have to do with the plan to kill Zapunyo?"

Hilo sighed as if giving up. "That Uwiwan coward won't leave his hotel room to meet at the place we've arranged. It's too risky for Andy to try anything now. The plan's been called off. We can't get to him this time, Wen."

"Not this time," Wen repeated. "When, then? You promised me, on the day that Kehn was murdered, that we would get the people who did this. *All* of them. It's been more than a year."

"You think I don't know that?" Hilo made a frustrated noise. "You're upset right now because while you were away, I wasn't paying enough attention to the boys and so this accident happened. But when have I ever failed to do what I promised? Have I ever left an offense against our family unpunished? Sometimes it takes longer, is all."

There was some distraction in the background of the hospital and Hilo turned away from the phone to speak to someone briefly before coming back onto the line. "I have to go; they're discharging Ru and I have to fill out some paperwork." A pause. "I didn't want to trouble you with bad news. It's not even that bad. Could've been a lot worse; we should be grateful it wasn't. And don't worry about the clan things. We'll talk when you get home. I love you."

"I love you too," Wen said. "Tell the boys their ma loves them." After Hilo hung up, Wen stared at the silent receiver for a long moment before putting it back in its cradle. She felt leaden. Mechanically, she got up and changed into more comfortable clothes, drank a soda from the minibar, then wandered her hotel room in a daze, before sitting back down on the bed.

She felt as if she wanted to cry, but the sensation was too indistinct, everything was happening too far away. If she were with her family, it would feel more real. She thought, *My son is a stone-eye.* She imagined Ru lying in a hospital bed, calling out for her, and with a surge of instinctive maternal desperation, she wished she was there to hug him tightly and comfort him. But she was also strangely relieved she was not there, that she did not have to look into his trusting face and lie to him by telling him everything was fine, because of course it was not fine. She felt herself detaching in a way, pulling away defensively from all the unkind thoughts that came to her: Ru could not attend the Academy, he could not be a Green Bone like his father and his uncles, he could not hold any significant rank in No Peak. He would be like his mother, ignored and dismissed, fighting the stigma of bad luck his entire life, only he was a boy so it would be even worse for him, because men needed to command to be respected, and who would follow a stone-eye?

With painful, revelatory honesty, she admitted to herself why, from the moment she'd seen Niko's baby picture in the letter among Lan's papers, she'd been so invested in bringing him back to Janloon, why she'd insisted that Hilo go in person to Stepenland to retrieve the boy so he could be raised with their own children. Perhaps she had suspected it all along; certainly the possibility had troubled her during her first pregnancy: Her son, Ru, could not be his father's heir.

Niko was the child she couldn't bear herself; he was the true first son of No Peak. It was an irony that he'd been born to a woman as ungrateful and faithless as Eyni, but the gods had a cruel sense of humor, that was something even Hilo and Shae agreed on. All that mortals could do was accept the lot they were given, and yet still fight to better their own fate and that of their loved ones. Alone in the hotel room far from home, Wen was overcome with such a baffling mixture of pride and shame that her vision finally did blur with tears.

She dried her eyes and began to think clearly again. She understood that her value in the clan, her value to her family, to Hilo, and most of all, in her own mind, lay not in what she could accomplish herself—because a stone-eye was always something of a blank space amid the strong auras around them, a void where gazes and expectations slid off like oil—but in what she made possible for others. She was unable to wield jade herself, but as a White Rat for the Weather Man, she had taken jade to those who could and would use it for the clan's gain. She had not borne the Pillar a son who could follow in the family's footsteps, but she had ensured that Niko was brought back to be raised in his rightful place. She could never be a Green Bone herself, as much as she felt she was one at heart, but she could think like a Green Bone. She was an enabler, an aide, a hidden weapon, and that was worth something. Perhaps a great deal.

Wen picked the phone back up and called the Weather Man's office.

———

Shae was silent for a long minute after Wen finished speaking. "I can't agree to that."

"You want Zapunyo dead as much as I do," Wen said. "You've spent months preparing for this opportunity and you know it's the best one we're going to get. If we don't take it, Zapunyo will disappear back into his fortress."

The arguments were not dissimilar to what Shae had said to Hilo over the phone less than an hour ago, but now Shae made excuses. "We don't have time to change the plan."

"Have you canceled the interview yet?" Wen asked. Shae had not. She had been delaying, trying to think of a way to handle the situation that would salvage the cover identity that had been so painstakingly crafted for Anden.

Wen said, "We still have five hours before the interview. I can be on a bus to Port Massy in less than thirty minutes. It takes three hours to get there. That leaves an hour and a half to spare." Wen paused. When she spoke again, her voice was calmly entreating. "Have I let you down before, Shae-jen? When I first told you I would be your White Rat, did you not believe I could do anything that you asked of me?"

Shae closed her eyes and leaned her head back, the phone cord pulled taut. "Wen," she said, "this is more dangerous than what you've done before. Even if it succeeds, there will be no way to hide it from Hilo. You would be risking your marriage, as well as your life."

Wen was silent for a minute. "I'm prepared for that."

"I'm not sure that I am," Shae admitted. "You have your children to think of."

"I'm thinking of them now. As long as this man breathes, as long as the family's enemies go unpunished, I'll fear for their lives." Wen asked, "Do you trust this man that Anden has told us about, this Rohn Toro?"

"Anden trusts him. And Hilo said that he was the greenest man he met in Port Massy."

"Then he truly is our best hope," Wen said. "Hilo made the decision to call off the plan without considering all the options. I'm giving you an option now, a good one. Zapunyo is the reason that Kehn and Maro are dead, and we're all still in danger from him. Let me do this, Shae-jen—let me do this for my children, and for the clan."

Shae felt as if she were staring at herself from somewhere else, unable to discern her own mind. Hilo was the Pillar, and he'd made his decision. It was her responsibility as Weather Man to follow his wishes. *The clan is my blood, and the Pillar is its master.* But Wen was correct: Hilo did not have all the information, and there wasn't time to go back to him now, to track him down at the hospital while he was caring for his son, and to explain everything she and Wen had done in the past, things he would never have agreed to but that had been of secret help to the clan at vital times, without which he might not even be Pillar, might not even have a clan at all.

Zapunyo and his barukan allies had maimed the Kaul family; they had killed Maik Kehn and nearly killed Wen and the children, including Niko, whom Shae had sworn on her knees to the gods she would protect. They'd done it by going after Maro, by threatening his family and manipulating him into treason. Because of them, Shae had been forced to execute her friend and lover, a good man, someone gentle at heart who'd truly been the better side of Kekon. The smuggler Zapunyo—like the Shotarian barukan, like the Espenian Crews—epitomized power without honor, jade without restraint, violence without principle.

You lead the clan as much as your brother. Maro had said that to her once, a long time ago, even before she'd believed it was true and nearly died to prove it. She clung to those words now, molded them into a spear of decisiveness as strong as the resolve she'd once needed to face Ayt Mada with a clean blade. She said to Wen, "I'll have Anden and Rohn meet you at the bus station when you get to Port Massy."

CHAPTER

59

From the Kaul Family

Just under five hours later, Wen sat in the back seat of a gray Brock Parade LS sedan outside the Crestwood Hotel in downtown Port Massy. The car was parked in a no-loading zone directly across from the hotel's main entrance, but the two police officers standing on nearby street corners did not bother them. They were well known to the Dauks as Southtrap beat cops who had reliably taken money for favors before and were sympathetic to the Kekonese, who rarely dealt drugs or committed violent crimes and took care of their own problems when they occurred. One of the cops was half-Kekonese himself. They were being handsomely paid to be the first ones to respond to any report of disturbance—and to look the other way while the gray sedan left the scene in a hurry. They were aware that Zapunyo was staying in the hotel, but what did they care if a foreign jade smuggler known for atrocious human rights violations happened to meet an unfortunate end?

Anden turned in the front passenger seat to look at Wen with concern. "It's not too late to change our minds," he insisted. "This is dangerous. Hilo wouldn't want you involved."

Wen checked her makeup in a hand mirror, tucking a stray strand of hair back into the knot it had escaped from. "We've planned this for too long to walk away now, Anden. The Weather Man agrees and is counting on us." She smiled at him reassuringly. "Besides, my part is simple."

From the driver's seat, Rohn Toro said, "Remember, just hit the ground and stay there. Don't get up until I say so." They hadn't had much time to rehearse, but it would have to do.

Anden said to Rohn, "Thank you for agreeing to do this."

"Thank me after it's done and we're safely away," Rohn said. "Preferably to somewhere warm and on another continent." He got out of the car and opened the trunk. Anden and Wen got out as well. Wen was still amazed by Anden's changed appearance: He sported a short beard that made him look five years older, bold black glasses frames, a suit cut in a trendy style with thin lapels, and a blue-and-white striped tie. He looked the part of a Port Massy urbanite, nothing at all like the earnest Kaul Du Academy student that she'd known him as back in Janloon. Anden fidgeted with his tie. She could tell from his frequent glances at her that he remained unsure about the decision to bring her in, but he was not about to ruin the plan now by disobeying. She only hoped he would quell any signs of unease once they were inside. From the trunk, Rohn Toro took out a professional SLR camera, which he slung around his neck by a leather strap, a camera bag, and a tripod. Wen straightened her skirt, picked up her leather folio, and carefully tucked her capped fountain pen into the breast pocket of her blazer.

Inside the lobby of the Crestwood, they waited in the cushioned seating area near the bar. One of Zapunyo's guards was supposed to meet them, but Uwiwans were never punctual. After thirty minutes, Wen began to worry. She saw Anden looking at the clock on the wall, anxious with what she suspected were similar thoughts: Zapunyo had backed out of the interview after all and they would be ignored or eventually sent away. She couldn't decide if her disappointment or her relief was greater. If the smuggler escaped back to the Uwiwa Islands, she would continue to spend every day fearing another attack on the family. On the other hand, she had done all she could. Her husband would never have to know how she'd gone against his wishes. Maybe they would eventually find another way to get to Zapunyo, just as Hilo had promised her.

A man came out of the elevators and walked toward them. Wen had never met a barukan in person before, but this man, dressed ostentatiously in a silk shirt and chunky nephrite rings set in gold, looked every bit the stereotype. Wen wondered, with wry contempt and curiosity, if perhaps it wasn't the barukan who took their cues from cinema as opposed to the other way around. As he approached, Anden stood up. Wen was relieved that he showed no outward sign of nervousness at all, speaking in confidently articulate, if accented Espenian as he shook the barukan man's hand, identifying himself as the journalist Ray Caido and introducing Rohn Toro and Wen under false names as his photographer and his assistant.

The man nodded and led the three of them to the bank of elevators. They ascended to the twelfth floor, where the premium suites were located. There was another barukan waiting in the elevator lobby, a younger man. They indicated by spreading their arms that the journalists would be searched before being allowed to proceed further. They patted Anden and Rohn down for weapons and examined Rohn's camera equipment. The younger barukan man looked uncomfortable as he stood in front of Wen. Shotarians were a prudish people. Wen held her arms out and the man ran his hands down her sides, back, and legs and stepped away. Wen noticed that the green stones hanging around his neck were nephrite but the studs in his ears were jade. He paused for a moment, Perceiving that none of them possessed jade auras before leading them down the hall to the door of the suite at the end. He knocked and they were admitted inside.

Zapunyo was seated in a wide fabric armchair in the center of the suite's sitting area. Wen was struck by how short he was; he looked almost childlike in the large chair and opulent hotel room. He wore a slightly creased tan linen suit with a folded white pocket square that suggested an attempt at formality. Wen could see the tops of his puffy veined feet bulging from brown loafers. Surprisingly, Wen's first emotion upon finally seeing him in person was pity, almost sympathy. Zapunyo might be a rich man with an ambitious and dangerous mind, but he was trapped in a frail body. It was not right that such a man should control jade or challenge Green Bones.

Zapunyo's eldest son stood near the window behind his father's chair along with another bodyguard, bringing the total number of men to five, three of them barukan.

Anden said in Espenian, "Mr. Zapunyo, thank you for agreeing to this interview. This is a rare opportunity and I feel privileged that you would trust me to share your side of the story. Would you prefer that we have our conversation in Espenian or Kekonese? I can speak either."

Zapunyo wetted his lips. "My Espenian is not so good. Let's speak in Kekonese."

"I promised to take no more than an hour of your time," Anden said, switching instantly to Kekonese and sitting down in the chair across from the smuggler. "While we're talking, my assistant will be sitting off to the side making notes for me, and the photographer will be taking some pictures. You can ignore them and pretend it's a conversation between just the two of us."

Wen smiled and nodded, pulling a chair to the side and sitting down in it. She opened her folio to an empty pad of paper and took the thick fountain pen out of her pocket. Near her, Rohn Toro began setting up the camera tripod. Zapunyo glanced at them before turning back.

"Where are your parents from, Mr. Caido?" the smuggler asked.

Anden said, "My mother was Kekonese. My father is Espenian."

"But you have a Kekonese family name," Zapunyo said.

"My parents didn't stay together; I was raised by my mother." Anden added, with a hint of forced amusement, "Are you planning to interview me, instead of the other way around, sir?"

"I'm curious about the background of any journalist who is so persistent in requesting a meeting with me," Zapunyo said. One of his bodyguards placed a glass of sparkling water with a straw on the side table next to him. He took it and sipped before speaking again. "Were you born in Kekon or in Espenia, Mr. Caido? Why did your parents come to this country?"

"I was born in Kekon," Anden said, "but I came to Espenia as a child." It was the first half-truth that Anden had told, and even though Wen doubted any of the barukan were skilled enough in Perception to detect such a minor deception, with each subsequent falsehood, the subtle tension in Anden's body would grow until it became suspicious. Wen uncapped her fountain pen and held it poised over the blank pad of paper. She glanced at Rohn Toro, crouched down on the other side of Zapunyo, snapping photographs.

"As for why my family came to Espenia," Anden went on, "I think they believed there was opportunity here. They thought I could make a better life for myself in Port Massy, because I was born looking Espenian, and because Kekon was a dangerous place at the time. What about you, Mr. Zapunyo?" he asked, pivoting the conversation. "How did you get to where you are now?"

"That is the question we're all asking ourselves every day, isn't it, Mr. Caido? How did we get to where we are now?" Zapunyo smoothed the top of his dark, coarse hair, looking thoughtful. "How is it that in my family, there were seven children but only four of us survived, and out of the four of us, I was the one who made it out of the ghetto, who made something of myself even though I was always the smallest and the physically weakest of all the boys?"

Each of the barukan and Zapunyo's son were armed with handguns and two of them carried *durbh* blades as well. Rohn Toro had circled back to where Wen sat. He attached the camera onto the tripod. Anden said, "What do *you* think is the reason, Mr. Zapunyo? Do you believe that perhaps it was your fate, being directed by a higher power such as the gods?"

Zapunyo held up a stumpy finger and his eyes glistened with satisfaction. "I do believe the gods have some say, that is true, but men set their own destinies. For example, who's to say what brings any two people together at a certain time and place for them to change each other's lives?"

The smuggler turned a shrewd look on Anden. "I have many enemies, and naturally, before I agreed to meet with you, I had to check your credentials. Mr. Caido indeed works for the *Kekon Journal* and has written many articles and conducted many interviews. But you are not Ray Caido, are you?" Zapunyo fished a small black-and-white photograph from the front pocket of his suit and held it up. It appeared to be a yearbook photograph. "You don't look like him. But you insist on meeting me, unarmed and on my terms, so you're not here to kill me."

Wen felt sweat break out on her back. She twisted the barrel of her pen and dropped it. It rolled off her lap and onto the floor. Rohn bent to retrieve it for her. Anden didn't look at them; he sat completely still and stone-faced, not speaking. Zapunyo, looking smug, said, "Who sent you to seek me out? The Mountain clan? Or is it the Kekonese here in Espenia who want jade?"

Wen's fountain pen broke easily. As Rohn pulled the thin string of tiny jade stones from inside the barrel, Anden leaned forward. "You're wrong, Zapunyo. I *am* here to kill you."

All of Zapunyo's guards drew their guns at the same time, ready to unload a dozen bullets into Anden's body. Two of them began to turn toward Rohn, detecting the sudden flare of a jade aura a split second before the Green Bone unleashed a Deflection that tore through the small confines of the hotel room. It knocked over the camera tripod, sent the water from the glass spraying, and slammed into the men who were standing, shoving them into the walls and furniture.

Gunshots rang out. Wen dropped flat to the ground, ears ringing, heart in her throat. She saw Anden throw himself onto Zapunyo, covering the smuggler's body with his own. As he dragged them both out of the chair and onto the floor, Anden maneuvered behind Zapunyo and wrapped his arms around the man's neck and thin shoulders, pinning him, then rolling over and ducking his own head so the smuggler lay struggling with his back on Anden's chest, trapped as an unwilling shield; the bodyguards couldn't shoot Anden without hitting their boss as well.

With her face against the carpet, Wen saw Zapunyo's son shout, "No, Pap!" His eyes widened with panic as he tried to decide where to aim his gun. With a burst of Strength, Rohn Toro flew at him and struck him in the throat, crushing his windpipe. As Zapunyo's son collapsed, Rohn twisted the gun from his grip and whipped it up, firing it—one, two, three times. One of the bodyguards went down; another brought up a desperate blast of Steel and Deflection that sent the final bullet into the hotel room window. The two remaining barukan returned fire; Rohn dove to the ground and fired twice, blowing out the kneecaps of the nearest man, who screamed as he fell, before Rohn's next two shots silenced him.

The final barukan guard raced for the door, firing again at the Green Bone in a panic. In such close quarters, Rohn barely Deflected the shots; one of them tore the fabric of his jacket at the shoulder; another bullet embedded itself in the carpet next to Wen. The barukan reached the door and yanked the handle. Rohn flew Light across the length of the room and tackled the man, shoving him back into the closed door with a crash. They fell to the floor and grappled, Strength against Strength, the sound of thuds and labored breathing reaching Wen even as the two men disappeared from view behind the sofa.

Wen clambered to her hands and knees. There was a gun lying not far from her reach, dropped by one of the barukan as he fell. She crawled to it, grasped and lifted it; it was heavy, much heavier than the compact pistols she'd practiced with before. She had to hold it firmly with both hands as she got to her feet.

Rohn and the last guard were still struggling. Rohn had his hands wrapped around his opponent's neck, squeezing and Channeling at the same time until blood began bubbling from the man's mouth as he spasmed and kicked, clawing at Rohn's Steeled hands. Anden was still on the ground, holding Zapunyo in a choke hold from behind. The Uwiwan flailed in a continuing effort to get free, but physically he was no match for Anden. Wen walked toward them. She could still hear the barukan's dying gurgles behind her, but she paid them no attention. Zapunyo's face was red, and his mouth worked in astonishment and fear, as if he could not believe that after so many years, and as sick as he was now, someone had gotten to him at last.

"Let go of him, Anden," Wen said.

Zapunyo fell choking to the ground. He crawled to his knees and held his hands up, the blood draining from his face at the sight of his dead son and his slain men. "I'm a rich man, a powerful man," he wheezed. "I can pay more than whatever you've been offered. Who sent you?"

"I sent myself," Wen told him, "from the Kaul family of No Peak." She pulled the trigger. The handgun bucked in her grip, jolting her wrists. Zapunyo fell back against the carpet, legs splayed out at an awkward angle, blood spreading under his head. Anden stared at the body, then at Wen. He got to his feet, shaking his head as if to clear it. Rohn Toro came over and looked down at the smuggler. Zapunyo seemed even smaller and more frail in death; it was hard to believe that he was responsible for so much evil in the world.

Rohn Toro glanced at Wen. "No wonder I've been told people fear the Maiks." He bent over, catching his breath. A layer of sweat stood out on his brow. "I'm getting old," Wen heard him mutter to himself. Taking a lens cloth from the camera bag, he wiped off the grips of the pistols he and Wen had handled and left them lying next to the bodies. The sleeve of his torn jacket was stained with blood; he took it off and threw it on the ground as well.

"Be quick, Rohn-jen," Anden said. "We need to get out of here." He crouched over the body of the nearest barukan guard, the younger one who had searched them out in the hallway. He tore the studs from the man's ears and held them out to Rohn.

"What are you doing?" Rohn asked.

"Collecting your jade so we can get out of here faster."

"Are you out of your mind?" Rohn said. "Don't take anything that might link you to the scene of a murder. If we take the jade off their bodies, it's a dead giveaway that Green Bones were responsible. Leave it. Take only the jade we came in with." He handed the thin string of jade stones back to Wen, who once again hid it away in the empty barrel of the false fountain pen and pocketed it. For a few seconds, Rohn's face contorted with the discomfort of jade withdrawal. He placed a hand on the back of the chair Zapunyo had been sitting in, steadying himself. Then he straightened and went to the door. Cracking it open, he looked down the hall and said, "Quickly, now."

Anden stared at the jade studs in his palm and gave a small start, as if suddenly realizing what he was holding. He dropped them hastily. Wen saw him cast a backward glance around the room as they hurried to join Rohn at the door. She wondered if the disbelief on Anden's face was because of what they'd done, or because it bothered him to be leaving jade behind on the bodies of their enemies, something no Green Bone in Janloon would ever do.

They shut the door behind them and walked quickly down the hall. Perhaps Zapunyo's guards had taken the precaution of renting out the neighboring rooms as well because no one opened their doors out of curiosity at the commotion. Wen picked up her pace to keep up in her wedge heeled shoes. She felt giddy from adrenaline, and even though she was still frightened and her pulse was racing, she had to fight the urge to smile. They might yet be caught and thrown into an Espenian prison, but she was certain Shae would find a way to get them out. The important thing was that they had done it. *She,* a stone-eye, had done it. For once, she had not relied on Hilo to mete out the clan's justice, but had delivered it herself. Not even all Green Bones could claim such a thing.

They rode the elevator back down to the second floor, then took the stairs down to the main level. There were people milling about in the lobby, bellmen coming and going, guests checking in or out, all of them oblivious to anything that had happened twelve stories above them. Wen suspected the sound of gunfire had been heard and reported, however; behind the check-in counter, two hotel staff were talking in an urgent manner to one of the policemen that had been on the street outside.

Rohn Toro slowed; he picked up a newspaper and tucked it under his arm as he ambled casually toward the main entrance. Wen looped her hand around the crook of Anden's elbow as if they were a couple heading out for dinner. The two of them followed Rohn at a distance. The policeman did not look at them or give any sign that he noticed them at all. They exited the hotel with no problem and got into the illegally parked sedan. Rohn started the car and pulled away from the curb. As they drove away from the Crestwood, he kept glancing in the rearview mirror, but no police lights or sirens followed them. Wen allowed herself a cautious sigh of relief, but still none of them spoke.

As they had planned, Rohn drove fifteen minutes away to Starr Lumber & Supply, the hardware store where Anden used to work. The store had closed an hour ago; the alleyway parking lot behind the strip mall was almost empty except for a black hatchback that Rohn and Anden had left there earlier in the day. Rohn parked the Brock nearby. From the rear of the hatchback, Rohn removed a duffel bag containing a change of clothes for each of them.

Anden had an employee key he'd long ago forgotten to return but that he now used to let them in through the back entrance and into the garage of Starr Lumber. He flicked on the lights; fluorescent tubes flickered to life over pallets of recently delivered lumber and boxes of merchandise. Anden let out a long breath, his shoulders finally coming down. Wen glanced at the clock on the wall. In a few hours, she and Anden would be on a red-eye flight home. "Are you coming to Janloon with us, Rohn-jen?" she asked.

Rohn shook his head. "I wouldn't like to be in an unfamiliar place like Janloon with so many other Green Bones around," he said. "I'm going to find myself a warm beach in Alusius instead. I have people I've trained here who are green enough, who I trust to keep things in order and help the Dauks while I'm gone."

Anden said, "I'll call Dauk-jen now and let him know we're ready to be picked up. The two of you get changed; the bathroom is right over there." Anden dropped the duffel bag on the ground and went into the manager's small office, where he picked up the phone and began to dial.

Wen unzipped the bag and pulled out casual clothes for traveling. Underneath were fresh shirts and pants for Rohn and Anden and in the bag's side pocket, a pair of black men's leather gloves. Rohn gestured for Wen to use the bathroom first; she gathered her items and was about to do so when the door of the garage flung open behind them and six men piled into the room.

A tall man with a felt hat and a gun stood at the front of the group. "You kecks," he said, "have been stepping on the wrong crewboys."

Wen screamed as he shot Rohn Toro in the legs.

CHAPTER

60

~

End of an Agreement

Shae had not slept the entire night. She'd unplugged the phone in her kitchen, brought it into her bedroom, and plugged it in next to her bed, then climbed under the covers and closed her eyes for a few hours, knowing that everything had been set in motion and there was nothing she could do now except wait for news. Anden was supposed to call as soon as the task was done and he and Wen were safely back with the Dauks and had access to a phone. If everything went according to plan, that would be early in the evening in Port Massy, which was just before sunrise in Janloon. Shae sat two bedside clocks next to each other on her windowsill, displaying the local times in both cities, and throughout the night the steady tick of their minute hands seemed as ominous as the countdown timer on a doomsday device.

The tepid glow of dawn began lightening the sky; across the court-yard, the lights in the main house came on. She saw Kyanla's figure moving in the kitchen, drawing open the blinds over the patio door. Shae's mother came out of the guesthouse and did her slow stretching exercises in the garden. The phone next to Shae's bed did not ring. Anden should've called by now. Something was wrong. Shae sat with her back against the headboard of her bed, knees drawn up, a feeling of dread gathering in her chest and spreading into her throat, her limbs and extremities.

"Get him off the phone," ordered Skinny Reams, twitching his gun toward where Anden stood in the office. Rohn Toro had collapsed to the ground in agony, but he lunged for the duffel bag and his jade-lined gloves. Reams strode forward and kicked the bag out of his reach. Wen pulled the fountain pen from her pocket, but before she could pass it to Rohn, one of the crewboys seized her from behind and lifted her, shouting and struggling, off her feet.

Anden dialed the last digit of Dauk's number and grabbed the base of the phone, pivoting behind the half-open office door, out of sight and out of the line of fire. He flattened his back to the wall; the rotary spun and clicked. The phone rang on the other end: once, twice. The receiver was shaking in his hands. *Hurry, hurry!* The call picked up, and then the phone was smashed out of Anden's hands and went flying. The cord was yanked from the wall. Anden recognized the reddened, freckled face right before Carson Sunter punched him in the stomach and then in the face. Anden had forgotten how hard Sunter could punch, but he remembered now. He tasted blood on his tongue as he fell to all fours behind the office desk. He searched wildly for something, anything, to use as a weapon and grabbed for a silver letter opener lying on the desk. The butt of a pistol came down on his fingers; Anden howled as he felt two of them break. The circle of the weapon's muzzle pressed against his cheekbone. "Didn't I tell you?" Sunter demanded. "Didn't I tell you I'd find you and kill you, you half-keck bastard? Did you think I'd forget?"

"That's all over, there was an agreement," Anden said, mumbling through the pain.

"You made an agreement with Boss Kromner, but Kromner is locked up, and we don't work for him anymore. It's Skinny's word now and Skinny figures you kecks have been behind all this trouble from the start." Sunter seized Anden around the back of the collar and, with the gun still pressed to his head, steered him back out into the garage of the hardware store.

Anden's heart was already slamming against his ribs, but now he felt his legs go weak. Rohn Toro lay on the concrete, blood from his gunshot wounds pooled around him. He'd been kicked and beaten; his eyes and lips were swollen. Skinny Reams and three of his men stood in a circle over him. "The demon who can kill five men with his bare hands in less time than it takes to have a piss," Willum Reams said, in a dry tone, almost disappointed. "Turns out you're made of flesh and blood after all."

Rohn coughed and winced. "How did you find me, Skinny? Who sold?"

"The cops at the hotel, of course," Reams answered. "Told us exactly which car to follow." Another of his men snorted and added, "You're amateurs, you kecks. The Crews have been as tight on the PMPD as a pimp on a virgin since before any of your race touched these shores."

"What do you want me to do with this one, Skinny?" Sunter asked.

"Put him over there next to the girl," Reams said. "Tie them both up."

Rohn's blackened eyes caught Anden's briefly with something near to apology but much closer to regret. Wen was kneeling on the ground by the wall, her face drained of color and expression; another one of Reams's men held a gun over her. As Anden was forced to his knees a couple of meters away, her eyes flicked to him, then to the open duffel bag that had been kicked aside on the floor. The fountain pen that had fallen from her grasp lay nearby.

"Put your hands behind your back or I'll shoot you in the knee-caps like your friend," Sunter said. Anden's mind ran seemingly in time to the throbbing of his broken fingers. Even as his wrists were tightly bound together, he tried to think of how he might create a distraction, get either the gloves or the pen with the hidden jade over to Rohn, possibly give them a chance of survival.

"Did his phone call get through?" Reams asked his coat. "Is anyone coming?"

"I didn't hear him talking to anyone, but I can't say for sure," said Sunter.

"Skinny." Rohn spoke from the floor, his voice strained with pain, but calmly, urgently reasonable. Perhaps he thought he could talk his way out of the situation, reach his jade somehow, or at the very least, delay what was coming. "We've known each other since way back. We grew up practically around the corner from each other in South-trap. We've been on different sides before, but the two of us, we've always worked things out between our bosses."

"That is true," said Reams. "We were good foremen, weren't we?"

"We can still work things out," Rohn said. His face had gone chalky, and his pants were soaked with blood. "Kromner was greedy, he got rich and fat, but you're practical, Skinny, you always have been. You're Boss of your own Crew now. Why make enemies instead of friends?"

Skinny Reams took off his felt hat and turned it around and around in his hands. "You make a good point, Rohn, but I'll tell you why," he said, as solemnly as a schoolteacher at a lectern. "Because I don't like you kecks at all. Everything was going fine before Boss Kromner got it into his head to get involved with you people over jade. I don't care how much they're worth, those rocks aren't natural. They don't belong here, and neither do you. Since I'm the new Boss in these parts, I have to make it clear that I differ from Kromner on this point. So it's got to be this way."

Reams's biggest, strongest-looking man produced a white plastic bag and double loop of cord. Rohn knew what came next; he surged upward, away from his executioner, toward the duffel bag with his jade gloves. Blood loss, the bullets in his legs, and the two other men who grabbed his arms ensured that he did not get far; the bag went over Rohn's head and the cord around his neck.

Anden lunged forward with a shout of sheer desperation but could do nothing with his arms tied behind his back; Sunter eagerly kicked him to the ground and put a boot in the small of his back. His glasses were knocked off his face and went skittering across the floor. The other guard took a cloth rag from the hook on the wall near the garage cleaning supplies and jammed it into Anden's mouth, muffling his cries. He gagged on the taste of grease and cleaning fluid, felt the corners of his mouth burning as the fabric was pulled tight.

Rohn Toro fought like an ox. His body heaved and crashed against the concrete. He twisted and tried to slacken the pressure on his windpipe, but injured and without jade, in seconds his movements began to weaken. Reams's coat continued tightening the garrote with the impassive deliberation of a piano tuner. From where he was pinned with his face against the cold concrete, Anden watched the most formidable Green Bone in Port Massy, the man who'd defended the grudge hall from machine gun fire and single-handedly taken out a room full of barukan, grow feeble, his legs beating against the floor, the plastic clinging to his face cutting off what little air remained to him. A stench rose from his body as his bowels gave out in the last few seconds of his life. The executioner stepped away; the plastic did not flutter against Rohn's open mouth.

Reams touched the tip of his forefinger to the center of his brow and raised it in the sign of the One Truth. "God uplift his soul," he muttered. His men followed suit obediently.

The garroter stepped away from Rohn's body and toward Wen and Anden. "Do we have to kill the peach, Boss?" Sunter asked, looking at Wen. "She's pretty; couldn't we just—"

Reams gave his coat a sternly disappointed look and Sunter stopped talking. Anden's vision was blurred and he thought his heart might pound itself to death before the crewboys killed him. When Wen turned her head to catch his eyes, he tried to speak but the gag was still in his mouth and he could only look at her in mute panic. He thought she made an attempt to smile at him, as if in solidarity, telling him to be brave, that at least they were facing this together.

Wen turned to Reams and tilted her chin to stare up into his face.

"Do you know who I am?" she asked in accented Espenian. Her hands were clasped together tightly and it was clear she was frightened, but her voice was shockingly calm. "Do you know the name Kaul? Or the name Maik?"

Reams looked down at her with dispassion. "Sorry, peach. Who you are doesn't matter to me. If you're important among your own people, then so much the better for my purposes."

Wen spat at Reams's feet. She straightened and spoke in Kekonese. "The clan is my blood, and the Pillar is its master." The man with the garrote stepped behind Wen and slipped the plastic bag over her head. He looped the cord around her neck and began to tighten it. Wen did not struggle. She had seen Rohn Toro—a man, much larger and stronger than her—beaten into submission and murdered before her eyes and saw no point in repeating the indignity. Wen's face remained turned slightly upward, and she kept reciting the single line, over and over again, until she had no access to air and only her mouth was moving. *The clan is my blood, and the Pillar . . .*

Wen's legs kicked, stiffened, went limp.

Anden was screaming endlessly around the gag in his mouth; his mind was filled with nothing but the sound of his own screaming and when the bag went over his head and the cord around his neck, he couldn't muster any of the composure Wen had displayed. He was sobbing with impotent, burning, grief-stricken rage, cursing their killers with every ounce of vitriol in his being. He couldn't believe he was going to die in such a low way at the hands of such scum, helpless, *here* of all places—on the floor of a garage in fucking *Espenia*. His vision went red, then white.

Shae took out her address book, picked up the phone, and told the operator that she needed to place a long-distance call to Port Massy. The number that Anden had given her for his apartment rang without response. She had been advised not to use the number for the Dauks' residence, as it was possible that the Espenian authorities might still be monitoring it, but she called it anyway; there was no answer there either. Her final attempt was the Weather Man's branch office, just in case for some reason Anden had gone there, but as expected, it was closed for the evening. Shae depressed the receiver cradle, then released it and called her own office to tell her secretary that she would not be coming into work this morning and to cancel her appointments.

She thought about the small prayer room in the main house, but she didn't dare to leave earshot of her phone. She placed three sticks of incense in a cup, set it by her window, and knelt. Thin tendrils of fragrant sandalwood smoke rose and mingled against the glass. Shae touched her forehead to the ground three times and whispered, "Yatto, Father of All. Jenshu, Old Uncle. Gods in Heaven, please hear me. My cousin, Emery Anden, was adopted into our family and raised as my youngest brother. He could've been a powerful Green Bone but he refuses to wear jade because he didn't want a life of killing and madness. My sister-in-law, Kaul Maik Wen, is a stone-eye but she's never let that stop her; she's risked her life and her marriage for the clan, and she's the mother of three small children who need her. Anden and Wen are green in the soul, and now they're in danger in Espenia because I put them both there. Please protect them and bring them home safely."

The silence that followed her words was so absolute that her growing panic spiked into anger. "Why are you always so *cruel*?" she demanded in a harsh whisper. "Every week, I come to you on my knees. If you even exist, then *help us*. We're not a family that can claim to adhere to the Divine Virtues all the time, but who can? Who in our position could stand a chance? Please, I'm begging you, don't punish Wen and Anden for anything my brother or I have done in the past." Shae felt her hands trembling against her thighs. "On my honor, my life, and my jade—I'm begging you."

Anden didn't hear the noises at first. When he did, he didn't identify them as the crunch of tires and the slamming of car doors. The one thing he heard was Carson Sunter exclaim, "*Shit*, they're here." He heard that part clearly—and then Reams's sharp order: "Out the front."

The circle of pressure around Anden's neck abruptly slackened and he was dropped to the ground on his stomach, the pain in his throat and chest so bad it felt like fire inside his lungs.

A great deal more noise erupted—gunshots and shouting, running feet, more gunshots reverberating in the enclosed space—he had no idea where they were coming from or how many there were, and then crashing sounds farther away in the front of the store. He couldn't see anything except shadow and movement through the film of white plastic over his face, which was still suffocating him. He was fading out, his consciousness sliding away like hot oil.

Hands seized him and rolled him over roughly; the plastic was torn off his face. Air flooded into Anden's nose and mouth and he gasped violently, blinking and heaving for breath. Shun Todorho knelt over him, his face ashen and horrified. He had a gun in his hand, but he set it down and worked at removing Anden's gag. Anden coughed and spat, the corners of his mouth raw and stinging. Someone else—Sammy—cut the bindings around Anden's wrists, and they sat him up, steadying him. Three other Green Bones that Anden recognized from the grudge hall were crowded into the garage. "The phone call was cut off—we thought we were too late," Tod said.

"We were," Sammy said, turning to where Dauk Losun knelt beside Rohn Toro's body. The Pillar of Southtrap rocked back on his heels, tears running freely down his rough face.

Anden shot to his feet, swayed, and stumbled to where Wen lay motionless on the concrete. He tore the bag off her face and pressed his ear to her chest, praying he would hear a heartbeat. He had learned basic first aid at some point in his life, and he struggled to remember what to do if a person was not breathing. He tilted Wen's head back and opened her mouth, sealing it with his own, and breathed out in two hard puffs. He began doing chest compressions. How much time had passed? It couldn't have been more than a few minutes... perhaps... He breathed into her mouth again. "Please," he begged all the gods, "please."

Wen remained limp.

Sammy crouched down beside Anden and put a hand on his

shoulder. "She's gone, crumb," he said. Anden stopped in midmotion. In desperate epiphany, he whirled, his eyes wild, and scrambled to the duffel bag still lying open on the floor, out of reach the whole time that Rohn Toro had needed it most. Anden grabbed Rohn's black gloves and hurried back to Wen; before anyone could even ask him what he was doing, he shoved his hands into the jade-studded lining.

Sharp, physical pain radiated from his broken fingers all the way up his arm and he whimpered, clutching his wrist, curling his body around his injury and bracing impatiently for the more profound pain to come. It had been so long since he had worn jade that he expected the rush to arrive like a sledgehammer, and he readied himself. In his mind, he coiled, the way a man might crouch, arms extended, balanced on the balls of his feet, optimistically hoping to catch a boulder hurled in his direction. Anden breathed in, then out, and for the second time in his life, sensation and awareness engulfed him in a maelstrom of energy. It was not as much jade as he'd once handled in the final battle against Gont Asch, but it was still enough to make his skull feel as if it were being blasted apart. He threw his head back, mouth open and gasping, but he did not cringe from the onslaught; through it all he was aware of the passage of time. Every second he took to adjust to the jade rush, every instant of delay, was one he could not afford.

He had only one chance, and it was *now*.

With a wrenching force of will, he grasped the jade energy with skills that were ill-used but not forgotten. He bent the flow of energy to his will; he pulled it into a single focus. His eyes were closed, but he could sense the presence of the people around him, breathing, pulsing, living creatures, and he ignored them all. He concentrated only on the form beneath him, the body that had been alive only a few minutes ago—and he saw it for what it was—an organism that had once throbbed with energy but in which the current was now stilled and rapidly draining.

Anden pressed his clenched fists down over Wen's chest and Channeled. The energy surged into Wen's heart and lungs. Anden hung on to it the way one might with shaking arms control the shaft of a thrust spear. With his jade abilities straining to their utmost, he *squeezed*.

Wen's heart convulsed in his grasp. It gave a juddering spasm and beat once, twice, and then continued to beat, forcing blood through vessels and organs, back into her brain. Anden's entire body trembled with unbearable effort; sweat bathed his face as he continued to press. Wen's lungs contracted. She gave a great, heaving gasp, her back arching on the floor. Her eyes flew open.

Anden released his hold on her, turned away, and vomited. His hands were shaking too badly for him to remove the gloves; he tugged them off with his teeth and let them fall to the ground. Wen stared up at him in abject confusion and pain, and then tears sprang into her eyes.

Jade energy crashed out of Anden like a weight dragging him through his own body toward the center of the earth. He was utterly drained, exhausted and empty, as if he'd run for days or crawled through a desert. He pulled Wen into his lap and began to sob, and she clutched him and they rocked together on the floor of the garage, only dimly aware of Dauk Losun and the other Green Bones of Southtrap standing around them, staring and silent with astonishment.

CHAPTER

61

~

Lines Crossed

Shae scrambled across the floor of her bedroom and grabbed up the receiver as soon as the phone rang. Anden's voice, dampened by the long-distance connection, sent her sagging against the bed in relief at first, but he sounded so strange that her alarm surged again. "Shae-jen," he said, "sorry I didn't call you on time. It's done, it worked as we planned, but we were ambushed afterward, and...the Crews..." Anden's voice caught audibly in his throat. "Rohn Toro is dead."

"Are you and Wen all right?" Shae demanded.

A pause. Her cousin was breathing hard. "I'm not sure yet," he said, almost too quietly for her to hear, even with the phone pressed hard against her ear. "If I give you a number, can you call me back? I'm on the pay phone at the hospital and running out of coins; I think this call is going to cut out soon."

After Shae returned Anden's call, he told her what had happened, with enough faltering throughout that she could tell he was still in shock and having difficulty grappling with his emotions. "How will we tell Hilo?" he cried. Shae told him not to worry about that, she would handle it, and to call her again in two hours so she would know he'd made it safely home.

Shae was reeling when she hung up. She took several minutes to compose herself, then placed yet another long-distance call to the personal residence of Hami Tumashon, catching him before he went to bed and instructing him to go to the hospital at once and spare no effort on the part of the Weather Man's branch office to make all the urgent and necessary arrangements.

Shae dressed and walked across the courtyard to the main house. In the kitchen, Kyanla was sitting at the kitchen table, coaxing Jaya to eat from a bowl of porridge. The toddler banged her fists on the high chair and flung a spoon onto the ground. "Where's Hilo?" Shae asked.

The housekeeper's brows rose in worry at the tone of Shae's voice. "The Pillar is in the training hall, I think. Is everything all right, Shae-se? Are you not going into the office today?"

Outside the training hall, Shae paused and leaned her forehead against the door. Her dread was worse than it had been in the cabin with Doru, worse than standing across from Ayt Madashi, knowing she might die. She could Perceive her brother's aura and her nephew's small presence and she hesitated, reluctant to take the next step, to ruin the moment, to destroy everything.

She slid open the door. Hilo and Niko were sitting on the floor playing Blind Miner, a game that Shae recognized immediately, one that every Green Bone family played with their children. A piece of cloth was spread on the floor; it covered a dozen small rocks, only one of which was a piece of jade. Niko was feeling the cloth and the hard objects underneath. He tapped one of them and Hilo whisked the cloth away and grinned. "Another point for you." It was a silly, simple game to pass the time, but it was also a way to expose children to jade and begin to attune them to its physical effects. *Which one makes you feel good when you touch it—a little warm, a little tingly?*

Niko looked up and said, "Do you want to play, Auntie Shae?"

"No, Niko-se, not right now," Shae said. "I need to talk to your uncle."

Hilo scooped up the rocks and the single piece of jade, depositing them into a cloth bag with a drawstring and putting them into a drawer. "Go play outside," he told Niko. "I'll let you and your brother watch television later." The boy ran off and Hilo turned to his Weather Man.

"How's Ru?" Shae asked.

"He's still sleeping. We didn't get home until past midnight last night." Shae already knew this because she'd still been wide awake at that time and had seen the lights of the Duchesse come up the driveway. "He's groggy from being put under and his throat's sore, but he'll be fine." Hilo looked as if he would say more, but instead his eyes narrowed and his chin tilted to the side; Shae knew there was no way he could fail to Perceive the roiling agitation of her aura.

"What is it, Shae?" he asked.

"Zapunyo's dead," Shae said. "After I spoke with you yesterday, Wen phoned me from Adamont Capita. We decided to go ahead with the plan, because we might not get another chance. Wen carried the jade into the room. She, Anden, and Rohn Toro—they killed Zapunyo and his guards—but they were ambushed afterward. Anden and Wen are alive, but they're in the hospital."

Afterward, Shae couldn't recall how much and what else she told him, she couldn't even remember if she explained it all calmly, or if she stammered and struggled. What she remembered later was the contrast: the way Hilo's face grew wooden, as if each muscle was locking into place, while his aura built in heat and intensity, began to roil and heave, bubble, smoke, and burn, as if it were subsuming her brother's physical energy, turning him into a statue even as he swelled in her Perception to a bonfire.

She remembered, strangely, that for years she used to take a secret cruel pleasure in angering Hilo. As children and even as teens and into their adulthood, she'd always been able to provoke him and inwardly smirk at the spectacle he could make of himself. She was ashamed of herself now, for all the times she had done that.

She kept speaking, as if facts could dull reality. "Anden's hurt and in shock, but he'll recover. They're not sure about Wen yet. It depends on how long her brain was without oxygen. The Espenian doctors are running tests, and once she's back in Janloon—"

Hilo crossed the space between them in a heartbeat and struck her across the face. Shae reacted with instinctive Steel, but even so, the Strength of the blow crumpled her to her knees. She put a hand to her cheek, blinking at the pain. Her head felt as if it were vibrating on her spine like a beaten gong. She Perceived rather than saw Hilo about to hit her again, his eyes alight with insensible fury, and she threw a reflexive Deflection that sent him staggering backward.

Shae got to her feet. She didn't think she could talk; her face was throbbing and felt frozen. She tried anyway; "Hilo—" but her brother launched himself at her with an inarticulate noise. His enraged blows fell on her Steeled arms and shuddered through her frame; their jade auras crashed against each other, shrill and explosive, rippling and grappling like tangled, sparking wires.

"How could you?" Hilo might have whispered the words; he might have screamed them—Shae was not sure. She could only feel the force with which they landed, harder than his fists. *"How could you?"*

Shae staggered from his maddened blows. In desperation, she planted a thrust kick in her brother's stomach, following it up with another Deflection that flung Hilo into the training room's cabinets. The force of the impact snapped hinges and buckled the wood. Hilo shook his head, dazed, but was on his feet again in a second, and Shae was suddenly afraid—not of Hilo, but of what might have to happen: One of them would have to beat the other unconscious for this to end—but then the door of the room slid open partway with a rasp. Ru and Niko stood peering inside, their eyes wide, mouths open in confusion and astonishment. "Da?" Ru ventured.

Hilo spun toward his sons, his face contorted. *"Get out!"*

The boys were so stunned at their father's sudden and inexplicable wrath that they froze like rabbits. Ru's mouth trembled, then he turned and ran toward the main house, crying. Niko ran in the other direction, into the room and to Shae, grabbing her tightly around the waist and burying his face against her stomach as if to hide. She put her arms around him without thinking.

Something in Hilo's expression shifted and collapsed like a crumbling tower; he sagged and slid to the ground, his back against the broken cabinets. He put his face in his hands.

"Go back to the house with your brother," Shae whispered to Niko, her voice strained but as reassuring as she could make it. She rubbed his back. "Your uncle and I are training and can't be interrupted right now. He's not angry at you, I promise. We'll be out soon." Gently, she loosened the boy's arms. Niko glanced uncertainly at Hilo, wanting to go to him, but his uncle, who was usually so quick to smile and roughhouse with him, neither looked up nor made any move to rise from his spot on the floor. Reluctantly, the boy shuffled out of the room. Shae closed the door quietly behind him and turned slowly back around.

Hilo lifted his face from his hands and stared up at her, and she was startled to see tears in his eyes. "You once asked me if I trusted you, do you remember?"

"You said that you didn't have a choice," Shae said.

"I didn't," Hilo agreed. "Even though I knew all along that you never wanted to be in the clan, never wanted to be a Kaul, never really wanted me as a brother either." His voice deadened, turned cold and remote. She'd seen it happen before: the explosion of fury and hurt, then the rejection, the pulling away. "Get out," he said. "You're not my Weather Man, not anymore. You're free, Shae, like you always wanted."

Shae put a hand on the door of the training room. For a second, she imagined obeying her brother—sliding the door open and stepping out, returning to her house and packing a few items, walking down the long driveway and through the iron gates of the estate her grandfather had built, not looking back. She had done such a thing once before, years ago. She'd been a different person back then. A young woman who'd not yet lived abroad, suffered heartbreak and terrible loss, or wielded power over clan and country. She had not yet fought and nearly died in a duel of clean blades, taken lives out of vengeance and one out of mercy, or rocked her niece and nephews to sleep in her arms. She could not have imagined such things, not back then.

She took several steps toward her brother. "I'm not leaving, Hilo." She spoke unsteadily, but with no uncertainty. "I've given as much for No Peak as you have. I've worked and sacrificed and bled and killed. After everything we've been through, how can you believe that I don't care every bit as much as you do? I'm guilty of having gone against you, but never against the clan."

"Now you sound like Doru." Hilo's mouth moved in a half-hearted sneer when he saw how his words cut her. He leaned his head back against the cabinets with a light thud. He appeared bitterly defeated all of a sudden, in a way that she had never seen him, not even in their most dire moments when it seemed their enemies would destroy them. "Maybe I don't believe in the gods like you do, but I do know that some things are the way they are for a reason. We're Kauls. We were born for this life, whether we like it or not. The clan can claim everything I have—my time, my blood and sweat, my life and jade—but it can't have my wife. She's a stone-eye. *She's the one thing in the world that jade can't touch.* You knew that was a line I would never cross."

Shae glanced the way Niko had gone. "We've both crossed lines we never meant to. We've made decisions that we'll have to live with the rest of our lives. We have that much in common." She touched her face gingerly; her jaw still felt numb and it hurt to talk. She went to where Hilo sat and looked down at him. "I never encouraged Wen, never forced her to do anything. She came to me years ago, Hilo. All you wanted was for her to stay out of clan affairs, and all she wanted was in. She knew you'd never approve, but she's too green at heart and was willing to risk even your love. Without her, we wouldn't have established jade sales to the Espenians when we most needed it during the war with the Mountain, we wouldn't have gained valuable information from the spies she managed, or transported jade to the Green Bones in Espenia and created our alliances there. We wouldn't have been able to get to Zapunyo and kill him."

Shae lowered herself to the ground next to her brother and rested her bruised back against the splintered cabinet. "Hate me from now on if you have to, but you need me to stay, Hilo. And you need Wen and Anden. You said it yourself years ago: We have each other, and maybe that's the one thing we have that our enemies don't." Hilo's aura gave a dark pulse, like an angry sigh, but he didn't move or open his eyes. Shae slumped back and closed her own eyes. "The clan is my blood and the Pillar is its master," she whispered. "I have a lot of regrets in life, but those oaths aren't one of them."

CHAPTER

62

~

Still at War

Shae had been sitting in the sanctum of the Temple of Divine Return for some time when she Perceived the unexpected presence of Ayt Madashi's dense, molten jade aura pierce the fog of her thoughts, intensifying like a heat source against her closed eyes as it approached. Ayt knelt on the green cushion next to her. "I'm told that you visit the temple every week at the same time," she said, conversationally. "Unwise from a security standpoint."

A sense of oddly poignant déjà vu kept Shae motionless for a moment. She imagined reaching back in time with her mind and looking down at herself nearly five years ago, meeting Ayt Mada in this same place, unsure of whether she or her clan would survive the encounter. She felt no fear this time, though the puckered scar across her abdomen prickled. She opened her eyes, and for a second, her gaze slid involuntarily to Ayt's bare arms. The coils of silver encircling them were more densely set with jade stones—jade that had once been part of Shae's two-tier choker.

She raised her eyes calmly to Ayt's face. "You've had your chances to kill me."

"True," Ayt agreed. "We'll both know when the real time comes." The Pillar of the Mountain was as formidable a presence as ever, but a few fine lines were visible around her eyes as she turned them on the younger woman. Over the past years, with all her public speeches and television appearances, she had taken to wearing some makeup. Shae was all of a sudden self-conscious of her own appearance; her face was still visibly bruised from where Hilo had struck her.

She brought her gaze back to the front, to the mural of Banishment and Return and the circle of meditating penitents. "You don't bow in the sanctum," she observed. "Do you ever come here to ask forgiveness from the gods? Do you even believe in the gods, Ayt-jen?"

"I believe in them," Ayt said, "but I don't need to explain myself to them. When I was eight years old, they destroyed my town and killed my family and everyone I cared for. In the orphanage, I was told that it wasn't the gods that caused the landslide; it was the Shotarians and their bombs. Which goes to show that the gods don't determine fate. People do. Powerful people." Ayt gazed impassively at the penitents, who were, it was believed, carrying all their words to the ears of the gods in Heaven. "I've never killed or ordered someone to be killed out of anger or a desire for personal vengeance. When I've taken lives, it's been out of necessity, for the ultimate good of the clan and the country. Can you say the same for yourself and your family, Kaul Shae-jen?"

Shae wondered if perhaps Ayt resented her in some way—if, beyond her simple ambition to see the Mountain prevail over No Peak, she harbored an ongoing desire to punish Shae specifically. The last time they'd met in this temple, Shae had spurned Ayt's fratricidal offer that they rule together under one clan, and chosen instead that they should struggle against each other at every turn. She'd offered Ayt a clean blade, and by all rights, she should be dead, yet here she sat.

"I congratulate you on assassinating Zapunyo," Ayt said, not expecting or waiting for Shae to answer the rhetorical question. "Perhaps you acted out of retribution, but you acted correctly for us all. Zapunyo was a blight on the world—an untrained foreigner, an *Uwiwan*—selling our jade to other foreign criminals. As Kekonese, as Green Bones, we can agree that he had to die. Zapunyo's sons are dead as well. Iyilo and the rest of the barukan saw to it that same night."

The casualness with which she said this shifted something in Shae's mind. Suspicions revolved and fell neatly into place. "You were collaborating with them the whole time."

Ayt said, "Your brother wanted to destroy the enterprise that Zapunyo had built. I wanted to *take* it. You and I came to the same conclusion, Kaul-jen: If we hope to extend our influence beyond the borders of our island nation, we need allies abroad. Allies with jade. Iyilo leads the barukan in the Uwiwas and has influential friends back in Shotar. They now control Zapunyo's estate and all his considerable assets."

"Which means that *you* control them," Shae amended. "What did you pay to the half bones in order to secure their allegiance?" She made a noise of understanding before Ayt could answer. "Of course. The passing of the Oortokon Conflict Refugee Act. You whispered Chancellor Son's name to ensure that the vote in the Royal Council would go your way."

"We think of them as petty gangsters, but the barukan are human beings as much as any of us. They want to get their families out of war-torn Oortoko." Ayt brushed a stray bit of lint from her smooth black slacks. "The Royal Council has voted to allow seven thousand Shotarians of Kekonese ancestry to immigrate to our country. Opponents of the Refugee Act have argued that it would be a security concern and a costly burden on the government. Fortunately, Green Bones will come to the aid of the country, as we have in the past."

Ayt's smile was cold and satisfied, the expression of a snake that has successfully swallowed a great meal. "Lawyers in my Weather Man's office have already been clearing the way in anticipation of this important legislation. The Mountain clan will be reviewing applications and sponsoring refugees, helping them to find new homes, gainful employment, and a place in our society. We'll teach them to leave behind their foreign customs, to learn our ways and integrate into Kekonese society—including accepting the authority of the clan."

Shae nodded. Up to seven thousand additional sworn members of the Mountain clan, selected and brought in by Ayt and her people. New barukan Fingers who already wore jade, who romanticized the Green Bone way of life, who had strong connections to the black market jade trade and other criminal enterprises throughout Shotar, the Uwiwa Islands, Ygutan, and the rest of the region. The Mountain had been busy. While No Peak had been growing its international businesses, strengthening relationships with the Espenian government and the Green Bone community in Port Massy, Ayt had been building a base of power closer to home.

"You've always had visionary strategies, Ayt-jen," Shae said, not attempting to hide the grudging admiration in her voice, "but do you really believe you can control the barukan you're bringing in? They might wear jade, but they're not Green Bones; they weren't trained at Wie Lon or the Academy, nor raised with aisho. The local criminals you supported years ago, the ones you used as informers in No Peak territory and then cast off—they turned into a social rot in Janloon, one that the barukan themselves took advantage of in order to steal jade from our shores."

Perhaps she and Ayt Mada had something else in common, Shae thought—the arrogance to rationalize their own worst ideas, to commit to a course of action out of pride without truly understanding the possibility of disaster. "You claim to be a patriot, a protector of Kekon and our way of life. But you're willing to bargain it all for your own gain. You're willing to ally with anyone who gets you closer to your ultimate goal. Even if you achieve it, even if the Mountain comes to rule all of Kekon, it won't be the Kekon we recognize. If you have your way, being a Green Bone will mean nothing."

Ayt appeared to consider Shae's words. "It will mean something different, something even more powerful than before. Change is inevitable, Kaul-jen; the only question is whether we control its direction or become victims of a landslide. There will always be people who resist, who try to drag us backward. People like Ven Sandolan, who believed that family pedigree and wealth meant he was untouchable." Ayt's dense jade aura emanated the deep heat of old coals. "Now that Ven and his heirs are dead, K-Star Freight has been acquired by an Ygutanian transportation conglomerate that has made assurances that K-Star will continue to be run independently in Kekon. We're all biased against foreigners, but the world is opening up more each day, and I'll take foreign allies over Green Bones who insist on standing in the way."

Shae said, "Did you seek me out here in the temple just to gloat, Ayt-jen?"

For the first time in their conversation, Ayt showed irritation. "I want to make it clear that even after all these years, No Peak remains in the weaker position. You've expanded your own businesses and cultivated your own allies, but the Mountain once again possesses more people and greater resources. Both of our clans have interests spread well beyond our borders; we have international networks and stakeholders. We're past the point we were at five years ago, when one of us might have won the war in the streets and conquered the other through superior exercise of violence."

Shae said nothing, knowing that what Ayt said was true. The Pillar said, "Surely you've seen the news that an armistice has been declared in Oortoko. The western half will be governed by Shotar and an independent eastern state will fall under the 'protection' of Ygutan. Nearly four years of conflict and gods know how much money and lives spent by both sides, and the result is exactly what anyone could've foreseen when two powers of equal determination clash." Ayt shifted on her cushion to face Shae more directly. Shae saw up close, for the first time, the woman's left ear, the top third of it cleanly sliced away. A permanent disfigurement that was ambiguously a mark of atonement or a badge of combat. Either way, Ayt wore it without shame, making no effort to hide it.

"We sat in front of the cameras in the General Star Hotel knowing the peace we were declaring between our clans was a temporary measure based on necessity," Ayt said. "Now the foreign proxy war is over but the necessity is no less. The military tension between Espenia and Ygutan continues unabated. The Oortokon War might've been an unfortunate thing for the world, but it has benefited the Kekonese economy and our importance in the world. The foreigners still want our jade—but now also our goods, our money, and our influence.

"So let this moment be one of true agreement between us, Kaul Shae-jen. Our own private armistice. We both tried to win the war covertly by manipulating agents. They failed, which only goes to show that outsiders are not reliable when it comes to Green Bone matters. I've whispered Kaul Hilo's name enough for it to have become a predictable habit, and I tire of the game. In Oortoko, the global powers came to the realization that they had to check their feud or risk dragging the entire world into another Many Nations War. Your brother may not be able to think in such broad terms, but you can. Prevail upon his better judgment, as limited as that might be. There are small children in your family now, and I imagine you don't want them to lose any more fathers or uncles." Ayt's voice took a softly menacing turn. "If you move against me again, or simply fail to keep Kaul Hilo's vengeful nature in check, then remember that Ven Sando was the patriarch of an old and powerful Green Bone line, one that should've thrived for generations to come, but because of his treachery, he lost everything: his business accomplishments, the lives of his loved ones, the very existence and legacy of his family name and bloodline. It could happen to anyone."

Yes, Shae thought. *Even you.* Ayt had not come by her victory unscathed. She'd been beleaguered by fractiousness within her clan—fractiousness abetted by No Peak at every turn. She'd sold the Mountain's largest company to foreign interests, made allies of the criminal barukan, broken aisho by murdering Chancellor Son, and stained her hands with the blood of her own Green Bones yet again. She'd been forced to recognize the claim of an unproven twelve-year-old boy and elevate the undistinguished Koben family into a position of power she had never intended to share. Shae suspected that for all of Ayt's smugness over her renewed position of strength over No Peak, she had not wanted to do any of these things.

Shae felt, in that moment, a curious empathy for her mortal enemy. What Ayt had said to her was correct: No one was untouchable. She felt the other woman's aura pressing against her like an expanding solid surface. She remembered the critical moment in their duel when their energies had grappled, neither able to overcome the other, and the sense of elation she'd felt when she'd succeeded, for an instant, to bring her rival to a standstill. She'd done so again. Ayt would not be threatening her if she did not on some level, even with all her considerable victories, fear the fact that the Kaul family was still alive. *Damaged*, yes—but alive, and growing, with its own allies, resources, and implacable vengefulness. As surely as the division between East and West Oortoko would fester like an infected scar, the history of violence between No Peak and the Mountain meant that in the end, one of them was bound to prevail, perhaps by the finality of the blade, perhaps by other means.

Shae bent at the waist and touched her forehead to the ground in front of the cushion. "Yatto, Father of All," she said, "I beg you recognize all the Green Bones who came before us, especially my grandfather Kaul Seningtun and his comrade Ayt Yugontin, and all the jade warriors who've fought for Kekon while striving to be true to aisho and the Divine Virtues."

Shae straightened and said to her enemy, "Everything you say is true. We have more at stake now, and it's in everyone's best interests for our clans to keep the peace. But we will never be *at* peace. You'll pursue your ruthless agenda—and my clan will pursue ours. Make no mistake: We're still at war, in a different way." She stood up, feeling the stiffness in her back unclench. "I have to pick up my nephews from swim class. If you'll excuse me, Ayt-jen, my family needs me."

CHAPTER

63

Home at Last

When Anden landed in Janloon International Airport, a car and driver were waiting for him. Crossing the Way Away Bridge into morning traffic, Anden stared at the skyline of the city he'd left three and a half years ago. The view was deeply familiar yet different; there were buildings that had been there as long as he could remember and new ones that he did not recognize. Construction cranes balanced like orange storks along the waterfront, stretching their arms toward Summer Harbor. Anden rolled down the window and breathed in the heat and smell of Janloon, letting the urban music of car horns and shouted Kekonese wash over him. The car carried him past the dense tenements of Coinwash and Fishtown, the condo buildings and upscale shops of North Sotto, the urban parks and trendy eateries between Green Plain and Yoyoyi, the manicured estate fronts of Palace Hill. He saw trees broken from recent typhoon damage, newspaper stands proclaiming the end of the Oortokon War, red Autumn

Festival lamps and grass streamers adorning eaves and street posts. Green and white paper lanterns hung from storefront windows in their respective districts.

A nameless and profound ache gathered in Anden's chest. Janloon was warm and dangerous, it throbbed with life and hot-blooded movement, it knew that it was special, that there was no other place like it in the world. Other places deceived; in other places, people hid their jade, they exchanged money under the table, and they killed in the dark. Janloon wore its savagery on its sleeve; it was a proud Fist among nations, it did not hide what it was. Janloon was honest.

When he arrived at the Kaul house, Anden took his suitcase out of the trunk, careful not to jar his splinted fingers. Two men were walking down the driveway on their way out, perhaps having concluded a meeting with the Pillar. It had been so long since Anden had seen jade worn openly that his eyes were drawn to the green around their wrists and necks even before he recognized their faces. Juen Nu and Lott Jin paused when they saw him. "Emery Anden," Lott said after a moment. "Welcome back."

Lott looked older; he was dressed in a collared shirt and smoke-gray jacket, talon knife sheathed at the hip, wavy hair cut short to show off the jade pierced through the tops of his ears. He didn't smile, but the adolescent sulkiness that used to hang around his bow-shaped mouth was gone; he spoke slower and more seriously. Unmistakable as a Fist of No Peak.

"Juen-jen. Lott-jen." Anden touched his forehead and inclined in salute. He took his suitcase and went into the house.

Like Janloon itself, the Kaul family home overwhelmed Anden with its familiarity and yet there were signs that things had changed. Some of the furniture was new and old pieces were rearranged. Anden glanced into the study and did not recognize Lan's old space. The desk was cluttered, there were more chairs, family photos on the walls, a television playing on mute. Most striking of all were the signs that this was a house with small children: a playpen in one corner of the family room, a half-assembled train set on the floor, a stack of children's books on the coffee table, pairs of small shoes near the door. For a long minute, Anden stood in the foyer, unable to move, until Kyanla came through the kitchen with a joyful shout and ran to greet him. "Anden-se, finally you've come home!" She'd aged visibly; her hair was gray now, her soft face wrinkled.

Anden went out to find the Pillar sitting in the courtyard. A cigarette dangled from the fingers of one hand, but he did not seem to be smoking it. Hilo's gaze was distant and tired, and there were circles as dark as bruises under his eyes. Anden approached and stopped in front of his cousin, but he didn't sit down in the seat opposite him at the patio table. Hilo looked up at Anden as if rousing to the realization that he was there, even though Anden knew he must've Perceived him arriving several minutes ago. Neither of them spoke at first; they took each other in silently.

At last Anden said, "How's Wen?"

Hilo stubbed out his unsmoked cigarette. "She's recovering in Marenia. Dr. Truw says it could take a long time, because of the brain damage. She's partly paralyzed on the right side of her body. She can understand what people are saying, but has trouble talking." Hilo's voice was factual and expressionless, his sunken gaze nowhere nearby. Quietly, "She's alive, at least. It could've been worse."

Wen had been flown home from Port Massy as soon as she was able to be transported. Hami Tumashon, working under Shae's orders, had swiftly made a number of discreet but persuasive and costly arrangements on behalf of the Weather Man's office. The staff at the Crestwood Hotel conveniently failed to remember seeing anyone go up to Zapunyo's hotel room. The police report concluded that the smuggler had been assassinated by bodyguards in his own inner circle during a shootout that left everyone in the room dead. Several members of the Kekonese community testified that Wen was Anden's cousin and Rohn Toro's recent girlfriend from Janloon, which was why the three of them were together on the night of the brutal revenge killing by Willum Reams's reestablished Southside Crew. Wen, who was in no state to answer any questions from local authorities, was medically evacuated to Janloon within forty-eight hours. It took another week and a half for Hami and the clan's lawyers to extract Anden—long enough for him to recover in the Dauks' house under Sana's care. Exhausted and shaken, he'd slept for days, huddled under blankets and fed bone broth like an invalid, but he wasn't as sick as he'd been the last time he'd handled too much jade.

At Rohn Toro's funeral, he'd folded the Green Bone's black gloves and laid them in the man's casket. He wished he could've saved Rohn as well on that terrible day. He'd tried, but Rohn's throat had been crushed in his violent final struggles and too much time had passed; by the time Anden crawled over to him, the life energy was gone from his body. He wondered if the Dauks blamed him for failing, but when he tried to apologize, Dauk Losun only shook his head and put a heavy hand on Anden's shoulder. "A man as green as Rohn Toro, he wasn't fated to leave this world peacefully," Dauk said sorrowfully. "Let the gods recognize him." Anden had always thought of Rohn Toro as the most Kekonese man in all of Southtrap, and yet he'd been as much a part of Port Massy as the Iron Eye Bridge. Without him, Espenia once again seemed like a foreign place to Anden, one that he was relieved to say goodbye to. Even bowed down with grief, the Dauks were there at the airport along with Mr. and Mrs. Hian to see Anden off on the day of his departure.

Cory was not there; he'd come into town to attend Rohn's funeral but stayed only for the day before returning to Adamont Capita. Although the circumstances were tragic, Anden was grateful for the chance to see his friend one more time. And to apologize in person.

"When you said you were busy with clan things, you didn't mention it might get you killed." Cory looked unusually somber in a black suit and tie, his eyes fixed on Rohn's casket. He rubbed a hand over his face and turned to Anden slowly. "My da always says you're green in the soul, as if that's a good thing to be. It's not, crumb."

"Did you get my letter?" Anden forced himself to raise his eyes from the yellowing grass at his feet. "I meant everything I wrote."

Cory's long expression was not warm, but had enough familiar softness to make Anden's chest hurt. "I haven't forgiven you, or my da," Cory said. "But I'm glad you're all right, and I'm glad you're going home. I know it's what you wanted."

Anden was not certain if that was still true. Standing in the Kaul courtyard, he wished he had just enough jade to be able to Perceive his cousin's aura, because Hilo's face was unreadable. "I'm sorry, Hilo-jen," Anden said. "I shouldn't have agreed to do anything if Wen was involved."

Hilo didn't answer for so long that Anden wondered if he'd even heard. "Wen made her own choices," the Pillar said at last. "I know how persuasive she is, how she gets her way when her mind is set on something. You're the only reason my children aren't motherless right now." A wounded and confused expression flitted across the Pillar's face. His voice turned hoarse and fell almost to a whisper. "She disobeyed me, went behind my back for *years*. How can I ever forgive that?"

Anden dropped his gaze to the paving stones. "It was never about going against you, Hilo-jen—for me or Wen. I know what it's like, to not be the person your family expects you to be. And how hard it is to act for yourself after that." He cleared his throat; his voice had gone scratchy. "It's not your forgiveness we need. Just your understanding."

Silence fell in the courtyard, disturbed only by the warm wind that stirred the leaves in the cherry tree and the surface of the pond in the garden. "You have to move back home, Andy," Hilo said quietly. "I've missed you."

Anden had been waiting to hear those words come out of his cousin's mouth for years. Now, however, he felt no great relief or happiness—only the sort of heaviness that comes from wanting something for so long that the final achievement of it is a loss—because the waiting is over and the waiting has become too much a part of oneself to let go of easily.

"I'm enrolling in the College of Bioenergetic Medicine," Anden said. "I've already spoken to their admissions department, and if I get my application and fees in this week, I can start in the coming year. Channeling was always my strongest discipline at the Academy. Killing Gont Asch made me feel like a bloodthirsty monster, but—" He tried, for the first time, to put his decision into words. "This time, when I used jade, I didn't want it for myself. I wasn't trying to overcome anyone else. I was only thinking of Wen, and the jade was just a tool in my hands that I could use to pull her away from death."

Anden let out a shaky breath. The memory of those few desperate seconds was etched indelibly into his mind, more recent and vivid than even Gont's death or his mother's madness. "Maybe I can wear jade in a different way. If I've learned anything in Espenia, it's that there's more than one way to be a Green Bone. I'm coming back to Janloon to stay, and I'll wear jade again, like you always wanted me to, but only to heal, never to kill." Anden paused; Hilo hadn't said a word to interrupt him the entire time. "I wouldn't ask the clan to pay my tuition," Anden finished.

Hilo's mouth went crooked halfway between a grimace and a grin. "You think I care about the school fees? You haven't changed as much as you think you have, Andy." The Pillar rose from his chair at last and walked past Anden to the patio door. When Anden turned around, he saw the Kaul children standing at the glass, staring out at them. Hilo slid the door open and said, "Come out, you three." They ventured out shyly. Ru ducked his face and went behind his father's leg. Jaya toddled forward with an excited screeching noise and fell to examining bugs on the pavers.

Anden crouched down. "Hello, Niko. Do you know who I am?"

The boy gazed at him with large, calm eyes full of interest and mild skepticism. "You're my uncle Andy," he said.

"The one I've told you so much about, who was studying far away in Espenia," Hilo added. "He's come home to stay now, so you'll get to know him. Would you like that?"

You've Come to the Right Place

Bero got off from his shift in the kitchen of the Double Double. He'd been working there for almost a year now, the longest he'd ever held any kind of job in his life, and he finally had enough money saved to move out of the charity home for recovering addicts. Eiten-jen had agreed to provide a reference letter so Bero could get an apartment of his own again. He hung up his apron and walked out of the casino where not long ago he'd contemplated ending his life by jumping from the penthouse level. Strolling down Poor Man's Road, he passed the glittering lights of the Palace of Fortune and the fountain in front of the Cong Lady. Across the street, a new casino was being built. Posters on the chain-link fence surrounding the construction site advertised the opening of the Green Lotus casino by Enke Property Group in ten months. The influx of Espenian servicemen on leave had kept Janloon's gambling tables busy over the last few years, and although most of them would soon be gone, the business owners in the Armpit district were optimistic that with the end of the Oortokon War, high-rolling foreign tourists would return to the city in greater numbers than before.

Bero walked south until he reached the end of Poor Man's Road and crossed into Dog's Head. The difference was stark; on one side of Janto Avenue, the Armpit swarmed with commercial activity and well-dressed people spending money; on the other, small brick shops looked down on narrow streets, laundry hanging from the open windows of their second-floor apartments. Bero stepped over a sleeping dog to enter an unmarked door on the right-hand side. He climbed the narrow stairway to a lounge on the upper floor. In the evening, people would fill the small dance floor and sweat to jiggy music or sit on the red benches and converse over brandy, but that would not happen for several hours yet. Right now, the lounge was empty except for three men who sat around a table, playing a game of cards and smoking while the bartender polished glasses behind the counter.

The card players glanced up when Bero approached. One of them, a man with a square hat and a thick beard down to his chest, said, "Ey?" He looked disreputable, almost certainly of mixed blood. Bero pulled out the crumpled single-page leaflet from his pocket, the one that demanded, in bold black font, *Join the Revolution!*

"You handed this to me on the street the other day," Bero said.

"Aha," said the man, brightening at once, and shifting his chair over to make room for another seat at the table. "If you're here for the meeting, you've come to the right place." He spoke with a foreign accent, introducing himself as Guriho, and his companions as Otonyo and Tadino.

"I wasn't expecting shotties," Bero said, looking at the choker of bluffer's jade around Otonyo's throat. He'd had enough of the barukan.

The men bristled, and Bero felt he'd made a mistake. Tadino said, "Call us shotties again, and I'll cut your fucking balls off and salt them." He looked like the sort that might do it, too, his face all angles and hard lines. "We're Oortokon, which is an independent country of the Ygut Coalition."

Bero shrugged; geopolitical distinctions didn't matter to him. "You're barukan, though."

"Ex-barukan. Did my time already and starting life anew." Otonyo placed a finger under the chain of nephrite links encircling his neck. "I wear this because it's symbolic. It's to show that jade is a tool of oppression, allowing those in power to stay in power and keep the rest of us imprisoned. Here in Kekon, it's the Green Bone clans. In Espenia, it's the military and the merchant class. In Ygutan, the aristocracy. As jade spreads, it'll be the same story all over the world."

"Unless people rise up," Guriho said, tapping the edge of a playing card against the table. "Jade in the hands of the people could also break chains and free the world."

"I don't want jade. Jade ruined my life." The words came out of Bero's mouth so quickly and without thought that he was surprised at himself. Yet as soon as he said them, he knew they were true. For so long, he'd lusted after jade more than anything else in the world; he'd risked everything to gain it, worn it for such a short while, then lost it in equally dramatic fashion. For the past two years he'd been an empty shell, unsure of what meaning remained in life. Most everyone he knew was missing or dead—Cheeky, both of the Mudts, Soradiyo, Mo and Shrimps, the scrap pickers, the new green in the Rat House. All because of jade and the clans that controlled it.

The fact that he, Bero, was still alive when they were all dead was a lucky joke of the gods. Or it might have some purpose. Bero said, "Taking down the clans, though, that sounds good."

Acknowledgments

This isn't the first time I've written a sequel, but nothing quite prepares you for the seemingly impossible task of following up the biggest, most ambitious novel you've ever written with an *even bigger and more ambitious* novel, the second in a trilogy, no less. My great pleasure in delivering this finished book to you, dear reader, is eclipsed by sheer *relief* that it all worked out.

My appreciation once again to the team at Orbit, and most of all to my editor, Sarah Guan, who never fails to push my writing in ways that add nuance, deepen the layers of the story, and make things worse for the characters. If you have suffered distress on account of the traumatic ordeals borne by the Kaul family, it is in no small part thanks to Sarah's encouragement.

Thanks once again to the marketing and publicity team of Alex Lencicki, Ellen Wright, Laura Fitzgerald, and Paola Crespo, design wizards Lauren Panepinto and Lisa Marie Pompilio, editor Jenni Hill and publicist Nazia Khatun in the UK, production overseer Andy Ball, ever-observant copyeditor Kelley Frodel, mapmaker Tim Paul, and everyone else who had a hand in putting my book on physical and virtual shelves.

I shared an early, messy draft of *Jade War* with my agent, Jim McCarthy, before I allowed any other soul to set eyes on it, and his excellent suggestions and continued optimism convinced me that not all hope was lost. (He's good at doing that.)

Thank you to beta readers Curtis Chen, Simone Cooper, Vanessa MacLellan, Carolyn O'Doherty, and Sonja Thomas for the feedback and brainstorming sessions. Tina Connolly spent a car ride with me to Seattle helping to solve a section of the story that resulted in the best fight scene in the book.

My husband, Nathan, has acted as reader, proofreader, sounding board, and regular emotional support provider. I couldn't do it without him. Our two children are a continual reminder that there's much more to life than how well the writing is going on any one given day.

The marvelous reader enthusiasm to the Green Bone Saga has motivated me through every day of working on this novel. I'm grateful for every appreciative and encouraging email, tweet, review, and in-person interaction I've received from new clan loyalists, and I hope you all keep coming back because there's more where this came from.